A SHIELD
IN THE
SHADOWS

L.A. RACINES

xulon PRESS

A Shield in the Shadows
by L.A. Racines

Printed in the United States of America.

ISBN 9781498428729

Unless otherwise indicated, Scripture quotations are taken from the New International Version (NIV). Copyright © 1973, 1978, 1984, 2011 by Biblica, Inc.™. Used by permission. All rights reserved.

www.xulonpress.com

DEDICATION

This book is dedicated to the six wonderful young people who spoke God's dream for me in December 2003 in Toronto. Their first names are Amber, Blake, Brook, Catherine, Trish and Flo. I never could find out their last names, but to them I would like to express my gratitude for your obedience to your calling as prophets.

It is also dedicated to my husband Philip, for his support and patience through this very long process, and to my children, Shannon and Lydia, and their spouses, Elias and Doug who have supported and encouraged me. Sorely missed from our family is Joshua, an intelligent, valiant and fiercely loving little white dog. 'Gideon' is my tribute to Joshua, and to the other animals who have shared my journey through life.

And finally, *A Shield in the Shadows* is dedicated to all those people struggling right now to understand why terrible things can happen to good people. My dear brothers and sisters, you are not alone and you are not forgotten.

"The race is not to the swift
or the battle to the strong,
nor does food come to the wise
or wealth to the brilliant
or favor to the learned;
but time and chance happen to them all.
Moreover, no man knows when his hour will come:
As fish are caught in a cruel net,
or birds are taken in a snare,
so men are trapped by evil times
that fall unexpectedly upon them."

Ecclesiastes 9:11, 12

ACKNOWLEDGEMENTS

No historical fiction worthy of the name is written in a vacuum. I have spent years researching the Roman Empire, and am grateful for the careful, tedious research done by scholars who love this period of history and have devoted their lives to it. I am especially grateful to Dr. Thomas Burns, S.C. Dobbs Professor of Late Roman History [Emeritus], of Emory University in Georgia. He has answered questions, sent pages and pages of relevant historical documents to me, challenged, corrected and encouraged me, and read every chapter for accuracy. That is an unimaginable gift.

I am also very grateful to Drs. Ron and Roseanne Kydd for reading the manuscript in its early stages and believing in it, and to Nicholas Harris, a former publisher of Collins Canada, who read the manuscript as a personal favor, and then telephoned to offer extraordinary encouragement, advice and endorsement. For a first-time novelist, this was pure gold.

I also have received helpful advice and guidance from Larry Willard, a publisher and supporter of Canadian Christian writers, and from the team of Ray Wiseman and Mary-Lou Cornish. They encouraged me to keep going, be patient, get the tedious work of editing done, and get this book out to a wide audience. This encouragement came at a time when I was weary of spending so many long hours at the computer every day, and impatient to "just get it done". Thanks, also, to Geraldine Lightfoot and Leila Mason who took the time to read the manuscript for errors.

I want to express my gratitude to my husband Philip for getting us both to Germany and Italy to visit the key places I have written about in this book. Thank you for that memorable trip, Phil! Along the way I met a few other people who added valuable information about the background. Thank you, Marco, for telling me about the aqueducts and springs of Montefiesole, and to a gentleman at the German Roman Museum in Mainz who helped me with the placement of the fortress of Moguntiacum.

Thank you to Professor Thomas Burns for the use of two of his maps, and to Steve Masson, who adapted them to fit the needs of this novel. Thanks also to Philip Bristow, who produced the map tracing Marius's and Theona's journeys, no easy task. All the maps will help readers understand the scope of the book a little better.

Last but not least, I need to thank God in this very public way. I found the whole process of writing this book an astonishing journey. I learned to wait when I was stuck, write when the scenes started flowing, edit and re-edit until some scene felt "right", go back and delete entire scenes when something in my gut felt "wrong", and follow through on practical suggestions from other people that helped to overcome gaps in my own research.

INTRODUCTION

I have been a Christian since the first time I realized that the story of the coming of Jesus into this world as the Son of God demanded a response. That was at the age of eleven. Over my lifetime I have come to know many other believers from places around the world. Amazingly, the cultural differences between us melt away whenever we compare our shared experiences of the Kingdom of God that Jesus established.

When I consider the history of Christianity as a whole, an even wider gulf opens up between the Christians of our age, and the Christians who lived long ago. Languages have changed, borders have changed, and customs have changed. Countries, empires, fashions and ideas have come into existence and disappeared into history. As the decades of my own life and experience have slipped away, I began to wonder what I would have in common with those who loved Jesus and who lived in earlier times. This led to the question of how to find God's fingerprints in human history. Is He sovereign in the affairs of man?

The questions formed a good beginning. As I read and studied, I found the kinds of stories that were amazingly similar to what I hear from Christians in my own time and culture, and from other groups of believers around the world. I conclude that the one thing we have in common with those distant fellow Christians is God Himself, eternal, unchangeable, and an ever present help to those who call upon Him in times of trouble.

I began to study the period I write about in this book in January 2004. I started to write this book in 2011, and it has taken me four years to complete it. It has been a long, but wonderful experience, and I have felt God's guidance throughout the process.

Radagaisus was a real Gothic leader who lead a massive invasion of the late Roman Empire sometime in the year 405. He was, according to St. Augustus of Hippo, one of the writers who mentioned him, a 'worshipper of demons' who hated Christians and looked forward to crucifying the members of the Roman Senate who had voted to remove the ancient statue of the goddess of Victory from the Curia in Rome. What would induce any sane Christian to travel with such a leader? Dire circumstances? Great hopes for the future? Theona and her father are my homage to these crazy people.

Radagaisus's nemesis was the great Roman general, Stilicho, whose method of defeating him is recounted here. The details of Stilicho's relationships with the Imperial family are accurate.

Radagaisus's sons, Prince Roderic and Prince Vitiges are my own creations, although it is likely that King Radagaisus did have children. Marius is also a fictional character, though his illustrious ancestor, Decimius Magnus Ausonius, did indeed write both *Bissula* and *The Mosella*, was a tutor to Emperor Gratian, and served for one term as Roman Consul. He established a very successful dynasty, and Marius's career could fit right in there.

About place names: in general, I have used modern place names when those names are well known, and kept the Roman names for lesser-known sites. I have included a couple of maps, a glossary and a list of characters to help readers who like such things.

Enough said. Enjoy!

TABLE OF CONTENTS

CAST OF MAIN CHARACTERS

* Indicates Historical Character

NAME	BRIEF DESCRIPTION	BASIC INFORMATION
Theona	Daughter of Pastor Rhodus	Can read and write, loves to fish
Wolfric	Theona's little brother	Killed, or kidnapped by the Huns?
Gideon	Young black and white dog	Heroic, good-natured, and loyal.
Fiona	Theona's mother	Mother, teacher, killed by the Huns
Darric	Pastor Rhodus's deacon	Recent Christian, calm and principled.
Pastor Rhodus	A Vandal missionary to the Goths	Founder of a Christian settlement in the forests of Germania
Marius Ausonius	Young Roman military tribune from the top level of Roman Gallic society	Good at many things, but not sure what to do with his life.
Paulus Ausonius	Wealthy landowner, Marius's father	A horse breeder, businessman, and father of four.
Constantia Ausonius	Marius's mother	A churchwoman with a keen eye out for her children's best interests.
Julian Ausonius	Marius's oldest brother	His passion is the farm and the horses.
Lucius Ausonius	Marius's other brother	Sociable, interested in the law and politics.
Priscilla Ausonius	Marius's younger sister	Fun-loving, spoiled and with a mind of her own.
Count Jovinus*	A Gallic aristocrat, Marius's godfather	A Gallic nationalist who, for a short time, took matters into his own hands and was executed for it.

NAME	BRIEF DESCRIPTION	BASIC INFORMATION
Marcellus Cavillicus	Garrison Commander of Trier defenses	Genial, proper, a part of the establishment in Trier.
Quintus Carausius	Legate of the fortress at Mainz	A big man with a very big responsibility
Flavius Eucherius*	Marius's fellow military tribune and friend	Son of General Stilicho and Princess Serena, brother of the Empress.
Sr. Tribune Barbatio	Charged with turning two gentlemen into officers	An excellent mentor and trainer.
Socrates	Marius's former grammar teacher	Late twenties already, but still young enough to want to see the world.
Bauto	Marius's optio	Capable young Frank with ambitions.
Bishop Aureus*	Bishop of Mainz (Moguntiacum included)	Killed in January 406 during the infamous barbarian crossing of the Rhine.
Anna	Darric's mother	Her hatred of violence had brought her with her family to Theona's village.
Edrica	Darric's younger sister	Theona's friend eventually.
Bishop Sigeseric*	A Gothic missionary and bishop to the Christians of Wodenvale	Historically recorded with Alaric and Ataulph during the years of wandering after the Sack of Rome in 410.
Duke Helerix	Warlord of Wodenvale	Leader of the Goths in his area.
Rue	Duke Helerix's lovely wife	Hospitable and spirited.
Enoch	A young ox	Strong, docile, calm with Gideon.
Radagaisus*	An Ostrogothic chieftain and a devout pagan.	Led a large collection of peoples across the Danube in 405 AD. Executed August 23, 406.
Anarilka	His grand-daughter	Imaginative and willful, loves stories.
Roderic	Radagaisus's younger son	Leader of Radagaisus's messengers, a bit thoughtless and self-centered.

NAME	BRIEF DESCRIPTION	BASIC INFORMATION
Goar*	An Alan prince.	Crossed the Rhine River into Gaul on December 31, 406.
Viteges	Radagaisus's older son and Anarilka's father	A good and brave leader.
Phaedrus	Radagaisus's chief advisor	A pagan priest of Roman birth.
Clothilde	Wife of Viteges, mother of Anarilka	Struggling to do her best for her child.
Bulleus	Military tribune and deserter	From the Veldidena (Innsbruck) area.
Severus Cantarcchio	Bulleus's second-in-command and fellow deserter	From the Pons Drusi area of Northern Italy. A Granny's boy.
Rumbert	A Christian Gothic chieftain	He requests to team up with Duke Helerix and his people.
Arnulf	A Gothic chieftain who also joins forces with Duke Helerix	His wife and many of his people were Christians.
Puella	Captured in Pannonia by a Wodenvale farmer	Her husband killed, her children abandoned, herself mistreated
Ptolemy	An escaped Gladiator	North-African origin, Roderic's man
David	Marius's slave, sent by Constantia to take care of him	Formerly a free man and landowner, now a widower wanting to regain his freedom.
Limenius*	Provincial Administrator for Gallia Belgica	Killed, along with many others at a military uprising two years later.
Cornelius Olybrius	Legate of the fortress at Augsburg	An intelligent and responsible commander with a passion for the mountains.
Granny Cantarcchia	Severus Cantarcchio's grandmother	An old Gothic woman, blind, cantankerous and often surprising.
Sarus*	Leader of the Gothic contingent of the Roman Army	An Amali nobleman who played a pivotal role during his time serving Emperor Honorius.
Legate Merula	Legate of the fortress at Bologna	A decent man with a good heart.
Zenobia	His six-year-old daughter	Sweet and generous.
Prunella	His four-year-old daughter	Sympathetic and helpful.

NAME	BRIEF DESCRIPTION	BASIC INFORMATION
Lady Julianna	Legate Merula's wife	A lady of grace, style and kindness.
Stilicho*	Guardian of the Emperor, head of the Western Empire's army, Eucherius's father	A Roman general who handled crisis after crisis for the Western Empire until he was abandoned by his own protégés.
Thaddeus	A lonely Roman orphan	Looking for love, playmates, and food.
Athanaric	Edrica's husband, a Christian	A farmer from Wodenvale
Bishop Zenobius*	Bishop of Florence	First bishop (337 – 417)
Wieland	Ostensible leader of a rogue Suevi clan, widowed	He has a tough family to lead.
Mathilde	The clan matriarch	A determined and unprincipled woman.
Meinrad	Wieland's brother	A bully with ambition.
Gerlinda	Meinrad's wife	Theona's fellow gardener.

HISTORICAL INTRODUCTION

T he Sea of Azov is the topmost part of the Black Sea and is separated from it by the narrow Strait of Kerch. With Ukraine rising along its western shore, and Russia along the east, it is shaped rather like a retreating rhinoceros. It is the shallowest sea in the world.

More than a hundred years before the story told in this book, bands of fierce nomads who may have come from as far away as the Mongolian steppes, migrated to the Russian side of the Strait of Kerch. Today we call these people the Huns.

On the opposite side of the narrow channel dwelled the Ostrogoths, a Germanic people who had come to the region from far away in the north-west. For a time, neither knew about the other's existence.

According to a legend, one day a cow belonging to a Hun was stung by a gadfly. She panicked, charged into the strait and swam across it, hotly pursued by her owner. A second version says the man was hunting a deer through the marshy area of the Strait of Kerch, and it eluded him by fleeing into Ostrogoth territory. The Hun followed, and found a land that was rich and inviting. He returned in great excitement to tell his people. Roused by the prospect of wealth and conquest, the Huns galloped westward into conflict with everyone they met, and entered Western history.

Everywhere they went, they brought terror and desolation along with them. Eventually some of them found their way to Theona's village, eight hundred miles away.

CHAPTER ONE

HUNS!

A village deep in the forests of German Barbaricum[1]
(Modern Poland)
Late June, 405 Anno Domini

The attack on the little Gothic settlement came on a peaceful summer afternoon.

The stout wooden door of the Great House swung open. Eight students burst out and down the steps. Three older women chatted together as they headed for their small wattle and daub homes. The other five students ranged in age from an eight-year-old girl to a seventeen-year-old boy. He passed the teacher shyly. Theona was a pretty blond, and a year younger than him.

She closed the door behind them, and walked back into the room. Her students' leaf tablets and pieces of charcoal were still scattered on the tables. She picked up the tablets and looked at their work again. All of them were progressing nicely. The oldest lad had been copying from the *Book of Proverbs*, and she could see only two mistakes in the transcription. She smiled with satisfaction.

She put the *Book of Proverbs* into its tin box with the rest of her father's precious Gothic Bible and closed the lid, and then put the charcoal and tablets into their wooden chest. Just before she left, she scanned the big room quickly. Six tables were neatly spaced down the middle, their benches pushed underneath. The loft above was empty right now—the newest people to seek asylum in the village had just moved into their new house, so the loft, too, was in order.

She went out the door, closing it behind her, the heavy tin box in her arms.

The goats in the shaded enclosure at the bottom of the stairs were restless. They bleated at her as she passed them.

"Bleeeee."

"Bleeeee!" she retorted. She grabbed a handful of oats from a wooden box at the base of the steps, and tossed it into the pen. They were snatched up in seconds.

Another young goat emerged from the shed under the stairs, and ran toward her, tossing his head playfully. Theona had witnessed its birth the year before, a difficult one, but the kid had grown strong and healthy. Bramble had already fathered several of his own kids.

---

[1]   The Romans referred to all the areas outside the Empire as 'barbaricum', the homeland of foreigners.

Theona grabbed some more oats. The kid wolfed them down and raised his bony head again, munching and eying her owlishly. The other goats crowded back toward her.

"Enough, you little bullies!" she complained cheerfully, and walked off.

The afternoon had been hot. A pungent fragrance wafted through the air, a mixture of animal scents, cooking smells, human waste from the village's dunghill, and the lovely scent of summer grasses and flowers. It signified home.

Theona's house was not far from the Great House. She headed there to drop off the tin box and pick up her fishing gear.

A little boy with dark golden hair, the same color as her own, ran out the door, shouting and waving his little bow and arrow. Close behind him ran a young black and white dog, barking excitedly.

Theona's mother, Fiona, shouted from inside the house.

"Be careful when you are running with that, Wolfric. You could hurt yourself!"

"I will," he promised. Seeing Theona coming up the path, he ran to her, sweetly hugged her legs, and grinned up, his little face smudged with dirt. Then he ran off again, followed by the dog. Fondly, she watched them disappear around the corner of a neighbor's house.

As she entered her home, her mother got up from her knees. She had been kneeling beside a broken spinning wheel that Wolfric had knocked over weeks ago, trying to fix it.

"How did it go today?" Fiona wiped her sweaty hands down her long tunic. Her hair, almost the same color as her children's, was tied back from her face with a yellow band.

"Good," responded Theona. "Turtik is reading a bit now, and I'm told the twins have been copying letters and runes all over their father's shed. Abraham was complaining to me about it yesterday. I told him that at least they're keen!"

Her mother laughed.

"Tell Darric," she said, referring to her husband's young deacon. Theona's father was the village pastor. "He'll be pleased. He's always looking for new readers. Are you going fishing?"

"Yes, it's too nice to work. I'll do some weeding in the vegetable garden this evening. You don't mind?"

"Not at all. Bring back supper. I'll wait to see if you are successful before I kill the fatted calf."

Theona chuckled. The little Gothic village had only one cow that they had named Abigail. She had recently been impregnated by a bull from another village. No one would willingly slaughter the calf she was carrying; they had great hopes for it. A bull would establish a herd. A heifer would double the little community's supply of milk.

Net and bucket in hand, Theona left the house. She passed half a dozen other homes before she reached the edge of the village. A man waved at her from the nearest field. Theona called back a greeting, and kept going toward one of the paths leading into the thick forest.

From spring to autumn everyone's workload was heavy. They had to prepare the fields, sow and tend the crops, care for the animals, and maintain their homes and gardens. In addition to the animal husbandry and fieldwork they all did, the women had the preparation of skins and clothes, and the care of the children, while the men handled construction, the defense of the village and the need to keep clearing new land. Newcomers might arrive at any time and would expect to be given a field of their own to work with. When they had leisure, the people liked to hunt and fish and gather the wild crops of the fields and forest for additional sources of food.

Anyone who lived this far north had little leisure in the constant struggle to sustain life, because winter was coming. Winter was always coming. Even at the height of summer it hovered like a cold threat; long, dark, lonely and sometimes dangerous. Once one was over, another loomed.

In neighboring villages there wasn't much to do in winter, especially for the men. They would sleep a good deal, and tend the livestock. In the evenings they would gather to feast and drink, and gamble and argue, and get into fights. And they would tell their stories. These were often retellings of ancient tales passed down from generation to generation, tales of the old gods and their epic feuds, of famous heroes and their worthy quests, of enduring romances and bitter betrayals, of mythical creatures and manly adventures, and of deadly battles which could last for days. In the gloom of cold winter nights, the story tellers and their avid listeners longed for the day when they, too, would have the chance to show the world their mettle. Most of the men hoped that when the spring came, their overlords would summon them to war, and they would be able to leave the seasonal drudgery to the women and old men, and go off to gain glory, wealth and immortality for themselves.

Theona's village was different. It was the only Christian one within forty miles. Fugitives from pagan persecution and new converts moved here to begin a different kind of life.

Her father, Rhodus, was one such fugitive from persecution. He had fled his Vandal village somewhere to the east and moved into Gothic territory to bring the Gospel to a new area. Fiona, his wife, was the daughter of a local farmer who had become Rhodus's first convert from paganism. Together the couple had founded the village, begun their family, and pastored the growing community. Here, newcomers not only learned how to read and write, but how to rebuild their shattered lives and reshape old patterns of thinking.

Theona left the clearing that surrounded the village and took the dirt path into the woods. She followed this for a while, and then left it to head into the heart of the forest.

There was one place where she particularly liked to fish. She often came here when she had a break, and frequently managed to come home with a fish or two. The twisting, tumultuous brook slowed down and lingered awhile before rushing on. The trees here were tall and leafy and the subdued lighting was perfect for eliminating shadows. Centuries of humus had made the ground spongy underfoot, and muffled her footsteps so she was able to approach the edge of the stream without alarming the large brown trout who liked to shelter under an overhanging lip.

Once she reached it, she eased her body into position and peered into the crystal-clear water to look for her wily prey. This required some awkward maneuvering. She was filling out now, and was not sure how long the overhang would continue to be able to bear her weight. She sighed. She was growing into a woman, and she wasn't ready for whatever that meant.

Occasionally animals would come down to drink beside the stream while she fished. They had learned to ignore her, and she them. Only once had she had to face a threat, and then it was in the form of a youth from another village.

He had seen her leave the path, and had followed her into the woods. When he approached her, Theona yelled at him and threw stones. He backed off quickly. To her chagrin, her noisy reaction had scared not just the youth away, but the fish as well.

Word came back to her village that the young man was an admirer, and had just seized the opportunity to try to get to know her. Until her vehement reaction to him, he had thought she might make a suitable wife, and if things had gone well, he had planned to kidnap her at some later time and take her home. Bride-napping was an old custom and a presumed honor. To the people in his village, the Christian pastor's daughter had behaved in a most unbecoming way. The young man was humiliated, his family and village were offended, and, for a time, there was bad blood between the two communities.

Her own people were equally outraged, though not at Theona. They had their own plans for the pastor's daughter. It was fortunate, they said, that the young man had not come with the usual gang of co-conspirators, or they might have lost her. Theona must marry one of their young men—it was just a question of determining which one. Most people thought that Pastor Rhodus's deacon, Darric, would be the best choice.

Theona was not ready to become anyone's wife, and would certainly have made the would-be bride-napper sorry had he succeeded in getting her away. She was perfectly content with her life. She loved being the pastor's daughter and the village teacher. Life was good. She was not interested in a change.

A large brook trout swam over to lie below her in the shadows of the overhang. It turned to face upstream, waiting for whatever food might come floating on the current. Once she was satisfied the fish was intent on its own hunt, Theona slowly raised her net and flashed it down hard and fast, jerking the fish back in toward the bank. She had it!

Jubilantly she placed the brown trout on the grass near her. It flapped there desperately, its silver eye staring at her. She quickly stunned it and settled back.. Now she could choose to wait for the other fish to settle down, or she could move on to a different spot farther upstream. She knew several good places, but this one was close to the main path, and the summer afternoon was so peaceful. It was too much trouble to move on. Anyway, the fish she had caught was big enough to make a meal for all four of them.

A gentle wind stirred the leafy canopy high above her. Fingers of flickering light illuminated a purple raspberry cane, a fallen pine cone, a tiny cluster of yellow flowers and a spider's web glistening against the dark green leaves of wild flowers.

Theona stayed. Only her eyes moved. Within minutes, they began to close.

She was roused by the sound of hooves pounding. There were horses coming along the path she had left, many horses from the sound of it, and all of them galloping fast toward her village.

Theona was alarmed. No one in her village owned a horse. They were few and far between in the thick forests of her land.

She sat up, her thoughts racing, and placed the fish into the bucket. Could this be a raid from another village? Had the local pagan overlord decided to come to call? He had tried twice before to conscript the men from her village and to seize some of the girls and children. Perhaps it was a group of enforcers from the distant Gothic warlord, sent to punish them for their faith!

Throwing the net and fish into her bucket, Theona stood up and yodeled a high-pitched warning, then grabbed her bucket and ran back toward the main path. Branches snagged her long hair, and scratched her face and neck. She scarcely noticed.

Whoever they were, these horsemen were coming fast. By the time she reached the path, she was already too late. There was no way she would be able to outrun the horsemen. Instead, she needed to find a hiding-place urgently. She saw two large intertwined fir trees a dozen feet ahead. She reached them and dropped down just as the horsemen swept around a bend and galloped straight towards her. Theona peeked through a gap and gasped.

She had never seen such men before in her life. They were hideous creatures—swarthy and muscular with narrow, misshapen heads, sloping black eyes, and dark scars carving their cheeks. Some of them were wearing rags and furs; others wore clothing like hers. All of them were wearing several of the bright, jeweled brooches typical of those made and treasured by her people.

Huns!

She had never seen a Hun before, but she recognized them from the vivid descriptions she had heard from visiting hunters and traders.

These Huns were riding strange-looking, swaybacked horses with very long manes. They carried bows and arrows over their shoulders. Their intent seemed clear—they were going to attack her village. She crouched lower behind the trees until the last rider, a black-eyed youth, had passed by. As soon as he had, she stood up, her legs and hands shaking, and yodeled another frantic high-pitched warning. Seconds later an arrow passed close by her head. She squealed and ducked as the youth sneered back at her and carried on. He was already preparing to launch another arrow in her direction. Theona dropped to the ground again, trembling violently.

The sound of the thudding hooves died away. Theona leapt to her feet and hurtled onto the path, running between the columns of trees, her bare feet nimbly avoiding sticks, stones and animal droppings. She heard shouts of alarm from the village and then a series of unnerving war cries. That's when the screams started.

Wolfric! Her mother! Her students!

The bucket with the trout in it was slowing her down. She abandoned it and ran faster.

The screams were becoming intermittent. Finally, even the yelling stopped. Theona stood in horror on the path close to where she had entered the forest. The voices she could hear were foreign ones, exultant and boisterous. There were a few other voices, too. Wails, moans, groans, one defiant shout, children crying, and then silence.

A voice she recognized called softly to her from the forest.

"Theona, get over here. Quickly."

It was Darric, her father's young deacon. She glanced around to locate him. His voice had come from the left. All she could see there was a web of branches, deep shadows, and the high, prickly grasses and brambles lining the path.

A Hun on horseback came around the far edge of the village. He was riding slowly in her direction and carrying a lighted torch.

Theona froze. Her world was about to go up in flames and she could not move.

The man suddenly veered toward one of the houses. He thrust the torch into the thatched roof and held it there until it caught fire. Theona cringed.

He began to move again, coming in her direction. He would pass her in less than a minute. Still she could not get her brain to connect with her feet.

She had to move, or she was dead. "Help me!" she prayed.

Another voice called out from somewhere in the village. The man with the torch shouted back in his guttural, staccato language and dismounted. He walked back into the village, torch high. Soon afterward, Theona heard a chorus of frantic bleating. A minute later, the goats, led by Bramble, came charging out from between the houses. They raced into the clearing chased by the youth who had shot the arrow at her. He was screaming and waving his arms. The frightened goats rushed around looking for somewhere to escape to. They suddenly veered as one into the oat field. The young Hun turned back, laughing, into the village.

A great noise began in Theona's head. She felt faint.

Out of the corner of her eye, she caught a brief glimpse of Darric. He had risen to his feet from the dense greenery in the forest, and was making wide circles with his arms to catch her attention. His knife flashed in one hand.

"Theona!" he called softly. "*Move*. Back up to that clump of birch trees and go behind them. Follow the little trail there."

His words got her brain going again. She moved quickly back to the birch trees, and swung her legs high over the tall grasses onto the little deer trail. She followed it until she could see Darric's broad shoulders and long sandy hair. He sat astride a large, moss-covered fallen oak and was peering through the web of leaves in the direction of the village. Theona hurried toward him and dropped down at his side. Darric gave her a brief, hard hug, and then turned back to his surveillance. Gratefully, she settled down to wait beside him. She clasped her hands together tightly to stop their shaking.

From where they sat, they had a very limited view of the village.

The foreign voices were muted now by the sound of roaring flames. A dog barked. A man yelled, and there was a squeal of pain. A high-pitched voice cried out in protest. Could that have been Wolfric? She stood up abruptly, but Darric pulled her down again.

"You can't leave. They'll kill you. Where is Pastor Rhodus?"

Her father. Where was he? She remembered.

"He went to visit a family in another village."

"When will he be back?"

"He said he would be back tonight."

"Which village did he go to?"

"Halodin's village. It's two roads over toward the sunset."

"I know where it is."

Darric's calm grey eyes searched hers thoughtfully. He was older than Theona by several years. He was a pleasant-faced young man whose tousled, sandy hair grew down to his shoulders. His reddish beard was already several inches long.

"Theona, I don't know if anyone in the village is still alive. I do know that quite a few of our people were away when this attack came. Some of them will be heading home, and they do not realize that our little village is now in the hands of Huns. One of us has to go spread the warning, and one of us has to stay. It is I who must go, and you who must stay."

"I can't!" Her wail was whispered.

Darric took one of her hands in his bigger ones, cradling it. His straight gaze steadied her.

"Listen to me, Theona. I have heard that the Huns usually do not stay long. They come, they attack, they look for gold and other precious things and then they move on taking what they want. The rest . . . they destroy," he added morosely, glancing at the flames spreading in the village. "If you stay here out of sight and they leave soon, you may be able to help anyone who is still alive there. You're good at that. But I *have* to go warn others from this village and the villages nearby. I can go faster without you. Your father must be told, too. I will try to find him, and I will tell him where you are. Stay right here. You must be strong."

"When will you come back?" she asked.

"As soon as I can."

"Then go," she whispered, her frightened eyes fixed on his face. She wanted to add "I'll be alright", but did not. It might not be true.

He touched her cheek tenderly and left, heading back to the main path. She knew that Darric could run fast, and he was a good woodsman. His brown leather jerkin and pants blended well with the forest. She listened intently for a long time. It seemed he had managed to get away without discovery.

Darric, his mother Anna and his two sisters, Edrica, who was her own age, and Edwina, two years older, had been baptized at the same time as her at a pool in the forest. They were all new converts. Darric took his faith and his call to ministry seriously. Her father and mother both liked him very much. Sometimes Theona thought that they hoped she would marry him one day and carry on their work. She wondered if Darric thought the same.

She settled into the place where he had sat and gazed through the leafy gap. At first, the only things she could see moving were the flames from the nearest houses. Then the Hun's horse wandered into view, munching unconcernedly. Theona leaned closer to stare. She had heard about such beasts, almost as strange-looking as their masters. They were smaller than any other horses she had seen. They were said to be nimble and fearless in battle, and they would forage and fend for themselves.

Their country is the back of a horse.

Where had she heard those words? She could not remember. Probably from one of the traders who passed through the area occasionally. The Huns' skill at riding was legendary. She remembered her father mentioning that they had a mystical bond with their funny-looking mounts; that they lived, slept, ate, fought, and held council meetings on horseback. She wondered if it were true.

The one she was looking at was thin and had broad hips. Its mane flowed down to its knees. The large hooked head had bulbous eyes. The animal suddenly lifted its head and looked straight in her direction, twitching its ears. She held her breath, terrified it could somehow alert its master to her presence. The horse stared in her direction for a minute, then lowered its head and began grazing again.

As the evening drew near, a breeze began to whisper through the treetops high above, and the air grew chilly. Theona heard footsteps quickly approaching the village from the path behind her. Someone was returning home—someone who was unaware of the disaster that had befallen the village.

It was Gruda, large with her latest child, hurrying home with a full basket of berries. Theona rose to her feet and hissed a warning, but the woman, though she looked around for the voice, did not pause. She had scarcely taken a few steps into the clearing when a Hunnic arrow hit her in the throat. Gruda dropped onto the ground, clutching at it, her berries spilling out around her. Theona cried out, and immediately clamped her hand over her mouth. She could not see Gruda's assailant. Where was he?

Her neighbor was writhing on the ground in the open clearing, blood streaming from her throat. Theona wanted to go to her but was too terrified. Cursing her cowardice, she sank to the ground, sobbing and gulping and trying not to make any noise. She bit her arm until it bled to control the sounds she was making. The pain distracted her: Gruda was dying nearby, or was dead already. Every impulse within her wanted to go to her aid, and every sane thought warned her to stay where she was.

Where had the archer been standing? Had he heard her call out? Did he know she was there? Was he sneaking up on her now? She could see so little from where she hid! The Hun must have been posted to kill anyone coming down the path.

She lay flat on the ground behind the tree trunk, unwilling now even to raise her head to look out through the spiky green keyhole. Instead, she concentrated on listening. Below the gentle rustle of the treetops, she could hear the sharp crackle and snap of flames, the excited exclamations of exploration and discovery, and the occasional gleeful howl of the raiders as buildings collapsed. The horrible smell of burning flesh marked the end of a good and godly dream. Theona accepted then that there was absolutely nothing she could do.

No one else came along the path. Darkness descended, lowering the shades on the devastated village. Eventually Theona's tense, aching body relaxed. She fell asleep, lying on the ground beside the log.

Her father returned a couple of hours later. Pastor Rhodus nearly despaired of finding her in the dark. He groped past the birch trees Darric had mentioned, and stumbled through the dark woods, unable to see the deer trail. His feet on the twigs underfoot made so much noise in the quiet night that he was almost frantic. He tripped over a log and hit his forehead against a heavy branch. His desperate prayers to find Theona were answered when a large flare from the village illuminated her pale arms and he was able to make his way to her. Her sleeping body lay exactly where Darric had told him it would be.

Weary but thankful, he settled himself alongside his daughter and put his cloak over them both to keep the dew off. He lay there for a long time, praying and listening to the noises from the village, torn between frantic worry for his beloved wife and young son, and the need to protect himself and Theona. Eventually he too fell asleep. Neither of them heard the Huns when they departed early the next morning.

CHAPTER TWO

A SPIRITUAL QUEST INTERRUPTED

❧

A villa near the Roman city of Augusta Treverorum, Gallia Belgica
(Trier, southern Germany)
Late June, 405 AD

Decimius Marius Ausonius looked both ways down the hallway before ducking into the villa's library, now shadowed and quiet. There was no one in there. He hadn't expected there to be, but what he was looking for was a little embarrassing, and he didn't want to draw attention to himself. He was looking for something that might help him connect with Almighty God.

Everyone else in the household was busy with the final preparations for the party. Slaves rushed around doing last minute chores. The head gardener passed the doorway carrying an armful of flowers to the kitchen where Marius's mother was overseeing their arrangement. Wiry Dorcas, a kitchen girl, trudged grimly behind him with one of the urns she had just polished. Two men could be heard arguing quietly as they struggled up the stairs from the wine cellar with a heavy amphora between them. In the office at the front of the house Marius's father and his two brothers were discussing business matters they meant to bring up with a few of the influential guests that would be coming.

Marius alone had no responsibilities. He felt like the bride who did not have to lift a finger on her special day. The party was in his honor. Tomorrow he would be off to join the Roman army—a big step for the eighteen-year-old. Tomorrow his life would change dramatically, and everyone in the household knew that and meant to give him a fabulous farewell.

The library's inventory was quite respectable. Succeeding generations of Ausonii had contributed to it, most especially his grandfather. Decimius Magnus Ausonius had been a celebrated poet, a tutor to the Emperor Gratian, and even, once, a Roman Consul, one of the highest honors in the Empire. That was back in 379. The library contained cubbyholes full of both scrolls and parchments, and, lying flat on some shelves, a few dozen of the modern parchment books. Scanning these, Marius quickly located the one he had come for, one of the four Gospels. It had a highly decorated leather cover and was a work of true beauty. Marius hastily shoved it into his leather satchel, glancing guiltily toward the door. No one was passing.

His eye fell on a new acquisition a bit farther along the same shelf. It looked like another interesting prospect. He opened it, and stood there reading for a moment.

It was a fairly new book, published only five years before, and had been written by the Egyptian-born court poet, Claudian. It was entitled, *On the Fourth Consulship of Stilicho*, and eloquently eulogized the man who was the current generalissimo of the Western Roman Army.

His brother Lucius must have bought it, thought Marius smiling. He was the one most interested in politics. Or perhaps his father.

He decided to take it, too. It might be advisable for him to learn something about General Stilicho. After all, from tomorrow on his life was literally going to be in the hands of both God and this man. It seemed almost providential to read these books together.

Paulus Ausonius, Marius's father, shouted from the front of the house, and everyone within hearing distance stopped to listen.

"Someone's coming! They're too early. Get ready. Where's Marius?"

Marius's mother, Constantia, raced past the doorway of the library, her hair half unpinned, her face flushed, a bunch of leaves poking, forgotten, from one thin blue-veined hand. He knew she was heading for her bedroom to change. Jamming the second book into his pouch, Marius looked cautiously into the hallway for an escape route.

"Marius!"

He turned. His fourteen-year-old sister, Priscilla, was coming through from the atrium, her freckled face earnest. "Father . . ."

"Later!" he shouted, and ran in the opposite direction toward the nearest exit. He wanted to get out of there fast. *Who on earth was coming this early?* he thought crossly.

Running to the stable, he feverishly saddled up Troya, his beautiful black mare. Seven-year-old Peter, their steward's only son, ran into the stable to greet him. Peter would have to come.

"Come on, Peter, we're going to the river," said Marius, and Peter, whooping for joy, scrambled up behind him, hugging his waist. Troya tossed her head and trotted eagerly to the back gate and on out of the walled compound. She cantered off along the farm road toward the Moselle River[2].

"Yahhhh," yelled Peter from behind him, and Marius, smiling, let go of the reins and clapped both hands over his ears.

"Hang on to the reins, lord," commanded Peter, and Marius obediently grabbed them again.

He always sought opportunities to give Peter a break from his daily chores. The boy loved to ride and loved to pretend. Today Peter would be his watchman on the ramparts, his spy against invading forces. Peter always made the most of it, and so far, no one back at the villa rustica had ever objected when the youngest Ausonius son bore him off.

They moved rapidly down the vineyard-lined road, and turned along a riding path that ran beside the river. Marius was heading for his childhood sanctuary, a small cave halfway down the steep bank of the river. The cave had been special to all the Ausonii children. It was shown to Marius by his two brothers when he turned eight. He, in turn, had introduced Priscilla to it on her eighth birthday.

When they reached the meadow above the cave, the two of them dismounted. Marius took Troya's saddle off and lightly slapped her rump. Troya wandered away to graze. A steep, rocky trail led down the embankment toward the river's edge. Clutching his satchel, Marius began the descent to the cave below, leaving Peter watching for boats, butterflies and unwelcome visitors.

---

[2]   The Moselle River (Mosel in Germany) originates in the Vosges Mountains and flows through northern France, Luxembourg and part of Germany before it empties into the Rhine River at Koblenz. It is 339 miles long. In Roman times it was called the Mosella River.

An overhang guarded the mouth of the cave. Marius cautiously peered into the shadowed interior. It seemed empty. Carefully, he turned his long body around and dropped down onto the earthen floor. The roof seemed lower than he remembered—he had to stoop now. He bumped his head and some of the rich brown soil brushed off onto his hair and shoulders. He winced; it was not good for the guest of honor to show up at his party looking grubby. The cave seemed smaller than he remembered, but then he had not been here in a year.

Awkwardly, Marius sat down on the dirt floor with his back to the wall. He laid the two books on the pouch on the floor beside him and looked out, sighing with pleasure. From where he sat at the mouth of the cave he could see the shimmering Moselle River not far below him. There was always traffic on the river at this time of the year, many small boats and a few ships. Swans could swim by, and gannets and gulls would swoop along near the water below. Puffs of cloud laid irregular patterns on the river and the fields beyond.

He watched contentedly for a few minutes, and then sternly reminded himself of his reason for coming. Bishop Mauritius had said on Sunday that God had created every man with a destiny. It was time to check into that. His heart pounding, he opened *The Gospel of John*, and began to read.

"In the beginning was the Word, and the Word was with God, and the Word was God. He was with God in the beginning. He came to that which was his own, but his own did not receive him.[3]"

The words stared up at Marius. They seemed important but obscure. He wasn't sure they were particularly relevant to his quest. Where in this book did it talk about personal destiny? For the first time in his life, he felt a deep need to know about things he had never bothered with before. With the river winding past, and the season changing to summer, his own life was about to change direction. Which way would it go? He felt as though he was "meant" for something. The question was *what*?

Of course, he and his friends had sometimes talked about the so-called 'meaning of life', but their conversations ended up going in circles. Even when they agreed they had found a reasonable and noble answer, it only seemed to satisfy them for a short time. It seemed that the need to understand one's own significance was unquenchable.

This new bout of introspection had come unwanted. For the last few months, Marius had been haunted in his sleep by fierce dreams that left him in a sweat. He was fighting something, he was cornered, he was dying somewhere alone, and he didn't know why or how he had got there. And what happened next?

He stared down at the next words in the beautiful little book again. The author was saying: "Through him all things were made; without him nothing was made that has been made. In him was life, and that life was the light of men. That light shines in the darkness, but the darkness has not understood it."

He frowned. Well, he clearly belonged among those who did not understand 'it'. He looked out at the sky beaming blue just outside the cave, and at the sun, just emerging from behind a soft, fleeting cloud. *There* lay the kind of light he knew, the reality he understood. The questions he had, the words he was reading, seemed as insubstantial as that cloud in the light of such a beautiful summer day. Nevertheless, tomorrow would still come tomorrow, and the questions struggling to be heard for so long had been persistent and relevant.

He decided to use the direct approach, prayer. If the sacred book was too obscure for someone in a hurry for answers, maybe prayer would help. He would just tell Almighty God what he wanted.

---

3   The Bible: The Gospel of John, Chapter 1, verses 1 and 11

Right away Marius realized that he had a problem. He had no idea how God was going to speak back. He decided to put his heart out there anyway. That was what faith was all about, wasn't it? His mother had said it was a muscle you had to use for it to grow strong, and if it did, you could move mountains.

Pushing back a lock of auburn hair from his face, he closed his eyes and imagined SOMEONE who sat on a big throne and looked a little like the icons of Christ you saw everywhere, and a little like Bishop Mauritius with his long grey beard. It was the best he could do. He plunged in.

"Almighty God, I'm sorry to bother you but I'm afraid I have to. I need to know if my life has a purpose, if it really matters to . . . you." He exhaled. Already he was feeling better. Lifting up the book he complained, "And God, if I'm going to understand this, you will have to help me. It feels like I'm wading through mud here!"

He became worried. How had the Most High God received that? He hastened on.

"Will you please help me? I'd like to believe you will be with me, even if I am . . . a soldier."

There, it was out. He squirmed, and then waited, listening.

Somewhere outside the cave a tiny creature scuttled through the grass. Downriver, two dogs started barking at each other. A crow cawed. God did not seem to say anything. Still, it was early days. Maybe you got better at this sort of thing with practice.

The truth was, he still had mixed feelings about becoming a soldier. The closer to leaving he got, the more urgent his questions became. Could he really fight and die, or kill on an order from someone else? Could he really turn his life over to the whim of his officers and the happenstances of fate? What kind of man would the army make of him? What kind of man did he want to be? It brought him back to the bishop's words: "For we are God's workmanship, created in Christ Jesus to do good works which God prepared in advance for us to do."[4] Was being a soldier considered a 'good work'? There were an awful lot of bad ones out there!

Where was that passage anyway?

He bent back over the little book, continuing to read.

"The true light that gives light to every man was coming into the world. He was in the world, and though the world was made through him, the world did not recognize him . . .

"He came to that which was his own, but his own did not receive him. Yet to all who *did* receive him, to those who believed in his name, he gave the right to become children of God—children born not of natural descent, nor of human decision or a husband's will, but born of God."[5]

Marius frowned. The 'true light' had to refer to the Christ. After all, the Gospels were all written about him. He knew that much. There was something hugely significant in all these thoughts, but it didn't seem to be what he was looking for. Something began to niggle at him though.

"Master!" Peter's little voice chirped his name over the edge of the riverbank. Marius poked his head out of the cave to hear better. Hooves were thudding along the riding trail in his direction.

"Not now!" thought Marius, annoyed. A new thought, a question, was beginning to form in his mind. He wanted to see where it led—something about the connection between "children of God," and that business about God preparing in advance good works for us to do. That sounded like it had to do with personal destiny!

It was not to be. The horses slowed down, and his sister's voice called out. A small stone sailed past the cave opening, and bounced down the hill. Peter was discretely warning him that visitors had arrived.

---

[4] The Bible, Letter to the Ephesians, Chapter 2, verse 10

[5] The Bible, Gospel of John, Chapter 1, verses 9-13

"Where is he, boy? Speak up. I saw you toss something. Is Marius down there?"

Marius recognized the distinctive baritone voice of Count Jovinus, his godfather. He knew that Peter would be in agony about whether to betray his whereabouts, or face the anger of one of the most prominent noblemen in all Gaul. He cursed the day he had ever brought Priscilla here.

"He's down in the cave, probably writing poetry."

Her voice.

"Is it any good?"

"I don't know. He never lets us read it."

Marius resigned himself to calling off his spiritual quest for the moment. He closed *The Gospel of John* in frustration.

"I'm here," he called out. His muffled voice must sound hollow to the three standing on terra firma above him.

"Get up here, lad. You have visitors at the house, and more coming all the time. As the guest of honor, you ought to be there. Everyone is waiting to greet you, and your poor mother is very worried."

Marius swiftly stowed the books in the pouch. He hadn't even opened the second book, the one about General Stilicho. It would have to wait. He wondered if his father would mind if he borrowed them both for a while.

As he emerged from the cave, a sheet of light from the sunlit river blazed into his eyes, nearly blinding him. He cast a regretful glance at the vine-covered hills across the river. It might be a very long time before he was here again. Sighing, he started the steep scramble up to the meadow. As he neared the top of the embankment, he slung his pouch ahead of him onto the grass. Clambering over the edge, he was dismayed to see that Count Jovinus had dismounted and was reaching out an elegant, bejeweled hand to pick it up. His godfather calmly opened the pouch and lifted out the two books, and then ostentatiously dusted them off and glanced at them before returning them to the pouch. Priscilla watched anxiously from her horse.

Marius scowled.

Jovinus acknowledged him with a friendly nod.

"I'm impressed!" he said. "One of Claudian's panegyrics on our great Generalissimo Stilicho, and *The Gospel of St. John*. Nothing wrong with your tastes, young man." He handed the pouch to Marius.

Marius said nothing; just put the pouch into Troya's saddlebags. Secretly, he was pleased by the compliment, but his godfather had been most impertinently invading his privacy. Stony-faced, he lifted Troya's saddle back on and gestured to Peter to mount up. Jovinus grabbed the boy's shoulder and turned to Priscilla.

"Priscilla, would you mind riding ahead to tell your mother that Marius is on his way and will need a few minutes to clean up before he meets his guests? That's my girl. And would you kindly take this child with you? I need to talk to Marius. Alone."

"Of course, Uncle Jovinus," she said. "Come on Peter," she snapped. "I guess we're not wanted."

With the seven-year-old perched behind her, she turned her horse back toward the farm road, and urged him on to a canter. Her long auburn hair flew behind her. They watched as Peter swatted at it and then hid his face against her back.

Marius noted her irritation with satisfaction. He turned to the count in somewhat better temper.

"I apologize for our rudeness," he began. "You must think . . ."

"No matter," interrupted Jovinus. "I have always been aware that you children got your own way most of the time. Perhaps a little too much, even for an Ausonius."

They mounted and set off along the track across the meadow, Marius in the lead, his head high.

The count and Paulus Ausonius, Marius's father, had been friends all their lives. Marius did not know if the choice of Jovinus as his godfather was based on friendship, a sense of obligation, or respect for the man's piety. Every time the nobleman had come to the Ausonius villa before, Marius had been able to pay his respects, answer a few questions about his interests and opinions, and retreat. In all Marius's life, they had never had a private conversation, or explored the obvious spiritual connection between them.

What could the count have to say to him that demanded such high-handedness, such secrecy even? They barely knew each other. For all Jovinus knew, Marius might have been a secret pagan. They rarely saw him now that he lived far to the south in Arles[6]. Still, the Gallic aristocrat seemed to have come a long way to wish his godson 'Godspeed'.

Marius decided to be generous. He owed the man the benefit of the doubt.

When they reached the farm road, the Gallic nobleman trotted forward to come alongside him. His little goatee glinting in the sunlight, he reached across to pull on Troya's reins and stopped both horses. Marius looked at him in astonishment.

"Let's just walk the horses for a little while," suggested Jovinus. "I know that you have to get home, but I have something to say to you."

"Alright. What is it?" asked Marius. It occurred to him that perhaps God was going to speak to him through his godfather.

Jovinus glanced at Marius's saddlebags.

"As I said before, I am delighted to see you making such fine choices in your reading," he began. "As your godfather, I am, of course, pleased to see you reading one of the Gospels. . ."

"The Gospel according to St. John, sir," said Marius, primly.

There was a pause.

"I know," said Jovinus. "I said that before. By the way, does your father know you brought it to that cave? Books are expensive. It takes a very long time to make one, and I noticed you managed to get some dirt on that beautiful leather cover. I tried to get it off, but there's still a smudge. You had better not let Paulus see that."

Marius's jaw tightened. He glowered at the man. The count seemed to have the unhappy knack of making him feel like a little boy, and him about to become a military tribune!

Jovinus ignored the tension.

"But I was really struck by the other book, the one written by that ridiculous poet, Claudian, about General Stilicho. That scribe has no sense of proportion. He makes Stilicho sound like Alexander the Great, or Julius Caesar, or the Lord Christ Himself!"

"Have you read it then, sir?"

"I have not, but I've read some of his other writings. I know all about how the general has faced down all the enemies of Rome and wheedled his gorgeous yellow head right into the Emperor's own family. For goodness sake, Stilicho is not the Emperor, just his guardian! If someone doesn't shut Claudian up, he will probably try to tell us next that his hero has walked on water!"

"You know, count, that I am about to join the army myself. I was just trying to learn something about my future commander-in-chief. I heard he has had a most distinguished career. If I may ask, what do you have against him?"

"In my opinion he is a dangerous man because he holds far too much power and influence for one who is not a true Roman. Stilicho is a flagrant opportunist. His mother *may* have been a Roman, but his father was a full-blooded barbarian, a cavalryman, and a Vandal at that! People cannot

---

6 During the days of the Roman Empire, Arles was known as Arelate.

change their basic natures, Marius, everybody knows that. Vandals are liars to the core. Even other barbarians say so. It is wrong to have such a man in such a high position of influence. This Stilicho is acting head of the whole Western Empire, and, it is said, has always had designs on the Eastern half, as well. He has the backing of the army, and is guardian of our Emperor himself. Don't bother reading Claudian's trash. He's hardly unbiased, and is almost certainly on the General's payroll."

Marius was shocked. He stared at his godfather, his resentment gone.

"Lad," Jovinus lowered his voice although the nearest farm slave was a field away and the house still several minutes away, "we are all here to celebrate with you as you head off to join the army. It is a brave thing to do. Your family has served Rome well. They've done very well by it, too," he commented with irony, glancing around him. "But always remember, you are first and foremost a *Gaul*. Some of your ancestors, and mine, were here for a thousand years before Julius Caesar arrived. Be proud of that."

"I am, sir."

Jovinus smiled, acknowledging his vehemence.

"We are citizens of Rome, but we are not Romans. You must do what you are ordered to do, go wherever you are ordered to go, and serve the Empire and the Army as well as you can, but only insofar as what you do does not hurt us here in Gaul. Rome frequently has to be reminded that they are working for us, as well as us working for them, but even when they forget, we must remember. Always. Right?"

Jovinus's pale brown eyes searched Marius's face. "Rome does what Rome does for Rome's sake. That is always their priority. You and I are first and foremost Gallic. Do not forget that, ever. We here at home expect that from an Ausonius."

Marius nodded, his eyes shining.

"Also, I have high hopes of you, young man. You have a great future, and Gaul needs good men in high places. It would be good to hear from you from time to time. I'd like you to write to me. Perhaps my connections can be useful to you. Your father certainly thinks so, and it would be interesting to hear how you are getting on, especially if you end up in Milan, or Rome, or even Ravenna. Do you understand me?"

No, sir, Marius thought.

"Yes, sir," he said.

"I have an idea—whenever you write to your family, include a note to me as well. Your father can forward it on to me. I'm interested in the goings-on of the Empire. Always have been. Let me know how you see things. Alright?"

Marius nodded uncomfortably.

Jovinus's teeth gleamed whitely above his red goatee. "Now hurry up, lad. Your party is upon you."

Without a backward glance, he spurred his horse to a canter and rode ahead down the road. Marius followed, keeping Troya to a walk for the last part of the ride home.

Joining the army had not been his own idea.

As the youngest son, his role in the family business was not obvious. His father was still vigorous and involved with the daily running of the family estate. He was a part owner of two of the warehouses near the harbor in town, and he managed the local and international sales of their famous wines and Treveri horses. Marius's oldest brother, Julian, was well able to run the farm and manage the herds. His second brother, Lucius, was the lawyer and burgeoning politician of the family. Lucius was fast becoming a familiar face around the city of Trier, and Marius suspected his brother had his eye on provincial politics.

Marius's aptitude was more of a mystery, even to himself. He seemed to do well at everything, but had no particular drive to do anything much. His boyhood had been privileged and happy. He had worked in the horse barns and training grounds alongside his father, his brothers and the farm workers. He was reasonably knowledgeable about the running of the estate, but he had no passion for it. Once he finished his schooling, he had no idea what to do with the rest of his life. He had certainly not wanted to leave the beautiful, happy home he had grown up in.

It was his father who had decided that Marius needed to be pushed out of his cozy world. He would enter the boxing arena of an international career, a family tradition of sorts, one that could well lead to promotion to high places in any of the provinces of the Western Roman Empire, and the first rung on the ladder for Marius would be the army.

At first he had no interest in an army career, but he had had a year to get used to the idea. In the last few months he had begun looking forward to the changes and challenges that lay ahead.

It was not as if life would be easy for him—the army was still the army—but as an aristocrat, he would have a reasonably comfortable life and an officer's rank right from the beginning. As a military tribune, he could have his own house and servants. He would be a commander of men, adored by the ladies, deferred to by civilians, and respected by the officers above him. He would learn how to protect himself and his country, and make his family proud. It was a good Roman tradition that had brought other men to the peak of greatness, and shaped a thousand years of Roman history.

Becoming a military tribune had become a vision Marius now felt he could embrace, but there were other possibilities that came with life in the army, and it was these that had been giving him the nightmares.

Back inside the compound, he dismounted. He took a moment to rub Troya's nose and look into her beautiful black eyes.

"I will miss you," he said. "Will you miss me?"

Troya looked at him and nickered.

A stable slave led her away, and Marius slipped into the house. He headed for his bedroom, hearing along the way the distant sounds of laughter and raised voices. Someone with a ripe tenor voice started singing. He must be really late!

There was no sign of Count Jovinus. Either he had gone to change into his toga, or he was checking on his brother, Sebastianus, who would be well into the wine by now.

Priscilla was waiting for Marius in his room, his mother's newest choice of party garments laid out on the bed for him.

"What was that all about?" she asked.

"I'm not sure," Marius replied. "He doesn't seem to care for General Stilicho. He wants me to remember that I am a Gaul first and a Roman citizen second."

"He went to a lot of trouble to tell you that!"

"He also told me to write regularly."

"That goes without saying!" she responded, losing interest. "Mother says to go straight to the party room when you are dressed. Almost everyone is here already."

Marius nodded absently. He was remembering that Jovinus had told him to send those letters via his father. Arles was actually much closer to Italia[7] than Trier!

What could the man be up to?

---

[7] Italia is the name of one of the provinces of the Roman Empire. The country of Italy did not exist until more recent times.

CHAPTER THREE

THE LEGATE'S SHATTERING NEWS

Imperial city of Augusta Treverorum, Gallia Belgica
(Trier, Germany)
Late June, 405 AD

The Villa Ausonia, Marius's home, was located several miles north of the city of Trier along the Via Ausonia, the main Roman highway connecting the city to the Rhine frontier, seventy-six miles away.

The long lane between the Via Ausonia and the Villa Ausonia was lined with beech trees and passed through a stretch of woods and a series of gardens. A large, timber-walled compound at the end of the lane contained the main house and servants' quarters, the family's own stable and carriage house, and a variety of sheds and installations appropriate to an active farm house.

The main stables and more farm buildings lay outside the walls. Ausonius lands included pastures, hay fields, vineyards, a small orchard, gardens, a large exercise and training ground for the horses, and some wooded areas. On its longest side, the estate stretched a couple of miles along the river, and even included one parcel of land on the other side. A few small homes had been built along the river for the families of freed slaves, men and women who had elected to stay on and work for a share of the estate's income. Residents in these houses saw ships traveling down the river from the loading docks and warehouses of Trier on their way to the Rhine River, the North Sea, and distant ports, and occasionally, these ships would be transporting amphorae of Ausonius wines, a source of satisfaction to everyone who worked on the estate.

The wide wooden gates into the compound were open today. In truth, they were rarely closed except in times of alarm along the frontier.

No farm work was being done today except for the care of the livestock. Everyone was busy with Marius's party. Paulus Ausonius and Constantia Ausonia had had slaves and artisans refurbishing for months. They had replaced chipped tiles, painted walls, touched up wall murals that had started to fade, and spruced up every room open to straying guests.

The largest room had been transformed into the party room. Constantia had ordered the statuettes in the wall alcoves removed and filled with artistic arrangements of garden flowers. Domestic slaves had placed pots of trees and decorative statues in strategic places here and in the vestibule and atrium. Intricate fans dangled and twisted from the ceiling. Some had been in the family for generations. A few had come all the way from Antioch, Jerusalem and beyond.

Adjoining the party room was the peristyle, an enclosed outdoor garden with porticos along its four walls. These were common in warmer climates but rarer in this area. The gardeners had attacked this area with vigor months ago, pruning and fertilizing the shrubs. The pool in the middle of the garden had been cleaned up and restocked with carp. These were swimming lazily among the water lilies. The red-tiled roofs of the porticos had been replaced, and the walkways underneath supplied with new wrought iron benches and large urns of flowers. At the corner most distant from the doorway into the party room, a few children were taking turns twisting and swinging on several braided rope swings.

On both sides of the doorway into the party room, old marble tables held large amphorae of wine, white on one side, red on the other. Two stalwart servants served this to the guests passing in and out through the doors. The big hall was full of people. So was the peristyle.

Cleaned up and wearing a white toga, Decimius Marius Ausonius halted diffidently in the hallway just outside the party room, shy to become the focus of attention. The party seemed to be a noisy success already, but he knew that his entrance would be the signal for the official farewell to begin. Amused house slaves who had known him all his life grinned at him as they passed into the room. They were dressed in their finest livery, their large silver platters piled with finger foods.

Over in a corner the trio of musicians loudly strummed their instruments. Animated conversations around the room almost drowned out their valiant attempts to be heard.

"Hey, you!"

The vocalist, a heavy man in a blue tunic, wiped his sweaty brow and beckoned in the direction of a passing platter. The slave bearing the tasty treats did not notice him. The singer turned and said something to the flutist behind him, who snorted.

Marius's oldest brother, Julian, stood against a wall, holding one of the platters and eating from it absent-mindedly while his eyes scanned the room. He laid a heavy hand on the slave's shoulder and sent him back. He had not bothered to change from his working clothes, and his stalwart farmer's body looked oddly out of place with his patrician features.

Marius noticed his other brother, Lucius, holding court out in the peristyle with three young women and two of his friends. A fourth young man, hurrying to join them, called a greeting to Marius.

There were others there whom he recognized, including the prefect in charge of the Trier city garrison, a tall, grey-haired man named Marcellus Cavillicus. He was just re-entering the house with two cups of wine and was looking around for someone. A pretty woman inside the room waved to him, and he carefully maneuvered his way across to her with the wine.

The legate from the great fortress of Moguntiacum[8] up on the Rhine River had also been invited, but had not come. His aide had declined on his behalf, stating that Legate Carausius was away in Italia.

Marius was relieved. He had seen the man on a few occasions when he was in Trier. He was usually surrounded by his bodyguards. Quintus Carausius was formidable to look at, big as a bull, and reported to have no sense of humor. Marius knew he would soon be seeing much more of the legate. He was heading north to Moguntiacum tomorrow to begin his basic training.

---

[8] The fortress of Moguntiacum was located in present-day Mainz not far from where the Main River joins the Rhine River.

Paulus Ausonius's loud voice drew Marius's attention to a circle of men in full toga standing in the middle of the crowded room. The Garrison Commander, Marcellus Cavillicus, had heard him as well, and headed over to join the group, leaving his wife with her wine and her own friends.

"Jovinus, my friend," his father was saying, "Surely you cannot be suggesting that Rome pull any more men out of Gallia Belgica! The Alemanni, Franks and Burgundians are quiet right now, but no one can tell when something might get them excited again. And then there are the Saxon pirates. They have made it up the Rhine all the way to Bonn. It's only a matter of time before those long boats of theirs reach the Moselle. The navy and our border troops are all that keep them away! We need *more* military strength up here, not less."

Jovinus was shorter and slighter than the other men in the circle, but his rich, authoritative voice and superlative self-confidence always seemed to give him an edge.

"That is not what I said, Paulus. You must have heard the rumors that General Stilicho is hoping to reassert his authority over Emperor Arcadius and the Eastern Empire. You know he thinks he is entitled. I was merely pointing out that until the Court at Constantinople and the Court in Ravenna stop glowering at each other, we would be naïve to expect Stilicho to leave our troop allocations untouched. There are hardly any troops left in Italia except for the field army stationed at Pavia. Stilicho was recently up in the Alps trying to enlist more Rhaetians to join the army, but I heard he wasn't very successful. It is simply a matter of time before he looks elsewhere for more troops."

"But not at our expense." Marius's father ran his hand through his thick salt and pepper hair, his jaw jutting stubbornly. "He knows we must keep the frontier strong here. Even without the threat from pirates, there is always someone up in Barbaricum trying to make a name for themselves. If the High Command withdraws any more men, and word reaches the barbarian chieftains across the river," he paused, "then God help us."

"We need more protection in the south too," said the count. "We have been getting pirate raids along our coast as well. We have sent several delegations to Milan and Ravenna asking for help. The bureaucrats and generals haven't promised us anything. I guarantee you, though, if all the regions of Gaul stood together, we'd get further with the Imperial Court. They need to see that Gaul is united when they talk to us, or they won't take us seriously."

"Forget that!" growled one of the other men. "Rome controls by dividing and conquering. Whenever we do take a stand, they send an army against us. If it's our goods the pirates want, it's up to us to protect them. You southerners too, Count. We'd do better to arm ourselves and form local militias. If the Army does remove any more of our regiments and jeopardizes our safety here, let's reinforce it."

Commander Cavillicus had been listening quietly. He spoke up then.

"I don't think you'd better go there, Magistrate. That kind of talk would be seen by Rome as a greater threat than the Saxon pirates!"

"You've got that right," murmured another man.

"I meant no treason by my remarks, Commander," protested the magistrate. "Protecting our holdings and our property is just good business. You have to admit, Rome is making it harder for you to do your job all the time."

Paulus Ausonius clapped the Garrison Commander on the back. "My dear Marcellus, you know we're just talking. It is a chronic problem that needs a solution. Perhaps Count Jovinus is right. If we could form a Gallic business owners' coalition for the entire diocese[9], we might be able to hold our own against the bureaucrats in Milan and Ravenna."

The manager of the siege engine factory who owned several farms in the area, spoke up. "Any business coalition with the south usually results in us losing even more ground."

There were a few murmurs of agreement.

Sebastianus, Jovinus's slower, fleshier brother now bent forward, beaming around the group. "Yes, indeed. We ought to stick together."

Several of the men cast a frosty look at him. From the doorway, Marius grinned. He did not know if the man was stupid, drunk, or insensitive to the old north-south rivalries the siege engine plant owner had alluded to.

His mother had positioned herself close to the doorway where he stood so she could inspect the slaves and their cargos coming out of the kitchen. Constantia was a tall, slender woman with a wide mouth, bony nose and long-lashed hazel eyes. Her beautiful auburn hair, going grey now, had been inherited by all four of her children, but only Marius and Priscilla had her eyes. Today she was elegantly dressed in a graceful, dark blue stola with a gold band around her hemline and neckline, and was in a distracted conversation with Bishop Mauritius, an old friend. When she spotted Marius, she smiled and excused herself from the bishop to move through the crowd toward her husband.

A large group of young men and women poured noisily into the room from the atrium. This was the crowd Marius had grown up with, the children of the local privileged class. What good times they had had together; studying, partying, flirting, hunting, boating on the river, and watching the Reds and Whites compete in the local chariot races.

Priscilla was with them. She must have been watching for them from the vestibule outside. She had changed into a softly flowing green stola, belted in the same fabric below her breasts and again at the waist. The gown emphasized the woman she was becoming. Her auburn hair was now plaited and pinned high in some complicated pattern, and her lips and cheeks were red. It was an astonishing change from the tomboy who had charged home across the meadow earlier in the afternoon.

Several of the young men in the group were staring at her. Marius noticed Julian frowning. Big brother did not like this new direction either.

Priscilla was smart and fun-loving, legally of an age to marry, and from one of the top families in the Diocese, but Marius and his brothers were swift to discourage any signs of interest in her. She was the youngest child and the only girl. She belonged to them. No one was going to marry their little sister any time soon and without their wary approval.

It was time he made an entrance. Marius started into the room toward his friends.

"Marius, my son, come with me."

Paulus Ausonius grabbed his arm and steered him to a position directly in front of the musicians. Marius regretfully glanced at his friends, several of whom smiled and waved.

The slaves, ever alert to their master's intentions, quietly exited. The musicians stopped playing. The people in the peristyle and the stragglers who had been lingering in the atrium pushed into the room as the hum of conversation died down. Sebastianus hurried out to the peristyle to refill his wine cup. Some of the newcomers followed him, knowing that a libation would soon be called for.

Paulus Ausonius did not wait for them. He began his prepared remarks in his usual loud voice.

---

[9] In late Roman times, the Empire was divided into large territories called Prefectures. For more effective administration, these were broken down into dioceses, and then into provinces.

"Friends, thank you for coming. Today is a great day for Marius, but a very sad day for us, his family and friends. We are all here to say goodbye and good luck to my son, who will be leaving tomorrow to join the Roman Army. His mother and I are thrilled for him, and very proud."

Constantia, back beside Bishop Mauritius, discretely wiped a tear from her cheek. The Bishop patted her arm.

"You all know I'm a horseman," continued Marius's father. "Have been and always will be. I raise them and train them and sell them at a fair price, many times to the army. This young man is a colt of my own breeding. I am shipping him off up the Via Ausonia to be stabled at Moguntiacum where he will be broken in as one of their new military tribunes."

Marius felt his face go hot. Julian guffawed. There were a few other appreciative chuckles as Paulus smiled fondly at his son and threw an arm around his shoulders.

"Indulge me, folks. We have our little family jokes. To make this young man saddle-ready, he will be put through his paces and trained by some of the best military men in the world. Once he can go the distance, he will be ready to serve our Emperor and our Empire as many in the Ausonius family have ably done before him."

There was a commotion at the entrance from the atrium. A big man with white hair and a heavily muscled body pushed into the room. He was wearing a general's crimson wool cloak over his white dress tunic and trousers. It was His Excellency, Quintus Carausius, the legate from the fortress at Moguntiacum. It seemed he had returned from Italia after all.

Right behind him strode a tall young stranger with curly blond hair and level brown eyebrows. He wore a navy blue tunic and matching trousers. A large silver buckle on his belt gleamed against the dark fabric. Behind them in the atrium, several of the general's bodyguards were heading back out the front door. They would be fed in another part of the house with the servants and carriage drivers on a not-so-lavish scale.

Decimius Paulus Ausonius's speech came to an abrupt halt.

"Oh, here is the legate himself. Welcome, Excellency. We understood you were not able to make it today, or we would have waited."

He abandoned Marius and hurried over to greet his latest guests.

The legate clasped arms with his host. The young stranger stood a pace behind them and looked curiously around the room. He seemed entirely at ease.

"Please do carry on with your speech," said Carausius, "and then if I may have a word?"

"Of course."

Somewhat awkwardly, Paulus Ausonius walked back to Marius and placed his hand on his son's shoulder. Gone were the clumsy horse jokes.

"As I was saying, Marius will receive excellent training as a military tribune up at Moguntiacum. We will miss our boy very much. This young man, as many of you know, is no mean horseman, an excellent student, a considerate son, and a good judge of character."

Really? thought Marius.

"He has great gifts to share with the Empire, and for that reason his mother and I send him out with our blessing. He will join the ranks of the brilliant men who have built this vast Empire and enabled it to stand supreme for a thousand years. When you raise your cup to Marius, please raise your cup also to all those brave Roman soldiers who have gone before him, and who still serve the Empire today in peace and in war."

He raised his cup high, "A toast to my son Decimius Marius Ausonius."

Turning to Marius, he said "Marius, may you do yourself and the family name proud, and may God protect you and guide you in all you do."

He turned back to face the crowd. "And to the men in the Roman Army who serve so valiantly."

All over the room voices echoed his father's sentiment as they sipped their wine, the finest the Ausonius estate had produced in recent years. Marius stood awkwardly, longing for the moment to end. His eyes happened to meet those of the young man who had come in with the legate. As the youth raised his own cup, he seemed to smile at him sympathetically. Weakly, Marius smiled back.

"And now," said his father, "I believe his Excellency, the Legate of the Twentieth Legion and Commander of the fortress of Moguntiacum, has some words of his own for us all."

His Excellency strode up to stand with his host and his newest tribune-to-be. Marius started to steal away, but a firm hand gripped his shoulder and held him in place. He froze and glanced at the legate. Someone in the room tittered. It sounded like Priscilla. The General waited politely until the brief interruption was over. When he finally spoke, he did not raise his voice. Years of parade ground experience had made that unnecessary.

"Distinguished guests, I am pleased to find so many of you here on this special occasion. I recognize many whose families have been in the area for generations. You have been able to build good lives for yourselves. Rome has provided the peace and the good government to allow that to happen."

He waited. People nodded.

"I am from Gaul myself, though I have served with the army in both Britain and Italia. It is a wonderful privilege to live in Gallia Belgica, which is so fertile and beautiful. You have much to be grateful for."

"Here, here!" said Jovinus.

The legate continued. "Apart from a few raids, there hasn't been serious trouble with the Alemanni, the Burgundians and the Franks for a long time, thanks to the treaties worked out with them by our great Commander-in-Chief, General Stilicho ten years ago. Going even further back, there has not been an incursion as far as Trier for a generation. Instead, we have had good trade relations and mutual defense treaties with the Celts and Germans on both sides of the Rhine[10]."

One of the musicians yawned loudly. Marius turned and scowled at him.

"But that may be about to change."

The room suddenly got quiet.

"This young man, Marius Ausonius, soon to be a tribune in training with me, is joining the army at a most crucial time. There is a huge invasion coming upon us as I speak, an invasion that will dwarf all previous ones. I have just returned this day from the army's headquarters in Pavia where I have been meeting with General Stilciho and the rest of the High Command of the army. For months there have been rumors of trouble north of the Danube. These have been confirmed by Roman citizens in Pannonia and Noricum as well as our fort commanders along the Danubian frontier. A huge assembly of people is gathering on the far side of the river, preparing to cross.

"My fellow citizens, this is not just an army coming our way. This barbarian invasion includes the warriors' wives and children with all their belongings and livestock. They have abandoned their homes and are looking for new ones inside the Empire. They are going to be crossing into Roman territory soon, and they mean to stay. Their leader is an Ostrogothic[11] king called Radagaisus."

He looked around the room at the polite, puzzled faces.

"We had not heard of him before. He is from somewhere far to the north. We only know that he is a pagan and ignorant of civilization and our great faith. Although he calls himself the King of

---

[10] At the time of the Roman Empire, the Rhine River was called the Rhenus River.

[11] The Ostrogoths (east Goths) were so called because they were the eastern branch of the Goths. The Visigoths were so called as they were located further west, but both people groups moved from place to place over the centuries.

the Goths, there are other people with him as well, including large numbers of Suevis, Vandals, and even Alans[12] from beyond the Black Sea. There may be smaller groups with him as well."

"For fear of this invasion, many of our citizens in Pannonia have already fled west into the provinces of Noricum and Rhaetia. Unfortunately, we no longer have as much military strength in those areas as we used to. We have lost over eighty legions during the last fifty years due to previous invasions and the civil war, and it has taken a long time to rebuild them. The way General Stilicho and the rest of the High Command see it, our defenses will be seriously taxed to stop such a horde."

The people in the room stared at him, alarm on every face.

"How many of these barbarians are coming?" asked Paulus Ausonius, his voice shaky.

The legate acknowledged the questioner with a brief nod while continuing to face the crowd. "We don't know for sure. Some of our sources have estimated perhaps as many as a hundred thousand men, women and children with more groups joining them daily."

A buzz of consternation broke out all over the room. Many horrified eyes moved to Marius. He suddenly saw himself as they saw him—the lamb to the slaughter. He planted his feet farther apart, clasped his hands grimly behind his back, and willed himself to meet people's eyes.

"As you know, in 377 we had another such huge, unauthorized crossing of the Danube by Goths. That time it was mostly Visigoths. The next year at the Battle of Adrianopolis near Constantinople, we had to fight large numbers of their warriors, and as you know, it was a disaster. For us. We lost several legions, some top generals and, of course, even Emperor Valens[13], who commanded the battle himself. It took years for the army under Emperors Gratian and Theodosius to bring Roman dominance back to that area again."

A few of the older ones glanced at each other and nodded. They remembered.

"Those Goths are still here, right inside the Empire. Many of their sons have attended General Stilicho's Military Academy and become officers in the army. I must acknowledge that they have given us invaluable service in fighting the Emperor's enemies. For such loyalty we gave them the Valeria region of southern Pannonia as territory to settle in and defend.

"However, there were large numbers of Goths who did not enter the Empire at that time. They stayed north of the river in their own lands. Radagaisus seems to be leading many of the clans who stayed behind."

"Then why are they coming now?"

"The Huns. Again."

A thrill of excitement rippled around the room.

"In 378, the main body of the Huns was still far away to the east. They were more a problem for the Sassanid Empire[14] than for us, but since then they have continued to journey west and in doing so they have created havoc for the people they have encountered on the way. The stories you may have heard about the Huns' greed for gold and taste for destructiveness are true. They advance in their own disorganized way, destroying the settlements they encounter without mercy."

"A large number of them have got as far as this side of the Carpathian Mountains, and they have been attacking the Marcomanni and Suevi who live on the great plains north of the Danube. That is their kind of land."

He paused. They all remained quiet, waiting.

---

[12] The Alans originated in the vicinity of Iran.

[13] Valens (328-378) was Emperor of the Eastern Roman Empire, while his brother Valentinian ruled the Western provinces.

[14] The last Iranian Empire before the rise of Islam.

"A generation ago, the Gothic king, Athanaric, put up a prolonged fight against the Huns, but in the end he had to give up and leave his traditional lands. Today, there is no real, organized resistance that we can detect. It seems that this new king, Radagaisus, and the groups coming with him believe that it is easier to take on Rome than to face those vicious sub-humans. We have to prove them wrong. We have to show that the same power and determination that forged this great Empire is still here to protect it."

He seemed to have finished. There was a long silence.

"Where do your spies expect them to cross?" called the man who owned the siege engine plant.

"Our guess is that Radagaisus is going to try to get through the lowest pass in the Rhaetian Alps. That route will bring them west across Pannonia and Noricum and on down the Isarco River Valley toward Verona. From there they can easily reach Ravenna, Milan, Bologna, Florence, and Rome itself. These are still only guesses. There are other passes they could use, and they might split up. We won't know until they start to move."

The siege engine manufacturer looked relieved, until General Carausius added a warning.

"Don't assume that you are safe here, that Gaul is not threatened by this invasion as well. We believe that they are intending to go straight to Italia, but some of them may well try crossing the frontier at any undefended place they can find. They will soon discover that there are good Roman roads they can use on the other side of the Rhine River, roads built by our own soldiers centuries ago. They are still used by the Franks, Alemanni and Burgundians, and are still in good condition.

"Of course we have defensive fortifications and troops all along the frontier, but the sheer numbers of invaders is what makes this situation so bad. This is a serious threat to all of us. My job is to keep this area safe, while preparing to deliver new recruits to the Italian army to confront Radagaisus when he finally arrives."

Marius's mouth was dry. He glanced at his mother. She had gone pale and was leaning against the wall. Bishop Mauritius was looking at her with concern. He saw fear and worry on the faces of many of the guests. The legate had noticed, too. He shrugged.

"Young Marius may be in for more of a challenge than he had counted on, but a soldier's life is never free from the possibility of danger. We have lived through many crises in the last fifty years, and it seems that whenever we get through one, another comes knocking. The army will need every man it can get now, experienced or not. There is one more thing."

His audience seemed to hold its collective breath.

"We are beginning a major recruiting drive right away. The sons of veterans will be called up, and volunteers will be actively recruited everywhere, including from our allies in the areas across the Rhine. If Radagaisus decides to come in this direction, their lands and people will be threatened as well.

"I urge any patriot who wishes to enlist in the army to do so quickly. Emperor Honorius has signed a decree that in this instance, even the slaves of soldiers may enlist and fight alongside their former masters. That hasn't happened in hundreds of years. Those slaves who accompany their masters to battle are at risk anyway, and might as well have the chance to earn their freedom. Upon completion of their service, such men will receive their manumission as well as two pieces of gold to help them begin their new lives. That is how seriously Emperor Honorius and General Stilicho view this situation. And, of course, regrettably, all of us will have to face an increase in taxes. That is all."

There was a burst of discussion around the room. The General seized the opportunity to turn to Marius. He spoke quietly, but his voice carried.

"Young man, I need you to collect your things and come with me now. We are leaving for Moguntiacum tomorrow at dawn and I want you with me."

"No! " Constantia implored, hurrying across the room. The hum of conversation hushed again.

"Sir," Paulus Ausonius looked at his white-faced wife and son. "We needed some warning for this. This is Marius's farewell party, and as you can see, everyone here has come to bid him Godspeed. Can he not show up at the garrison as planned tomorrow morning? I will guarantee he will be there as early as you wish. Or, failing that, could he not meet you on the road out front as you and your men head up the Via Ausonia toward the frontier?"

"I apologize for not giving you previous notice, Ausonius. That was not possible since I did not arrive in Trier until this afternoon. I did not think I would even be here today, but this party was a good opportunity to speak to everyone. Unfortunately I cannot change my request. The matter is urgent."

He frowned at Paulus Ausonius, and then switched his gaze to Marius, who looked him in the eye and silently nodded.

"It's alright, Father. I will go with His Excellency now. He has big things to worry about, and I am, after all, under his command. Give me a little time, sir, and I can be ready. I just need to pack a few more things."

CHAPTER FOUR

STILICHO'S SON

~

Romulus Garrison, Augusta Treverorum
(Trier, Germany)
Late June, 405 AD

Marius sat alone inside the Ausonius's best carriage. It was driven by an elderly stable slave everyone had always called 'Stud'.

Up ahead, General Carausius and Garrison Commander Cavillicus rode side-by-side on horseback. They were followed by the bodyguards and the young stranger who had accompanied the legate to the party. Unlike him, Marius reflected glumly, they had all enjoyed some of that wonderful food at his party. As soon as he had reappeared with the two slaves carrying his trunk, Legate Carausius had rushed him away. He barely had time to embrace the members of his family and wave to his friends before the military party was off. Back at the house, his family and their guests would be carrying on with the party, eating, drinking, and talking a mile a minute, probably about the ominous news they had just heard.

By the time the legate's entourage finally reached the walled city of Trier, a few evening stars were beginning to poke through the dusk.

The city they were heading for had been one of the great Imperial capitals of the Roman Empire for most of the last hundred years, and as a result it was magnificent, unmatched by any other Roman city in the province.

When the Emperor Diocletian first divided the huge Roman Empire into four, more manageable sections, the Caesar governing the north-western quadrant was one of his generals, Constantius Chlorus. In 293 Constantius Chlorus, the father of Constantine the Great, chose Trier as his residence and the new capital of Gaul. Constantine the Great lived here and raised his family here. His sons, Crispus, Constantine II, Constantius II and Constans, as well as several of their successors, continued to rule the Empire from Trier for at least part of the time.

The city walls that surrounded Trier were ten feet thick and had crenelated battlements. Soldiers patrolled the walls from the four fortress-style city gates and from the circular watchtowers which rose above the walls at intervals. City planners had built in a wide buffer zone of parkland between the walls and the city itself. The amphitheater and the circus, both with the capacity to hold huge crowds, were located in this area on the eastern side of the city, while at the south end, one of the main temple districts had grown up in it.

Major decisions had been made in Trier that affected every part of the life of the Empire. As a result, in its heyday the city was larger and far grander than any other city north of the Alps. Many famous men, even Roman senators, had had homes in the area, while others had made the long trek here from Rome and more distant places to appear before the Emperor and his court. Such a visit was by invitation only, and arrangements would have been made months ahead of time. This required an extensive complex of government buildings in the heart of the city.

Like Sirmium, Antioch and Constantinople, its counterparts elsewhere in the Empire, Trier had to have institutions and buildings worthy of imperial patronage.

The preeminent example in Trier was the magnificent palace complex, and the most awe-inspiring part of it was the imperial audience chamber and throne room, the Aula Palatina. Here, the emperors came to receive visitors, reports and petitions. This long and very high vaulted basilica was ornately decorated from floor to ceiling, and had two tiers of large, arched, glazed windows high above the courtiers and citizens waiting below. Once the Emperor entered the room, everyone would have to fall to their knees, and from this lowly position observe him take his place on the raised throne at the end of the hall. The light from the windows high overhead outlined him with a halo of light, subtly hinting that he was more than just a man among men, but closer to the level of the gods whose statues surrounded him.

Other grand buildings in the city included the Barbara Baths and the Imperial Baths, vast complexes of heated pools and gymnasiums that were fed by aqueducts from the hills beyond the city walls. Many of the streets had arcades to provide protection for the citizens of Trier in stormy weather. Ordinary buildings along the orderly streets of the city gleamed with sandstone walls and red tiled roofs, while white marble clothed the imperial edifices, giving them a glorious luster in sunlight and moonlight. Even the cathedral[15] was a fair match in size and splendor to St. Peter's Basilica in Rome—Constantine the Great had been the driving force behind them both.

Few visitors were aware of another colossal construction beyond the city.

Mindful of the envious and ambitious barbarians across the Rhine who had a history of raids and invasions, the emperors built a massive land wall to surround the area. Immensely tall and more than thirty feet thick, this wall was guarded by Palatine soldiers, the best-trained men in the Roman Army. With the city at one corner of the base, the wall's irregular and elongated shape extended for fifty miles, following a natural line of hills. Within its protection lay cemeteries, government buildings, many private villas and some prime, agricultural land.

Trier had not always been so heavily fortified, but raids from the barbarians across the Rhine had changed Imperial defense strategy. Just in the last fifty years there had been several serious breaches of the frontier. Marius remembered the excitement in 395 when General Stilicho had secured peace in Germania by signing treaties with the Alemanni, the Franks and the Saxons. Instead of confronting the barbarians with demands and threats, he had broken with tradition, made friends with their chiefs, and persuaded them into a productive peace.

Trier was a glamorous and important city, but the tide was turning. By the beginning of the Fifth Century, it was deemed easier for much of the court's business to be handled from Arles, on the Rhone River. Arles was much closer to Milan, Ravenna and Rome, and it had a more agreeable climate. Count Jovinus and several other major landowners in the area had abandoned their local villas, and moved south to remain close to the politicians and imperial bureaucrats.

---

[15] The Roman Catholic Cathedral complex is still in use and is visited by thousands of tourists every year.

Because of the Moselle River, Trier would always be a major supply center for the frontier. It still had one of the most important imperial mints in the empire, an armaments factory which made siege towers, and a pottery industry. The climate was wonderful for agriculture and viniculture, and there was a long-standing history of horse breeding in the area. Still, its importance was beginning to ebb. It was galling for the locals to have to make the long trek down to the south of Gaul or even to Milan to present their petitions and business applications, when formerly it had been the other way around.

The legate's entourage finally reached the city gates. This massive structure, a three-story fort with high round towers on each side of it, had been built right into the city wall. It had been nicknamed Romulus[16] after one of the mythical founders of Rome. Its twin, Remus, stood guard on the south side of the city. Two other gates into Trier, the west one which guarded the bridge and the fortified harbor from the opposite bank of the Moselle, and the east gate at the amphitheater, were similar.

Romulus had two arched gateways, each so high that three men standing on each other's shoulders might just be able to touch the top. Traffic entering Trier used one gateway, traffic exiting, the other. Guards closely inspected visitors and carriages coming and going. Once through, the road continued straight for some distance across the buffer zone and then passed under a triumphal arch and into the city proper. Arcades along this road effectively screened from view Marius's destination, the city's garrison.

Stud halted the horses pulling the Ausonius carriage just inside the gate. Marius climbed down onto the cobbled road and looked around. Ahead of them, the riders were dismounting.

Behind him stood the imposing Romulus fortress with its offices, armory, and guard rooms. At this time of day, most of it was dark. Lamplight shone from torches that lined the walls of the long stone archway and from the guard's office inside the gates. Above him, soldiers on lookout duty would be facing out into the dark. Very soon, the guards would be lowering the portcullis and closing the gates for the night.

Through the arcade, Marius could see soldiers moving around the garrison. Lamps were being lit in several buildings. One blaze of light Marius knew came from the base's own small bathhouse.

Just ahead of him, General Carausius was talking to Commander Cavillicus. He handed his horse over to one of his men, and walked back to the Ausonius carriage.

"Tell your slave to take out your trunk and leave it on the road here," he instructed. "It will be taken over to where you are staying tonight. Two of my men will accompany the old man back to your home in case there are any robbers around."

Light from a passing torch briefly touched his white hair and illuminated his lined face.

"For tonight you will have to share accommodations with that young man." He pointed toward the blond stranger now chatting with one of the soldiers. "He's going to be leaving with us in the morning as well."

He seemed to want to say something else, but only added, "I'd like you to join us right away in the Garrison Commander's house. It's over there." He pointed to the left. "I'm sure you're hungry. Commander Cavillicus has agreed to arrange for some food for us, although it won't be up to your mother's standards."

Before Marius could reply, he had turned and walked away, disappearing through an arch in the arcade.

---

[16] Romulus still stands. It is now known as the Porta Nigra, and is a main tourist attraction in modern Trier.

Stud was grasping the heavy brown trunk with his skinny old arms. He had only managed to move it a few inches. Marius hurried to lend a hand. Together they heaved it onto the cobbled road. Two soldiers came over, lifted it easily between them, and walked off through the arcade. The young stranger with the natty navy tunic and trousers was gone. Everyone seemed to be disappearing.

"Nay worry, young master."

The old slave was smiling, the few teeth left in his mouth yellowed and worn. "We'll take good care of yer family while yer gone. Everthin' will be awright. Ye'll see."

His words were meant to be reassuring. Marius swallowed. Evidently news of the coming invasion had made it all the way to the slaves' kitchen.

Marius had not realized how uncertain and lonely he had begun to feel. Impulsively, he seized the old man's wrinkled hand in both of his and squeezed it hard, then hurried away down the road, furtively rubbing his eyes. Behind him, he heard the clatter of horses' hooves on the cobbled road and the squeal of the wheels as the carriage turned. Two minutes later the portcullis dropped with a thud..

At the end of the road, just before the triumphal arch, Marius passed through the arcade into the dark garrison. He stopped to orient himself, and stood listening to the sounds of the night. From the direction of the city came indistinct voices followed by raucous laughter. Closer by, he heard the low, melodic sounds of the Cathedral choir intoning a psalm. On the far side of the field, a watchman called out from the city wall. A voice answered from somewhere below. Wood smoke and cooking smells drifted toward him from the city.

Commander Cavillicus's real home was in a villa somewhere on the other side of the river. Marius wondered idly how often he got home to his family. His pretty wife had been with him at the party that afternoon, and Marius knew two of his children by sight.

The Garrison Commander's 'house' stood within its own fenced enclosure about two hundred feet in from the road. A guard stood at attention at the enclosure gate, barely visible until Marius was close to him. He waved him through, telling him to knock and walk in. Hesitantly, Marius did so.

The front room of the building was empty and in darkness, but beyond it there was a second room, large and well-lit. He ventured to the next doorway. The center of the room was clumsily furnished with couches and chairs and assorted tables, including a long trestle table which had been placed against the wall to his left. Lamplight flickered from bronze lamps in niches along the walls. At both ends of the room he could see two hallways leading away. The one on the right was brightly lit; the other was in darkness. As he stood there, a slave emerged from the lit hallway and crossed the room to place a small box on the trestle table. He inclined his head to Marius, and went back.

Marius could smell roast pork and the pungent scent of garum, a popular sauce based on salted fish blood and intestines that had seasoned in the sun. His mouth began to water.

"Would you like a cup of mulsum[17]?"

The voice came from the young man he was to room with. He was pouring himself a drink from a glass pitcher on top of a cabinet. It appeared that he knew his way around and felt comfortable enough to take liberties here. Neither the Garrison Commander nor the Legate of Moguntiacum was anywhere in sight.

"Yes, please."

Marius waited until he had the cup in his hand, wondering how long it would be before the two officers arrived. It was already late, and he was starving.

---

[17] Mulsum is a mixture of wine, water and spices. The one they drank here had a touch of anise in it.

"My name's Eucherius." The young man raised his cup in salute. He had an accent, a cultivated Italian one.

"Oh! That was the name of the first bishop of Trier. I'm Marius Ausonius".

"Yes, the grandson of Decimius Magnus Ausonius, the great poet who wrote *Bissula,* and *The Mosella*."

"You know them?"

"Of course! I studied them with my tutor."

"I'd heard that they were well-known. They are required studying around here, of course, but then you don't come from this area, do you?"

"No, but lots of people know *Bissula*; it's quite famous. How's this?" Eucherius struck a dramatic pose, his hand on his heart.

"Bissula, born to know the Danube,
Beyond an icy Rhine you leave your gods and home,
Enslaved but freed, Bissula, by your master,
He whose prize of war you are, whom you master. . ."

Marius, delighted, assumed the same pose and took up the verse.

"Missing mother, needing nurse, you never knew the power of a lady,
Your land's disgrace you know not, now that I've freed you, my slave.
Thus a Roman makes you to remain a German . . ."

Eucherius, grinning, chimed back in, joining Marius for the next few lines.

"So lovely, blue-eyed and golden-haired.
Your tongue calls you one girl, your body another:
Speak like a Latin, but flow as the Rhine. . .
My rustic little nursling,
You excel, Bissula, the doll-faced girls of Rome. . ."

"My sisters hate that part." interrupted Eucherius, grinning.

Marius frowned. "*'You excel, Bissula, the doll-faced girls of Rome. . .'.* I can't remember what's next!"

Eucherius shook his head sadly.

"Next is business."

The legate and the Garrison Commander had come in quietly and were smiling.

"Sit down, men. Bissula can wait."

Embarrassed, and smirking, Eucherius and Marius hurried over to sit on two of the chairs facing the General. Tall, spare Marcellus Cavillicus went to the drinks cabinet to pour two more cups of the spicy water-wine drink. Having placed one in front of his visiting commander, he hurried down the hallway to call to someone for refreshments, and then took a seat on a couch.

"You've met?" asked the legate.

Marius and Eucherius looked at each other, and nodded.

"It has been a long day, Marius," said Carausius. "Eucherius and I just arrived here this afternoon, and we had to leave almost right away to get to your party. Tomorrow we are leaving at first light for Moguntiacum. As you can imagine, I have a great deal to do up there. I know you are a rider, and I hope you are up to it. It's a three day trip."

Marius had never in his life ridden for longer than four hours, and his worry must have shown in his eyes.

"Eucherius hadn't ridden for long periods either, but he managed to make it from Rome to here just fine, didn't you son?"

The young man massaged his thighs, wincing. Marius laughed.

The legate smiled. "Eucherius is going to train with you as a tribune. I suppose he told you he is General Stilicho's son?"

Marius stared at them both with shock. Eucherius reddened.

"Oh come on, it's not that bad. I'm actually a good guy."

Commander Cavillicus snickered, and then winked at Marius, who grinned sheepishly. He was, frankly, stunned. General Stilicho was, next to the Emperor, the most important man in the Western Roman Empire! He had to force himself to concentrate on what Legate Carausius was saying next.

"You'll be sharing accommodations, so you'll have ample opportunities to compare your saddle sores and illustrious relatives, but I'm afraid we have no choice, any of us. When we left Italia two weeks ago, we knew that the barbarian invasion was halted, gathering strength on the far side of the Danube. Who knows when they will be ready to cross over into the Empire? They may have done so already. There is no time to lose.

"When we get to Monguntiacum, you will remain there for a time to receive your basic military training. As tribunes you will be given officer's responsibilities as well, under strict supervision, of course. I have to recruit as many soldiers as possible from both sides of the river, all the way to the coast. Many of these will be under your direct command. As soon as you are all ready, or sooner, you will set out for Pavia[18] to join the army in Italia. Any questions?"

He took a long quaff from his cup.

Marius could not think of one, although he knew by morning he would have a hundred of them. He did not think he would sleep a wink that night. Even the physical challenge that lay ahead of him dwarfed in comparison with the idea of rubbing shoulders with General Stilicho's *own son*, and there would be no opportunity to tell his family.

"In that case . . ." The Garrison Commander seized the chance to ring a bell.

The slave Marius had seen before walked in carrying a tray with hard boiled eggs, bread, cheeses, some garum sauce, and the pork they had smelt. This, he placed on the table in front of them. Another slave followed with large pewter platters and some knives and spoons. Once they had left, Commander Cavillicus invited them to eat, which they did eagerly.

As soon as the legate had finished eating his light meal, he wiped his mouth and banged his cup down on the table, causing Marius to jump.

"Time to begin the ceremony," he announced.

"If I may, General . . .," interrupted Commander Cavillicus, with a quick glance at Marius's plate.

"Go ahead," grunted his superior.

"Some of the local businessmen were asking me questions concerning the strength of this garrison and the frontier troops. The citizens were worried about recent Saxon raids down the Rhine River. Will the strength of the army in this area be at all affected by the troop build-up in Italia?"

Marius immediately pushed his plate aside to listen politely.

Legate Carausius sat back and looked at him apologetically.

"I'm afraid so, Commander. You have some of the best trained troops in the Diocese right here in Trier. A couple of years ago we had to pull complete legions away from Britannia, Pannonia and Gallia to fight Alaric when he rampaged through Italia, and it was only on account of General Stilicho's treaties with the people across the river and their dependence on trade with us that we got away with it. General Stilicho is counting on those treaties to continue to protect us, although I assure you, he is well aware that the western frontiers are under-guarded right now.

---

[18] The city of Pavia in Roman times was called Ticinum. It is located on the Ticino River in the western part of the Po Valley.

"As I said before, we've lost eighty legions since the invasion in 378. It's not just here that our troop strength is down. We are running out of places to look for more men. All along the Danube, the forts are operating with fewer men than they need. Now, with the Huns controlling more and more territory on the north side of the Danube, it is getting harder to recruit men from that area, too."

He inhaled, and then exhaled gustily.

"So the Army has a very serious problem—where to find men, let alone good men. The High Command, including myself, tried to think of some other way to raise troops. Allowing the army's own slaves to enlist is a serious decision, but the Emperor and General Stilicho do not see any other choice. And yes, some of your men will have to be withdrawn for the fight against Radagaisus. That is the reality we all face if the Empire is to make it through this latest crisis."

He did sound regretful.

"To tell you the truth," he continued, "if we were able to draft these Goths and their allies into the Roman army, it could be the answer we need for our own manpower problems. It's been done before. But first, we have to conquer *them*. Well, that's all I have to say. Is that all?"

The Garrison Commander nodded glumly.

The legate stood up and crossed to the trestle table. He picked up the box the slave had left there, and brought it back.

"Stand, Flavius Eucherius. Stand, Marius Ausonius."

The young men stood at attention as the legate took two small leather pouches from the box. Inside were their identity tags which they would wear henceforth around their necks.

The two recited an oath of loyalty to the Emperor, and then the legate handed them their new tags. Proudly, Marius slipped his around his neck. General Carausius handed him a pouch of coins, the traditional "viaticum", an allowance to help him defray his expenses until he received his first salary. He glanced at Eucherius who had not been given one. His fellow tribune must have received it before he had left Italia.

General Carausius saluted them. They saluted back smartly. He put on his red cloak, said his farewells and departed.

Marius and Eucherius looked at the Garrison Commander for instructions.

"He's staying in town overnight. Off you go, men," he smiled. "You had better get some rest before tomorrow. Good luck and congratulations."

He led them outside and pointed to a small house just a few doors away within the enclosure. The little building was dark when they entered. It smelled dusty. In the dim light it resembled the building they had just left.

Eucherius sneezed, and sneezed again.

Marius looked around him for a tinderbox to light the lamps along the wall. He could not find one. He felt along the windowsill and even above the doorframe. Nothing there but grime.

Eucherius hurried back out the door, rubbing his eyes and muttering something.

Marius waited inside for his vision to adjust. Something scuttled past him. Something else landed lightly on one arm. Alarmed, he brushed it away, wishing he were at home in his comfortable bed. Now he could make out the bulky form of a heavy trunk in the middle of the room. His own, he presumed.

He blundered toward the pitch black hallway on his left and followed it down to another hallway, moonlit from a couple of end windows. He turned right and found he was in another hallway with rooms down one side. Walking into the first room, he tripped over a trunk and stubbed his toe, almost losing his balance. He steadied himself and felt it quickly. The straps were in the wrong place, and it felt more worn than his. It must belong to Eucherius.

He left that room and went searching for another bedroom. There were three more little rooms along the same hallway and the one at the end contained a second bed. This room, he presumed, would be his. Something ran quickly past him on the dark floor. He jumped and yelped, retreating to the front room again.

He arrived just as Eucherius came back, accompanied by the two slaves whom he had seen in the Garrison Commander's house. They were all loaded down with candles, lamps, bedding, some pots and pans, cleaning supplies, and even a platter of food.

"Apparently someone forgot to give the order to clean this place up and get it ready for us," griped Eucherius. "But these men will have it in good shape in no time."

He sneezed.

The slaves lit lamps and busied themselves dusting, cleaning, and preparing the beds. In a short time, the house was presentable, though not necessarily bug- and mouse-free, and the food had been put away in the kitchen. Finally, the two of them were alone again.

"Give me a hand with this trunk, will you?" said Marius.

They struggled with it down the hallways, and eventually got it into the narrow room next to Marius's bedroom. The smaller rooms between the two bedrooms seemed to be for storage—weapons, uniforms, extra chairs, trunks and other odds and ends. Each bedroom had a small table with a lamp on top, a chamber pot stowed underneath it, a chair, and a narrow bed.

Eucherius left the room, claiming to be exhausted. A few minutes later, rough snores erupted from his bedroom.

Marius got into his sleeping tunic, but he was too excited to sleep. *What a strange co-incidence!* he thought. *This must be God answering my prayer.*

If he was about to become the close friend of the only son of the great General Stilicho, then his future prospects were very bright indeed. He must prove himself worthy!

He took the lamp, went into the storage room and opened his trunk. His pouch was on top. Pushing *The Gospel of John* aside, he carefully lifted out the other parchment book, *On Stilicho's Fourth Consulship*. His own illustrious relative, Decimius Magnus Ausonius, had achieved that elevated status only once! He lit two more lamps and sat on the chair.

It was not just information he was after now. This book had become personal. The more he knew about Eucherius's father, the better off he would be. He started to read.

Much of it was, as Jovinus had said, a mixture of extravagant praise poetically put—favorable comparisons between General Stilicho and Rome's previous great heroes, with unsubtle allusions to Stilicho's beneficial and godlike influence over Emperor Honorius and the grateful people of the Roman Empire. According to the poet, even his enemies regarded him as a brilliant general—selfless, tireless, and fair-minded.

There were even occasional glimpses of Stilicho as a family man.

One such mentioned Stilicho as a father: *"He was always with the army, seldom in Rome, and then, only when the young emperor's anxious love summoned him thither. Scarce had he greeted the gods of his home, scarce seen his wife when, still stained with the blood of his enemies, he hastened back to the battle. He did not stay to catch at least a kiss from Eucherius through his vizor; the anxieties of a general o'ercame a father's yearning and a husband's love. How often has he bivouacked through the Thracian winter and endured beneath the open sky the blasts that slow Boötes sends from Mount Riphaeus. When others, huddled over the fire, could scarce brook the cold, he would ride his horse across the frozen Danube and climb Athos deep in snow, his helmet on his head, thrusting aside the frozen branches of the ice-laden trees with his far gleaming targe. Now he pitched his tent by the shores of Cimmerian Pontus, now misty Rhodope afforded him a winter's bed. I call you to witness, cold valleys of Haemus that Stilicho has often filled with bloody slaughter; and you, rivers of Thrace, your waters turned to blood . . ."*

It was stirring stuff, if you were a soldier, but what if you were that son? He reflected on what he already knew about the famous general.

Eucherius's father was the son of a Roman lady and a dashing young barbarian cavalry officer. After graduating from the Roman military academy, Stilicho had come to the attention of Emperor Honorius's father, Theodosius the Great. While they were both young men, they had fought side by side against invaders and one usurper to the Western imperial throne. A genuine friendship developed between the two comrades in arms.

After Theodosius became Emperor, he gave his favorite young niece Serena to Stilicho as a wife, and by all accounts the beautiful and popular princess had gladly agreed. It had been a happy marriage. The two had three children, Maria, Eucherius and Thermantia.

Emperor Theodosius and his own beloved wife, Aelia Flaccilla, had also had three children—two sons, Arcadius and Honorius, and a daughter who had not survived. The families were close, connected by Princess Serena's royal blood and the friendship and shared military experiences of the two men.

After Aelia Flaccilla died in 386, Theodosius married a second time. His second wife, Justina Galla, was the beguiling daughter of a previous emperor, Valentinian. Justina Galla also bore three children to Theodosius—one daughter and two sons, but this time, only the daughter, Princess Galla Placidia, survived. Her younger brother John died at birth in 394, taking the Empress, Justina Galla, with him.

Two-year-old Galla Placidia was now motherless. Although she had her own staff and household to take care of her, whenever her father the Emperor was ill or away from Constantinople, her cousin Serena and her uncle Stilicho kept a close eye on her.

Then, in 395, a year after the passing of his second wife, Theodosius the Great also died.

Galla Placidia, daughter, grand-daughter and sister of emperors, became an orphan at the age of three. By then General Stilicho had become the most powerful military man in the whole Empire, his position seemingly unassailable. He emerged from the Emperor's bedroom claiming that Theodosius's dying request to him was that he act as guardian for his surviving children, Arcadius Augustus, Honorius Augustus, and the little orphan princess, Galla Placidia.

No one disputed Stilicho's right to be guardian over Honorius and Galla Placidia, both still very young, but Arcadius was eighteen, shortly to be married, and had already served as co-Augustus with his father in Constantinople. He and his courtiers strongly protested that he did not need a guardian.

Honorius, however, was only ten. Days before his death, the Emperor had elevated the boy to the status of co-Augustus over the Western half of his Empire, so General Stilicho, Princess Serena and their own three children set off for Italia with the child Emperor and his younger half-sister, Galla Placidia.

Three years later, in supposed compliance with another of the deceased Emperor's alleged dying wishes, Serena and Stilicho's oldest daughter, Maria, was married to the Emperor Honorius. Both of them were only fourteen years old.

Seven years had since passed, and they were still childless. It was even rumored that Maria, a quiet, pretty blond, was still a virgin. Some blamed Princess Serena for that. She had told the young couple when they were first married that there was no hurry to consummate the marriage, and Honorius, an indolent young man, seemed to have taken that to heart. Now twenty and sheltered all his life from both danger and unpleasant business decisions, he seemed to have little drive to do much of anything.

A couple of years later the palace announced the engagement of Serena's and Stilicho's son, Eucherius, to Galla Placidia. Uncomfortable jokes began to circulate that if Arcadius Augustus, the Emperor of the Eastern Empire, had not rushed into marriage with the beautiful daughter of General Bauto, Stilicho and Serena would have tried to marry him off to their youngest daughter, Thermantia, many years his junior.

A brave and wise hero of the Empire? An ambitious schemer with his eye on the Imperial throne? Who was this man?

Now Marius knew why his godfather had sought him out. Wait till Jovinus learned that he was closer to the centers of power than any of them could have imagined! It was a long time before he finally got to sleep.

CHAPTER FIVE

THE WAKE OF DISASTER
∾

Pastor Rhodus's Village in Barbarian Germania
(Modern Poland)
Late June, 405 AD

Theona awoke after a night of troubled dreams. The sun was up, and the birds were singing blithely in the trees overhead.

At first she thought she must have fallen asleep beside the brook, but her father's worn brown cloak lay across her, and his pouch had somehow ended up under her head. Groaning, she sat up. One swift glance around her brought it all back—the Huns, the torched village, Gruda!

She was heartened by the sight of the cloak and pouch. Her father was alive. He had come and had been with her, but where was he now? His sturdy walking staff was gone and he was nowhere in sight. Had he gone into the village?

Her body was itchy from insect bites she had received, and her stomach was growling, reminding her that she had not eaten for a long time. With the horrors of the previous day still so fresh in her mind, she decided she could bear the itchiness, the hunger, and the thirst. Discomfort was no great hardship when compared to an arrow through the throat!

Pushing herself up onto her knees, Theona peered through the gap in the trees. The buildings she had seen flare up the night before were now blackened ruins. Smoke was still rising from them. A few, miraculously, were still standing. She could not see any sign of the Huns. She sat back against the log, trying to decide what to do. Apart from the birds' songs, it seemed to be quiet.

Hunger and thirst reasserted themselves insistently. She tried to ignore them and think. The only sounds she could hear were the normal ones one would expect from a tranquil forest on a summer morning. Perhaps it would be safe to move after all. Awkwardly, she got up, collected her father's cloak and satchel, and began her exit. The previous evening's breeze had stopped. Sounds would carry.

Carefully, she picked her way along the deer trail, pushing the undergrowth aside and bending to pick up tiny twigs and dry leaves in her way, trying to keep her balance and plant her feet as soundlessly as possible. The trail had not been made by humans, and she found herself grabbing at branches before they could swing back and strike her. Her father's cloak kept snagging on branches.

One snapped off. She froze. A startled bird flew suddenly out of the bushes a few feet from her, but there was no matching human alarm.

After a while, she reached the birch trees beside the path and cautiously leaned forward to look down the path. No one was in sight in either direction, so she stepped out. Through the clearing ahead she could see the village, but now she could also see the body of the neighbor who had been killed the evening before.

Gruda had two children already, twin boys who were in Theona's class, and another youngster on the way. She and her husband had been members of Pastor Rhodus's Christian community for a year and were real assets to the village. Gruda had been a seamstress, and had taught Theona and the other women some of her fancy stitches. She, in turn, was excited to be learning to read and write.

Theona hovered a few feet from the entrance to the clearing, watching and listening. She moved closer. No-one was in sight in the clearing, and nothing was moving. She crossed to the woman's body and bent down to say goodbye. Somberly, she wondered about the fate of the unborn child nearing term inside the woman's body. It would surely die too, was perhaps dead already, a double tragedy. She grieved for them and for the rest of the family. Had any of the others survived? She would soon know.

It was now or never. She rose, and started toward the village, twisting her head from side to side and whirling around every few feet to look for Huns. No-one challenged her.

Signs of the attack were everywhere. A few houses still stood, their turf roofs showing signs of having smoldered and gone out. The Huns had not bothered to try torching them again. The contents of all the houses were strewn around. What the raiders did not want, they had tried to ruin. They had broken pottery, axed furniture, stamped on food supplies and urinated on clothing. Theona passed snapped arrows and broken bows. Outside her own house she recognized the spinning wheel her mother had tried to repair. It had been hacked to kindling. She stared at it blankly, hardly able to fathom such malice.

A man's arm lay on the path in the middle of a large blood stain. The rest of his body was missing. Theona shrank past it, recognizing the arm of the farmer who had greeted her from the field when she had gone fishing.

He had stayed. She had left. If she hadn't gone fishing!

Wolfric's companion of the previous day, the young black and white dog, limped toward her, whining. She fondled his head, then stooped and gave him a comforting hug. His name, she remembered, was Gideon. When she moved on, the dog followed her.

From the direction of the Great House she heard voices, Gothic voices, and hurried on. She found her people near the Great Hall. It had been badly damaged.

Losing the Great Hall, not that large in spite of its name, was going to be harder than losing her own home. It was the heart of the village where most of their community life took place—the worship, the laughter, the dancing, the stories they told, and the knowledge they had shared with one another. It was where her father had preached, and where people went just to be together, and it was where everyone who arrived to join their ranks stayed until a new home had been built for them.

The structure was not completely gone, but the loft had collapsed, the roof had been torched, and the animal stalls underneath them had been broken down. They were empty, of course. The goats had been chased away. Abigail was probably gone, too. She was a prize the Huns would most certainly take.

The bodies she had been dreading to see on her walk through the village were here. Survivors were busy retrieving the dead and ministering to the wounded. She watched as several men began to prepare a mass funeral pyre in the village square.

Abraham, Gruda's husband, passed her carrying the body of young Turtik. His twin boys were holding hands and following him, their eyes and noses streaming. Theona averted her eyes. She was not ready yet to tell them about Gruda. She saw several other children, including one of her students. They must have been working in the fields or playing in the forest when the attack had happened. They followed close on the heels of the distracted adults, their misery and confusion ignored by their silent elders in the midst of mind-numbing activity.

One little girl saw Theona and headed hopefully towards her, holding her arms out, but Theona shook her head and turned away. She had to know about her own mother and brother.

Pastor Rhodus stopped in front of her, his blue eyes dull, his beard dark with tears. His trousers and tunic were heavily soiled with blood and dirt.

"Did you find mother?" she asked, "and Wolfric?"

"Mother, yes," he affirmed. His chin quivered. "She's over there."

He pointed.

Her eyes followed his finger. Her pretty mother lay at the end of a row of bodies, all of them with their arms crossed neatly over their breasts.

"She seems to have tried to get Wolfric and herself to the root cellar. They didn't make it." His voice was flat.

Theona frantically scanned the row of bodies for her brother. She didn't see him.

"Where's Wolfric, then?"

"We haven't found him yet. Perhaps he got away."

Theona suddenly remembered the sounds she had heard the previous evening. A dog had yelped and a child had cried out.

"Or perhaps the Huns took him with them," she said. "They do that, don't they? Don't their women like pretty blond children as slaves?"

"Theona!" He held his hand up sharply to stop her from talking.

She had never heard such agony in a human voice. She could not endure his grief. She left him and ran to her mother's lifeless body, dropping to the ground beside it.

The beloved face still wore a look of terror. The rope marks around her mother's arms and the axe wound in her chest told how she had died. If she had been running with Wolfric, then she had turned to face her killer at the end. Her frightened brother must have seen it all!

Theona gently lifted her mother's head onto her lap and began rocking back and forth, massaging the pale cheeks and forehead to try to erase that awful grimace, afraid that that look would remain seared in her memory for the rest of her life. The futile act of love she was giving seemed to help her, if not her mother.

She was suddenly very angry. Why had this happened? This was so utterly wrong! She was infuriated at the stupidity of it all. If she could face the man who had done this outrage, she would have hurled his axe back at him without a second thought.

Had anyone in the village heard her warning yodels? Had she been too far away? Had they all taken their safety too much for granted? Because the village had been unprotected, because no one had stayed to guard it, because she had gone so far, her mother and many others were dead, and perhaps her little brother was, too. She knew in her mind that the disaster was the fault of the Huns, but she could not stop herself from wondering if there was anyone closer she could blame. Anger and vengefulness might compensate a little for the loss of two of the three most important people in her life.

Wolfric had been their special delight. There was such an age difference between them that she had been more like a second mother to him than a sister. Sometimes she and her parents had speculated whether Wolfric actually knew which was which. After all, mother and sister were just words to a young boy who had always had them both at his beck and call.

She watched her father continuing with the grim job of searching for bodies. Occasionally he would stop to pray with someone. Darric appeared around a corner and spoke to him. Pastor Rhodus pointed in her direction. The young man walked over toward the growing line of bodies, among which lay his younger brother Hartman, and his sister Edwina. He stood in front of them for a few minutes, his shoulders heaving, and then crossed over to crouch in front of her.

"Theona, I am sorry about your mother and Wolfric," he began.

She did not answer him and did not look at him. Sympathy would threaten her composure. She felt safer with anger.

"He was a beautiful child, so sweet, so full of life. And Fiona. . ."

"We don't know that my brother is dead yet, Darric," she interrupted in a hard voice.

"No. You are right. We cannot give up. Gandric watched the Huns leave. He thought they had a couple of children in tow, as well as Abigail."

"Why didn't he stop them, then?" she shouted. A few people glanced her way and hurried on.

"He couldn't, Theona. They had got him already. I was with him when he died."

Theona was ashamed. Gandric had been an old man, a secret Christian most of his life, and he had begun to blossom in the little village under the protection of her father's leadership, but she *needed* someone to blame, someone to hit out at.

"Does he know for certain that it was Wolfric?"

"No. He couldn't see who the children were—you know his eyes haven't been so good lately, and he was badly wounded and terrified. But it gives us hope. The best thing you can do for your brother now is to pray for him, Theona."

"For what?" she stormed. "You saw them, Darric. If Wolfric is not dead, then he is their prisoner, which might be worse. Maybe the Huns sacrifice children to their gods, if they have any. Maybe they hurt them for entertainment. I saw them, Darric—even the young ones were scarred. They believe in pain. They will sell him into slavery, or teach him evil ways. If only I had taken him with me!"

"You could not know what was about to happen."

"But God knew, and God should not have let this happen!" Her voice was rising. She lowered it. "At the very least He should have given us some warning that this was going to happen!"

"Perhaps He did, and we didn't want to know."

"And now I have lost two of the best people in the world." The tears she had tried to suppress slipped down her cheek.

Darric leaned across to wipe them away. "Theona, someday, God willing, you will have children of your own. Maybe we will have them together. Life is not over. We are still alive and we have to keep living. We will begin again."

She glared at him. How dare he say such a thing at a time like this!

"I don't want to begin again," she said stubbornly. "I want life back the way it was."

She knew he was trying to find something, anything to say to her that would help. She could have written his next words herself.

"If Wolfric is dead," he said at last, "then perhaps he has been spared something worse, and if he is alive, and with the Huns, there is hope. Perhaps he'll get away from them. Maybe someone will rescue him. Maybe there are some good people among them who will adopt him, or maybe he will be sold to a kind master. We don't know, and we have to pray. It's all we can do. Keeping up hope is better than yielding to despair."

His eyes moved to where some of the men were just lifting the bodies of his brother and sister to be carried to the pyre. He stood up, watching. Theona knew he wanted to go and felt a twinge of compunction.

"You have lost Hartman and Edwina. I am sorry."

"Thank you."

One of the older women, the portly village potter, came over.

"Come on, Theona" she said. "There's work to do. People need to eat. Your mother would be helping us with the food. Why don't you come help us, too?"

Theona ignored her, and stubbornly continued to rock her mother.

"Come," said Helga firmly, placing a hand on her shoulder, "You cannot help your dear mother. She's gone to be with God."

Theona hit the hand away angrily. "Give me a little time," she snapped. "I just want to be alone with her. It's the last time, Helga. Go away."

The older woman looked at Darric in appeal. He nodded. She turned and left. Darric left as well.

Alone once more, Theona noticed her father and another man watching from a distance. She guessed that they were waiting to take her mother's body to the funeral pyre. Fiona's merry blue eyes were now lifeless, the mobile mouth still frozen into that grimace. Her mother was gone. Really gone. She was holding just her empty shell.

She gently bent to kiss the dear face for the last time and carefully wriggled out, laying her mother's head and shoulders back onto the ground. Then she got up and walked over to Pastor Rhodus and the other man.

"Gruda's body is at the entrance to the path into the woods," she said.

"We know," her father replied. "It's been dealt with."

"What about the baby?" she asked, anxiously. "Is there anything we can do to save it?"

"I don't know," fretted her father, glancing at the other man. "Perhaps."

He frowned, thinking.

Theona wandered away. She spent a few minutes questioning everyone she could find about Wolfric. One of the other children, a beautiful little six-year-old girl, could not be accounted for either. The girl's young father was distraught. Together they set out to explore the fields, the orchards, and the areas of the woods where the children liked to play. Finally, Theona gave up and returned to join Helga and the other women.

She found several of them working together in one of the houses. It was made of stone, and was from a much older time. Today it had become the focus of activity as several of the women and one man tried to put together a communal meal. Soon Theona was busy stirring pots and chopping vegetables.

Little by little the level of conversation rose. It became clear that the members of her community were all considering abandoning the village for good. Except for her own father, all of them were Goths. Most of them expected they would have to return to their former villages, although when they left as Christians, they had made a clean and public break from their pagan culture. Though disaster had decimated their numbers and ruined their village, none of them really wanted to go back to their former homes. Most of them devoutly wanted to stay, but that option did not seem possible.

They did not know where the Hunnic camp was, or if they would be back. All they knew about the Huns was that they were nomads, virtually homeless. Their behavior had spoken for itself—they were malevolent, destructive, and very, very good at what they did.

The survivors were in no position to defend their territory. If they stayed, they would need larger numbers, strong walls, and a skilled military force. These, they did not have. Their former warlords would be able to give better protection for such a situation. It seemed that this experiment in Christian community was about to fail.

The children had been given the task of rooting through the gardens for vegetables and transferring out the contents of the root cellar. They were sorting everything into piles for each family. Almost all of the goats had been found and brought back, and many of the chickens and geese had survived and been found as well. The crops in the field would just have to be abandoned.

An elderly couple, Badwila and his wife Gildefarica, decided to remain behind. Their youngest son had suffered serious wounds during the attack, but he was still alive. He could not be moved, and they would not leave as long as he survived. It was a heroic decision since the man had little hope of a good recovery, and there was always the danger that the Huns would return, but the couple had insisted. Their fellow villagers spent time fortifying the stone home and carrying in provisions. They also left what weapons they could spare, just in case.

At noon the women served up a huge meal with a generous quantity of ale to wash it down. There was none of the usual joking and laughter. Soon they would have to torch the funeral pyre and leave forever.

Pastor Rhodus had one final message to them as their spiritual leader.

He urged them to release their loved ones, their anger, and their dashed hopes and dreams into God's hands before they left the village. He reminded them that Jesus, the Head of their little community, had also experienced death and separation from loved ones. Their Lord and Leader, like them, had had his life and his world come to an end, but that was not the end of the story. God had a glorious future planned for His Son and the ones he had redeemed. A new Kingdom had been started on that day, and their loved ones were a part of that. God would avenge their untimely murders, and He was the only one who could bring good from such horrific evil.

"Do not risk your soul or your faith by holding on to unforgiveness or bitterness or thoughts of revenge," he said. "Those are traps that will steal your joy and wound your soul and even your body. Forgiveness is the best revenge," he said. "Forgiveness alone allows you to keep your freedom, and it has the power to change everything, even the hearts of our enemies."

The adults listened intently and took a little comfort. They knew that what he was saying was true, but hard, very hard. However, living without the peace and joy in their lives that they had as followers of Jesus would be harder still. This was just one more battle they had to fight.

Theona was in no mood to listen to any message about faith and forgiveness. Her mother might be alright, but she was not, and her brother was not. Her innocent faith was rocked to the core. If this could happen, anything could happen. It felt right to be angry, at least against God since she could not reach the Huns. It was not fair!

One by one they lit a piece of kindling and poked them into the gaps in the funeral pyre. The flames took hold, and then flared to begin cremating the bodies so lovingly laid on top. Sobbing and wailing broke out again. The pyre would take hours to burn, and few people had any stomach to stand watch to the end. One by one, the families made their preparations to leave.

Gruda's husband, Abraham, loaded her body onto their wagon, and he and the twins set out for the home of a wise woman Pastor Rhodus knew of in another village. Abraham was drawn and red-eyed, but determined to find out if the baby could be saved. Theona hugged the boys and waved goodbye to them as they left. As other groups became ready to leave and headed down the paths into the dense forest, she sadly waved them off, too.

It was early evening before Pastor Rhodus was ready to leave, and they had been breathing in the smell of burning flesh from the funeral pyre for hours.

Theona fled into the woods to look for her bucket and fishing net. When she came back, she brought two trout. These she left with Gildefarica. She and her husband had never had so much food in their lives!

While Theona was away several families, including Darric, his mother Anna and his surviving sister, Edrica, had made the decision to travel with Pastor Rhodus and try to rebuild their community somewhere else.

Theona was pleased. It meant she still had a family of sorts, and perhaps there was safety in numbers. She wondered, though, if it would ever be possible to resume life as it had been. All of them were different people today.

CHAPTER SIX

FRIENDS IN ADVERSITY

Poland
Late June, 405 AD

Twenty-two people left the village with Pastor Rhodus, the survivors of five families. Everything they could bring was piled high on every cart they had left. They were also able to bring along a few of the chickens and goats, and Gideon, the young black and white dog who had limped up to Theona when she first returned to the village.

She had lost sight of him for a while, but during their final meal, she had seen him again as he eagerly snatched up the scraps of food her neighbors threw to him. When she had left to go fishing in the afternoon, Gideon had gamely limped after her into the forest. Once she had settled herself beside the brook, she took a look at his lame foot, but could not see any burrs or cuts. She thought the limp would pass.

Gideon had a long drink and a joyous romp in the brook, and then settled down beside her and went to sleep. When they returned to the village, he stayed nearby and watched her pack their cart. It seemed he had made his choice. Now, as this last group to leave the village headed into the forest along one of the paths, Theona called to him. He wagged his tail and followed her, his warm brown eyes trustful.

After some discussion, their group had decided to head south toward a range of mountains they knew about. Perhaps the Huns had not reached that area yet.

That evening they did not go far. The first village they came to had heard about their misfortune, and gladly put them up for the night. Wherever possible, they avoided the better known roads and river fords to follow lesser-known trails recommended by local people they encountered. These routes were often narrow and more arduous, but they felt safer. The last thing they wanted to meet was another fast-moving band of Huns.

The group also went out of its way to avoid having to spend nights in the forest. There were other dangers there and little comfort after a day of walking. In this vast wilderness of forests, hills and marshes, there were no big towns and few fortified villages, just a myriad of scattered settlements along the roads and rivers. The Celts and Germans who lived in here were all free farmers trying to eke out a living from the hard clay soil, trusting in their own resourcefulness to keep their families alive, and in their clan connections for protection and a wider sense of belonging.

With hardship and loneliness their normal lot, most of them were happy to offer lodgings in their homes, their barns or their community's Great Houses. Hospitality was a fundamental Germanic value, so much so that in many villages the refugees would have been welcome to stay until their hosts were themselves destitute.

The fugitives were often invited to stay and settle nearby. Pastor Rhodus, as the leader, politely refused. An inner urgency drove him to keep moving, so Theona and the others tramped doggedly after him.

They heard about a walled town named Wodenvale in the hill country to the southwest. Here, they were told, they would find another Christian pastor, a Goth named Sigeseric. Perhaps they could stay there for a while until they could decide what to do next.

They decided to head to Wodenvale.

A high, wooden stockade with gates on three sides protected the town. The road running past Wodenvale was the artery that had given it its prosperity, and its need for the walls.

Inside the town, one-story, wattle and daub buildings crowded together in narrow streets. Outside the walls, the farms and pasturelands belonging to the people of the town spread out in all directions. It had not been a good year for the crops in this area. Blistering sunshine had been blazing down for weeks. The horses and cattle huddled in the lee of the forest, which stretched in every direction.

The Christians were coming down the road toward Wodenvale when the second Hunnic attack occurred. Fortunately for them, the raiding party approached the town from the opposite direction.

It was market day. Dozens of families were selling their wares in the central square just outside the village gates. The new band of Huns, a much larger group than the one which had attacked their own village, tore up the road from the south and bore down at full speed toward the open gates yelling their war cries and launching deadly volleys of arrows.

People started screaming. Panicky vendors and shoppers swarmed towards the open gate, abandoning their livestock and stalls. The townspeople barely got the big gate closed before the first Hun reached it. A dozen men, women and children caught outside did not make it in on time.

A horn blared from the nearest watchtower, and was joined by blasts from the other three. At the first distant sound of the savage yells and blaring horns, the Christian refugees fled into the forest beside the road. Theona and her father hid behind a massive, rotting tree trunk that lay on the forest floor. Her father held her slight, trembling body close to him, his brown cloak pinning her down and covering them both. Gideon crawled in beside them, and they laid their hands on his trembling flanks in silent comfort, and waited.

Others in their group hurried deeper into the forest. Darric and one of the boys climbed a tree, and hid in the leafy canopy. From their concealment, they could hear the fearful din—the thunder of hooves, the yells of the Huns, the uproar from the terrified people and animals left outside in the marketplace, and the shouts of the town's defenders.

The Huns were unable to breach the walls of the town, but they were adept at setting fires. Flaming arrows soaked in pitch soared into Wodenvale, setting some roofs on fire. Residents raced from building to building in a desperate attempt to smother the flames before they took hold. A few people were injured by Hunnic arrows shot blindly over the walls.

When the town's defenses proved too stout for their impatient temperaments, the Huns turned to ravage the land. They fired an unguarded grain field close to the town, and stampeded the horses and cows. The women and children rushed to deal with the fires inside the town while the men prepared for battle. By the time they were ready to emerge and put up a fight, three of the grain fields were on fire, and the attackers had charged off up the road, heading for the next ill-fated settlement.

The market square was devastated, animals and people lay dead and wounded, and every coin and bright trinket abandoned in flight had been seized as booty. The Huns pounded down the road right past the hiding Christians, and on out of earshot.

From the roots of the fallen oak, Theona had one brief glimpse of the war party riding by. She hung tightly on to her father until they had passed. After a few moments of silence, Pastor Rhodus pulled her up, called to the others, and they hurried toward the shaken town. Already residents were running out with buckets of water and blankets to fight the flames destroying the grain crop. The new arrivals ran to help. Everyone understood that the loss of the crop would be catastrophic.

People poured into the area from the surrounding fields and forest, dozens of them, rushing to help wet down the blankets and smother the fire. There were no questions and no explanations while they all worked together to save the crop—it took everyone's determined effort to stop the advance of the flames and keep the fire from spreading to the town walls or to other fields and the forest. Only when the danger was past did the people of Wodenvale stop to welcome the new arrivals.

Their host for the next week was the village warlord, a man named Helerix. He insisted on putting the newcomers up in the loft of the Great Hall attached to his spacious home inside the town walls. The twenty-two newcomers joined his extensive household for meals every day, and grew accustomed to hearing his warriors coming and going in the room below where they all slept. They were just glad to be safe behind the town's walls, and have a bed at night.

Sometimes Theona sat with Darric and Edrica and watched the duke's henchmen as they practiced their wrestling and swordplay. At other times they joined the spectators outside the gate to watch the competitions in archery and axe tossing. Duke Helerix encouraged this: the men of the town were worried and disheartened, and new spectators, especially the two unmarried girls, seemed to stiffen their morale.

A pagan himself, Duke Helerix now had eight Christian families under his protection. He sent for the man Pastor Rhodus was seeking.

Sigeseric was a Gothic bishop who had travelled a long way from his monastery in the province of Moesia in the Eastern Roman Empire. He had brought with him three copies of the books in the Gothic Bible, and was teaching Duke Helerix to read. The warlord enjoyed spending time with the bishop and learning about the outside world, and was proud of this new ability to make meaning out of symbols and encounter new thoughts.

The good bishop embraced Pastor Rhodus and his people, and welcomed them into Wodenvale's small Christian fellowship. He insisted on giving Theona's father one of his precious parchment Bibles to replace the one that had been burned in the raid on their village.

For the first week after the Hun's attack, the newcomers joined the townspeople as they cleaned up the damaged fields and market place and did odd jobs around the town. Most of them did not attend the funeral pyre for those killed in the raid. Their own losses were still too recent.

Pastor Rhodus and Bishop Sigeseric began to spend time together in discussion and prayer. In the warmth of this new friendship, Theona watched her father begin to emerge from his stoic grief. One night as she lay trying to sleep, she overheard her father talking to Sigeseric in the lower room of the Great Hall and he began to cry. His muffled whoops of sorrow were audible for several minutes before the bishop led him outside and there was silence once more.

Theona lay in the darkness struggling to keep her own grief pressed down. She had never tried to push her pain onto her father because he had so many other people to stay strong for, but she missed

Wolfric and her mother dreadfully. Now, her sorrow erupted in a torrent of tears. She writhed among the blankets, muffling the noise as best she could and sobbing until her stomach and her head ached.

She longed to talk to her mother about everything that was happening. She ached for the comfort of her arms, the chance to share a laugh, a new accomplishment, a thought. But her mother could not come; Fiona was gone from her life forever, and so was Wolfric. She would never again be able to cradle him on her lap until he fell asleep, to tease him and chase him around the village, and to teach him all the things she knew.

He was probably waiting for them to come save him. How would he feel if he knew that his father and his big sister were moving away from him, not closer? This thought was the most unbearable of all.

Where was he now? How was he doing? Was he being treated well? Were they misusing him or teaching him to be as violent as they were? Had they carved their scars into his soft cheeks? She would storm a Hunnic camp single-handed to get him back if she could.

She was helpless, and felt useless. There was absolutely nothing she could think of to do to change the past, the present, or the future. She cried until there were no more tears, just a weary despair.

Her fear of the Huns had gone deep. She still had nightmares haunted by the youth whose arrow had passed so close to her in the woods, and the faceless man who had lassoed, and then axed her terrified mother. Now she wanted desperately to get as far away from all that as she could. Only then, she thought, would she be able to forget and build a new life. But by doing so, she was leaving her little brother behind.

The people of Wodenvale were struggling with their own future. Everyone talked constantly about what to do. Somewhere in the area they had an elusive and savage enemy. Many times the Christians from Pastor Rhodus's community were stopped by the townspeople and asked to recount their story. The enquirers listened carefully, shook their heads, and moved on without comment.

In the evenings many of them came together in the Great Hall to debate their options. To stay or to leave was just the start of the heated discussions. If they stayed, how could they protect themselves, their fields and their animals? If they left, where would they go? The people would argue, approach a decision, and then change their minds. Opponents even came to blows over the right strategy, and had to be separated by some of Duke Helerix's henchmen.

"Why should we leave? How can we leave? These are our homes, our land," a man would lament.

"That's right," another man would reply, "Our families are buried here. My great-grandfather started our farm. To leave without a fight is out of the question. We've been raided before, and we've survived. We just rebuild and go on. That's what we Goths do."

Someone would then turn to glare at Pastor Rhodus, clearly accusing him of cowardice.

Someone else would shout out, "The Huns are different, you ox head! They are wolves. They do not farm the land or build anything. They don't want our land. They only want to destroy everything we've built. Do you want your children to die here because you are too stubborn to leave?"

"If we banded together with the other clans and villages in the area, we might defeat them." This suggestion would inevitably come up, and be rebutted quickly.

"How do you protect yourself against people who have no homes or villages, no fear of death, and no other purpose in life than to destroy what other people have built?" the rebutter would protest. "No, no, my friends. Banding together won't help—we don't know where they are, but they know where we are. They will come back. Our crops will be destroyed, then our orchards, and eventually the town itself. They will drive us out by war, or starve us off the land."

"Perhaps we could make a treaty with them?"

This would be said tongue-in-cheek, and everyone would laugh. The idea was preposterous, but it lightened the tension. Many of them had heard the harsh sounds the Huns made to one another, and very few thought that it could be a real language. These people were clearly too different, and perhaps not fully human. There could be no treaty.

Into the circular discussion at last came a moment of clarity. The road past Wodenvale began to fill up with more fugitives. They told of other towns and hamlets which had been attacked. These people were heading south to join a Gothic chieftain, a king named Radagaisus. He was planning to lead an invasion across the mighty Danube river and on into the fabled Roman Empire. Radagaisus's camp was reported to be southwest of them on the banks of a great river. Among the thousands of Goths with him were large numbers of people from other places, groups they had never even heard of.

According to the rumors, Radagaisus and this multicultural multitude were thought to be already on the verge of crossing, but if the people of Wodenvale hurried, they should be able to reach the safety of this massive exodus before it moved out of reach. Time had now become a factor in the decision to leave.

The townspeople met once more, and voted to leave. A few families chose to stay in the town, knowing that their own future might well be death. The ones who were intent on going faced the same risk. The Romans had always proven themselves ruthless toward previous invaders. This was not an easy choice.

Pastor Rhodus and his fellow believers had no stake in Wodenvale, so their decision was easy. They would go with their new friends until God blocked their way.

On a cold, rainy day in early July, Duke Helerix, head high, led his people out through the gates of Wodenvale, abandoning it forever.

Dozens of families followed the mounted warriors. Most of them walked, or drove covered wagons. Into these they loaded everything they held dear as well as the necessities for a long journey. For Pastor Rhodus's people, it was history repeated.

Bishop Sigeseric managed to procure a wagon for Theona and her father. It had belonged to a farmer who had been killed in the marketplace attack. They were fortunate in the ox they were given— he was young, and calm enough to handle Gideon's frisky presence nearby. They named him Enoch.

Other townspeople provided wagons for the rest of their group. Wodenvale now had its own caravan heading off to join "the King of the Goths" somewhere to the south.

They followed the ancient dirt road toward the south. Eventually it led them to and through a gap in a mountain range. On the other side lay flat lands. Here the going became easier until it was just an ancient hard-packed streak across a vast plain. This was perfect territory for marauding Huns, but they encountered none. Local cowherds and shepherds pointed the way toward the great Danube River, which formed the boundary between Barbaricum and the Roman Empire.

They met other caravans heading in the same direction and fell into line together. This was Suevi territory now, flat and seemingly featureless, with occasional vast, sandy patches. Radagaisus's camp was said to be somewhere along the north-south axis of the river where there were fords they would be able to cross.

One day they saw an aura of light to the west. Word spread that the light was reflected from the great river ahead. One day more, they were told, and they would find Radagaisus's camp.

Excited, they surged forward.

CHAPTER SEVEN

MARIUS REPORTS HOME

Moguntiacum Legionary Fortress
(Mainz, Germany)
Early July, 405 AD

E*steemed Pater and Mater, Julian, Lucius and Priscilla,*
I finally have a minute to myself to write to you. Since this is also the first opportunity I have had, I think you ought to be proud of me!

Your son and brother is now officially a military tribune. You should be glad that I was made one before we even left Trier, because, based on what I have experienced so far, I may very well have backed out of the whole thing and run home with my tail between my legs.

The legate and Commander Cavillicus made Eucherius and me tribunes in a private ceremony the evening of my party. Eucherius is the young man in civilian clothes who came with His Excellency to my party—you may have noticed him. It turns out that he is training with me at the Fortress of Moguntiacum, and you'll never guess who he is! He is General Stilicho's son! He is good company, and we are becoming friends. He seems very popular with the soldiers he meets. Everybody likes him. Our senior tribune suspects he is part of the General's recruiting drive for the war with the Gothic king, Radagaisus.

It is good to have an active, varied life again, because the three days we were on the road to get here were torture. How I missed my own saddle!

We left the city at dawn after taking some food in Commander Cavillicus's garrison quarters. It felt very strange to ride past the Villa Ausonia without stopping or seeing you all. For the few long moments we followed the property line along the road, I was tempted to buck and bolt, but with the legate's body-guard close behind and beside me, I dared not. I felt like one of the young colts we break and train. More accurately, I felt like a sheep being guided to the shearer.

We rode on to Noviomagus Treverorum where we stopped to take some lunch and a break. Then we left the river behind and cut across country. We got all the way to Dumnissus before stopping. I was ready to fall off the horse, I was so sore. Eucherius says you get used to it. He has been riding since he left Italia a few weeks ago, and he is a city boy. When we finally make the long journey to Pavia, I will probably remember the one from Trier to Mainz with fondness.

We stayed the night at the military guest house in Dumnissus, and then left on fresh horses the next morning. I said to His Excellency that I wished I could substitute a fresh me, but he didn't laugh. One of his men told me he's heard too many such silly jokes before. I hate to be boring.

We rode to Bingium that day, and arrived at the fort in the middle of the afternoon. The Bingium fort stands at the intersection of the Rhine and the Nava Rivers, and you have to cross a bridge to get into it. General Carausius wanted to meet with the officer in charge to discuss their defenses and warn them of another possible major invasion. Eucherius and I were left on our own, so we wandered around to take our first look at the Rhine and the fort. It was an eye-opening experience, one I wanted to share with you all.

The Rhine is wider than the Moselle and the current is quite fast, especially farther upriver toward Mainz. Looking downriver toward Koblenz, we could see solid cliffs on both sides of the river. These cliffs make it impossible for an army to cross from the barbarian side. From here on upriver, though, the land gets flatter, although the current is stronger.

His Excellency says that if the Gothic invaders were to cross the Rhine, it would be somewhere between Mainz and Worms, which is farther upriver. In the past, groups of barbarians have been able to assemble upstream on the Main River and come by boat down to where the Main intersects with the Rhine. Then they storm ashore at Mainz where the land is flatter. Occasionally, when the Rhine freezes, people can even walk across it there without too much trouble. That happens quite rarely, so that, at least, is one possibility that is remote.

Now I understand why the fortress of Moguntiacum is so immense—it used to have two full legions housed in it to defend the frontiers and this weak spot in particular. It was the first time I realized how vulnerable we are in Trier, and I really understood the importance of the land wall around the area. You can be grateful that Radagaisus is set on going to Italia. Pray he doesn't change his mind!

Eucherius and I got to talking to some of the soldiers at Bingium. A lot of them seem to be of barbarian origin themselves, mostly Franks and Burgundians. They live on our side of the river in their own villages. When we told them about the coming invasion, they got quiet. It seems they have been undermanned for a few years and are already struggling to cover all the territory they have to guard. They are really stretched and there is no back-up anywhere close.

Their concern got me really worried, too. The legate told Commander Cavillicus that the generals are going to pull even more Palatine guards out of our area and send them off to Italia for the fight. I thought I had better not mention that to these border guards. If the barbarians ever captured these forts and fortresses, the people of Mainz could be cut off from retreat, and the way to our own city would be open at least as far as the land wall. After that, the next line of defense would be the soldiers within the Trier garrison.

The next day we rode to Mainz thirty miles away. Sometimes we could see the river from the road, but most of the time it was somewhere out of sight on our left.

It was an amazing experience to ride into the fortress of Moguntiacum. There is just one legion here at the moment, and it is not at full strength. Some parts of the fortress are not used at all.

As soon as we arrived, His Excellency started shouting for his senior officers, and they all hurried straight into a meeting. We were not invited to join them. Our own officer training starts tomorrow.

We turned our horses in at the stables, and spoke to one of the legate's aides. He told us that our house was not ready yet—some slaves were still cleaning it up. Our trunks hadn't arrived either, so we were at loose ends. The town of Mainz? Or the fortress? We decided to explore the fortress.

Moguntiacum is huge, near a hundred acres, I believe, and we are about twenty minutes away from the river. On one side, where the Twentieth Legion have their quarters, it is quite busy even when the patrols are out, but once you leave that side of the base it gets quiet. There is some activity beginning *there now as soldiers and slaves clear out the empty barracks and prepare them for the new recruits, but when we first walked through it, it felt eerie. You could almost feel the ghosts of soldiers who had been stationed here centuries ago. It made the hair on the back of my neck stand up.*

Eucherius found an old army knife under a cot. The blade is rusted, but it has some bright bits of glass in the hilt. It looks to be of barbarian design, probably bought with some soldier's hard-won wages. It is not particularly valuable; nevertheless, he is keeping it as a souvenir. I am going to look for a new one in the town and buy it with some of my viaticum. There will be a place for such a knife on my new army belt when I get it.

After looking around for a while, we walked back to the Porta Praetoria gate and on into the town itself. It is actually closer to the river than the fortress, and has walls and watchtowers along the river bank. The harbor is fortified, as you would expect.

Mainz is not anywhere near as large or impressive as Trier, of course, but it is a good size, though a little rundown. We were pleased to see that it has public baths, an amphitheater, a circus, a decent-sized cathedral and lots of shops and tavernas. There are some interesting things to buy here, including old weapons, helmets and shields, souvenirs of distant postings and some decent barbarian products, including pottery and glass. Very few luxury goods, though. I did see a fur cloak I might buy.

I spotted an obelisk to Isis, Queen Goddess of Egypt, and got excited. It has been here for centuries! There were a number of other pagan temples in the same part of town. They aren't used much anymore, of course, although there is an active Mithraum somewhere out in the countryside. Apparently some of the country boys still kill bulls and conduct ceremonies in secret there, even today. There is so much to see, even in a place like this! Moguntiacum itself is named after an old Celtic god. Did you know that?

We walked over to the bridge that spans the river and went some distance across it. There were Roman soldiers guarding both ends. On the far side of the river you can see Roman-style villas and several of our old roads built during the days when the frontier was a lot farther away to the north. We were told that many of the Roman villas on that side are now owned by traders and veterans, both Romans and barbarians. There are even tradesmen in town here who make their living building Roman-style homes in Barbaricum. I must find out if we are allowed to go across the river to explore on our own.

When we returned from our explorations, the carriage with our trunks had arrived, and our new house was ready. Eucherius and I are staying on the empty side of the fortress not far from the Praetorium. The house is quite large, and although the legate is happy to give us two houses, one each, we have decided to stick together, at least for now. All that empty space around us is a bit disquieting. Besides, we like each other.

We have also been assigned a slave, a brute of a man whom I've yet to see working. We think he drinks full-strength wine. I wonder if they are expecting him to train alongside us. That will be interesting!

Legionaries from the Twentieth Legion say the legate is apparently expecting to put all the new recruits in the empty barracks on the same side as us. They are not at all ready for all of us. There really is not enough food, uniforms or weapons here and the officers and legionaries of the Twentieth Legion are busy with their own full-time responsibilities. Our overall impression is that the army is hard-pressed to keep up with the needs. According to one of the bodyguards I was talking to on the journey here, the legate has his hands full. There has been peace for so long that the provincial governors are unwilling to spend more tax money on defense maintenance and improvement. There is mounting concern about how he is going to do it. Maybe this threat of invasion will help them loosen their purse strings a bit more.

To tell you the truth, I am astonished and worried by how weak the whole frontier area seems to be. Take note, dear family, the land wall notwithstanding. When the High Command pulls out more troops from Trier, how will the ones left behind manage to patrol the full length of that wall, let alone defend the towns beyond it?

I hope to be able to make it home before we leave. It will take a long time for us to recruit and train a good sized fighting force. It is thrilling to think that I will be a part of such an important operation. I can only hope I can give a good account of myself, as Pater said.

I forgot to tell you that I have a couple of books I borrowed before I left. They have been useful, but I don't want to take them any farther without your permission. Write soon, and let me know.

Your favorite brother and son,

Marius

CHAPTER EIGHT

THE ROMAN ARMY

Moguntiacum Fortress on the Rhine Frontier
(Mainz, Germany)
Early July, 405 AD

There was a loud noise somewhere. Marius ignored it. One of the slaves would take care of the problem. The banging continued. He rolled over, and almost fell off the narrow bed.

He became conscious of voices talking—they sounded far away. The next minute someone was hitting him. Who? . . . What?

Angrily, he sat up. Eucherius, still wearing his sleeping tunic, was looking anxiously down on him, lamplight flickering behind him. Marius looked around in confusion at the small bedroom with its plain, whitewashed walls. Then he remembered where he was.

"What's the matter? What was that awful noise?" he demanded, grumpily.

"The door, Tribune. Me, pounding it. Get up out of that bed now! You are not going to be late for the parade ground on your first morning here."

The voice was not his new friend's. Someone else was standing in the doorway holding a lamp. Marius swore, and leaped out of bed. In the lamplight he could see a handsome man with curly dark hair and a mustache. Dimly, he discerned an officer's uniform.

"This is Tribune Barbatio, Marius. He is the man assigned by His Excellency to train us."

Marius glanced out the window. It was still dark. It must still be very early, way too early to be up. His whole body was aching from the three day ride.

He walked, yawning, over to his new leader. Tribune Barbatio's eyes narrowed. Marius straightened up and saluted just in time.

"Sorry, sir. I haven't slept so deeply in years. I don't think anyone told us you would be coming to visit so early."

Had he seen a brief smile? In the wavering lamplight it was hard to tell. Perhaps not. The man's voice when he spoke was definitely unsmiling.

"You are a Roman soldier now, Ausonius. No excuses unless you are asked for one. And this is *not* a visit."

"Yes, sir."

"There is water for your ablutions in the kitchen. And towels. I also sent your slave—the lout was hung-over by the look of it—to fetch some food for you. He should have had that arranged last night. I'll have a word with the officer in charge of him."

He glanced around. "You need to get yourselves set up properly in this . . . this mausoleum. You can speak to the quartermaster about whatever he can provide and get the rest in town."

"Yes, sir!"

"The bathhouse is on the other side of the base, but you won't be able to use it until at least tonight. Do what you have to do here, and be ready as soon as you can. You have a big day ahead. I'll wait for you outside. You can eat later. And, by Jove, you need to throw the fear of God into that slave. You won't have time to look after your own needs. I wonder if . . ., yes. I think I had better be moving into the house across the road to keep an eye on you."

He turned and walked briskly away. Marius and Eucherius rushed to get ready. Marius, in particular, did not want to be last out the door after such an inauspicious introduction. They dashed out onto the empty street together. It was still dark. In the quiet morning they heard two roosters crow, one after the other. Tribune Barbatio was nowhere to be seen, but in the house across the road they could hear doors opening and shutting.

"Come on," said Eucherius.

They found the senior tribune, still holding the lamp, prowling upstairs. There was no sign of anyone else around, and the place was largely unfurnished.

"Not too bad," he commented. "It will do until you have to leave. I'll speak to my wife and the legate."

He marched them ahead of him through the deserted street. The red tiles of the barracks roofs fired with the first rays of the sun. When they reached the parade ground, the grassy field was empty. They looked at it, perplexed.

A trumpet sounded a few streets away.

"Where is everybody?" said Marius.

"The legionaries of the Twentieth will be out here shortly," Barbatio replied. "For the sake of efficiency, you and your men will have to train ahead of them, at least for a few weeks. The men of the Twentieth Legion don't need clumsy beginners getting in their way. They have a lot to get through in the course of their regular duties, and for them parade ground is just the routine start of a new work day.

"It will be your responsibility to make sure your men are up and here by the time I arrive in the morning. I don't care how big or bad your fellows are, insist on promptness and obedience from the start. It will help you maintain discipline on the long marches when you are alone with them."

He must have noticed their anxiety, because he grinned. "Don't worry. You will have the force of the whole army behind you. I understand that by tomorrow, some of your men will already be here on the base, so I will drill you again in the first routines tonight. I see no point in letting the new recruits know just how raw you really are! Once they hear your names, some of them will be eager to find your weaknesses. Don't let them find any. Even you, Eucherius, won't get far on your father's name alone."

"Sir!"

"In two weeks I want you ready to conduct parade drills on your own. If you find good potential optios among the new recruits, you will eventually turn this duty over to them. But not too soon. No one, especially me, respects a shirker or someone who does not put everything he's got into the performance of his duty. Is that clear?"

"Yes, sir."

"In the mornings you and your men will receive training in basic procedures and strategy, and weapons and combat training. In the afternoons your men will all have work assignments around the base. Make sure you get reports from their supervisors. Tribune Eucherius, you will be spending the last three hours of the day with the recruiting staff until further notice–I believe the Army plans to broadcast your name far and wide to attract ambitious upper class officers, not to mention fortune-seekers. Legate Carausius will be taking you off base with him fairly often for a while. You'll get to see something of this area. Marius, you will work with me.

"Right. Now I want you to run around this parade ground six times. When you have finished, go home and eat whatever that fellow has managed to find or fix for you. I have something I need to do. I will meet you there in an hour."

He saluted and left.

They set off around the perimeter of the field, well-matched in height and speed, but Marius had the edge in stamina. After the second lap, he was slowing down to stay with Eucherius. By the end of the fourth lap, even he was panting, and Eucherius was struggling to keep going.

Soldiers began to appear from the side streets. They stood on the periphery and shouted insults and encouragement at the two youths pelting past them, sweating in their civilian tunics. As the number of spectators increased, so did the din of their conversations.

Marius and Eucherius pushed on. By the end of their fifth lap, officers were purposefully walking towards the center of the parade ground, and the watching soldiers followed, lining up in formation. The two new tribunes struggled on until an officer waved a frustrated arm in their direction and they staggered off the field. Immediately, orders rang out and the legionaries' parade drill began.

Chests heaving, legs wobbly, they stood and watched for a few minutes, impressed as the soldiers moved in unison to the shouted orders. All too soon *they* would be the ones calling such orders.

"Do you know how to do that?" asked Marius, admiring the precision of the men performing before them.

"I've seen it done a few times," panted Eucherius, "but I hear it is more difficult than it looks."

"Oh, great."

"We'd better go."

Weary and hungry, and still sore from the long ride to Mainz, they trudged back to their house. Tribune Barbatio was waiting out on the street. Inside, on the triclinium table, they found two plates of sausages, bread and cheese.

"From my own kitchen," the senior tribune said. "Your man isn't back. I've eaten."

He took a chair and straddled it.

Marius and Eucherius quickly began to eat, afraid that he would order them up and out before they had finished.

"By the way, well done," Barbatio said conversationally. "I'm impressed. I wanted to see what condition you were in, and what effort you would put into the run when you thought I wasn't looking. I really did not think you would be able to complete six laps, but I'm pleased you did. We might actually manage to make decent tribunes out of the two of you."

Marius cast a sidelong glance at Eucherius. This man was tricky!

"From now on," Barbatio continued, "I want you, Marius, to run at your own pace. Eucherius needs competition, not company. There are bound to be things you are better at than him, and other things he is better at than you. That is true of everybody, and as officers you will need to remember that. Find out your men's strengths and weaknesses and use that knowledge judiciously."

"Yes, sir."

"Parade drill and battle training, though, is all about learning to work as part of a team. The Roman Army has vanquished its enemies over the last thousand years precisely because we have been capable of forging units from men whose backgrounds and inclinations are different. Most of the people we have defeated could not, or would not, do what it takes to make that happen. That is one of the reasons we almost always win against bigger men and stronger forces. That and our own stubborn refusal to accept defeat."

"Why couldn't we win at Hadrianopolis, then?" asked Marius. General Carausius's reference to the disastrous clash between the Goths and Emperor Valens's legions in 378 had been bothering him.

Tribune Barbatio made a face.

"The men in charge were too confident and more interested in making their reputation than in protecting their soldiers. The Generals should have insisted that Emperor Valens wait for Emperor Gratian's armies to arrive—they were not far. Instead they went ahead and began the battle without him. They also underestimated the enemy—not a good thing to do. The barbarians have been learning our ways for centuries, and they are getting to be pretty good at using our own strategies and tactics. Now we even take some of their best men and train them in our own military colleges. If they ever get their own warriors to work together the way we do, we will be in trouble."

He stood up. They hastily rose as well.

"Come on. Let's go get you both kitted out with your uniforms and weapons. Tomorrow when you do your laps, you will be wearing armor."

Marius and Eucherius looked at each other in horror.

The quartermaster grumbled the entire time they were in his domain.

"I don't suppose you brought any cuirasses or helmets or weapons with you, did you?" he scowled, noting the cut of their clothes.

Marius shook his head.

"I brought one of my father's winter cloaks and a dagger," replied Eucherius.

"Good. God knows how many new recruits may be coming," snorted the man. "I don't have near enough equipment in stock to outfit them all."

They said nothing.

He eyed them both expertly and brought out several tunics, both long-sleeved and short-sleeved, and several pairs of tight-fitting long trousers. From a nearby crate he lifted two padded leather jackets and tossed them carelessly on top of the other items. Then he disappeared into the back and came out with a cart full of metal armor. After rummaging through these, he dumped two chain-mail cuirasses on top of the counter.

"Here. Try those on. Put on the leather jackets first, of course. You'll also need leather caps to protect your heads under your helmets. I've got some here."

He pried open a wooden crate and fished through a supply of leather skull caps, then stared at their heads and disappeared into a back room to reappear with two helmets, different from each other.

Eagerly the tribunes put on the padded jackets and chainmail coats that would cover their midsections. They did up the leather ties and tried on the helmets. Everything fit perfectly—the man had a good eye.

Tribune Barbatio slouched in the doorway, watching.

The quartermaster began searching through some drawers built into the wall.

He slapped down two broad leather belts with loops on them for carrying tools and weapons. Each of them already had a leather pouch. Long leather straps tipped in bronze dangled front and center from this tool belt.

"To guard the Theodosian dynasty," commented Barbatio, a smile curving his attractive mouth.

Eucherius shot him an embarrassed look, and then smiled to himself as he put it on. Barbatio winked at Marius, who laughed.

From a back room, the Quartermaster brought one dagger and two swords which he placed carefully down on the crowded counter, then found scabbards for them.

"You attach these to your belt like this." He demonstrated. Once the scabbards were secure, the tribunes cautiously inserted their swords and daggers.

Foosh.

The quartermaster tossed cloaks onto the counter. These fell off immediately. He placed them back more carefully.

The man was a natural fussbudget. By the time they were fully kitted out, they knew all about the troubles he was facing because of the coming recruitment drive. He would have to place orders to several different factories for more clothing, armor, and weapons, and who knew how long it would be before those supplies arrived.

And then there was the matter of food and accommodation. He had been told to expect a cohort or three. That was a big range! Where was he supposed to get the extra blankets and bedding for everyone? The pallets in storage had not been used for years and some were likely moldy or moth-eaten. The new recruits would each need cooking pots, tools, and provisions. He did not know when the next shipment of shields would be coming in. He had sent that order months ago! He only had a handful of soldiers working under him. He needed months of notice for such a situation!

"They were much better equipped to handle this kind of thing in the old days," he complained. "I just found out yesterday that the army brass have decided to let our own slaves enlist. Foolishness! You don't give weapons or weapons training to slaves. You hand them a shovel and a cooking pot. You leave the fighting to the professionals."

"Maybe the High Command is hoping to turn them into professionals," suggested Eucherius meekly.

"Or maybe the army brass are really desperate for troops," added Marius.

The quartermaster glanced at them scornfully.

"You two are too new to have opinions. Why don't they get those idle scroungers in Rome to defend their own province, then?" he retorted. "General Stilicho has no idea the trouble he could cause if slaves are taught how to fight the way we legionaries do. Look at Spartacus. There'll be nasty repercussions for a generation from this."

"You've said enough!" snapped Barbatio, striding forward to glare at him. "You've got a job to do, and so do we. Keep your opinions to yourself, my friend. You might be interested to know these young tribunes are Marius Ausonius, grandson of the late Consul, Magnus Ausonius, and Flavius Eucherius, son of General Stilicho and Princess Serena."

The man blanched and would not look at any of them again. They left feeling extremely guilty, carrying a pile of new clothes and wearing their helmets, belts and cuirasses. They offered to fetch the rest of their supplies later.

"Humph," muttered the quartermaster, scratching studiously away at a tablet. "Don't bother. I'll send a *slave* over with them."

Tribune Barbatio accompanied them as they carried their new uniforms home and changed clothing. Afterwards, Marius and Eucherius followed him back to the buildings where the fortress's administration was handled. In one ground floor hallway, a series of rooms was being set up to handle the recruitment process. The soldiers working in there saluted as they entered. Tribune Barbatio put them at ease.

"Legionaries, meet the two tribunes who will be heading up the new cohorts you will be recruiting. I know they look raw, but they're not fools, so remember—no blind octogenarians or three-fingered millworkers."

The legionaries chuckled, and began showing them around the recruitment center. It was clear that they, at least, were confident in their ability to handle the influx of men Moguntiacum was expecting. They were setting up interview rooms, medical examining rooms, a literacy and numeracy testing area, and a couple of offices. It was reassuring.

Barbatio then gave them a tour of the entire fortress. The first stop was the Principia. He pointed out the offices of the legate, his officers, aides and staff. They saw the Twentieth Legion's standards and ceremonial emblems, and the statue of Emperor Honorius and Queen Maria.

The Treasury was located here as well, in a secure underground area which they were not allowed to see. They would be able to deposit their viaticum with the staff who worked there, however, and these men would also handle their pay and expenses from now on. Already the Quartermaster had sent over his account for the items he had given them. The total cost of his uniforms and weapons took a sizable chunk from Marius's viaticum, and the Treasury officer told him not to be too hasty to indulge in an expensive household. His salary would be stretched to cover the slaves and provisions he would need until he received his next pay, and that would not be for months.

Outside again, they went to take a look around the Praetorium district where the top officers had their homes. They visited the stables and admired the horses, took a quick look at one of the granaries, toured a barracks building and the hospital, found where the armory, weapons repair shop, blacksmith shop, carpentry shop, and storage buildings were, and took a look around the bath house, an immense complex run by slaves. As usual, it had a gymnasium.

Along the tour they noticed a few soldiers whitewashing some of the buildings and stacking sacks of grain. Barbatio told them that such menial tasks would be assigned to soldiers who were under discipline for various minor offences. A whipping post and the prison behind it suggested more dire punishments.

Tradesmen driving delivery wagons passed them in the streets. Groups of soldiers trotted by in formation. Army slaves pulled wagons full of supplies for the vacant barracks.

Moguntiacum was a busy place. It seemed to Marius that whatever a city needed, the legion needed.

The legionaries of the Twentieth had multiple responsibilities within and around the area on this side of the Rhine. Some of them specialized in investigating crimes or maintaining the peace in the area. Others fought fires, carried messages, escorted visiting dignitaries and collected taxes. Many worked full-time on the base as clerks, cooks, tradesmen, and engineers.

At the end of the tour, Tribune Barbatio left them again. Marius and Eucherius noticed a man in civilian dress leaning against the wall of the recruitment office. One of the legionaries they had met before emerged, and directed the man back to the main gate. Was he hoping to enlist? Curious, they followed him. The man left the fort. Eucherius waited while Marius hurried to the gate to see where he had gone. The civilian was just disappearing into a crowd of men waiting outside the fortress. The news about the recruitment drive was widely known already.

Big, bearded Burgundians and Franks, some in leather jackets and trousers, some in modern Roman clothing, chatted together as they waited their turn to get into the fortress. Marius saw men from the town dressed in natty, semi-military style tunics talking to rough-looking men who could have been bandits or farmers or the town's drunks. Even a couple of young dandies who might have been from Marius's own social class stood quietly together, while off to the side of the road their drivers waited with the carriages to conduct their young masters home, or take back the news of their acceptance into the Roman Army. No doubt these young men carried superlative letters of reference to show their future value to the Empire.

One of the men in line spotted Marius and saluted. Several others noticed, and saluted as well.

Startled, Marius looked around. No other soldier was anywhere in sight. Thrilled, he saluted back. He wore a grin off and on for hours after that. Eucherius was amused.

"You're such an important man, Ausonius," he teased. "Give us a recitation. *Bissula*, perhaps, or *The Mosella*."

"Give it a rest, Curly. You must get this kind of treatment all the time. It's new to me. Just wait until the news gets out that General Stilicho's son is in town. I won't be able to go anywhere with you. We'll be mobbed. I'll have to take myself and my minor fame into town alone. Anyway, I think they were saluting the uniform, not the Ausonius in it."

CHAPTER NINE

BECOMING A SOLDIER AND AN OFFICER

Moguntiacum Fortress
(Mainz, Germany)
July, 405 AD

His second night at Moguntiacum, Marius slept badly. In his dreams he kept rehearsing what he had learned the day before. His mind was buzzing with excitement and plans, but he had vowed not to risk sleeping late again, and as a result, woke up several times. The moment he heard the first rooster crow, he got up, bleary-eyed and yawning. His head was aching, his neck felt stiff, and his body was still sore. He and Eucherius dressed in silence.

The sullen fellow who was supposed to look after them was still asleep on his mat in the kitchen. A line of ants was marching in under the back door, crawling across his body and up onto the counter.

Angrily, they kicked him awake and ordered him to get them breakfast. He belched, and struggled to his feet, eying them sourly, then foggily began opening and closing boxes and doors and mumbling incoherently. Marius and Eucherius stamped on the determined ants. These seemed to be more familiar with the kitchen's contents than their slave. Eventually they gave up and brushed the ants off the plates of bread and cheese the man banged down onto the triclinium table.

"We've got to get somebody better in here," muttered Marius. "This one is hopeless. Maybe we could force him to become a soldier."

"No chance," replied Eucherius. "He would never make it through the selection process."

"I'll write home and ask my mother to send someone up," said Marius. "She might be able to spare someone from the kitchen staff at our house."

They headed out the door to begin pounding on barrack doors.

So far, forty-two men had been provisionally accepted into the new cohorts. Some of them were already up. A few had been to the grain storage building and were preparing porridge. Others had gone to the bathhouse. Everyone was excited. They had passed the initial interview and the physical. They were now on probation, but their spirits were high. The tribunes heard a good deal of laughter and joking.

According to Barbatio, the recruitment office had been surprised by the number of candidates who were lining up to enlist. So many were interested that in the end Marius and Eucherius might find themselves each commanding a full cohort. It left the two young tribunes dry-mouthed and excited. No one had expected so many.

Over the next several weeks a steady stream of individuals arrived at the base to be evaluated. The best of them were men from across the river or from the barbarian villages on the Roman side of the Rhine. They were seizing the chance to join the army and eventually earn citizenship. A number of the base's own slaves had left their grumbling masters to cross over to the barracks. At first they were shunned by the free men who had been accepted, but they were so much better than the others at parade drills, and knew so much more about what to expect in the army, that their status improved fast.

Tribune Barbatio ordered Marius and Eucherius to keep their eyes open for possible optios, men they would select themselves to become their lieutenants.

Among the men from the town was a thin, red-haired man, energetic and ambitious. Rufus had started life as a slave in the home of a local landowner. He had done well and been promoted all the way up to the role of supervisor of several of his owner's business interests in the town. When his master died, the family sold off the businesses and Rufus was given his freedom. With the money he had saved and a small inheritance from his master, he was able to open a sewing shop in the center of town.

Rufus had five children now by three different women, all slaves in his former household, and he was immensely proud of them all. He was determined to buy their freedom. Rufus made good money from the sewing shop, but not enough. He left the shop in the hands of his own slaves and enlisted, determined to survive life in the army and with his earnings eventually purchase the freedom of his "wives", and maybe even their children.

His ambition had amused them all. How did the man expect to earn so much in one lifetime? But it was his intelligence and determination that had really impressed the tribunes. They all agreed that Rufus would make an excellent optio.

Instead, Marius decided to choose a man named Decius Claricus, a classmate of his brother Lucius. Decius Claricus had arrived at Moguntiacum on his own horse, followed by a wagon with his luggage on it. He had been at Marius's farewell party, and claimed to have been inspired to enlist by the legate's speech and Marius's brave example. He was fit, had good references and a good education. His credentials were fine, but Tribune Barbatio was suspicious.

"Why him?" he asked, his upper lip slightly curled. "What makes him better than, say, Bauto, the Frank?"

Bauto was a handsome young man whose father was a veteran and a member of the local Frankish nobility. He had won the respect of everyone with his open manners, adventurous spirit and quick intelligence.

Marius was sheepish. "I thought it would be nice to have someone from my own background to talk things over with," he admitted.

Barbatio scoffed and made a rude gesture.

Bauto became Marius's optio. Eucherius took Rufus. The decisions were Barbatio's.

A few days later, Marius's old grammar teacher arrived on foot. Socrates was a thin, quiet man with brooding eyes and angular features. He looked older than his 28 years.

Socrates's father had been a tutor to the children of one of Trier's wealthiest landowners, and had been given his manumission when he was no longer needed. He became a teacher for many of the children of the townspeople, at first among the arcades around the city forum, and later in a room he rented above a store. Socrates had been one of his father's best students in the grammar class, and had done so well that he went on to take on students of his own.

Marius knew him well and was thrilled to see him. Tribune Barbatio and Eucherius watched as the two embraced.

"Socrates! How good to see you! When and why did you decide to sign up? You don't seem the type."

"It was an impulse, Marius," beamed the grammarian. "I got tired of dreaming about all these exotic places I teach about and never hoped to see. I just thought I had better grab this chance while I'm still fit and see what more life has to offer."

"But a soldier! It's a whole different life. Can you fight?"

"I really don't know. I've never been interested enough to find out, but Commander Cavillicus thinks the army can use me anyway." He smiled. "I'll just have to learn to fight, won't I? It will be worth it to see more of the world. I'm not afraid to die. I'm more afraid of not having lived before I do."

"It takes all kinds, Tribune," said Barbatio as they watched the grammar teacher head down the hall for his interviews. He glanced at Marius's worried face. "He should be fine."

Soon the empty barracks at Moguntiacum were bustling. Barbatio moved into the big house across the road from his junior tribunes. He claimed he needed to keep a close eye on them both as they were such important people. If he hadn't been so darned likeable, they might have bridled, but his lack of deference towards them was bracing.

Barbatio was soon joined there by three officers from Cologne who arrived in Mainz by ship. Their junior officers would follow in a few days with hundreds of men from the naval and army installations farther up the Rhine. All of them would be leaving for Italia shortly afterwards.

By the second week of July, two full cohorts had been recruited. The double legionary fortress was now almost fully occupied.

The recruits' first task was to learn how to do parade drill.

In the evenings, on the far side of the fortress where it was still usually empty, Tribune Barbatio drilled Eucherius and Marius over and over until they knew exactly how to follow the moves and give the orders. Each morning he would watch from the sidelines as they rehearsed their men on how to move forward, backward and sideways as a unit. It was, as Eucherius had suggested, harder than it looked. The recruits grew tense with the effort not to bump into each other. Chronic failure would mean disgrace and expulsion. They learned to pay close attention.

In every fort there was always a broad space between the outer fortress walls and the buildings. This area served several purposes. It provided a convenient place for units to form up before marching out. It provided protection against enemy projectiles such as javelins, arrows and metal bolts. The army's heavy equipment, its catapults and battering rams were usually stored here, and in frontier zones such as Moguntiacum, piles of weapons were available at intervals, ready to hand in case of attack.

Marius had also noticed a number of puzzling clusters of six-foot high posts here. These were inserted in concrete bases and stood apart from each other. He had wondered what they were for. The answer came one morning right after parade drill. Tribune Barbatio ordered the tribunes to march their men through the streets to the back of the base where they stopped in front of one of these sets of posts. Wooden boxes filled with javelins, spears, and swords had been placed nearby.

Far down the buffer area they could see more sets of posts and other, similar boxes. In between were archery targets with crates of bows and arrows.

Marius looked at them with anticipation. Here was his chance to learn some important new skills.

"Soldiers," bellowed Barbatio, waving to the nearest set of six-foot high posts, "meet the Carthaginian, the Persian, the Briton, the Scythian, the Saxon and the Hun. They are going to teach you how to deal with Radagaisus's Goths when you come face to face with them. These are the enemy and you will learn how to destroy them."

"I don't think that Radagaisus and his warriors will be standing still, do you?" murmured Eucherius to him quietly.

"And here are your weapons instructors."

Barbatio gestured toward a group of men approaching them from the nearest street.

Their trainers, all veterans from the Twentieth Legion, had brought their own weapons. They set about demonstrating proper techniques of attack and parry.

The javelins were long and skinny—they were meant to be thrown, and you had to be prepared to carry several at a time.

The spears were shorter—they could be used for both thrusting and throwing.

The swords were spathas, now the standard sword in the army. They were longer than the outdated gladius.

Finally it was the recruits' turn. Marius eagerly lifted the first sword he could reach. To his surprise, it seemed much heavier than the one he had been given. The other recruits were swearing. These weapons were made of a very hard wood. Their instructors were grinning.

"Those weigh more than the real ones. Get good with them, though, and you will develop muscle *and* skill."

They split up into groups, and began to practice. Some of the posts became the target of the men with javelins. Others were rushed at by the men with the wooden swords. The spearmen practiced with both groups. The exclamations turned to grunts and cheers. The recruits slowly began to center their thrusts and throws.

Marius stayed with Barbatio at the first set of posts. Eucherius followed an archery instructor toward the nearest set of targets. Many of the recruits left for the posts and targets farther down the buffer zone.

Marius practiced with his sword until his arms and shoulder ached. Down the field he caught glimpses of Eucherius zinging the arrows into the targets time after time.

He walked over to watch him. "You've had practice," he commented.

Eucherius turned to him, pleased, "I can do this as long as the targets don't move. It's when it does, or when both of us do, and someone else is coming at you from behind, that it gets tricky."

Marius agreed. To stay alive and unharmed would take luck, skill and good cover by his fellow soldiers.

A week after beginning weapons practice, their instructors ordered the men to bring their shields along with them. Suddenly they had a whole new set of moves to coordinate with the throwing and thrusting. Their instructors began to pit them one on one against each other using blunted, leather-tipped weapons. Then they divided them into teams and they fought against other teams. The fights became hard and dangerous, and many of the men suffered injuries.

More and more the practices were becoming like war itself. All of them were being challenged physically, mentally, and emotionally. Not everyone could handle this level of aggression. The training officers ordered Marius and Eucherius to send some of their men home.

A few weeks into their training, they had to learn how to handle all day marches and make overnight camps. At first legionaries from the Twentieth Legion accompanied them to coach them through this.

On the day of his cohort's first expedition, Marius and Bauto had their men form up inside the fortress and march briskly out of the gates and head south along the road beside the Rhine for twelve miles. After a short halt at one of the smaller forts up the river, they marched back to Moguntiacum. By the time they reached their barracks, everyone was exhausted. Marius trudged wearily home.

On their second sortie, the legionaries had them do short spurts of marching at double the speed. Over time, these periods became longer and longer.

Eventually, they had to prepare to camp overnight. Wagons followed them with the supplies they would need to set this up, and several of their instructors rode alongside them to show them what to do.

When they reached their destination, a field almost twenty miles up the river road, their trainers demonstrated how to lay out a temporary camp complete with palisade, latrines, campfires, and their orderly rows of eight-man tents. After that long, uncomfortable night was finally over, the recruits had to dismantle the camp, load up the wagons, and march back to Moguntiacum. Weary was too weak a word this time.

Once they had mastered this, they had to do it on their own. Tribune Barbatio did not accompany them, nor did any of the men from the Twentieth except the wagon drivers. Marius, Bauto, and their men were on their own. When they returned after a successful journey, they were exultant and very proud. The only incident they had to relate to the members of the other cohort was about a wolf pack that had howled at the moon from the hills behind their camp site.

There were regular trips after that. Each time they marched out the gates, the wagons accompanying them carried less and less. Instead, their trainers would order a new item to carry, until finally they were marching out the gates in full armor, carrying everything they needed for living off the land. It was exhausting and challenging, but still new enough to seem like an adventure. They all knew they were being prepared for the long march to Italia, and they had a growing confidence that together they would be up to the task, no matter what dangers lay around them.

On the parade ground they had begun practicing the testudo, or 'tortoise'. Using their shields to form a tortoise-like shell over most of their bodies, a group of soldiers could creep right up to enemy strongholds or city gates to use assault equipment or other tools with much less risk of injury from the boiling water, javelins, or arrows being pitched at them from overhead. This training, too, was becoming dangerously real, but all of them were stronger, faster, more experienced, more skillful and better able to react instinctively to any threats around them.

Marius could feel his confidence growing along with his muscles and weapons skills. He was now comfortable enough in his role on the parade ground to pass the task along to Bauto. He was getting good comments from his weapons instructors, and he found he was able to function and think, even in the heat of a mock battle between his cohort and Eucherius's.

Every day he was learning more about military protocol and the workaday running of the monster fort, and little by little, he was getting to know the men under his command. He no longer questioned his decision to join the army. The two little books he had brought with him remained unread on a shelf in his bedroom. Things were going well.

After their first few weeks at Moguntiacum, he and Eucherius began to receive dinner invitations to the homes of some of the officers of the Twentieth Legion. Barbatio, their minder, was always there as well to keep an eye on them.

Often the officers would share their stories, and discuss and dissect battles going back centuries to the days of General Marius's patient tactics against the Teutones, or Pompey the Great's forced night march and ambush against King Mithridates of Pontus, or Julius Caesar's campaigns in Gaul, or Caesar Titus's sieges in Palestine. And occasionally their hosts and hostesses would encourage Eucherius to share any tidbits and tales he had gleaned from his father. He would give lively, and increasingly theatrical, versions of his famous father's adventures. Marius enjoyed these evenings as much as anyone, and would often tease Eucherius about how much embellishment he suspected had landed into these accounts. His friend just grinned.

One evening General Carausius invited the three tribunes to join him for dinner. He apologized for the plainness of the fare, explaining that his wife was away visiting her sister in Marseille, and she was the one who usually fussed over the meals and the entertainments. At the last minute he had called in a dancer from the town that Barbatio had recommended. He hoped that would be alright. He was sure that Eucherius had seen far better dancers in Italia . . .

"I'm sure she will be quite competent Your Excellency," replied Eucherius with a gleam in his eye.

The woman was more athletic than graceful and made up for her lack of ability with her lack of modesty. Eucherius admitted later that his father and mother would never have allowed such a creature into their home, and he had never, ever seen such a dance in his life! He appeared to have enjoyed it. Marius had not—he kept thinking about his mother and what she would have to say if she knew he was being fed this kind of entertainment. Neither, apparently, did the legate, who seemed restless and bored. He dismissed the girl abruptly after the sixth course. She slunk away with relief and a small purse in her hand.

General Carausius immediately reverted back to his role as commander-in-chief.

"My officers and I have been considering the matter of what to call your cohorts," he said. "Someone suggested—actually it was me—the names *Mosella Cohort* and *Rhenus Cohort*. We thought it appropriate for Tribune Ausonius to call his unit *The Mosella Cohort* and Tribune Eucherius to call his, *The Rhenus Cohort*. How does that seem to you?"

They looked at one another.

"Of course, I was thinking of your grandfather's poem about the Moselle, Marius, and it seemed only right to name your cohort in his honor. I believe he would be proud of you."

"Thank you, sir."

"And then the other name just made sense. Eucherius is doing his apprenticeship as a tribune here on the Rhine. Two rivers, you know . . ." His voice trailed off.

Marius repressed a smile. It seemed the legate had a poetic side to him.

"I don't think there could be a better choice, Your Excellency," said Eucherius. He clearly meant it, and Legate Carausius beamed.

Every day was busy, so busy Marius had little time to think. Sundays were different. On Sundays there was no parade drill or weapons practice, and only essential duties. The men all had some time to themselves. Marius could catch up on his sleep, go to the cathedral in town for a morning service, catch up on his weapon's practice, or read. Such luxury!

It was on one of these Sundays that he re-opened Claudian's panegyric on General Stilicho. It had beckoned to him from a shelf from time to time and each time he had ignored the pull. He knew he had to take the time to read it; he was going to have to get it home to his family soon.

He carried the book out to the front room and settled onto a couch to read.

Described in Claudian's poetic terms, General Stilicho seemed to be almost mythical.

"Ever from thy cradle did thy soul aspire, and in the tender years of childhood shone forth the signs of loftier estate. Lofty in spirit and eager, nothing paltry didst thou essay; never didst thou haunt any

rich man's doorsteps; thy speech was such as to befit thy future dignities. A mark wert thou even then for all eyes, even then an object of reverence; the fiery brightness of thy noble countenance, the very mold of thy limbs, greater even than poets feign of demi-gods, marked thou out a leader of men. Whithersoever thy proud form went in the city thou didst see men rise and give place to thee; yet thou wast then but a soldier. The silent suffrage of the people had already offered thee all the honors the court was soon to owe.. Happy is our emperor in his choice; he judges and the world agrees; he is the first to value what we all see. Ay, for he has allied to his children and to his palace one who never preferred ease to war nor the pleasures of peace to danger, nor yet his life to his honor."

The more Marius read, the more he was amazed at Eucherius's humility. He was deep in thought when his fellow tribune walked in the door.

Eucherius had gone into town to the fanciest bathhouse for a bath and a shave. "What are you reading?" he asked.

Wordlessly Marius showed him the book.

"One of Claudian's. Which one is that?"

Marius looked at the title again. *"On Stilicho's Fourth Consulship"*, he said.

"Oh, that. My favorite is the Sixth. He's a good poet, isn't he?"

"Is it true that your father pays Claudian to write these?"

"Pays him! No, I don't think so. Claudian sells many copies of these books, and he makes a good living out of it. Father isn't the only patron he has. Just the most glamorous."

Marius looked at him. Eucherius waited.

"What does it feel like to be the son of someone so famous? So . . . perfect?"

Eucherius laughed. "My father is not perfect. Only almost. He enjoys these poems as much as anyone. Mother teases him about some of the more florid descriptions of him, but he did actually live through all these things Claudian writes about. It's amazing, really. His father was just a cavalry officer, a Vandal at that, but a good one. My Roman grandmother was the brave soul who married him. Stilicho is the result."

He paused and looked out the nearest window where some soldiers were tossing dice.

"He just seems to move smoothly through everything life throws at him. It's not always easy being his son, but I'm very proud of him. I just wish I could be more like him."

"Perhaps you are!"

"I don't know. Sometimes I think I could be, but I can never achieve what he has achieved, no matter how good I am."

Marius looked at his friend warmly. "I don't see why not. You are a good soldier. Your father is a hero, and your mother is a royal princess. I would think anyone with sense would fall over themselves to help you."

Eucherius shook his head.

"Lots of people admire him, but there are powerful people in the army and at court who do not like him. He rose too high too fast for their tastes, and many would like to see him fall. They don't trust him. I can even see their point of view. He swears that marrying Honorius to Maria, and Placidia to me, was the Emperor Theodosius's idea, but no one else knows if that is true. My sister Maria tells us about the poisonous looks she sometimes catches from the patrician ladies in Rome. Some of them have daughters of their own. They can't forgive my family for marrying Maria to Honorius first."

"The Emperor believes your father though, doesn't he?"

Eucherius nodded. "I think he does, but I don't think he dares to believe otherwise. He needs Father too much. He has always relied on him since we were children, and Father encourages that. In fact, without my father, Honorius would be lost."

He stared out the window with a worried look on his face, unaware that what he had just said could be construed as treasonous. Marius decided that he was just saying things the way he saw them, without malice.

CHAPTER TEN

A PROPHETIC STORY

ᕲ

Radagaisus's Camp City
End of July, 405 AD

The people from Wodenvale set up their camp on the outskirts of a vast wagon city. They were fully two miles away from the Danube River, the way forward blocked by thousands of other wagons, most of them grouped in laagers[19], the traditional defensive circles.

Pastor Rhodus tucked his wagon in alongside Sigeseric's and got down, stretching, before he unhitched Enoch and tethered him. Theona threw down some straw for the ox, and then let the chickens out of their baskets. All of them needed a good, long drink. She wondered where to find water. Someone in the next laager would likely know.

The next laager turned out to belong to Asding Vandals from somewhere to the east. Their dialect was not very different from hers, and their accent was similar to her father's, which she could imitate quite well. They had arrived a few days before. An old woman directed her to a little market manned by the local Suevi people a short walk to the east. There was a spring on the near side of it which her people had been using.

Theona hurried back to spread the word. Many of the Wodenvale travelers set off to the Suevi marketplace with excitement to see what kind of goods were available. Others grabbed buckets.

"I'll get the water this time," said her father, hoisting their water buckets. "I'm going to find out what they are using for trade here."

He headed off, whistling. Theona looked wistfully after him.

"Do you want to go exploring?" Darric had come up behind her.

"Yes," she exclaimed. "Just a minute. I'll get my shawl."

She clambered up into their wagon and grabbed it. Her fishing bucket and net were at the back. She grabbed them, too. Maybe she and Darric would get as far as the big river! If they did, she'd be ready.

Gideon got up from the shade of the wagon and followed them.

---

[19] Author's note: Laager is a term used by the trekkers of South Africa many centuries later. I have borrowed it to avoid using 'circle' and 'wagon circle' too many times in the following chapters.

The huge camp was overwhelming. Theona had never seen so many people in her life! For a girl from a small village, the atmosphere was exhilarating. As they made their way through laager after laager, some of the people shouted and scowled at them, but others called out friendly greetings. Most of the people they passed were busy with their own concerns and ignored them.

They saw wagons and carts of several sizes and shapes, some old, some quite new. Campfires blazed in front of many of them, and the smell of the wood fires and the tantalizing foods being prepared accompanied them from laager to laager. Children ran past them, chased by other children, all of them shouting with excitement. Several dogs barked at Gideon, and in one laager, a goose ran at them. Darric hurried Theona away.

They saw boys and young men competing with one another in wrestling matches and axe-throwing contests, while young girls stood around and cheered them on. Hawkers passed them selling chickens, cloth and jewelry. A few farmers trudged by leading ponies loaded down with buckets of water, bags of barley, and baskets of vegetables for sale. Theona stopped to gape at one highborn woman with bright, stylish clothing and heavy jewelry who was bossily ordering a couple of slaves around as if they were all still back in their former home. When she saw Theona staring, the woman angrily waved her away.

Amidst the chaos, domestic animals looked dumbly on, munching on tufts of grass they were able to find.

A group of horses was grazing in one clearing, and Darric walked over to take a closer look. Theona hovered well back, afraid the huge beasts would decide to approach her. Only after coaxing from Darric did she move closer. She decided that horses were beautiful animals, but they must belong to men who were both very brave, and very rich. They looked like they would need plenty of food.

Soon after, they passed a couple of wagon-borne blacksmith shops and an area where several men appeared to be repairing wagons. They stumbled into a small marketplace where a group of men and women were sitting around doing nothing much at all. A tavern keeper was ladling out beer to anyone who came with a coin and a cup. Several customers seemed to have had too much to drink, and a few had passed out, leaning against the wheels of nearby wagons. Theona and Darric hurried past, trying not to stare at the degenerates.

After a half hour of fascinated wandering, the two of them realized that they were lost. A low, tree-covered hill stood some distance away. It might be possible to see the river from it and get their bearings from there.

They walked over and climbed it, discovering at the top a dozen men, Goths and Alans, seated in the shade of some large trees in friendly conversation with each other.

The two groups were vividly contrasted. The light-skinned Goths wore their mostly red and blond hair cut short, Roman style, while the Alans, swarthy horsemen from the distant plains to the east, wore their black hair long. All of them were avidly examining something one of the Alans had brought.

Darric stopped Theona to take a look. Gideon patiently lay down on the grass.

The center of attention was a large and very elaborate bow that the owner claimed to have retrieved from a Hun he had killed. He had one broken arrow and several good ones to go with it. His companions were debating how the bow must work.

This was the first time most of the Goths had seen such a bow close up. In the heat of battle, they were more focused on the rider coming at them, than on the details of his weapon.

This was a war bow, not a hunting bow. It was smaller than the ones used by their foot soldiers, but quite a bit larger than the ones used by their warriors who fought from horseback. The bows used by the mounted warriors were small so that the body of the horse would not interfere with their aim. The Huns, though, were able to ride bareback and use these big bows with great accuracy and velocity over long distances. The men had often wondered how their enemy managed to do this.

Now the mystery was solved.

The bows they used were symmetrical; the section above the arrow rest was the same size as the section below it. This bow was asymmetrical. The bottom curve was considerably shorter than the top one, and the support where the arrow rested was well below the half-way mark, so the bow would not interfere with the reins or the horse's body. They conjectured that the archer would have to learn how to compensate in his aim in order to hit his target.

It was also a composite bow, the first most of them had ever seen. It was made from wood, sinew, and bone laminated together. The sinew was glued to the outside ends of the frame and the bone was glued to the inside belly facing the archer. These structural changes greatly strengthened the bow and accounted for the increased velocity of the arrows shot from it. They were impressed by the quality and artistry of the weapon. How long had it taken to make it? Theona overheard remarks from several of the Goths who were revising their opinions about the quality of the Huns, as well.

The Alan owner demonstrated, and the other men watched as his arrow flew far and fast, its bone tip thudding into a tree across the hill. This weapon packed enormous power, and they had plenty to say about it. Darric, fascinated, eagerly joined in the discussion.

Theona listened for a few minutes, but then grew bored and wandered away. She prowled the hill looking out over the wagon city. Soon she spotted the Danube, glinting in the distance. She stared. It was much broader than any other river she had ever seen.

Radagaisus's followers were spread out along the river bank, seemingly forever. The growing camp was dissected in several places by roads set up to allow wagons to pass back and forth. On the opposite river bank, low hills stretched into the blue distance.

She took a moment to get her bearings and then went back to get Darric. The men were just about to experiment with the angle of flight, and Darric was in no mood to leave.

Theona tugged at his sleeve and pointed to her bucket and net. He nodded absently and turned back to the discussion. She shrugged and left again, this time descending the hill on the side of the Danube, taking note of the sun's position to keep on course. Gideon followed her.

A while later they reached the great river. Across it was Roman territory, the Province of Pannonia[20] in the Diocese of Illyricum. It seemed very quiet over there.

A cool breeze blew her hair around her face. She walked to the edge and sat down, grasping her knees, her shawl and fishing gear on the ground beside her. Gideon lay down again, watching her.

The Danube, formed by many spring-fed rivers in the mountains to the west, had a brown hue from the sediment it carried. Pretty stones glistened close to the shore, and occasionally fish shimmered by. Gulls swooped and scooped from the wavelets on the water.

Theona watched them for a few minutes, delighting in their harsh cries and sunlit whiteness. Absently she combed some order into her long blond hair. The sounds of the wind and waves softened the noises from the camp behind her.

She was not the only one on the riverbank. Up and down the river other people were walking, fishing, and even swimming. In the distance she saw two horsemen riding along the shoreline in her direction.

---

[20] The Danube River formed Pannonia's boundaries on the north and east. The Roman province of Pannonia included modern day western Hungary, Slovenia, eastern Austria, northern Croatia, northern Bosnia-Herzegovina, western Slovakia and northwestern Serbia.

Theona sighed, feeling the tension seeping out of her body. It was the closest she had come to contentment since the day the Huns had swept into her village. She knelt to drink, cupping her hands in the brownish river water.

"Stop! What are you doing?" asked a childish voice.

She turned quickly. Behind her stood an indignant little girl, her tight red tunic covering a plump body, her arm clutching a straw doll that had been dressed the same way. The child seemed to be around five years old.

"I'm just having a drink," she exclaimed. "Why? What's wrong with the water?"

"You didn't ask me," answered the little girl, scowling. "I'm the Queen of this river. Everybody knows that. They all have to ask me when they want to drink or fish."

"Are you? I didn't know. I just got here. May I have a drink from your river?"

"You may," replied the little girl grandly, "if you tell me a story."

"Oh," Theona frowned, pretending to think. "Why don't you sit down beside me for a while? If you let me fish, I'll tell you a good story. I know lots of them. But you have to let me fish at the same time. I want to take one home to my father for dinner."

The little girl nodded and settled herself comfortably beside Theona, her bright blue eyes fixed on Theona's face. Gideon moved closer and lay down beside her. The child leaned over and pressed her face against his, then began idly stroking his coat. Theona glanced around to see if any adult was taking special notice. No one seemed to be.

"What's your name?" she asked.

"Anarilka. I'm a water goddess. Do you like my river?"

"Oh yes. It's very pretty and it's so big! I enjoyed my little drink, too, but you should try to keep the water cleaner, don't you think?"

"I do try, but the boats mess it up again every day."

The little girl shifted her weight so that she faced Theona.

"My story!" she said. "Make it a good one. Put lots of heroes and adventures into it. Those are my favorites."

"Do you know the one about Shadrach, Meshach and Abednego?" asked Theona.

"Who are they? Those sound like dwarves' names."

Theona smiled. "No, they weren't dwarves. They were three heroes who lived far, far away in a country called Babylon. That was not their real home, but they had been forced to leave their real home and go to live in a brand new place."

"Like what we are going to do," nodded the little girl knowingly. "Why did they go? Were they on a quest?"

Theona fished a string from her tunic pocket and looked around. There was a thorn bush not far away. She rose and broke off one of the smaller twigs with a fierce thorn on it, then trimmed it to form a hook. She wove green leaves into it to make it more appetizing, and studied it critically. Anarilka watched in silence. Satisfied, Theona tied the hook to the string, and tossed it into the river.

"No. They were all boys from noble families who had good lives in their own country. One day though, a ruthless king called Nebuchadnezzar conquered their country and forced the children of the nobility to go back with him to Babylon."

The little girl's eyes widened.

"Was he really a bad man?"

Theona considered the question.

"He was bad!" she decided at last. "He didn't care whom he hurt, so long as everyone feared and obeyed him."

"Did the men with the funny names fight him and free their people?"

"Well, no, not in the way you are thinking."

Anarilka looked disappointed. "So, what adventures did they have?"

"Well," said Theona, "they were hostages in Nebuchadnezzar's kingdom. That meant that they were sort of guests, and sort of prisoners. They couldn't go home again, so they decided to make the best of it and do such a good job working for the king that he would think kindly of them and the friends and family they had left behind. Shadrach, Meshach and Abednego worked hard, and were so good at their work that they became important leaders in one of Nebuchadnezzar's lands. They did so well that some other men became jealous of their success and wanted to make trouble for them."

"Ohhh. What happened?" Anarilka's eyes were sparkling, now.

"Back in the big town where he lived, King Nebuchadnezzar decided to test all his people. He took all the gold he had stolen from all the people he had conquered, and turned it into an enormous gold statue. He ordered the men making the statue to make it look just like him, but it was as big as a giant. Maybe bigger! Then he called all the leaders of the people, and told them to worship that statue as if it was a god. In fact, he thought that if everyone worshiped that statue that looked like him, they would believe that *he* was a god and be afraid to do anything to make him angry.

"He got all his musicians together and told everyone in the crowd that when the musicians began to play, they had to bow down and worship the huge golden statue as they would all their other gods. If not, he would kill them."

Anarilka sucked in her breath.

Theona continued. "Everyone was afraid of him, so they did it."

"Did the heroes fight him then?"

"No, Shadrach, Meshach and Abednego were not there. They were still far away in the place Nebuchadnezzar had sent them, but the men who wanted to make trouble for them *were* in the crowd, and they told the king that they were certain that Shadrach, Meshach and Abednego would refuse to bow down and worship his big statue."

"Ohhh." Anarilka looked up at Theona in perplexity. "Why not?"

Theona looked at her in exasperation. She gestured at the scenic view before them. "Look at all that, Anarilka. That was made by the real God. He made everything and He does not like it when people ignore Him and worship something they have made instead. Did you make that doll?"

The little girl looked down at her toy and back at Theona in surprise. "No, my Uncle Roderic did."

"Would your Uncle Roderic want you to think the doll was more important than him? After all, if he made that doll, he could easily make another one even better, couldn't he?"

"Oh, yes. Uncle Roderic is very clever."

"Well, you see, that's the point. The heroes knew that the real God had made the gold in the ground, and the miners who dug it up, and the man who shaped the gold into the statue, and even King Nebuchadnezzar himself. All their lives Shadrach, Meshach and Abednego had never worshipped any other god but the real One, and they were not going to pretend to do so now. God was real to them, not someone you could ignore or someone you dared offend. God would care if they worshiped something he had made instead of him."

"So what happened?"

"King Nebuchadnezzar had heard good things about the heroes. He knew they were good men who worked hard and did their jobs honestly. He thought they did that because they wanted to please him, so he thought they would agree to worship his statue to please him, too. But just to be sure, he ordered them to come to Babylon, and there he ordered them to bow down to the golden image of him.

"Shadrach, Meshach, and Abednego told him that they would gladly serve him, but they would never worship him or his statue. The King was not used to people not doing what he ordered them to do. He got angry, and threatened to kill them. They answered that if he tried, then their God would save them, and even if God didn't, they would still refuse to worship his big old statue because they thought it was wrong.

Anarilka had begun stroking Gideon vigorously. One of his legs was pumping up and down.

"What happened then?"

"King Nebuchadnezzar got really angry with them. He got his biggest warriors to tie them up tight, so that they couldn't move, and then ordered them to make a great big fire that was seven times hotter than usual. When it was ready, he had his soldiers throw the heroes into it with all their clothes on. His men died just getting close enough to the fire to throw the heroes into it. 'So there!' he said. 'Your God is not going to be able to rescue you from that!'"

Theona tossed her makeshift fishing line out into the river again.

Anarilka was enthralled.

"Then what happened?" she demanded. "Did they die in the fire, or did their God come and save them?"

"He did!" said Theona triumphantly. "How did you know? But he did not take them out of the fire. Instead, he got right in there with them."

"Why? Why would he leave them there? Why didn't he just kill the bad king and get them out of the fire?" Anarilka was agitated. This story was not going the way she had expected.

"Oh. I think he wanted to show them how proud he was of them for their courage and loyalty to him. But there was another reason . . ." Theona had told the children of her village the story often, but new implications were dawning on her this time.

"Well," she said, "God had a big plan, bigger than the King's plan. As King Nebuchadnezzar stood there watching, he saw with his own eyes that even though the ropes on their hands and legs had been burned, their clothes were not on fire, and Shadrach, Meshach and Abednego were still alive, even though his own soldiers were dead. He could even see them walking around, fully clothed, in the middle of the flames. And then he thought he saw a fourth person in there, someone his men had not thrown in. He rubbed his eyes. Yes, there was another person in the fire. This person was talking with the three heroes as coolly as if they were all old friends, as coolly as though the flames were not burning hot and high all around them.

"The king started to shake with fear. He realized that Shadrach, Meshach and Abednego had been right, and that no matter how much he wanted to believe he was a god, he could not do what their God was doing right before his eyes. The God they had stayed true to had stayed true to them. The king became afraid for himself, and sorry that he had ever tried to kill them. He shouted for the heroes to come out of the fire, and when they did, he saw that they were not burned at all. They didn't even smell smoky! They were as fresh as a spring breeze."

"Did the fourth man come out with them?"

"He disappeared. If Nebuchadnezzer was hoping to meet him, he was disappointed. Whoever was in there with the heroes did not bother to come out to speak with him. But Nebuchadnezzar had learned a big lesson. He never again tried making anyone else worship his statue of him. Instead, he announced that the God that Shadrach, Meshach and Abednego worshiped was the real God, and everyone could worship Him instead."

"And is that important?" Anarilka was genuinely curious.

Theona looked away across the river, remembering the fire at the Great House, the line of bodies, the uncertainty about her own future.

"Yes, Anarilka. It is very important. People need to know that there really is a powerful and faithful God who will get into the fire with them. They need to know that God really is there, really is watching, and really does care what happens to them."

"I still think he should have taken the heroes out of the fire and killed the bad king. The heroes had not done anything wrong."

"No, but God needed Shadrach, Meshach and Abednego to help Him teach the king a lesson. King Nebuchadnezzar was not looking at their God, just at Himself and at them. It was a hard lesson for the king to learn, but harder still for Shadrach, Meshach and Abednego."

"And just what lesson was it that the king needed to learn?"

The voice that asked the question was deeper, a man's voice.

Theona, startled, looked around to see a handsome young Goth with shoulder-length brown hair standing a short distance away, his arms crossed over a muscular chest. A jewel-studded sword hilt and a new leather jerkin indicated wealth. Beyond him, a princely looking Alan with long, shiny black hair sat on a beautiful bay mare. He was holding the reins of a second horse, a handsome black stallion with a long silky mane and a little star on his forehead. The Alan was unsmiling, but he had a sardonic lift to his bushy eyebrows, and there was mirth in his eyes as he watched her. The two were clearly men of rank.

Flustered, Theona stood up and snagged her homemade fishing line on a branch poking over the edge of the river.

The little girl scrambled to her feet and pulled at her tunic. "Don't mind him," she said. "It's just my uncle Roderic. Go away Uncle Roderic. I want her to tell me another story."

"I can't stay, Anarilka. I have to go home," said Theona.

"What's your hurry?" asked the young nobleman, taking a couple of steps toward them. "I hope it's nothing to do with me? My friend and I like stories, too! So I repeat, what did the king have to learn from three stubborn idiots?"

Theona frowned at him, looking up into amused brown eyes.

"The king was missing an important truth. Kings have a great deal of power. They can do good or harm to people. Nebuchadnezzar was blind to everything but his own reputation. If he thought someone was putting anything else, even God before him, it worried him."

"Naturally," he replied. "That's what kings do. Even the gods do that. They have to be on guard all the time, or someone will move in to take their place. It's just the way things are."

"What you believe about God is the most important lesson in life," she said. "It affects everything! The king in my story and all his people too, did not know what the real God was like. They were doing things to themselves and to each other that were bad, believing that this is what the gods expected from them. God had given Nebuchadnezzar a very important position, and all of his people needed him to be a good man and give wise leadership."

"And from that day forward, that king always gave wise leadership?"

She raised a troubled face to look at him. Was he laughing at her?

If so, he was hiding it well.

"I'm afraid my father will be worried about me," she said. "I've been gone too long. Anarilka and I were just getting acquainted."

She looked back at the child, who was staring at her with a mouth that suggested she was working up a good cry. *What a little schemer*, she thought. She had to smile. She'd seen that act a few times before.

"Don't worry, my Queen, I'll find you, and tell you another story sometime."

"It might help if you know where she lives," suggested the young man.

"Isn't she from around here?" asked Theona in surprise.

"No, she has been waiting for me to come and get her. She was under strict orders to stay here. That man over there has been keeping an eye on her." He pointed toward a man with wild grey hair and battle scars who appeared to be mending a net near one of the wagons at the nearest laager. "If Rilka were in any danger, which she probably is not—there are consequences—then he would have been here like a flash of lightning along with half his clan. He's an old friend of the family."

Theona looked where he had pointed and saw the man wave at her. She waved back, deciding not to ask about the 'consequences' Anarilka's uncle had mentioned.

"How can I find her again, then?"

"I'll bring her to you when she wants to see you next."

She frowned at him. "That won't do. I have responsibilities. It might make a wasted trip for you both if I'm busy or not there. It's better if I come find her when I have the time. After all, she's the child."

Beyond him, the Alan grinned.

"Perhaps you are right," replied the other. "Well then, what's your name? You can send word through that warrior when you have time for Rilka. I'll fetch you myself on my horse."

"I can walk."

"Of course. You have two good legs, I see, but why should you walk when you can ride with me? It will save wear and tear on your boots and feet." His eyes had been casually taking in her old tunic and worn boots.

Theona lowered her eyes, suddenly self-conscious. The young man was appraising her shabby clothes and scratched arms as though she were a heifer he was out to buy. His casual self-confidence was getting to her. She stared dumbly at the ground, wishing she had never left Darric.

"However," he continued, "I'm afraid I must know where you are staying, and it has nothing to do with Rilka. My friend Goar and I," he glanced back at the Alan, "have responsibilities within this camp. We work for the King. We carry messages for him to all the clans and leaders. It's part of our job to keep tabs on the groups who are coming to join us. I have never seen you before."

His voice became teasing. "Where have you been hiding?"

Theona hesitated. "Our caravan just arrived today," she said. "Our leader is a warlord named Helerix. From Wodenvale."

"Is he a Goth?"

"He is a Goth."

"Where is he located?"

"At the very back of the camp. I can't tell you more than that. Is that all, then?" She looked up at him demurely.

He looked uncertain. "Does Rilka know your name?"

Theona looked at the little girl, who shook her head emphatically.

She stooped down. "I guess I forgot to tell you, Rilka. It's Theona."

"Well, it was good of you to keep her entertained. I suppose she told you she was Queen of the River?"

"Yes," smiled Theona, straightening up again. "She has a powerful imagination."

"So do you! What was that story you were telling her?" he asked. "I haven't heard those names before, Shadrix, Meshix, and the other man. Were they dwarves?"

"No. It's a story I used to tell the children of my own village," said Theona. "She asked for one with heroes and adventures, so I told her the first one that came into my head."

"I want another one." Anarilka had decided that she wanted the attention back.

Theona bent and picked up her shawl, her bucket and her net.

"Anarilka, I have to go home," she said. "My father will be worried about me."

Quickly, she unhooked the thorn and poked the string back into her pocket. Then, giving the little girl one last smile, she passed the two men shyly and headed off across the grass toward the nearest laager, Gideon at her heels.

"Wait," the nobleman called out. "Let me get you a fish to take home."

He hurried past her to have a word with the grey-haired net mender, who stooped and pulled a large fish from a wicker basket. The young man handed him something and then carried the fish over to Theona. He seized her bucket and dropped the fish into it, then handed it back with a gallant bow.

"Thank you," she murmured. She did not look up at him. She knew she was blushing. "Well, goodbye then."

She walked off. Just before she disappeared into the obscurity of the nearest laager, she glanced back. He was still watching her. Beyond him, Goar had dismounted and was lifting Anarilka onto his horse. The little girl was squealing.

It was two hours before Theona reached her own wagon circle. Pastor Rhodus was not around, though signs of his success at the market were evident in the buckets of water and containers of grain beside their wagon. No one was in Bishop Sigeseric's wagon or Darric's mother's wagon, either. In fact, she could not find anyone from her own Christian community. Where had they all gone?

Worried, she approached one of the Wodenvale women whom she knew slightly, and asked if she had seen Pastor Rhodus. The woman glared at her, and informed her that her father and "that nice young man Darric" had gone looking for her long ago, and had not yet returned. Her tone implied that if the two men had suffered some terrible fate while out searching for her, Theona would be to blame.

Theona was mystified by her antagonism. Head high, she turned to walk away, but the woman had one parting comment for her.

"You've got us *all* in trouble, girl. Two of Radagaisus's messengers came by a few minutes ago. One of them mentioned that you had been telling one of your stories to Radagaisus's granddaughter. I knew it was you. That's the last thing we need—Christians in our camp and the unwanted interest of the overlord who hates you people. The King has asked to meet Duke Helerix now."

Theona looked at her in horror. She hurried over to Helerix's large leather tent. It had been erected close to his family's three wagons. The warlord was in there with his wife, Rue. Theona could hear angry words as she approached. She called out, and there was a sudden silence.

Rue looked out, her pretty face drawn. She bit her lip when she saw Theona, then looked back and whispered to her husband. Helerix's fierce eyes were shadowed as he climbed out. He stood there with his arms crossed and regarded Theona grimly.

"Your father needs to keep you close to home, Theona. You left Darric's protection and wandered off. Wandering around alone in this camp can be very dangerous. You don't know these people. If anything happens to you, how would we know where to find you? I want you to promise me . . ."

He was interrupted by Pastor Rhodus and Darric who had just come back. They rushed over.

"Theona!" Pastor Rhodus threw his arms around her, and gave her a fierce hug. "You gave us a scare. Where have you been?"

"Why did you leave the hill?" demanded Darric, angrily.

"You wanted to stay with those men. I wanted to go fishing," she replied. "You knew that."

Silently, she held up the bucket with the big fish in it.

Pastor Rhodus turned to the warlord.

"Don't you worry, Lord Helerix. We've heard that the High King has sent for you. I and my people will leave your laager immediately. We will go elsewhere in this camp so that you will not have to answer for us. We will be fine. I thank you for your generous hospitality and protection these past weeks."

He bowed.

Helerix glared at him, lifting his head proudly.

"Rhodus, stop. You are underestimating me. I will not let you leave. I will never forget how your people so generously rushed to our help back in Wodenvale. We have come this far together, and I will not abandon you. If there is any problem about you being Christians, I will make my position clear to Radagaisus. After that, if we must fight to defend you, we will do what we have to do. I only require that you and your people fight for yourselves, too."

Pastor Rhodus looked at Darric, who nodded.

"Agreed, my Lord," he replied. "Though I cannot vouch for all my people, my deacon and I will set the example, though warfare is no sport to us. We would rather give our own lives than take another's willingly."

"So I understand," replied Helerix, "but so it has to be while we are this dangerously outnumbered."

The Wodenvale wagon circle was gloomy that evening. There was tension between the Christians and their pagan neighbors. Many of the people would not look at, or talk to Theona. Even some of the other Christians were angry with her. One simple story to a child had placed them all on the horns of a dilemma.

Theona cried herself to sleep that night. Why had this happened? Had she been wrong to leave Darric? Wrong to tell her Bible story? Wrong to tell that man where she was staying? None of it had felt wrong. How could she know that Rilka was Radagaisus's grandchild?

Her nightmares were different that night. For once they were not of Huns racing towards her, or Wolfric being torn out of her mother's arms, or her mother facing danger alone. This time she lay bound and frightened while accusing faces, familiar faces, prodded at her and taunted her with hateful accusations.

She sat up sweating, and began to pray. It was the first time she had wanted to pray on her own since leaving her village. Even now, she could hardly prevent herself from accusing God of faithlessness and neglect. They had walked in His presence in times of peace. Had he turned his back on them in times of war? Then the lessons she had learned while telling her story to Rilka came back to her. The three heroes had trusted God in the worst of circumstances, and He had come through. She would try to do that, too.

When she went back to sleep, her accusers did not return.

CHAPTER ELEVEN

PREPARING TO MEET RADAGAISUS

The Barbarian Camp on the Danube
(Modern Hungary)
End of July 405, AD

The morning after Theona's chance encounter with Radagaisus's granddaughter, Anarilka's "Uncle Roderic" rode into the Wodenvale laager followed by a dozen Gothic warriors, all wearing braided green and yellow armbands. They had come to conduct Duke Helerix to meet the King.

Bishop Sigeseric and Pastor Rhodus called the Christians together for prayer away from the camp. Their anxious prayers moved from urgent petition to peaceful trust. They returned to the camp chatting calmly.

Two hours later, Helerix was escorted back by Roderic and his men. He was in a very good mood.

The meeting with Radagaisus had gone well. The king had been gracious and welcoming, and had introduced the Wodenvale lord to some of his advisors and a few of the other chieftains. The King was delighted to have the Wodenvale community join him in his invasion of the Roman Empire. Duke Helerix' men would be joining thousands upon thousands of fighting men already pledged to him. With such a massive fighting force, the Roman Army didn't stand a chance.

Radagaisus had grand plans for the future. He assured the Wodenvale warlord that there would be land and plunder enough for everyone. He might even give Duke Helerix part of a province to rule! Helerix had knelt and sworn allegiance to the Gothic king, and they had departed with mutual declarations of support and good will.

"King Radagaisus wishes me to bring all my fighting men to this afternoon's meeting of the Grand Council," he announced proudly. "This is our chance to show off who we are to every leader in the camp. Men, full battle attire. If you own a horse, ride. If not, you will march in formation. We will march out right after we eat. The king's men will escort us—the place that the Grand Council is meeting is away from the camp."

The subject of Christians had never come up.

Duke Helerix bore down on Pastor Rhodus and Theona as they were heading back to their wagon.

"Rhodus, wait! Your daughter has been invited to come along, too. Apparently there is a little girl who is eager to see her again. The king was most insistent that Theona come, too."

He looked at Theona questioningly.

Pastor Rhodus and Theona froze.

"She insisted I tell her a story before she would let me fish in the river," she admitted sheepishly. "She's only little, so I went along with it."

Duke Helerix laughed, and left.

"What story did you use?" asked Pastor Rhodus urgently.

"The one about King Nebuchadnezzar and Shadrach, Meshach and Abednego," she answered.

"If she asks you for another one, you'd better think carefully. The king must not suspect we are Christians, or we will put everyone here in danger."

She nodded. "I don't like to hide my faith," she said glumly.

"Neither do I, daughter, but I'm not ready to lose you, either."

The men hurried to prepare for the march to the Grand Council while the women rushed to prepare a communal feast for their menfolk and the king's men.

Pastor Rhodus dug out his axe and began to sharpen it. Theona sat beside him for a while, polishing and rubbing grease into his quiver and straightening the feathers on his arrows. There weren't many good ones left. They needed to buy more but did not have the money. She stuffed a cloth into the bottom to try to make the arrows look more imposing. They still slumped to one side.

Darric came by, lamenting that all he had was his axe and his hunting bow. Duke Helerix's wife, Rue, ran up and tugged on his sleeve. In her hand was one of her husband's spears and a dented shield. Pleased, Darric set to work polishing them, and then threw the spear expertly at a knot in a tree trunk. It hit and bounced off. Pastor Rhodus passed him his whetting stone.

All through the camp men honed their weapons and buffed their leather belts, jerkins and saddles. Many of them hurried to the Suevi market to purchase additional arrows from the fletcher, or new axes and slings from the armorer. Some of the horses needed the urgent attention of a blacksmith. Theona noticed one young man searching for stones for his slingshot. She scrambled down from her wagon, and set to the task of helping him find more of the right size and shape. Soon, several of the children were helping look as well.

She felt eyes on her, and looked up. "Uncle Roderic" was squatting near Helerix's tent, watching her. Gideon sat beside him, practically purring as he got his head rubbed.

She was startled. Gideon had adopted her, and made no bones about it. He slept in their wagon and accompanied her whenever she let him.

She left her pebbles on the growing pile and walked over to him. Around his neck she noticed a green and yellow scarf, and remembered that the men he led had armbands in those colors.

He rose to greet her, topping her by a hand's length.

"Gideon is my dog," she said, smiling. "He seems to have taken to you."

"As Rilka is my niece," he replied with an answering smile. "She certainly has taken to you. She has been telling her little friends and a few people in the family that story you told her."

Theona frowned slightly. "How did she do? She's pretty young to remember it all. Did she get it right?"

"How would I know? I didn't hear it all myself. Her mother told me about it. It seemed to be a good story, even if she didn't get it quite right. We didn't recognize it. She can't wait to hear another one, and the rest of us are all out. She's lying in wait for you. I'm afraid she can be a pest. She's the King's only grandchild, so far, and he adores her."

"What's he like?"

"The King? You'll probably meet him yourself. Rilka likes to hang around him, because he gives her rides on his back and lets her get away with things he never let his own children do."

"Does he have many?"

"Many what?"

"Many children?" She was trying to put together some picture of the man, in case she had to meet him.

"Two," he replied. "Two sons, both of them poor imitations of their father."

"What do you mean?"

"He's tough, a natural leader, absolutely certain of himself, or so it seems. A little like the one in your story."

That was awkward! They looked at one another, each waiting for the other to speak.

"I couldn't get you out of my head, yesterday," he said at last. "Your eyes, are they dark blue or grey?"

This was too personal. Theona lowered her eyes in rebuke.

"I understand you have been invited to come to the Grand Council, too. Why don't you put on something prettier? Surely you have something that will show off those pretty eyes."

She looked at him in astonishment. Show off her eyes! What a crazy idea. Eyes were for looking, not for being looked at. Who did such a thing?

"I just mean," he stammered, "it would be a good idea to wear your best dress today. I expect Rilka will be dragging you all over the place this afternoon. There will be many people there, and you will be the only woman to represent Wodenvale."

He had a point. She looked down at her tunic. "I only have this, and one other gown," she said. "I save it for . . . special occasions."

"Well, go put it on then," he said. "This is one."

Theona ran to her wagon, conscious of the brown eyes following her. Inside, she crawled over to the box which held her Sunday gown. It was much the same as the one she wore every day, but it was clean and had no tears or worn patches on it. She knew it was not beautiful—she was not blind to what other women had to wear—but it was very precious to her. It was one of Theona's few personal items. Her mother had woven the cloth and sewn it by hand the previous winter. When it was finished, Theona herself had embroidered clusters of yellow and blue flowers around the neck. The yellow ones had a blue center, and the blue ones had a yellow center. Right under her chin was a simple white cross. Gruda had taught her the stitches and had given her the pretty threads in exchange for extra reading lessons.

The gown was larger than the one she was wearing, which was, in truth, getting to be too tight across the chest and a little short in the legs. The new gown had been made large—her mother had said it needed to be roomy enough for her to grow. Whenever she wore it, Theona tied a rope around her waist.

She washed her face from the bucket, stripped off her tunic, and pulled the newer one over her head, smoothing it over her hips. Then she fluffed her hair, wishing her mother were alive to come with her to the great assembly.

Her everyday dress lay in a heap. She plunged it into the water bucket, and worked it vigorously—she would need it later. Then she stretched it over a nearby bush to dry. She threw out the dirty water knowing that she would have to fetch more when she came back.

A gong clanged. People hurried past her wagon toward the big pots of food the women had cooked up.

Roderic was still waiting near Helerix's tent. Shyly, she stopped in front of him, wanting his approval. He looked the gown up and down and nodded, and then he looked at her embroidery. His lips tightened.

Theona's spirits plunged. She had done what he wanted, but it obviously wasn't good enough. He was disappointed in her. They walked in silence to the crowd of people near the cooking pots, while she wondered how to get away.

"I have something else I must do before I eat," she said, and hurried off.

The young nobleman went to join his men who were standing around eating and talking, enjoying the adulation of the Wodenvale youths and girls.

Theona pretended to check on the animals one last time. All seemed well. Enoch was snoozing on his feet; the chickens were roosting. It was time to go.

Gideon got up to follow her.

"Gideon, you are going to have to stay here," she said firmly. He hung his head, his brown eyes begging.

"Not this time, little friend."

He lay down with his head between his paws as she set off. Darric met her half-way with a bowl of some stew.

She shook her head, gesturing to her dress. "I don't want to get this dirty," she said.

"You put your church dress on," he exclaimed. "I thought you were just going along to visit with the little girl you told us about."

"Roderic suggested that I wear my best dress in case I had to meet the King."

"Roderic!" Darric's tone was disgusted. He made a wry face and lowered his voice.

"Don't let him put you off-guard, Theona. He's Radagaisus's man and reports to him. I suspect he's fairly high up, too. Never forget that the king hates Christians. They say that he has boasted that when he gets to Rome, he intends to crucify the members of the Senate because they voted to remove the ancient statue of their pagan god Victory. Stay away from the king's men. They will be his eyes and ears. If you must come along, stay with the child. She is your best protection, not Roderic."

There was no denying the conviction in his voice.

"I suppose you are right . . ."

She stopped abruptly as Darric raised a hand in warning.

Roderic had come up behind her, leading his elegant black horse. Darric bowed deeply, looking pointedly at Theona as he did so. Roderic nodded, apparently missing the sarcasm in the courtesy, and then ignored the other man.

"Theona, I've been thinking. You're the only woman going to the Grand Council. All the men will be riding or marching. It's a long way, and you won't be able to keep up. You can ride with me if you like."

"Excuse me," muttered Darric. He marched off, carrying the bowl of food.

Theona watched him go, frowning.

"What about it? Would you like to ride with me?" asked Roderic insistently.

"Thank you, but no. I have never been on a horse before. I'm afraid I will fall off." She looked up at him, then quickly away so he could not look at her eyes.

"You won't fall." His voice was gentle. "Just hold on to me. It is not right that you should have to march through the camp with all the men."

He was right. She smiled at the thought. It would look silly.

"I will ask my father. If it is alright with him . . ."

Roderic had been following Darric's retreat with his eyes. The deacon was now having an agitated conversation with Pastor Rhodus.

"I think your father would probably prefer you to ride with one of Helerix's men," he said abruptly. "I will be around if you need to take me up on my offer."

He bowed politely, and led his horse away.

Surprised, Theona wondered what she had done to disappoint him this time. She sighed, and went over to join her father. Darric was standing stiffly beside the pastor, his eyes angry. The food bowl he had been carrying was now on the ground, and one of the dogs was wolfing down its contents.

"Theona," began Pastor Rhodus, "Darric has told me about that young man's offer to carry you on his horse. I'm sure he meant well, but I hope you did not accept. He is a nobleman and one of Radagaisus's own men to boot, and if you are seen riding behind him, you will become an object of interest. That attention is the last thing we need. I will speak to Duke Helerix. Perhaps one of his men can give you a ride. No one can misconstrue that."

"Yes, he said you'd say that." She sighed gustily and walked away.

The pastor and deacon stared after her. "I think, my friend, we've got trouble," muttered Pastor Rhodus.

Darric nodded.

If she had to sit on one of those big horses, Theona would need to wear her trousers. She headed back to the wagon to put them on, rolling her tunic up to bunch at the waist.

They were all confusing her. She did not want to worry her father, but the attraction she was beginning to feel towards the attentive and handsome young nobleman was becoming a problem. He was, indeed, dangerous. This was unknown territory for her, and her mother was not here to give her advice.

Regretfully, she said good-bye to Gideon again, and ran back to join the others.

When everything was ready, the men who owned horses mounted up and formed a column, two by two. The marchers lined up by fours. Darric and Pastor Rhodus took their places in line with the others. In spite of his reluctance to classify himself as a warrior, her father had a gleam in his eye. To watch a Grand Council in action was not an everyday experience. He grinned at Theona, now garbed in her trousers, her tunic folded high and bulky around her waist, and waved.

Helerix mounted his powerful bay horse last and looked around.

"Where's our Theona?" he called loudly.

Her cheeks burning, Theona hurried over. An old man came over to give her a boost up behind the warlord. Awkwardly, she gripped the saddle. The horse tossed his head and shifted position. She gasped, and grabbed at the warlord's arms.

"I'm afraid I'm going to fall off," she whispered to him.

"Hold onto my waist," he hissed. "You'll need to once we *really* start moving."

Gingerly, she put her arms around his waist. The horse danced ahead and she grabbed him more firmly. The Duke seemed unworried. One day, God willing, she might even try to ride a horse herself.

Roderic, on his own black horse, turned to face his men. Thrusting his arm straight up, he shouted, "Hah rah, hah rah, hah rah."

"Hah rah, hah rah, hah rah," they yelled back. He wheeled, and led them out of the Wodenvale wagon circle.

Helerix faced his own excited infantry and cavalry. Wodenvale manhood was on parade. The women and children watched their husbands, sons, and fathers with pride.

He too thrust his arm up into the air. "Hah rah, hah rah, hah rah," he shouted, and all his men yelled back with savage joy.

Theona almost lost her seat again as the bay horse strained forward eagerly. The women and children cheered, and ran with them to the edge of the laager where the escort party had halted.

They were off.

The initial thrill did not last. High above the ground, Theona felt very insecure. She hung on to Duke Helerix's waist, trying to relax and get accustomed to the rhythm of the horse's movements, but then, to her consternation, Roderic's men broke into a trot. For a few minutes she bounced around on the horse's broad back, grimly hanging onto the duke. Eventually, she was able to hold on without doing damage to his ribs. She glanced backwards. The Wodenvale infantry were still in formation but were struggling to keep up. Two of Roderic's men turned around and headed back.

In due course they re-entered the huge camp by one of the dissecting roads. Soon they turned down a wider road heading toward the river. This seemed to double as a massive marketplace; one she had not known existed. Tables and carts, livestock, produce and merchandise had crept right into the center of the road. Roderic's men yelled and swore at the people in their way, knocking down some of the tables as they passed through. The infantry managed to catch up here, and marched stolidly along, trying hard to maintain their dignity and formation in the midst of furious insults, and the occasional lobbed vegetable.

Slowly they threaded their way through the clutter down to the waterfront.

Radagaisus's men turned left and followed the shoreline until they were beyond the huge camp.

From her vantage point high on the horse, Theona could now see that there were islands in the river. Men and women hurrying on foot in the same direction turned to stare as Lord Helerix, his cavalry and panting infantry followed the King's escort past them. Once again the men on foot began to fall well behind.

It was with relief that Theona finally saw Roderic and his men turn into a wooded area near the water. Behind them, the men on foot were just coming into view around a bend.

A group of boys was waiting in a clearing to look after the horses. There must have been several dozen horses there already, and more up in a pasture they had passed on the way in. From the river, now hidden by the trees, Theona could hear muffled voices and the sound of waves slapping against wood.

Roderic got off his horse and handed the reins to one of the boys. Duke Helerix's men started to dismount, too. Roderic ran over to stop them.

"No, Lord Helerix," he said. "You and your men need to keep with your horses. Only this one time. The King and the Grand Council will want to see the strength of your cavalry as well as your infantry."

"Of course," agreed Helerix. "Where do we go then?"

"The Grand Council is meeting on the big island beside us here. There is a ford some distance ahead where you and your men can cross quite easily, with room to line up again on the other side. My men will guide you there and give you further instructions until I can get there myself."

He turned to Theona. "Come on, Theona. This is where you get down."

Duke Helerix would have none of it.

"Theona is staying with me, young man. I am responsible for her welfare."

Roderic's teeth flashed. "And is she to stay behind you up there until you meet the Grand Council? I'm sure the girl has had enough of a horse's back for a while."

Theona could feel the Duke's body stiffen with anger.

Roderic changed tactics right away.

"I meant no offence, Duke Helerix," he said in a chastened voice. "There is a boat crossing just down the path here. That is how the women and children get to the island. I will take her over on one of the boats and we will walk the rest of the way. I will take her straightaway to find the little girl she was with yesterday—she will be with her mother at the Council meeting. I give you my word that she will be safe, and I will return her to her father as soon as possible."

"She can wait here, then," said Helerix, stiffly. "Her father will be along soon enough. He can accompany her."

"As you wish. Theona, let me help you down."

Her people were being a little rough on the poor man today, thought Theona. Unhappy and embarrassed, she swung her farthest leg over the horse's rump as she had seen others do, and cautiously started to slide down the warm body of the horse, holding onto the saddle. Her bunched up tunic rose up, exposing her midriff. She could not tell how far below her feet the ground still was. Frightened, she looked up at Duke Helerix.

"Let go and drop the rest of the way," he said. "You'll be fine."

Roderic stepped forward, catching her around the waist and lifting her down the last few inches. She stumbled backward and he steadied her, then released her and stepped back. Her skin burned where he had touched her.

She turned and pulled down her bulky tunic. "Thank you," she said quietly.

The nobleman's expression was unreadable. She became aware that Helerix was glowering at the two of them. Roderic nodded to the lead rider. His men turned and trotted back out of the glade, followed by Helerix and his men.

Theona barely noticed them go. She was glancing furtively at Roderic. She felt oddly confused. What had just happened? Something indefinable.

He had started walking down the path toward the river.

"Come on. We had better get the next boat, or we'll be late."

"I have to wait here for my father," she said. "You heard the duke."

"Your father does not know you are here, does he? The Duke has gone on ahead to the ford, and I cannot wait. I have duties at the Grand Council. The men in your lord's infantry will have seen the riders leaving here and will surely follow them straight to the ford. I'm afraid the crossing can be a rather wet experience when you are on foot, but if you want to run after them, you can get wet too."

Theona still did not move. He looked at her anxiously.

"Of course you can wait, Theona," he said, "but you really should come with me. I don't want to leave you alone here. I promised Duke Helerix that I would keep you safe. At least let me keep my promise."

He started to walk again. Theona stood there uncertainly and then noticed the boy who was holding Roderic's black horse winking at her. She hurried after the nobleman, rolling down her tunic from its bunched-up position around her waist as she went, and smoothing it out again.

She followed him down a short path through the woods to a wooden dock. Two Goths wearing the yellow and green braided armbands stood guard there. They bowed as Roderic and she approached.

Out on the river a short distance away and parallel to the shoreline stretched a long, narrow island. Directly across from where they stood was another dock with more of Radagaisus's men. Theona thought she glimpsed others among the trees along the shoreline.

Two Suevi boatmen poling a shallow-bottomed boat were approaching them from the island. A group of women whom they had just taken over could be seen disappearing up a path from the opposite dock.

The Suevis silently waited for Theona to get into the boat. Roderic held out his hand to help her aboard. Theona refused to look at him. She was angry at how he had managed to manipulate her, and her warlord.

Her legs still felt wobbly after the long horse ride, and the movement of the little skiff on the water was disconcerting. She took the extended hand. Once again, she felt that mysterious spark between them. It felt as though her own hand had become the essence of herself, highly honored and warmly embraced. She sat down in the boat and stared around her, still refusing to look at him. She wondered if the pleasure she had felt represented some disloyalty to Darric.

The two Suevis poled the boat out. In a few minutes they had reached the island. As she climbed out, Theona glanced back at the mainland. She noticed the Wodenvale riders downstream from her. They were coaxing their horses through thigh deep water. Duke Helerix was shouting at one of his men whose horse had balked at entering the river. It occurred to Theona that the warlord could very easily have sent one of his henchmen back to let her father know where to find her. In fact, knowing him, she felt sure he had done so. He was not one to neglect his responsibilities. She suddenly remembered that as the riders were leaving the clearing, Duke Helerix had been speaking to the rider on his left. He might have been telling the man to carry a message back to her father. Pastor Rhodus would be coming for her and she would not be there. For the second day in a row she had given her father cause for concern.

This time, her own feelings made her feel complicit. Roderic was keeping her from thinking straight. It was very worrying. She hated it and liked it at the same time.

Her companion again preceded her along the path through the woods. He too was quiet.

They came out onto a road, one wide enough for two carriages. It was lined on both sides with tall trees and paved with flat stones, and it ran straight ahead and then disappeared to the right. This was the first Roman road she had ever seen.

Roderic had stopped to wait for her here. He walked beside her on this amazing road. Far ahead they could see the women who had crossed before them walking. They were absorbed in their own conversations. It emphasized the unhappy silence between them.

In a few minutes they rounded a bend and reached the first of a series of large brick homes, now abandoned and overgrown. She suspected that these must belong to the fabled Romans. They seemed enormous! No wonder the men were so excited about the coming invasion. The Romans must be very rich, but if they were so rich, maybe they were formidable fighters as well.

"Theona, are you betrothed?" The question startled her.

"No, why do you ask?"

"That young man you were talking to back at your laager . . . he acted like he owned you." The brown eyes were watching her carefully.

She stopped walking, and looked at him, puzzled by the question. "Darric is my friend."

"But not your intended? Does he think he is going to marry you?"

"There may be some understanding between him and my father about that, but neither of them has mentioned it to me. I am not ready to marry anyone yet. Why?"

He looked at her sheepishly.

"All of them, your father, Duke Helerix and especially that man, are acting as if I were an interloper. Me!" he raged. "It is insulting. I have offered you nothing but courtesy and respect, have I not? And yet they act like I am a villain they have to protect you from. Why is that?"

His eyes were hurt and accusing.

"They only wish to protect me. Perhaps they are afraid you may have an interest in me yourself," she answered calmly.

"And what if I do? I am not married, I am of noble birth—I am from the highest noble clan, an Amali, in fact. I am well-respected. I have excellent prospects, and I try to be a good man. There are many families among our people who would consider it an honor to have their daughters linked with me. Why don't they?" he demanded in exasperation.

Theona giggled. Roderic looked at her in surprise, and then started to laugh, too.

"I suppose that if I *were* interested in you, I have just done myself an injury," he said.

"You are right" she agreed. "Your injured pride seems to be more of an issue than any serious interest in me."

"Maybe," he admitted. "Pride is a fault of mine. Let's forget it, shall we? I am just not used to being the subject of so much suspicion. And by men I could like."

The frozen silence had been breached, but built up between them again as they walked, lost in their own thoughts. They walked past more Roman villas and saw larger and even more impressive buildings at the end of the road.

"I wish we had time to go into some of these buildings," said Theona at last.

"And so we shall. When we get to Italia, perhaps I'll give you a palace myself." Roderic's expression was warm and friendly once more.

"I think I would like one big enough so that I could teach classes in it, but not so big that I would feel lost or better than other people."

"So, no palaces for you?"

"No. I don't think so."

"Maybe you'll change your mind about that."

"I don't want to change my mind about that."

"Why not? Lots of slaves, fancy food, gold and silver plates, an easy life—it's all just over there."

"I'm not a thief!"

"That's not stealing," he said indignantly. "We're going to fight for it. That's the spoils of war!"

Theona went silent again.

They entered a large paved square surrounded by low-slung buildings. This had become a center for wrestling and gymnastic displays, as people waited for the Grand Council to begin. Gothic soldiers wearing King Radagaisus's colors were everywhere.

On one side was their destination, an outdoor amphitheater. Roderic led Theona into the amphitheater and to a seat part way down.

"Who built this?" she asked.

"The Romans. This used to be the Governor of Pannonia's summer home."

"Did we fight them to get this?"

"No. They abandoned it some years ago."

"Why?"

"Perhaps they heard we were coming. Don't move from this seat, Theona. I have to go find Duke Helerix and give him his instructions. I'll bring your father back with me."

He hurried away.

CHAPTER TWELVE

THE GRAND COUNCIL

∾

The Barbarian camp on the Danube River
End of July, 405 AD

Theona looked around her in wonder. The amphitheater was open to the elements and carved into the side of a hill. Row after row of wide stone bench seats curved around to form a semi-circle, the rows broken by aisles of steps descending from the top, two steps for every bench row. At the bottom was the paved semi-circular theatre itself. There appeared to be rooms or waiting areas built into the amphitheater at each side.

She was facing a wide, two-story high whitewashed building with glazed windows and a red-tiled roof. Along the upper story was a spacious verandah with its own tiled roof supported by slender white columns. A door at the back of this opened into the building. A second set of doors, these ones wide and plain, opened at ground level into the theater. The whitewashed building glowed in the afternoon sunlight, and the bright red roofs stood out boldly against the tall green trees behind the building.

A long elevated walkway stretched out from the verandah into the theater to a large, raised podium that had stairs leading down to ground level. Both the walkway and the podium floor had designs on them, and Theona leaned forward to look. They seemed to be complicated patterns with people and animals displayed in them.

So much work had gone into creating this whole area. How could the Romans just walk away from all this? She wondered what the purpose of such a big building had been. It was almost certainly a Great Hall of some kind. Roderic had to be wrong about its being someone's summer home.

At ground level men were setting up a large semi-circle of chairs, some of which were plain and some fancy. Many had brass or gold ornamentation. Several were intricately carved. Two of the fanciest had plush, embroidered cushions. Two men carried out a large square chair and set it up at the front of the podium. The back of this chair was topped by the carving of a bear's head, its mouth open in a snarl. Theona guessed that these were all thrones of some kind, and the one on the podium was for the Gothic king, Radagaisus. The men then brought out more modest chairs and placed them in rows behind the king's throne.

The seats were beginning to fill up with spectators. From their clothing, hair styles and complexions, Theona recognized several different nationalities. Their leaders, equally distinctive, were arriving and settling into the semi-circle of portable thrones in front of the podium. Sometimes they were accompanied by other men who squatted behind them, and decided that these must be interpreters or perhaps advisors for the chieftains on the thrones. One of them was Roderic's companion, Goar, from the day before. He was talking to a big Alan who had taken his seat on one of the elaborate thrones with the gorgeous cushions.

Roderic was suddenly beside her again, standing on the nearest step.

"Come on, Theona, we're changing seats. I've brought your father. We have to hurry. The Grand Council is about to begin," he said.

He hurried ahead of her down the aisle between the steps.

Delighted, she rose to welcome her father. He was damp and looked tired, but his eyes warmed to see her. They followed Roderic down the stairs. Lower and lower they went until they reached the bottom row. The young nobleman led them across the pavement to seats near the end of the first long curved row. From here, they had a good side view of the podium and the members of the Grand Council. Theona sat down beside her father and looked around. No one else was sitting near them. Quickly she whispered an apology. Pastor Rhodus gave her an odd look and seemed about to say something, but Roderic gave him no chance. He stood close in front of Theona, and pulled a blue shawl from inside his jacket and handed it to her just as a group of elegantly dressed people began to pour out of the building onto the verandah.

"Put this on," he ordered. "It's my sister-in-law Chloe's."

"But I don't need it," protested Theona. "It's not cold."

"Yes, you do!" said her father shortly. "Put it on, Theona."

He glanced pointedly at her neckline. Theona understood.

Without a word, she draped the shawl around her neck and tied it in place, surprised at their collusion. Satisfied, Roderic sat down beside her.

"Where's Anarilka?" she asked. "Does she know I'm here? I thought . . ."

He moved a little closer to her, now relaxed and smiling. "I'm afraid I forgot to mention you were here. I'm sure she'll be along sometime. This is my time with you."

The admiring look he gave her was unmistakable.

Theona glanced at her father, her eyes shining and her cheeks pink. He did not seem to have noticed.

A chorus of "Hah rahs" began. Louder and louder it rose. All around them people were rising to their feet. A tall, bare-chested man wearing a heavy gem-studded gold crown walked out of the building. On his chest and face and arms were displayed the proud scars of battles survived, the proof of his personal courage. Around his neck and down his back hung a bearskin fur. Two large amber beads filled the eye sockets. In one hand he carried a wooden club, and in the other, a large silver shield bearing the image of a bear, its mouth opened to take a bite from the sun and the moon.

He crossed the verandah and strode down the walkway to the podium, followed by a dozen other men who jumped down to the floor of the arena and faced outward, their arms crossed. All of them were armed.

Last to come out of the building was a group of women, led by a tall woman with large, dark eyes and a long yellow gown. She was holding Anarilka's hand and they took their seats on chairs in the front row. The other women seated themselves behind and around her. Theona watched with interest as the woman begin scanning the amphitheater. When she spotted Roderic in the front row, she shifted her attention to Theona, sitting next to him. For a few seconds she looked at her, then bent down to whisper to the little girl, pointing in their direction.

Rilka squealed, and flew down the walkway and onto the podium, past all the dignitaries, and down the steps. Every eye must have followed the excited little girl as she tore across the ground to Uncle Roderic and his two guests. Radagaisus watched too, smiling fondly from his own seat on the large wooden throne. Theona's heart pounded as his gaze settled on her. Uneasily, she remembered Darric's warning about him and his son.

"Theona, you're here!" Anarilka was jumping up and down in front of her. "I told Uncle Roderic to bring you."

"And as you can see, I did," he grinned.

"Move over," she ordered, and wriggled in between her uncle and her new friend. He looked at Theona and sighed. She giggled. Her father frowned at her.

The Gothic king stood up and waited for silence. Everyone on the podium and below in the semi-circle of thrones stood as well. He held the silver shield out in front of him. When everyone was quiet, he hammered it with the wooden club. When the echo stopped, he struck it again. Other men with shields joined in. The rest of the audience began to stamp their feet and clap their hands in time with the metallic thuds. Roderic and Theona pulled Anarilka to her feet to clap along with the crowd.

After a hesitation, Pastor Rhodus began to stamp his boots and clap his hands, too. The pace increased, and the volume with it. Finally, one of the men standing behind the king came forward and raised a huge horn to his lips, and blew. The deep note blared out and the crowd cheered.

The Grand Council was now in session.

"What's going to happen now?" asked Pastor Rhodus, leaning across Theona to Roderic.

"The Council will begin judging offences committed by people from different factions here. Their judges normally deal with any crimes committed in their own jurisdiction, but since all the groups have different laws and different penalties, serious differences and offences are brought before the whole Council for justice. Otherwise, there could be revenge killings and feuds, and everyone would be fighting one another instead of the Romans."

The lower set of doors opened at the base of the Roman building, and a man walked out, a thin man with white hair, an unlined face, hooked nose, and hooded eyes. He wore an impressive looking draped white garment, and carried a brass gong and its hammer. Two men in peasant clothing walked on either side of him to the space between the podium and the thrones of the chieftains. Here they halted and bowed, first to the High King, and then to the seated rulers.

"Who is that man wearing the Roman toga?" asked Pastor Rhodus.

"That's Phaedrus, one of our priests. He's the king's advisor, a Roman by birth, they say. He's been around for as long as I can remember. He has no say in the decisions—that's up to the Council members, but he is an important man. He decides who gets to present their case before the Grand Council and when they get to appear."

"What is the offense?" demanded Radagaisus, as chief judge.

Phaedrus's words were clipped and slightly accented.

"This man, Dieter, claims that this other man, Ecke, sold him an injured ox."

"Under what circumstances?"

The shorter of the two men bobbed his balding head all round to the dignitaries, and nervously defended himself.

"Sire, I am Ecke. I told Dieter when he bought the ox that it had stumbled and hurt itself on the last day of our journey here. I told him that, because of that, I would let him have it for a very good price. He took it, knowing there was a possibility the ox was injured. I bear no blame for his decision. He knew what he was getting."

The other man spoke up hotly. "My lords, I could barely get the ox home before it collapsed. Ecke did not tell me that the injury had opened up a cut and that the wound had gone bad. The leg was badly infected, and the poor beast could not stand on it or walk. It collapsed and broke its leg before I even got it to my camp. Now the beast will not be any good at all to my family. Ecke has cheated us, and we need our money back to buy another ox. If we don't, how will we ever make the trip to The Roman Empire with our kinsmen?"

"Are there any witnesses?" called the king.

"Yes, Sire," answered Phaedrus. "Both men brought witnesses to appear before the Council."

"Summon them."

Twenty men and women pressed forward down the aisles to stand before the Council. One by one, the friends of Dieter acknowledged that the ox he had led home was fit only for eating, and one by one, Ecke's friends insisted just as hotly that the ox must have injured itself on the walk back to his laager, because the first injury, which they had all witnessed, had not been serious. Dieter was dishonestly trying to get compensation from Ecke for an accident that was not of Ecke's making.

Before long the witnesses were shouting at each other, and there was some shoving. Around the amphitheater, discussion also became heated as everyone expressed opinions.

"Silence," roared the king, glaring at the witnesses. He raised his spear. Some of his guards rushed towards them, separating the crowd of witnesses, and enforcing order among the spectators.

"Who are your chieftains?" demanded Radagaisus.

Two warlords stood up from among the seated judges, and crossed over to confer with Radagaisus. His advisors also crowded around him. The discussion did not last long.

Once everyone was seated again, the king turned to Ecke.

"You must give Dieter another ox. It was the first injury that weakened the ox, so that the second injury, if there was one, became serious."

Ecke fell on his knees and threw his arms wide. He was close to tears. "What will I use to travel with, then? I cannot give away my other ox, or my own family will not be able to go."

"Your chief will help you buy a new ox. You will repay him from any plunder you take from the Romans. You can work out what that will be between yourselves."

"Then I want the first ox back. I can at least sell the meat."

"Agreed."

The two men and their supporters headed amicably up the aisles of the amphitheater. It seemed that they were all satisfied with the decision.

There were two more cases to be heard. A Suevi man had been injured by a Gothic man in an axe-throwing contest. The Suevi had lost much of the use of his left arm. A fine was levied against the Gothic clan leader, who agreed to pay it. He did not look surprised, and was clearly angry with his warrior, but seemed relieved that the judges had decided not to charge him the full cost of a complete left arm.

In the last case to be heard, a Marcomanni husband brought a charge of adultery against a handsome young Alan. His wife was already dead, killed by the women of their clan, but he wanted the seducer killed as well. The Alan had already fled the camp and was nowhere to be found. He was sentenced in absentia to permanent exile.

Radagaisus announced that, there being no further cases that day, there would be a break while he and the Council members inspected some new troops that were waiting outside in the field. Everyone in the audience stood as he left the podium to cross to the stone staircase leading up to the exit. As he passed them, he beckoned to Roderic to come with him. His sharp eyes raked Theona and her father. She knew he would not forget their faces.

Roderic leaped to his feet and followed the King up the steps and out of sight. After they were gone, other people began moving out, too.

Anarilka grabbed Theona's hand, her eyes bright with anticipation.

"Now you can tell me another story."

Pastor Rhodus stood up.

"Theona, I'm going out to line up with Duke Helerix's men," he said. "Why don't you tell her the story about the giant and the brave boy who fought him with only a slingshot and five smooth stones? That's always been a favorite of mine."

Theona nodded, amused. King David's impetuosity and death-defying courage were just the kind of story that the Gothic people loved.

The Grand Council resumed within the hour. This time, when the Gothic king re-entered the amphitheater, he brought a beaming Duke Helerix with him. For the few minutes the amphitheater was filling up again, the Wodenvale warlord moved around, introducing himself to the leaders. Theona saw him looking upward into the crowd from time to time. She waved from her seat on the side, but did not catch his eye.

Many of the Wodenvale men started to enter the amphitheater, filling up seats left vacant by people who had already left. Darric was among them. She saw him high up toward the back. Again she waved, but stopped when she noticed King Radagaisus watching her from the podium. Of course! She was new to him, and she was sitting alone with his only grandchild. She smiled nervously at him. He continued to contemplate her without smiling back.

Where was Roderic? Radagaisus's steady gaze made her nervous. Was he staring at the girl who told his beloved grandchild unfamiliar stories, or at the girl who seemed to have attracted the attention of one of his top men?

Her father came down to join her again, followed soon after by Roderic. She was ridiculously glad to see him. So was Anarilka, who screamed with excitement when he snatched her up and held her high above his head.

"Shoo. Shoo," he said to her, lowering her to the ground with a grin. "It's time to go back to see your Mama."

Anarilka giggled, and darted off across the field to climb the steps onto the podium. She ran to sit with the women on the verandah. Roderic sat down beside Theona just as the man with the big horn blew it again. The audience grew quiet. The king stood up.

"In preparation for the invasion, I sent my son Vitiges with some of our men across the river into the Roman Empire. You may have heard that they have returned. They bear good news, though not unexpected. The people in the lands across the river are abandoning their homes, and leaving their fields for us. They are shaking with fear and running away even before we begin the invasion."

People laughed.

Radagaisus held up his spear for silence and continued.

"The Roman Empire is not as well-defended as it used to be. There have even been rumors going around that some Roman troops are willing to desert to our side."

Shouts and knee-slapping broke out across the amphitheater. This was gratifying news indeed. Radagaisus held his spear up for silence.

"As it turns out, those rumors are true. There are valiant men inside the Roman Army who want to join forces with us. Some of them are here with us today."

The audience murmured in surprise as he turned and shouted to Anarilka's mother. She hurried inside and came back immediately, followed by a man who bore a strong resemblance to the king. Theona noticed that he was wearing the same kind of green and yellow neckerchief that Roderic had on. Behind him walked two men in Roman uniform. There were some rude noises from the crowd and a few half-hearted cheers as they strode down the walkway onto the podium.

The younger of the two men was tall and pale, with a thin face and broken nose. His white-blond hair was long and beginning to thin on the top. The other man, older by about twenty years, was red-haired, muscular and a little shorter. His face was tanned and deeply lined. They carried no weapons, yet did not appear to be particularly nervous.

The three of them bowed to the King, and then to the other leaders sitting on the thrones below. Then the first man, Prince Vitiges she assumed, walked back and took a seat on the podium, leaving the Romans to face the crowd alone.

Again, Radagaisus raised his spear for silence.

"Vitiges and his men intercepted these officers and their men coming our way. They were carrying a white flag, and apparently making their way to our camp. My son and his men escorted them back. They claim to represent many soldiers on the other side who would like to join our cause. Unfortunately they are Celtic-speakers. . ."

He pretended to spit, and there were a few indignant shouts from the audience. The king grinned.

"However, they do speak Latin as well. And these two, especially the young one, also speak some German. My priest, Phaedrus, has been invaluable in helping us understand each other."

The white-haired priest got up from his seat on the platform and went to stand beside the two soldiers.

"Roderic," called the King. "You should be up here with me for this, too."

Roderic hesitated, and then stood up.

Theona grabbed his sleeve. "Why does he want you?"

He looked at her.

"I'm his son." he said. "I have to go."

"You're his son? You're a prince? Why didn't you tell me?"

His eyes twinkled. "I didn't think I would need to," he replied, calmly. "At first I thought you must know it, but then, when it seemed you didn't, I enjoyed being just another brave, handsome nobleman." He bowed, and walked away.

They stared after him in shock. From his throne on the podium, the king was watching, fascinated.

In spite of herself, Theona started to chuckle. She understood now Radagaisus's scrutiny, and why Roderic had placed them so far away from the rest of the crowd. This area must be reserved for only the most distinguished visitors. She found she was not angry with the prince. The man was too charming by far. She was getting used to him, in spite of the dangers he represented and she was subtly succumbing to his obvious interest in her.

She wondered if Duke Helerix had known. She turned to look at him, and found her father doing the same. The warlord had been watching them. He met their gaze, shrugged, and shook his head. Perhaps he hadn't known himself. After all, all of them had only arrived yesterday.

Only yesterday! She had learned a great deal in a day, though not that the young nobleman was the son of the pagan king himself. But Roderic did not know her whole story, either. He may have guessed that she was a Christian, but surely did not know that she and her father were on a mission to convert his Goths to a new faith. They were well on their way towards their own fiery furnace!

CHAPTER THIRTEEN

THE DESERTER'S ADVICE

The Grand Council Meeting
The Barbarian camp on the Danube River
End of July 405 AD

Roderic took a seat near his brother on the platform as Radagaisus's priest led the senior soldier onto the podium to face the members of the Grand Council. The younger soldier stood stiffly at attention in front of the podium, eyes front, his face expressionless. The amphitheater grew quiet, and, within a minute or two, he was forgotten as everyone listened to the words of the officer and his Roman-born interpreter.

"My name is Bulleus," began the Celtic officer in Latin. Phaedrus translated.

"I am a tribune with the Third Italian Legion. For the last ten years I have been the garrison commander assigned to the fort at Veldidena[21] I am married and have seven children, all boys, all destined for the Roman army. My wife comes from the same area.

"This other soldier is my optio, Severus Cantarcchio. He is from Pons Drusi[22], a little community a few days south of Veldidena. We are mountain men from a long line of mountain men. We know the area you are going to pass through well, better than anyone else except other local men and women. Better than them, in fact, because in the army, we have to move around. I have been as far south as Pavia, and as far west as Regensburg."

The chieftains sitting below him looked mystified. They did not appear to recognize the names he had mentioned.

"My men are like me," he continued, "mostly local Celtic farmers, but proud to be Roman soldiers and part of the great Roman Empire. Up to now we have been willing to risk our lives for the Empire, because we believe in the Pax Romana and the Roman way of life. Our job is to protect the frontiers, keep peace in our areas and collect taxes for the Emperor. We are not traitors. It has been a good life, and we are proud of what we do.

---

[21] The fort at Veldidena is in the town of Wilton, on the outskirts of Innsbruck, Austria.

[22] Pons Drusi (the Bridge of Drusus) was located in the vicinity of Bolzano, Italy.

"This past year though, our supreme commander spent months in our province of Rhaetia trying to recruit more men for the army. If you heard this, you may have thought that he was recruiting out of fear of all of you.

There were some laughs and jeers.

Bulleus nodded respectfully.

"That's what we thought too, at first. Not at all! We began to hear from several army sources that our supreme commander wants to build up his own field army in order to begin another civil war. The rumors say that he intends to march on Constantinople in the name of the Emperor, Honorius, to force the other Emperor, Arcadius, to allow him governing power in the east."

There was a surprised murmur around the amphitheater. It was clear that many people in the audience had some knowledge of the Roman Empire and its two sections. The kings, dukes and chiefs sitting in the circle of thrones were listening carefully.

The tribune continued, "The men we represent believe that the rumors are true. It is hard to keep such suspicions quiet, and I have been told that even some members of the Senate in Rome believe this rumor."

His voice rose. "Why else do you think the General would take our best men out of our province, when the entire world knows that the great Gothic king and the chieftains who support him are waiting to cross into the Empire?"

The King looked pleased. All around the amphitheater people began hitting their shields and stamping their feet. Radagaisus raised his spear. The pause gave Tribune Bulleus a chance to compose himself.

"This man's evil plan is to take experienced soldiers like us out of our own area and force us into his field armies. His plan is to appoint other, less experienced men, even slaves, to defend *our* mountains in any invasion. He expects us to march out and abandon our families, while the new men he is recruiting will be left to guard them and the frontiers against you."

Bulleus stopped. They waited.

"We want *no* part of that. When Roman armies fight other Roman armies, nothing good comes from it. There is too much death, and it weakens the whole Empire. Many of my soldiers do not want to leave home, do not want to die in foreign parts, and do not want to kill other Roman soldiers, some of whom they have served with before.

"Many from my Legion, the Third Italian Legion, and the legion in Noricum have decided that we would rather defy our orders and join your invasion than leave our families and homes to march off against Emperor Arcadius.

"The men with me here today represent many other men who will join you at the right time, or at least not stand in your way. Those who stand with us will let you pass safely through our land to Italia. We see this as our best chance to protect our villages and our families. We are asking you today for a treaty that will protect our people, and in turn, we will provide you with guides and assistance."

When Phaedrus finished translating this, there was a roar from the crowd.

One of the Vandal leaders rose hastily and turned around to shout at the spectators. There was a lull, and he spoke into it. "Don't be fooled by this Roman Army officer. Since when can you trust the words of a representative of Rome?" He turned back to glare at Bulleus, "Roman filth, enemy of the ancient gods, what makes you think we need your help. Or your empty promises?"

Phaedrus translated this, leaving out the insult.

Bulleus had his answer ready, and answered calmly.

"It will take you many weeks to get your people to Italia. You do not know the mountains. We do. There are very few roads that will lead to Italia. Others lead only to the mines, or to remote villages and dead ends. If you take one of those, you will have to turn around, a hard thing with so many people and wagons coming behind you, yes?"

A few of the leaders nodded reluctantly.

"Without us, your people will get lost. If you get lost, you will lose time, maybe so much time that winter will come and people will die. And do you know where the passes are? Some of them will lead you deeper into the mountains and then the road will run out. Others are almost impassible, even to a man on foot. The passes are very high—only a trained guide would know how to find his way to them and through them. There are very few ways to get from here to Italia, but my men know them all."

He paused to give them time to consider this, and then continued. "Winter comes early in the high mountains. There is little food available, and many dangers. Your people will lose their confidence in you unless you can get them to Italia safely. Without our help, the bodies of your people and animals will be littered along the way. The wolves will grow fat on them. The Roman Army need not raise a hand against you. The mountains will get you."

A broad-shouldered young Goth stood up from the audience, and banged his shield to get attention.

"King Radagaisus," he shouted, "It is my opinion that these men are spies. We know the Romans are aware we are coming. How do you know this man is not luring us all into a trap designed by his superiors?"

Phaedrus translated. King Radagaisus turned to Vitiges and said something. The Prince nodded, and stood up. His deep voice boomed out.

"My fellow warriors, these men are brave fighters, like us. They are family men, like us. And now they are deserters. If they are caught, they will be killed. Tribune Bulleus and his men knew that in coming here they faced death—from us, or from their masters. Yet they came."

"They are still Romans," shouted the Goth. "And if they were sent as spies, they will not face death, but rewards and advancement."

The man beside him also stood up.

"Romans will say anything to you. They have no honor and no loyalty even among themselves. In my country, they have massacred women and children just to punish us for raiding a few of their paltry market towns. I will not work with such men. It would be like trusting my people to a pack of wild boars."

Shouts erupted from all over the amphitheater. Radagaisus signaled to the guards. They began to move down the aisles and take up positions beside each row. The men and women seated near the ends looked at them in alarm. The king raised his arm for silence.

Vitiges spoke directly to the two men: "You will get your revenge. Just not on them."

He raised his voice to the crowd. "Listen to what the Roman has to say. Then make up your mind whether you think he speaks truth or not. As for my father, my brother, and I, we believe him."

He sat down. So did the two Goths.

"Speak, Tribune," said the king. "What have you to say?"

"Your majesty," said Bulleus, "We would *never* have come to you at all if we had not been faced with fighting an unwinnable war against other Roman armies for no good reason. It is death to talk such treason as I am doing here, and yet many of our men have been talking about this quietly for the last six months. If they obey General Stilicho's orders, they may die fighting the soldiers of the Eastern Empire while their farms and families remain unprotected back home. If they disobey those orders, they are traitors and will be killed. Only if we join you, will we have a chance to save our families and our own lives."

"So," said the king to the Grand Council. "What do you think, councilors? Do you trust these men?"

One of the Vandal chiefs stood up.

"Your majesty, I, for one, would trust any one of my brothers here rather than a Roman. If these men accompany us, we dare not trust them. Anyone who accompanies my group will be kept under guard and killed at once if there is any problem."

"King Radagaisus, may I have permission to speak on my father's behalf?"

The question came from Roderic's companion from the previous day. Goar had been whispering to the older man on the ornate throne throughout the leadership council. Theona wondered why the older man did not speak for himself. Perhaps he could not understand the language.

"Go ahead, Prince Goar. What does my good friend, King Respendial, wish to say?"

The young Alan stood up, his shiny black hair and lithe form a striking contrast to the big men around him.

"Sire, as Drevus says, it could be a trap, but having guides through the mountains would be a huge help to us. Let's hear what their plan is so we can gauge better. Perhaps it is true that they are dead men if they desert. Any man under my father's command would be."

There was laughter.

The Roman officer had been watching and listening carefully to the exchange. Perhaps he was interpreting their body language. Or, perhaps in spite of what had been said earlier, he had more than a rudimentary understanding of the dialects being spoken around him.

To Theona, his fearlessness was remarkable. She glanced at his companion. The young man was still standing motionless, his posture stiff, only his eyes moving. Their eyes met. Hers widened and he looked away quickly. Whatever he was thinking was off-limits to her.

The tribune was addressing the tough-looking leaders facing him.

"You have a multitude of people with you, women and children, not just warriors," he said. "Rome has heard of your misfortunes, and many people there have sympathized with your plight at the hands of the Huns."

Someone on the stage behind him snorted.

"The Emperor understands that many of you just want safety and a chance to build a new life for your families. This, he is unlikely to allow at this time. You cannot just demand to get land and support from the Emperor without proper permission. Even if many of you have peaceful intentions, your invasion will be considered an act of aggression towards the people of the Roman Empire. You must understand this—your parents and grandparents learned it to their cost. However, if you are determined to go, you must go right away. Do not wait a day longer."

The King thumped his spear to interrupt.

"Tell him that we have to wait," he said firmly. "Other chiefs have told us they may join us. Some of them may be on the way."

Phaedrus translated.

Tribune Bulleus turned to Radagaisus.

"Your Majesty, *when* you cross the river is your decision to make, and what happens once you get inside the Empire is between you and the Emperor," he said, loudly. "But listen to me, my lords. It will take you weeks to reach the mountains from here. If you do not want your people to starve, you must leave now. There is little food in the mountains. My people will not work with you if you try to deprive us of what we need to get through the winter. If we work together, and if you follow my advice, you will make it to Italia alive."

Phaedrus translated what the tribune had said. When he had finished, the amphitheater was quiet. The king said nothing.

Bulleus looked around and seemed satisfied that he had been heard.

"So here is what you must do, my brothers. Across the Danube in Pannonia, and farther away in Noricum, the farmers have been bringing in the hay and harvesting their early crops. They will be hard at work for weeks, knowing you are coming. Local government officials have been threatening them, and urging them to hurry. Everyone is rushing. Soon the food you need will all be safely locked away behind city walls and in fortified storage facilities and your chance to get this food supply will be gone.

"You must give your people the chance to stock up on food and grain *before* they get to the mountains. If you wait for other chiefs to join you, there will be very little food to be found. Your people will die of hunger before you face a single Roman soldier."

The Council members listened, and nodded.

"And there is something else I have to say, even if your High King does not want to hear this."

He turned, and looked apologetically at the King. Radagaisus's eyes narrowed.

"This is something you must *not* do. You must *not* stay all together, even if this was your plan. If you all travel together, the people in the rear will have no food supplies at all. The ones ahead of them will have taken all the food. You will do better to split up."

Theona looked at Duke Helerix, who was thrumming his fingers on the arm of his chair, thinking.

Radagaisus rose and spoke to the Grand Council.

"It is true we had thought to stay together. We must be able to form an army when we enter Italia. If we separate, the Romans will be able to pick us off like deer at a waterhole. But the Tribune's words make sense. There must be somewhere safe where we can reunite."

Bulleus had an answer for him.

"My men and I have been talking about that. You will face no great danger across the river in Pannonia. Much of the army there is away in Macedonia now. There are three main routes you can take from there into Italia. Two of them meet in the valley of the Isarco River south of one of the passes. There are places farther down which are wide enough to accommodate you all for a short time. Perhaps you can gather and wait at Tridentum. Then you can move south toward Verona as one army."

"Verrrona," repeated the king, rolling the word around his tongue. "Verrrona. Where is this place?"

"When you come out of the mountains, there is a great and fertile plain with many cities in it, sire. Verona is a large town on the edge of that great plain."

Some of the Grand Council members were nodding their heads. It seemed that Bulleus's plan pleased them. They were beginning to trust him.

The red-headed officer had noticed. "We have conditions for our co-operation, sire."

The Gothic king nodded graciously. "And what are your conditions, Tribune?"

"We will guide you through the mountains on the condition that your people do no harm to our homes and villages. Nor to the crops and animals we need to take us through the winter months. Our daughters and sons, our wives and parents, are as precious to us as yours are to you. Your fight has to be with the Roman soldiers who face you, not with us or our communities.

"Secondly, once we have led you safely through the mountains, you must not prevent us from returning home to our families. Some of the men wish to stay with you and fight, but most do not. You and these other chiefs must each give us your word that you will treat us as respected allies and not break these terms. Is that agreed?"

Prince Vitiges stood up and came around to speak to his father quietly. Radagaisus listened and nodded, and his son came forward to stand beside the Rhaetian tribune to address the Grand Council.

"Tribune Bulleus and the men with him—there are eight others—represent garrisons from six different forts guarding the passes through the Alps. He has told my father and me that the men in these garrisons are waiting for word from us that we will keep their conditions. As you can understand, they are anxious to help us all get through the mountains as quickly as possible. When you agree to spare their families, their villages, and their farms, they will not oppose us, and they will give aid to any groups who get lost or in trouble in the mountains.

"It is a good plan. All you have to do is make sure you have everything you need *before* you enter their territory, that you do not molest the villages or forts whose garrisons allow us passage, and finally, that any soldiers who travel with us will be allowed to return to their homes without harm. We, on both sides, must be men of our word."

He turned and walked back to his seat.

Radagaisus looked down at the chieftains seated in front of him.

"What do you say?"

A distinguished looking duke stood up. He was wearing quality clothing and wore his long yellow hair shoulder length. He moved stiffly, even though he did not appear old. Two of his fingers were missing.

He looked around at his fellow leaders.

"King Radagaisus, and fellow members of the Grand Council," he began. "All of us are going for our own reasons. We are having to trust one another and forget past grievances even though at different times some of us have been at war with each other. It is no different for these soldiers. The reasons this man has given are sound ones. He is right. We will have serious difficulties if we do not have experienced guides for this journey. I confess I am more afraid of the mountains than I am of the Emperor's men."

He sat down.

There was a brief consultation. One by one the chiefs rose to declare their backing for the proposal.

"It is agreed, then," announced Radagaisus. "Bring out the rest of the tribune's men."

The lower doors opened and eight more Roman soldiers marched out. Their uniforms were soiled and worn, their shields and helmets ill-matched, and they appeared tired and badly shaven, yet they marched proudly in step to the front of the podium and turned on command to face their senior officer with barely a glance at the crowd or the Gothic king. They saluted Tribune Bulleus and his junior officer and were saluted smartly back.

Bulleus gave an order and they relaxed, looking around curiously at the big Roman amphitheater and its barbarian crowd. Their expressions ranged from apprehensive to curious.

"Know these men," said Bulleus to the crowd. "Everyone is an experienced mountain guide. All of them know all the routes into, and out of the high mountains. They know which roads are paved, where the forts and bridges are, which places are particularly dangerous, and where to find emergency supplies. They know where to hunt, and how to survive in bad weather. I will assign one of them to each group. They will guide you to your destination as safely as they can. After that, as agreed, you must let each of them go home. They have no wish to harm the Roman people or their fellow soldiers. If you fail to keep these conditions, you will find the mountains can be evil places should you try to come back through them again. Mountain people have long memories.

"Be assured that we wish you success in this venture. If you do not succeed, then even our children will suffer the consequences. The Romans do not forgive betrayal. From this day forward, my men and I have no future if you do not succeed. We will do our best to make sure you do."

As Phaedrus translated, there was a murmur of respect from the crowd. Someone began to hammer their shield across their knees. Others followed. All over the building, people stood up and stamped their feet, paying homage to the courage of the ten Roman soldiers standing in front of them. The Rhaetians looked around, grinning and relieved.

Once the din had subsided, Radagaisus became the gracious host. "Tell the tribune he and his men are free to go now. They are invited to join all the leaders at a great feast I am giving here tonight. We will need to decide on our route and assign the guides to lead them. The first to depart will leave the day after tomorrow."

He signaled to the horn blower, who raised the great instrument to his lips and blew.

The Council was over.

All over the building, people headed up the stairs, eager to spread the news that their long journey to Rome was about to begin.

Up on the podium, Bulleus saluted the king and the other members of the Grand Council, and nodded to his optio. The two turned and marched their men back through the lower doors. Roderic got up and prepared to jump off the podium. His father stopped him briefly. The prince smiled and jumped down. He ran lightly across the ground to where Theona and her father were waiting.

"Good news!" he smiled. "My father would like to meet you and your daughter after the ceremony. He has invited you both to stay for the feast."

CHAPTER FOURTEEN

PASTOR RHODUS PROVOKES THE KING

∾

The Grand Council Meeting
Radagaisus's Camp on the Danube River
End of July, 405 AD

"Please thank your father for his kind invitation," replied Pastor Rhodus. "We do not belong in such fine company, as I'm sure you know. My daughter and I have a long way to walk to get back to our laager. We will perhaps meet your father on another occasion. Come, Theona."

He turned and started across the grass towards the steps.

Shocked and embarrassed by her father's rudeness, Theona didn't move. She had no wish to hurt the young man whose attentions and conversation she had so enjoyed. Roderic turned to her, his smile a bit stiff, the hurt showing in his eyes.

"Oh come on, father. Please let's stay," she implored. "It's not every day we get invited to a king's feast. Can we not stay at least for the ceremony?"

She had enjoyed the opening ceremony of the Grand Council as much as the rest of the crowd. The martial chants and rhythms had been rousing to the young girl whose life had normally been quiet and orderly

"What kind of ceremony is it?" asked Pastor Rhodus, suspiciously.

"Find out for yourself. It's just about to begin. Look, lots of people are staying for it."

They looked around. It seemed that half the spectators had indeed chosen to remain, although the amphitheater was still emptying. Reluctantly, Rhodus sat down in the seat beside the center aisle. Theona hurried over to join him, and Roderic followed.

Radagaisus had begun speaking again.

"It is time to see if the omens are favorable for this grand adventure of ours. Tribune Bulleus says we should leave now. We will see if the gods agree, and if our adventure will be successful."

The high priest hurried down the steps from the podium, and headed back to the wide doors. He knocked. Someone opened them and he entered.

Pastor Rhodus quickly stood up and grabbed his daughter's hand. "Come on, Theona. We need to go."

"But, why?" Theona was disconcerted. She had thought she had won the battle.

"This is a pagan ceremony. We cannot be here."

Roderic stood up too, and physically blocked the entrance to the aisle. "You can't leave now," he insisted. "It will look disrespectful, and my father will be offended if you reject his hospitality. It is best to wait at least until you meet him."

"I mean no disrespect to King Radagaisus, young man, but Theona is innocent of these things, and I, as her father, wish her to remain so."

Roderic hesitated, and then shook his head stubbornly. "Perhaps she should get used to it."

"Indeed she must not!"

"Why not?"

The prince's voice, too, had taken on an angry note. The question was a direct challenge to Rhodus to declare his loyalties.

"Get used to what?" Theona was becoming frightened. She knew her father would not lead her astray. Roderic, she was not so sure about.

A number of people nearby were watching and listening. One of the guards was approaching. The King's attention was elsewhere, but Duke Helerix had twisted around and was watching from his 'throne'. He looked up and gave a signal. Many of his men were still in the building and Theona saw them take their seats again.

Pastor Rhodus, becoming conscious of the attention they were drawing, looked at his daughter in anguish, and sat down.

Theona sat, too. Roderic waved the guard away, and sat beside her.

Phaedrus reappeared, this time in his role as priest of the Gothic gods. He had taken his sandals off and was carrying a long, elaborately carved pole with a packet of twisted vines and feathers tied onto it. He walked with dignity to the podium. Everyone in the auditorium rose to their feet and waited.

He began to wave the sacred pole through the air in some kind of symbolic picture language and at the same time began to chant, invoking the presence of his gods. The sonorous voice rose and fell. After several such incantations Radagaisus raised his shield and struck it. A few people in the stands struck their shields as well. Once, twice, three times. New people, drawn by the noise, entered the amphitheater and came down the rows to find seats. The place began to fill with sound again, the noise rising to a fast, fevered pitch.

Theona noticed that a few of the leaders were not participating. One had conspicuously crossed his arms. Goar's father, King Respendial, was looking around, mystified. One Gothic duke made a wry face to his neighbor, a Marcomanni judge. In spite of their distaste, they did not leave. What was going to happen? Her father had his eyes closed, and his lips were moving. He looked miserable. His unease was infecting her as well.

"What's going to happen?" she hissed.

He didn't bother keeping his voice down—the din covered his words. Only Roderic was close enough to hear.

"The priest is going to kill some poor creature as a gift to one of their gods, and then examine its entrails to see if there is anything unusual about them." He glared at Roderic. "How can that help?"

He looked back at Theona. "Pray that their black master does not come. Pray that the entrails look satisfactory. Just pray for everyone here to be protected against the powers of darkness. We will leave as soon as we can."

"It would be best if you stayed for the feast," said Roderic coldly. "My father has requested it."

This was too much for Pastor Rhodus. He whirled on the prince.

"Because he noticed your interest in my daughter, Prince Roderic," he accused. "You think my daughter is pretty? Look around you. There are many beauties in the camp." He grabbed Theona's hand. "You have a problem, young man. My daughter is not available to you."

Roderic glared at him.

"You'd best be careful, old man. Remember whom you are talking to," he hissed. Impulsively, he seized Theona's other hand, staring angrily at her father.

Theona tried to pull her hand away, but Roderic held on tightly, only once glancing at her in this contest of wills.

Rhodus turned, and looked up into the seats above them. Darric started to make his way down. Several other Wodenvale men followed him. Roderic noticed, and waited tensely. Darric calmly moved into a seat two rows above them. The other men, almost all of them skilled warriors in the Duke's service, settled into other rows nearby.

Radagaisus's guards watched uneasily. Because of their earlier presentation to the Grand Council, the Wodenvale men were still fully armed.

The wide doors opened again. A naked man walked out leading a white lamb with a rope around its neck. The little animal was bleating and balking, frightened by the crowd and the noise. He strained against the rope, not at all a willing victim.

The man and the struggling lamb were followed by two men in white robes carrying a tall black-curtained litter with occult images carved on it. Inside, dimly seen though a veil, sat a woman with a large headdress on her head. Pastor Rhodus swore, and sat down again releasing Theona's hand. She bent closer to his ear.

"What is it?" she shouted.

"Nerthus! One of their goddesses. One of the most blood-thirsty!" he shouted. "The sacrifice is to her."

Theona abruptly sat down too, almost pulling Prince Roderic over.

He released her hand and reached across to her father, pulling him on to his feet again.

"Get up, old man," he shouted. "Are you looking for trouble?" His eyes darted meaningfully to the podium and back.

King Radagaisus had noticed the exchange and was staring at them. Other guards were crowding onto the verandah behind the podium where Rilka's mother and the other women had been.

Pastor Rhodus reluctantly stood there, his shoulders tense.

Theona was becoming deeply frightened. She stood up shakily, and put her arm around her father's waist. He looked at her with a grateful smile. She could feel his thin body relax under his woolen shirt.

What was going on that would make her gentle father and Prince Roderic become instant adversaries?

She had seen animals slaughtered before many times. It couldn't be just that.

She suddenly remembered her story about David and Goliath. Perhaps that was what was going on here. Her father believed they were in the middle of a battlefield between the forces of good and evil. Roderic's anger was probably his darned vanity again. She turned and smiled at him. He looked at her, troubled.

"What?"

She continued to smile at him, but didn't answer. After all, he had held her hand against her will and called her father an old man! That had to be punished!

The two priests carried the litter and its occupant to the front of the podium where they stood erect. Phaedrus walked around to the side, bowed deeply to the priestess inside, and knelt down on the ground. The woman got out, stepping barefooted onto his back and then onto the ground. The two priests carried the litter away some distance and laid it down.

Nerthus's priestess wasted no time greeting the King or his Grand Council. She was dressed in a long black robe with occult symbols embroidered all over it. Her long black veil was bizarrely held in place by a bear's head perched on top of her own. Theona smiled in spite of her nervousness; balancing that thing must be the reason why the priestess held her head so rigidly and moved so slowly.

She seemed almost remote as she pulled a long ceremonial knife with a black and silver hilt from a leather scabbard attached to her belt and walked over to the little lamb, still struggling against the rope that the nude man was holding.

Him, the priestess did acknowledge, bending her head ever so slightly in his direction. He was looking at her with horror. It looked as though he was putting every ounce of his courage into not shrinking away from her.

Ever so gently, the woman stooped to embrace the little white animal. For a minute it struggled, and then at last relaxed into her deadly cuddle. Expertly she slashed the knife across the submissive animal's throat. Blood gushed onto her black robe and onto the pavement. The crowd grew very still.

Carefully, she knelt down and placed the little body on the ground. With three expert strokes, the priestess slit the animal's belly, laying open the insides. After a solemn examination, she stood up. Phaedrus hurried over and she spoke to him, gesturing down at the mess on the ground. He, too, looked at the entrails, and then walked back to the podium to speak to Radagaisus who was watching attentively. They had a whispered consultation. Once again Radagaisus raised his spear.

"The omens are not favorable," he shouted. There is much trouble ahead. The goddess has sent us a warning. Her servant says that Nerthus requires human blood to protect us. Otherwise we are walking into a disaster."

There were shocked exclamations from the audience. The chieftains who had not wanted to participate in the ceremony exchanged glances. Everyone's attention now switched to the man who had brought in the lamb. He swayed, and the two priests reached out to grab his arms to hold him upright. Suddenly, Theona realized why her father had been so desperate to get her out of there. She looked at Roderic in shock. He looked at her sadly.

"Give her one of the Romans," shouted a hoarse voice from the crowd. A few others echoed the suggestion.

"There is no need for that," replied the King. "We have the blood sacrifice we need, a volunteer. This criminal has chosen this way to pay for his crimes. His family has refused to support him, and his clan head will not pay the tribute for the life he has taken, that of his own brother!" he shouted, pointing an accusing finger.

There was a gasp from the crowd. Fratricide was a terrible crime. A few people got up and raced for the exits. Council members and many in the crowd began to hammer their judgment on their shields. Those without such luxuries stamped their feet and shouted. "To the goddess. Death to the criminal!"

The naked man straightened up and faced the priestess. She handed him some leaves which he took and began to chew. One of the priests sliced the rope that he had used to lead the lamb into two parts and used one to bind his hands behind him, while the other priest tied his feet together. He was pale and sweating profusely. His hands, bound as they were, were shaking.

The priestess stood there waiting quietly, bright drops of blood from her previous victim slipping down the blade of her knife and pooling on the ground.

When they were ready, the king began to beat his shield. The din started up once more. The sound had now become hateful to Theona. She covered her ears, but continued to watch in fascinated horror.

Phaedrus walked over to the murderer and grabbed his hair, forcing his head back. The priestess took a step toward him, her bloody knife cocked up and ready to do its job.

"No."

Pastor Rhodus started running toward them. Everyone in the crowd, focused on the fatal stroke to come, looked at him in shock. Few had heard his shout, but everyone could see the thin pastor running like a crazy man toward the priestess and her 'volunteer'. The amphitheater hushed briefly and then exploded into sound. Phaedrus and the other priests watched him come but did not relinquish their hold on their human sacrifice. Radagaisus stopped pounding on his shield and yelled at Roderic.

Theona grabbed Roderic's arm and hung on grimly.

"Get off me. I'll not hurt him," he yelled. He yanked his arm away and turned around to find Darric there, blocking his way, axe blade towards him, his gray eyes deadly serious. Roderic stood there, uncertainly. A few guards started toward them and the Wodenvale men stood up and came down to stand around the group. They were at a stalemate.

Pastor Rhodus reached Nerthus's priestess and made a grab for the ceremonial knife. He inadvertently knocked her bear's head headdress and it began to fall, taking the long veil with it. The priestess raised her knife to defend herself. Pastor Rhodus knocked her down. She dropped the knife. Phaedrus finally let go of the fratricide and rushed to help his priestess. The other priests continued to hold the fratricide's arms to prevent him from hobbling away. He appeared to be as much an avid spectator now, as everyone else in the amphitheater.

Pastor Rhodus grabbed the long knife and rushed straight at the podium. Everyone there hastily drew their weapons. Guards leaped to stand in front of the High King. Radagaisus pulled out his own sword.

To everyone's surprise, the crazy man did not attempt to climb the stairs. Instead, he stooped down and rammed the sacrificial knife into the soil beside the concrete base of the podium. Using all his strength, he tried to bend the knife sideways against the concrete to snap off the blade.

Phaedrus, guessing his intention, roared and ran to stop him. He leaped on Theona's father and tried desperately to reach the sacred knife. Rhodus strained to break the blade, covering his efforts with his body. The priest grabbed at the pastor's arms, but Rhodus hung on to the knife grimly. Frustrated, Phaedrus went for his eyes. Rhodus let go of the knife at last, and shot his fist sharply up into his attacker's face. Phaedrus screamed, his nose broken. Blood rushed down onto his white toga.

Pastor Rhodus, his own face bleeding from the priest's nails, ignored him. He had gone back to bending the knife hilt away from the concrete base.

Phaedrus leaped on him again just as the blade suddenly snapped. Rhodus lost his balance and fell backward onto his adversary. They both scrambled to their feet, snarling.

Theona started to run.

The other priests abandoned the fratricide and pulled knives from their robes, silently closing in on the angry missionary. Pastor Rhodus turned, defiant and weaponless, to face them. His daughter raced in to stand in front of her father. Roderic and Darric looked at one another and took off after her. So did Duke Helerix, who let out his war cry and got there first, sword drawn, determined to protect the Christian pastor who had befriended his people in their own time of trouble. His men hurried down to stand near the guards.

Roderic and Darric reached Rhodus and Theona together and stood in front of them. With Duke Helerix, they formed a protective barrier, three grim faces wielding two swords and one axe. The deacon and the warlord faced out towards the crowd, their weapons holding back the three furious priests.

Roderic faced the podium, his eyes fixed on his father's face, his mouth set. There was a sudden rush from behind the row of seated Council members, and Goar hurried in to stand back to back with his friend, his jeweled scimitar flashing dangerously, a huge grin on his face.

Now they were four. Theona shrank back to stand against the podium, her eyes on Phaedrus. Both she and her father were unarmed and defiant.

All over the auditorium the audience watched in delighted horror. The man intended to be the human sacrifice stood there, color returning to his face. His hands and feet were still bound, but he seemed to have decided that today would not be his last day—whoever's blood might be shed to satisfy Nerthus today, it likely would not be his.

The king's men poured into the amphitheater from the square outside, trying to assess the situation and waiting for their orders. There were at least as many of them as there were Wodenvale warriors, but they wavered. They were facing two princes and a warlord. Although the odds were good, the politics were not. Radagaisus still had not decided what to do.

Nerthus's priestess signaled to the two priests and headed for the litter, her bear headdress and veil in her arms. The frustrated priests abandoned vengeance for expediency and hurried to get her out of there, leaving only Phaedrus to represent them.

More and more Wodenvale men were pouring down the aisles from the field outside. There was shoving and shouting as Helerix's Goths and Radagaisus's Goths vied with each other to get down to ground level for the fight.

Three members of the Grand Council looked at each other, stood up, and turned to face the other kings, princes and dukes, swords drawn. Their pagan counterparts stared at them in anger. Most of them had no idea what was behind this insanity, or what was motivating the different players. Onlookers ran from the amphitheater, whether to escape the danger or to get reinforcements was not yet clear.

Radagaisus made up his mind. He hit the silver shield hard.

"Stop!"

A few seconds more and his Grand Council would have dissolved into a bloodbath.

"Everyone back off."

He waited until people showed signs of complying with this command.

"Members of the Council, all of you, take your seats again. We need to investigate this matter and find out what is the source of this trouble. It seems we have a problem, or else we have a madman in our midst."

The three chiefs remained standing, but lowered their weapons. Wary warriors slunk back to the periphery of the theater or took seats on the nearest benches, waiting to see what would happen next. Theona could see far more weapons displayed than were probably allowed.

"Escort the criminal back to his cage," ordered the King.

One of the guards cut the ropes binding the fratricide's feet and hands. He bent down and gently picked up the disemboweled carcass of the little lamb and carried it back through the lower doors. Theona watched, deeply moved.

Phaedrus wiped his bloody nose with his sleeve. His snowy robes were now filthy with blood and dirt. He walked past them, glaring at Prince Roderic. He stopped in front of Pastor Rhodus, his eyes narrowing. "You stopped an important ceremony and broke a sacred knife. Why? What did you hope to accomplish?"

"That man will go to hell if he dies in his sins."

"That man is not your concern. You think you have saved him from death? He chose this way to die to atone for his fratricide. He will still die, and rightly so, but perhaps he will not be able to atone for his sin next time."

"Nobody can atone for their own sin. Not you, not him. Not ever."

"Ah. You are a Christian? Because of your foolish interference, you have aroused the anger of the goddess. There will be more suffering on this trip, not less, and it will be on your head."

He switched his gaze to Theona. She glared at him.

"If I were you, I would keep away from Prince Roderic."

"Phaedrus!" exclaimed the prince.

"I will gladly do so, if you will promise to do the same," she said.

Phaedrus's eyes narrowed, then, ignoring the rest of them, he limped around to the stairs and painfully climbed to the podium to speak to the King.

"Get her out of here," Roderic muttered to Darric.

"I'm not going anywhere without my father," protested Theona.

They looked at her, then at each other, and then at Pastor Rhodus, who was attempting to explain his behavior to his furious warlord.

"Get them both out of here," said Roderic, resigned.

"And just how am I supposed to do that?" Darric's eyes were sweeping the amphitheater, taking in the guards, Phaedrus, the people on the podium and the warriors on both sides. Goar raised an eyebrow. Roderic flushed.

He glanced up at his father, frowning down at them all from the podium, while he listened to Phaedrus's muttered comments. The king clearly was angry with him and waiting to talk to him. All the Council Members were on their feet now, swords put aside as they argued with one another. From his throne, Respendial was vehemently signaling to Goar to come back and explain what had happened. With a shrug of his elegant shoulders, Goar left, winking at Theona. She grinned, and watched him go. She saw several of the chieftains watching her. A couple of them caught her eye and smiled in fatherly reassurance. Others eyed her father and her coldly, or with sour curiosity

"Come with me," said Prince Roderic.

The Wodenvale four followed him around to the steps of the podium. A dozen guards with yellow and green armbands surrounded them and followed close behind. The Wodenvale men kept abreast of them. It would have been comical if so many lives had not been at risk.

Roderic paused at the stairs, and turned to face his uneasy companions.

"Duke Helerix," he said quietly, "You will need to make things right with my father, and this is your best opportunity. Will you trust me to get these people safely away from here? You can sort this out back at your laager."

He waited as Helerix's sharp eyes studied him.

"See that you do, Prince Roderic, or you will answer to me and my people. I have given my word to protect these men and Theona, and I keep my word. My men, as you can see, are also loyal, and ready to follow my lead."

"Yes sir."

There was no irony in Roderic's tone. Lord Helerix's men, for all their loyalty and skill were a tiny force compared to the vast military resources the High King now commanded.

He turned to speak to the guard who stood closest to them. "Hold them here," he ordered, "while the Lord of Wodenvale and I speak to my father."

To Pastor Rhodus and Darric, he said, "I will be right back." He met Theona's anxious eyes without comment, and then turned to climb the stairs with Duke Helerix behind him.

Darric, Pastor Rhodus and Theona stood at the foot of the stairs, surrounded by dozens of soldiers and warriors, the focus of curious eyes from all over the amphitheater.

Darric reached up to scratch his quiver shoulder. The guards stepped closer. So did Duke Helerix's men.

The camaraderie that had been there before was now severely strained. All of them were trying to hear the conversation between the High King, the warlord, the pagan priest, and Prince Roderic.

Roderic was there for only a minute, then left Duke Helerix to sort things out with Radagaisus and an indignant Phaedrus, and returned to the others.

"Follow me," he said. He led them to the two wide doors the Roman soldiers, the fratricide, and the priest and priestess had gone through. Theona, Pastor Rhodus and Darric followed him, closely shadowed by the guards and Helerix's men. Roderic knocked. The door was opened by one of the priests. Roderic held the door open for them and they walked in. He blocked the entrance into the building with his body to prevent anyone else from following.

"Thank you," he said to the guards following them. "I will take it from here."

The leader saluted, and Roderic closed the door, leaving the guards and the Wodenvale warriors standing outside.

They passed the fratricide, who was now clothed, and sitting in a cage with a guard nearby. He was shaking, and looked in bad shape, worse than he had when he had first walked out leading the lamb. Theona recognized the look on his face. She had seen it before in her own village after the massacre and in Wodenvale after the second Hunnic raid. He was in shock.

He had had to face death and accept it. Now that final end to his ordeal was gone. He was still alive and facing an unknown future. He did not smile or say anything as they passed, even though her father smiled at him. Theona did not smile. The man had killed his brother. In her opinion, he deserved to die.

The prince led them through a hallway lined with cubicles. Some of the Roman soldiers were bunked down on pallets in these. They came to a heavy wooden door that opened into a new section of the building. Roderic lifted down a key from a hook on the wall. On the other side of the door the rooms were nicer, better furnished. The smell of fried and boiled food drifted down a hallway from somewhere. Guards' quarters, perhaps?

Silently Pastor Rhodus, Darric and Theona followed Prince Roderic down the hallway and into another set of rooms. This area was finer still.

At last they came to an unguarded outside exit and walked out into a peristyle. It was in sad shape, the pond was empty and the flower beds were a mass of weeds. Bulleus's young optio, Severus Cantarcchio, was sitting on a bench enjoying the sunshine and a large tankard of beer. He inclined his head to the prince, but did not rise, just watched as the four of them hurried past him down the weedy path.

At the back of the peristyle was an ornate, wrought iron door in a stone wall. Roderic removed a key from an alcove beside the door and used this to open the old lock. Beyond the wall a path led through a wooded area to the river a short distance away.

"There's a boat down there," he said. "Take it, and go back to your camp. Theona knows where one of my father's men has his tent. Leave the boat there. He will bring it back here. I must go and try to help your lord with my father and Phaedrus."

He turned and hurried back through the garden and into the building.

Pastor Rhodus led the way to the boat and they climbed in. There were three sets of oars. Theona stepped forward to the middle seat and Darric prepared to jump in last. Just before he pushed off, a voice called to them in heavily accented Goth.

"Wait!" Tribune Bulleus's junior officer, Severus Cantarcchio, was coming at a run down the path toward them. "I will come with you. It will go faster."

"There is no need. There are three of us. We can manage fine," replied her father.

"Prince Roderic told me to go with you," he insisted. "I can bring the boat back."

They looked at one another. It was possible.

"He is my patron. Trust me," he added.

Wordlessly, Theona moved to sit on the bottom of the boat in front of her father. Darric reluctantly let the Rhaetian soldier climb past him to take Theona's place at the middle set of oars.

Darric pushed the boat out and jumped in. They rowed hard to the end of the island and headed out toward the middle of the river, past the men standing guard along the shore. They were not stopped, perhaps because the boat was recognizably the High King's. They had a long way to row, and then a two hour walk to their camp. They did not talk at all because of the presence of the stranger with them, but concentrated on covering the distance. It was almost an hour before they landed near the center roadway through the camp.

Other hands reached out to help pull the boat in, and Theona saw the grey-haired fisherman, the prince's "old friend of the family," leisurely walking toward them, his bare legs knotted with muscle. Darric climbed out first, followed by the optio and Theona. Pastor Rhodus was the last to exit.

Cantarcchio had a heated, if broken, conversation with the fisherman which involved much gesturing, and then both of them climbed into the boat for the trip back to the island. As Pastor Rhodus and Darric were pushing it back out onto the river, the soldier leaned forward.

"Your name, sir?" asked Cantarcchio. "I see you are a friend of the King's family."

Pastor Rhodus frowned. "We were merely guests of Prince Roderic today," he replied curtly. "My name is Rhodus."

He gave the boat a final shove and walked quickly away with Theona and Darric hurrying after him.

The last part of the journey was the hardest. Theona had had almost nothing to eat that day. She felt sick from hunger, and reaction was beginning to set in. None of them had brought food or money, so they would have to wait to eat till they got back to the Wodenvale laager. Her steps grew slower and slower. Darric put his arm protectively around her waist with one eye on her father. Pastor Rhodus, worn out and worried, did not object.

There was much to talk about, too much. As soon as they reached the laager, Darric said goodbye and left for his tent, his own exhaustion showing in his face and step. Gideon was ecstatic to see them. Theona cooked some eggs and vegetables, while her father fetched more water. They ate, put out the fire, climbed into the wagon, and went straight to sleep.

Duke Helerix rode into the camp, drunk and singing, with most of his mounted warriors several hours later. The rest of his men continued to straggle in over the course of the long, summer evening.

The next day their laager, indeed the whole camp city, hummed with the news about the events at the Grand Council. The scandal of Pastor Rhodus's bizarre behavior and Prince Roderic's protection of him and his daughter was tantalizing and titillating, but it was overshadowed by the news that they were all to get ready to leave for Pannonia immediately. The other incident became a juicy morsel to be dissected once the main work was done.

Duke Helerix called for a council to be held at midday. Everyone stayed around the camp waiting for this. He arrived with a dozen of his henchmen looking pasty and tired, and regarded Theona and Darric sourly when they, along with the rest of his men, women and children, showed up to hear what the plans for departure would be.

They learned they were to move their oxcarts out of the circle formation and form a line in the grassland beyond. They would be joining two larger groups of Goths who would be traveling with them. A Roman guide had been assigned to them, an officer by the name of Cantarcchio. Everyone would be heading south down the Danube to a place where there were said to be fords they could use. Once they reached the other side, their guide would lead them through Pannonia towards Noricum and the mountains. They would need to post guards every night, especially if, and when, they became separated from the main caravan. Some of King Radagaisus's men would act as messengers and attempt to keep the caravans in touch with one another and with the High King. This effort would be headed by the King's younger son while the elder son, Prince Vitiges, led the way with the Roman leader. King Radagaisus and some of his men would guard the rear.

Helerix warned his people to be strategic about what they took with them. They would be able to raid farms and gather food along the way. He advised them to collect as much food, firewood and blankets as they could for the passage through the mountains. The lives of their families would depend upon it. He dismissed them.

Darric and Theona waited to see if the warlord had any special word for them. He had, but he waited for them to speak first.

"My lord," began Theona, "we want to say thank you for your defense of my father yesterday. You have been a good friend and protector. We honor you for it."

"Then you will honor my wishes by keeping your impetuous father out of trouble, young lady. King Radagaisus was deeply concerned about the trouble he caused yesterday. He thought at first your father was a madman. Once he understood that your father is a Christian pastor, he immediately wanted to ban him from the trek altogether.

"Prince Roderic and I interceded for you, reminding the King of what you have already suffered, and begging that you be allowed to continue with me. King Radagaisus agreed, provided that you do not tell any more of your Christian stories to anyone, and that your people, including your father, not talk about your religion to anyone who is not already a believer. The King says he will not tolerate any exceptions. If he hears of anything different, he will expel you from the caravan, wherever we may be. Or worse. I had to swear to him that if I learn of any transgression of this rule, I will report it to him on pain of my own, and my people's expulsion from the caravan. I hope that is clearly understood."

They nodded glumly.

"And since Prince Roderic seems to have taken such an interest in this girl, Darric, may I suggest that you marry her as soon as possible. Life is complicated enough for all of us."

CHAPTER FIFTEEN

THE INVASION BEGINS

The Danube River, Pannonia
(Modern Hungary)
End of July 405, AD

Two days after the Grand Council, the great migration got underway. The King's men and their tired horses galloped back and forth for miles trying to orchestrate the disassembly and reassembly of the various factions. Laagers all over the camp began to break up, move out and realign themselves into long caravans.

There was a last minute flurry of activity in the temporary markets before the vendors began taking down their stalls and packing away their supplies. The wagon repair men and blacksmiths were busy to the end making last minute repairs. Men shouted and swore as they pushed and hauled their wagons around to face in a new direction. Cart wheels and pigs squealed, oxen bellowed, goats bleated, and chickens and geese ran in every direction to get out of the way. The women packed and repacked, while their children rushed around returning borrowed items and retrieving lent ones. The older ones wandered in search of family members, new friends, and lost animals. Firewood, grain supplies and smaller livestock were loaded onto the wagons, and, finally, the oxen were hitched up.

With the camp configuration changing all the time, some children got lost. Theona found three from her own laager in one morning and managed to get them back to their families. She wondered how Rilka was coping with the chaos.

Then came the restless hours of waiting for the order to move out. The wagon drivers and their family members hung around their campsites, grumbling as other oxcarts moved past them to the outlying areas. The huge camp spread out, then shrank as it reformed into strings of caravans. To add to the misery, a rain began late on the first day and lasted through the night. The Danubian shoreline and surrounding grasslands became churned up and muddy, clogged with wagons and disgruntled people.

The Wodenvale caravan had been one of the smallest laagers within Radagaisus's camp. That changed after the Grand Council. Two warlords approached Duke Helerix at the feast and asked if they might travel with him. One of them, Rumbert, was a Christian. The other, Arnulf, had a large contingent of Christians among his people, including his own wife. They wanted access to the pastor who had shown such steadfast courage and conviction in the face of great odds. They would be proud to serve with Duke Helerix who had stayed loyal to him.

Helerix's stature was immeasurably enhanced, and many Gothic fighters showed up at his tent to request permission to join his retinue. A number of Suevi families decided at the last minute to join the invasion, and attached their wagons to his caravan as well. The warlords met frequently and began to build common bonds. Rhodus and Sigeseric were startled to discover that they suddenly had a much larger fellowship of believers to look after.

And one by one the Roman guides were escorted by Prince Roderic's men to their new assignments.

The Roman optio, Severus Cantarcchio, brought his leather tent along and demanded an ox-cart and an ox to pull it. One of the Suevi newcomers managed to scrounge one from some relatives, and the young man's thin, inscrutable face became a fixture in the growing community. He quickly made himself known to all the leaders, and began to spend as much time with them as he could. They found him impertinent and reticent at the same time. No one really wanted to have him around, but hospitality and need mastered hostility most of the time. When Theona passed him in the camp, he gave no hint that he even recognized her.

That scarcely worried her. She was much more interested in seeing Roderic, and kept an eager eye out for him. She half expected him to show up at their laager to visit, but that did not happen. Twice she saw him riding his black horse through the camp. Once she saw him on foot at the local Suevi market. He merely nodded and smiled at her, and kept talking to the armorer. Warm with her feelings for him, and aware of others watching, Theona kept walking, hoping he would try to catch up with her. He did not, and her spirits sank.

Ever since he had sent them away in the boat, she had been eager to find out what had happened between the king, Phaedrus and Lord Helerix. Of course, she could easily tackle the warlord. He would understand her avid interest. Duke Helerix seemed to be in a better mood now that the alcoholic fuzz had lifted, and his standing in the wider community had taken a big leap forward. She had questions, many of them, but recognized that most of them were an excuse to be with the handsome young prince again. Somehow during their short time together she had developed dizzying feelings for him. His attentions had been exciting, yet she had held back from encouraging him, worried about trusting him too much. It was disappointing to realize that any choice she might have had, had evaporated before she realized there was a choice to be made.

Sadly, she decided that the Prince himself had had a change of heart. He had opportunities to seek her out, but chose not to. She was beneath his social standing, was someone from a rival religion he had been taught to hate and fear, and she and her father had already alienated his father, the King. Probably he thought her too willful and impetuous, too. Or perhaps she had been mistaken about his interest in the first place. It was only his vanity that he valued. Ruefully Theona decided to put the whole episode behind her. They were all moving on.

The first group to move out was led by Prince Vitiges and the Roman tribune, Bulleus. They headed downstream, following the Danube shoreline. Other caravans crowded in behind them, passing those still mired in the muck and confusion. Everyone was eager to get on with the long journey, aware that for every day a rider on horseback would need, their oxcarts would need three. It could be a month before they even reached the mountains, much longer before they reached the passes to the south and west, and meanwhile the days of good weather and dry roads would be slipping away.

Some of the leaders chose to take a different route. King Respendial and Goar with their huge Alan following, and most of the Vandals and Suevis decided to continue westward on the barbarian side of the Danube for as long as they could, and then fight their way across some Roman bridge. No guide had been assigned to them, nor would they accept one.

Every day whole sections of the camp left the area and the lines of caravans stretched out along the Danubian shoreline, sometimes parallel to each other, sometimes snaking along in single file.

With a sigh of relief, the local villagers waved goodbye to their uninvited guests and set to work. Their economy had prospered greatly with all the visitors, but they had little food and no wood left to tide them through the coming winter. Their own warlord and even the Suevi king were looking for a cut of their newly-acquired wealth, and the Roman Army might yet descend on them to take revenge on them for giving aid to the invaders. If that happened, they would need their own people to protect them, so they would have to pay up. There was a good chance they would be able to get away with their venality, though. Roman dominance in the area was not as strong as in previous generations.

On the third day, Duke Helerix and his fellow leaders received the signal from one of Prince Roderic's men that it was their turn to move out. Within the hour, the Wodenvale wagons began to move. They were followed by Dukes Arnulf and Rumbert, and the Suevis.

Theona hurried to chase down all their chickens and load them back into their baskets. She and Gideon walked alongside the wagon as Pastor Rhodus on the driver's seat tapped their ox, Enoch, with his long stick and shouted. Enoch strained and the wagon lurched forward over the hardening mud ruts. They set off.

Darric drove the wagon behind them, while his mother Anna and sister Edrica walked beside it.

Edrica had pestered Theona with questions about the events at the Grand Council and Theona's impressions of the people she had met, especially Prince Roderic. What had started as indirect questions about the man had grown more direct and insistent.

Theona was evasive. The time she had spent with Roderic was a source of private pleasure for her. The memory was fragile, and she was still picking it apart herself. She did not want to discuss it. So she described the island, the Roman buildings, and the proceedings of the Grand Council with careful attention to detail, but about Prince Roderic and their time together she said little.

Edrica looked at her shrewdly. She had heard stories.

"My brother is, of course, by far the better man for you. Don't you agree?" she asked.

Theona pretended to give it some thought, and then nodded emphatically. "Most definitely," she answered.

Pleased, Edrica left her alone. Anna looked at Theona with compassion and smiled. She understood.

That first day they did not get far. Any delay up ahead delayed everyone behind. The caravan stopped for the night just ten miles downriver, blocked by the congestion ahead. Theona fed Gideon, Enoch, the chickens, her father and herself, then grabbed her fishing gear and headed for the river. She had heard it was full of carp, catfish and other varieties of fish. Perhaps she would be able to catch one.

She settled herself along the river bank and cast her line. Others were doing the same. A few of the fisher folk had even gone a little way out from the shore and were standing in the water with their nets and spears waiting for one of the bigger fish.

Bishop Sigeseric came up behind her and sat down. He plucked a long grass, pulled it tight across his lips, and blew. It squeaked weakly.

Theona laughed, and he grinned. He was a delightful man, big and strong, with sky blue eyes and dimpled cheeks. His sense of humor and quiet dignity were what had attracted Duke Helerix to him. She knew they met regularly, ostensibly so that the warlord could learn some Latin, but she knew the pastor was also teaching him about Christianity. Helerix claimed to be curious, but not personally interested. According to her father, Sigeseric did not believe him.

"What's the Roman Empire like?" she asked him after a while. She knew he had come from Moesia, one of the Roman provinces to the east.

He stared across the river.

"I have never been inside Italia, but I have been through other Roman provinces and seen several cities. It will be like nothing you have ever seen," he said. "Nor dreamt of. People come from all over the world and speak different languages. In the towns there are many buildings, some of them four or five stories high and packed with people like goats in a shed. There are great churches with roofs of gold, large market places inside long buildings and arcades, and huge places of entertainment. Many people are very, very rich. Some of them live in great palaces and have hundreds of slaves, but there is great poverty there, too."

"What are the Romans like? Are they great fighters?"

"They used to be. Now they have people in the army from all over the world that do the fighting for them. They all fight together on the battlefield under Roman officers. That is a marvel! But the Emperor has to pay them." He pinched his lips in disapproval.

Theona waited.

"Where we are going, the Romans have not had to fight for a long time. I am told that large parts of the Army are men from the north, like us. Many of them are Goths. I know Duke Helerix and his men are hoping to be accepted into the army and be given land somewhere to settle on, but I have heard that Radagaisus thinks the Romans are soft and will be easily defeated. He and some of the other chiefs expect to get everything they want through fighting *against* Rome, not for it. I think the High King is hoping for a fight. He is eager to prove that he is more of a man than the Emperor, and he will gain glory and immense wealth for himself if he can humble the Roman Empire. Very few men have ever done that."

His words alarmed her. "So what will happen to us?"

"Only God knows. The best we can expect is that they will let us settle somewhere as one people and then leave us alone." He looked doubtful.

"I was looking forward to being in a place where there are so many Christians," lamented Theona. "It's hard when there are so few of us. I thought it would be like Heaven to be in a place where everyone knows Jesus, and his teachings are honored as they should be."

Sigeseric made a face. "Well, that's the thing, Theona. I am afraid you will be quite disappointed in that, too. It has been a long time since our Lord was here and taught us how he wants us to live, and many people who call themselves Christians have never known what life was like for the people who lived in earlier generations. They did not choose Christianity for themselves. They were born into it, or just adapted to it, so they have never been born 'of the Spirit' the way you and I were. For that reason, they can't understand and don't value what a difference that makes. They act like Christians because that's what they see around them, but they are not moved by the Spirit of Jesus.

"There are also still pagans in the Empire who never stop trying to undermine the Kingdom of God. Sometimes there have been battles on the streets between Christians and pagans, and there is a constant struggle even now between Christian and pagan scholars about who is right. Sometimes the pagans win, sometimes we do. In Moesia and Illyricum I met many people who tried to worship both Almighty God and their family idols—sort of keeping a foot in both camps. They are too lazy to try to find out which is right."

Theona thought about the first story she had told Anarilka.

"So, nothing much has changed," she said soberly. "Is the Emperor a Christian?"

"I believe so. There are actually two emperors, both still young men. They rule from two different cities and have not lived together for the last ten years. One lives in a big city called Constantinople, way to the east of here, and the other lives in a city called Ravenna in Italia. Their father and mother were both devout followers of Jesus, but died when their children were young. The boys grew up with other people advising them how to think."

"At least the Empire is headed by men who do not hate us."

"Maybe, but the Romans, even if they are Christians, are not that interested in whether we are Christians or not. They call us heretics. The Emperors may think that way, too."

"What do you mean?"

"For a long time there was division and even riots inside the Roman Empire over the issue of whether God is Supreme and the Christ and the Holy Spirit less so, or whether they are all equal in their authority and identity. Most of the bishops there recently decided that they are all substantially the same. We Goths do not believe that. The church inside the Empire has changed its beliefs on this issue many times and they could soon change it again."

She pondered that. "Are you saying that we believe that the Lord Jesus is a lesser being than Almighty God?"

He smiled.

"It is complicated. Jesus was sent by God, and the Gospels say he prayed to Him for guidance and did what the Spirit led him to do. He showed us what God is like, but when He died, Almighty God withdrew from him because Christ had become the Lamb of God, the sin-bearer. Also, it was God who raised him from the dead. Jesus did not raise himself, even though he was able to raise other people from the dead and equip us to do that, too."

"But the Bible says He deliberately emptied himself of most of his divine powers," she protested. "He became like us in order that His full glory would not blind the people He came to serve. And he was killed by the rulers because he said outright that he was God, wasn't he? And he accepted the worship of men, even though he knew that would be idolatry in any other form."

It sounded like the kind of debate that would give her a headache.

"I don't understand it myself, Theona. I just have to trust that the teaching I received from Bishop Ulfilas is true. For myself, I am grateful just to be my Lord's servant and to do what He tells me to do. That is enough for me in this life."

It was time to change the subject.

"What do you think will really happen when we get over there?" she asked, indicating the other bank of the river.

"Rome will not welcome us, Theona. We are not invited and they don't want us. Not the Christians, and not the pagans. They will fight us every inch of the way. Even if King Radagaisus and his followers win, the Romans will not give up until they have got rid of us. They never do."

They sank into silence. A large fish seized Theona's bait. Together they struggled to land it. People up and down the shore cheered when they had the big carp finally flopping on the ground. They were both laughing and much more cheerful when the bishop put the fish into Theona's bucket and picked it up.

They started back to their laager.

"So why are you going, Bishop?" she asked. She knew *she* was going because her father was going, and that *he* was going hoping for a new, safe place to rebuild his community. Bishop Sigeseric's vision of the future was bleak and unsettling.

"God called me to bring the gospel to these people. Where they go, I go. If I did not, I would be disobedient to the Lord. I learned years ago not to do that."

"But these people are leading you into danger and perhaps death. You are a man. You have a choice. There are other Goths you could minister to."

"These are the ones I am called to be with, Theona. I cannot abandon them until God Himself leads me elsewhere. Perhaps the Goths will be more open to the message when they find danger and death pressing them closely."

She nodded, impressed. That danger and death would press on him, too, but he didn't seem to care.

☙❧

There was a further delay downriver at the first ford. Silt regularly collected in this area, allowing this part of the Danube to become passable for the wagons and animals. Here the river ran wide and shallow.

Once Theona's caravan reached the ford, she hurried down to the river to see what was going on. A Roman fort confronted them across the river, but she did not see any movement there. In the event, no one was making any attempt to stop the barbarian caravans from crossing.

Roderic's brother Vitiges and his caravan had been the first to arrive. They had been gone for days, and the people crossing now were part of the larger Gothic community behind them. Theona saw wagons in the muddy river pushed by men and hauled by the oxen and other animals hitched to them. Women and children carried, dragged, and attempted to float the other domestic animals across to the other side. There was a general air of nervous excitement. Once across they were committed to the invasion

It looked like it would be days before it was their turn to cross, so she headed back to the caravan and helped her father stake out their campsite and set up their tent. Once that was done, they had their first real opportunity to relax. For the next three days they swam, bathed, fished and assisted the work on the river for hours at a time. Some of the Wodenvale people walked inland to see one of the sand dunes they had heard about, while groups of hunters set out to find game birds in the marshes along the river. Some of the more daring ones crossed to the other side to explore the farms and fields that had been vacated by their occupants. They came back exhilarated and encouraged, bearing their first plunder.

On the fourth day, a hot and sunny one, Pastor Rhodus and Darric moved their wagons into the queue to begin the crossing. Enoch, usually so patient, began bawling in sympathy with the oxen already being forced into the river. Theona stood beside him, her legs eaten up by ferocious tiny insects, trying to calm him, aware that the chickens, their legs tied together, were beating their wings and clucking within their baskets.

Men from their caravan helped support and push the wagon down off the bank and into the river, and then passed them on to other men, farther out, who walked with them through the cold silt-laden water. Gideon swam beside Enoch and occasionally nipped the ox's leg gently. The ox struggled forward, seeming to draw comfort from the dog's presence and the sight of the wagons ahead of him ascending from the cold river bed onto the opposite shore.

Theona trudged along beside the wagon carrying one of the neighbor children, anxiously watching Gideon valiantly swimming. One of the men steadying their wagon at length lifted the little dog up and carried him to the opposite shore where he lay on the grass, panting.

A group of their neighbors helped pull their wagon up onto the shore and directed them to the location of their new campsite. Pastor Rhodus unhitched Enoch and led him away to graze, Theona released the chickens, which, though stressed, seemed to be all alive and accounted for. Then she hurried back to the river, followed by Gideon, to see if she could help with the flocks of animals.

Vitiges's men had rounded up every boat they could find on the Roman side of the river and brought them back to the ford. Goats, sheep, and pigs that could not be herded across the river were loaded into these and tied securely and then rowed or dragged across the river. The motion of the lapping waves and their precarious positions terrified the helpless animals, and they struggled to escape. Some fell into the river and could not be rescued. A few of the most crazed and unruly ones had their bindings unfastened, and were thrown out of the boats to save the others. The horses and cattle were forced to enter the river and wade across, guided by men with prods. Occasionally, even some of these got away and swam with the current downriver. Some were later recovered wandering on the shore. A few drowned when they lost sight of the shoreline and became exhausted.

The transfer took many days, and as new caravans arrived in the area, caravans that had completed the transfer moved on. For a time it seemed that the huge camp city was being restored here, but that illusion ended as caravans got ready and moved off across country with their Roman guides.

It would take three more weeks before the hindmost caravans were across, and the last of the wagons brought in to shore. Radagaisus ordered the destruction of all of the boats. There would be no turning back.

The Gothic caravans travelled along a Roman road in a north-westerly direction. This road would bring them straight to the town of Savaria, two weeks away.

The waggoners quickly learned to drive the ox-carts beside the road, not on it—the cobbled Roman roads were bumpy and could twist delicate ankles and wagon wheels. Theona tried walking along the road, but gave up quickly; her boots were wearing thin and walking beside it was often easier when the ground was dry.

They were moving ever deeper into the rich agricultural farmlands of Pannonia Superior and could see for miles in every direction. Great swaths of the countryside appeared to be suffering from neglect. One of the women in their group told her that for hundreds of years the farms here had produced good harvests—wheat and barley, wine, dairy cattle and produce, but high taxes, invasions and imperial armies had done immense damage to the local economy. Many of the smaller landowners had walked away from their land, unable to pay the Emperor's or their local taxes. By the time the Wodenvale caravan arrived, the local farmers and then the caravans ahead of them had already stripped bare many of the fields, orchards and storage facilities.

One of Prince Roderic's messengers assigned to their stretch of the trek encouraged them that there was still much food to be had—they would just have to spread out in different directions to find it. The men began to form foraging groups and head out together to try to find farms, communities and hunting grounds which had so far escaped notice. Whenever they spotted a distant farmhouse or hamlet, whenever they crossed another road or even a country lane, entire groups rushed off to investigate. It became dismally clear that not much had been left behind, and soon they began to see burning farmhouses and outlying buildings. The migrants in front of them had begun venting their frustrations in a rampage of destruction.

Occasionally they passed clusters of wagons belonging to people who had been ahead of them. Their owners were off raiding somewhere. They heard from the messengers that entire caravans had broken away from the main group to head toward rich towns, prosperous country villas, army supply depots and granaries they had heard about. One large group of Suevi had gone south-east, lured by the mines in the mountains, and the gold, silver and iron to be found in them.

With all the wagons and animals ahead of her and behind her, Pastor Rhodus had his work cut out keeping Enoch moving steadily forward. They did not know how they would have coped had they had other animals to look after as well, but there was only Gideon, Enoch and their few chickens.

Theona could not help but worry about food. For now they had enough, but what happened when they ran out? Unlike most of the people within her own caravan, she and her father had very little to trade with. They had left home with not much more than their lives and they would not steal; at least she hoped that would not be their only option. She did not want to be ashamed before God when she went to him in prayer.

Pastor Rhodus encouraged her to put her worries aside. "God knows our needs," he said. "If we ask in faith, he will look after us."

Theona wanted to believe it, hoped it was so, but could not stop worrying. The desolation of the farms they passed was not encouraging. No animals or crops were to be seen in what had recently been rich countryside. The only people they saw were beggars, men and women so destitute they were willing to beg from their enemies. Not for the first time Theona wondered just how long this journey was going to take. They were part of a massive body of migrants, all with bellies to fill and animals to feed.

Part of her answer came a few evenings after they had crossed the Danube. As they were making their camp, one of the Wodenvale farmers approached them. He and his wife had nine children and many chickens. He came up to Pastor Rhodus and asked if it might be possible for him to carry some of his chickens in their wagon. During the day his children could walk, but at night the youngest children needed room on the cart. They all would, when the weather got cold.

He had noticed that Rhodus and Theona were alone in their wagon apart from their dog and a few chickens. Would they consider keeping his chickens with theirs? Rhodus bargained with him: boarding and transportation for the birds in exchange for one of every five chickens. The farmer agreed, relieved. Rhodus whistled cheerfully for days, his attitude almost unbearably triumphalist. Theona asked him how they were going to feed the chickens once the grain ran out, but her father told her not to worry. He and his "partner" had it all worked out. It would be her responsibility to look after them and sell the eggs they did not use themselves.

Whenever the Wodenvale caravan stopped to take part in a raid, Theona, Edrica, Anna and the other Christian women would go looking through deserted fields and orchards to glean. They avoided the farmhouses, a main target for many other people, in case there was still someone hiding within them, and also because they did not want to plunder someone's home. The harvested fields and orchards were, however, fair game. They usually found enough grain and fruit to make these excursions still worthwhile.

The miles rolled on and the trek got farther and farther into Pannonia. They passed deserted military outposts at intersecting roads. A rumor spread that a few miles down one of these roads there was a good-sized town that the first migrants had missed. A confederation of warriors banded together to try their luck. Fifty wagons peeled off down that road to see if there was anything left to scavenge. Theona lost sight of them after that. Another caravan caught up to close the gap.

The raiders came back with plunder and food from the undefended country villas and farms, but with no success at gaining entry to the town where most of the people in the area were hiding.

She had become acquainted with many of the people in her caravan through the long journey from Wodenvale. One of them was a sad-looking young farmer whose wife had been killed in the market massacre. Theona had had several brief conversations with him, but he seemed to resist her attempts to comfort him. The young man had gone on a few raids that she knew of, and she could see him changing before her eyes, his depression finding an outlet in rage.

One day he came back from a remote farm driving a wagon full of food. He had a local woman with him. She stumbled along behind the wagon, attached to it by a rope lashed around her wrists. The white apron pinned over her long blue robe was stained with blood, although it did not appear to be her own, and tears streamed down her lovely face.

Two children, a boy and a girl, walked beside her. The girl, like her mother, was crying, but the boy was angry and shouting invectives at the farmer. The man, his face stony, unloaded the pony, left the food on the ground and then smacked the pony's rump to drive it away. He untied the mother and forced her into his wagon, yelling at the children to leave. When they would not, he threatened them with his whip. Still they would not leave their mother. Finally he got down from his wagon and threw rocks at them, swearing, and they ran away. He glared at Theona, who had watched in horror.

The children hung around for hours until the caravan started to move again and the farmer emerged from the wagon to take up his long stick. He ran at the children who were still sitting beside the road where the boy was comforting his exhausted sister, and they fled. The boy turned back and shouted curses and threats at all the Goths as Theona drove her oxcart past. She hid her face from their accusing eyes, deeply ashamed and grieved. She was learning just how quickly her neighbors were willing to embrace unthinkable behavior.

CHAPTER SIXTEEN

PRINCE RODERIC MOVES IN

∾

Lake Pelso, Pannonia
(Lake Balaton, modern Hungary)
August, 405 AD

On the tenth day after Theona's caravan left the Danube behind, they camped beside a large and beautiful lake. As the people were settling into their evening routines, Prince Roderic rode into the camp. Theona, who was plucking a chicken, saw him and took a few eager steps in his direction and stopped, angry at herself. It had been almost two weeks since she had seen him.

He dismounted, and looked around. Darric, who had been in conversation with a group of men standing around one of the wagons, left them and sauntered over to her, squatting beside Gideon to give him a stomach rub. Gideon rolled over onto his back blissfully, his eyes half-closed, his legs poking into the air. Edrica had just washed her hair and was combing it with her fingers beside their wagon a short distance away. She straightened her torn gown and began to comb faster.

They all watched Roderic cross toward Duke Helerix's tent, which was just being erected. Their leader emerged from behind it, tent pegs in one hand and a hammer in the other. He looked surprised to see the prince. He wiped his damp forehead with his sleeve, laid down his hammer, and bowed. They stood together talking for so long that Darric got impatient.

"Where is your father?" he asked, looking at Theona.

"He's gone to look for Cantarcchio. Papa thinks he might know where he could find a Christian church in the area that might be willing to help us with warm clothes and blankets."

Darric snorted. "That's not likely. All doors will be closed against us from now on. Who can blame them? They're all furious at us." He sounded depressed.

Theona knew how much her friend loathed what he saw happening all around them. Nevertheless, after the Grand Council he had insisted on teaching Edrica, Theona and the children in his catechism class how to use a slingshot. He said it was for hunting, and that it was fun, a diversion. His students' skills were improving all the time. Theona could hit a target three out of ten times, about average for the group. Darric kept pushing her to aim for five out of ten, and warned them all that soon he would want to see seven hits out of ten and a rabbit in each family's stewing pot. Theona didn't practice very much—there were many other things to do, but she did practice. You never knew . . .

Darric continued to squat beside Gideon watching the two men talking for a while longer. Then he left to collect his bow and quiver of arrows to go hunting for ducks on the lake. He wanted to borrow Gideon to retrieve any fowl he managed to hit.

"I doubt you'll find him much use for that," said Theona, grinning, "but I know he'll enjoy the swim."

She finished plucking the chicken, and put it in a pot to boil over the fire. She and her father were joined by another family to eat it, and they would join that family for a meal another night. Even though food was still reasonably plentiful, no one wanted it to be wasted or go bad. Every scrap saved now might mean another meal another day.

Afterwards, Pastor Rhodus left to visit an elderly man from Arnulf's caravan who was dying. Their dinner companions headed off to their own wagon.

It was a warm, overcast evening and still light. Theona gathered her fishing gear, and set off for the river with Gideon beside her. She had to pass Helerix's tent, and was surprised to find that Roderic was still there. He was having dinner with the warlord and Rue. Theona greeted them shyly as she passed. Rue chuckled, and she rushed on, blushing.

She had to go quite far before she found a good fishing spot; many other people were also trying their luck. Theona spread her shawl on the ground, cast her line out into the stream, and sat quietly. Gideon wandered off to explore for a while, and then came back and lay down, his body warm beside her.

The sky darkened. A chill breeze sprang up. Clouds scudded across the sky, and a few waves broke white out on the lake. She decided that fishing was a lost cause for the day and pulled her line in. Other fisher folk were packing up as well. Few appeared to have been successful in their hunt.

She heard footsteps behind her and turned, expecting to see another fisherman coming to see how she had done, and was surprised to see Duke Helerix descending on her.

"Theona," he said, as she stood up hurriedly, "I have been looking for you. I had to ask several people along the way where you were. Why do you go so far?"

He was clearly irritated with her.

"The shore closer to our camp was full of people fishing, my lord. I have to go where there is room for me, and where I think the fish may want to be."

"You take too many chances, my girl. You may not have noticed, but this venture of ours gives ordinary people courage to try things they would never normally do. Some who used to be decent men and women have become thieves and murderers. I have overheard rude remarks from men who know better about what they plan to do with the Roman girls they meet. Some have already committed such offensive acts. They won't say it in front of you or the other women, but you had best beware."

"I will, my lord, but Gideon always watches out for me."

"Gideon cannot protect you from someone who is determined to have you. The prince is not the only man to think you attractive, although his interest has been noticed and is probably a deterrent to others. Next time you have to go away from my caravan, take someone you know and trust with you."

She nodded shyly. "I am grateful for your concern, Lord Helerix. We are not even from Wodenvale, and you treat us like your own."

His expression softened.

"You are good people. I don't always understand you, but I see the good you all do every day. As long as caring for you does not endanger my own people, I will not shirk my responsibilities to you. Come now. It's far from our camp and getting dark. I will escort you home."

He appeared thoughtful as they started off. They followed the shoreline for a little while, listening as a few bullfrogs and tree frogs sang. Somewhere she heard an animal cough, and a flock of small birds fluttered from one tree to another. The wind hushed and a deep silence descended on the big lake. They could hear the quiet voices of people a long distance away.

After a few minutes they left the shore, and he led her back toward the Roman road.

"Prince Roderic has asked me if he may stay with us in our laager," he said abruptly.

Theona's throat closed. So that was what Roderic's visit had been about. She looked up at him in alarm. In the poor light his expression was hard to read.

"Did he say why?"

"Yes, he did. He said that my laager is close to the middle of the caravan as a whole, and therefore in a good position for all his messengers to reach him with their reports."

"But he placed us here himself!"

"I know. That is what I said to him. I asked him if perchance your being in the camp had anything to do with that."

She looked at him expectantly.

He smiled. "He was evasive. And then he told me outright that he was not certain of his feelings for you, but that you had caught his fancy. He said that he wanted to place himself where you would have the chance to get to know him better, and he you."

Theona felt a smile creeping onto her face. She lowered her head quickly, wondering if Helerix could see it. "And what did you say, my lord?"

"That as far as I knew, you already had a suitor and one your father and I liked very much."

"That was brave of you. I do not wish to see him take a dislike to Darric though, my lord. Darric is a wonderful man, and will make a good husband someday."

"So you have no interest in the young prince yourself?"

Theona's cheeks burned. She looked up at him, frowning and smiling at the same time.

"I admit I like him, but it is not a good idea for us to be together if there is no future for us. You know I cannot ever marry him. My father would never permit it, nor would I even give it a second thought were the prince not around to persuade me otherwise."

Helerix laughed. "You are a funny girl. Sometimes you seem to be wiser than I expect from such a young woman. One day I think you can handle this, but the next day I think you need to be protected."

"It will be hard for me to say no to the young man. He already knows my reservations and your father's. His final word was that this is the most central place for him and his men to meet. He is stubborn. He is staying with me and my wife tonight. I will have to talk to your father and the other leaders."

Theona felt uncomfortable. She was going to be the focus of discussion. Her personal feelings and the prince's would be the subject of public debate.

"My father and I have already brought worrying attention to this laager, my lord, and I don't know what would make it worse, saying no, or saying yes. But I must remind you of this—Roderic has also taken a risk for us all. He is perhaps our best ally in his father's household. If we say no to this request, he would likely be welcomed by the leaders of the laagers on either side of us. They would have no reason to say no. The High King's good will is important to everyone."

Beside her, the warlord nodded. Briefly he closed his eyes and rubbed the back of his neck. They walked in silence. He seemed to be in a reverie. He did not speak again until they rounded a bend in the road and saw their own camp looming black against the darkening sky. Her father was standing just outside the laager looking down the road. He waved when he spotted them.

"So what do you advise me?"

"I want him to stay, my lord," she faltered. "But I fear it."

"Exactly my thoughts."

He left her with her father.

Late that night there was a meeting down by the lakeshore. Duke Helerix invited Pastor Rhodus, Bishop Sigeseric, and some of the other leaders of their church community to meet with him and the other chieftains.

Theona, as nervous as one of her own chickens, wrapped her shawl around her shoulders and slipped down from the wagon, ordering Gideon to remain behind. She followed her father at a distance, staying in the shadows as much as possible. He had not told her not to come, but she knew he would not expect her to try. It was her first flagrant disobedience in many years, but she had to know what was said.

The men were meeting along the shoreline of the lake at a place where the land jutted out into the lake to form a little peninsula. There were no trees here, so Theona could not get close, but voices carried clearly through the cold night air. A clump of bushes provided the only possible hiding place, and she squeezed in under the thick, scratchy branches, well hidden from view, and waited.

A few of the Christian men she knew passed by, talking quietly. Duke Arnulf and Duke Rumbert walked past together. Both were armed. Nobody looked her way. Her position grew painful, but she dared not move lest the crackle and snap of the branches and dead leaves give her presence away. She scarcely dared breathe in the quiet night. After twenty minutes it became clear that no one else was coming. She crawled out and sat on the ground, listening hard.

Duke Helerix's voice carried clearly. He was explaining why he had called them together at such short notice. To a man, the Gothic Christians were alarmed at the idea that Radagaisus's son, even one as popular as Prince Roderic, wanted to turn their laager into his headquarters.

"Does this have anything to do with Pastor Rhodus's daughter?" asked Rumbert heatedly. "I remember well how he and his friend rushed to stand with them both at the Grand Council."

Duke Helerix looked at Pastor Rhodus, who looked distressed.

"It might," he admitted.

"Has she been encouraging him?"

"I don't think so," said Helerix, "but she does like him. She admitted that."

"This is a dangerous situation indeed. It must be handled with great care, or she is lost, and perhaps all of us."

"O come now," protested Helerix. "He's just a man trying to find the right woman. At the moment he thinks she might be the one, but that could change. She's very young still, but she's not a fool. We just have to give her any support she needs while they work this out. Perhaps she *is* the right one for him after all. She has the makings of a wise woman. The prince seems to be a good man, better than . . ." He did not complete his sentence, but they all understood what he was not saying.

"But he is not a Christian," said one of Bishop Sigeseric's men with an apologetic look at the warlords. "She must know she cannot marry a man who is not a fellow believer, and how can he become a believer if we are forbidden to tell him about how to become one, and what it all means?"

"God will take care of that if it is His will," replied Bishop Sigeseric. "I am willing to risk my life to tell him. It would be a great triumph if a prince of the royal household gave his heart to Jesus."

"You will not speak of this to him, Bishop," declared Helerix firmly. "I am honor bound by my word to the High King to keep all of you from talking about your religion as long as we travel under Radagaisus's leadership. If you cannot speak about it to any other follower of the Gothic gods, you surely cannot speak about it to the king's own son! We are at an impasse."

"But God is not," said Sigeseric. "Let's tell the prince he can come with us, and then see what God does. Surely He is able to take any situation and bring his redemption into it."

Theona saw Duke Helerix and Duke Arnulf get up and leave the group when the others moved into prayer. She dashed away ahead of them, flitting low and fast, so as not to be seen by her sharp-eyed warlord. The trees lining the Roman road soon hid her from their line of sight. She hurried on back to the laager, unaware that she had passed another figure hiding near her who had also been watching and listening.

The next day Roderic was given the permission he sought. He was gone all day, riding out in mid-morning and returning at nightfall with a wagon and a couple of slaves.

Soon the slaves had pitched a large leather tent near Duke Helerix's. A tall green and yellow pennant waved from the tent pole in the center, instantly granting special status to the privileged laager it graced. After that, the two slaves began to carry in the prince's bedding, weapons, supplies and clothing. One of them remained to prepare Roderic's food and see to his domestic needs. The other left with the wagon.

Most days, the Prince was gone all day, returning only for supper. Sometimes some of his men would be waiting for him near his tent with news from far-off sections of the caravan. Occasionally, Helerix, Arnulf and Rumbert would invite Roderic and these messengers to join them for a feast or a beer, and they would be swarmed by people with eager questions or offered information. On one occasion Rue threw a dinner for twenty men. She scurried around their wagon circle asking everyone for herbs, ideas and their best ceramic dinnerware for the occasion. These days she was less testy with Theona, nervous of the girl's influence on their royal visitor.

On days when there was no messenger waiting for him, and no urgent errands to be done, Prince Roderic often wandered around the camp from group to group, talking with the women, practicing his skill at weapons with the men and boys, and passing on information and helpful advice. He was friendly and casual, but did not approach Pastor Rhodus's oxcart once. Nevertheless, Darric and his sister took pains to spend time with Theona whenever the Prince seemed to be on the loose. She found their protectiveness touching, irritating, funny, and stifling. Occasionally, she was even grateful for it. She needed time to find her own balance in this new state of affairs.

Four days after Roderic had joined them, they were on the move again.

For those on foot, there wasn't much to do during the long days of walking except gossip with neighbors, comment on the scenery, and watch for danger, opportunities, and sources of food. By the end of the day, they were almost too weary to look after their needs and the needs of the livestock, but this, too, had to be done.

It was almost as physically taxing trying to steer the wagons. Drivers had to avoid obstacles, and keep a safe distance from their neighbors ahead and behind. The driving was complicated by the increasing numbers of dead animals, discarded household items, runaway fowl or other domestic animals and abandoned wagons. Occasionally, they would even pass bodies in various states of decay. Roman or Gothic—it was impossible to tell, but it was worrying proof that violence and personal tragedy had hit someone hard.

When he was around, Pastor Rhodus would drive the oxcart, but he was often called away to deal with families who were in difficulty. The travelers might have wagons filled with growing piles of plunder and stored food, but there were also an increasing number of casualties and distraught people to minister to.

When her father was away or needed to sleep after being up half the night, Theona drove the ox cart. The muscles in her back would ache from the continual rattling they got from the movement of the wagon. Her head and arms would ache too, and her bottom grew sore.

Along with every other caravan on the trek, the Wodenvale caravan had its own troubles. Once they had to pull off the road for a time when one of Duke Helerix's oxen stumbled and broke a leg. It had to be put to death and another found before they could all proceed. It was a tense moment, followed by a laager-wide feast with ox on the menu.

Theona and her father began to baby Enoch from that day forward—the animal made all the difference between carrying your own possessions, and the relative security of having a place to keep them and be able to sleep out of the elements.

One day they heard about a raiding party ahead of them that had been ambushed by a small troop of Roman cavalry veterans. The skirmish ended with the Gothic raiders bloodied and defeated, while the crowing veterans took back everything that had been stolen. The chagrinned raiding party was jeered, and warned to be less greedy and better prepared next time.

Cantarcchio did not laugh. He warned the Goths that this was the kind of gutsy fighting they could expect from the Roman army. The common people scoffed at this, but their leaders took it to heart. They had heard too many stories like that one.

Up to now the ground had been flat, but they could all see mountains directly ahead now.

They were also approaching the autumn equinox. The days were growing shorter. Soon they would have to start the day later and end it earlier. They could not risk breaking a wagon axle or injuring their precious beasts of burden traveling in the dark.

Shorter days, difficult conditions, increasing risks and dangers—that was the future they all faced. There were bright spots. Gifts of food and clothing were sometimes brought to the Pastor by kind or grateful people. Early one morning, Theona and her father woke to find that someone had left a long, warm red cloak for her. Delighted, she put it on and danced around the wagons, showing it off to Anna, Darric and Edrica.

"I wonder who gave you that?" asked Edrica, jealously. "I heard the prince was on a raiding party recently."

"Theona, dear," said Anna gently, "Did you ever wonder who wore that before you?"

Mortified, Theona took it off and carried it back to her wagon. She could still use it as a cover at night, but she stopped wearing it outside. She did wonder if, perhaps, it had been a gift from Roderic, as Edrica had suggested. But then, she would not ask. It warmed her to think that perhaps her friend had been right. At any rate, someone had dropped it off specifically for her. That was something.

The gift of the cloak had been a happy surprise. The rest of her wardrobe was not going to hold up through the coming winter. Her boots were almost worn out, and she secretly hoped someone would notice and find a pair that would fit her. If so, she would ask no questions, nor draw attention to the gift.

One afternoon, as she was driving the wagon, Roderic suddenly appeared beside her on horseback. He looked tired. He told her to move over and let him sit beside her. When she did, he swung easily from his horse to the moving wagon and took the long stick from her. The horse, as if accustomed to this behavior, walked alongside, waiting until the prince was ready to remount.

"Hello Uncle Roderic," she said. His arrival had been so sudden she was unable to hide her pleasure in seeing him.

He turned and smiled. "Where is your father?"

"Right here." Pastor Rhodus pushed back the leather hangings and looked out, yawning. He, too, looked tired. He had been up most of the night with the family of the old man who was nearing the end of his life. The daughter had promised him the man's fur coat when he died. Her father would not live to wear it himself.

141

There was not enough room for the three of them in front, so Pastor Rhodus took over the driving, and Theona climbed back into the interior of the oxcart. She tied back the hangings so she would be able to listen to their conversation.

It started to rain again. The steady thudding raindrops, together with the squeaking and splashing of the oxcart's wheels, made it hard for her to hear. She settled down among the furs and chickens, and dozed off, using the red cloak for warmth. She woke up again when the cart stopped moving. There was another delay somewhere up ahead.

Theona looked out, rubbing her eyes. The rain had stopped, and Roderic was remounting his horse. He waved goodbye cheerfully, and rode back the way he had come.

Pastor Rhodus and Theona climbed down to stretch. More rain appeared to be drifting their way. Down the line the carriages had begun to move again. They climbed back up and waited to start.

"What did he want?"

Pastor Rhodus looked shifty.

"Someone told the prince that I could speak Latin. He wants me to teach him how to speak it too." He looked at her defensively. "That makes sense, Theona. It will ease his dependency on the Roman guides. He wants me to teach him between here and Italia whenever both of us are free. I suggested that it would be useful to teach it to some of the other leaders as well. He thought that was a good idea, so we are going to start a class."

"Why can't he learn it from one of those Roman soldiers? What about Cantarcchio?"

"He and the prince don't seem to like each other very much. At least, I have rarely seen them talking in spite of what the guide said about Roderic being his patron. I think he lied about that, though I can't think why. Besides, I live here where he has his tent. Why shouldn't I help him?"

"When will you start?"

"Sometime soon. He'll let me know."

"What if you get called away?"

"I'll go when there is a serious need, but most things I can do during the day, and there is always Darric and Sigeseric. It should work out. Don't worry."

Theona scowled.

"I wish I had something to do too, father. I'm so tired of this trip."

"And we've only just begun!" he exclaimed. "But I know what you mean, daughter. Everyone feels that way. The journey goes on and on. The wagons bog down, a child or an animal goes astray and we all have to look for it. We don't get enough rest. People are bored, worried and out of sorts. Fights start. This weather doesn't help. I've told the Prince that his messengers should tell the leaders to organize games and competitions for the evenings to keep morale up."

He was silent for a few seconds.

"Prince Roderic has something for you to do, too, Theona. Someone told him that you know how to read and write the Gothic language. He wants to learn that as well. I told him I was too busy to do that, too, so he asked if you might be allowed to teach him. I said I would ask you."

Theona looked at him in astonishment. He looked sheepish.

"I have two motives, daughter. There is no use pretending he is not interested in getting to know you. He has said as much. I want to watch him with you. And secondly, how else are you going to teach him to read and write but by using the Bible? It's the only book there is in our language."

Theona was impressed, but remained silent, thinking. It was true. The book could speak for her, for all of them. It had the power to change hearts and lives. It truly was an exciting thought. But there were risks . . .

"Father, you need to know that I like him too. What happens if we continue to like each other?"

"Suppose you do. Suppose he remains a pagan. Then you could not marry him. But suppose this is all God's doing, and Roderic learns to love God and wants to live the way Jesus taught us? Is not this the best way to find out if that is even possible?"

"I thought you wanted me to marry Darric?"

He looked surprised.

"I love Darric like a son, but I would not presume to push two people I love together for my own sake. If this long trip does nothing else, it will surely test whether you belong together. How will you know if Darric is the right man for you if you never look at another? The Prince may be a good test for you both."

He sounded confident, but later as Darric dismounted from his own ox-cart, Rhodus hurried over to have a private word with him. They argued for a few minutes, and then Darric gave Theona a hard stare and turned to unhitch his ox.

Theona, watching anxiously, was stung. She had no wish to hurt him, and he seemed to be saying that he did not trust her. Well, it was her life. Still.

She dug out her leaf tablets and charcoal from a box at the back of the wagon. They were old friends to her, a sign of normalcy.

Around her, things were anything but.

CHAPTER SEVENTEEN

THE GLADIATOR

Savaria, Upper Pannonia
(Szombathely, Hungary)
Late August, 405 AD

In the third week of August, the first of the caravans reached Savaria, the capital of the Roman province of Upper Pannonia. Savaria was on the ancient Amber Road that traders had used for centuries to bring furs, slaves and amber from as far away as the Baltic Sea. At times, the city had also served as an Imperial residence for the Emperors' traveling court.

During the reign of Emperor Marcus Aurelius, a pagan by tradition and a stoic by conviction, it had also been the site of intense persecution against Christians. Saint Irenaeus, an early church father, had been one of many put to death within its stony walls. Constantine the Great had ended the last of these sporadic, life-threatening persecutions less than a century before.

The mountains now loomed ahead, a wall of ancient rock hundreds of miles thick that extended north and south as far as the eye could see. They were an awesome sight to the migrating families, an immense barrier they had to conquer before they could enter Italia.

The plan was to go from Savaria north along the Amber Road towards the Danube again. They could then cut west across the foothills of the Alps, bypassing at least part of the mountain fastness blocking their way. This route would take them close to several of the major military bases guarding the Danube frontier, but this route would make it much easier for them to get to and through the pass they were heading for before winter weather locked them out. The pass was deep into the mountains and was 4500 feet high, and they would likely have to battle the Roman legions to get there, but other wagon trains had managed this route before. Once past Tribune Bulleus's own fort at Veldidena, there would be few soldiers to stop them.

Six miles before Savaria, some of the king's men stopped Duke Helerix's caravan and instructed him and his co-leaders to join a large, defensive laager forming up ahead, and then await orders. There was fighting in the suburbs outside of the town, and the area in between was jammed with wagons.

A man wearing the King's colors rode fast toward them from the direction of Savaria. It was Roderic, breathless and excited. He dismounted in the center of the laager and was immediately surrounded by dozens of people.

Helerix, Rumbert, and Arnulf ran forward to meet him. Cantarcchio emerged from his tent and walked purposefully over to join the group. Theona, along with many of the other women, hurried over as well. Her father was meeting Bishop Sigeseric for prayer off in an adjacent field. For once, she would have the latest news before him.

Roderic said that Savaria was shut up tight against them, with most of the people from the area in hiding behind the city walls. So was most of the harvest, to the frustration of the people who had arrived before them. Food for the animals as well as for humans was beginning to run short for the invaders.

So far, the legionaries from the XIVth Gemina had been successful at repelling every attempt to climb the walls or break down the gates. The Romans understood siege tower technology, but Bulleus and his men stubbornly refused to teach their newest allies how to build one. Vitiges's men had improvised with beams and ladders they found in the suburbs, but their attempts had not worked. The warriors had tied ladders together to scale the city walls, but these were unsteady and never quite the right height. The jeering soldiers manning the ramparts above them poured boiling water onto them and tried to set the ropes, the warriors and their ladders on fire. It was a mess. The bodies of Gothic attackers had begun to collect at the foot of the walls.

The warriors had also attempted to ram the gates of the city, but without the siege towers, they had no protection except their archers. The soldiers rushing forward with the heavy beams had only their armor and shields to protect them. With their arms full holding the heavy beams, they had no way to avoid the javelins, arrows, boiling water and pitch hurled at them by the defenders. Good men were being injured and killed.

Bulleus and his Roman guides were advising the Goths and their allies to keep moving. It would take too long to storm Savaria, they said, or to wait around for the people of the town to surrender.

This was something the warriors did not want to hear. They were salivating over the probable riches within such an important city. Any newfound camaraderie and sense of common purpose was dissolving in the tensions building up between the uneasy allies.

Tribune Bulleus and the two princes decided to ride back to meet King Radagaisus at the end of the long column of wagons to prepare him for the decision he would have to make. There would be a Council at the arena which lay outside the city walls as soon as he arrived in the area. The warlords were all invited to come and present their arguments.

Roderic's messengers carried this message to every part of the huge laager and to every caravan along the long column still coming. They needn't have bothered. The news had already spread like a wild fire.

The Goths and their allies who were already at Savaria withdrew to take out their frustrations on the unprotected suburbs and countryside. Thousands of men, women and children combed through the villas, museums, temples and factories of the suburbs looking for things to take. Others rode out in every direction to find outlying farms and villages. There would be little left for the ones coming behind.

One piece of good news caused excitement up and down the line. The gladiators from the arena outside the town had seized the opportunity to overthrow their jailers, and had escaped to join the invaders. This news was received with great excitement. The gladiators had waltzed out of their barracks holding their weird, assorted weapons high, beaming and prancing with joy.

Within hours a few of them could be seen strutting down the road, going from camp to camp looking for accommodation. One barrel-chested man in his mid-twenties, his wiry black hair and bronzed skin suggesting a North African origin, came into the Wodenvale laager and spoke to one of the women in a slow, gravelly voice. Frightened, she ran to fetch her husband, who went to fetch Duke Helerix.

While they waited, a crowd started to gather around the fighter. Two innocent lads grinned at each other and threw punches at him. The man grinned back, and floored them both. They got up, laughing along with the rest of the crowd.

Duke Helerix approached the gladiator with veiled reluctance, asking him what he wanted. The gladiator replied in Latin using confusing gestures. Helerix shook his head and sent for Cantarcchio. A few minutes later, Cantarcchio strolled up in his usual surly fashion, and the duke asked him to interpret. The guide looked the newcomer up and down with distaste, and then spoke to him in Latin.

"His name is Ptolemy," he said. "He wants to know which is Prince Roderic's tent. He says Prince Vitiges has assigned him to be his brother's bodyguard."

"Take him there, then," replied Helerix.

"I think I'm going mad," Theona heard him mutter as he passed her.

Cantarcchio crooked his finger insolently, and stalked off. The gladiator followed. A dozen people trailed along behind, and one big fellow took a daring swing at the fighter. It didn't connect. Ptolemy, several inches shorter, grabbed him and hoisted him onto his shoulders, pinning his legs tight with his powerful arms. When the astonished man could not get free, he began to pull Ptolemy's hair and beat him about the head. Ptolemy promptly plucked him off his shoulders, and stuck him head first on the ground, his feet seized in a tight grip and his beard painfully caught under the gladiator's foot. The young man now had his hands fully occupied clutching the ground with one hand and the muscular leg of his opponent with the other, while his tunic flapped around his head. The crowd roared with laughter.

Even Cantarcchio smiled. He said something in Latin, and pointed to the tent with the yellow and green pennant. The gladiator let go of his attacker's legs, and stepped away with a bow. His prisoner flopped over onto the ground in a heap. He quickly sat up, scratching the dirt from his hair. His audience helped him up and pounded his back in appreciation of the fun they had had at his expense.

When they reached Prince Roderic's tent, Ptolemy jauntily waved goodbye and entered. They heard a furious exclamation from the slave inside, followed by a burst of excited conversation in two languages.

Cantarcchio hurried away chuckling, and soon after the small crowd drifted away as well.

They learned later that the gladiator had been seized as a child by slave-raiders in his native North Africa, and sold to a gladiator school where he served first as a servant, and then as a fighter with the travelling troupe. His specialty was in fighting with net and trident, but he had become a top-draw wrestler, and could turn his body to other combat skills as well. He had had years of hardening, and Theona suspected he had known little kindness.

When Roderic rode into camp that night, he was furious to find the fighter sleeping inside his tent, and the slave pouting outside. He sent for Pastor Rhodus to interpret for him, and once again a small crowd gathered to watch. Roderic sent one of his men for Prince Vitiges. They all waited until the messenger returned with instructions that whatever Roderic decided to do with Ptolemy, he needed to provide hospitality for the man. The discussion ended with the North African firmly ensconced in the Prince's tent and Roderic agreeing to send the slave to join his brother's entourage. Ptolemy would have to assume the man's domestic duties. None of them looked very happy about this. Prince Roderic rode off with the slave behind him. He did not return that night. The word around the Wodenvale wagon circle was that he had gone to persuade his father to reverse his brother's decision. The gladiator enjoyed the luxurious tent and his first nights of freedom alone.

Two days later, very early in the morning, a large group of horsemen rode up the road and into the middle of the dense wagon circle. Duke Helerix's laager was now quite far inside the perimeter of the laager. Theona was taking a basket of eggs to the wagon owned by her father's 'partner', when she heard a familiar childish voice calling her name.

"Theona, where *are* you?"

Several voices answered at once. Theona stopped and looked back. Several people were pointing in her direction. Excited, she turned back.

Anarilka was perched in front of Roderic. His handsome gelding sported a thick black blanket under its saddle. Its edges were embroidered with a vine of heavy gold threads.

His niece grinned down at Theona. Today she wore a clean blue tunic and her blond hair was braided. Impatient as usual, she started to squirm off the horse. Theona raced to catch her as Roderic made a grab for her arm. Between them, they held a breathless little girl suspended in mid-air.

"Now suppose I hadn't been able to get to you, young lady," scolded Theona. "You might have broken your neck."

She lifted the child to the ground. The little face shone with pleasure.

"Don't worry, Theona. Uncle Roderic and you wouldn't let me fall."

Endearingly, she embraced Theona, beaming up at her as Wolfric had once done. Tears sprang to Theona's eyes.

"O, how I've missed you!" said Anarilka. "Mother says to say hello. She says she has missed you, too."

Theona laughed. Roderic's presence on the horse above her was beginning to have its usual effect. She wanted to get away before she did something silly.

"Well, come on, then. Let's go for a walk. I have to deliver these eggs."

"Not far," warned Roderic. "Don't leave the camp. You never know who could be hiding in the fields nearby. My father would not hesitate to skin you alive if anything happened to Rilka."

"We'll find something safe to do here, then," smiled Theona. "If that's the king waiting for you out on the road, you'd better get going. Everyone is wondering whether we fight for the city or move on."

"What do you want?" he asked seriously.

"A home and peace," she answered soberly. "No fighting. No wagons. No running."

He looked at her. "What about a husband and children?" he said at last.

"Certainly. Someday. When we have no fighting, no wagons, and no running."

"You know, Theona," he said soberly. "We might be dead in a year. Perhaps you had better rethink that."

She nodded a little, shyly, and then watched him ride back to join his companions.

"What are we going to do?" Anarilka was waiting expectantly.

"Let's take these eggs over to the man who owns them, shall we?"

For the next hour she and Rilka played hide and seek with some of the Wodenvale children, including six belonging to the farmer whose chickens they were boarding, and other children who joined them. After that, Rilka pestered her for a story. She settled all of them down on the ground, and stood in front of them, thinking.

The yellowing fields around them and the migration itself had had her thinking about the biblical Joseph and his nightmare journey to a strange land, only to face more suffering there, until finally the doors of a happier destiny opened for him.

She could see no harm in telling such a story if she changed the names, so she began. With her rapt young audience hanging on every word, Theona told the story more dramatically than she had ever done before, changing her voice, adding gestures, putting everything she had into the story of Joseph and his eleven jealous brothers to bring it to life. By the time she had finished, she found she had a much larger audience watching and listening. The children's older brothers and sisters, and some of their mothers and grandparents were watching from the sidelines. They said they had been mesmerized by her story, and thanked her for the entertainment. Theona was thrilled.

One of the spectators had been standing quietly by a large wagon a little distance away. She was the young mother who two weeks before had been forced to accompany the Wodenvale widower who had murdered her husband and driven her children away. The woman was hobbled and tied by the waist to the wagon like an animal. Her master was making sure she could not escape, and had threatened everyone who complained to him about her treatment.

Theona looked at her sadly, wondering how much of the story the woman had been able to follow. She alone of all the spectators might have been able to recognize it. The Pannonian woman turned away as the gathering broke up, and climbed with difficulty back into her master's wagon. She had lost weight and looked haggard. Theona would have liked to go see her, but Rilka and the children were already demanding another story.

"That's it for today, I'm afraid," she replied. She no longer had the heart for it.

"Awwwwww."

"Come on, Rilka. Let's go see if we have anything to eat at my wagon," she said.

"Food! Let's go!" Anarilka placed her hands on Theona's waist, and the others lined up behind her.

"Not all of you, I'm afraid," she said. "Just Rilka. I'm sure your mothers have some food for you somewhere."

They nodded, and ran off.

The wife of her father's "partner" was sitting on the seat of her wagon polishing some bronze lamps. "Don't forget your basket," she called. She had filled it with vegetables.

"Thank you," said Theona, delighted. "My father and I will enjoy this. I will make soup from some of these and roast the rest."

"Enjoy them while you can," said the woman. "It's pretty slim pickings around here with so many people. My husband was saying that he wished we could travel farther up the line or take another route. By the time our caravan gets anywhere, there isn't much left to take."

It was a reminder to Theona that she and her father would be eating stolen food. She clamped down on her conscience and nodded.

Roderic did not come back for Rilka until the early afternoon. When he arrived, the little girl was asleep on the bed of furs inside the wagon, the red cloak covering her. Gideon snored beside her, his front paw on her leg.

Theona had taken the opportunity to read her Bible on the driver's seat. She looked up as the prince rode into the camp and made straight for her wagon. She could feel her face go warm. It was very annoying.

"Well?" she asked.

"It was a fight, but Bulleus's reasoning triumphed. We are moving on tomorrow. Many of the warriors hate the idea of walking away, but we don't have anything like the machines the Romans use, and our guides still refuse to show us what to do. Besides, it would take too much time and cost too many lives. Italia is still the goal and apparently there are many towns there that are not well protected. The smaller ones don't even have walls. Savaria is safe for now."

He looked at her Bible. "Are you reading?" he asked eagerly.

"Do you have a few minutes for your first lesson?"

"Where is Rilka?"

"In there. Sleeping."

Roderic dismounted, and tied his horse to the frame of their wagon. Theona hurried to get the horse a drink and an apple. She was finally getting used to the large beasts. She still could not understand them, but they intrigued her. She reached up to pat the gelding's nose and then withdrew her hand quickly when it swung its big head over to touch her bare arm. When it did not bite her, she tentatively reached up again and this time managed another small pat.

She climbed back into the wagon to sit beside Roderic, grinning from ear to ear. Roderic was leafing through her book, a scowl on his face.

"I don't know how anyone can make sense of this. It's a bunch of symbols. How am I going to learn this? It looks hopeless."

"Not at all," she said. "There are really only twenty-seven of them. You just have to learn how they work together."

She showed him the combination of Greek letters and the few runes designed by Bishop Ulfilas fifty years before, and then sounded them out for him. He repeated them. She reviewed them a second time, and then a third time. After that she showed him a few small words and sounded them out as well. Roderic got the concept immediately.

"I think I can do this!" he said with deep satisfaction. He reached over and gave her a quick hug, relief and pleasure in his eyes.

"I know I don't have quite the same fascination to you as Theona," said Darric dryly, appearing beside them, "but I have a great deal more experience at teaching the Bible than Theona does. Perhaps you would allow me to continue as your teacher? It would be my pleasure."

His kind, grey eyes were disapproving, his smile forced. He was angry, but trying to hide it. Theona looked at him in dismay. He had misread the situation, and was embarrassing them all.

"I wasn't teaching the Bible, Darric," she replied quickly. I was teaching Prince Roderic the Gothic alphabet. He is learning to read."

"The Bible? The Christians' book?" Roderic's recoiled from her. "You didn't mention that this was a Bible, Theona! You know I can't be seen reading it. Perhaps this is all a mistake. Or perhaps even a trick!" He was furious.

He turned to Darric and glared. "Excuse me. Rilka and I are leaving. I think I can do without your lessons, both of you. Rilka!"

Gideon grumbled in his throat. Rilka woke up, rubbed her eyes, and crawled out and into her uncle's arms, the red cloak falling away from her sleepy body.

Theona, flustered, reached for the little girl to kiss her goodbye, but Roderic whisked her away. Without another word, he hoisted the child up onto his horse, and mounted behind her.

And then they were gone, the clip-clop of hooves audible for several moments to the silent couple they had left behind.

Darric looked at Theona apologetically. "I'm afraid I made a bad mistake, Theona. I let my worry for you get in the way. I misspoke."

She was annoyed and upset with him. "Are you sure it was your worry for me and not your jealousy of him, Darric?"

Hurt, he turned away and walked back toward his carriage. Theona saw Edrica ask him a question, but he shook his head and kept on going. Edrica gave her a cold stare.

Theona stared defiantly back.

As soon as Edrica turned away, she crawled into the wagon and curled up on the soft furs beside Gideon, crying her heart out. Gideon licked her face several times and snuggled closer. He even allowed her to hug him.

When they were eating their supper, she told her father about the incident.

"Why are we doing this?" she exclaimed, angrily. "What's our reason for being here? We're not along on this trip for plunder, or conquest, or revenge. Where do you expect all this to end?"

"I don't know. I really don't know," he sighed. "I haven't felt in control since we left home. I have nightmares about being carried along like clouds in a storm and I can't break away."

"We should go back before it's too late."

"I think it's already too late." He sighed again, and poked at the fire, then looked at her.

"Even if we could go back, Theona, what would we go back to? Do you want to live every day waiting for the Huns to come again? Every time you have something to live for, they could race into your life and destroy it. They seem to be everywhere. You saw them yourself. What chance do settled people have with such lovers of violence? Every time I think of going back, I think of you and say 'No, not yet'. In fact, if there is anything I want out of this trip, it is to keep you safe. That is my hope."

"But this trek isn't safe either, Father. Bishop Sigeseric has little hope things will go well in Italia. He says the Romans won't care to distinguish who is their friend and who an enemy. We're all the same to them. How will you persuade them we are good people who just want a safe place to live?"

She looked at him and saw a tired man with thin cheeks and anxious eyes. He had aged since they had left, and she knew it was not the work, or the journey—he had always worked hard and travelled a lot. He was lost without his beloved partner in life, his adored wife, and their son, his heir. Like her, he probably regularly berated himself for not keeping them safe.

"Don't ask me these questions, Theona. As I say, I don't have any answers. All I do every day, all I suspect most of us do every day, is keep going forward. Sometimes I think only the High King has a plan. The rest of us are just people on the run from the grim realities of our lives, hoping Radagaisus can make it all work out."

He seized her hand and kissed it, staring at her.

"You're becoming very pretty, my love. You look like your mother did at your age, but perhaps even prettier. No wonder the prince lost his head for a while."

He dropped her hand and became thoughtful. Theona felt the sting of tears threatening again. That reference to "for a while" sounded like a death knell on the most exciting friendship she had ever known.

Her father had already forgotten his comment. He had gone back to thinking about her questions.

"Even if we make it to Italia, we have no means of support except other people's generosity. I would like to go back to Gothia, but we can't. I want to stop and stay in some of these places we are passing through, but we can't—if we were on our own, they'd kill us for what we are doing to their countrymen. I just go along trusting in God. I don't know what else to do. I've never felt so adrift, or so dreadfully uncertain of myself and my life. We have nothing left now but faith and hope. And each other." He reached out an arm, and she went and sat within his embrace, staring into the fire.

"Not true, Father," she said after a while. "Faith and hope are not just words. Haven't you always said that they are the handles that open the door for Almighty God to come in? Didn't Mother always say that they are muscles we have to use? We keep asking God to be with us and protect us. He's coming along on this trip too, and surely He is big enough and loves us enough to look after us, even in this dismal situation."

Roderic stalked past with his new bodyguard beside him. Ptolemy was holding an iron pot stuffed with smaller items, while the prince ostentatiously carried a pile of rugs. He glanced over towards them and met Theona's eyes. Abruptly dropping the rugs, he said something to the gladiator, unhitched his horse, remounted, and rode out of the laager. Ptolemy looked wistfully after him and then picked up the rugs and added them to his own load.

The two by the fireside watched as he began taking everything out of the Prince's tent and then dismantled it. Sometime later, a wagon driven by one of the slaves pulled into the laager, and the slave and the gladiator silently loaded the tent and all of the prince's household goods onto it. A short time later they were gone.

The stars came out and the cold night pressed down as father and daughter continued to sit there, staring into the flames. The cold air and the sleepy clucking of the chickens finally roused them. It was time for bed.

It took a day before the laager managed to unwind itself and get moving again, and it was late in the afternoon of the second day before the Wodenvale wagons finally saw the walls of Savaria.

Hard-faced soldiers on the battlements of the city stared down at them as they approached the north-south turn. Theona could feel their implacable anger towards the endless caravan of folk moving steadily past their city. She walked on the far side of the wagon as Pastor Rhodus turned onto the Amber Road. Gideon walked beside her, occasionally barking at other dogs in the long column, or rushing to round up a straying goat.

To the north, once again, lay the Danube. They were now closer to its sources, fast and icy streams and rivers surging down from the mountains over hundreds of miles. Ahead lay the line of Roman fortresses whose main task for centuries had been to keep out barbarians like them, and to enforce Roman rule throughout this vast territory.

The first stop they would make after Savaria was the walled town of Scarbantia[23], less than two days away. Thousands of warriors ahead of them had thundered into Scarbantia and taken it by force. By the time the Wodenvale wagons arrived, the town was in ruins, and the warriors, Suevis and Goths, were drunk with success and the liquor they had found. The warriors had rushed through the streets looking for food, livestock, clothing, furniture and treasures. Anyone who got in their way was fair game, including, once they were inebriated, each other. It was impossible not to see the outrages committed by her people this time— the route they were following went right past many of them.

Some of the people she was traveling with went into Scarbantia out of curiosity to look around. Theona was warned by her father not to go—the grisly sight would be deeply upsetting, but she went anyway, taking Gideon for protection.

She was passed by a group of Suevi warriors in war paint, their topknots in disarray, their faces red with drink. They were loaded down with armfuls of silver statuettes, expensive ceramic crockery and glass bottles, woolen blankets and weapons. Two of them were leading animals. A few of their comrades had pigs slung over their shoulders. The swineherd, a mere boy, lay in a pool of blood just down the street. Theona gasped and felt faint. She dropped quickly to her knees. Gideon whined and stood close beside her.

"Oh look, there's a pretty thing," she heard one of the last Suevis call out to his friend.

---

[23] Scarbantia is modern Sopron, a city in Hungary on the Austrian border.

Another man, a Goth she recognized, had been standing at the intersection of two streets lined with two-story apartment buildings. He was wearing two leather jerkins and had a Roman helmet on his head and an extra sword in one hand. Something metallic rattled from an overstuffed pouch on his belt.

"Let her alone," he said. "She's one of ours."

"One of yours, you mean," snapped the Suevi. "And who's going to stop us? You, Goth?"

His friends stopped in preparation for a fight.

"If you want a fight, take it up with Prince Roderic," replied the Goth. "He has first claim on this one."

Disappointed, the Suevis staggered off. One of them winked at Theona as he passed, as if to imply that the whole thing had been just a joke.

"Thank you," gasped Theona as the Goth helped her to her feet. She was trembling and felt sick inside. She knew she had had a close call.

"What are you doing here?"

"I shouldn't have come, but I was curious." She pointed toward the body of the swineherd. "Are there many others like him?" Her voice was shaking. She didn't know why she was persisting, but she had to know.

"No. I'm told the town was almost deserted. A few people were hiding and they got it, but it seems most of the Scarbantians are somewhere ahead of us. I don't know why that young fool stayed behind with his pigs."

"I was afraid to know what's been going on here, but I had to know."

"You've seen enough," said the man. "A woman like you should not be here. Go home. I'll let the prince know you were here, but that you are alright."

"I really don't think he'll care," she sighed.

"Well, if not, I'm sure someone will," he said kindly. "Go home."

She ran, and the dog ran with her.

After Scarbantia, the road divided. Each branch went toward a different important city, each about two days away along the shores of the Danube. Both were large and relatively prosperous, and both were heavily defended by the legionaries of the Tenth Gemina.

Directly north lay Carnuntum[24], a pivotal fortress guarding the bridge across the Danube and the Amber Road. It had been weakened during the Alemannic wars and was somewhat reduced in size, but the military base was still powerful.

Radagaisus and most of the Goths determined to head for it. Alarmed citizens from the area hurried ahead of them carrying as much of their worldly treasures as they could fit onto their wagons or their backs. Many of the people who fled Carnuntum headed toward the second city, Vienna. Most of them would go right on past it and head for Italia, or Rhaetia, the next province to the west.

One large contingent had opted to bypass Carnuntum and head straight for Vienna[25] which was almost as large, and closer to the pass. The route would take them near the city, but then they could continue west for hundreds of miles on ground that would be easy on the wagons, though dangerously close to the thousands of legionaries guarding the Danube frontier. There were several major roads near Vienna, all of them under the protection of the soldiers of the Tenth Gemina, but the fortress there, once a powerhouse, was, according to Tribune Bulleus and his men, now much

---

[24] Carnuntum, in present day Petronell-Carnuntum, lies between Bratislava, Slovakia, and Vienna, Austria along the Danube. It was the capital of the Roman province of Upper Pannonia after the 1st Century AD.

[25] During Roman times Vienna was called Vindobona.

reduced in strength. Their guides believed that the Tenth Gemina would not be able to protect the city and guard all the roads as well.

Cantarcchio had a third route in mind. He wanted Dukes Helerix, Arnulf and Rumbert to follow the road toward Vienna, but then break away and head right into the mountains, following the river valleys to the plain on the far side. That way was more difficult but they would avoid coming into contact with any Roman armies.

His route, he said, was a shortcut. They would be ahead of most of the other caravans, and be ready to enter the pass before the main horde of invaders brought the legions down on them all. He assured the three warlords that even though they would miss out on Carnuntum and Vienna, they would be first to reach Cetium[26], a small walled town on the far side of the mountains which would not be heavily defended. They could sack it to their hearts' content.

The Gothic warlords were uncertain. Without the presence of the other Goths who were accompanying the king, Rumbert, Helerix and Arnulf felt more vulnerable.

Cantarcchio assured them that the soldiers of the Tenth Gemina would have their hands full with Radagaisus and his allies farther north, adding that he thought the farmers along the new route were unlikely to have hidden their crops and they might have better luck finding new sources of food.

They did not altogether trust him, and met alone to discuss it. After debating the points he had made, they decided to take the chance.

Cantarcchio kept an impassive face when they gave him their decision, but seemed relieved. He advised them to go easy on the area they would be passing through. These, too, were mountain people, and they could cause problems if they were riled enough. The leaders agreed to pay for whatever food and animals they 'took' along the way. The towns beyond the mountains, including Cetium, offered a much richer target anyway.

In due course, Cantarcchio guided them away from the Amber Road and into the hilly terrain leading to the river valleys he had described.

The crags, though not yet the mile-high massifs to come, were high enough to seem menacing. When the sun wasn't directly on them, the valleys were shadowy and cold. The travelers crept along through the river valleys, awed by the dark and lonely landscape. The canyons, overhanging cliffs and sloping roadways were fantastically mystical. It was very easy to imagine that, not just mortal enemies, but trolls, goblins and giants lurked around the bends or peered down at them from the heights above. It was an introduction to what Cantarcchio told them lay ahead in the long pass to Italia.

They crept along, exhausted and anxious. This part of the journey was much harder going than what they had experienced so far, and if anyone had wanted to attack them, there were times it would have been easy to do so. The caravan was stretched out for miles, and they passed through many places where an enemy might waylay individual wagons or set dangerous booby-traps.

Occasionally the path they followed narrowed to next to nothing, and then would dramatically widen to encompass pretty farming communities huddled beneath the peaks. Whenever they reached one of these, they would set up their wagon circles and then the raiding parties would set out. The three warlords ordered their men to leave payment behind for everything they took. It was an opportunity for some of them to unload bulky, heavy and useless items they had plundered in moments of careless greed, and replace them with food and fodder. The news of their coming had gone ahead of them. The people had concealed their animals and fled farther into the mountains.

Eventually the last of the wagons made it through the mountains and onto the plain beyond. Ahead lay their easy target, Aelium Cetium. The relieved and exuberant warriors fell on the town

---

[26] Aelium Cetium is the modern Sankt Pölten, in Austria.

153

and ravaged it. This was the first opportunity any of them had had to plunder a Roman town before any other group got there. It was easy pickings, as the walled town was poorly guarded and largely deserted. The frightened citizens had fled.

In high spirits, the Wodenvale caravan set off again, eager to be the first to reach the next town, Ovilava[27], five days away, and Iuvavum[28], a day farther south. Perhaps, they boasted, they would be able to catch up with the fugitives from Cetium and relieve them of their remaining treasures.

Then they would be on to Rosenheim[29], far away to the west.

Rosenheim was still a month away. By then it would be dangerously close to winter and they would begin the hardest part of their journey, the tortuous route through the Alps to, and through the pass.

---

[27] Ovilava is the modern town of Wels, on the Traun River of northern Austria

[28] Iuvavum, or Juvavum, was the Roman name for modern Salzburg. In Roman times it was an important town in the Roman Province of Noricum.

[29] Rosenheim, in southern Germany, used to be known as Pons Aeni, meaning bridge on the Inn River.

CHAPTER EIGHTEEN

EUCHERIUS VISITS VILLA AUSONIA

~

Legionary Fortress of Moguntiacum
(Mainz, Germany)
September, 405 AD

On a beautiful September evening, the mail wagon from Trier was escorted through the gates of the Moguntiacum fortress bringing mail for the soldiers and officers.

Marius and Eucherius both had letters. Eucherius eagerly hurried off to his room clutching three of them.

Marius had received a letter from his father. He spread it out on the table in the triclinium, and sat on one of the couches to read it. The remains of the last meal they had eaten had still not been cleaned up, and there were crumbs on the table and floor. This happened so regularly that the two tribunes had stopped commenting.

Paulus Ausonius reported that the family was well and hard at work around the farm. The harvest was going to be quite good this year. They had taken on extra labor, neighbors who were leaving some of their fields fallow that year and who needed the income. His father and Julian had heeded Marius's warning about the weaknesses of the frontier defenses (Marius now wondered if he had perhaps stressed that a bit too much), and they were taking steps to reinforce the walls around the villa and the horse barns. They were going to replace the spiked wooden walls with stone ones, also spiked. Paulus had always intended to do that, ever since the last Alemanni invasion, and now he had hired a master mason and ordered stones for the job. It would take time and a great deal of money, but it would at last get done. Not that it would stop the barbarians if they were really determined to break into the compound, but all of their consciences would rest easier if they did what they could. He had passed the word along to others in the area.

There was more news about the farm, his family and his friends in town.

They all enjoyed receiving Marius's letters. The family was excited and thrilled that Marius had had the good fortune to team up with General Stilicho's son, and they were all eager to meet him again, but then his father had added a warning: *"Certain people who were unaware of Eucherius's identity when he was at your party, plan to form a delegation and come to see him before you two march out. They have a message that they want him to convey to his father and his brother-in-law, the Emperor.*

Your godfather is planning to come up from Arles to join the delegation. He mentioned in his last communication with me that he has not heard from you yet. Can you drop him a line? I suggest you ask His Excellency for permission to bring Eucherius home for a few days if the General's son is willing. It would be easier all around, and we would love to see you.

After we read your first letter, I went looking for a book I bought a couple of years ago, but I was unable to locate it. Priscilla suggested that you might know where it is. I remember you mentioned in your first letter that you had borrowed a couple of books from the library when you left here. I presume one of them is a panegyric about General Stilicho I bought last year. You are welcome to keep the books if you like. Consider them my compensation for the party you missed.

Your mother wants you to know that she has been thinking about your request for a domestic slave. She is sending you one of our slaves, a Hebrew man named David. He was married once, and had a small vineyard up the river towards Bingium. His wife died giving birth to their first child, and he did not take care of the grapes properly. He lost his freedom when he could not pay the taxes on his land.

He is better now. He is clean, an apt worker, and eager to join you in the Army. He was under the misapprehension that any slave who joined would automatically be set free. (I promised him that I would give him his manumission if you returned home safely to us after your own service is done.)

We gave him your saddle to bring and money to stay at a couple of inns along the way. He should be there in a week or so.

If he is not acceptable to you, or if you no longer need him, you can send him back. He is a good worker, though kind of quiet. I don't know whether he can cook much, but after what you said in your last letter about the slave you have now, David should be a change for the better.

❧

Eucherius was on his bed by the window, reading aloud one of the letters he had received. He looked up, frowning, when Marius entered his room.

"From one of your many admirers?" asked Marius, dropping into the chair.

"You might say that," replied Eucherius. "My extensive female fans always seem to have the same idea—write to the boy and tell him to come home soon."

"Anyone special?"

"Yes. This one is from Placidia." He indicated the one letter he had not yet opened. He had placed it on the little table beside his bed. It was lined up neatly with the edge.

"And this one is from Mother—she always writes most elegantly and tells me what to do in the nicest way. She's very bossy, and very sweet. This one," he waved the one he was reading, "is from Thermantia, my little sister. I think she is the same age as yours, maybe a bit younger, but she writes the kind of stuff I like to read. It's full of complaints and cheeky gossip and innocent ideas about how the rest of the world should behave, and she always has lots of questions about my life in the army. She's the happy-go-lucky one among the three of us."

He smiled. "Probably because there are no more Theodosian princes and princesses Father and Mother can marry her off to." There was irony in his light tone.

Marius did not comment. Eucherius looked up at him, suddenly aware.

"I love them all, really. They're good people. It's just that I never did have many choices in life. Neither did Maria."

The Empress. Marius did not know how to respond.

"I notice you haven't opened the Princess's letter yet?" asked Marius. "Saving the best for last?"

Eucherius looked haunted. "I always read her letters last. I never know what to expect from her. Sometimes she sounds like she is only writing because she has to, as if she sort of resents having to write to me at all. She can be almost hurtful, and at other times she is just like she used to be growing up, my third sister. We used to have fun as children, but it is harder now. The older we get, the more aware we are that we . . ."

He stopped and looked apologetically at Marius. "It feels like we are part of some grand play written by Homer. You know, lives orchestrated by fate to fulfill some cosmic plan. I've never said that to anyone else, Marius, just thought it, so please keep it to yourself. Some people would think that sounds ungrateful. And I don't always feel this way. Just sometimes."

He stared at the floor, and sighed. "Placidia has it the worst, I think. I am lucky to be able to get away from it all, even for a time. She *can't* get away, ever! I know she resents that, and she takes it out on all of us except Thermantia. It's not my fault she feels trapped. So do I, sometimes."

"Have you ever said that to her?"

"No. She has the ear of the Emperor, and anything I say to her is just as true about him and my sister. It would cause trouble within the family."

It was true. It was time to change the subject.

"Well, your destiny has come knocking again," said Marius. "I had a letter from my father. There are some people back home who want to talk to you before we leave the area."

Marius read the excerpt from his letter out loud and looked at his friend expectantly.

Eucherius made a face.

"Don't worry, Marius. It happens all the time. Some ambitious soul always tries to use me and my sisters and even my mother to get to the Emperor or my father. Almost every time I go into town, I have to listen to someone's complaint. It's so tiresome and useless. Whatever I say, Father always does what he thinks is best anyway, and Honorius listens to him. I can't change anyone's mind, so why do they keep hectoring me? I can ignore the spontaneous complaints, but not this kind of organized delegation. I guess I'll have to meet them."

"Father suggests we ask Legate Carausius if we could go to Trier rather than having them all come up here."

Eucherius brightened. "That's a great idea. I liked your family, what I saw of them, and I'm looking forward to talking again with that pretty little sister of yours. Priscilla, right? I'm sure His Excellency will give us no trouble about going."

Legate Carausius was home. The soldier on duty ushered Marius and Eucherius into his office where he was reading his own mail.

"Ah, Tribunes! I have been intending for some time to get together with you. I have been hearing good things about both of you. Tribune Barbatio has told me that you have stepped up to the parapets quite nicely. I plan to write to both your families to let them know that before you go."

"Thank you, sir," they murmured.

"I understand your men have done rather well, too, considering the shortness of their time here. I don't think we will be able to keep any of you here much longer. My last communiqué indicated that the High Command has made the decision as to where to send your cohorts."

"Do you think they will keep us together, sir?"

"I expect so."

The legate went behind his desk and fished around among a pile of scrolls, then found what he was looking for.

"Sit down, men," he said.

They sat down.

"This letter is from one of General Stilicho's aides. It was written just over a week ago. It says that Radagaisus's invasion is underway. The main force crossed the Danube weeks ago and is now in Noricum. Pannonia and Noricum have been pillaged again. I'm amazed anyone still tries to keep farming there," he commented.

"Apparently the barbarians have split up into different groups. Radagaisus's main force has headed across Pannonia toward the mountains. The commander of the Tenth Gemina is convinced they are making for Innsbruck and the pass that leads south through the Isarco Valley toward the Adige Valley. If they make it as far as Pons Drusi at the bottom of the Isarco Valley, they can walk right into Italia.

"There is another large group that has stayed north of the Danube—we're not sure where they intend to cross, but they are staying away from our fortresses and bridges for now. Our Alemanni and Burgundian allies are watching them. My personal nightmare is that they might be coming here!

"There are two other groups, both headed south. The generals think they may be trying to get to the pass near Emona, the one used by people going to and from the Eastern Empire. The army is determined to block that route. Extra troops are being sent to reinforce it. I expect that those barbarians will have to turn around and try another way, most likely the road that leads into the Alps west of Poetovia. That's where the last group has gone. The legion there will try to block them, of course. As long as they can."

There was a long pause.

"I do not know why your father does not send for General Alaric and his troops," he said to Eucherius. "That area was assigned to them to defend, but right now they are a long way away sitting in Macedonia doing nothing."

Eucherius looked uncomfortable, but did not reply.

The legate sighed.

"Anyway, we're into it now. The forts along the upper Danube and the Amber Road have been recruiting locally and stocking up on supplies. They will take the brunt of the invasion, but they are understaffed. It's going to be a long winter."

He sounded glum.

Marius spoke up quickly.

"Sir, this may be a bad time to bring this up, but I wonder if I might have leave to take Eucherius and go home for a few days."

Legate Carausius looked up with a scowl.

Marius explained the situation.

"My father thinks it would be better for everyone if we went back to Trier, rather than have the delegation come all the way up here."

"That's good thinking," replied the legate quickly. "I don't think I can face them when I have so much to do right now. I don't suppose you are just looking for an excuse to go home? Though your father couldn't have known about these new developments . . ."

He looked at Marius, who shook his head. "Your orders have not come yet," he reflected. "How are your optios doing? Do you think they can cope in your absence?"

"Yes sir. We think so, sir."

"Tribune Barbatio seems to think so, too."

He smiled at last. "We've talked about it. I've made a point of watching Rufus and Bauto. They both seem keen, and smart enough. Good men. Well then, you two make your preparations and go. I'm giving you ten days. I expect your orders will be waiting for you when you get back."

"Yes, sir. Thank you, sir."

Marius was excited. A chance to go home, to be with his family, and to take Eucherius with him! He wondered whether they might be allowed to use the military inns they had stayed at on their trip up from Trier, and then wondered how much it would cost to go home by boat. Freedom! He could taste it.

They hurried down the Via Principia and rounded the corner, excitedly discussing the trip and the latest news.

A soldier was standing in front of their house. He had a message for Tribune Ausonius: the duty officer had requested that he come to the guardhouse at the main gate as soon as he could. Someone was waiting for him there.

Marius hurried back to the main gate. He walked into the guardhouse and found the duty officer talking with the new arrival, a tall, dark-haired man with deep-set brown eyes in a long, thin face. His travel clothes were dusty. Beside him were a worn travel bag and a large awkward looking package. He stood up as soon as Marius walked in the door, a warm smile on his face. Marius appraised him. He looked familiar.

The duty officer saluted him.

"Tribune, this man says he is your new household servant. Do you know anything about this? Were you expecting him?"

Marius was astounded.

"No. Yes! I just got the letter today that he was coming. I didn't expect him here so soon."

He looked at the man in amazement. He now recalled seeing him in the gardens and doing odd jobs around the kitchen back at the Villa Ausonia.

"How did you get here so fast?" he asked. "Father said you would be a week."

The man gave the ghost of a smile.

"Your father gave me money to stay in inns, but I used some of it to hitch a ride with a merchant I know who was coming up here. I slept in one of his wagons at night. I couldn't wait to get here. Here is the money I didn't use."

He handed over a flabby grey purse with some coins in it. The gentle smile widened a fraction.

"Keep the rest. So glad you are here. Is that my saddle?"

Marius pointed to the awkward looking package he had brought.

David nodded.

Marius picked it up, and led the way out of the guardhouse and on to his home. He dumped his saddle inside the front door. David looked around.

"The kitchen is that way," said Marius, pointing. He smiled. "Tell the chap in there that he is no longer needed here. He can report to his supervisor for new duties."

"Yes, Master Marius." The slave gave him that same ghost of a smile, and started toward the kitchen and scullery.

Marius looked after him thoughtfully. "Welcome to your new home, David."

The man turned and grinned, warmth flooding his face.

"Yes Master Marius. It is good to be here."

"Can you cook?"

"Yes." The man waited, his body half-turned.

"Good. The other man who lives here is the Emperor's brother-in-law. He is used to good food."

159

David's eyes widened, and the smile vanished. He disappeared down the corridor. Marius chuckled.

"Marius?"

Eucherius had been standing at the top of the stairs. Marius turned to him with delight.

"Rejoice, my friend. We have been rescued from the abyss. We have our new servant."

"I thought you wrote weeks ago. I wonder why it took so long. I'm getting used to eating bad food. I shall miss it."

"Maybe my mother couldn't decide which servant to release. She takes as much interest in them as in her own family."

"Did you mention that we're about to leave for Villa Ausonia ourselves? What do we do with him?" asked Eucherius, nodding toward the kitchen. "Take him back with us?"

"No, leave him here. He's just come and will take some time to settle in. I'll give him money to shop, and tell him to fix up the kitchen and the garden and do some cleaning. The other slaves can tell him what to do and where to go. That ought to keep him busy."

"And what do we do with him when we leave here? Send him home? Sell him?"

"Father says he wants to earn his freedom and is willing to fight. Maybe they'll let us bring him along. He's miles behind all the other men."

"I don't think it can be done, Marius. He has missed too much. It would be nice to have him as a servant, though. I hope he can cook better than that other slob. Maybe we can teach him some skill in weapons, so he can at least defend himself. You can buy him a shield, a belt and some tools to go on it. Do you think he'll be content with that?"

"I don't know. My father is going to give him his manumission when I leave the army for my political career. That's years away. A lot can happen between now and then."

Two days later, they left for Trier. This time, Marius rode on his own saddle. That familiar mold kept him reasonably comfortable on the three day journey. They were able to stay at the military guesthouses along the way and to change their horses for fresh ones each day. With only each other as company, they were relaxed and enjoyed the journey.

Their visit to the Villa Ausonia was a happy occasion. For the first few hours Paulus Ausonius, Constantia and Lucius were on their most patrician behavior; then, warming up to their son's new friend, they became more bold, discussing politics with him, beginning with local and moving on up to international.

Julian said little, clearly more interested in getting back to the business of the farm: the grapes in the vineyard were at their 'bursting with flavor' best. Priscilla was shy at first, and then as Eucherius flirted with her, she became coquettish and teasing.

The family loaned their esteemed guest one of their prized young geldings to ride, one destined for an Iberian cousin of the Emperors'. Marius and Priscilla rode with him down to the river and along the shoreline. To Marius's surprise, Eucherius started quoting some stanzas from *The Mosella*. He was having a wonderful time.

They clambered down the bank to the little cave. Their guest was enthusiastic.

"If I ever need a place to hide, I'll come here," he exclaimed with satisfaction.

"It might get a tad crowded if you do" said Priscilla. "The rest of us plan to be here, too."

"Well, beautiful, you had better get busy and make it bigger, because I will definitely be back."

"With your bride?" she asked sweetly.

He grinned. "Somehow I can't see Placidia in this cave, can you? Besides, she'd need a host of servants to look after her, and there's hardly room for all of us."

Marius bumped his head against the roof of the cave, and rubbed it.

"While you're making it bigger, Priscilla, could you make it higher, too?" he complained.

"No need, brother. There's room in the slave cells of the old silver mine for you," she teased. "I haven't been there for nine years, but they seemed high enough back then."

On the way back, she and Eucherius rode side by side, while Marius, riding ahead on Troya, fretted at their slow progress. After a few minutes, he gave Troya her head and they galloped swiftly up and down the road until the other two caught up and they all raced for the back gate.

Julian proudly escorted Eucherius on a tour of the foaling barns, mare and foal pastures, and the training areas. They watched the stable slaves and hired workers exercising, grooming, and racing some of the horses. Eucherius was next shown around the deep wine cellar below the house with its organized amphorae of Moselle wines, most of them from the estate. He tasted a couple, and told them they were as good as Sicilian wines and were all the rage in Rome. They knew that, but beamed to hear him say it.

Four of Lucius's friends showed up at the house the day after their arrival, then twelve more dropped in the day after that, and finally Lucius asked if they could perhaps throw a big party for their celebrity guest. Marius put his foot down. He suspected Eucherius would be up for it, but he was not.

Constantia fussed over them both, feeding, lecturing and quizzing them until they fled the house. On the third morning, Marius found his mother sitting in the peristyle with his friend singing her son's praises, and urging Eucherius to press for Marius's advancement with the Emperor. He was mortified.

Eucherius winked at his friend and skillfully avoided making any promises. It was clear he had had plenty of practice. Constantia cheerfully changed subjects, inviting him to go with her to visit her favorite charities in town, and have lunch with the Bishop. This, Eucherius was happy to do. Marius went with them to protect him.

On the way back, they stopped at the Romulus Garrison to visit Commander Cavillicus. He eagerly invited them in to talk with him and his officers who were avid for news and gossip. It was an altogether different level of conversation than they had had with him that first evening in the garrison. Both had matured in profound ways over the last few months.

On the fourth evening, all the Ausonius men accompanied Eucherius to the home of Limenius, the Provincial Administrator. The dinner would be the meeting with "the delegation" Paulus Ausonius had referred to in his letter.

Jovinus was there, looking weary from his journey north. The other guests included a number of important landowners and imperial bureaucrats from the area. Characteristically, it was Jovinus who got right to the point.

"Young man, we are concerned about protecting our provincial economy, and we represent hundreds of other landowners in Gaul, men who have loyally supported Rome with taxes, food, soldiers, and economic opportunities for almost thirty generations."

Eucherius raised an eyebrow. Some of the other men at the table looked worried.

Only twenty years before, Gaul had raised a usurper to the imperial throne, and Emperor Theodosius and Eucherius's father had led the army against the usurper, Eugenius, and the Frankish general, Arbogast, who had supported him. Every one of the men sitting at that table was well aware of this, including Jovinus. Paulus Ausonius gave an exasperated look at his old friend. It was a bad beginning.

"Barring the occasional mistake, of course," added Jovinus smoothly.

"Act of treason, you mean," muttered their host.

"Would you like to take over, Limenius?" demanded Jovinus, turning on him. "Perhaps you would do better?"

Limenius nodded calmly, and turned to Eucherius, "As the senior spokesman among this group, perhaps I might be allowed. . ."

Jovinus, offended, folded his arms, and gritted his teeth.

"I have not taken offence, gentlemen," cut in Eucherius. "We all know that Gaul has a very long history of cooperation with Rome. There have been mistakes on both sides. No one is perfect." He smiled and met their eyes.

The men around the table relaxed.

"You may not know this, young man," began Limenius, "but it was your excellent father who appointed me Provincial Administrator for Gaul, and I have been proud to serve him and the Emperor here ever since.

"You must have seen for yourself that much of Gaul and Gallia Belgica are not as prosperous as they used to be. Many farms have been lying fallow for years instead of being productive. Ours, of course, the big estates," he waved an arm at the men seated at the table with him, "are still doing fine, but in my position as the Emperor's civil administrator, I have seen a big decline in overall income. The taxes Rome needs are now harder to come by than they have been in a long time."

"These men and the ones we represent are afraid to lose what previous generations have worked so hard to achieve.

"As you may have heard up at Moguntiacum, Tribune, there is a growing threat from pirates who are attacking along both coasts and up the Rhine. There are also more bandits on the loose, even in this area. Meanwhile, thousands of soldiers have been pulled away to serve in other arenas, and some of the Palatine regiments have been ordered to leave their duties here and go to Italia to face this new crisis. Our historic enemies are taking note. They think that we are rich. Indeed we are, by their standards, but not so rich we can spare our declining wealth to them.

"We have an old suggestion to put forward to your father and the Imperial Court. Give us the right to bear arms and defend ourselves. We are proud Roman citizens, and such an exemption will pose no threat to the Emperor. If we cannot defend our land, our businesses and our shipping routes, then we will lose even more ground and we will not be able to continue paying Rome the same level of taxes. It does not serve any of us to lose this income. We all agree that under the current circumstances, this is the best way for us to be able to prosper and pay the taxes Rome needs. But we are losing time."

He looked grim, as did the others sitting around the table.

Eucherius promised to make a strong recommendation to his brother-in-law, the Emperor, and to his father on their behalf. The meeting ended, and the men broke open an amphora of a ten year old local red wine. Food and drink flowed freely, and the Ausonius men and their guest were driven home in a state of pleasant euphoria. The subject raised at the meeting was not raised again for the rest of the visit. That was only good manners.

Before they left to return to Moguntiacum, the family dined informally in their private dining room, the one with the best view but the most shabby floor and wall mosaics. Eucherius was thrilled. He was getting to be treated like one of the family. But one feature puzzled him.

"You call it a 'triclinium', but there are no couches!" he said.

"Couches are the Roman way to dine," smiled his host. We are Celts, you know, and in the past we Celts always used chairs. It is one custom many of us have chosen to keep in our own private dining areas, although we do have couches in our formal dining room."

The talk over dinner was all about the renovations to the villa's defenses, the quality of this year's grape harvest, the army's unwillingness to pay more for top quality horses, and speculation about their impending departure from Moguntiacum.

As they rode out of the gates, Eucherius looked wistfully back. "You don't know how good you've got it," he commented. "If I ever have a choice, I want to live in a place like this and have the kind of family you've got."

Marius could not agree more. Eucherius's personal life seemed increasingly bizarre to him.

"Your sister is wonderful company, Marius. Does the family have anyone in mind for her?"

"She's only fourteen, Eucherius!"

"My sister Maria and Honorius were married when they were fourteen."

Marius looked at him indignantly. "You know fourteen is ridiculous, Eucherius."

"But legal."

"Legal, yes. Wise, no. Nobody knows what they want when they are fourteen."

The thought made Marius quite angry. He knew that the Emperor and Empress still had no children of their own. Seven years had now passed since Princess Serena had advised them to wait before consummating their marriage. Everyone wondered, but dared not ask, whether the Emperor had continued that platonic relationship with his pretty blond Empress. They were both shy and submissive by nature.

"Why are you so irritated?" demanded Eucherius. "I'm not saying everyone should marry that young. I wouldn't want to myself. But I was really only asking if your parents had an understanding with another family about her."

"No they don't," replied Marius shortly. Eucherius looked pleased.

"You already have a betrothed, remember?" Marius said evenly. "Princess Galla Placidia."

Eucherius looked dubious. "Yes, but . . ."

"There is no 'yes, but', Eucherius. You may like my sister, and she may like you, but please understand that my family will not appreciate it if you get us in trouble with the Emperor. Besides, Priscilla is the only girl in our family, and we are determined that when she marries, she must marry the right man for her, and, moreover, be ready for it."

Eucherius pulled ahead haughtily. They rode on in silence.

After a few minutes Marius caught up with him and asked, "What did you mean when you said 'Yes but . . .' to me a minute ago? You *are* betrothed to the princess, are you not?"

"Officially, yes," answered the other tribune, staring straight ahead.

"And unofficially?"

Eucherius turned to him in exasperation. "You still don't get it, Marius. She's practically my sister, for God's sake. How would you like to be betrothed to your sister? We grew up together. She and Honorius spent more time at our home than they did at their own. It kind of dulls the romantic interest!"

"What's she like?" As soon as he had said it, Marius wished he had not.

"A bit stuffy and formal. Not bad looking. Quite pious, thanks to my mother. Usually bad tempered, at least with me, although she can be quite funny at times! You'll probably meet her. She's had her own household since she was a little girl, but she visits quite often. I'll introduce you when we get to Rome. Now can we drop the subject?"

They rode together in a stiff silence.

"Well, no one is going to choose a wife for me," said Marius emphatically.

"That must be a good feeling," sneered his friend. "Are you waiting for Bissula?"

"Naturally."

CHAPTER NINETEEN

MARIUS BEGINS TWO JOURNEYS

Legionary Fortress of Moguntiacum
(Mainz, Germany)
Mid-September, 405 AD

On the Ides of September, Marius and Eucherius received their marching orders. Ready or not, it was time to move on. There was no longer time for further training. The barbarians were already pillaging at several locations in the foothills of the Alps. The passes were full of refugees fleeing ahead of them.

Tribune Barbatio brought them the news with the request that they report immediately to the legate's office.

General Carausius handed them their orders and told them to be ready to leave in three days.

To their great disappointment, the two friends received altogether different orders. Marius's were to take the Mosella Cohort to Augusta Vindelicum[30], a fortress strategically placed in Rhaetia, north of the Alps. Eucherius's orders were to lead the Rhenus Cohort to Italia where they would join up with the Italian Field Army at Pavia, south of Milan, the administrative center for the Western Empire.

The two cohorts would travel together up the Rhine past the fortress towns of Strasbourg[31] and Augst[32]. From there they would move on to Bregenz[33], a Roman naval center at the far end of Lake Constance. There they would separate. Marius and the Mosella Cohort would march northward to the fortress of Augusta Vindelicum in the province of Rhaetia, while Eucherius and his Rhenus Cohort would march south through the mountains into the heart of the Western Roman Empire.

---

[30] Augusta Vindelicum is now Augsburg, Germany

[31] Strasbourg in Roman times was called Argentorate.

[32] The Roman fort at Augst, Switzerland used to be called Augusta Rauricum. The Roman settlement was abandoned in AD 260, but the road remained.

[33] Bregenz, in Roman times known as Brigantium, was a major center for the Roman navy on Lake Constance (Bodensee), a large lake at the northern end of the Alps.

"Come with me," the legate said. They followed him down the hall to another room where there were several long tables and a large library of scrolls and parchments. On one of the tables were two hefty scrolls. "They're for you," he said. "One each. Open them, and take a look."

Marius fumbled with the long document, trying to open it wide enough to see what it contained. It seemed to go on and on.

"They're maps!" exclaimed Eucherius. "I've seen these before, and have always been fascinated by them."

"It's more information than you need for this trip, because that's the whole map," said His Excellency. "I had my scribes make several of them last year. I don't usually give the whole thing away, but you may as well see the full extent of the Empire you have chosen to serve. I'm sure you will find them useful. Tribune Ausonius, lay yours out on the center table here and we'll take a look at it."

Together they stretched the scroll out along the long table, and put weights on each end. The document, a road map used by the army and government administrators, was a little over a foot wide and stretched to more than twenty feet long. It showed every Roman road and major fortress in the Empire. Many settlements were also shown on this map, with the distances between them and the roads connecting them. Even forts and supply depots had been marked. The three most important cities of the Empire, Rome, Constantinople and Antioch received special iconic decorations.

Marius was in awe. He had heard such maps existed, but unlike Eucherius, had never seen one. It might be awkward to work with, but at least it would be easy to carry.

They walked along the table looking down with fascination. General Carausius spent a few minutes demonstrating it.

"I find these useful when planning long journeys and campaigns," he commented. "You will see that your routes have been marked on the ones I have given you. I want you to spend some time here this morning learning more about how to use them."

"This is Moguntiacum." He pointed to a dot. "And this is Augsburg, where you will be taking your men. The quickest way to it is to use the old roads across the Rhine"—he pointed vaguely out the window—"That used to be the most direct route."

They knew he was referring to the series of old roads built by Roman soldiers centuries before, when the frontier had been miles farther away.

"That route is out, unfortunately. Even with the current treaties, it would be considered an act of provocation by the Franks, Burgundians, and Alemanni if you were to take your men through their territories without permission. I can't risk that, and since your soldiers are not yet seasoned veterans, I would just as soon not let the people on the other side get too close a look at them."

They winced.

"The second quickest way to Augsburg is by boat up the Rhine, followed by a short march across country, then by boat again on Lake Constance[34] to Bregenz[35] at the other end of it. With so many men, that is out of the question—much too expensive!

"That means, unfortunately, that your men will have to walk the whole way. You should be at Bregenz in two weeks, and then you, Tribune Ausonius, will need a few more days to get to Augsburg.

"Eucherius, from Bregenz, you and your men will be conducted by army guides through the Alps as far as Comum. From there, you will take your men on to Pavia. There are forts marked along the route where you can stay. Your father does not think you run much danger of meeting any of Radagaisus's people along that route—it's quite far west. You should be in Pavia about two weeks

---

[34] Lake Constance, a large lake touching Austria, Germany and Switzerland

[35] Modern Bregenz, Austria, at the eastern end of the lake

after leaving Bregenz, except, of course, if you get caught in an early blizzard or an avalanche. It's unlikely, but always possible. I suggest you learn everything you can from your guides on the journey south. The mountains are unpredictable and dangerous."

"My father has told me some terrifying stories, Your Excellency. I'll be on my guard."

"Being on your guard might help. It would be nice to see you again the next time I get to Italia."

"Yes, sir."

"Tribune Barbatio will accompany you both as far as Bregenz. He has requested it."

They looked at each another, pleased.

"So, young man," continued Legate Carausius to Eucherius, "from time to time I have kept your father aware of your progress. He tells me that your family is eager to see you again. How do you feel about going home?"

Eucherius sunny face clouded. "I really don't feel ready to go home yet, sir," he said carefully. "I know I still have so much to learn."

Legate Carausius nodded. "You are right, but duty calls, and we are never quite ready when it does. You will learn much on the journey, and more when you get to Pavia, where, I believe, your father plans to use you."

"Yes, sir." Eucherius sighed and stared at the map, his attention elsewhere.

The Dux looked at him with compassion.

"I'm sure you will see action, Tribune," he said. "We are at war, even if you haven't seen the enemy yet."

He saluted them.

They saluted back, and he walked out.

Another man entered, a short, bald man with an encyclopedic knowledge of the geography and fortifications around the Empire. He began to explain the maps in more detail, including the geography and cultures behind the names. They listened carefully, conscious that at any time they might need to know how far away the next town or fort was, and what kind of help might be available there.

It was an hour and a half before they left. They were quiet during the walk back through the great fortress. They each had a good deal to think about.

For the next two days they and their men prepared for departure. They would be accompanied by a small group of auxiliary cavalry, army slaves and a baggage train. Food, clothing, armor, weaponry—all had to be collected and loaded. There were goodbyes to be said on the base and in the town, monies to be reclaimed from the Treasury at Headquarters, last minute letters to write, debts to repay, and shopping and packing to do.

The legate had suggested that Marius and his men would reach the fortress at Augsburg in about three weeks. Once there, he would be turning over command of his cohort to the legate of that fortress and receiving new orders for himself. Tribune Barbatio thought it possible that he would stay at Augusta Vindelicum over the winter.

"It's a good life, Marius. Augsburg is the capital city of Rhaetia and it is in a beautiful area. As a tribune you will be in high demand socially. The Rhaetian women are lovely—I met my wife there. So is the scenery, and there is good fishing and hunting in the area. If you get to stay there, you are going to enjoy it." Barbatio's eyes sparkled.

"Lucky you, Marius," said Eucherius sourly. "All that snow and ice, and wondering every day which you will meet every time you leave the fort, wolves or Goths."

"Want to trade places?" asked Marius.

"Yes! You're going to be having all the fun and adventure, while I am stuck at a desk during the day, and entertaining the sons of senators and the Spanish cousins of the Emperor at night."

Marius met Barbatio's eyes. Eucherius had summed his own future up well. There wasn't much they could say. The legate had known it too. Stilicho's son, and the future husband of Princess Galla Placidia, was an asset to be used, not risked.

"Maybe you'll be fighting Radagaisus on the plains of the Po while I am having a glass of spiced wine with a fur merchant's wife," said Marius consolingly. Eucherius grinned.

"Hey, maybe!"

"What are you going to be doing, sir?" asked Marius, turning to the senior tribune. "With all of us gone, it's going to be pretty quiet here again."

"I'll be returning here. In style, I might add. The navy will take me to the end of Lake Constance, and then I'll catch a ride on another ship up the Rhine. His Excellency wants me to help him smarten up the frontier troops down the river between here and Bonn."

They looked surprised.

He grinned. "Just in case any of the invaders get this far. If the army won't give this area more troops, we'll try to give them better ones. I'm heading for Italia myself as soon as this crisis is over and I have a break. I'll look you up, Eucherius. I'll get you out on the town one way or another."

"You promise?" The young man's eyes lit up. "You won't be intimidated by my Mother?"

Marius and Barbatio laughed. The young man seemed fearless, except when it came to the members of his own family.

Along with many of the men from the two cohorts, Eucherius and Barbatio went out into the town that night to visit their local haunts and say goodbye to new friends. When they returned home that night, they were both as drunk as dock slaves and singing bawdy songs. Marius and David undressed Eucherius and got him to bed.

Marius went into town too, but headed for the cathedral. It was windy and dark when he got there, but the door was standing open. An acolyte who had been lighting the candles in the lamps along the wall slipped away when he entered. He stood in the semi-darkness, letting his eyes adjust.

The basilica, with its massive marble columns, distant chancel, flickering lamps and dimly glinting choir stalls did not feel as conducive to prayer as his little cave on the hillside had, but he wanted to try once again to make a connection with God. Tomorrow he would be going even farther away from home, and he could not know when, or if, he would return. He was also soon to lose two good friends, one of whom felt like another brother to him. And unlike Barbatio and Eucherius, Marius was heading directly towards danger.

In spite of his outward confidence and all the training and practice he had received since June, he still had a lingering worry that he was not really ready to take command of his cohort. For at least the week when he would be leading his men from Bregenz to Augsburg, there would be no one else to fall back on. Even Bauto and the centurions, his junior officers, were new. Normally the men in such positions, career army men, would be much more experienced than a brand new tribune. But they were all new, and he, their leader, was younger than many of them, although he knew he had won their respect.

Marius had brought *The Gospel of John* with him to the cathedral. It had not been opened since that day in June when he had taken it down to the cave. He had left it on the shelf in his room, and little by little the beautiful book had become covered by other items until it was out of sight and almost forgotten.

Now he pulled it out of his pouch and opened it at the beginning again. In the dim light the beautiful script was hard to read. He crossed to one of the lamps along the wall to take advantage of its flickering golden light, and peered at the page. Where had he left off?

167

"The Word became flesh and made his dwelling among us. We have seen his glory, the glory of the One and Only, who came from the Father, full of grace and truth. No one has ever seen God, but God the One and Only, who is at the Father's side, has made him known."

Oh, yes. He remembered. The "Word"—it was coming back to him.

"Can I help you?"

A priest had emerged from a doorway at the altar end of the cathedral and approached him silently.

Marius looked up. "That's kind of you, but . . ."

"You're Marius Ausonius, are you not?"

"Yes, but . . ."

"Bishop Mauritius asked me to keep an eye out for you. I have seen you here on Sundays but have never been able to get to you before you were gone. I understand you and your men are leaving soon, are you not?"

"Yes, but . . ." Marius laughed at himself. "Who are you, Father?"

"My name is Aureus[36]. I am the bishop for this area. My authority covers the fortress too, in fact, although I know you have a chaplain there. Do you need help with anything?"

Bishop Aureus. Yes, his mother had mentioned that name. He knew nothing about the man, but he seemed kind, the sort of priest you could talk to.

"Well, Father, I have been trying to understand the symbolism of this poetry in *The Gospel of John*. I am not sure I really see it, yet."

"How far have you read?"

Marius was grateful for the dim light which hid his embarrassment. "I'm just at the beginning, and I'm already confused."

Bishop Aureus did not laugh.

"I know it well. It does seem like poetry, doesn't it? But it's theology. And ultimate truth. What do you want to know?"

"Well, it says here that the Word became flesh and dwelt among us." Marius held up the leather-bound parchment Gospel. "*This* is the Word of God, is it not?"

"Oh, I see your difficulty. That is the *written* Word of God. It tells the story of how God has tried to reach mankind and teach us about Himself. The Bible is actually a library, Marius. It contains many books written in several languages by people from different countries over many centuries. The marvel of it is that when you read it from the beginning through to the end, you begin to perceive that there is really only one Author behind it all. It is one continuous story which starts with the creation of man and ends with the restoration of mankind to our original relationship with God.

"But beyond the Holy Scriptures, there is another Word, the Author who inspired the book, the Person the Bible tells us was with God from the beginning, the One who existed before time began, long before the written Word came to be.

"I am finding it hard to get from this," said Marius, pointing at the Gospel, "to Him. He always seems to be out of my reach, and the words I am reading confuse me. It's harder than I thought it would be."

"That will change the minute you receive him yourself. John says that we have to welcome Jesus into the center of our lives. When we do, the Author Himself comes and lives in us and helps us to understand it. People who seek to know God with an open heart are transformed this way. The

---

[36] Bishop Aureus of Mainz was killed a couple of years later during the invasion of Vandals, Alans and Suevis that crossed the Rhine River on December 31, 406 AD.

Bible, which starts out being big, scary and something you *should* read, then becomes a feast for the soul. Come with me. I want to show you something."

He led Marius through a door at the back of the basilica. They went along a hallway and into another room. It was dark, so Bishop Aureus took a few minutes to light all the lamps along the wall with a taper. Marius found himself in a beautiful little chapel with mosaics on the floor and on the wall above the altar. The picture at the front of the chapel showed Jesus at the Jordan River being baptized by his cousin, John the Baptist. A dove hovered over his head. The sky above him was filled with an angelic host, and there was a rainbow above them all.

"This is where the other priests and I come to pray," said the bishop. "We use it all the time for our private devotions."

"It's beautiful."

"It was done by a master artist from Milan. Now look at the floor."

Marius looked at the floor. It was a complicated pattern of interconnecting tree branches, with songbirds singing in the spaces between. It looked as intricate, if not as colorful as the mosaic on the wall.

He looked back up at the priest, puzzled.

"This was done by the same man. It looks fine, now, but it had to be repaired a few years ago. Over there." He pointed to an area near the entrance. "It wasn't any fault of his—we had a few incidents with some fanatical pagans. I don't blame them—we've done worse to some of their temples.

"We tried fixing the damage ourselves, but we just made it worse. Then we brought in some of the local men who have experience with mosaics, but it didn't look right. Some of the pieces weren't the right size, some of the shading was not there, and sometimes they had not bothered to set the tesserae as flat, or line them up as carefully as the original work. You could see the difference between the good areas and the repairs. The mosaic artist who had done the job in the first place heard about the damage and our difficulties, and he made a special trip here to fix that one area. He came and tore out the damaged area and replaced it with his own work. In the end, it looked even better than in the beginning. Here, look at this."

He took one of the lamps from the wall, and bent low over the repaired area. Marius stooped to look. The pattern here was the same as elsewhere on the floor, but the artist had added slight colored accents to the birds, and flakes of gold to the boughs surrounding them.

"We didn't notice the enhancements for months. It is subtly done, and we did not ask him to do this, nor did he request payment for it, but now we are very conscious of this section whenever we gather here to pray. The master artist not only repaired the pattern, but improved it, and occasionally, when the sun is at just the right angle, this section catches the light and glows, just like the pattern on the walls. That's what God intends for us, too, Marius. "

"The Bible says that God created us in His own image. We were like the floor the artist made, but of course, much more beautiful and valuable. The Bible says that God was very, very pleased with us, and for some time He was able to enjoy our company and we His, but we chose to go our own way, and without Him beside us, we got lost and broken. We lost our glory and our joy, as well as our sense of direction. So the Master Designer came back.

"That chapter in John you are reading says that the Word became flesh—that means that God became man. John was referring specifically to Jesus whom he had known and followed closely for three years. As a human himself, Jesus could reach people and show them what God was like in a different way than just reading about what God said to do and not do. His life spoke for him. He was supremely loving, full of wisdom, able to heal and command the rapt attention of crowds, and yet empty of pride and selfishness. Jesus showed us what God is like, His sense of right and wrong,

His mercy, and His deep commitment to us. In his death he showed us we are more loved and more valuable than we can possibly understand."

In this quiet little chapel, Marius found his unspoken thoughts flowing easily. "I never did understand why, if Jesus was God, he allowed them to put him to death on the cross."

"Do you know what Gospel means, Marius?"

"It means one of the books about Jesus, doesn't it?"

"No. It means good news. Good news has to be good news for everyone, not just educated people or religious people. If God came as Savior to the whole world, then the good news has to be something that anyone can experience, not just the very good or the very smart.

The issue is not with our theology, Marius. It is with our basic nature. The biggest problem common to man is sin, and sin erects an impossible barrier between us and God. God and sin cannot co-exist, and when we are sinners, we are separated from Him, and our lives are very different from the way it used to be when God first made mankind to walk with Him. Everyone has sinned, so everyone has experienced this wall between them and God, although not everyone cares to find a way around it.

"The Word became flesh, not so much for the purpose of teaching us about God and showing us what God is like, as to deal a death blow to that impossible barrier. His disciples said Jesus was without sin, something none of us can claim. When the Savior was crucified, he took with him on the cross the sins of everyone else—those who were alive at the time, those who had gone before, and those who would live in later generations. He came as God incarnate, and died as sin incarnate.

"On that cross he felt for himself what it was like to have that wall blocking him from perfect fellowship with the Father. That separation from God, and that awful burden of shame, guilt and condemnation that sin brings, they were probably the worst part of the torment he experienced which was already horrendously cruel.

"Jesus's death on the cross became the Way for the rest of us to get back into that intimacy with God He created us for, and that Jesus himself enjoyed until he became our Sin Bearer. The minute you welcome him into your heart, the wall separating you from God is behind you, not in front of you. It is a mystery that people can only understand experientially, not through their intellects. It is a pathway designed by God Himself, and the only one that gives us back the intimacy with God we crave.

"That is the beginning of your freedom, and the start of a great journey through life. You will begin to hear God's quiet voice and feel His loving Presence more and more, and you will also become aware of the things He wants you to do. Best of all, He will give you the power to help you do everything he is asking you to do with surprising ease. You can spend a lifetime growing closer to Him, learning to hear His 'voice' from the nudges and checks the Holy Spirit will use to teach you, and even from your mistakes when you make them."

Marius was listening carefully. Something was stirring within him, but he didn't know what to do with it.

"Bishop Aureus, suppose I want to become one of God's children? How do I do that?"

"It's not hard, Marius, so don't make it hard. You read it yourself. John said that to everyone who received Jesus he gave the power to become a son of God. You have to receive him."

"But how?"

"How does a child receive a new toy? This isn't something you have to figure out. It's a conversation you have to have. You simply bring your flawed life to Jesus and offer it to him. Then just invite him to take over yours. He suffered a great deal for you. As a human being he gave up his own life, and as God, He became Sin, the thing He hates the most, in order to destroy its power over us. He did what He had to do. That was the hard part. Now you should do what you have to do. That's the easy part. Just receive Him into your life and follow him forward."

"Thank you, Bishop Aureus. I will try."

"The only thing you have to 'try' Marius, is to be sincere when you invite the Lord in. Jesus described Himself as the Way, the Truth, the Life and the Door. Don't try to figure it out. Walk through and keep going. And keep reading this," he pointed at the Gospel, "and the other books in the Bible. They will help you go in the right direction."

He bowed and walked away.

Marius's heart was pounding. He had the sensation that even though Bishop Aureus was gone, there was still Someone standing there in the little chapel with him. He wondered what to do. He was not at all frightened, even though he felt something momentous was happening in the atmosphere around him. He felt excited, as though he was on the verge of a great discovery, or on a bridge crossing into a new land. The air around him was electric.

"Alright," he said, "You can come in."

Nothing happened. That amazing presence was still there, waiting, majestic and patient.

Marius got down on his knees. Humility, bending the knee to the One who most deserved your respect and devotion—that was the right and proper way to do this, not the previous immature and careless invitation he had just flung out.

"Please, Lord Jesus," he said. "I know you are here."

He faltered. Did he? He did.

"I want to receive you and become a son of God. I only understand a little of the cost you paid to give me that chance, but I am really grateful for the love that made you do it. I know I need you. Please, let me enter into your Kingdom and make me one of your sons. I will do my best to serve you if you teach me how."

A deep warmth and peace spread through his body, and an unimaginable joy began to rise up within him. He sat back against the wall, receiving the blissful outpouring of love and cleansing flooding through him. He felt as though he was being made new from the inside out.

He could hardly believe it. Almighty God had heard his puny prayer and was answering it with a storm of mercy. If this was becoming a "child of God", it was amazing, and whatever happened in the future, he was alright with it.

CHAPTER TWENTY

MARCHING TO PONS DRUSI

Fortress of Augusta Vindelicum, Province of Rhaetia
(Augsburg, Germany)
Mid-October, 405 AD

The fortress of Augusta Vindelicum in Augsburg was home to troops from the Third Italian Legion. Their predecessors had built Augusta Vindelicum and the other fortifications in the area to enable their masters in Rome to hold and expand their territories north of the Italian peninsula. The most important of their projects were the military roads and bridges.

In 15 BC, Augustus Caesar ordered his stepson, Nero Claudius Drusus, to conquer the feisty Alpine Celts once and for all, and then put a road through their formidable alpine landscape, one that could be used by troops, traders, and travelers. It was no easy task converting a pack-animal trail on steep-sided mountains to a durable, usable road, especially when the builders were subject to avalanches and enemy attacks, but Drusus and his successors were up to the job. The project was completed sixty years later by Drusus's own son, the Emperor Claudius.

The road that Drusus and Claudius built, one that could carry an army on wheels, was the great Via Claudia Augusta. It began in Italia at the Adriatic Sea, pushed up through the Adige River Valley past Verona and Trento[37], and on to Bolzano[38]. There, the road and the river veered west past Merano[39], north over the Reschen Pass and on down through the foothills of Germany. It passed the fortress of Augusta Vindelicum on its way to Regensburg[40] on the Danube, where the legionary headquarters of the Third Italian Legion was located. Here it intersected with the main east-west road that supplied the frontier fortifications.

Augusta Vindelicum was close to the confluence of the Lech and Wertach Rivers. They both raged down from the Alps on shallow, gravelly river beds to converge in Augsburg and rush on to the mighty Danube River.

---

[37] Trento, at that time was known as Tridentum.

[38] Pons Drusi, the "bridge of Drusus", is located in the area of Bolzano.

[39] Merano, at that time was called Statio Maiensis.

[40] The fortress on the Danube at Regensburg in modern Germany was formerly known as Castra Regina.

The fortress was situated at the intersection of several key routes, east-west as well as north-south, and these connected to more roads and other mountain passes. The city had grown around it, becoming the thriving capital of the Roman province of Rhaetia.

Four days after leaving Lake Constance and the naval center at Bregenz behind them, the Mosella Cohort finally reached its destination.

The thought of a real bed, even one in a barracks with seven other snoring men, spurred on the tired soldiers. The journey had been routine, no problems except for broken axle wheels, one broken arm, two fights, a theft among the ranks, and forty-five cases of diarrhea.

Marius was relieved. That had been eventful enough. The aching muscles in his calves, his tired shoulders and back, and the occasional glimpse of distant, snow-capped peaks had been regular reminders of the longer, more difficult journey Eucherius and his men were now taking.

As they approached, they could see that the gates to the fortress were wide open. There seemed to be a great deal of activity going on. Hundreds of soldiers were lining up along the wide buffer road. They could hear shouting over a din of carriage wheels, horses' hooves and hammering. The activity looked like more than an exercise. The soldiers of the Third Italian Legion, most of them big blond men bristling with arms and determination, appeared to be getting ready to march out. Their gear was on their backs and they were fully armed.

The air of urgency affected Marius's men; it took shouts from his centurions to keep them from losing their focus. Marius and his officers wanted to make a good first impression on these Rhaetian legionaries.

A man wearing the uniform of a high-ranking officer sauntered out the gates to wait for them as they drew closer. This, as much as their own centurions' barked orders, motivated the men from Moguntiacum to march briskly and in step.

Marius went forward to present himself. The officer, who identified himself as Magnus Generis, the second-in-command at the fortress, was a big, jowly man with thick, blond eyebrows.

Once the introductions were over, he led them through the lines and on down the street to the fortress's headquarters. Everywhere they looked, they could see further signs of preparations for departure. A squad of cavalry trotted past them. A wagon packed with javelins, arrows and boxes of ballista bolts came around a corner pulled by four large horses. Three others with similar cargos followed behind.

From the area which would contain the fortress armory and workshops, they could hear the sound of hammers hitting anvils, and the rapid rasp of weapons being sharpened. A few seconds later a group of soldiers came down the street wheeling a double-armed carroballista[41] and hustled it past them towards the front gate. Two lighter ballistae, the so-called scorpions, followed. This was looking more and more like preparations for war.

Tribune Magnus Generis led them into the courtyard of the Principia. Here, it was quieter.

"Your men can wait here until you come back," said Generis. "They can use the latrines and get water and rest awhile. The legate wants to see you right away. We won't keep your men waiting long. The barracks will be available presently. Tell your men not to get too comfortable. I understand you will not be staying here."

Behind him, Marius heard exclamations, and then mutterings as the officer's remark was quietly passed along.

"Our legate's name is Cornelius Olybrius. He's in his office now. Follow me, Tribune."

---

[41] A carroballista is a large bolt-throwing catapult used to hurl rocks and bolts long distances.

Mutely, Marius followed Tribune Generis across the pavement and up the stairs into head-quarters. He was badly shaken by the man's comment. He hadn't realized how much he had been looking forward to a quiet room with a warm bed and someone else to give the orders for a while.

Marius knew the base commander of the fortress by reputation. He was of equestrian rank from a prosperous, land-holding family in Macedonia. As a young soldier, his first assignment had been to Rhaetia, and he had fallen in love with the area. He'd never left it. He had married the eldest daughter of a prominent Rhaetian merchant and fathered two children, but his true love and passion were the mountains, and the army was his means to gain access to them. Legate Olybrius had become so adept at mountaineering, and so knowledgeable about the highways and byways through the Alps, that he had become a legend.

The High Command and the head of his legion took note. Soldiers who showed the intelligence and toughness needed to be an Alpine spy, were sent here to train. Tribune Barbatio had served under him for a short time, and admired him greatly.

"General Stilicho himself has gone climbing with this man, Marius," he had said. "He has trained hundreds of our best alpine couriers, guides, and spies. The men of the Seventh Alpine Cohort are famous, but they lose good men every year. Legate Olybrius, though, thrives on it. He even goes along on missions once or twice a year just to keep in practice. I've heard he subsidizes his men's pay out of his own pocket and looks after their widows. He says he knows how tough the life is that he trains them for, and how precarious."

When they reached the base commander's office, Tribune Generis knocked at the door. It was opened by a tall man with alert, black eyes, a strong jaw, and curly, grizzled hair. His gaze took in Marius's dusty clothing and tired face.

"Come in, come in, Tribune" he said. "We have been waiting for you. I should have allowed you time to rest and clean up, but as you can see, we are in a bit of an uproar here."

"Yes sir. Looks like some of your men are getting ready to leave."

"Hmmmm. Do you have your letter of introduction?"

Marius opened his pouch, and pulled it out.

"Good, good. Sit down, Tribune . . . Ausonius?" He gave Marius a sharp look, and then addressed his second-in-command.

"This will be a short meeting, Generis. I believe Tribune Ausonius has been assigned to the fourth house in the Praetorium. It's empty now, I expect. The other tribunes are all getting set to leave. It's not very homey at the moment, but it will do for today. There should still be a slave or two around."

Generis left the room. They were alone in Olybrius's large inner sanctum. Legate Olybrius shut the door and went back to reading the letter of introduction from Legate Carausius.

Marius looked around. The office furnishings were functional and covered with normal administrative clutter. The rest of the room, though, was unique. The wall panels were decorated with Alpine scenes of peaks and lakes under cloudless skies, the rocky ground and high meadows showing occasional tiny flowers. Some of the mountain peaks disappeared at the ceiling line, but most were visible, diminishing into an endless invitation to explore. Marius stood there wishing his mother could see this unusual display of artistic decor. This was in the modern style. Even so, whoever had painted it had broken several conventions. The mosaic on the floor, though, was plain black and white. It obviously predated the work on the walls.

In a minute the base commander looked up.

"Seems alright."

"Who painted this, sir? It's quite wonderful."

"Do you like it? I did. I love the mountains and I miss the big peaks when I'm away from them for long, so I painted them in myself. It's not any particular landscape. All my favorite mountains are in there. That one's called The Tetrarchy, and that one is The Bowl, and that one . . ."

The legate's voice was fading. Marius was almost beyond thought. He stood up, trying not to sway with the effort. The heat in the room was starting to undo him.

"Yes, sir. It's amazing." He felt a yawn begin and suppressed it painfully.

"Would you like something to drink?" The legate's voice sounded clearer, louder. He looked up. The man was standing right in front of him, and looking concerned. "The water here is pretty good. You can trust it without needing to add any wine."

"Thank you, sir. We drank from the local streams and rivers on the way here. The water was usually exceptional."

But then, there had been some place along the route that had caused the diarrhea. He smothered a smile—it had not been funny.

Legate Olybrius walked to the door and shouted to someone in an adjacent room.

Marius used the opportunity to rub his eyes like a child and yawned. The legate heard him and shut the door again.

"Sit down, son, sit down." He waved Marius toward a leather-covered couch.

"I'm afraid if I sit down, I will fall asleep, sir. We had rain the last two nights, and none of us got much sleep," he confided. He sat down anyway. The material the couch was covered with felt soft and warm. He ran his hand over it appreciatively.

"Chamois," said the legate.

Marius looked bewildered. He didn't know what that meant.

There was a knock on the door. Olybrius went back to receive a tray with two pewter mugs and a glass jug. He poured water into the mugs and handed one to Marius. It was icy cold. Just what he needed. Apart from hours of sleep, that is. He drank thirstily.

The legate eyed him sympathetically.

"Tribune Ausonius, you look exhausted. I'll give you the news straight, and then you have twenty-four hours to rest and recover from your journey. Then, I'm afraid, you and your men will be marching out again."

"New orders, sir?"

"Yes. From me. The Third Italian Legion is sending every man it can spare to the east to guard the pass south of the fort at Veldidena. Know where that is?

Marius nodded.

"There are already thousands of barbarians in the vicinity of Rosenheim and farther east, and they are wreaking havoc there and farther north and east. Some areas they seem to be leaving suspiciously alone, and my spies say that there are some Roman soldiers with Radagaisus. We don't yet know how many, or where they have come from, but we are checking.

"My men have orders to keep the barbarians from getting through the pass, and they are leaving immediately to get to Veldidena ahead of Radagaisus's main force. Your job is to march your cohort down the Via Claudia Augusta to Pons Drusi at the other end of the valley and harass the hell out of anyone who manages to get that far. Know where Pons Drusi is?"

Once again, Marius nodded. He was almost asleep. The couch was too comfortable. He stood at attention to concentrate better.

There was another rap at the door. Olybrius glanced at it and then back at Marius.

"The good news for you is that I am coming with you. Along with one of my best cohorts, the Seventh Alpine. We will be joined at Pons Drusi by at least one regiment from the Italian Field

Army, or some of the foreign federate troops under General Sarus. That should lift our numbers to at least two or three thousand men, enough to deter any of Radagaisus's people who make it past the Third Italian Legion in the Innsbruck area. You and your men can spend today sleeping and resting. My men will look after getting everything ready for you. We are leaving tomorrow as soon as we can be ready."

He walked to the door and opened it. Tribune Generis was standing there, waiting. He held up the key and waved it invitingly. They both looked at Marius.

"Take him to his lodgings and tell the slave to spoil him," said Olybrius. "He needs to be back in shape by tomorrow. I may as well go out to give the news to his men myself. Let's see what quality of soldiers the tribune has brought us."

The soldiers of the Mosella Cohort grumbled, but only to each other. The legate was an unknown quantity to them, but many knew of his reputation and were excited to serve with him. Another ten days of walking, though! Another ten days of blisters, sore backs and tired legs. Ten more days of temporary camps and standing guard duty at night. Not to mention eating hard biscuits on the march.

"By the gods!" swore Bauto, when he met Marius much later in the day, "I enlisted to fight, not to walk the skin off my feet."

"You'll be that much closer to a fight once you get there," responded Marius.

"I don't know how much of me will be left to throw at the barbarians," retorted Bauto. "And I'm not very good with heights, either. I get dizzy just climbing a tree!"

"You'll live," said Marius, tiredly. Bauto stalked off.

Marius was sorry. He admired and liked the young Frank, a noble by birth, but they had never been able to bond the easy way he and Eucherius had. He wondered if it was jealousy that kept them apart. Or competitiveness. After all, they were both new at the game, and it wasn't his fault that the army automatically placed members of the Roman aristocracy into positions of authority while others had to work and wait to get to the top. There were historical precedents for that going back centuries. Bauto should know that!

As it turned out, he and his optio would each be able to ride. Legate Olybrius and his senior officers would also be on horseback. He hurried to share the good news with Bauto, who was visibly relieved.

They were told by the officers of the Seventh Alpine Cohort to instruct their men to leave all non-essential personal possessions and luxuries behind. There were a few guffaws from the ranks at that, but as the experienced Rhaetian soldiers carried in their new supplies of heavy hiking boots, additional layers of clothing, walking staffs and mountain helmets, they ceased to complain and quietly repacked. That night they were served the best hot meal they had had since leaving Bregenz, knowing full well that such a meal might be their last for a long time, perhaps their last ever.

The next morning the two cohorts marched out of the main gates and retraced their steps down the Via Claudia Augusta.

The soldiers who had left the fortress the day before had taken a route toward the south-east. They were heading straight for the beleaguered province of Noricum to guard the entrance to the pass into Italia from the top end.

Legate Olybrius and the men with him were heading directly south. Their journey would be longer and much harder. Pons Drusi was close to two hundred miles away. If they were allowed to walk at a normal pace, the trip would take twelve days.

They were not allowed to walk at a normal pace. The legate wanted them there in ten days, and it would be uphill most of the way.

Along with the marchers and the men on horseback came a baggage train pulled by tough, army mules and a contingent of army slaves, their hewers of wood and haulers of water. The slaves would be responsible for the baggage, the main domestic chores, and the animals. They, too, were armed and had their orders, and were quite capable of defending themselves and their areas of responsibility.

A few of the slaves belonged to the officers. Among them was David, quietly excited, and watchful always over Marius's welfare. He had begged not to be sent back to the Villa Ausonia, claiming he had known of the dangers when he had agreed to come. Marius had become used to the man's thoughtful efficiency, and gave in easily. David and Socrates had struck up a friendship, and the grammar teacher was attempting to teach his friend some of the finer points of swordplay and self-defense.

The first stage of their long march was relatively easy. Epfach[42] lay at the intersection of the Via Claudia Augusta and the road that connected Bregenz on Lake Constance in the west with Rosenheim to the east. There was a Roman garrison at Epfach to guard the roads with accommodations available at the fort and in the town.

Marius and David were assigned to the home of a veteran's widow. Marius was given a clean, relatively comfortable room with a good new mattress and warm blankets, and invited to join the family for dinner. David was handed a thin pallet and a thinner blanket, and told dismissively to sleep on the kitchen floor with the lady's own slaves. Marius intervened, and the thin straw pallet got transferred to the floor of his room and reinforced with extra bedding from the trunk in the corner.

Beyond Epfach they entered higher country. The road began to twist and turn and their journey became a steady climb.

Occasionally, carriages would catch up to them from the rear and frustrated drivers would sullenly fall into line behind the two cohorts. Some were merchants, frantic to get through to Italia before the barbarians blocked their route. Others were people from the areas threatened by the barbarians. They were hurrying home to protect their livestock and movable goods, and get their families out of danger.

The long column of soldiers also met riders, pedestrians and carriages coming from the other direction. Whenever this happened, the officers would ask for news. They continued to hear that the area around Pons Drusi was quiet.

The mountains grew steeper and began to crowd in on the road. Broad slopes became overhanging cliffs, so high that you could get a crick in your neck just trying to see the top, so high that they cut out the nourishing sun and shortened the daylight.

Their eyes grew weary from staring at the brooding peaks around them, gritty from the gusts of dust-bearing wind, and dazzled by the sudden transitions from deep shadows to brilliant sunlight, but the occasional sight of snow-capped peaks, the stubborn growth of trees and bushes in impossible places, and even the animals moving through the valleys far below or high above provided memorable moments of beauty and inspiration.

The settlements they passed on this part of the route were mere hamlets often well below or high above them. They were few and far between. Occasionally, they heard cowbells ringing in the

---

[42] In Roman times, the modern town of Epfach in southern Germany was known as Abodiacum.

distance. A threesome of wolves passed below them on a slope and disappeared into a fir forest, and once, Marius noticed a small herd of mountain goats climbing up an almost vertical cliff high on an adjacent mountain. Excitedly, he pointed them out to his riding companion.

"Chamois," Olybrius commented. "Those are chamois."

Marius looked at him blankly.

"Don't you remember the couch in my office? That wonderful leather? If we can, we'll go hunting for a couple of them. Perhaps you can have a couch of your own made."

Marius watched the alpine goats until they had reached the top of a cliff and disappeared out of view. The chamois's amazing surefootedness astonished him. How could they walk up cliffs like that? The legate's idea was tempting, but he was sure he would never be able to get close to one. But then, that incredible soft leather would make a wonderful gift for his mother. A trophy he could be genuinely proud of!

The scenery was spectacular, but after one perilous slip, Marius learned to keep his attention on the road ahead. Sometimes the Via Claudia Augusta would turn sharply, and the men would find themselves looking down at a forest floor hundreds of feet below. Sometimes they would come around a corner and be struck by winds that pushed and pulled at them. Sometimes rain that felt like sleet would bite at their faces, blinding them.

The Via Claudia Augusta, like the mountains it clung to, continued to climb, Marius and his men became uncomfortably short of breath and headachy. The air was thinning and their bodies were struggling to adjust.

One afternoon they walked into a snow blizzard. For half an hour the going was very difficult. They could see only a few men ahead of them. Those on horses or driving mule-carts had to lead the frightened animals. The road grew slick, and their formal march turned into a shambles as men bumped into each other, and slipped and fell. One misstep sent a soldier plunging over the edge of the road. They found him alive below, but with a broken leg. He had to be carried by mule litter back to the last military post and left there. One of the searchers, a Mosella Cohort man, got lost, and trackers from the Seventh Alpine Cohort had to find him. Olybrius called a halt for the day. The presence of so many novices among them made proceeding too dangerous. It was clear that the Mosella Cohort had much to learn.

They passed military outposts and supply depots along the way, but none of these were equipped to handle so many soldiers, and the terrain made it difficult to build their normal temporary camps at night. Increasingly, the soldiers of the Mosella Cohort began to rely for help on their Rhaetian companions who seemed to take these conditions in stride.

Olybrius's men had, at first, kept their distance from the newer soldiers, but began to respond to the respectful inquiries they were receiving. Little by little they took Marius's men under their wings. They taught them how to walk so that every step could refresh their weary calf muscles, how to use their walking sticks, how to avoid starting a rock fall or an avalanche, and where to find water that was safe to drink. The men from Gaul learned that the cause of the diarrhea on their previous journey could have come from melting glacier water which would cause stomach problems that fresh spring water would not.

On several occasions, the Via Claudia Augusta passed across solid Roman bridges suspended high above icy rivers. The legate and Marius stopped and dismounted on the far side of one of these bridges, and climbed a hill as their men crossed the bridge below them. Two of Olybrius's scouts were waiting for them there.

The first man reported that thousands of oxcarts and warriors had managed to break free of the battles going on around Rosenheim, and were descending the Inn river valley towards Innsbruck.

The second scout reported that there still was no sign of any disturbances in the area of Pons Drusi. It might be a little over two weeks before the main body with Radagaisus made it that far. They had an excellent chance of beating the barbarians to the bottom of the pass valley and organizing a defense. They were only a week away.

During the days, the effort to walk and keep the baggage train moving kept them all focused on the road they were following , but in the evenings, the men from the two cohorts began to sit together over shared campfires, find common interests and tell their stories. The Seventh Alpine soldiers used the closing moments of daylight to demonstrate rock-climbing and rescue techniques, and taught the men from Moguntiacum survival skills that could be incredibly valuable in the capricious mountains.

As the grueling journey drew to its close, they began to keep a cautious eye on the hills around them, particularly the lower tree-covered slopes where ambushers might hide. There was no sign of the enemy just yet, but the scope of the battle ahead was beginning to become clearer.

"How in the name of God can anyone fight on this terrain?" grumbled Bauto to Marius as they sat around a campfire one evening.

One of the Rhaetians, a rangy centurion named Hannibal, overheard him.

"Watch and learn, tribune," he said. "Armies have had to fight on all kinds of terrain, and the men of this area know how to fight on this one. No lining up in nice formations on the battlefield here. We have our own ways."

"But have you ever fought against such numbers as we hear are coming?"

"Not for centuries, but we have stories and tactics going back a thousand years, and legs and feet that are almost as sure as the chamois."

He stretched out one of his well-muscled legs and studied it admiringly. Bauto and Marius obligingly stared at it too. It looked ordinary, but they had seen Hannibal scale a cliff. It was not something they could do.

"I'm not sure my men and I will be equal to the task," admitted Marius. "We know how to fight, but this will be like nothing any of us has ever faced."

The centurion bent closer to Marius. "Be careful what you say, Tribune," he whispered. "My people believe these mountains are gods and have ears. They can take a shine to you or get bad-tempered in a hurry. Don't let them know you're afraid." He poured some of his wine out on the ground and looked up at the peaks around them.

Marius was amused. He winked at Bauto, who shook his head. Hannibal had noticed.

"Make fun of me if you want," he said. "I know I'm not as educated as you, Tribune, but I'm a survivor. Whatever gods there are, I make sure they're on my side."

He swatted at a lone fly near his face. Another one settled into his pewter cup. They waited.

"You and your men, you'll have a couple of days, maybe four, to get ready. If your men work with ours, they'll get some solid training. There's nothing much else you can do after that except trust the officers and obey orders. We know more about fighting on this kind of terrain than Radagaisus or any of his people. They just want to push through. We'll just push back a bit, and then disappear. You'll see."

They left the Reschen Pass behind them and followed the Adige River. In a few days the valley began to widen. They were getting close to their destination now. They looked around in wonder as farms, orchards and vineyards began to reappear along the valley floor and adjacent slopes. This area was renowned for its pleasant climate and hot springs, an oasis in the center of the massive alpine peaks, a welcome change for travelers on an arduous journey, an invitation to stop and dally.

179

They crossed a Roman bridge to bypass a waterfall that was in their way, and then a second Roman bridge a little farther on. Finally they reached the little Roman fort of Statio Maiensis. Pons Drusi now lay sixteen miles ahead.

Two rivers converged at Statio Maiensis, the Adige which they had been following, and the Passiria, a smaller river that drained into it from the mountains to the north-east.

While the soldiers were setting up camp, Marius and Legate Olybrius went in to talk to the prefect on duty at the garrison. He was a big man, a blue-eyed farmer with a bushy beard and huge forearms who was in conversation with another soldier when they walked in.

He saluted them smartly enough, but seemed oddly casual. The soldier with him withdrew. Marius heard a door shut, and through a slit hole in the wall saw him walking away.

Legate Olybrius introduced himself and Marius. His first question, as always, was whether the barbarians had reached Pons Drusi, yet. The answer, as they expected, was negative. Marius exhaled and felt the tension in his body drain away.

"How close are they?" continued his commander.

"The last thing we heard was that they were just over a week away from here."

"And when was that?"

"A couple of days ago, sir. One of the soldiers based at Pons Drusi came by."

"So they could be only five or six days away now?"

"Yes, sir."

"What else have you heard?"

"Well, Your Excellency, a traveler from Aguntum[43] got here a few days ago. According to him, there is a second large force of barbarians coming along the Aguntum-Teurnia[44] road from the east. He estimated that there were many caravans of people in that group alone, mostly Suevis, and reported they have attacked the mining communities and administrative towns all along the way. Many of the people in the east have been hiding out in caves or retreating farther back into the mountains to wait until it is safe to come out. The traveler reported that they were approaching Aguntum when he left."

To Marius, Olybrius murmured, "That would mean that they could be getting to this area around the same time as the main body coming with Radagaisus from the north."

"Have any other Roman troops passed through here?" he continued.

"No sir. You are the first. We have not heard of any coming up from the south to Pons Drusi, either. It is encouraging that the High Command has not forgotten us here altogether. We were beginning to think they had."

That was alarming, but Olybrius gave no sign of concern. "How many men do you have under your command here?" he asked.

"There are sixty of us in the area, Your Excellency, but most of the men are hard at work in their fields right now. Everyone is hurrying to get their crops in before the barbarians arrive."

"What are your plans for defense?"

The farmer-soldier laughed heartily.

"We have no plans for defense here, sir. There may be a hundred thousand people coming this way. What do you expect the sixty of us to do against so many?"

---

[43] Aguntum is 2.5 miles from Lienz, Austria on the Drau River which runs between the north-south axis of the Danube in Hungary, and the Italian Alps.

[44] Teurnia was, at one time, the capital of the Roman province of Noricum. It is close to modern Lendorf in Austria and is also on the Drau River, farther east from Aguntum.

"No plans except to protect your own farms and families, you mean," said Olybrius, outraged. "But you have no plans to evacuate the people, or defend the bridges and the supply depots? No plans to burn your grain fields and pastures so that they and their animals have nothing to eat?"

"We have no plans that would antagonize them, Excellency. The sooner they are through here, the sooner we can get on with our lives again. People around here *are* trying to harvest what crops they can and hide them and their animals. Many of them have gone—toward Italia, or up into the hills to the caves where they always go in times of crisis. They took their livestock with them, but nobody is burning their fields. There has to be something for us and our animals to eat after the barbarians have passed through. You can't blame us," he said defensively. "We are ridiculously outnumbered."

"Tell me, prefect, what orders did you and the garrison at Pons Drusi receive from the High Command about preparing to receive two or three regiments of your fellow soldiers for the fight against the invaders?"

The man hesitated.

"We received no such orders."

Marius stared at the prefect. He thought he was lying.

"What do you suggest my men and I do about that? Where do you usually put up regiments when they are in this area? In your homes?"

The man's eyes narrowed.

"This is a small community, Your Excellency, as you must have noticed. We don't have barracks for all of our own men, only those who are on duty. We have guest houses for visitors in the area, a supply depot, of course, and we do try to provide visiting units with food and guides, but that is all the High Command usually requires of us. As for Pons Drusi, the town has some inns and guest houses where officers can stay, and I know the locals have billeted soldiers in times past, but not on a regimental scale, sir. The garrison there is also pretty small."

"What, then, do you suggest?"

"If you set up camp in the pasture across the road, we will try to find food for your men and your animals."

"And what have you heard about the local soldiers stationed at Pons Drusi?" he asked the prefect. "Are they also looking after their own self-interests?"

The prefect's jaw clenched and his eyes blazed. All friendliness was gone from his expression.

"Well, sir, there're only a few men there. Mostly farmer-soldiers like us. Their job with the army is to collect road tolls and keep the peace in the area. People from outside can't expect them, or us, to put up a serious fight against thousands of barbarian warriors."

Olybrius glared back. "Have you heard about Roman soldiers from this area who have deserted to Radagaisus?"

There was a short pause. "Yes, sir. There have been rumors about that, but they are just rumors, sir." For the first time, he seemed nervous.

"The Army, too, has heard such rumors. They have been circulating for months. I think you would know by now if there was any truth to them. Are all your men present and accounted for?"

The man's eyes flickered and he seemed at a loss as to how to answer. "As I said, sir, many of them are in their fields bringing in the harvest, or taking their families to higher ground."

The Legate's voice grew quiet, though his face was red. "You and your men are now under my command, prefect. I want a full list of all the soldiers in this garrison and the keys to the supply depot. Within the hour. My tribune will collect them from you. Also, send word that I want all your men to come in immediately for further instructions. Have as many of them as possible here by the time my tribune comes back for the list and the keys. Good day to you."

He marched out with Marius right behind him.

"Sir, I think he's compromised."

Olybrius nodded glumly. "Let's go for a walk while I think."

They strolled down the road in the direction of Pons Drusi. For the first few minutes, the legate kept silent. It wasn't until they turned back, that he spoke.

"Listen to me carefully, Marius. There is going to be a change of plan. Tomorrow morning my men and I will be leaving you."

"Going where?" Marius was alarmed.

"A couple of hours north of here, there is a route that will take us across the top of the mountains to the valley that Radagaisus and his people will be using. It is a ridge known as Jove's Pass—I guess because it must seem to the locals like a highway made by the god himself. We have to climb a fair distance to get up to it, and then travel at a good speed for miles along it before we reach that other valley. Your men would not be able to attempt this, but my men are well trained, and we can handle it.

"By tomorrow night we will be in a good position to see what is happening along the valley of the pass. We will need to find out where the nearest barbarians are, and then do whatever we can to weaken them and slow them down before they get to Pons Drusi. They must be stopped before they get there, because from Pons Drusi on, the whole area opens up and the going gets easier.

"The wagons and the families travelling with Radagaisus have to stay in the valley, but the warriors might attempt to climb the mountains to get a good look around. I want to prevent that so they don't dare come at you from any other direction. My men will try to keep them close to their caravans, afraid to leave their families unprotected. We will attack the wagon train before the warriors can get down to this area, and then join you in Pons Drusi as soon as we can.

"Now here is what I want you to do. . ."

CHAPTER TWENTY-ONE

PREPARING FOR WAR

~

Pons Drusi, Rhaetia, Western Empire
(Bolzano, Italy)
Late October, 405 AD

The next morning the Seventh Alpine Cohort set off, following the Passiria River into the mountains. Soon after, Bauto and some of the best riders in the cohort left for Pons Drusi. Their task was to take charge of the garrison there and keep the local men in custody until Marius could arrive with the rest of the cohort. That would not happen until the next day.

They all now knew that these fellow soldiers were traitors. Not one of the local men had shown up for duty, and by the time Olybrius had gone in a rage to see the prefect they had spoken to, he had fled taking the keys to the supply depot.

Bauto and his men were warned not to discuss their plans with anyone in the area, or mention the desertion of the garrison in Statio Maiensis.

Even more alarming to Marius was the information that there was no sign of the other troops the High Command had promised to send into the area. For now at least, they were on their own.

The Mosella soldiers dismantled their camp, loaded up the baggage train, and set off down the road. Along the way they passed a continuous stream of people going in the opposite direction, their carts, carriages and wagons piled high. Shepherds and goatherds passed them driving their animals toward safer highland meadows. The news of their arrival seemed to have propelled people out of their homes. No one wanted to stick around for the fight.

Marius and his officers stopped some of them to ask the latest news. They were told that the nearest group of Radagaisus's barbarians was about three days away, and the second large group of invaders had been seen approaching the Brixon area. It seemed both groups would be converging north of Pons Drusi within a day or two.

That afternoon they made camp in a meadow just above the Via Claudia Augusta. Marius ordered double the number of guards, placing them at several elevations. With David looking after his domestic arrangements, and with several hours of daylight left, Marius decided to climb to the top of the nearest mountain and have a look around.

He found a footpath and began to climb. By the time he reached the top, he was sweating. Far below, he could see the town, the camp, and people moving around on distant farms. The view of the mountains around him was breathtaking. These peaks were different from the ones they had passed through earlier. The rugged, light grey cliffs and spires were more jagged and barren, but streaked with vertical patches of pink and orange. He stood there for a few minutes composing lines of poetry to fit their stark and bleeding beauty, and then turned to continue on through the forest.

The footpath he was on was soon intersected by another one. He paused indecisively, and then continued straight ahead. Twenty minutes later he came out of the forest and into a broad meadow. It was part of an upland plateau whose backdrop was another tier of peaks. Across from where he stood, he could see terraced fields, farm buildings, and a few stone fences. The only sign of life was a boy herding goats or sheep along a road some distance across the meadow. He could see a piece of that same road about a mile away before it disappeared down a hill and re-emerged across a valley.

Quickly he shrugged out of his red officer's cloak and hid it and his weapons and belt behind some trees in the forest. He shivered. It was cold, but if he ran he might be able to stay warm. He set off at a run to see what lay in that distant valley where the road had gone.

The dirt road was packed hard and deeply rutted by centuries of hooves and heavy wagons. The farmhouses along it seemed to be deserted—there was no smoke rising, and he saw no animals in the fields. The exercise was invigorating, though, and the experience an eye-opener. The road was crossed by multiple trails. Some of them led to homes and farms. Others carried on and disappeared into woods and around bends. At one point, his road intersected a drover's trail which climbed to a meadow hundreds of feet higher up. He kept running until he reached the place where he had seen the road dip down into the next valley. Here he stopped.

Opposite him and in the valley below there were more farmhouses and cultivated fields, all apparently deserted. The road meandered past them and kept going. He had no time to explore farther. He would have to get back.

Just before he turned around, Marius spotted movement. A dozen chamois were grazing in a meadow across the valley. He watched for a few minutes until the lead goat suddenly raised its head and then began to run straight at the cliff that rose behind them. The other chamois followed, and Marius watched, fascinated, as they ascended the rock wall most of the way to the top and then took a side trail along it, disappearing around a corner. He could not see what had startled them. Perhaps it was the pair of eagles drifting along in the sky above.

Marius hoped the eagles were a good omen for his cohort. Eagles had always been the proud symbol of the Roman Army and of the Emperor himself. He watched them circling and gliding for another minute, and listened to the stillness around him. Then he turned thoughtfully back.

The area was far more densely settled than it had looked from the Via Claudia Augusta. How many people lived up here? How many of them were complicit with the local rogue soldiers? He wondered how Olybrius and his men were doing, and wished that the legate had left him with even a handful of his skilled alpine troops. They were so much more experienced than anyone in his own cohort.

It was nearly dark by the time he reached the camp again. A couple of guards were preparing to take their place on sentry duty, and Marius warned them to keep their eyes on the areas above them as well as below. He visited all of the sentries in turn, and passed on the same message.

That night his men were quiet; they were getting nervous. A few months ago, they had been bakers and barbers, farmers and army slaves, the sons of veterans called into service, and the sons of barbarians from villages across the Rhine. Now the reality was sinking in—they would be facing an assault by countless experienced fighters determined to prove their supremacy, and they had enemies within the local populace that did not like their presence there, and who were opposed to what they were there to do. Even the mountains looked threatening.

The next morning Marius force-marched them right to the outskirts of Pons Drusi. Bauto was waiting for him at the point where the Adige River was joined by the Isarco, and the Via Claudia Augusta turned south. He had been watching for them and seemed ready to burst with his report.

Marius dismounted and they saluted.

"What news, my friend?"

"Tribune, when we arrived, there was no one guarding the bridge, no one in the toll house, and no one in the fort. In fact, someone had set fire to it. It was still standing, but the walls have been damaged. The supply depot was open, and most of its contents were gone. They left almost nothing behind."

"What about the toll bridge?"

"It would take a month to demolish that, Tribune! That bridge is as solid as a rock. The barbarians won't even have to get their feet wet crossing the gorge."

One of the main criteria in choosing an army camp site was defensibility. Another was making sure it was near a supply of drinkable water. In the end, Marius decided to place his camp close to the toll house at the Pons Drusi bridge and use the river for drinking water. The location would give them some natural protection on three sides and a possible escape route behind.

Once again, his weary soldiers began to lay out their camp.

He sent a large group of men into the town. They were to bring back anything useful that had been left behind, especially weapons and food. He was so angry that he had decided that any of the local people who were still there could not to be trusted. His soldiers came back with armfuls of blankets and food for the animals. They had also scavenged through the supply depot.

"We found some large catapults the Pons Drusi soldiers left behind," one of the centurions reported. "No bolts, though, and if there were any scorpions, they must have taken them, too."

"Go get the carroballistas, then," said Marius. "We're going to be using them."

For the rest of the day as the soldiers worked to repair the fort and set up their camp, they spotted people watching from the hilltops across the river. Neither group made any attempt to approach the other. Marius sent tent groups of eight up the mountain to patrol the top and the sightseers rapidly dispersed.

After a while some local children came down the valley toward them and stood watching their preparations from a distance. The soldiers waved and called to them, and the children waved back, shouting out their names, asking the soldiers for theirs, wanting to see their weapons and their muscles. The grinning men of the Mosella Cohort obliged, reassured by the heavily accented Latin they were hearing. These were not barbarians, and their parents would surely not allow the children such freedom of movement if the barbarians were nearby.

By the evening their camp was ready and fortified. There was still work to be done in the garrison, but at least they had begun and knew what still had to be done. Tomorrow most of the men would go upstream to carry out the rest of Legate Olybrius's orders.

Once again Marius posted guards at several elevations. He insisted that every time anyone left the camp, even to wash their clothes in the river or to fetch water, they had to use a password. For tonight it was 'Constantia'. Wearily they headed for their tents.

The constant noise from the river and the bright moon shining overhead kept Marius restless for hours. His mind was busy with plans and worries, and he found it hard to relax. Several times he was tempted to get up to check on the sentries. He fought against his concerns, reasoning that surely someone would raise an alarm if anything went wrong. If only it wasn't so noisy down here by the river!

Come morning, two of the sentries were found dead on the hill above the camp. The attackers had killed the first guard, and then waited to kill his replacement when he arrived. They were being sent a message—*we know this area and you don't. Never for a moment think you are safe, or have the upper hand.*

The bodies were brought back into the half-burned fort and laid out on benches. After roll call, when everyone else was present, Marius had the two dead soldiers carried into their camp. His men were deeply affected—by now they all knew each other.

"Someone local did this," said Marius. "The barbarians may be close, but they are not here yet. This was not done by Goths, Vandals or Suevis. There are traitors among the local soldiers. If any of them approach you, do not trust them. Send them to me. Trust only each other, and watch each other's backs. From now on, there will always be four men on guard at each station. Stay alert.

"You know the odds. They're not good, but Legate Olybrius and his men are somewhere up the valley fighting already, and they are counting on us to do our job here. If we are going to die, let it be honestly and valiantly, in battle with the enemy, not from our own carelessness or someone else's treachery, as happened to these two men. Use your anger and grief for these, our comrades, to keep you wise and alive. Do not let traitors and invaders intimidate you. Let men everywhere know that the soldiers of the Mosella Cohort are true Roman soldiers. We may lose the battle, but we will win the war."

He had spoken fervently and there were fervent cheers. They would do their best.

They left fifty men behind at the camp to continue rebuilding the burned fort. The rest of the cohort marched up the river carrying tools, supplies, and some of the tents. Marius left the majority of the weapons they had brought with them under guard back in their camp—he was not willing to risk bringing them upriver just yet.

Legate Olybrius had ordered Marius to prepare an ambush for the wagons coming down the valley. He had described a spot a few miles up the Isarco River, and Bauto's men thought they had found it.

At one point along the tortuous route and uneven terrain in this lower part of the valley, the river did a sharp zigzag. The Mosella Cohort could do enormous damage here with its catapults, javelins and archers. The invaders would be forced to make their way slowly in single file, pressed, at times, even into the river itself. The wagons would be spread out for miles.

Anyone coming down the valley who tried to run the gauntlet would be exposed over and over again, and casualties here would cause a backup for miles. If the drivers turned around to flee, they might find the Seventh Alpine Cohort blocking their way.

Olybrius had thought it would be easy enough to set up. All they had to do was build stable platforms on the steep slopes and near the base, set up an obstacle course to direct the wagons, and fortify their own positions.

Marius and Bauto looked at the area dubiously. Yes, this would be a good place to concentrate their attack, but preparing it would not be easy. They would also be exposed on the dangerous terrain all the time they were trying to attack the warriors and wagons.

For the rest of the day Marius's men worked to prepare their ambush. Marius instructed them to stay within their eight-man tent groups. He wanted no more soldiers to go missing.

His men felled trees and dragged them to the river bed to slow the wagons—the barbarians would have their work cut out removing such obstacles while trying to keep their oxen moving forward under a hail of arrows and bolts.

Some of the soldiers placed or loosened boulders high above the river, ready to be shoved over the edge onto the wagons passing below. Marius warned the men to take careful note of where these were located for their own safety.

They created paths where there were none. Placing logs between trees gave them more traction and maneuverability on the steep slopes. They also hung ropes between trees to grasp onto while they were working. These proved to be so valuable that Marius ordered a second raid on the town to find more rope.

They carved out steps and spaces for wooden platforms above the double bend to hold the torsion artillery called *onagers*. These catapults, nicknamed "wild asses" because of their fearsome kickback, had single upright throwing arms and could lob rocks with terrifying force. Soldiers were assigned to look for the right size of rocks along the river bed, and a relay was set up to carry these to the platforms where the onagers had been placed. They also placed bins to hold the arrows and javelins as close to the platforms as they could.

Some of the men went up and downriver for miles looking for paths up the mountains. These they camouflaged with bushes and brush. It would not fool the local men, but their efforts might prevent barbarian warriors from climbing the mountains and getting above them.

A few hundred men could do a lot in a day.

The centerpiece was the S-shaped bend in the river. This would be where they used the two carroballistae, the large catapults left behind by the local men.

The ideal place to locate them was at the second bend. The mountains pressed in close here. Carroballistae placed on each side of the valley and aiming along this stretch would have deadly results. The barbarians would have no choice but to turn into that second deadly bend, or retreat back to the first bend and face the soldiers behind them. They would be trapped, and there would be chaos. In such a situation, Marius's soldiers knew that the sheer numbers of the invaders would prevail, but they tried not to think about that.

The decision made, his men prepared the platforms high enough up the slopes so that his artillery men could strategically maneuver the ballistae and coordinate their aim. This meant more trees had to be felled, more logs and planks prepared and more niches carved out of the mountain side. They also prepared pits to hold the bolts. These deadly weapons could blow a man or beast apart on impact.

By the time the two platforms were ready and rough ramps up the steep slopes had been prepared, the men were exhausted. Once again they all became aware of curious eyes watching from above them, but whoever was up there was too far away to chase. The watchers must be seeing much of what they were trying to accomplish. Any friendliness the soldiers had felt the previous day had vanished with the murder of the two sentries.

Marius sent back to the camp for the carroballistae, and late that afternoon a large group of slaves and soldiers appeared downriver helping the mules drag the sleds and the heavy catapults to their new location.

The most dangerous part of the job was getting the machines up to their platforms. This required a very slow advance up the hillside using braced logs and massed muscle power. The strongest men worked in teams, moving the first heavy catapult up a few feet at a time. There had already been injuries, most of them sprains and strained muscles, cuts and scrapes, and here there were more. A log suddenly slipped and broke the arm of one of the soldiers. Another lost his balance and fell backward into the trees below when his foot slipped, just as his teammates were responding to an order to push the ballista in his direction. A branch took out one of his eyes.

Marius kept one eye on the sun and another on the platform fifteen feet above them. His admiration for the army engineers and soldiers who had gone before him shot up. If only he had more experienced men with him!

It was dark before they got the first of the catapults into place on its platform. They would have to leave the second one for the next day.

Socrates nicknamed the ambush site "Thermopylae" after the most famous battle of the Persian wars. It had been fought between King Leonidas of Sparta and King Xerxes of Persia. That original Thermopylae had also been extremely narrow and readily defensible. It was an apt choice.

The grammar teacher reminded Marius that a small minority of Greeks had held off over a hundred thousand Persians for three days. Marius reminded him that King Leonidas had had over a thousand men supporting him in his final stand against King Xerxes, and that the Persians had won, killing most of the Greeks. Socrates shook his head sadly.

Marius left eighty men with their tents at "Thermopylae" to guard their preparations overnight. They had orders to change the guards on outpost duty every two hours. He and the rest of the men trudged back to their campsite to prepare their meal and try to sleep.

They reckoned the barbarians to be now only two or three days away. From tonight, sleep would be a thing of the past.

CHAPTER TWENTY-TWO

CANTARCCHIO MAKES HIS MOVE

From Veldidena through the pass into Italia
(Innsbruck, Austria to Vipiteno/Sterzing, Italy)
Late October, 405 AD

The fort of Veldidena was deep into the Alps. It was the last one before the pass the barbarian invaders would take into the heart of the Western Roman Empire. It lay within the beautiful valley of the Inn River which here was fast-flowing and milky-green. Much of the valley and the lower slopes of the mountains surrounding it were cultivated. High above the fields and vineyards soared the mountains.

The fort guarded the junction of two important roads, one coming from Augsburg to the northwest, and one coming from Rosenheim and the frontier cities of the northeast. The town of Innsbruck was here. It provided shops and inns and a central market place to service the army, the local farmers, and any travelers passing through.

Duke Helerix and his people reached Innsbruck at the end of October. Behind them lay miles of alpine peaks and prosperous farming communities. They were in the forefront of the migrants battling their way south. Their caravan was growing larger by the day as families rushed to come under the protection of the Wodenvale warlord and his fellow chieftains. Many were fleeing the violence of the Rosenheim area on the Inn River farther north. A large contingent of mounted warriors was reported to be somewhere behind them, dashing from place to place to defend caravans under pressure from local militias or organized units of the Roman Army. These men were part of the King's personal army, and were on the move all the time. They had been seen a few days ago heading back the other way.

For the people with Duke Helerix, the journey had so far not been difficult. The weather had stayed comfortable. The Inn Valley was wide and lush, wide enough to allow them to form defensive circles at night, and lush enough for them to buy food and fodder from the Celtic farms and villages along the way.

To everyone's surprise, some farmers from valleys connecting with the Inn Valley had hauled cartloads of their own produce and fowl to the Roman road and were setting up impromptu markets along the road. This part of the province of Rhaetia was protected by the warlords' pledge to Tribune Bulleus and his soldiers, a pledge that depended on the barbarians keeping the peace. It galled some of the people to have to pay for their food now, when they had become accustomed to just taking whatever they wanted, but the cooperation of the local frontier troops was still important: they did not want trouble from their allies here, or on the other side of the pass. Moreover, their leaders had given their word and were watching them. It may have hurt their hubris to pay, but it was not hard—they now had plenty of Roman coins and excess plunder to trade with.

Somewhere ahead in the forest of white-topped mountains was the thirty mile long pass. Once into this part of the Alps, they did not know what they would find. The weather could change from valley to valley and from day to day. If it snowed in the pass ahead, their journey would become much more difficult and dangerous. This next phase would be the most challenging part of the journey for all of them, especially the animals pulling their wagons, but once through the pass, they would begin the descent into southern Rhaetia and Italia.

The warlords hesitated. They could wait for more caravans to join them here where there was room and provisions, or press on. This interminable journey was finally nearing the end.

Optio Cantarcchio, their young Roman guide, was impatient to press on—he knew the area beyond the pass well, he said. It was where he had been born and raised. Any delay just made their misery last longer. He would see them safely through.

Still the leaders hesitated. They were the first of Radagaisus's followers to get this far, and they were unsure of themselves. Their men had not yet been tested in battle against the Roman army. Besides, they did not trust Cantarcchio. They had never trusted him, even though he had never yet led them astray or into danger. Anything he wanted them to do had to be scrutinized closely.

The huge caravan halted on the outskirts of the town, while Cantarcchio and the warlords made the obligatory trip to the local authorities to pay their respects and acquire information. The forum and much of the town was deserted. High above them, anxious eyes would be watching their homes and shops and fields with jealous attention. They might have an 'understanding' with the barbarians now arriving in their neighborhood, but these Roman citizens were not going to trust the reckless ruffians any more than they had to.

The Roman military presence in Veldidena was not much to look at. Although towers jutted out from the four walls of the fort, there were no ramparts on top of the walls or trenches dug around it. This fort, and the others like it scattered throughout the mountains, were supposed to represent a second line of defense against invaders, but there was no way they would be able to stand against a sizable enemy force. Under normal circumstances the fort served as a supply depot, a guard post, and a shelter for refugees in times of trouble. There was only a small garrison here, and their duties were mostly administrative and policing.

Cantarcchio and the warlords came back from the fort with sobering new information. Thousands of soldiers from the big fortress at Augsburg were approaching Innsbruck along the other road into the area from the north-east. The prefect on duty advised them to leave immediately.

The warlords were not ready for a serious fight with the Romans. They could wait for reinforcements to arrive, or they could move on into the mountains. They decided that waiting was too much of a gamble. Cantarcchio was in hearty agreement.

Once again the caravan staggered forward, this time off the cobbled road and onto the dirt track leading toward the pass.

As they climbed higher, Theona watched with regret as the town, the road and the farms faded from view. The relatively easy rhythm of recent days was gone, along with any chance to buy more food. No matter—she and her father had run out of anything to trade with. They had been surviving on the fish she caught in the Inn River, gifts from some of the hunters, especially Darric, meals at other people's campfires, and gleanings from harvested fields they passed.

The pass they were heading for was the lowest one in the area that would actually get them through and out of the mountains. To get to it they would have to get their wagons and animals up steep mountains and across deep ravines.

They were entering a barren area with no convenient paved roads and bridges. The prefect in Veldidena had warned that there were bandits in this area that preyed on travelers that were not as numerous or as well protected. She had heard that a hundred miles away on the Via Claudia Augusta, there was another pass with a solid Roman road, and a much better chance for honest travelers to get through the mountains. But the Goths and their allies were not honest travelers. They were not welcome here. They had to use the back door.

Her attention immediately became fully occupied with the difficulties of following the ribbon of track through the mountains. It was very difficult terrain. Their wagon had to follow the ox-carts ahead and keep out of reach of the ones behind as Enoch struggled uphill and downhill with their wagon, over grass, over snow, over rocky slopes, and across fast moving mountain streams.

Sometimes she and her father would have to rush to catch up with wagons that were disappearing out of sight. Sometimes they would have to wait for the congestion ahead to clear so they could continue.

Many times they had to cross and re-cross the same mountain slope to climb ever higher to reach the next leg of the journey. Then they would begin an equally difficult descent. Even such a young, strong ox like Enoch could pull a tendon or break a leg. The danger was that they might lose control of the wagon on a steep slope and be dragged over a cliff. Everyone who was not driving wagons, shepherding animals, carrying children, or leading their horses, had to help. They steadied the wagons and encouraged the straining animals as they labored up and down the mountain slopes.

There were casualties. Several animals suffered serious injuries. A few had heart failure.

Many of the families were now short of food. Stopping on such terrain to camp or go hunting was rarely an option through these days. They had faced desperate situations before, but the climb to the top of the pass was the worst yet, and they were all exhausted and ill-tempered, and becoming famished.

Families who still owned goats or chickens started losing them. Their fellow travelers blamed wolves, and swore that they had heard howls during the dark hours. Everyone had heard the howls— it was feasible, though not likely.

One night there was a snowstorm. The inches piled up, covering the ground.

After the snow storm a goat was discovered to be missing, and footprints, not paw prints, were found. The furious family from Duke Rumbert's caravan followed them back down the caravan looking for their last goat. It was found, still in the process of being cut up, in the wagon of one of Duke Arnulf's families. A blood feud was only averted when the thieves promised to pay back ten times the value of the goat. The warlords got together then, and decreed that migrants who still had animals must share them with their envious and hungry countrymen. Everyone had enough trouble getting themselves and their wagons safely through this frightening journey without the added worry of infighting. Even so, for a few days plenty of suspicious and angry looks passed between the followers of Duke Arnulf and those of Duke Rumbert.

Eventually, Cantarcchio told them that they had reached the top of the pass. This was something to celebrate! However, any celebration had to be postponed until they could reach easier terrain. The journey downhill was just as treacherous as the journey up. It started to rain, and the rain continued on and off for several days, making the going more dangerous yet. The families slipped and splashed despondently along. When the last of the rain cleared away to the south, it left so much moisture in the air that fog became a problem, an icy fog dense enough to make it difficult to see.

During this terrible part of the journey, Pastor Rhodus often left Theona alone in order to track down the Christians within his growing flock. He would return to the wagon exhausted and dispirited. No one was happy. There was nowhere to wash, no comfort or cheerful conversation, little to eat, and nothing much to look forward to from day to day. Theona was resentful. She needed help, too. The two of them would fall asleep at night with barely a word to each other.

A week after they left Innsbruck, the caravan emerged into a valley, one large enough for them to be able to form a defensive wagon circle. There were houses here, and farms, but once again no one seemed to have stayed around to welcome them. At least now they could find firewood, and root crops, and even shelter in some of the abandoned homes in the area. It was a chance for a respite, isolated, apparently deserted, and wide enough to hold them all.

The families begged their leaders to let them stay for a few days so they and their animals could have time to recuperate before they had to press on. The warlords, too, wanted to stop. They needed time to check on the needs of their people, time to search the area for much needed tools and food, time to rest their exhausted animals, and time to give other caravans the chance to catch up.

Cantarcchio argued with them. Pons Drusi was not much farther, and from there the journey would be easy. To wait ran the risk of the weather changing, an avalanche or blizzard filling up the valley ahead, or even the Roman Army charging in from the pass behind them.

The leaders met again, and they decided that their people needed at least a day to rest. The optio gave in, but warned them all to continue to respect their agreement with the Rhaetian farmer-soldiers: their people must not destroy or steal anything.

There was some muttering at that. Many of the men in the laager felt in their bones that their warrior destiny was drawing close now. They wanted action, something more exciting than this slow, awkward, exhausting daily grind. They resented the guide's influence over their leaders. Besides, who were they to pay? But the war lords and their henchmen kept a tight grip on them. It would not be long now before they would be free of Cantarcchio and the restraints they had agreed to months before.

On the mountain high above them, Legate Olybrius and the Seventh Alpine Cohort watched.

The trouble began before dawn the next morning. Theona, her father, and Gideon were asleep inside their wagon home. Enoch was tethered nearby. During the night, the fog had returned and lay like a thick white veil over the sleeping community, muffling sounds.

They were awakened by a scream, followed by shouts coming from several directions. Pastor Rhodus sat up, pulled on his boots and grabbed his new fur coat.

"What's happening?" asked Theona. Gideon raised his head and sniffed the air. He suddenly barked loudly, and scrambled to the tied-down covered entrance, pushing through the bottom. In an instant he was gone.

More shouting was heard, and the bawling of an ox.

"This could be it!" said Pastor Rhodus, grabbing his axe and fumbling with the rope bindings. "Get dressed, get under the wagon and stay there."

He, too, leaped down from the wagon, but reappeared immediately.

"Enoch's been killed," he said tersely. "Someone has slit the poor beast's throat. We're under attack. I'll come back as soon as I can."

He was gone.

Frightened, Theona struggled into her long trousers and battered boots. She was now wearing her best tunic everyday—she had outgrown the other one. She shrugged into the scarlet cloak and seized her pouch with her flint, her knife, her slingshot and stones and a few other personal items. At the last minute she grabbed her fishing net too, just in case.

Cautiously she pushed open the wagon's cover to peer out. All around, there were shouts and people running, but nothing that indicated actual fighting. A figure ran past her wagon, but in the dark and the fog she could not make out who it was. All the sounds she could hear now were indistinct. Then, close by she heard a woman scream and some children begin to cry. A man yelled at them, and then there was silence.

Enoch was dead? She jumped down to find him, and tripped over him. Her hands followed his body along to his head, and felt the sticky touch of blood. He had been killed, his throat slit, as her father had said. Someone had killed him within feet of where they were sleeping. She shuddered, suddenly glad for the fog which hid her from her enemies, as well as her enemies from her. She must get under the wagon.

"Theona?"

A figure strode out of the fog toward her. She recognized the voice of their Roman guide, Cantarcchio. She had not exchanged more than a few words with him since their boat journey together back in July.

"Yes?" she quavered.

"I see you lost your ox. I am sorry. Come with me. Your father told me to get you to safety. These your things?" He seized her hand, and grabbed her bag.

She nodded, noticing that he was fully armed and dressed for travel.

"Hurry," he said urgently.

"What's going on?" she asked.

"Roman troops," he replied. "They're attacking the camp. We've got to get you out of here."

"What about the others?"

He looked at her, his body grey with the swirling mist. There was impatience in his voice. "Just you, princess. Your father only mentioned you. We cannot let the enemy get their hands on Prince Roderic's girl now, can we?"

Angrily Theona tried to pull her hand away from his, but he was ready and held on tightly. He pulled her along through the wagon circle, stopping to listen whenever they heard sounds of fighting, and then changing direction.

No one tried to stop them. Men ran past, their spears and axes in their hands, but recognizing her and their Roman guide, they kept going. Soon she was lost among the crowded wagons, not knowing where they were or which way they were headed, but Cantarcchio seemed to have some kind of map in his head and hurried her on. She remembered that he had been raised somewhere in this area.

The night seemed to be ending. No colors could yet be discerned, but it no longer felt as though they were moving quite so blindly. They passed the bodies of several other oxen, and she thought she saw evidence of axe damage to the wheels of some carts. Cantarcchio kept her moving so fast she could not be sure. In the fog everything seemed unreal.

The whole camp was now awake. People were scrambling in several directions. You could no longer tell where the fighting was, or where the danger lay. Somewhere, enemy soldiers were moving through their camp. Or had they done their damage and already left?

A rooster crowed somewhere in the neighborhood, its dawn call rising above the other noises. After that several others crowed in the new day. It would be light soon. Suddenly, Theona wanted to get away from this weird battleground before the sun came up. She did not think she was brave enough to face a Roman soldier or watch the fight. She would come back as soon as it was safe. Her escort, sensing her mood change, lessened his grip.

In front of her, Cantarcchio suddenly lost his balance and swore. Theona, right behind him, bumped into him. They had tripped over a body, a human one. She recognized the Wodenvale farmer who had kidnapped the Pannonian woman and kept her prisoner all these months. Theona had seen her several times, and always felt pity for the woman, who seemed to have diminished further each time.

She looked around frantically to see if they were near the man's wagon. They were. It was only feet away. The farmer must have caught one of the Roman attackers in the act of slitting his beast's throat. The animal was alive, but bleeding, its legs trembling, its head lowered. The Pannonian woman was sitting on the driver's seat, her shoulders bare, her ankles still tied with the rope. She was staring ahead into the fog, and shivering. Did she even know her tormenter was dead?

"Wait!" insisted Theona, pulling away from the soldier.

"No waiting," replied Cantarcchio, grabbing her arm again. The sky over the mountains to the east was showing a faint strip of white. Daylight.

"We have to untie her."

"There isn't time. I've got to get you to safety."

"Let me help her, or I won't come with you."

He sighed, then pulled his knife from his tool belt and stepped over to the young woman. He sliced through her ankle bonds, and then cut a second rope that held her hands together. The woman looked at the rope pieces incuriously and rubbed her wrists together. She did not even glance at them.

"See. She's crazy. Come on," said the Roman guide urgently.

She turned to the woman who did indeed seem to have lost her mental focus.

"Do you have a cloak?"

The woman raised her head and looked at her. Theona pulled off her own "new" red cloak and tossed it over. "Go home," she said, pointing back up the valley. "This is your chance. Go home to your children."

It seemed to Theona that the Pannonian was looking directly at her now—there was a tension about her that had not been there before.

Swearing under his breath, Cantarcchio waved the knife at Theona.

"Walk!" he commanded. Startled, she nodded and turned away.

He shoved her in the back. She shot him an outraged look, but said nothing.

"Run home to your children," he mimicked, as they walked. "How do you suppose she is going to do that on her own, with the entire population of Barbaricum coming this way?"

Theona was silent. He wouldn't understand. It didn't make sense, but it was something she had to do anyway. Maybe it was to relieve her conscience. Everyone needed a friend at times.

The greatest danger should have been at the edge of the circle of wagons where soldiers from the Seventh Alpine Cohort who had become trapped were battling shoulder to shoulder with a growing cluster of angry Goths. Hundreds more could be heard screaming their battle cry as they headed from the center of the camp towards the battle. They wanted their revenge on the remaining Rhaetian troops for the damage done to their animals and wagons.

Cantarcchio ignored them all, even when someone called his name. He strode calmly around the battle line, pushing Theona ahead of him, his Roman uniform granting him immunity from the other Rhaetians, his familiar face protecting him from the Goths he had been leading.

Past the battle zone, the valley seemed eerie. Thick fog lay on the valley floor, hiding anything or anyone in it.

"How far are we going?" whispered Theona.

"To somewhere where you will be safe."

It wasn't an answer, but he clearly was not going to supply another one.

Distance and fog combined to mute the sounds from the barbarian camp disappearing behind them. Theona could not see far in any direction, but the dawn light indicated they were going south. Soon the mountains began to close in on them again.

They walked silently, as daylight gradually overtook the night. A morning breeze arose, causing the fog around them to shimmer and swirl. The sun and the wind would soon get rid of it all, but the battle behind them would continue. There was little hope that the attackers still in the camp would be able to escape alive.

She began to hear the familiar sound of rushing water. The river had come alongside them once more, and this time, there was a road. They followed this down the valley for a short time, and then the guide stopped.

"Wait here."

"Where are you going? Is this the place you are taking me?"

"No. Just wait here."

He ran up a wide lane on one side of the road and disappeared around a bend, leaving her alone. His presence had given her some sense of protection against the Roman soldiers in the area, but now she felt vulnerable. She looked uncertainly back up the valley, wondering if she should go back to the laager. She was beginning to have misgivings about this journey. Why had he taken her? And since when had he cared what her father thought or wanted? She hovered there uncertainly, desperately wishing for someone to advise her.

Something moist pushed into her hand. It felt like an animal's nose. Theona whirled around to see Gideon standing facing her, his tail wagging. He had followed them all this distance, and was only letting her know now that he was there. She fell to her knees and hugged him, murmuring her appreciation.

Cantarcchio came back down the path leading a horse, a big black farm animal which followed him docilely.

"My dog!" she said happily, standing up. "He followed us!"

He frowned.

"Send him back. There's no way he can keep up with us."

She looked dubiously at the horse he had brought. Its head was hanging and it looked old.

"Of course he can. He has come with us all the way from my home!"

"I don't want him coming. Go!" Cantarcchio pointed sternly back in the direction they had come. Gideon tensed, and growled at him.

"There's only one way to settle this." Cantarcchio pulled his sword from his belt.

"No!" cried Theona. "What's the matter with you? Leave him alone. He's trying to protect me, just like you."

"Tell him not to come, or I'll take care of him my way. I don't like dogs, and you don't need protection."

She knelt down again and held Gideon's head between her hands, looking into the bright brown eyes. She whispered to him, and he lay down on the grass.

"What did you tell him?"

"I told him to stay," she said.

"Smart girl," he said. He did not put his sword away immediately, but stared warily at the two of them.

"Get on the horse," he ordered. She hesitated, and he brandished his sword at the dog. There was no mistaking the threat. She mounted the horse quickly, frightened. Her instincts had been right: Cantarcchio could not be trusted. He had chosen his time well, luring her away when everyone's natural suspicion of him had been blunted by the more immediate fear caused by the sudden dawn attack.

Cantarcchio continued to stare at Gideon for a moment, then picked up a stone and threw it sharply at him. Gideon yelped and ran off, then lay down again out of reach. The soldier swung himself easily onto the horse behind Theona, and struck its side with the flat of his sword. The horse obligingly trotted off. Theona, outraged, held herself stiffly away from him.

Gideon did not move as they disappeared around a bend.

CHAPTER TWENTY-THREE

THEONA ABDUCTED

The Brenner Pass area, Northern Italy
Late October, 405 AD

Olybrius stood on a hill looking down on the valley in the light of the rising sun. He was satisfied. Before the fog had got too thick, half of his men had descended the mountain into an adjoining dead end valley. Another large contingent had descended the mountain well south of the laager and moved north up the valley towards the large barbarian camp. They had instructions to encircle it. He had also sent a dozen of his scouts farther up the valley to learn where the next group of invaders was.

His men had had a good hour to get into position to move into the barbarian camp, and then another fifteen to twenty minutes to do as much damage as they could and get out. The fog covering the area prevented the legate from seeing what was going on in the valley, but from the sounds of alarm, their work had been detected. It was time to get them out.

He gave the order to his trumpeter to sound the retreat, and then he and his companions began to jog back towards the alpine corridor they had used to get here. Any of his soldiers who were caught would fight as well as they could against the maddened warriors. The rest had orders to make their way in groups down the valley towards Pons Drusi to link up with Tribune Ausonius and his men. By the time the fog had lifted, the Seventh Alpine Cohort, or most of it, were well away. In the valley, the fighting continued until the last Roman was dead or gone.

The warlords sent their men around the camp to inspect the damage. Sixty oxen had been killed. Many others had been badly injured. They would have to be put down. A few wagons had had their wheels sabotaged.

The bodies of eighteen Roman soldiers were found. There was some satisfaction in that. Only a few of their own people had actually been killed, thank the gods, but without their oxen, the journey for many families would become extremely difficult until they could find replacements.

The people were angry.

"Where's Cantarcchio?" they began to ask. "What happened to his promise that we would be safe in this area? He must pay for this."

Duke Helerix sent some of his men to find the optio. They came back a while later with reports that his guide had last been seen heading out of the camp with Pastor Rhodus's girl. Helerix sent for Rhodus, who was once again saying prayers for the dead and bereaved.

"Where is Theona?" he demanded.

Her father looked haunted. "I don't know. I told her to hide under the wagon. I came back to it, and she was gone. I have been up and down the camp several times looking for her, but I keep getting interrupted. She is probably helping people somewhere around the camp. I haven't seen her since this all started. The dog is gone, too. I am sure he is with her. That's been my main consolation."

"My men have heard that she left with our guide. Has she taken up with him?"

Duke Helerix was a very angry man. He did not know what to think. He had liked the girl, and thought she was above deception.

Pastor Rhodus was indignant.

"Indeed not! If she went with him, it would only be because he lied to her to get her away, or he is acting on someone else's orders. She doesn't like him."

Two men hurried toward the little circle pushing the Pannonian woman. Everyone turned to look at them. Pastor Rhodus gasped.

"That woman's wearing Theona's red cloak!"

The men bringing her thrust her forward. She looked confused and a little frightened.

"Where did you get that cloak?" Pastor Rhodus asked in his heavily accented Latin. "That belongs to my daughter."

She fingered the clasp at her throat and did not raise her eyes.

"She gave it to me," she mumbled.

Duke Helerix stepped forward and slapped her hard. The young woman winced, and licked at the blood that began to trickle from her mouth. Color came back into her face, and so, somehow, did her dignity. She glared at the warlord, and then proudly turned to look straight at Theona's father. Lifting her hands up in front of her face, she showed him the rope ends, still dangling.

"She did this."

Pastor Rhodus smiled at the Duke, lifting his own arm to prevent a repeat blow.

"I knew she would be off helping people if she could. That sounds like Theona," he said proudly. "Perhaps she gave her the cloak as well."

He turned back to the woman to thank her, but she was not finished. She seemed determined now to tell them something, and would not be satisfied until she had done so. Between her rudimentary Gothic and Pastor Rhodus's rusty Latin, and with lots of acting out, they got her story.

She pretended to sit, her feet and hands tied, staring straight ahead. They nodded, knowing the cruelty of her captivity. She pretended to be Theona, entreating someone, and then changed positions, acting out the role of the soldier, imitating his walk and his sneer to perfection. She demonstrated Cantarcchio drawing his knife, slicing her ropes, and turning to drag someone away. Then she switched roles and was Theona, ripping off her cloak and throwing it at Pastor Rhodus. "Go home," she said in Gothic. "Go home."

And then the woman stood there mutely.

Pastor Rhodus put an arm around her, and gave her a hug.

"Theona did not go willingly, and now she has no cloak!" stated the Duke.

"No," agreed her father, looking worried.

"He has taken her for some reason," mused the warlord. "Perhaps Prince Roderic gave him orders privately to get her to safety if there was any danger. Maybe he thought she'd be safer with Cantarcchio than with anyone else."

Pastor Rhodus looked doubtful. "Perhaps, but I don't think the Prince liked him, either. I thought they seemed to avoid each other most of the time."

But it was still possible, and it certainly was a consoling thought. Perhaps the runaway couple was safe and would reappear soon. And then there was Gideon. The dog would certainly try to protect his daughter.

"We'll have to wait and see," he said. "If you are right, they should be back soon. The fog has lifted, and the fighting has been over for a while."

Hours passed with no sign of Theona or their Roman guide, hours in which more sentries were appointed, funeral pyres were started, graves were dug, a makeshift workshop was set up to repair the wagons, and oxen meat was cut up and distributed to all the families. In the late afternoon they heard cheering from the top end of the wagon camp. People ran to see what the excitement was all about.

Pastor Rhodus ran, too, hoping the cheer was for Theona, returning safely to them. The cheers grew louder as more and more people joined in, and soon he could see the cause for himself.

A long procession of warriors on horseback was streaming into the valley. On and on they came, dozens of them, then hundreds. They were drooping with fatigue, but when they heard the cheers from the people, they straightened up and pushed their horses into a gallop, rushing down the valley led by Radagaisus's two sons, Vitiges and Roderic. Banners flying, hair streaming in the wind—it was a magnificent entrance. After such a bitter day, many of the people wept for joy and took courage. The High King was coming through for them.

The warlords walked purposefully to the edge of the crowd and waited. As soon as the princes saw them, they reined their horses in and dismounted. The crowd rushed forward to surround their followers, greeting them with their news, questions and invitations. The valley was suddenly a vastly different place than it had been only an hour ago.

The warlords exchanged glad greetings with the two princes.

"We heard there was fighting here," said Roderic. "We've brought about eight hundred men with us. There are more coming down the pass all the time on foot. You should not have gone off on your own, my lords. As you can see, it isn't safe."

"Our guide hurried us through the pass to avoid an army of Roman soldiers that was approaching from western Rhaetia," replied Duke Helerix. "This is the first time we have been attacked."

"Where *is* Cantarcchio? I don't see him with you." Roderic scowled, scanning the crowd.

"He's gone off with Theona," said Pastor Rhodus, pushing into the discussion.

"What!" The comment seemed to have shocked Roderic. Vitiges looked at him in surprise.

"We do not believe she went of her own accord. Did you instruct him to get her out of harm's way if anything like this happened?"

"No," exclaimed Prince Roderic. "I've barely spoken to him. My brother and I deal with his tribune. Bulleus gives the orders, but I am certain this is not of his doing. He would not know your daughter."

"Then he has taken her for his own reasons, and she has gone along, trusting that one of us is behind this. In truth, she did not care for him much."

"Were they on foot?"

"Yes."

"Then perhaps a few of my men and I can find them before they have gone too far. I believe he has family somewhere down the valley. He travelled with you. Perhaps you have already asked around? He must have talked to somebody."

The warlords looked at one another, and shook their heads.

"I never thought to do that, my lord," admitted Duke Helerix "We have been busy with this crisis all day, and I thought they would be back by now, thinking it safe to return."

"How long have they been gone?"

"Since dawn."

"It is too late to leave today. We must learn what we can of his destination, and leave in the morning when there is light to track them. In the meantime my friends, our men and we need food and accommodation for the night. We will be going ahead of you from now on. If there are more Romans waiting down the valley, they will have to deal with us, first. We will leave you enough men to deter any other attacks until the foot soldiers get here. The rest of us will be gone tomorrow. Take the time you need to recover even if that means letting other groups go ahead of you. Come down the valley after us as soon as you are ready."

Cantarcchio kept Theona and the horse moving all day.

The valley now bent toward the south-east. The horse seemed to know it well, automatically crossing the river at select spots, and ambling toward the places where the grass was most succulent and accessible.

A few times they dismounted to stretch and give the nag a rest, and when the sun was high overhead, they stopped to eat some hard biscuits that Cantarcchio had brought with him. Theona wondered where he had got them, and how long he had had them, but stopped wondering when she almost broke a tooth on her first bite. Cantarcchio laughed as he dipped his biscuit into the cold river to soften it. After that, she did the same. The biscuits weren't bad, taken that way. He let her try fishing, and she caught a one-pound trout which he stowed in his own bag.

As the day wore on, they had to stop often to let the horse rest, but they still made better time than they would have done on foot or by wagon, especially with nobody else to slow them down.

Late in the afternoon the narrow valley widened again and Theona saw farms, and villas on the vineyard-clad hillsides. The river they had been following all day was joined by a larger one coming from the east which ran beside it for a while, and then merged with it. There was a fairly big town here. It, too, seemed to be deserted. All around were places to stop and stay, yet Cantarcchio kept going. Once again the mountains closed in on them and the valley grew narrow. The sun disappeared out of sight behind the western slopes.

Cantarcchio stopped a short time later, and dismounted.

"Get down," he said. "It won't be long now."

Theona awkwardly dropped down from the horse, sore from her back and shoulders to her thighs and bottom. They were beside a wide path that wound up a hill and out of sight.

"You might as well come with me," he said. "We're leaving the horse here." Wearily she trudged behind him as he led the horse up the path. They rounded a couple of bends and came to a farmhouse which appeared to be as deserted as the town they had left behind. Among the farm buildings here was a stable.

Cantarcchio brought the tired horse inside, covered him with a blanket that was hanging from a hook on the wall, and fed him oats and water. When the animal had been looked after, they left the stable and headed back down to the road. They kept going in the same direction on foot for a few minutes, and then crossed to a footpath on the other side which seemed to be taking a tortuous route up the mountain.

Theona looked uneasily at the darkening sky.

"How far now?" she asked again. She no longer cared where he was taking her. At this point it was the 'when' that mattered.

"We're almost there."

It was the same thing he had been saying for hours. She glanced back in the direction of the town. Cantarcchio grabbed her arm grimly and pushed her toward the path. For someone who seemed to dislike people as much as he did, he had an amazing sensitivity to their moods. His taller body crowded her up the path.

As they climbed, the dark woods closed in around them. Soon, they could no longer see the valley floor. The pleasant scent of pine trees accompanied them up the mountain. Their path connected with another one and they continued to climb. Before long, Theona's legs were aching with the strain and she was out of breath.

She reached for Cantarcchio, now climbing easily ahead of her. He was carrying both their satchels.

"How far?" she gasped.

"To the top."

She staggered on.

The path became less steep, and a gap in the trees appeared ahead. They came out at the edge of a long, narrow field, bristly with tree stumps and stubble. It sloped gently southward from somewhere higher up, and ended half a mile away at a line of trees which dropped away to a lower plateau. Opposite them stood a small round hill. Beyond it Theona saw high, pale grey peaks glowing orange and blue with the last rays of the setting sun. There wasn't a building in sight.

"How much farther?" she said irritably. By now any distance was too far. She was ready to lie down right on the field and be done with it. It occurred to her that the young man might have brought her to this remote place to kill her and dispose of her body. Why he would do such a thing hardly mattered. She would be able to rest in peace.

"Not far now. Just walk," he snapped, pointing toward the round hill across the field. "Where we're going is just behind that hill."

Theona tripped and stumbled across the field over rocks and upturned roots. Partway across, she glanced back to locate the path they had climbed. She saw the valley they had left discernable now as a long wavy black gap through the deep green landscape in a sea of mountains.

Somewhere far away up that valley, her father would be worried sick about her. Probably her friends had given up trying to find her by now. She hoped they were all uninjured, and that Gideon had made it safely through the battle zone back to their wagon. How, she wondered, was her father going to continue the journey without Enoch? Would Darric and his family take him in? Had their ox been spared? Everything had happened so fast that she had no idea what had happened after she had left the laager.

It was growing dark even here on the plateau now. A couple of the brightest stars were already visible.

They reached the far side of the field. There was a wide dirt track here, and Cantarcchio turned along it and followed it downhill beside the hill they had seen. On the far side of this the land opened up to their right. There was a barely discernable foot path here that led down a long gentle slope toward a little lake. Its still surface was already a deep blue and mirrored only the black images of trees overhead and a few bright stars.

Near the far end of the lake she saw the silhouettes of a house and a couple of farm buildings. This scenic dell, their destination, nestled in a natural dip in the alpine terrain. Once they had reached the level of the lake, all you could see were sky-high mountain peaks and behind them, the little round hill and a piece of the road.

As they drew close to the house, Theona could see that it had stout, stone walls and a thatched roof. No light was visible within it, but there was smoke drifting lazily from the chimney, and the smell of food cooking. Her mouth began to water.

"Wait here."

Cantarcchio ducked through the doorway into the house and closed it behind him.

The heat from Cantarcchio's body followed by the steep climb to this lonely starlit place had kept Theona warm most of the day, but now, with the last bit of daylight gone, the chill of the alpine night began to bite into her. She rubbed her arms, almost regretting her impulse to give away her red cloak. It wasn't very warm, but it was better than nothing. At the time, though, she had had no idea what Cantarcchio was planning for her, or how far they would be traveling. She still did not know why he had brought her here, but right now she didn't care. She was cold, exhausted, sore, and hungry. Warmth was what mattered now, and rest.

She shifted from foot to foot, hugging herself, wondering when the Rhaetian soldier would re-emerge from the house. A multitude of stars was now blossoming in the sky overhead.

A light sprang up in one of the windows: someone had lit a lamp. Still no one came to open the door. She looked longingly at the barn and the shed. The barn had boards across the doorway, and the shed bore an iron lock.

The stars filled the landscape with cold, silvery light. Off in the distance she heard a fox bark. A wolf howled. Its haunting cry sounded miles away, but wolves had legs.

It seemed like a long time since Cantarcchio had gone into the house. Theona decided she would wait no longer—going inside could not be worse than staying out here in the cold with no coat. She eased open the door and looked inside. The silver starlight revealed a tiny vestibule with coats and boots and other things on shelves. Beyond it, she could see a crack of yellow light outlining a second door, the real entrance into the house. Theona stepped inside the vestibule, and quietly closed the outside door.

Now she was in total darkness except for the crack of light at the top and bottom of the inside doorway. The tiny space she stood in was still cold, but less so than the frosty night outside. She stooped down and felt around her in the darkness, waiting for her eyes to adjust. There were two pairs of boots on the floor, one of them still warm and damp—Cantarcchio's assuredly. She fingered some soft furs and coats hanging from nails farther up the wall, and higher still a shelf with boxes on it. For a farmhouse entrance, the tiny room seemed remarkably neat.

Her eyes and ears were both beginning to adjust now, and she stepped up to the inner door and pressed her ear against it.

There were two people in the room beyond, two voices, one female, quarrelsome and old, one male, conciliatory and young. She could not hear what they were saying through the thick door, so after a couple of minutes she stopped listening and sat down on the floor to wait. The delicious smell of her own fish cooking drifted out through the cracks in the door, tantalizing her.

What was Cantarcchio doing here? Who lived here?

As if on cue, the optio himself opened the door. He did not see her immediately, but as he reached down for his boots, she placed her hand on his arm. He jerked back in alarm, banging his head against the low doorway.

"You!" he said.

"You were gone too long. I was freezing out there."

"Is that her?" called the second person, speaking in Gothic.

"Granny wants to meet you," he said grimly. He seized Theona's arm, and yanked her to her feet. "Leave your ugly boots here."

"Don't be so rough," she complained. She pulled off her offending boots, and followed him into the main room.

Her eyes widened. Cantarcchio was wearing a fresh, rust-colored tunic, and his lank, thinning hair was damp and pulled back in a ponytail. The man had had the nerve to have a bath, while she stood outside in the freezing cold with no cloak on!

He saw her anger and grinned. His eyes mocked her.

She decided not to comment. He was a despicable lout, and she would not give him the satisfaction of gloating.

Apart from the light coming from a fire, there were two candles burning, lit, apparently, by Cantarcchio himself. She blinked and peered around the room.

She was standing near the doorway of the main room of the house. At the back of the room was a wall with two doors. These probably led to sleeping quarters or perhaps storage rooms. They were closed. Above them there was a loft with a ladder leading to it at one end. Coming from somewhere up there she could hear the lazy cluck of chickens settling in to sleep.

To her left was the kitchen area. There was a fire in the fireplace with a pot suspended above it; the delicious smell of fish stew was coming from that. Smoke escaped through holes in the walls just below the ceiling. Shelves above the wide wooden counter contained an assortment of food stuffs and cooking tools, all neatly laid out. On the floor of this area stood three amphorae of different sizes, some large bags of grains, and a window, a glazed window.

Theona had seen many by now, and no longer found them remarkable, but unlike the rest of the house, the window was filthy. It looked like it had not been cleaned in years. Underneath it was a large round tub, half-filled with water—Cantarcchio's bathtub.

Along the wall near the cooking area stood a table with four chairs, and elsewhere in the room she could see more furniture, including a spinning wheel shoved into a corner on its own. It was a grand home, far grander than hers had been. It was tiled throughout and seemed cozy and well-cared for.

"She smells worse than you did!"

The voice came from an old woman sitting in the rocking chair. Her face was in shadow and she was staring straight ahead. Theona saw her wrinkle her nose in distaste and press her lips together.

Theona looked at her in surprise and embarrassment.

"I'll bathe her, Granny," replied Cantarcchio.

"No you won't!" Theona jumped back toward the door.

The old lady cackled. "She sounds young. What does she look like?"

"Alright, I guess. Thin, blond, blue eyes. You know the type."

Theona shot him a look of annoyance. He did not notice.

"What kind of blond? What kind of blue?"

"What do you mean?"

The old lady sighed. "Sev, you disappoint me. You arrive with a young Gothic woman and expect me to keep her for you, and you can't describe her? Come here, girl."

Theona walked over and stood in front of the woman, who continued to stare straight ahead. She kneeled in front of her and took the old lady's hands, placing them on her face. The woman felt around her head, fingering her ears, her hair, her chin and her nose, and then suddenly dropped her hands to Theona's neck. Theona smacked her hands away, and the woman promptly smacked her back.

"Sit still, girl. I need to get to see you."

Cantarcchio guffawed unpleasantly.

"How is it you speak Gothic?" whispered Theona, as the woman's hands continued to explore her. She had to take her mind off the probing she was getting.

"I *am* Gothic," replied the woman. "I was raped by Severus's grandfather, and thrown out by my people when they found I was carrying his bastard. I followed the brute here and demanded he take care of his brat."

"Did he marry you?"

"Of course not. I never expected him to. He was already married, but his father, Sev's great grandfather, gave me this house to stay in, so I stayed and raised my son right here in front of all his kin and friends. The brute died of shame."

"He died when his horse kicked him, Granny. You know that."

The old woman chuckled. "And high time, too. Pour more hot water for her, Severus. If she is going to stay and we have to smell her, let's make her as nice as possible. And wash your hair, girl. It doesn't feel blond to me, just stringy." She gave a little yank to one long strand, and muttered something in Latin.

The old woman got up to feed her grandson. As soon as the kettle of hot water had been added to the bath, Theona stripped quickly out of her clothes and stepped into the tub. Cantarcchio sat at the little table where he could keep an insolent eye on her, and ate his fish stew hungrily, sopping it up with a large hunk of bread.

It was all Theona could do to take her mind off the food and wash herself. She had had precious little to eat for the last couple of weeks. If they did not share that stew with her, she would be beside herself!

She had also not bathed in weeks, and the warm water felt wonderful. She sat in it and swished it around her body, then dunked her hair in, rubbed her scalp a little, and settled in for a soak, not the least bit concerned about the watchful eyes of the young man devouring his grandmother's cooking a few yards away.

She no longer wondered why there had been no lights in the house when they had first arrived, or at the general neatness. A blind woman living alone would have to be able to lay her hands on anything she wanted without searching for it.

Theona had lots of questions, but some of them were being answered as she bathed. The pair in front of her continued to speak in Gothic, although Cantarcchio's, greatly improved since joining her caravan, was still not up to the level of his grandmother's.

"So. They really are coming."

"Yes, they're only a couple of days away."

"And why did you choose this girl, and why today?"

"It was the best I could do, Granny. I know you suggested seizing one of the king's children, but that wasn't possible. He is quite old. His own children are full-grown, and there is only one grandchild, a little girl, but I couldn't get at her. My caravan came through the pass ahead of all the others, so the main Gothic force is still somewhere behind us. When the Romans attacked this morning,

I just seized the chance to get this girl away. Radagaisus's youngest son is sweet on her. It has all worked out so far. I've kept my promise to you, haven't I?"

"Yes." There was a pause. "So far. So, she's the younger son's sweetheart. What do we do now?"

"Just keep her here. Tie her up if you want. Feed her occasionally."

He glanced at Theona sitting in the tub, watching them and clearly listening.

"If you want to eat any of this stew, you'd better get out of that tub," he said. "I'm hungry enough to eat it all."

Theona stood up hastily, and dried herself with the same cloth he had used. Her Sunday best tunic was filthy, but she slipped into it, then picked up her trousers and dropped them into the tub. Even with the poor light, she could see the water turn several shades darker.

"You are wrong about Prince Roderic and me," she said, dunking the filthy garment up and down in the water. "He lost all interest when he thought I was trying to convert him to Christianity. That's why he left our caravan."

"Don't take me for a fool, Theona. I've seen him with you several times, and I know he joined our caravan because of you. He may have lost his temper, but he will still care what happens to you. You'd better hope so, anyway, because if he has no interest in you, neither have I."

"Let the girl come and eat, Severus."

The old lady got up and crossed to the counter, reaching up when she got there and taking down a bowl from a shelf. She expertly ladled some of the fish stew into it and set it down on the table. Theona went to sit on one of the other chairs at the table, and hungrily began to eat. Cantarcchio stuck out his foot to fondle hers. She moved her foot away. He laughed mirthlessly.

"Don't flatter yourself," he said. "I do not find you in the least bit attractive. On the contrary."

"I have to admit" she said between bites, "I haven't heard such good news in days!"

He rose swiftly, and planted his fists across the table on both sides of her food bowl, his angry face mere inches away.

"Be careful not to anger me, Theona. You are a dirty Gothic bitch who fancies herself a princess, and you are no Christian, whatever you might believe. We Romans know all about your faith. You can't even get that right. If you think I trust your people to keep their word to protect my family and my valley, you must be crazy. Granny is my closest relative now, and I don't want any filthy barbarians hurting her or any other of my kind. You, dear Theona, will make sure of that."

"You are a cruel man."

"You're not so bad yourself. And by the way, once Prince Roderic gets an eyeful of our Roman girls, he won't give you a second look. I'm going to bed, Granny. I have to leave early in the morning."

"All right, Severus. Where will this one sleep?"

"Put her up with the chickens." He pointed up at the loft, and stalked off through one of the two doors at the back, carrying one of the two candles he had lit.

Theona slept upstairs with the chickens. The old woman told her where to find blankets, and where to find the chamber pot, and where the well was outside, and when breakfast would be available, and what she would do to her if Theona dared wake her up too early, and after that she cleaned away the remains of the meal, put extra wood on the fire, and tottered off to her own bedroom.

She had somehow remembered to leave the second candle burning, or perhaps she had not been aware of it, although Theona suspected little got past the woman.

Except for the crackling of the fire and the eerie shadow patterns made by her movements, the main room was now silent and empty. Theona stripped off her tunic and swished it, too, around in the dirty bath water, and then squeezed the water out of the two garments as best she could. She had no idea how to dry them without antagonizing her reluctant hosts. She thought about fetching more water from the well, but did not trust Cantarcchio not to come along behind her and bar the door.

When she had finished, she carried the candle up the ladder to the loft to look around quickly. It wasn't large, but it seemed clean and clear. The chickens were indeed up in the loft with her, but in a separate area through a closed door. She could hear a few gentle noises from them, a comfortable sound she had grown used to on the long trek from the Danube. Otherwise, the house was silent.

She rested the candle near the edge so there would still be some light below, and then climbed back down to get the blankets from a big chest near the spinning wheel. She was still hungry. Guiltily, she helped herself to some of the bread the old woman had put away in a wooden box. She hadn't been offered her any even though they had used her fish in that stew. The round loaf was fresh and tasted wonderful. At last she climbed back up the ladder clutching the blankets, her wet clothes, and her worn pouch.

It was warm up in the loft. She found some nails hammered into the wall that separated her and the chickens, and suspended her tunic and trousers there, hoping they would be dry by morning.

Three straw pallets were piled on top of each other in a corner. They seemed clean, and she looked forward to the extra softness three would provide. Eagerly she spread a blanket on top and lay down, pulling the other two up around her neck.

All day Theona had longed for a quiet moment to pray. The prayers she had sent like arrows to God during the disasters of the day were not enough. She began to pray. Her prayers were short, and increasingly confused. The Son of God, she thought, would have to enlarge them for her to the Father. She yawned, let it all go, and fell asleep.

The trail Gideon had been following ended at last at a large building up a winding country path. It was a cold trail, by now, as the night was cold, as Gideon himself was cold, but the strong scent of the horse he had been following was fresh and pungent. That horse was inside the building, but the scent of the people was less strong.

Gideon limped around the building trying to find an opening. The big stable door was closed, but it hung crookedly on its hinges. He pushed at it with his paw. It banged shut. He sidled around to the other side of the door and tried again, this time trying to pull it towards him with his paw. It moved creakily. After two more tries, he managed to get his shoulder wedged in the opening. The weight of the door pinched, one more pain in a sore, tired, hungry body, but the start he had made enabled him to push in a bit more, and at last he was through. The heavy door swung shut behind him. Little gusts of air ruffled his fur.

The stable was very dark. Gideon took a couple of steps forward and waited to gain a sense of the place, appreciating in his own canine way the lack of frost in the air, the relief to his tired, freezing paws. The smell of apples wafted sweetly from somewhere farther down.

There was no one else here but the horse. It had snorted when the door banged shut, and whinnied in its stall. All the other stalls appeared to be empty. Gideon padded across to the one where the old horse was standing, and lay down on the straw-littered floor, peering in. The horse sensed his presence and stamped its foot, backing up to the rear wall. Gideon continued to lie there until the horse, reassured, began to relax. A few minutes later the big head came down and large, damp nostrils sniffed at him. Gideon did not move. The bigger animal nickered and backed up a bit. Gideon inched into the stall and crept to the bucket of water the man had placed near the wall. He drank deeply, sniffed at the oats, and crept back out. He found the bin of apples farther down the barn, tipped it over, and eagerly ate a few.

In the stall adjacent to the old horse he found a matted pile of old straw and curled up on it, tucking his nose into his tail to keep warm. In a minute he had fallen asleep. Mice skittered around the barn all night long, a source of food for him, but they were perfectly safe—Gideon was exhausted. The old horse listened for a while, and then allowed himself to drift back to sleep.

Both of them woke up the next morning when the big door of the barn opened and banged shut. A man had come in. Gideon sniffed the air and poked his head out to take a quick look.

It was the same man who had carried off his beloved Theona. He tensed. The man smelled differently today, but it was the same unpleasant fellow who had thrown a stone at him and carried Theona off on the horse. Gideon eased quietly back into his stall.

The man was doing something to the horse, and in a few minutes he led the big animal out of the stable, and the door swung shut again. Gideon followed.

He loped after the two of them until they had reached the road, and watched as they turned to continue their journey south.

As soon as they were gone, he began questing with his nose for the scent of the man himself, alone and on foot. It took a little while, but his sensitive nose did not let him down. He found the path the man had come down and followed it up the mountain, hoping lunch would come hopping across his path somewhere along the way.

CHAPTER TWENTY-FOUR

GRAPPLING WITH GRANNY

~

The Isarco Valley of Northern Italy
Late October, 405 AD

Theona awoke to the sound of the old lady moving around below. There was a little more light in the loft—it must be daytime. She stretched and yawned, enjoying the coziness of her bed. Her body felt more relaxed than it had in ages, but she was still deeply weary. In fact, she felt ancient. She went back to sleep.

She woke up again sometime later to an uproar coming from the room down below, a frenzied mix of shouts and barks.

"Get out! Get out. Where are you anyway? Theona!"

The blind woman appeared to be in a panic. Theona sat up so fast she bumped her head against the sloping ceiling. She threw off the blanket, crawled to the top of the ladder, and looked down. Gideon was standing on his hind legs, his front paws on the rungs of the ladder, looking up at her, his tail wagging vigorously.

Gideon! The old woman was closing in on him, coming at him from behind, swinging a heavy broom in her scrawny arms. Her face was tight with concentration as she tried to locate the animal that had slipped into the house when she had opened the door.

"Stop!" yelled Theona. "That's my dog! Don't hit him. I'm coming. Wait."

She tugged on her tunic—it was almost dry—and began lowering herself onto the ladder.

Granny paused uncertainly, and then brandished her broom again.

"You get down here then, missy, and get him out of here. He frightened me half to death! How'd he get here anyway? Sev didn't mention a dog."

Theona didn't know. It was a mystery. It was a miracle. She quickly descended the rungs and dropped to her knees, hugging Gideon, crying with relief and joy. He accepted her homage, thumping his tail vigorously and licking her face. He had found her. His own delight matched his mistress's. They both completely ignored the angry old woman. She had stopped to listen, then quietly took her broom and walked back to place it in its own exact spot.

Theona stood up and faced her. "He's hungry. He probably hasn't eaten for at least a day. He's likely been out in the cold all night."

"How'd he find you?"

"He must have tracked us. The last I saw of him he was lying quietly, watching your grandson carry me off."

"Some guard!"

"Sev had threatened to kill him if he followed us, so I told him to stay."

"Sev will still kill him."

"No, he can't. He mustn't. Gideon has been with me since my family was killed."

The old woman raised her head and looked sightlessly in Theona's direction.

"Now that's a story I would like to hear," she said with relish. "You tell it, while I get breakfast for you and your dog."

Marius got up early. The roar of the river nearby had finally helped him fall asleep, but his first thought when he woke was to check on the guards around the camp. The sky was still dark when he came out of his tent, but there was a rosy glow to the east that reflected on the snow clad mountains in that direction. The fir trees in the forest were stirring, shedding the light snow that had fallen during the night.

He spoke to all of the men who had stood guard within the camp. Everything seemed fine. They hadn't heard anything unusual during the night, but the noise from the Isarco River might have covered the sound of an attack higher up. Several of them climbed with him to check on the sentries posted farther up the river and on the hillside above their camp. All the reports were free of complications. He breathed a sigh of relief. As soon as possible he wanted to get back up to Thermopylae and check on the eighty men he had left there overnight.

Before they returned to the camp, Marius and the sentries continued on up the hill to have a look around. From the top they could see a little way up both the Adige and the Isarco Valley. They looked quiet and empty.

His mind flashed briefly to the chamois he had seen the day before. He was itching to go hunting for them. Today might be his only chance. Apart from the placement of the second carroballista, most of the preparations for the coming battle had already been done. Once the big catapult was in place, they would just have to wait for the barbarians to show up.

Their quartermaster had met a farmer on the road who had pigs to sell. He had purchased several, and the cooks had slaughtered them. David had purchased some of the meat and prepared it for Marius to take with him. Marius offered some to Bauto. Bauto had no servant of his own, and no patience to cook. He eagerly accepted the gift and ate some of it on the spot.

"This is so good," he sighed. "Am I going upriver with you today?"

"Yes. I think Thermopylae will have to be our center of operations from now on unless something dramatic happens down here. We'll take most of the men up there now, and send the guards back here to rest. Our first priority will be to get that second catapult into place. We also need to test both of them to get the sightings right.

"I've also been thinking we should send men to explore the areas above both sides of the valley. I want to know about the roads and paths up there, and which ones descend to the valley floor. We may need to post men to watch these. It's possible the missing soldiers are hiding out somewhere up there. We haven't found them in Pons Drusi. You take charge of that. Tell the men to be careful. Approach any settlements and farms with caution. If they see anything unusual, they need to report back to me, and I'll send a good-sized squad up to follow through."

Bauto agreed and left.

David was clearing up nearby. Marius asked him if he might borrow one of his homespun tunics and his old cloak. The Hebrew paused and looked at him, his eyes narrowed and his mouth pursed. Marius knew better than to ask what the man was thinking--often he would look at him and see his mother's own anxieties reflected back. He was convinced now that Constantia had chosen David to be his servant because the man was incorruptible and reliable, and she could trust him to take care of her youngest son.

"I thought we could do some hunting later today if it's quiet," he added nonchalantly.

"We, master?"

"Wouldn't you like to come along? I'm sure you hunted when you had your own farm."

"Yes, master. I'm good with a hunting bow."

"Well, bring the change of clothes and your bow with you to the ambush site this afternoon. Maybe we'll be able to add more fresh meat to the menu."

"What are we hunting for, master?"

"Oh, maybe a chamois or two. Their leather is exceptionally luxurious."

David's face relaxed.

"Yes, master." He turned back to the work he was doing.

The Mosella Cohort headed back up the Isarco to the double bend. They reached the place where they had struggled to haul the first carroballista to its high platform, and found it nose down in the river with all the bolts and rocks scattered along the shoreline and in the water. They hurried around the bend, and found their comrades scurrying to rebuild platforms and restock the stones and rocks they had so painstakingly collected and carried up the mountain the previous day.

Marius was angry.

"What happened here?" he demanded of the centurion he had left in charge.

"At daybreak the men heard sounds of fighting up the valley. We left a few guards here, but most of us went to investigate, thinking it was the men of the Seventh Alpine Cohort under attack. When we reached the area, there was no one there. We heard the signal to come back here and ran back. When we arrived, this had happened."

The soldier, formerly a taverna cook in Trier, gestured at the pieces of broken platform and the strewn rocks and stones lying on the valley floor.

"Was anybody hurt?"

"Yes, sir. Two of the guards were pushed down the mountain, and one was knocked unconscious. They're going to be alright though, sir. They said that their attackers weren't wearing uniforms. It was still pretty dark."

"Is there anything else?"

"As you probably saw, tribune, someone pushed the carroballista we set up yesterday off its platform. They turned the second one around to face our tents and lobbed a bolt at them. It destroyed one of the tents, sir."

"Do you think they meant to steal it and gave up?"

"You saw the effort it took for us to get it here, sir. We think they just wanted to frighten us."

"They" had certainly done that. Marius sent the eighty men back to their main camp.

The soldiers spent the morning renewing their preparations and wrenching the big catapults into position. The second one did not take as long to set up, both because of their previous experience, and because the platform was lower on the slope.

Marius set up a series of javelins at several places in the narrow defile, and his artillery men practiced zeroing in on these as he called out the coordinates. The ballistae could rotate left and right, up and down, and by practicing, the men grew ever more skillful. At first the bolts hurled by the powerful wire "bowstrings" connected with trees alongside the river, shattering them. Shards from the rocks and other debris created a danger to the soldiers working nearby. After an hour's practice, the artillery men were able to hit closer to the targets, bringing cheers from the watching soldiers.

Bauto sent four parties of soldiers up the mountains to explore above the valley. Two of the groups were to tackle the terrain nearby, while the rest hiked five miles up the valley and worked their way back.

Later in the morning, the soldiers at Thermopylae began to see people coming toward them. Many were pushing handcarts piled high with household goods, or driving goats in their direction. The travelers stopped well back when they saw so many Roman soldiers blocking their way, and for a short while there was a standoff. After a while, some men came forward waving a makeshift white flag, and Marius, accompanied by some of his soldiers, met with them on a level section of grass beside the river.

These people spoke an unfamiliar dialect and bore a strong resemblance to one another. Only a few of them spoke Latin, and then not very well.

They said they had left their homes in the east and had been following the river valleys westward for several days, fleeing a multitude of barbarians approaching the area through the Drau River system. They repeated the stories of mining towns and Roman administrative centers that had been attacked and looted. The fugitives had not heard of any real resistance to the invasion from the fortifications along the way, and were relieved to see the Roman Army at last.

Marius felt his throat tighten. He was beginning to feel like the shepherd that had been ordered to lead a flock of lambs to the slaughter house. He desperately wanted Olybrius's confident presence back beside him.

The soldiers who stood with him listening to these reports glanced at each other uneasily. They were worried enough about the main throng descending this valley from the north. Now they knew that a second massive enemy force was approaching Thermopylae.

There appeared to be no harm in letting these simple peasants continue on their way, so Marius gave the order to his men to let them pass.

For the next several hours, other groups—some small, some large—continued to filter down the valley. Most of them had come from the east. A few others came from farther up the valley. They were local residents who had finally lost their nerve.

In the early afternoon it got quiet again and the soldiers sat around and rested. A few played dice or practiced with their weapons, while others restlessly collected stones from the river bed and carried them to the hillside platforms. Everyone roused again when soldiers from the Seventh Alpine Cohort came marching down the valley from the same direction as the fugitives. The soldiers sprang to their feet and cheered, excited to be able to meet up with old friends.

Marius counted the newcomers from his vantage on one of the hillside platforms—there were over a hundred. He looked for the legate, but Olybrius was not among them. The Rhaetian soldiers assured him that their commander was most likely heading towards them from the direction of Statio Maiensis. Marius did a quick calculation. The legate would not arrive until the next day.

Like his men, he was eager for details about their work up the valley. From the point of view of the Seventh Alpine Cohort, the attack had gone splendidly. They had successfully disabled many wagons or destroyed the animals that pulled them, and they had probably slowed the barbarians' progress by at least a day or two. Moreover, they had lost only a few of their own number.

The skirmish had energized them. They were eager to face the enemy again, this time fighting alongside their brothers in the Mosella Cohort. Their enthusiasm was contagious. Marius and his men took heart. They would need every good fighter they could get.

"Are there any more of you coming?" he asked.

"We don't know, Tribune Ausonius. Some of us did wait to see what would happen after we left. It looked like most of our fellows got away. There was one squad that the legate had sent farther up the valley to find out where the next groups of barbarians were. They were to go at least a day's journey past the first group of wagons. None of them has shown up yet. That might be a good sign. Most of the barbarians may still be fighting on the other side of the pass."

The Rhaetian soldiers marched off down the valley towards Pons Drusi, singing as they went. They were looking forward to a hot meal, a cold bath and a few hours of sleep to get them back into top shape.

Twenty minutes later a figure appeared up the valley. It was another Roman soldier. He, too, was wearing a uniform with Rhaetian insignia. This one, however, was riding a worn-out black nag. As he got closer, Marius saw that his uniform was shabbier and the colors and insignia not as bright or highly polished as the ones worn by the soldiers of the Seventh Alpine Cohort. He went down to meet the man.

He was young and lanky, and his blond hair was tied back in a ponytail. He dismounted and looked around with interest at the ambush preparations done by Marius's men, and then saluted.

"Severus Cantarcchio, sir. Reporting for duty."

Marius studied him. He did not recognize him, although he did not know every individual who had accompanied the legate. There were little details about the man's appearance that bothered him. Legate Olybrius's officers would not have tolerated such sloppiness. Besides, the man's uniform was more like that worn by the Prefect he had met at Statio Maiensis.

"Who is your commander?" he asked.

"Publius Cantarcchio, sir. He's in charge of the local garrison here."

"And will he vouch for you?"

The young man grew still. "I should hope so, sir," he smiled. "He is my cousin."

"And where will I find him?"

Cantarcchio stared at him.

"He should be at the garrison, Tribune, unless something has happened to him."

"And if it has," said Marius, "I should think you would know, since you serve under him."

"No sir. I have been away for a little while. I am just returning to duty."

"Then here is your first order, Cantarcchio. Go find your cousin and bring him to me, or bring me someone else who knows where he is. All of the soldiers who should be on duty here seem to have vanished into thin air."

Cantarcchio's eyes were shuttered. "Yes, sir."

He turned to remount the nag.

"Leave the horse," ordered Marius, more out of spite than for any logical reason. There was just something about the man that got his back up.

Cantarcchio looked at him with resentment, then nodded in resignation. He set off down the valley on foot, passing the watching soldiers stiffly.

"Follow him," muttered Marius to one of the slaves who had come up the valley with David, "and don't let him see you. If he is local, he could be a spy, and if he is telling the truth, he may help us locate those traitors who are causing us so much harm."

The groups of men who had gone out to explore that morning began to return. One by one they reported what they had seen. Marius and Bauto lost track after a while, and sent for Socrates, asking him to create a map from the reports, and put down on a scroll the interconnecting roads and paths that each group were describing. They had found foot paths, drover's roads, and farm lanes winding their way up and down and around every negotiable area on both sides of the valley. Very few of these went any great distance. Most led to dead ends such as pastures, farm houses, and farmers' fields. A few disappeared altogether when an alpine peak butted into them.

There were arguments between the groups and within groups. Socrates was becoming frustrated. So were they all.

After verifying that the scouts had not seen anyone who looked as if they could be one of the missing Roman soldiers, Marius stopped listening. He had had it. He needed a break, and since no one yet had seen any indication that there were any barbarians close to this end of the valley, he decided he would do a little "exploring" of his own.

He left Socrates and Bauto arguing with the men, and changed into the rough brown clothing David had brought. Leaving his optio in charge, he set off with his slave up a steep path toward the upland areas above Thermopylae.

At the top, the path continued a long way through a stretch of forest. Eventually they reached the end of the trees, but the path continued across a pasture heading north. They followed this for half an hour without seeing any sign of the elusive wild goats. Then David called his attention to a small, rounded hill off in the distance. There appeared to be some tiny animals grazing near it.

Marius squinted. Chamois! He began to run.

The morning passed companionably enough. The old woman had put together a simple breakfast of apples and porridge. She listened with interest as Theona described her village and the raid that had driven her people so far from home. She made disapproving noises whenever Theona described some of the sadness and horrors she had seen on the long journey, and nodded when the girl talked about her worries about the journey ahead, but when Theona asked her if she remembered much about her own home village, she shook her head.

"It was just a few families sharing fields in the middle of the forest. I remember the sacred grove of oaks and a big river, but that's it. There must be thousands like it, and it was a long time ago."

"What . . . what happened to bring you here?"

"I told you," said the old lady irritably, "I was raped by Roman soldiers who came to our village to punish our warlord. They killed the men they could find, raped the women, and burned our village. My father sent me away when he learned I was with child—I was the only one who was—and I set off to find the man who had ruined my life. It wasn't hard. The Romans left their seed behind all the way home."

Theona shuddered. But men on her side had done the same. Why, she couldn't begin to understand. Why take out your fury on the women? Going to war was not usually a woman's choice. Perhaps raping the women was supposed to be meant as punishment for their men! The woman's father's attitude, though, mystified her. She could not imagine her father ever treating her that way, no matter what she did.

"Do you have other family members in the area?"

"No. I raised my son up here. He married a local girl and moved into the town. I refused to let him bring her back here. She was one of *them*. They all knew my story, yet for years none of them came by to help me. Sev was raised by my son and that woman in town, but he liked to come up here. It suited his temperament, I think. He has cousins in the valley, but I didn't care to know them."

"Does your son look after you?" Theona looked around – the woman was clearly not destitute.

"No. He turned out to be more like his father than me. He died in a tavern fight. Serves him right. It was over some floozy from the valley."

"What about Sev's mother?"

"I heard she died a few years back. Sev never told me how."

"How do you manage here all alone?" asked Theona. "How do you get this food? *Someone* must help you. How do you buy things when you can't see? And aren't you lonely here all by yourself?"

The woman chuckled. "You'd be surprised. People come up here all the time. All the merchants know their way to my door. I pay them good money and they know not to cheat me. I may not be able to see any more, but my nose and my fingers never lie, even if people do. I always know when someone tries to cheat me. If they try it more than once, it's over. I won't buy from them ever again. I'd rather starve."

"But where do you get your money?"

"Wouldn't you like to know, nosy girl." She stood up and took a step towards her bedroom. "Where's that dog?"

"He's lying over near the fireplace."

"Put him out. I won't have him hanging around in here. I fed him. That's enough. Put him outside where he belongs."

She shuffled off to the bedroom. Theona sighed, and took Gideon to the inner door. She opened it and took one of the furs hanging on the hook and laid it down on the floor of the little vestibule. The dog curled up on it, and went back to sleep. Theona returned to the main room.

The old woman re-entered carrying several small woven sacks which were tied with ropes. These she placed on the little table.

"Here, come and help me with this, and I'll show you what I do," she said.

Eagerly, Theona moved to the table and peered into the first pouch. It was filled with human hair. She reached in and fingered it, then looked into the other bags. They were all full of hair, mostly shades of blond, light brown, and red.

"What's this for?" she asked.

"Have you ever heard of an ornatrix?"

The word was new to Theona. It sounded Latin, not Gothic. She shook her head.

"No."

"An ornatrix is a girl who does fancy hairdos for other women. Have you ever had anyone do your hair, girl?"

"What do you mean?" Theona had never heard of the concept.

"Bring me the brush on the shelf in my bedroom and that wire contraption next to it."

Theona fetched the brush and sat back down at the table. Granny shuffled around behind her chair and began gently brushing Theona's hair which was clean now, but tangled.

"What color blond is this hair?"

"My father says it looks like the color of an oat field in August. He likes it."

The woman sniffed. "So, it's a darker shade of gold. That's a popular color, and it's certainly long enough. When was the last time it was cut?"

"My mother cut it three years ago."

"What did she use?"

"Scissors. She brought them with her when she married my father. Only one other woman in the village had scissors, so we all shared them."

The old woman parted Theona's hair into sections and then began to braid many of the strands together. She took the "wire contraption" she had asked for, and placed this on top of Theona's head, and then she began to weave the braids and the unbraided hair in and out through the wires, tucking, pinching, and pulling until her hands told her she had achieved the design she wanted. She finished off her handiwork with bits of ribbon, and patted Theona's head lightly.

"I don't have a mirror anymore," she said. "Sev does, but I wouldn't know where he keeps it, and I wouldn't let you go into his room anyway, but if you go and look at yourself in the lake, you will get an idea of what a good ornatrix can do. Go."

Theona ran to the door and opened it. Gideon looked up sleepily and got to his feet. She looked around for her boots. They were not there, nor were the others she had noticed the night before. She opened the outside door to let in more light. Gideon slipped out. Theona scanned the little entranceway frantically. Her boots were truly gone and there was frost on the ground outside.

"My boots are gone," she accused.

The old woman laughed. "That's Sev. Smart boy. He thinks you might try to leave me if you could, so he's got rid of them."

"But what am I going to do?"

"Take two of those strips of cloth on the shelf there and wrap them around your feet. You only have to go as far as the lake and back. You're not going to freeze to death."

The little lake was smooth as glass, a thin layer of ice beginning to form near the edges. Theona knelt down and bent forward to look at her image. Her hair was piled high and looked way too fancy. She thought that if she moved her head too quickly, the whole thing would come tumbling down. She could see her ears, too, something she was not accustomed to. Disgusted, she pulled at the fancy hairdo and took it apart, leaving her long hair loose and slightly wavy. That was better!

She hurried back into the house holding the wire cage the blind woman had used to create her fancy design.

Gideon had been sniffing at the ground. He watched her go, but made no move to follow. He had found a new scent, a very interesting one. He wanted to investigate it.

"Did you like it?" Granny's voice was eager.

"It looked very nice, but it felt strange, and I didn't know how long I was supposed to keep it in, so I took it out."

"Stupid of you," snapped the old woman. "You may not have that privilege ever again!" She was clearly disappointed.

"I'm sorry to have ruined your work."

Granny glared.

There was a short silence.

"Well, I was an ornatrix for a while. It started with a few women, and then more and more came up the path. I wasn't always blind. My sight had been going for years before it finally died on me. I learned by myself by looking at the statues around town and studying old coins. I also watched what some of the fancy townswomen were doing with their hair. After a while, I tried making a wig for one of the dark-haired ladies who came to me from the town; some of them like to pretend they are blonds occasionally.

"For that first wig I used my own hair. Then I started buying hair from women who needed the money, and from some men, too. The wigs brought in more money than doing fancy hairdos for farmers' wives. I live alone and don't go out, so I have the time. I got so good at it that I can still make them, even without my eyes, but I can't see to sort the hair people bring me anymore. If I don't know the seller, I won't buy the hair, but I know most of the families around here, so I know the blonds from the brunettes. I pay them well, but I charge a lot more for my wigs."

She showed Theona three she was working on, the cleverly sewn thin strands of hair all attached to soft leather skull caps, and then styled.

Each wig must take weeks to do, thought Theona, but for a blind woman living alone, it made sense. She noticed that there were coloration mistakes in all three wigs, dark hairs mixed in with the light, but the wigs the blind woman was working on were still remarkable works of art.

"I have a few orders waiting, so you can help me by sorting all this hair out," remarked Granny. "Better still, you sort and I'll tend to my chickens."

She chuckled.

She instructed Theona to sort by lengths, and then separate similar hues.

Theona set to work sorting the first bag of hair, and the blind woman left to climb up to the loft. She heard a flurry of activity up there and the low sound of Granny's voice making clucking noises to the birds and talking to them. The table top and the floor around Theona's chair became covered with neatly sorted piles of hair. This job was tedious. It was going to take hours!

Granny came back down and passed her with a basketful of eggs which she stored in a wooden box filled with straw. She began preparing food on the counter near the hearth. Soon, there was the smell of some kind of herb-flavored bread dough, and a pot of soup simmering away. Theona enjoyed the sense of hominess in the little house as she worked.

She reached for more hair from the first bag. She would need more space. She got up and went over to the wash tub she had bathed in the previous night, and started to drag it over to the table.

"What are you doing?" snapped the blind woman anxiously.

"I need more room to put the piles of hair. I want to turn the tub over and use the bottom as an extra table."

"No. Don't move anything. I have everything just the way I need it. Just use the table and the shelves."

"What shelves?"

"The empty ones along the back wall between the bedroom doors. Didn't you see them? Sev built them for me especially to sort hair."

Theona was annoyed. She hadn't noticed the shelves. There they were, all three of them, one above the other, all several feet long, and all empty. She went to get a cloth to wipe them.

"What have you been using?" asked Granny accusingly as she listened to Theona moving about near her.

"The table, the chairs, and the floor."

"The floor! And suppose I had stepped on them?"

"I didn't know about the shelves," complained Theona. "I didn't see them, and you didn't mention them to me."

"Why should I? You have eyes. And they say I'm blind!"

They did not talk after that. Once she had cleaned the shelves off, Theona carefully transferred her piles of hair over to them and continued to sort, placing the longer ones on the bottom shelf, the shorter ones on the top shelf, and the middle length ones on the middle shelf. The work went more quickly, but soon she was tired. The day before had been very long and hard, and her legs and feet were starting to ache again.

After a while, the old lady called to her to come and eat. She had placed a bowl of soup, a piece of cheese and yesterday's bread on the table, and now she stood near Theona's chair, a pair of large pivoted iron scissors in her hand.

"Sit down and eat," she said.

Theona looked at her doubtfully. "What about you?" she asked.

"I will eat later."

Theona sat down, eyeing her warily, and reached for her spoon. She was hungry again and the aroma from the steaming soup was wonderful. She took the bread and broke it into quarters as she had seen Cantarcchio do the night before, and dipped it into the soup.

The old woman stood beside her, listening.

"Do you like it?"

Theona bit and swallowed. "It is very good. Thank you."

She took another bite. The woman stepped behind her chair and moved in close, grabbing Theona's long hair and pulling it sharply back.

Rrrrrrip.

The sound seemed to screech in Theona's ear. A lock of dark gold hair slid to the floor.

"Stop! You can't do that!"

She tried to move, pushing her chair back, but the woman had her trapped against the table, her long hair firmly pinned behind her against the back of the chair.

Rrrrip.

Another tress fell beside the first. Theona panicked. She had not known she was vain about her hair until it was threatened. The tresses lying on the floor were long. The woman meant to cut off all her hair!

She tried to toss her head from side to side. Granny gripped more tightly. It hurt, but the old lady was not going to get one more hair from Theona without a fight. Theona thrust the table forward and made a lunge after it. The soup, the bread, and the cheese spilled onto the floor, pooling around a cluster of loose hairs she seemed to have missed. Granny cried out and instinctively reached in the direction of the sound of the bouncing bowl. She almost lost her balance and grabbed for the chair. The scissors she was brandishing passed dangerously close to Theona's head. Theona leaped to her feet, and stepped away from the mess.

"Sit down or you won't get any more food," said the blind woman firmly.

"No. That's *my* hair. You have no right to take it."

"Of course I do. You are eating my food and you don't have any money to pay for it. Sev wants me to keep you here for I don't know how long. At least until your dear prince comes to rescue you," she sneered. "That's going to cost *me* money. You have nothing to give me *but* your hair. It's mine, missy. Mine, not yours. Sit down, and let me have it."

Theona ran for the door. The woman just stood there, waiting patiently.

Theona turned back. "Where did Cantarcchio put my boots?" she demanded.

"How would I know?" chuckled Granny. "He probably flung them into the lake."

Theona went cold. The young man was mean enough to do just that.

But then, she thought, if Cantarcchio expected to use her as barter, he would likely not have done anything so drastic. The Goths would make him pay for any damage to her person, and, she assumed, her meager property.

"I am sure he did not," she said. "And I am sure that you know all of his hiding places very well. If you do not tell me where my boots are, then I am going to move everything in your house to a different place. It will take you days to find things. After that, I will start mixing up or throwing out the hair I have just sorted, and after that, I will let your chickens out. So tell me, where are my boots."

The old lady had gone ashen. Her shoulders sagged. She lowered the scissors.

"The wood pile. They're probably in the wood pile," she shouted. "Get out of here you wretched girl, and if you and that dog come back here, I'll kill him myself."

Theona grabbed the bread and the cheese that lay damply on the stone floor, and then scrambled to the loft to gather her things. The old woman continued to stand near the table. She was shaking, and once again listening intently.

"Good day to you, Granny," said Theona, hurrying past her.

On the way out the door she grabbed the fur that she had used to make a bed for Gideon. Now where was the wood pile? It was behind the house. Feverishly she began to dig through it, her hands bruising against the cold, hard wood. Then she glimpsed the corner of one of her boots. She dug it out, and soon after located the second one. They had looked old and worn before. Now they looked worse, bent under the weight of the wood, and filled with splinters, but at least she had them. She pulled on her long trousers and then spent a few precious minutes trying to clean out and straighten her boots. Finally, she shrugged into the fur, pleased when she discovered that it was a coat and had long sleeves.

There was no sound coming from inside the house, but the walls were thick, and there were two doors between herself and the old woman. Already she was feeling guilty about her threats and the theft of the coat. What would Cantarcchio do when he came back and found out? Would he see it as she did—payment for the loss of some of her hair and his own treachery?

Oh well, she thought, *I may never see either of them again. I hope I don't.*

She just wanted to get as far away from the two of them as she could. Now where was Gideon?

He wasn't anywhere in sight. Then she heard him barking in the distance. The sound was coming from somewhere up past the road. Theona hurried towards the sound, glad of anything that would put off the moment she would begin to regret running away from food and shelter.

CHAPTER TWENTY-FIVE

MARIUS MEETS HIS FIRST BARBARIAN

Near Pons Drusi
(Bolzano, Italy)
Late October, 405 AD

Theona ran back up the slope past the lake and on to the road. She could not see Gideon any-where. She stopped to listen again at the edge of the field. On the far side of it was the steep path down to the valley. The barking was not coming from that direction.

At the bottom of the field was the line of trees she had noticed. The wooded area, like the road itself, plunged downhill to another plateau. The barking, now muffled, was coming from some-where over there.

She followed the sound and came to a path. It was steep and treacherous with rocks and tree roots, but wide enough to walk on. She made her way down this, catching at tree branches to steady herself. The bent edges of her boots rubbed against one of her legs and began to raise a welt, so she stopped to push the edges of her trousers into them again, aware that they would not stay put for long.

The path drew alongside a brook. It gurgled along beside her, interfering with her ability to hear Gideon who was now somewhere below her, then it veered away in a different direction. In the renewed silence she heard again Gideon's insistent barking. She called to him. He barked more frantically. Wherever he was, he wasn't coming, and he wanted her to hurry up.

The slope became easier and she saw green grass at the bottom. The dog's urgent woofs were near now. Theona emerged from the trees to find herself on the edge of a narrow meadow with a clear view of the plateau. Beyond it stretched a sprawling landscape of farms and fields.

She saw Gideon on the far side of the meadow, only his head showing above a fall of rocks and boulders. She could not see what he was barking at, but at least he had stopped moving away from her. Theona pulled her sling and a few small, round stones out of her pouch, and readjusted her trouser leg inside her boots, hoping the dog had not corralled a wolf or a bear.

She limped across the meadow until she could see her dog, his head lowered, his shoulders hunched up, his four feet planted defiantly on the ground.

He had managed to corner a family of wild chamois. They were caught between the determined little dog and a deep crevasse which stretched right across the meadow.

The chamois all had shaggy coats, some spotted, some grey or brown. The dominant ewe was a large mottled grey animal with the chamois' characteristic black and white markings on her face. She stood facing Gideon, her head lowered, daring him to come closer. Her companions had drawn together. A few of the young ones were watching nervously. The older ewes continued to graze, but kept an eye on the protagonists.

Gideon loved to herd. His insistent barking had been a summons to his mistress to come and take charge of these stray animals. He clearly meant the wild goats to come under his and his mistress's rightful authority. The crevasse here was a natural barrier, as wide as Theona was tall. In the winter, covered with snow, or in foggy conditions, it would have been particularly treacherous.

Someone had built a sturdy bridge across the crevasse not far from where she stood. It served an old drover's road that traversed, and then carried on up the steep hillside. Theona noticed two men on the road approaching the bridge at a run. They seemed to be coming to investigate Gideon's barking. She got there first.

As soon as his mistress neared him, Gideon began to sidle around to the back of the flock. Theona knew that he was attempting to maneuver the mountain goats towards her so that she could take charge of them. He knew she knew the routine. The dominant ewe circled to keep an eye on him.

"No, Gideon," said Theona firmly. "We don't want them."

Gideon wasn't about to give up, not after his excited hunt and chase. The more submissive chamois stepped nervously backward toward the crevasse. Gideon ran behind one of them and nipped near her legs. She leaped forward. The dominant ewe charged at him, her backward curving horns lowered.

"No!" shouted Theona, waving her arms in the air and flapping her fur coat to look bigger.

Out of the corner of her eye she saw something fly past her, an arrow. She squealed, and turned to see a handsome young peasant with auburn hair reaching for a second arrow.

The ewe veered and leaped for the gorge. Her family followed. All of them landed safely on the other side and sped away. Gideon raced after them, trying to imitate their graceful flight, but his legs were not up to it. His paws vainly scrabbled for the opposite side, but he could not grasp on. He plunged into the crevasse, bouncing against the sides on his way down.

Theona and the two men rushed to the edge to look down.

"My dog," she cried.

They looked at her, and nodded.

The younger hunter, his hazel eyes sympathetic, took off his cloak and handed it to Theona.

"Hold this," he instructed. "Drop it to me when I get down near your dog."

Confused by the foreign language, she took the cloak and gripped it tightly, her eyes wide and worried. She watched in silence as his companion, a thin, dark-haired man, pulled a rope from his pouch and handed it to the younger one, who tied it around his waist.

A large boulder poked out of the ground a few feet away. The older man hitched a knot in the rope, sank the knotted end around the boulder and pulled it tight, then looped several lengths of it around the boulder and stood stalwartly, his hands busy forming additional loops with the long middle section.

The younger man peered down into the gorge, and looked for the most strategic way to descend. Theona could hardly believe her eyes—he was going down there to try to rescue Gideon. She followed him over to his point of descent.

Marius carefully lowered himself down into the gorge. Sharp rocks hurt his hands and he hated to look down to see where to put his feet next.

He was astonished at himself: how was it that he was putting himself in danger by stupidly climbing down into this crevasse to retrieve someone's dog? True, the dog had been cute, and he certainly didn't want it to suffer, but it was likely badly injured, maybe even dead, and yet he had given that no thought at all! He had not hesitated to step into this, this crazy, difficult, dangerous situation. It was as if he had been spellbound by those large grey-blue eyes and that girl's worried face. He felt like a fool. He had a battle to lead, important, no, *crucial* responsibilities as the man in charge of a cohort at war, but here he was, descending below ground level to the increasingly dark and narrow place where the little dog lay. He wondered if David ever wrote back to his family to report on his activities. Could the man read and write? He was suddenly convinced that David could.

He saw now that the little dog was alive. Gideon had landed on a rough rock ledge about twelve feet down. One pain-filled eye was watching him descend. Marius could see that at least one leg was broken. There would be more damage internally. Compassion filled his heart.

"Don't worry, boy," he whispered. "You've been very reckless, but so have I. I'm going to get you out of this and back to your mistress."

He glanced upward, seeing Theona staring down at them, her long bright hair catching the afternoon sun.

"Throw down my cloak," he called to her.

She hesitated for a second, and then threw it down. He caught it just before it went sailing past—the act almost unbalanced him. Gently he tucked it around the little dog and tried to lift him. Gideon whimpered. He was a dead weight. There wasn't much chance of getting him to the top without injuring him further or losing his own balance. It was dark below him and he could not be sure where the bottom of the crevasse was. He suddenly had the inspiration to make a package of him.

"David," he called, "I'm going to need you to haul him up. Get the girl to handle the back of the rope, and you pull him up at the top. I'll do what I can to support this poor creature from my end. He's alive but is badly hurt."

David beckoned to Theona to come back and showed her how to reel in the rope and wind it around the boulder. She took his place and nodded to him. He crossed to the crevasse, rolled up his cloak and kneeled on it, ready to haul.

Marius had untied the lead end of the rope from around his own waist. Slowly, gently, he shifted Gideon's body onto the cloak, and trussed his "package" in several places to keep it stable. Gideon trembled through it all, and yelped once. He leaned over to lick Marius's hand apologetically.

What a wonderful dog, thought Marius.

When he was ready, he pulled his "package" toward him and lifted it gently off the ledge. His careful movements almost dislodged him—one foot started to slip off its tiny foothold. He let go of Gideon and grabbed for a better handhold. His "package" bounced against the rock wall and there was another painful yelp. As soon as he felt secure again, he reached out to steady Gideon and braced his foot against the opposite wall.

"Pull," he shouted.

The 'package' eased higher. Marius steadied it, and took another step up.

"Pull," he shouted.

David hauled again, coiling the new rope in his hand and releasing more of the back end to Theona who wound it around the boulder.

Slowly Marius made his way back up to the top, buffering Gideon as much as possible. David reached out, straining to support the weight coming toward him and not slip off the cloak. With every foot of rope that passed around the boulder, Theona felt her hope and gratitude build. These two hunters who had come along just when she needed them seemed like angels to her, especially the handsome young one who was risking his neck for her gallant, but foolish pet. Their act of extreme kindness meant the world to her after the treatment she had received from Cantarcchio and Granny. When the 'package' finally reached the top of the crevasse, she ran to help David lift Gideon the last few inches onto solid ground.

Soon it was all over. Gideon lay quietly on the ground, his eyes closed, while David picked away at the tight knots in the rope confining him within the cloak. Theona fed him bits of cheese and damp bread, stroking his head and murmuring to him. He was not much interested in eating, but swallowed when she coaxed him. He had started to shiver.

Marius sprawled on the ground nearby, watching and listening. He was utterly exhausted. If any barbarians were to come along now, he reflected, he would be unable to lift a finger to defend himself. It wasn't so much the physical exertion, but the stress level he had been through. He sincerely hoped he never met any other girls who could so bewitch him.

He sat up and contemplated the mountain peaks to the west. They were turning black against the sinking sun except where it spread fire on their snowy slopes. Facets of the pale rock glowed orange and pink, while the grassy meadows below glistened with a golden sheen. It was a moment of awesome beauty.

Nevertheless, he and David would have to hurry to get back to the camp. Reluctantly he picked up his hunting bow and got to his feet. He shook out David's old cloak again and put it on, and then turned to say goodbye to the girl. She had examined her dog with loving concern, and was now wrapping him up in her own warm fur coat.

She, too, stood up, lifting the dog tenderly, and murmuring words of comfort in that strange language of hers. Now her only protection against the chill mountain air was her long brown tunic and trousers. He noticed that the tunic had a tiny white cross and a border of little flowers embroidered around the neckline. He also noticed that there was blood on her trouser leg above one of her ankles. He wondered how it had got there, and hoped she didn't have too far to go to get home carrying the dog with that injury.

The girl glanced at him and smiled again. Marius felt flustered. Her pretty face was looking at him with something like hero-worship. Well, he thought, he was one, just a little. It had been a memorable episode, one to think about with fondness for the rest of his life. Never had he done anything so fine and brave!

"We'll be going now, Bissula," he said, smiling down at her. "I wish I could take you with me, but I have a battle to fight and things to do. Take care of yourself and your little friend there."

She didn't reply, just stood there looking at him, her eyes shining. David made a sound somewhere between a snort and a snicker, and Marius looked at him furiously.

"You are sworn to secrecy, David," he said. "I'll beat you if you mention this to any of my men or any other slave, or anyone. Promise!"

David grinned and nodded. The girl smiled too. She must have understood.

He turned abruptly to go back to the bridge over the crevasse, and started down the road. David hurried after him, waving goodbye to Theona.

She, not knowing what else to do, followed the two men at a distance, Gideon heavy in her arms. The two men noticed, but kept walking rapidly, aware of the setting sun. Before long, they were leaving the uplands and descending a steep path to the dark Isarco valley below.

Theona continued to follow them. It was getting chilly again, and she had no hope of food or shelter for the coming night. These two local hunters were her best and only hope, so she kept following them, even though the way they had taken was steep and treacherous, especially carrying the dog. She slipped several times, and fell once, twisting her ankle over a root and hitting her head on a low hanging branch. In her fall she almost dropped Gideon, and cried out in fear and pain just as the two men reached the bottom of the path.

Worried, they stopped and waited. A few minutes later she emerged from the path, still holding the dog, her face wet with tears.

David lifted Gideon from her arms and began to unwrap him. Silently he stuffed the little body into his own cloak, cinching it shut with his belt. Theona promptly sat down and dragged off her boot. Marius gasped when he saw her bloodied ankle. While she explored and cleaned her blistered leg, he took the boot and began to work it with his hands. They were cruder than any he had ever seen before, but strong and stiff, though in appalling condition. Gently he worked the leather and then tried to put the boot back on her. She winced. He pulled her to her feet. Theona took a few steps, and then a few more before she nodded. It felt marginally better. She reached for the fur coat and put it on.

"What are we going to do about her?" muttered David. "We can't very well take her into the camp."

"I wish we could talk to her," replied Marius, frowning. "I thought she'd be going home by now."

"I have an idea she doesn't have a home," said David slowly. "What language do you think she was speaking when she was talking to the dog?"

"Some local dialect, I suppose."

David didn't respond. They started walking down the valley again, much more slowly than before. It seemed that the girl was determined to go with them, and they were reluctant to chase her away. Soon after the valley took a turn to the southwest and a new vista lay before them. Marius thought he recognized the mountain scape. They could not be too far from Thermopylae now. Once there, he would send the girl into town on that old nag he had seized. David could go along with her for protection.

A figure was approaching them from the south, dark against the sinking sun. They, on the other hand, were clearly visible in the golden light.

As the man drew closer, they could see that he was in uniform, though his face was in shadow. His long light colored hair was pulled back in a ponytail.

The thin face became recognizable as the Rhaetian soldier he had met earlier in the day, the one who was supposedly a cousin of the head of the local garrison. Theona, hobbling along beside him, suddenly faltered.

"Good evening, Tribune, I see you have met my wife."

So, the girl was married! Marius looked at her, ridiculously disappointed, even though he had no intention of pursuing their relationship any further. They stopped and the Rhaetian moved to stand in front of the girl. She edged closer to Marius.

"I trust she's not in any trouble?"

Marius shook his head.

"Then I will take her home now. Thank you for your help, Tribune."

Cantarcchio stepped forward and took a firm hold of the girl's arm. She pulled away defiantly, shaking off his arm and saying something to him in her own language. He muttered something back in the same language, and she glanced in shock at Marius.

Cantarcchio pulled her toward him and placed a possessive arm around her shoulder. She suffered this stoically, and then smiled apologetically at Marius and David. Without a word more, the two of them began to walk together back up the valley. Gideon struggled weakly to get down.

"Wait. You forgot her dog!"

"Keep him. We don't need him," called back the soldier.

Marius was outraged. His hands curled into tight fists. He hadn't known he could feel so angry.

"Well, that problem is solved," he muttered to David

"Master!"

Marius turned around again just in time to see Cantarcchio jerking the fur coat off the girl. He casually threw it around his own shoulders and kept walking, leaving her once again with just her tunic and trousers for protection against the chill. She glanced back. They were too far away to see her expression, but sensed her distress.

He thought quickly. There was the matter of his earlier order to Cantarcchio when he had 'reported for duty'. He could ask about that. He could even order the man to accompany them back to the garrison, overruling whatever order Bauto had given him, presuming he had reported to the optio.

He wondered what the Rhaetian soldier was doing so far up the valley. Unless he had a believable reason, the man was blatantly out of line. Marius, as his commanding officer, would insist on answers.

"What do you think, David?" asked Marius grimly.

"He's a liar and she's not his wife, or if she is, he's a traitor," replied David. "I think she's a Goth."

It was enough. Marius set off after them, leaving David standing there with Gideon.

"Soldier!"

Cantarcchio grasped the girl's arm and hurried her up the valley. They rounded the bend again, disappearing from his sight.

Marius began to run. He didn't want them to disappear up any mountain trail before he could reach them. His fury was fuelled by the casual cruelty the soldier had exhibited toward the girl and the dog, an affront to Marius, who had already risked his life to help them both.

He reached the bend in time to see a group of horsemen coming slowly down the valley in their direction. There must have been a dozen of them. They were led by a tall, young man on a large black horse. Marius drew back quickly, and peered around the corner.

A voice rang down the valley, its echo bouncing off the nearby cliffs. "Cantarcchio!"

The Rhaetian soldier ahead pushed the girl to the side of the road, pressing her toward the path they had just descended. She resisted, looking up the valley at the newcomers.

The lead horseman urged his horse into a trot, and rode directly for the couple. Cantarcchio shoved the girl ahead up the path. She grabbed hold of a tree branch and hung on. The horseman was almost upon them, his sword in his hand. At the last second, cornered, Cantarcchio drew out his own sword.

Marius watched in amazement as the dark-haired rider leaped from his horse and landed expertly on the ground. He closed in on the Rhaetian who hurried to step away from the mountain wall behind him. The two began to fight. Marius heard the girl scream, and saw her ease down from her perch and jump out of the way, shouting at the two men. The rest of the riders arrived and dismounted, forming a semi-circle around the two combatants.

Unable to see much anymore, Marius continued to stare down the road in frustration, aware of David's presence right behind him. The struggle lasted only moments more and then was over.

Cantarcchio's challenger had won. The circle of riders broke up and Marius could see the girl now sobbing in her rescuer's arms. The Rhaetian soldier lay inert on the ground, his sword some distance away. One of the riders collected it, while two others stripped him of his chain mail and his tool belt. One by one they remounted. The distraught girl was eventually calm enough to climb up behind her rescuer on his big horse. Then they all wheeled and headed back up the darkening valley.

Marius turned to David.

"Goths," he said. "You were right. We've got to get back to camp. They're already here."

"What about that man?" asked David, jerking his thumb backward towards the body of Cantarcchio.

"He's dead."

"Master, you don't know that."

Marius looked at the Hebrew slave with exasperation, and then shrugged. David could have no idea how many things had to be arranged in the next few hours. On the other hand, his own conscience would not give him much rest until he checked.

They hurried back to the body of the young soldier. Cantarcchio had not moved. Marius bent over him and checked him. Blood was seeping through the man's clothing, out from under his leather jerkin and onto the ground. There were stab wounds in several places, including one that had pierced right through his chain mail and the leather undercoat.

"Is he alive?" asked David.

"Yes," murmured Marius, his hand feeling for the pulse, "but maybe not for long."

"We'll take care of him now."

The voice was not David's. Marius stood up rapidly, reaching for his sword.

Three grim-looking men stood blocking them. All of them had their swords pointed directly at him, and they were all wearing heavy army cloaks with the hoods up. The only set of eyes he could see were the stern blue eyes of the man closest to him.

"Where did you come from? Damn you, David," he swore.

The men looked at each other.

The leader pointed up and across the valley.

"We see most things around here. We know this man. He's one of us. We'll get him to safety, and if his life can be saved, it'll be to our credit, not yours. You'd best get back to your camp, Tribune. You have no idea what's coming down on you. If I were you, I'd take my men and clear out of the area now. If you stay, you've probably less than a day to live."

CHAPTER TWENTY-SIX

COLLIDING DESTINIES

Pons Drusi/Bressanone area
Early November, 405 AD

High above the valley snow-laden clouds scudded fast, catching the last bright rays of the setting sun. Marius and David took turns carrying Gideon. He had become very quiet, but his body remained warm. His presence with them was a constant reminder of the girl they had encountered, and of the battle coming with her people.

"Do you think he'll live?" asked Marius.

"The soldier?"

"No. The dog."

"That fall he took was probably too much for the poor creature. He is a brave one, though. Hardly a whimper now."

Marius was not sure this was a good sign.

It grew dark, and the moon rose.

David had brought along some army biscuits, and they ate these as they walked, grabbing mouthfuls of water from the Isarco from time to time. Several times they startled animals that had come down to the river for a drink. With the bright moonlit sky and such unexpected encounters, the walk would have been enjoyable but for Marius's sense of urgency.

They tried to cling to the shadows at the base of the mountains. Futile as the attempt might be, it was instinctive to avoid being seen by spies higher up—Marius was certain that the men who had surprised them over the body of Cantarcchio were part of the local deserters; they had had the unmistakable bearing and authority of Roman soldiers. There were probably more of them patrolling the heights above.

Gothic spies, too, could well be up top, checking out the strength of the opposition now before their descent down the valley in force. All eyes would be focused on this one twisting narrow stretch of land. He was grateful that he was not wearing his uniform.

At length they were able to pick out familiar landmarks, and then they saw the first of the platforms the cohort had installed along the hillside. To Marius's surprise, no one hailed them. He was tempted to challenge the sentry on duty, but that would have to wait. They passed three more sentry posts and still no one challenged them. It was as though the two of them were invisible. Marius began to worry. At last, just before Thermopylae they were hailed by one of his men demanding that they identify themselves.

"Tribune Ausonius and his man, David," shouted Marius.

"Password?" shouted back the sentry.

Marius thought quickly. He had gone through Constantia and Paulus. It must be Julian's turn. "Julian," he shouted back.

The sentry stepped out from behind his barrier and with him several other men. One of them was Bauto. The other two were centurions from the Seventh Alpine Cohort. Marius hurried forward.

"What has happened?" he asked. "Where is everyone? I was not challenged once coming back here."

"We've received orders to pull back," replied Bauto. "The barbarians are gathering in the next valley up. There are apparently thousands of them there already. They'll be here by tomorrow at the latest. Legate Olybrius is waiting for you back at the camp. Sarus the Goth is with him. He and his men arrived this afternoon. General Stilicho sent him to assess the situation and support the fight."

He fell into step beside Marius. The two centurions walked a few paces behind, while David and the sentry followed in the rear.

"Marius," whispered Bauto, "I'm glad to see you alive. We were afraid you were dead. I need to warn you . . . Commander Sarus was not very pleased to hear you had gone hunting. I'm afraid you may be facing arrest for deserting your post."

Moonlight silvered the ribbon of the narrow, fast-moving river as Prince Roderic and his men cautiously picked their way back up the valley beside it. The bright light came and went as fleets of clouds moving high above them sped across the sky. Whenever the clouds covered the moon, the riders had to slow down to a careful walk.

The warriors were in a good mood. On the whole things had gone very well. They had found the traitor Cantarcchio and seen justice done to him, and they had a wonderfully romantic story to tell of their young prince's valor in defense of his beautiful maiden. Now that their mission was accomplished, the men were able to chat and joke. Their proud leader rode in front; the girl he had rescued was behind him on his noble steed, the moonlight glinting on her freshly washed hair. They were certainly a handsome pair!

Perched on the back of Roderic's horse with her arms around his waist, Theona began to relax. She was so tired that she could barely think, let alone hang on. Only the cold air kept her awake.

Roderic was here! He had come to her rescue, had fought for her. That was so far beyond any romantic dreams she had ever had that she didn't know what to do with it. Cantarcchio was dead. Her gallant Gideon was once again lost to her. The two men who had saved his life and been so kind to them both were Roman soldiers. Roman soldiers! The handsome younger one who had risked his life for Gideon was the commanding officer! It was too much for her tired mind to grasp.

Her body felt more sore and weary than it had done since the terrible journey through the pass. It was insisting that she sleep, but she had to fight against it. If she slept, she would surely fall off the horse, a fine way to respond after her heroic rescue. The Goths would never let her live it down. She smiled to herself and gave Roderic's waist a little squeeze. He turned his head in acknowledgement, and she caught a glimpse of his smile.

How brave he was! How caring and handsome! How amazing his timing!

But then in her mind's eye she saw the shock on Cantarcchio's face as Roderic's blade had pierced him, and the desperation in his eyes as this had happened again and again. The man had been killed right in front of her! It brought back memories of Gruda's violent death on the path near her village. It was not something she would forget soon, and at least for the moment, it confused her.

Sometime later they began to see homes with lamps lit within them, and men, her own kind, walking up and down the valley. Then the mountains pulled away, and they rode into the wide valley and on into the town she had glimpsed from the back of the old nag the evening before. They passed the place where the two rivers converged. There were lights now in many of the windows in the buildings. Roderic and his men clattered along the road beside the river coming from the east. A few minutes later they all trotted up the lane to a large house on a hillside. Lamplight was coming from its windows, too.

In the courtyard the other riders dismounted, and two youths came running from the house to take charge of their horses. Roderic and she stayed on his horse until two of his men came over. They helped her down and then Roderic tried to dismount. Theona saw a grimace on his face and a dark patch on his leather jacket. He stumbled, and the two men caught him.

She was horrified. He, too, had been wounded in the fight. He must have been in pain all the way back. She glanced down at her own tunic—it, too, had blood on it—his blood, from the time she had stood weeping in his arms.

The front door of the villa opened and someone familiar came out holding a lantern. In its flickering light she recognized Ptolemy. He was now wearing a rather tight leather jerkin with a yellow and green armband on his sleeve.

He came over to help Theona down while the other two men assisted Roderic into the house. Against her protests, he picked her up and carried her into the house and on down a hallway into a small, richly-furnished sitting room before gently setting her down on a divan with a padded seat and blue pillows.

"Are you alright?" asked Roderic anxiously from another couch. His face was drawn.

"Yes." She yawned. "I'm tired, hungry and sore, but apparently not as bad as you. I didn't realize you had been hurt! How bad is it?"

He sighed.

"My arm is beginning to throb. It probably didn't help that we had to ride so far, but it will heal. Ptolemy knows about injuries. He'll take care of it."

A group of men trudged by the doorway. With them were three women, all with painted faces and fancy hairdos. They glanced at Theona and Prince Roderic, and one of them waved. Theona had never seen anyone with so much facial paint on. To her they looked like crude dolls. She shuddered. She had read about women like them in the Bible. They passed out of sight.

"Whose house is this?" she asked.

"It belongs to a wine merchant. He wasn't at home to welcome us, so we just took it over when we got here. Unfortunately all of his slaves ran away. Still, we're grateful for his hospitality!" He grinned.

"And who is staying in the other homes around here? There was light coming from a lot more of the homes than the last time I passed through here."

"The elite warriors who came with my brother and me, as well as a few of the local people who stayed to take care of us."

She looked at him and he colored slightly.

"Our men have been coming down the valley all day. There are thousands here already. Tomorrow we move on in force against the Romans. They have set up a blockade down the valley."

"Do you know if my father is here?"

"None of the caravans has come through yet. Maybe by tomorrow night. The warriors will be gone by then, and the families can take over these houses."

Ptolemy entered the room with a bowl of vinegar and some bandages. Roderic struggled to remove his leather jacket and went white. Theona leaped up and went over to help him get it off. Underneath, his shirt was dark with blood. She helped Ptolemy peel it back.

There had been only one wound, but it had bled enough to weaken him. Cantarcchio's sword had caught him in an upswing and the upper part of his left arm had taken a sharp swipe. It was still bleeding. She was amazed he had not fallen off his horse. In spite of herself, she grinned.

"What's the joke?" he asked sourly.

"I was hanging on for dear life on the ride back here," she answered. "I was done in when you found me, but I didn't want to disgrace myself by falling off your horse. I see now I had company."

He smiled, his brown eyes warming.

"Lie down," she said. "We need to give your wound a chance to stop bleeding." She eased a cushion in behind his back, and propped another under his injured arm and turned to Ptolemy. "Do you have anything to stop the bleeding besides these bandages?"

Ptolemy shook his head.

"What about flour or eggs?"

The gladiator brightened, and raced from the room. Roderic, recumbent now, closed his eyes, his legs extending beyond the end of the couch. Theona shoved a pillow under his knees and covered him with a blanket, then began to clean away the blood with the vinegar. He hissed and shrank from the sharp sting.

Ptolemy was back shortly with the items she had requested. Theona gently dabbed some flour on the clean wound. When the bleeding had dried up, she once again dabbed at the area with the vinegar. The men watched as she separated the eggs into two bowls and carefully set aside the shells. She spread egg white over the wounds, and then, removing the delicate membranes from inside the shells, placed them inside the wound and held the edges of the cut together while Ptolemy wrapped the bandages around Roderic's arm.

The prince sighed, and reached for her hand. "Thank you."

"Would you rather eat, or sleep?"

"I'd rather talk to you while I can. Can we have some food in here?" he asked.

"Yes, my lord." The gladiator picked up his medical supplies and hurried from the room.

"Tell my men to keep me informed about anything that happens," called Roderic after him.

"What are you expecting?" asked Theona.

"There are other chieftains arriving with their people from the east. My brother and I have already met with some of their advance party. The main body should be starting to arrive sometime tomorrow. Vitiges has gone back up the valley to see my father, and I am in charge until they get here."

He changed the subject abruptly. "Tell me, Theona, did you go with Cantarcchio of your own accord?"

Briefly she told him about Cantarcchio's ploy, her journey with him down the valley, his strange grandmother, and her eventful day.

"Why did he take you?"

"His grandmother had told him to grab one of Radagaisus's children to hold as a hostage, but you were too big to take, and Anarilka was too far away, so he took me instead. He told Granny that it was a last minute decision when he knew we were under attack."

He looked at her speculatively.

"I believe he had persuaded himself you still had feelings for me," she said, blushing.

"And who were those two men who helped you with Gideon, Theona?"

"Cantarcchio told me that they were Roman soldiers."

He tried to sit up and winced. "Roman soldiers! And they have Gideon!"

"Cantarcchio gave them no choice, Roderic. They will take care of him, I'm sure. They were good men."

He brooded on that.

"You need to sleep."

"I will. I have a room down the hall. You'll stay to look after me of course?"

A wave of heat passed through Theona's body.

"Ptolemy can do that"

"Clearly not as well as you! That was very impressive. Who taught you?"

"My mother," she said softly. "I learned from her. We don't have much cloth in our village, but we do have chickens. My father also knew some things about healing."

Several of his men came in carrying dishes of hot food and set them on a low table. Ptolemy followed with a delicately carved chair for Theona to sit on, and placed it where she could serve Roderic. Groaning, the prince struggled into a reclining position on his couch.

"Apparently it's the custom here," he panted. "I've been told that husbands recline on couches while their wives sit on chairs. I suppose so they can fetch a slave or whatever is needed. I don't know if all Romans do it, but we might as well get used to it."

"We're not married."

"But you've just been bride-napped!" He grinned.

"Is that what that was? I'd rather sit on the chair anyway."

"And I believe I would rather lean back again. This is really uncomfortable!"

She served him some of the food and they ate, her eagerly, him with effort. When he had finished, he reached for her hand again and lay back against the cushions, his eyes closing.

"I've dreamed about you, you know. I don't understand how that bastard knew I would still care."

"He just took a chance, Roderic. He couldn't be sure."

"Well, this little adventure has helped me make up my mind. We're going to be married." He folded his arms and dared her to contradict him.

She giggled. He was weak, pale, wounded, worn out and tucked into a blanket. Altogether endearing.

"Roderic," she said, "I think you're quite wonderful. I am really tempted, but I need to get back to my father. He must be worried to death about me, and I need to look after him. He doesn't take very good care of himself."

"You're not going back to him, Theona," replied Roderic, frowning. "He cannot protect you the way I can. You're safer with me and my men."

"I have to go back. He's already grieving because he lost my mother and my little brother. I'm all the family he has left."

"Then I'll send my men to get him. He can come and join you here, with me."

"But that is a crazy idea. Your father would never let you marry me, and you know he hates my father! We are Christians and we would have to continue to live as Christians if you and I were married."

"No," he looked stubborn. "I'm afraid you will have to give that up."

"You see? My Lord is a part of me. It would be like severing my head from my body. And I have to tell you that God loves me even more than I love him."

Roderic got agitated.

"That's nonsense, Theona. No god is interested in the likes of us. They are all too busy living their own lives. The only way any of them even notice us is if we do something so spectacular they have to stop and watch. That's what my father wants to do—get their attention and earn the right to enter Valhalla when he dies. You may think your God cares about you and what you do, but he doesn't really. I do. Trust me."

"You cannot be there to protect me all the time, Roderic, but He can."

"He should have protected you and your village, then. Think about the terrible things that happened to you while your God stood by and watched."

She thought back, remembering the massacre, the horror on her mother's face, her beautiful and beloved Wolfric, a little child stolen by cruel heathens and delivered to who knew what fate. She remembered Turtik, and Darric's brother and sister, and Gruda, a new believer who had been killed for no reason at all. These momentous and horrifying events had changed her and her destiny forever. Why *had* God allowed them? Roderic was only asking what she herself had often wondered.

But there had been countless moments when she had felt God strengthening her, clarifying her thinking, warning her. She remembered how the Hun had turned away into the village when she was frozen with fear at the edge of the clearing. She remembered how, in spite of the difficulties of the trip, she and her father had been looked after, more or less, while they tended to the needs of the people around them. She remembered Gideon, and the miracle of his finding her, and of the two soldiers who had showed up when she needed help to rescue him. Were all those things to be put down to chance, human kindness and canine loyalty?

"Other people did those things, Roderic. I don't know why God allowed them to happen. I don't think He wanted them to—if we think those things were terrible, then He would too, because He made us in his image—the Bible says so. But when these things happen, it doesn't help to get angry at Him."

"Your God is weak," he said flatly.

"What would you have him do? Open the earth and swallow the killers, the thieves, the deceivers, the fratricides among us? Where would you draw the line? At boys who pull spiders apart, or girls who pull each other's hair?"

"I cannot admire a God who does not show courage, and protect his people. The old gods show us how to live as men should, how to be strong!"

"The old gods teach you to fight and kill to make wrongs right!"

"Yes," he said.

She could feel the heat rising in her cheeks. "The old gods do what it takes to win," she said, "by might or trickery. Most of the time they are selfish and self-seeking, like the people who invented them. Our way is a way of love, Roderic. God is pure love. He is the one who prompts us to get in there and make a difference in the darkness and to try to help other people who are suffering."

"And what about punishing the evil and rescuing damsels or children who are in trouble?"

"He has his own ways of punishing the guilty, but he doesn't always do it immediately."

He shook his head in disbelief. "Face it, Theona. He wasn't there when you needed him most, was he? I was. I would do it again. What good is love alone when men with evil hearts want to harm you? Where would you be if I had not shown up tonight?"

"Perhaps he sent you," she said.

"No-one sent me. I went after Cantarcchio because I cared about you. That's what love does!"

He lay back quietly for a few minutes with his eyes closed. She thought he was going to sleep, but then he looked at her again.

"Theona, I believe your God is no threat to me or the old gods. Your god is a woman's god. I will speak to my father. He will let you worship your woman's god as long as you also respect the gods of our ancestors."

She looked at him in frustration. They were at an impasse. She would not be able to persuade him, nor he her. She would have to find a way to leave.

"We've really got to get you to bed," she said. "I'll get Ptolemy to help you."

"Come here, first." He had a certain look in his eye that indicated that now that he had dealt with the issue between them to his own satisfaction, he would turn his attention to other things. "You have not thanked me for saving you from Cantarcchio."

She got up and knelt beside him, her face close to his, her eyes soft.

He was dear, and near, and kind to her, and caring, and so earnest and brave, and they were alone. She was far from sure she should let him embrace her, yet she really did care for him, and after what he had done for her . . .

"Thank you, she said looking at him. "I really am grateful."

"Are you?" he asked, his eyes twinkling.

"Very grateful," she whispered.

"Show me," he said.

She glanced at the doorway—no one had passed for several minutes. She rested her face against his and felt his kiss touch her cheek. He was trembling, and to her surprise, so was she. She sat up to smooth the lines on his face with her finger. He watched her, his eyes as vulnerable as a young child's. That undid any resolve she had had. She leaned in and kissed him. Roderic made a painful effort to enclose her in his arm. She nestled in as comfortably as she could, happier than she had been in months. Their kisses became eager, sensuous, and then dangerously thrilling, and she felt a longing for a closer connection to him. She had never been so intimate with anyone in her life, nor felt so conflicted.

She withdrew as carefully as she could and went to find Ptolemy.

The gladiator had been waiting. He helped Roderic to his feet, and between the two of them they supported him down to his sleeping quarters and onto his bed. Roderic protested when she started to leave.

"Hush," she said. "I'll be right next door if you need more medical attention than Ptolemy can give you."

She smiled demurely, and Roderic grinned.

"I'll be needing lots of it. I'll make sure of it."

Ptolemy settled into the brocaded settee and pulled up a blanket.

The cubicle next door was occupied by one of the painted ladies she had seen earlier, energetically entertaining one of the Goths. Theona ordered them out, and sent the man for fresh bedding. After it arrived, she crawled onto the bed herself. She didn't move until morning.

When Marius and his escort arrived back at the Pons Drusi camp, they found it a busy place. Piles of weapons and supplies were being loaded onto the wagons. Members of the Seventh Alpine Cohort were dismantling the two carroballistas while some of his own men waited to load the pieces onto the wagons. It seemed they were going to make sure their enemies would not be able to use them.

In spite of the late hour, many of his soldiers were sitting around the campfires. They were probably waiting to see what was going to happen to their disgraced tribune, thought Marius.

They waved at him, and many came over to express their relief that he was safely back. From their faces he could tell that they were still worried.

He spotted Legate Olybrius crossing one of the paths between the barracks tents with another man, a big blond stranger with a prominent jaw and high cheekbones. He was wearing a quality crimson cloak, and presumably was Sarus, the leader of the Emperor's Gothic auxiliary troops.

Marius hurried towards them. They stopped when they saw him and waited. Bauto and the Seventh Alpine centurions who had escorted him back from Thermopylae stood at a distance, watching for further instructions. David slipped away toward Marius's tent with the dog still hidden inside his cloak.

"Tribune Ausonius," said Legate Olybrius acidly, glancing at Marius's old clothing. "It is good of you to join us at last. Did you come on your own, or were you apprehended somewhere?"

"My apologies, sir. I was not expecting you or any trouble today, or I would never have left. I trust that you and Commander Sarus have been well looked after by my men in my absence?"

Olybrius was not to be diverted. "Tribune Ausonius," he said, "Everyone here has been very worried about you. You have been gone for hours, and the Goths and their allies have been pouring into the next valley above us. When you did not return . . ."

"Yes, sir," interrupted Marius. "I've seen some of them, a party of a dozen riders about nine miles up the valley from here. We also met some of the missing local soldiers in the same place. My man and I hurried back as quickly as we could."

The two senior officers glanced at each other and then at him. Marius resisted the impulse to wring his hands and apologize. He set his jaw, straightened his back and waited.

"Perhaps we had better hear what the young man has to say," murmured Olybrius. The other man nodded once.

"Tribune Ausonius, Commander Sarus and his men were sent by General Stilicho to help us with the situation here. He was very angry when you were not here to greet him. As was I," he added. "And surprised and disappointed."

"Your men believed that you would not be here until tomorrow night, sir," said Marius defensively, "and I had no idea that anyone from High Command was still expected, or I would never have left."

"With the invaders so close to here, you should never have left anyway," said the Goth loudly in his thick Germanic accent.

"No sir. You are right, but we have had reports from several sources today that the enemy was at least a day or two away. Even the Legate's men thought so. I did not leave until late afternoon, as I'm sure my optio told you, and I did not intend to be long when I left."

They both glanced at Bauto who was standing watching from a distance.

"Tell us about these Goths you saw. Who were they?" asked Sarus.

"There were about a dozen of them, Commander, and they were all on horseback heading this way."

"You were on foot. How did you get here before them?"

"They seemed to be after a local man named Cantarcchio, who I believe, was in league with them. He seemed to know them, and they recognized him. They fought and almost killed him, and then they left again."

"I recognize that name, Sarus" said Olybrius to the other man. "There are several from that family around this area. One of them was the head of the local garrison, I believe."

"Not this one, sir," said Marius. "This Cantarcchio said he had been away for a long while. I believe he was with Radagaisus during that time."

"And what was he doing when you saw him?"

Marius hesitated. "He was taking away the girl I was with."

It sounded so foolish that he reddened in the dark.

Both officers were not amused.

"Tribune, you had better have a good explanation for that remark," replied Olybrius. "If you are not totally honest with me, I will whip your aristocratic hide myself. Spit out your story, all of it."

"Well, sirs, as you may remember, you mentioned once that we should try hunting for some chamois . . ."

He told his story, all of it. There was still no sign of a softening in their expressions. He got to the place where he had gone chasing back after the girl and her alleged "husband", and then described the violent encounter between the leader of the Gothic rescue party and Cantarcchio.

"And then what happened?"

"Then she got onto the back of the leader's big black horse and they turned and went back up the valley the other way."

There was a thoughtful silence. Finally Olybrius spoke: "Did you say the leader was riding a black horse?"

"Yes sir."

"Were there any markings on it?"

"Yes sir. There was a small white star on its forehead. The leader was a tall young man with a green and yellow scarf around his neck and longish brown hair. I couldn't see more than that from where we stood."

They exchanged glances.

"And why do you suppose these men turned back? Why didn't they keep coming this way?"

"It was clear to me that this was a rescue mission, sirs. As soon as they had the girl, they turned around and went back up the valley. I saw the leader and the girl embracing before they left."

"Who was she?"

"I've no idea, sir."

"Tell us about her. She may be important."

"Why, sir?"

Both men were silent. He was still clearly in trouble.

"She was very pretty," he began. "She had long golden hair," (he paused, remembering the section where the girl's hair was curiously short), "and beautiful grey-blue eyes, a pretty nose, some freckles on her cheeks, and," he fingered a spot on his neck thoughtfully, "a dark spot here. She was probably about sixteen or seventeen and she wore long brown trousers and a tunic with a rope belt, as they do. My man and I did wonder if she was a barbarian. She spoke a language we didn't recognize."

He looked up, and caught the two men smiling at each other.

"Were you so close to the riders that you could hear them talking?" demanded Commander Sarus. "I thought you said you were down the valley around a bend."

"No sir. I was too far away then. I meant when she was talking to the dog."

"Anything else?"

Marius thought. He suddenly remembered the embroidery on the girl's neckline.

"She had a little white cross embroidered on her tunic," he said. "I wondered at the time if she was a Christian."

The two of them looked at him in disbelief. Radagaisus was known to be fiercely anti-Christian. The legate pulled at his chin, his black eyes speculative.

"As you may have been told, we're pulling out of here in the morning, Tribune. After what your optio and I have told him, Commander Sarus has decided that staying here would be a suicide mission. We don't think even Radagaisus knows that there are thousands more people coming towards him from the east. We have decided that it is better to fight another day when we have a full army on our side. From what we have seen and heard, you were doing very well up to this point, but leaving your command was a big mistake. We will take over from here on."

"Yes, sir," said Marius dispiritedly.

"Fetch the dog to me," ordered General Sarus. "Bring him to my tent."

Dejected, Marius went to find Gideon. David had started preparing their dinner at their campfire. Gideon was lying quietly nearby, awake and watching.

"One more journey for you, little fellow," said Marius, stroking him. "And then you can rest. I'm afraid you're stuck with all of us for the moment."

He turned to David, "I'm to take him to Commander Sarus's tent. Did you feed him?"

"Yes, Master Marius. One of the men who knows about animals checked him over. He has some broken ribs. Some cuts, too. He'll have painful bruises but we can't be sure what he's like on the softer parts inside. Still, he ate a bit."

It was the only good news Marius had heard all day.

Sarus's men had erected a large leather tent within the garrison walls. His men had built their own campsite nearby, as had the men from the Seventh Alpine Cohort.

When Marius reached the big Goth's tent with Gideon in his arms, he found the man sprawled on a rug, tearing into a chicken leg. He had taken off his helmet and cuirass, and even his boots, a sight that startled Marius. Olybrius was seated on a folding chair, holding a goblet of beer.

Sarus signaled to a slave to bring him a drink as well, and told Marius to show him the dog. Marius laid Gideon gently down on the rug. Sarus leaned forward to look at him, his brow furrowing.

"Do you know his name?"

"The girl called him Gideon, sir," said Marius.

"That suggests that your guess that she is a Christian might be true," said Sarus. "That's a name from the Bible, is it not?"

"I believe so, sir."

The big man got down on his elbows and knees and inched close to the little dog's face, dangling the chicken leg near his mouth. The legate got up and squatted nearby to watch.

Gideon raised his head and sniffed. Sarus moved the meat slightly away and said something in Gothic. Marius watched in amazement as Gideon tried to struggle to his feet. He yelped, and collapsed again. The General said something else to him, and the dog weakly wagged his tail. Satisfied, Sarus held the chicken leg close enough to Gideon's mouth so that he could begin to tear off little bits and chew them.

There was a long silence that Marius dared not break.

Finally the Goth looked at him. "I think we'll just keep the dog around for a while. If he can lead us to his mistress, and if she is important to Prince Roderic—oh yes, he's the one on the big black horse, and he is Radagaisus's youngest son, then your little excursion today may well turn out to have been a lucky break."

He stood up, went over to one of several satchels, and pulled out a document.

"I have new orders for you, Tribune. Someone at headquarters wants you back there. You are being reassigned as a lowly clerk for a while. It seems you have friends in high places. I have almost decided not to mention this incident in my report on you, but do not think that I will forget this, Marius Ausonius, and if you do anything else that shows such poor judgment, I will have to expose this incident to the rest of the High Command. Is that understood?"

"Yes sir. Shall I keep the dog, sir?"

"By all means, but keep him safe. He may yet live to serve the Empire."

CHAPTER TWENTY-SEVEN

RADAGAISUS'S THREAT

~

Brixon/Bressanone, Italy
Early November, 405 AD

Theona woke to the sound of voices and heavy boots coming down the corridor. They passed her cubicle and someone thumped on the door next to hers, demanding the prince open it at once. She did not recognize the voice and jumped out of bed, anxious to protect Roderic from bullying while he was still so weak. She hurried across to the water basin, drank deeply from it, and washed up. As soon as she was ready, she rushed out into the corridor.

It was full of men wearing yellow and green armbands. No one commented when they saw her, but she received a few scandalized looks. Whatever they might think of Roman women, they would not appreciate seeing one of their own in a compromised position.

She heard voices coming from Roderic's room. There was an argument going on in there, and Roderic sounded defensive. Theona wondered what to do. She hovered in her doorway listening with the others and trying to make up her mind when the door precipitously opened, and Prince Vitiges stalked out, followed by three Gothic chieftains.

Roderic's brother's irate glance grazed her disdainfully as he passed. Roderic came hurrying after them. His shirt and trousers were on and he was struggling awkwardly to pull his neck scarf over his head. He held his jacket in his other hand. He grimaced when he saw her and tossed the jacket to her.

"Keep this for me, will you love? I don't have time to wrestle with it right now."

"What's going on?" she asked as he continued down the corridor.

"My father and brother just got here and it seems a delegation from our local Roman allies arrived at the same time. They are demanding justice for what I did to Cantarcchio, and my dear father and brother are determined that I give it."

"But you're injured!" she protested.

He shrugged, and disappeared after his brother and the chieftains. The other men all followed, leaving Theona staring after them.

Not knowing what else to do, she went back into her room and shut the door. The room was chilly. She sat shivering on the edge of the narrow bed wishing she had someone to talk to. Now even Gideon was no longer there to comfort her. There was only God. She pulled a blanket up over her shoulders, and closed her eyes, pressing in to that familiar, loving Presence.

"Lord, I need you," she whispered. "You've said in your Word that all things work together for good to the people who love you and are obedient to you. I have been holding on to that. I feel so alone and useless that I don't even know what to think or how to feel right now, and I have no idea what to do. I have no idea why you have allowed all this to happen to me! I don't belong in this place. I never wanted to leave home, or come on this journey. I don't know where I am going, and now I'm here in the middle of a dung heap.

"I'm worried about Roderic and myself. I miss my father! I miss all of them! Help me! I don't know which way to turn."

Tears welled up. "Couldn't you at least have let me keep Gideon?"

She was beginning to descend into self-pity, something she knew would get her in real trouble, so she got up and began to pace back and forth in the tiny space, trying to banish the disconsolate thoughts that kept coming.

"Dear Lord, I am your daughter. Help me to behave like one. I am going to continue to trust you, and I am going to choose to believe that all things will indeed work together for good for me. Help me to hear your voice, and please look after my father, and Gideon, and Roderic, and Darric and Duke Helerix, and our people, and those two men who helped me. You are the Redeemer. Redeem this awful mess."

She sat down on the bed again, and began to wait for her Lord to clothe her with his strength and love. It began with the sensation of a light touch on her head, and then her inner being began to fill up with a sweet and blissful energy. The experience was no surprise—she had felt God's Presence many times, and she knew that this strengthening, although it was always a mystery, would make the hard times coming much easier. It was God's way of telling her that even though she might seem alone and in a situation fraught with danger and complicated choices, God was there to help. She was not alone. She would never be alone. The blissful infilling lasted for several minutes and at last slowly lifted, leaving her peaceful and confident.

Theona yawned and stretched. It was time to get moving. She might as well get Roderic's jacket to him, wherever he was.

As she opened the door again, Ptolemy was coming out of Roderic's room carrying a bowl and some used bandages. He looked at the leather jacket over her arm in surprise.

"Where is Prince Roderic?" she asked. "He threw this at me."

He led her through the villa to a different part of the house. They passed a large room full of men. More were coming all the time.

Roderic was probably in there, too. She paused, uncertain.

Ptolemy gripped her arm. "Come," he said. "This way."

He led her past the big room and they entered a short hallway. It was a narrow serving area for the big room they had passed. Ptolemy began to put away the supplies he had been carrying. She noticed platters of food on a table and eyed them hungrily.

"Eat," he said, noting her interest. While she ate, he began to fill a leather pouch with additional food, and when she had finished eating, he pressed this into her hands.

"Take. For you."

She looked at him in surprise.

"Everyone is leaving here soon," he said. "You need food."

She was touched by his kindness, and smiled at him. "You are a good man, Ptolemy," she said.

To her surprise, his eyes welled up with tears. He turned away abruptly and rubbed a fist across his eyes.

When he had control of himself, he turned back to her. Slowly, his eyes on her face, he pulled up his tunic and began turning around. Almost every inch of his body was pierced, slashed or punctured. She looked at him in shock.

"Romans," he said. He pointed to himself. "Roman slave. I kill other fighters like me. Also slaves. Some were friends. I had no choice."

A dreary smile touched his eyes and he pointed to himself. "I have choices now. I kill *Romans* instead of slaves."

She reached out and laid her hand on his arm.

"There are other ways to live, Ptolemy. You don't have to kill or die."

He looked at her with disappointment. "Not for me. Stay here."

The last had been an instruction. He left the serving hall and went out, carrying two of the platters of food. Theona waited, unsure what to do next. She still had Roderic's jacket.

A little farther along the wall there was a door which opened into the larger room. She eased it open a crack. A man was speaking. She bent her head to the crack to listen.

A voice was speaking Latin. A second voice, one she recognized as that of Tribune Bulleus, followed it, translating the speech into Gothic. He now seemed totally fluent with her language.

"Your majesty," the speaker was saying, "We sent our representatives to you in the belief that you were a man who kept his word. Tribune Bulleus and his men have brought you safely this far, and given you good service along the way. We have kept our side of the treaty thus far, haven't we?"

Theona eased the door open a bit further and caught a glimpse of Radagaisus nodding his head. He was seated on his throne with the three Gothic chiefs she had seen come out of Roderic's room. Phaedrus and Vitiges stood behind the four thrones watching.

In front of Radagaisus and to his right stood a group of men, some wearing the uniforms of Roman soldiers, some wearing the rough clothing of local farmers. Their representative was a tall wiry man with flat grey hair, a sun-burned face and bright blue eyes. Roderic and the men he had ridden with the night before stood facing this group. The rest of the room was filled with warriors, with more trying to squeeze into the room every minute.

Theona had barely sized up the situation, a mini Council it seemed, before Ptolemy, scowling at her from the other side of the door, gently pulled it almost shut. She could no longer see or be seen, but he clearly meant for her to listen to the proceedings.

Radagaisus was responding to the leader of the local delegation: "Tribune Bulleus has been of great service to us along this journey, and to our knowledge the terms we agreed on have been honored. My people have done their best to cooperate with your people. We have tried to keep faith with you. We have protected the areas you asked us to spare. I cannot answer for the ones not under my own direct control."

Theona heard rumblings of assent all over the room.

"Then why did your own son attack the guide who came from this very area? Has the King decided it is no longer worth his while to honor the treaty? Are you not a man of your word?"

Bulleus translated, and there was an indignant eruption from the crowd. Radagaisus raised his hand warningly.

"I am indeed a man of my word," he said gravely. "I have no personal knowledge of the incident you describe. As you well know, my older son and I just arrived here a short while ago."

"Your Majesty," the level voice was Bulleus's, "Prince Roderic is here. He can tell us himself what happened between him and my optio."

The crowd of men pounded their shields and there were earnest nods from many of Roderic's own men. When the noise died down, Roderic's voice rang out.

"Tribune Bulleus, You know me, and I have great respect for you. My attack on your optio was in response to his desertion at the very moment of the attack by the Roman Army farther up the valley. He deserted the people you had assigned to him, and when the lords of the caravans tried to find him, they learned that he had tricked my future bride into leaving with him in order to hold her as a hostage for his own personal protection."

There were exclamations and more stamping of feet from the audience.

Bulleus quickly translated this for the benefit of the Rhaetian visitors. Theona heard murmurs of surprise and tense whispers among them.

"I was not aware that you were betrothed, Roderic," said Radagaisus coldly.

The room grew quiet.

"I have had this girl in mind for months, Father, and the feelings I had for her would not go away. However, my men and I hunted down the guide not only because he had taken Theona, but because he had to be punished for his treachery and desertion. When we found him down the valley, he had Theona with him and was forcing her up the mountain. We fought, and he lost and we brought her back."

"Theona. What kind of name is that? Is this, perchance, the daughter of that Christian meddler, the girl who went to the defense of her crazy father at the Grand Council?"

Theona could not hear Roderic's answer.

"And she ran off with one of the Roman guides?"

"She did not run off with him." Roderic's voice had an edge to it. "She left because Cantarcchio claimed her father had given him instructions to get her to safety if there was an attack."

"And you know for a fact that this is true?"

"So she says, sir, but her father has denied ever giving the guide such an order."

"And for that reason you tried to kill this man who has been trying to help us?"

"It was necessary, Your Majesty. He was about to escape, and he had proven he was a traitor by his behavior. Theona says he had first planned to seize Anarilka, but when he could not get to Rilka, he seized her instead. He got the death traitors deserve."

"Theona says . . . Where is this girl now, Roderic?"

"She is here, father. It is she who nursed me last night after my own injury." He tried to hold up his arm and winced.

"Fetch her to us," said the king to some of his guards. "Let's see what my son's Christian bride-to-be has to say about all this, and since we cannot be sure she will be telling the truth of her own accord, we shall use a little persuasion on her to make sure."

"No!" shouted Roderic.

Torture! Theona did not wait to hear more. She grabbed Roderic's jacket and the pouch of food Ptolemy had prepared for her and ran down the corridor away from the big room. She turned the first corner she came to and ran into a stream of warriors that were pushing their way into the house from a side entrance. Their topknots identified them as Suevis. After the first few pushed past her, there was a short gap, but then she met more and more of them. Trapped, she squeezed into an alcove and waited for them all to pass. Among them she recognized two of the chieftains she had last seen at the Grand Council. These men must have just arrived in town from the river route to the east.

It was a diversion King Radagaisus would need to attend to immediately, and Theona was not going to hang around waiting for his men to find her. She pulled Roderic's jacket on, pushed her hair underneath it and headed out the side exit.

From where she stood on the hilltop, she could see a long procession of wagons snaking into the town. At its head rode hundreds of Suevi warriors, just in time to join the Goths for the big push down the Isarco Valley towards Pons Drusi. While she hesitated wondering what to do, she saw a home on the opposite hillside go up in flames. Soon after, two others nearer the road were set on fire amid loud cheers from the mob entering the town. More and more flames erupted as this new crowd, their wagons already chock full of stolen treasure, vented their excitement on the homes and shops and churches of the area.

So much for the deal the Rhaetian deserters had made with the Grand Council on the Danube, she thought. The treaty was broken beyond repair.

She headed down the hill to join the newcomers. She needed to blend in with them for a short time. She knew now where she was going to go, and what she was going to do.

Ptolemy arrived at the door just in time to see her disappear down the hill and into the crowd.

During the next hours caravans continued to push into the town and the streets filled up with wagons. Anarchy reigned. Homes were plundered and burned; unlucky citizens found hiding were murdered. Even the hillsides and country roads began to attract the attention of the men, women, boys and girls looking for treasure, food, excitement and trouble.

It took hours for the situation to stabilize and the barbarian leaders to agree on their plan of action. By the early afternoon, however, they were ready.

With King Radagaisus and his two sons in the lead, thousands of Goth, Suevi and Vandal warriors swept down the valley towards Pons Drusi. Energized by the thought of battle and glory, they reached Thermopylae and found it abandoned. Excitedly, they explored the area, laughing at the futile preparations left behind by the Mosella Cohort. Not much was left of the preparations for the ambush, just piles of rocks and a few hillside platforms. A short time later they erupted into Pons Drusi. It, too, was deserted.

The Roman troops who had been sent to the area were gone, leaving no protection for the people of the region or their homes and monuments. Farmers and shopkeepers who had not already left now fled for their ancient hideouts in the hills. Even the Pons Drusi farmer-soldiers were not there to welcome them—their representatives had all been killed at the big house up the valley. The rest had gone into hiding.

Not one of the Roman guides who had been assigned to the Suevi caravans had survived the journey, and the outraged fury of Bulleus and the local Rhaetian garrison had brought bloodshed on their own heads.

Nothing now stood in the way of the invaders. The King of the Goths and his allies stormed down the valley toward Trento and Verona. The door was now wide open to the rich cities and countryside of the heartland of the Western Roman Empire.

CHAPTER TWENTY-EIGHT

A SURPRISING DECISION

Isarco Valley, Italy
Early November, 405 AD

Theona walked along with the crowds of migrants streaming along the road from the east toward the center of the town. The main streets were already clogged with wagons that had tried to thrust their way through the unfamiliar intersections of rivers and roads. Looters were abandoning their wagons to race towards apartment buildings and homes looking for new treasures to steal and places to stay. A few of them headed straight up the hillsides to get at the larger, richer villas there. Some of these were already on fire. All around her, people were shouting directions, insults and information at one another.

She reached the area where the two rivers converged and became one, and turned south. This was now familiar ground. She found a place to sit where she could watch the caravans passing her and scanned the crowd for familiar faces. She saw no one she recognized. Surely the Wodenvale caravans must be close by now—they had had two days to make it this far and it had taken her only one. Then she remembered Enoch and the other slain beasts of burden, and the battle she had walked through. She had no idea how bad things had been in her laager. It might be a while yet before her people got here. She would have to wait in the area for them for as long as it took.

She began to walk again, joining other people who were continuing south along the road. All around her, crowds of men, women and children chatted to each other in their native tongues, most of which she was able to follow. A few of the younger ones tried to engage her in conversation, but she shook her head. Theona did not want to chat with anyone. She was on a mission.

Eventually they reached the lane leading to the farm where Cantarcchio had left the old horse. Smoke billowed from up there—the farmhouse was on fire. Only this morning, it had been someone's home.

She heard horses coming up behind her, and moved with the rest of the pedestrians over to the side of the road to get out of the way. The Gothic warriors were coming through, on their way down the valley to clear the Romans out of the way.

Roderic, his father and his brother rode in the lead. The younger prince's injured arm was supported by a sling, and he was looking straight ahead, his pale face grim, oblivious to her presence a few feet away. The three of them were followed by a long line of mounted warriors. Running along behind them came thousands of infantry. Once they were all past the excited crowd surged after them, eager to be among the first to exploit the new area the warriors would be opening up farther down the valley. Theona hurried along with them.

A short time later she spotted the path she had climbed with Cantarcchio. She slowed her steps and eased toward the side of the road, and then casually began to climb the path. Those watching would assume she had to relieve herself and would rejoin them later. She kept climbing until she reached a bend and had moved out of sight.

Ptolemy, who had been following her, waited at the bottom of the hill for some time. When she did not come back, he too climbed the path. There was no sign of the girl. He began calling her name. There was no answer. Frustrated, and with no training in tracking except what he had picked up from the Goths, he had no choice but to follow the trail higher and guess which intervening paths Theona might have taken. He meant her no harm, but he did intend to keep an eye on her for the sake of his young master.

At the top of the mountain, Theona crossed the barren field, glancing to her left and right. There was no one in sight.

She wondered if she was being foolish, coming to the rescue of the old woman when perhaps no rescuing was needed. Nevertheless, it could still be a day or two before the Wodenvale caravan reached the area, so she might as well do what she could to protect the lonely homestead against the kind of conflagration she had seen back in the town. She went down the road beside the hill to take a look at it. The peaceful dell and the smoke curling idly from the house mocked her concern, but she still felt uneasy.

Theona wondered if Cantarcchio was inside. She had seen him badly wounded and thought he was dead, but the comments she had heard at the mini council had seemed to indicate that he was still alive. If so, then surely the men who had rescued him would not have carried him up here! But if they hadn't, then he would be somewhere down in the valley, and every home there was in danger from the destructive crowds. He might yet die.

In any case Granny had probably lost him, and her future without her grandson would be difficult. Her business would be affected by this invasion. If she lost her house, too . . . Theona did not like her, but she did not want that for her either.

There could be no harm in keeping watch from the top of the little hill. It had a good view in all directions, and with any luck she need not encounter Granny at all. She climbed to the top and sat down, opening the pouch of food that Ptolemy had thoughtfully prepared for her. She gave thanks for it and for him and began to eat. Far off, a bank of clouds was moving slowly in from the north, but where she sat, it was clear and windless, and the sun still had enough warmth in it to keep her comfortable while she waited. The fur coat was gone; she had left it behind at the site of the battle between Cantarcchio and Roderic—in truth, all thought of it had gone right out of her head when she left with Roderic and his men, but the prince's leather jacket gave her some protection from the cold.

She wondered how Roderic was doing. It seemed cruel to her that he had had to get right back onto his horse again and leave with his father. She desperately hoped that he would not have to fight the Romans. For a few moments she dwelt on the tender moments they had spent together at the wine merchant's house. From a romantic perspective, yesterday had been spectacular, but exhausting and stressful. All thought of marriage to her must have been driven straight out of his mind when he saw for himself Radagaisus's implacable anger towards her. He was learning quickly the stigma she carried as a Christian.

She was not the naïve girl whom Cantarcchio had tricked into leaving with him three days before. That girl had since experienced deception and dislocation, loyalty and loss, conflict and kindness, rescue and romance. She could not begin to understand the lessons she was learning, let alone steer a straight path through them. What was coming next?

A part of her felt glad to be alone again with no pressure from Roderic, Granny, Cantarcchio or anyone else. It was almost a relief to have some freedom of choice. For the last few days she had felt like a sprat in a cataract.

She heard voices coming from across the field. More people were coming up the path she had climbed. Quickly she hid herself, and peered over the top of the hill.

The first people to emerge were two men with top knots. One of them was wearing war paint and both carried battle axes. Seeing the farmer's field, they yelled to the people behind and began running across it. More than a dozen men and women followed clutching their own weapons and large, empty sacks.

Once they reached the hill, they would likely head downhill along the road, and would quickly discover Granny's home in the dell. Theona scrambled down the hill and raced for the house.

She burst into the main room, startling the old woman who was sitting at the table stitching at a wig.

"I need something green and yellow," Theona yelled.

Granny leaped to her feet.

"You! What are you doing here? I told you to get out! Where's that filthy animal of yours?" The old woman marched, fists clenched, for her broom.

"Never mind that! I need something green and yellow NOW, or they'll burn your house down."

"Who will? Don't you dare touch my house!"

"Give it to her, Granny," came a dozy voice.

"What?" Both of them turned to stare in surprise. The door to one of the bedrooms was open. It looked as though Theona had guessed wrong. Cantarcchio was indeed there. Pale, and covered with bandages and blankets, he lay stretched out on his bed.

"Those are Radagaisus's colors," he whispered. "It's a good idea. Wait. . . I have one of his armbands. Give her that."

"You idiot! I'm blind!" shrieked the old lady. "How am I supposed to do that?"

She was suddenly still. "Someone's coming, Sev."

Theona could not hear anything, but she had no doubt that Granny was right. She rushed over to the soldier's bedroom, taking in his pallor and the wrappings with a glance. She must find out where Granny kept her vinegar, eggs and flour. Whoever had done the job the first time might not be able to make it back up the mountain.

"Cantarcchio," she said. "Where is the armband?"

"In the trunk," he said. "In the corner."

They could all now hear noises coming from outside. The raiders had seen the house and were gleefully closing in. Theona pushed the lid of the trunk up, and began to rummage through it, tossing the items onto the floor. The little room was dark—she could barely see what was what, let alone tell what color it was.

"It's in there somewhere," the tired voice advised.

The instant he said it she saw it, lying twisted and dull among the items she had tossed out. She grabbed the armband and ran back through the front room, slipping it onto the sleeve of Roderic's jacket which she was still wearing. She flew out of the front door just as the first of the Suevi men reached it, his axe raised.

"This home is Gothic," she shouted, pointing at her armband, "and I am Gothic and Vandal. There are injured people inside. Go away."

The man lowered his axe, but looked defiant.

"It could be true," said one of the women. "Look at her clothes."

"I heard that there were Goths here already," muttered another woman.

"It is true," shouted Theona. "We are under the protection of Prince Roderic."

"What did she say? What's she saying?" The others were all arriving.

"She says that Prince Roderic is protecting the people here."

"Where is the prince, then?" asked the second man suspiciously.

"Ahead. Down the valley. Fighting against the Romans."

"That's true," said the first man. "How else could she know that if she wasn't telling the truth?"

They looked at one another and were silent.

"Are there other Goths staying in the houses up here?" asked one woman hopefully.

"Yes, many others. You never know who is now living in these homes. The Goths got here before your people."

"We didn't know. We just got to the area this morning," the woman replied.

"Then go in peace," said Theona. "And do what is right."

The woman nodded and turned away. The others slowly followed. One turned and waved back at her from the road.

Theona followed them back as far as the hillock and climbed it again. The remains of her meal had attracted ants. She brushed them off and began eating again. There would be more raids coming, she was sure of it, but the king's armband, her clothing and her knowledge of their languages were weapons she would use to defend Granny and protect Cantarcchio, little though they deserved it.

All day long Theona stood guard over the house. Half a dozen other groups, some small, some large, climbed the mountain or came down the field from the north. All of them were deterred by her from plundering and burning the little home. Most of them went back down the path to the valley.

At last the night came. Still she waited while the stars came out and the frost began to settle onto the ground. Even through Roderic's jacket, she could feel the cold. After an hour with no sounds but distant ones, it seemed safe to assume that she could relax her vigilance.

She wondered what to do. Would she be welcome back at the house? Would they feed her and let her sleep there out of gratitude for her efforts? Or would the two of them attack her in her sleep, cut off her hair, and trade her for safety to their enemy?

She had to admit that she did not know. Either reaction was equally possible with those two. She should just go quietly back down to the valley and find shelter with some kind family in one of the caravans, if any of them were still in the area.

She sat there a while longer, hoping for some kind of a sign. The moon came up high enough to throw a silver sheen over the landscape, throwing into relief the dark shape of someone new coming across the field. He was alone and heading directly for her hill. Whoever he was, she needed time to decide whether he was friend or foe. She began to creep backward down the far side of the hill.

"Theona!"

Chagrinned, she realized that her hair in the moonlight had made her a clear, bright focus. She was sitting on the top of the hill like a bee on a flower.

But whoever was coming knew her name. She waited nervously as the dark figure drew closer. At last she was able to recognize Ptolemy. With a cry of joy she stood up and waved. He waved back, stumbling over a root that stuck up from the field. Theona hurried down the hill to meet him, the pouch he had given her slung over one shoulder.

"Ptolemy," she said, "What are you doing here?"

He shook his head wearily. "Food?" He pointed to the bag

Theona handed it to him, relieved that there was still some food left.

He reached eagerly into the pouch, pulling up everything he could find and eating it quickly.

"I can't go back with you," she said.

He shook his head again. "I stay with you."

She brightened. "It's only for a few days. Once my father comes, I'll join him."

"Where we stay?"

"Here," she grinned. "There's a little house around the corner. You remember our Roman guide, Cantarcchio, don't you?"

He stiffened and glowered. "Him! Your lover?"

She was shocked. "Oh, no! What a dreadful idea! He's a fox, Ptolemy, not a good man. But he has a grandmother. We're here to help, you and me both."

His reluctance was nothing like that of the two residing inside the house. When Theona knocked on the door, Granny opened it belligerently.

"Are you still here? What do you want?"

"We need supper and a place to sleep."

"Aren't you the presumptuous one? So, you have the dog with you after all."

"No, I have a friend."

"And who might that be? Your prince?" she sneered.

"My prince is with his father, King Radagaisus, fighting the Romans farther down the valley."

"Go away. You've done your good deed for the day. Go back to your barbarous friends. Let them feed you."

"Granny . . ."

"Don't call me that. You can't call me that. Only Sev."

"What shall I call you then?"

"Nothing. Go away. I'm not letting you in."

"You don't have to let us in. Just give us two of the straw pallets from up in your loft and the key to the shed, and supper. You owe me that."

"And then will you go away?"

"I am staying here with my friend for a couple of days. You need me to check on your grand-son—I have some experience with wounds, and I can change his bandages."

"Oh, Sev will love that," she jeered.

"And also, I chased away quite a few groups of Suevi and Vandals from your house today. There are many, many more coming down the valley. If I left you, who would protect your home? Can Severus?"

"Sev's friends can protect us. I'll send for them."

"Tribune Bulleus and the local soldiers all dead." Ptolemy's deep voice cut into the conversation from behind Theona. Granny hastily slammed the door shut in their faces.

Theona pushed it open before the old woman could bar it.

"Go away," quavered the old lady. "Please, go away."

"Granny, we need supper and a place to sleep."

The old woman started to cry. "Who was that with you?"

"His name is Ptolemy. He serves Prince Roderic. He was a gladiator in Savaria."

"Really?" There was a thoughtful pause. "Come in, then."

It was some time before they were given supper. Granny needed to check over Ptolemy the way she had Theona, and after persuasion from Theona, the gladiator resigned himself to the exploration. Reassured by what she "saw", Granny quietly served them bread and a cold stew. Theona checked Cantarcchio and cleaned up the seepage from his bleeding wounds. He did not look good. Granny had no vinegar in the house, but she did have some local wine. Ptolemy held the soldier down while Theona dabbed at his wounds, demanding he remain still. The young man was too weak from loss of blood to fight them off, but he could still savage them both with his tongue. His grandmother laughed at his helplessness and his rude sallies.

"Serves you right, my boy!" she said cheerfully. "You brought her here yourself."

For the next three days, Theona and Ptolemy watched over the house. Most times, Radagaisus's armband and Theona's arguments dissuaded most of the foraging migrants, but when that failed, the sight of Ptolemy and his sword did the job.

At night they slept side by side in the old barn, covered by blankets and lying on the pallets Theona had pushed down to the gladiator from the loft in the house. Twice a day they nursed Cantarcchio, who cringed at their efforts.

There wasn't much food in the house to begin with, and after two days of feeding two extra mouths, Granny announced that she was almost cleaned out of fresh food. There was little point in begging from the caravans passing through the valley below; the people there were scouring for food themselves.

"Where would some of the local people hide their food stores in case of an emergency like this?" Theona asked Granny.

"I don't know," retorted the woman. "No one ever bothered sharing their little secrets with me. Ask Sev."

When she asked the Rhaetian soldier, he turned a cold eye on her.

"Why don't you ask all your Gothic and Suevi and Vandal friends?" he said. "By now, I suspect they have found far more than they need and probably destroyed the rest." He was listless and weak, and ate little himself.

Ptolemy seemed to have few skills beyond fighting and a little medicine, but he was willing to go searching for whatever was to be found. In the early mornings before the foraging parties began to ascend their mountain, he would go off and come back with whatever he could find from the farms and orchards on this upland plateau. He managed to chase down a stray domestic goat, and brought back an armful of apples from an orchard.

He killed the goat, and Theona made a stew and cooked the apples. Granny snorted in disgust at her efforts, but she ate what Theona cooked. Her precious chickens continued to cluck quietly in the loft. Their eggs were undeniably the best reason to leave them alive.

Cantarcchio turned restless and hot. Something about the Roman guide's condition did not feel right to Theona. Ptolemy was phlegmatic—he had seen wounds all his life and had seen many men recover from them or die—he could not predict which or guess why.

Theona couldn't tell whether he cared about the young soldier's health or not. She rather suspected he did not care, and was just waiting for the two of them to be able to leave together. He did what she asked, but no more. It seemed that she, and she alone of the four of them, seemed to care about the welfare of all of them, and she found herself becoming resentful.

Granny, though sometimes cantankerous with Theona, rapidly softened in her attitude towards Ptolemy. More and more she would start a conversation with him in Latin, and Theona would find herself excluded. Little by little, the two of them seemed to become easier in each other's company. Once or twice she heard them laughing.

"What do you talk about?" she asked.

"My life," he replied. "She always want to meet a gladiator, and here I am, a gift from God. She like stories and is interested in mine. Sometimes she talks about herself. Did you know she own land? That field is hers. Her son and Cantarcchio used to work it for her. She say if Cantarcchio die, she adopt me. I don't know. Is possible?"

He sounded wistful. Theona looked after him sadly as he went to fetch wood from the wood-pile. The man had had no personal life that she could tell. Killing and training to kill, and serving as a street thug for hire as he had done between bouts in the arena, seemed the antithesis of working the land and embracing the mountain life that Granny could be offering. It was surprising there was any good left in him.

Some days when no barbarians seemed to be coming up the path from the valley or down the field, Theona would go down as far as the lowest bend where she could see the continuous crawl of the wagon train below. Usually she would go close enough to determine whether the people were Goths or some other group—so many of them dressed similarly and had the same light hair and coloring. Sometimes she would even join the column of wagons for a while, walking with the people just to get the news. It was while doing this that she learned that there had been no fight between Radagaisus's warriors and the Roman soldiers. The Romans seemed to have run away in advance of the battle. It surprised her—the tribune she had met had been very courageous.

No one she talked to knew how far away the warriors were by now, or even where the tail end of the wagon train was behind them, for that matter. They were all tired and hungry, though, and thoroughly unhappy with this adventure. She could not find an optimist among them.

Theona met no one from Wodenvale or found anyone who had news of them, and she dared not linger long. Raiding parties might approach the house from more than one direction and she did not trust Ptolemy to protect the couple inside on his own. He and Cantarcchio never spoke to each other, and the gladiator seemed to be growing restless.

By the sixth day she was becoming frantic. Where was her father? Had she missed Duke Helerix's caravan altogether? She went back to the house in despair, and would not talk to any of them.

While she was re-bandaging Cantarcchio's wounds that evening, she noticed that one of them had begun to smell. She wondered if he could smell it too. His skin was clammy in spite of the cold air in his room. She swabbed his wounds with the wine yet again, but the blood was looking darker.

"What's the matter with you today?" he asked, tiredly.

She sighed. "I haven't been able to find our caravan. I'm afraid I might have missed it altogether."

"So, it looks like you've been abandoned," he said. "No rescue party this time?"

She shook her head and would not meet his eyes. At the moment, she hated him for his hurtfulness.

"Looks like you're going to have to stay with us after all." His eyes glinted. "Do you think dear Roderic will mind when he finds out you came back to me?" Theona laughed bitterly. Ptolemy said something rude in Latin, and Cantarcchio turned his face away. Granny, watching, allowed that maybe it was time for the two of them to move from the barn into the loft. Ptolemy ignored her invitation and chose to remain in the barn, but Theona moved her pallet back up to sleep near the chickens again.

Granny sulked.

After two weeks the migration through the valley seemed to have finally passed. There were no longer any wagons coming along, and the people of the valley were beginning to come out of hiding. A few of them brought food up to the house in the dell, and a doctor was sent for. He bled Cantarcchio, and suggested that they summon the local priest as soon as he returned to town.

The local people were shocked, at first, to see Granny's exotic house guests, but they did not challenge them directly. Theona heard whispered questions behind her back, but Granny enjoyed frustrating the visitors, and they learned to leave it alone. Cantarcchio, at first eager for news, now learned the fate of his cousin, his tribune, his comrades, and the bleak state of his hometown. He seemed to lose heart at last, and quietly surrendered to the infection that had spread through his body.

Theona found him dead one morning, and called in panic for the others. Granny let out a sustained shriek which brought Ptolemy charging in from the barn. The old lady stumbled to him for comfort, and he held her briefly before pushing her toward Theona.

"Where bury?" he asked briskly.

"Out by the road, you insensitive ox," sniffed Granny. "There are a few family graves there beside the hill. Sev can join them. I don't want him buried in the village with *her* or any of his father's other relatives. They never cared for him the way I did. We were true kin, he and I. So, he's mine now."

Theona had never seen a human body buried intact before. She found it barbarous. Before they put the Rhaetian, dressed in his military uniform, into the ground, she said prayers for his soul. Granny added a few Latin prayers she remembered "to make it official", and Ptolemy crossed himself. He then got down into the grave to receive the body that Theona pushed toward him. She saw him sneak a knife from his belt and place it into the soldier's hands, and then cover Cantarcchio's upper body with his shield. Together they filled in the grave, and trudged back to the house.

"I leave tomorrow," said Ptolemy.

Granny let out a pitiful cry.

"I come back," he said hastily. "I come back when I can. You keep Theona with you, and I let you adopt me. I must let Prince Roderic know Theona is alright. Yes?"

Theona looked at him in consternation.

"Why can't I come with you?" she asked.

"Stupid girl," said the blind woman acidly. "Do you think it will be a picnic trying to find your father or the prince in a war zone? You will be safe here, safer anyway, but down there you will be a target for anyone angry at what your people have done, and which you too, would have to do to survive. Is that what you want? Prince Roderic, your father and this dear man are better off without you for now. If I can put up with you, then you can put up with me. It's the best thing to do."

Theona looked at Granny in astonishment. She could not believe the old lady wanted her to stay. The sightless eyes glared back in her direction. She looked at Ptolemy. He was nodding.

"Be back as soon as you can, then," she said. "Send my father if you can find him."

"If he's still alive," chided Granny. "Ptolemy my boy, I'll have a magistrate I know prepare the papers. I must think of a good Roman name for you."

She looked up with a grin on her face, her excitement rather touching.

"I'll have a son again at my age. Fancy that." She turned sharply to where she thought Ptolemy was standing.

"You'd better take real good care of yourself, son."

Ptolemy looked at Theona doubtfully. She thought she knew what he was thinking. He had no citizenship papers—he had been a slave all his life. No Roman magistrate would allow Granny her wish unless he was venal, but then, they were a long way from the courts of Rome.

The gladiator left the next morning. Three days later it started to snow heavily. The valley became covered with a thick blanket of white which the sun melted, the wind froze, and the outside world could not reach.

CHAPTER TWENTY-NINE

PTOLEMY'S MOTHER

❧

Pons Drusi Area
(Bressanone-Bolzano, Italy)
Winter, 405 - 406 AD

The first days the two women spent alone together were awkward. Granny kept cocking her head to listen to whatever Theona was doing around the house. Whenever Theona tried to cook or clean or sort hair for her, Granny would be constantly asking if she knew what she was doing. At night and in the early morning, she would walk around and touch everything in the house to be certain it was back in the right place.

But exhaustion and then the snowstorm, and then Theona's growing competence and efforts to keep her calm and satisfied, gradually eroded Granny's anxiety and she began slowly to relax. By the second week she had clearly decided to make the best of the relationship, and use Theona as a volunteer domestic servant until Ptolemy came back or more trouble arrived on the doorstep.

Theona's efforts to fit in to the blind woman's demands were exhausting to her as well, but she believed she was there at God's call and did her best to fit in. It wasn't long before she realized that she had been given a golden opportunity to learn some valuable lessons from the old woman, starting with the Latin language and some useful skills.

She moved into Cantarcchio's bedroom and furtively packed up his clothing, much of which dated back to when he was a boy.

As she swept and cleaned, emptied chamber pots, and carried water and wood, she kept an eye on the old woman in the kitchen as she created her stews and the breads that always tasted subtly different. She begged for the chance to help and Granny grudgingly allowed her to try her own hand at cooking the meals. The few herbs and spices in the house became an exciting playground for her to experiment with, and Granny's still acute sense of taste became a challenge. The acid comments she received in the beginning become fewer and fewer, until the day came when she saw satisfaction on her face. Since Granny was unlikely to ever voice her approval, Theona watched for those moments with covert eagerness, and took them as confirmation that she was becoming more skilled in the kitchen. The one area she was never allowed to touch was the chickens. The old lady treated her birds with a gentleness Theona had never seen her exhibit to humans.

Each day Theona would spend some time sorting through the bags of hair, and eventually all of them had been dealt with. Then she could just sit and watch Granny's nimble fingers working with the wigs. She began to regale the old lady with story after story from her own life, from the lives of people she knew, and from the Bible. Granny interrupted her only to ask help in finding just the right match of red, or blonde, or occasionally brown hair to carry on her work.

At first they spoke only in Gothic, but there were many items in the house that Theona had never seen before, so she learned the Latin for these, and after a few weeks she started asking Granny to teach her other words and phrases. Eventually their conversations became a confusion of both.

They had a few visitors. Vendors skied in to the little glen to sell a meager assortment of useful items and some foodstuffs. It amused Theona to watch as Granny argued and bartered with them, unwilling to admit that the recent invasion had created just cause for inflated prices.

Some local women came by to sell their hair. One even came to place an order for a wig. Granny let Theona watch as she measured the woman's head for the leather skull cap. Theona helped the visitor to choose the color from the sorted bags of hair. A few of Cantarcchio's relatives who had survived the attacks climbed the mountain to pay their respects, timidly ask for money, and meet the young girl that was now taking care of the miserable old Goth.

Theona listened with growing understanding to the conversations and replied to direct questions with her halting Latin. On repeat visits they found her confidence and command of their language improving quickly, and the old lady's natural antagonism toward Cantarcchio's valley relatives made her push Theona more and more into the position of intermediary. Theona knew that they wondered about her and her intentions, but they kept their reservations to themselves.

Christmas came. Theona wanted to go down into the town to attend a service of celebration. Granny warned her not to—it would be years before many of the local folk forgave barbarians like her for the extensive damage and death they had inflicted on the area. Theona wept. She was by now very lonely. The weeks with no word about her father, Prince Roderic, her Christian and Wodenvale communities, and even Ptolemy were beginning to strain her faith and emotional stamina. Whenever she tried to share her pain with Granny, the old woman cut her off: "You're not the first to suffer in this world and you won't be the last," was all she would say.

She found Cantarcchio's skis in the shed. Theona put on the fur coat and tentatively tried them on one cold, bright December afternoon. She managed to ski down and onto the frozen pond before she fell, and although she was able to get up and ski around the periphery, she could not manage to get back up the hill to the house. Granny explained to her how to move uphill, and the next afternoon she tried it again.

After a few days she ventured farther. The majestic beauty of the area was thrilling and calming, and now she had something she could do outside, and could stay out longer.

She fell many times, and her occasional groans and complaints were a source of serious irritation to the blind woman, but once again, her growing skill gave her satisfaction. She would glide across the snow and thrill to the vastness of the mountains and the sky around her. When she returned, she was often so happy that Granny began to question her about whom she was meeting on these ventures. Theona laughed.

"Father God," she replied. "He always makes me feel so good!"

One day the local magistrate made his way up to the house. He was a youngish man, a part-time farmer whose house was in another valley and had not been touched by the hordes of invaders. Granny ordered Theona out of the house while she met with him. When the meeting was over, he came out and began fastening on his own skis, and then noticed her shivering as she watched from the shelter of the barn, her skis still on her feet. He skied over to Theona to talk to her.

"Who is this man she wants to adopt?" he asked.

"He is a young man who joined my people in Pannonia. He wanted to come along with us to Italia."

"The old woman is rich. Do you think he is after her money?" He was watching her eyes.

Theona met his gaze. "I do not know. This is all her idea, not his. That I do know. He told me that she has fields, and he would like to be a farmer. Like you."

"What are you keeping from me?"

She shrugged. "I don't know what she told you. He comes from Africa or Egypt, not Pannonia where he met us."

"She swears he is a Roman citizen. Is that true?"

Theona did not answer.

"The old lady is willing to pay me a lot to let her adopt him. What do you think of that?"

"I think you should do it."

"Why?"

"Then he will stay and they can each have a family. They both need that."

"What about you?"

"I will be leaving sometime soon, and Granny Cantarcchia knows it. If she cannot adopt him, Ptolemy will leave too. He respects her, but he does not love her, and he has friends elsewhere. I think he will be happiest here."

He studied her. She looked steadily back. Finally he nodded and left.

Theona put away the skis in the shed and went into the house.

Ptolemy returned to them in the middle of March, to the relief and joy of both women. He was quietly thrilled at their effusive welcome and allowed them both to embrace him. Theona was kicked out of the kitchen by Granny, and a chicken was sacrificed for the stew pot.

"Did you see my father?" asked Theona, excitedly.

Ptolemy put his feet up on a footstool and looked down his nose at her.

"No, but I saw Prince Roderic. He was happy to know you are safe here."

From the kitchen Granny snorted, and they looked at her and then at each other, and smiled.

"He told me to tell you to stay here until things settle down in Italia. It is extremely dangerous to travel right now, and his father still has not made any deal with the Emperor. Prince Roderic hopes the Emperor will assign land to them in the same way the Romans assigned land to the Goths who invaded back in 376."

A shadow briefly crossed his face. "Anyway, he sent you this."

He stood up and rooted in his purse until he found a cloth bag. He handed this to Theona. It felt heavy and clinked a bit. A red and gold braid closed the neck of the bag.

Theona fumbled to untie the knot, and pulled out a heavy gold chain with a locket attached. She gasped. It looked very valuable. She wondered what she was expected to say, or do with it.

"That chain is gold," said Ptolemy proudly. He reached across, took it from her and fumbled to open the locket. Inside was a little picture. He passed it back, smiling.

"What's that?" she asked, looking up at him.

"That's an icon of Jesus," he said decisively. "It's a copy of a picture made by a famous artist. The Prince got it for you. He thought you would be pleased."

Apparently Ptolemy had thought so too. He looked disappointed at her unenthusiastic reaction.

"Did he steal it?" asked Granny.

Theona looked at Ptolemy beseechingly. The same question had occurred to her.

"No, he didn't steal it. He bought it from one of his men."

"Did they steal it?" the two women asked in unison.

He looked exasperated. "I don't know. He insisted on paying for it, and now it's his gift to you. Don't you want it? He will be deeply hurt if you won't wear it, and I had to fight off two groups of his thieving Goths who knew I had it and followed me to get it."

Theona lifted it over her head, and dropped it solidly onto her chest.

"Yes. I will keep it until I know I cannot. Thank you." She smiled at him. He looked relieved.

"What did he intend by that expensive trinket?" asked Granny from her rocking chair.

Theona looked at her in surprise, and as if Granny could see her, she said, "O, don't be so innocent, girl. Such an important gift means that he thinks he has an understanding with you. Doesn't it, Ptolemy? You keep it, and you're done for."

In the weeks that followed, as the ground began to warm up, and the ice to melt, Ptolemy fit easily back into their way of life and made himself useful. Granny sent for the magistrate again. He returned with the documents, and Granny paid him double the normal fee.

Ptolemy's adoption papers were issued in the name of Quintus Cantarcchio Ptolemeus. The slave was now the quasi-legal adopted North African son of a Gothic victim of a Roman war party. They celebrated with a decent jug of wine purchased from a local farmer

CHAPTER THIRTY

FROM ONE VANDAL FATHER TO ANOTHER

Ticinum Military Base, Italia
(Pavia, western Italy)
End of May, 406 AD

Dear Pater, Mater, Julian, Lucius and Priscilla,
I greet you from sunny Italia and hope you are all well and enjoying life.

Thank you for your letter. It arrived yesterday and was passed on to me. If I get this letter written today, it can go back with the same messenger who brought yours. He is leaving tomorrow morning. I am thrilled that it got through—these are tricky times for any kind of delivery. This area remains pretty safe because the army is here, but there are bands of barbarians in many areas across the plains of Italia and everyone is fearful of attempting anything without huge military support.

In my last letters I have described to you my life at this massive military base. What I do each day has not been particularly dashing or inspiring. Someone assumed that because my family breeds horses, that I would fit best in the Cavalry Quarter-master's Department. I process requests for supplies and horses from all over the Western Empire. It is very boring. I have requested a transfer to join the training program for the Cavalry, but it has not come through yet. My former optio, Bauto, is being trained as a cavalryman and he seems to be very contented.

I have complained often about this so-called promotion to Eucherius. He is working with General Stilicho over in the main building, but he just chides me and tells me to be grateful I'm not facing Radagaisus anymore. I think he is jealous that I actually have had a bit more real-life adventure than him. To be honest, I exaggerated the importance and the impact of my contributions back in Rhaetia, so he thinks he has done me a great favor by bringing me to Italia. We remain very good friends and share a house with another tribune, a young man named Jason. He is a patrician, and his father Jovius is an important man in the court at Ravenna. David, the slave you sent me, is part of our household staff and looks after Gideon most of the time.

Do you remember Gideon? He's the dog I told you about a few months ago. Commander Sarus persuaded General Stilicho to let me keep him with me, and Eucherius, who is a major romantic, put in a good word as well, emphasizing the mysterious and beautiful "Bissula", Gideon's previous owner. I *think his father is rather skeptical of the whole thing, but he did say we could keep Gideon with us "for now". I'm not sure what I will do with Gideon when we have to march off to battle. Maybe the soldiers left behind to run the base here will look after him for me. Or perhaps I will send him home with David. He would fit in well.*

The poor creature has continued to recover from his disastrous attempt to leap across that crevasse back in the mountains. One of his legs is crooked now, and he seems stiff in the mornings, but he manages quite well. He has regained his health enough to accompany me on my long walks around the base and he even runs.

The camp here at Pavia is huge, as you can imagine, and it is very flat, which works for sports, parades, and cavalry training exercises, but is not particularly inspiring. The vegetation here is quite exotic, though. I have seen many trees and birds that I do not recognize, but I miss our hills.

Being here has given me a marvelous chance to learn what is going on throughout the Empire. I have met men from as far away as Britannia and Mauritania, but there are times when it feels like we are all prisoners on this base. As you can imagine, we don't get to leave the base very often. Eucherius, Jason and I sometimes go into the town with groups of other soldiers to attend the races or go to the baths or eat out. That is about the extent of our entertainment these days.

Every time we do go off-base, we get accosted by angry citizens wanting to know when the army is going to go after the barbarians and drive them out of Italia. They are sacking towns, destroying people's homes and farms, and now even besieging walled cities. Farmers here have had a hard time getting their crops into the ground this spring, and then protecting them against marauders, many of whom are not even barbarians. It is dangerous to do routine things if there are any such gangs in the area.

The citizens accuse us soldiers of not protecting them. The stories we are hearing are truly dreadful, and we do not blame them for being angry. The men here want to join battle as soon as possible. We are told we have to wait.

It is really embarrassing, but we do understand. The High Command is not willing to risk taking on Radagaisus until they are sure we can win. We are still waiting for additional forces to join us from several other provinces. There will then be a huge army here, and we have barbarian allies staying at other major bases.

I mentioned Commander Sarus to you in my last letter. He and his Goths are in one of the auxiliary camps, and there is a Hun named Uldin at another one. He leads his own warriors and works under General Stilicho. That surprised me at first. I remember you mentioning his name years ago, Pater—I couldn't sleep for several nights after that story you told. Well, he is in another camp somewhere to the east of us. We don't have much to do with the foreign units, apart from trying to get them the right breeds of horses, but I have seen Sarus and Uldin at headquarters on several occasions. Sarus always asks if I am taking good care of Gideon.

I digress.

General Stilicho has already sent Uldin and his Huns against one of the three armies under Radagaisus. The battle took place over towards Genoa, if you know where that is. Many of us wanted to fight alongside them, but the Huns do their own thing very well, and this Uldin was confident that his Huns could defeat those Goths. They did.

It was a glorious victory for our side, and won by Huns! It seems strange to me that the Huns, who started this whole mess, should now be fighting their victims here on Roman soil where those victims fled for safety.

The leader of that particular Gothic group was one of Radagaisus's own sons. He was killed in the battle, and the men under his command fled back to join Radagaisus and the main force.

Eucherius mentioned that the more people Radagaisus has with him, the harder it is going to be for him to find food for them all. That is why he initially split them up, and that is what he will need to keep doing. However, if they split up too much, we even the odds. I am proud to say that a small group of Roman soldiers can take on much larger numbers of barbarian warriors and beat them.

You asked if I had managed to get to Milan. No, I have not been there. In fact, I am far more likely to get to Rome soon than to Milan, even though Milan is not all that far from here. Eucherius has invited me to go home with him if we can get leave together. I am so excited! Guess where he lives. He lives in a palace on Palatine Hill! And he and his family dine with the Emperor and Empress quite often! He has even watched some races from the Emperor's own balcony.

I believe his idea is that we would go by ship from Genoa and stay for a month or even longer if General Stilicho gives us something official to do there.

I just had an interruption. Eucherius came in. We have been summoned to headquarters. I must go, so will say farewell. Know this, dear family, whenever I have time on my own, my thoughts turn to you all and our beautiful Villa Ausonia. I may be getting leave in the fall, and if so, I will be heading home as fast as I can.

Eucherius says hello to all of you, and hopes to see you again sometime. He also wants you to know that he spoke to his father about the request for the business owners in Gaul to be able to form a militia. The answer is no.

Respectfully and lovingly,
Marius

"Sarus says to bring the dog."

"What for?"

"They want him to smell something."

"You're joking."

"Would I joke about something like that? Well, yes I would, but this is for real. Just bring him."

Marius went to find Gideon. He was lying, as usual, on David's own pallet on the kitchen floor. Eucherius's slave, Bouticus, was pushing a batch of round bread loaves into the hot oven, and David was attempting to de-feather a bunch of thrushes. He looked frustrated. It looked like he was going to try to prepare a thrush pie for the evening meal. Gideon wagged his tail when Marius came in, and got stiffly to his feet, stretching and yawning.

The two tribunes took him to the main headquarters buildings and to one of the meeting rooms. Eucherius knocked on the door. They were admitted by General Stilicho himself. Marius saluted the generalissimo briskly, and then Commander Sarus, who was sitting on a chair in front of a long, document-strewn table. Two other men whom he did not recognize stood behind his chair peering over his shoulder.

"Good day, Tribune Ausonius," smiled General Stilicho. "How are you getting along?"

"Very well, sir. A bit restless on occasion, but eager to do whatever I can to help."

"And how is your family? What is your esteemed father up to these days?"

"He spends a lot of time supervising the training of the new foals, sir. He doesn't need to, but he loves it, and he tells me he is trying to replace the wooden fence around the central compound of our villa with stone walls."

"Wise idea. Tell him from me to take every precaution. Just in case. There is a situation developing north of the Rhine that he may not know about yet. Vandals, Suevis and large bodies of Alans are congregating there. The Franks living along the border are preparing for a big fight."

Marius stared at him. This was alarming news. He wondered if he could get a note about it into his scroll before it left the base.

The General stooped to pat Gideon.

"Eucherius has talked often about your beautiful estate. I have been in Trier a few times. I did meet your father once a few years ago when I was there to deal with the Alemanni chiefs, but I do not believe I have ever been up to your home."

Was there a hint of reproach in that? The General's face was hard to read.

"I am sorry, sir. I would have invited you, but they did not consult me at the time."

Stilicho laughed. "No. Well, you can rectify that someday I hope. In the meantime, I will set the tone and invite you to stay with us at our home anytime you are in Rome."

Marius was thrilled, and would have answered effusively except for the expression he noticed on Commander Sarus's face. Apparently, even as an esteemed leader and brother-in-arms, he was not on such familiar terms with his General's family as to be invited to stay at the palace. Marius would have to be careful.

"That is very kind of you, sir. I will look forward to that someday."

"Tribune Ausonius," ordered Sarus. "Bring that dog over to me."

Marius led Gideon over to the table where the big officer was sitting. Sarus bent down and spoke gently to the dog in Gothic. Gideon cocked his head attentively. He appeared to be listening carefully.

Sarus picked up one of the scrolls from the table and held it for Gideon to sniff. The dog looked at him and then away. Sarus pulled another one forward and offered it for Gideon's attention. Gideon looked at him and sniffed at it dutifully, but showed little interest.

Marius noticed that General Stilicho, Eucherius, and the other men were watching attentively.

Sarus ostentatiously lifted a third scroll from the table. He brought it close to Gideon's nose. Gideon at first appeared disinterested, but then seemed to change his mind. They all watched, fascinated, as he took a serious sniff at the document and slowly began to wave his tail. He took a step backward and cocked his head to look at the man holding it.

"Woof!"

"Well, what do you know?" said one of the other men in the room. "That is the one, isn't it Sarus?"

"Yes, that's the one."

One what? wondered Marius in frustration.

Sarus stood up and looked at him.

"Alright, Tribune Ausonius. Would you like to tell General Stilicho how you first acquired this dog?" he suggested. "Or shall I?"

Marius swallowed hard.

"I believe I did hear the story from Eucherius when you first arrived, Tribune, but I'd like to hear it again from your own lips," said Stilicho kindly.

Great. Marius's palms began to sweat. Sarus had promised not to put forward his own sour view of Marius's brief absence from duty the day before the army's withdrawal from Pons Drusi, and now he was ordering him to disclose the incident to the most powerful man in the Roman Army. Did that include the awkward timing of his chamois hunt? Would the Goth allow him to keep that much a secret?

"Eucherius, send for fruit and cheeses," said Stilicho. "Does Gideon like cheese?"

"Yes sir. He adores it," replied Eucherius, heading for the door.

"Fine. We'll share the cheese with him."

Marius decided to tell the truth, the whole truth. He felt decidedly uncomfortable knowing that Commander Sarus was in a position to destroy his reputation with the General any time he chose. He'd rather do it himself.

So, haltingly, he began to tell his story. He was interrupted several times by questions from General Stilicho, who seemed to have a clear grasp of the geography of the area, and once by Eucherius who came in followed by a slave with platters of cheese and fruit. Finally Marius got to his encounter with the girl. When he was finished, Sarus nodded approvingly, and turned to General Stilicho.

"You see, General, why I thought the letter might refer to the same girl?"

"Yes by Jove, and keeping the dog around seems to have been an inspired idea, my friend. Now all we have to do is get our hands on the girl. Perhaps this little dog will be the key to that."

He turned to Marius. "So, Tribune Ausonius, I know you must be curious about this scroll. My staff has had some fun trying to read it. Would you like to know what's in it?"

"Yes, sir, General."

"Well, so did we, and it wasn't easy. Take a look."

Sarus handed the scroll over to Marius, while Gideon followed the exchange with his eyes.

Marius took it and opened it out. He frowned over it for a minute and then looked at the other men.

"I thought this was written in Greek," he said, "but it's not. Most of the letters are Greek, but there are some symbols here that I have never seen before. Even the words that have only Greek letters in them don't make sense to me."

"You are right," said Stilicho. "One of my men thought it might be the kind of script you can find in Gothic Bibles, the script that Bishop Ulfilas invented sixty years ago to teach the Goths about the Bible. So I sent for Commander Sarus." He nodded toward the big man.

Sarus continued the story. "And I came in and took a look at it, and recognized that yes, it was written in the Gothic script, but I couldn't understand it. It wasn't written in the Gothic language."

"So," continued General Stilicho smoothly, "I asked him to read it aloud to me and to a few other officers with barbarian backgrounds, and once I heard it, it sounded more like my father's Vandal tongue. Being a bit rusty, I sent for Tribune Guntherus here—he was raised in a Vandal village—and asked Sarus to read the letter aloud to him. Tribune Guntherus, tell the young man what it said."

Guntherus, a serious man with iron grey hair and a sculpted beard, looked at Sarus, who began to read it phrase by phrase. The Vandal interpreted each phrase for them.

Most highly esteemed General Stilicho,

I am writing to you man-to-man, as one Vandal father to another, to ask for personal help. My name is Rhodus. I am a Christian pastor who, with some of my people, was forced to flee our village after Huns attacked it and massacred many among us and burned most of the buildings down.

We found protection with a Gothic warlord, the same man who has asked me to write the other letter. He, too, had to flee with his people after the Huns attacked, and we joined up with King Radagaisus, seeking safety and a new life inside the Roman Empire as others have done in the past.

Along the way I was separated from my only surviving family member, my young daughter Theona. This happened sometime before last Christmas in the valley south of Veldidena. I have not seen her since. I thought at first that she had been bride-napped by Roderic, the younger son of Radagaisus, but I know now that this is not so.

Theona is all I have left, and I am all she has left. I beg of you, as one father to another, to be merciful to us. If you or your soldiers should find her, please spare her. She is a most excellent daughter. She is kind, virtuous, educated and very pretty. I do not ask for clemency myself—these are difficult times and your people have suffered as much now as my own, but Theona deserves none of the suffering that has come on her head.

Again, if you or your soldiers find her, I beg you for her life and protection. She can read and write and teach, and may be accompanied by a black and white dog. He disappeared at the same time.

Most respectfully and fervently,

Rhodus, priest of our Savior Christus, and Scribe for Duke Helerix of Wodenvale

General Stilicho turned to Marius.

"Commander Sarus thought that it might be she whom you saved from that Rhaetian deserter. He thought that your dog might be able to recognize the smell of his former master even after all this time. And I think now that, since this does indeed seem to be the case, then you and Eucherius should take the dog and go back to Pons Drusi to look for this girl."

His smile widened as he watched Marius's reaction.

Marius could hardly breathe. He could almost feel the hair rising on the back of his neck. He could almost hear the Voice of God speaking into his ear. This was amazing! But . . .

"What if she *was* bride-napped?" he demanded. "I saw the Prince practically kill Cantarcchio, and I saw the girl get back up behind him on his horse and ride off. She may be still with him."

"We don't think so. This man, Rhodus says that he had thought so too, but has heard something that made him change his mind."

"What?"

"No doubt he has heard that the prince has no ladylove in his life at the moment. News that the King's surviving son had taken a bride would surely have reached his ears by now. There have been no such reports. We have our own spies in their ranks."

"But why?" he asked. "What do you want her for?"

"Tell him what was in the second letter," urged Eucherius, excitedly.

Sarus picked up another scroll from the table.

"This is interesting. It is a request from a group of chieftains who want to distance themselves from Radagaisus and are hoping for a deal from us. This one I can read with no problem. It is written with the same script as the first one, but the writer would have had to read it back to the dukes who attached their symbols to it, and they needed to understand it. It is written entirely in the Gothic language, not Vandal, though they are similar. This Pastor Rhodus must know that General Stilicho has Vandal ancestry, and he wrote his own private letter in a language he thinks the General can understand, but the official one he wrote in the language of the people travelling with him. It all makes perfect sense."

"What's in it?" Marius croaked. He reached for a piece of fruit.

"These Gothic chieftains are fed up with Radagaisus's bloodthirsty ways," said Sarus. "They say they never came along to do harm to the Empire or its people, but to find a better, safer life. It's the usual story—'give us land to settle on and we will serve you well', meaning fighting in the army, of course." He passed his piece of cheese to Gideon.

"For us," interrupted General Stilicho, "it is an enormous breakthrough. We just have to negotiate how and when we can receive these people, and on what terms, and our manpower problems are solved, along with the need to wait any longer for more troops to arrive from the provinces. These Gothic chieftains are in charge of thousands of warriors. Losing them to our side will be a huge blow to Radagaisus."

Marius had wondered if the son of Radagaisus whom Uldin's Huns had killed in battle was the one he had seen that fateful day in the valley. Now he knew it must be another one. These generals seemed to think that Prince Roderic was alive and well somewhere. It seemed that he was to go and find the girl who had become his personal Bissula.

"What's the plan?"

"We want you to take the dog, and my son who has been clamoring for an adventure, go back to where you first met Theona, and find her if you can. If you are successful in finding her, the two of you will accompany her with an army escort as far as Bologna. After that she will be transferred into the care of my legate there.

"These letters were delivered to us by the Gothic priest of a heretic congregation east of Bologna. We will send a reply to him to say that we are interested in working out a deal with them, and he will send it on to these chieftains and this man Rhodus. We will offer to meet somewhere—perhaps at his church, and discuss a plan to formally accept their surrender and incorporate their warriors into the army. We will turn the girl over to them as a gesture of good will. You just find her and we will take care of the rest."

It seemed like a reasonable plan, though "arresting" the girl was not exactly the vision Marius had had in his daydreams. He frowned.

"I have one more question, General. Will this girl, Theona, be permitted to stay with her father again?"

General Stilicho smiled.

"Of course! For now."

CHAPTER THIRTY-ONE

A PIVOTAL CHOICE

Florentia, Italia
(Florence, Italy)
June, 406 AD

The Apennines and the Alps surround the Po[45] Valley on three sides. The Alps spread across the top of it and curve right on down to the Mediterranean coast to straddle the coastline and stretch over to Gaul where they are known as the Maritime Alps. Towards the east they join the Apennines, not nearly as high and rugged as their northern cousins. The Apennines circle eastward along the bottom of the Po Valley almost to the Adriatic coast but then dive southward to form the spine of the distinctive Italian boot. Between these two mountain ranges the Po Valley provides a well-irrigated plain which is an agricultural gift to the people of Italia.

The city of Bologna[46] sits just north of the Apennines at the bottom of the Po Valley. Thanks to the Via Aemilia which ran all the way from Piacenza south of Milan to Rimini on the Adriatic coast, Bologna had become a major commercial and military center. The Via Flaminia Minor began here and crossed the Apennines to Florence, fifty miles away.

<hr>

The gates of Florence were barred. The roads nearby and the bridges across the Arno River were patrolled by men wearing Radagaisus's yellow and green arm bands. The large suburb across the river was now in the hands of the Goths. The Gothic king and his family had taken up residence in one of the larger homes along the riverfront. It had a fine view of the walled city opposite and flaunted a large banner bearing the image of a bear's head snapping at the sun and the moon. Tents and wagons covered the nearby hills and valleys as thousands of warriors and their families settled in to await the anticipated surrender of the despairing people within the city walls.

It was common knowledge in the Roman Empire that the barbarians were not equipped for siege warfare, and the Florentines, like the citizens of other walled towns, had assumed they would

<hr>

[45] The Po River in Roman times was the Padus River, and the Po Valley was the Paduan Valley.

[46] In Roman times Bologna was known as Bononia.

be left in peace. However, word of the rich treasures sheltered within the palaces and churches of the city had reached the ears of Radagaisus, and he had arrived with thousands of warriors and settled in to wait patiently for the people here to starve to death, or open their gates to their own peril.

Inside Florence, its residents and thousands of fugitives from the surrounding Tuscan countryside struggled not to panic. How long could they make their remaining food supplies last? Could they outlast these covetous, murderous enemies? When would the Goths and their allies decide to give up and move on, especially since even they must be running out of food? The soldiers on the walls reported that every day the groups of hungry Goths, Marcomanni, Suevi and others going off to search for food in the surrounding area would come back later and later.

The biggest question for Florentines was, where was the people's hero, General Stilicho, and the Army? Surely they would soon come marching vigorously to the rescue of such an important city, especially one so close to Rome. That's what they all paid taxes for, wasn't it? Protection and security?

Florentines had heard horror stories from other parts of the Province of Italia for months now, stories of theft and rape, burning and murder, widespread destruction and the aftermath of chaos. If the Goths got in, they were under no illusions about the dangers they faced. Hadn't the Gothic king threatened to sell them all into slavery? Hadn't he bragged about crucifying the members of the Senate? His dreadful people had been making free with their beautiful country for half a year already and had left it in ruins. Every patriot and everyone who had ever visited the area felt fear and fury in their hearts. Only sweet revenge would quench that anger.

Just before the city was totally surrounded, the Prefect had sent a frantic letter to General Stilicho to hurry to their rescue with his armies, and the sooner the better. Yet weeks had now gone by, and the Roman Army was nowhere to be seen. Florence was experiencing the same shocking lack of protection that other places had experienced. While they waited, the people within the walls fumed and cursed and doled out less and less food to their children and to themselves. They took long periods of rest to conserve their energy, and sent clamorous prayers to the Gates of Heaven. These, too, seemed to be closed. Many had died, and more were dying.

In the cathedral, Bishop Zenobius[47] led his people in fervent prayers for deliverance, for disaster to strike their enemies, for God to remember that *they* had responded to His Gospel message and were followers of His Son, the Christ, whereas their foe worshipped demons and had declared himself an enemy of Christ.

Bishop Zenobius had already raised several people from the dead—he believed that God cared, had heard their prayers, and that God was all-powerful and in charge. He had faith that God would come through for them, and begged his people to have that faith too. They tried, but it was hard, especially when their bellies were sore, their children were crying, and they had no comfort to offer them.

One of the devout women in the cathedral congregation came to the bishop, excited about a dream she had had: his mentor, the late Bishop Ambrose[48], famed and godly Bishop of Milan, had appeared to her and announced that God had heard the prayers of the people, and would bring swift and sudden deliverance to them.

Bishop Zenobius reported this message to his people, and some believed.

---

[47] Bishop Zenobius (337 – 417) was the first bishop of Florence.

[48] Bishop Ambrose of Milan, St. Ambrose (340 – 397), a powerful and influential cleric of his day.

Isarco Valley

The trip which in normal times would have taken under two weeks took Marius and Eucherius more than three. General Stilicho had his soldiers escort them to Cremona, and then up the Via Postumia to Verona. From here on, they would be on their own.

The two friends carried little, just their documents, weapons, money, and knowledge of the roads and military establishments along the way. The documents allowed them to find food and safety at night with the army, but they still had to walk. Using horses or a larger wagon would have made them too visible, too much of a target. These days, normal commercial traffic was rare and risky. Groups of barbarians were everywhere, and the local people had formed militias even though this was illegal. They all avoided or challenged strangers now, especially two young men travelling alone in peasant's clothing.

They left Verona on foot, pushing aa handcart piled high with turnips. These they would sell when they had to. Their awkward conveyance slowed them down, but proved useful whenever Gideon's legs began to give out. At times he had a royal ride up the valley while they tramped the whole way.

They travelled slowly up the Adige valley to Pons Drusi. The village, like every other one they had passed, had been devastated by bands of marauders. The residents eyed them sourly, two ill-clad strangers who might be up to no good. They headed straight for the local garrison, now in the hands of members of the Seventh Alpine Cohort.

The centurion in command recognized Marius and welcomed him warmly. He and his men had received their own orders from General Stilicho, a copy of which Eucherius also carried, and he assured them that the escort they required was ready to go as soon as they had the girl in custody.

Marius tried to explain that Theona was not exactly a prisoner, even if she was a barbarian. She was under the protection of the church and General Stilicho, and had an important role to play in the expected peace talks with the barbarians. She must be treated with respect and consideration. He caught Eucherius winking at the centurion, who nodded amiably, a glint in his eye. That evening they were treated to a good country meal and a few glasses of the local wine at a taverna that had just reopened, and they went to bed at their billet in town soon after nightfall.

They woke at dawn the next morning full of anticipation. This was the day the real hunt for Bissula, as they privately called her, would begin.

They followed the river as far as Thermopylae so that Eucherius could see the site of the planned ambush, and from there they climbed the path to the top of the mountain. Gideon pranced along ahead of them, stopping to sniff and leave his scent along the way. It would be a long day for him, so Marius had come prepared with a sling to carry the young animal should his strength fail.

They arrived, panting, at the top of the mountain, and set off through the forest. Once they reached the pasture, they discovered that low-lying clouds were resting on the plateau and obscuring the view. Undaunted, Marius led the way towards the drover's road which he knew must lie somewhere in front of them. They found it, and headed north while the sun burned off the clouds and a beautiful morning began to emerge from the haze.

Around them sprawled a fresh and brilliant alpine landscape. Fluffy clouds drifted across a royal blue sky. The grass sprang back under their feet. Birds called and sang from tree and meadow, and the inscrutable peaks crowned the skyline, erect and untamed custodians of the region.

Eucherius kept stopping and looking around, inhaling deeply, awed by the profound freedom and beauty of it all.

"No wonder my father loves coming up here so much!" he exclaimed to Marius. "It's enough to make you reconsider paganism! Everything is so full of life that on a day like this it is easy to believe there must be a god in every blade of grass and soaring eagle."

"It's beautiful, all right," responded Marius, "but it's not enough. The best they can do is point us to their amazing Creator."

"Well, that's as deep as I get," replied Eucherius carelessly. "I just want to revel in the sheer pleasure of all this."

Marius was remembering that first hike up the valley with David. First they had seen the chamois, then the dog, and then the girl. Where had she come from?

They reached the crevasse and the wooden bridge across it. They were near where Gideon had had his terrible fall. The dog, clearly uneasy, pushed against Marius's leg, so Marius stooped down beside him and ruffled his fur while just pointing silently ahead to his friend. Eucherius hurried over and stared down into the chasm.

"How far down did you go?" he called. Marius walked over and looked down. The dog hung back, watching them anxiously.

"You see that little shelf jutting out from the chasm wall?" he asked. "Gideon landed on that, and I had to get down there, pack him up, and get him back to the top."

"That far! I'd like to try that. Do we have time?"

"No, we don't know how far we may have to go today, and it wasn't fun, Eucherius. It was terrifying."

They crossed the meadow to the base of the next hill and found a path heading uphill.

"Theona may have come from up there," he said. "We didn't see her coming down the road. She appeared on the scene quite suddenly. Let's head up."

At the top of the climb they emerged onto a long field where a young barley crop was growing. To their left they could see the road running alongside it. Gideon suddenly pointed his ears.

"Look, Marius, he's recognizing something."

Before Eucherius could finish the sentence, the dog had bounded off across the field toward a little hill. Grinning excitedly, they raced after him. They reached the road, and saw him disappear down a slope. They followed as quickly as they could, and came upon an idyllic scene.

At the bottom of the grassy slope, a pond reflected the sapphire sky. At the far end of it they could see three buildings. One of them was a stone house, and a black and white dog, their dog, was barking excitedly and jumping around a young woman who had fallen to her knees just outside the door. A large market garden beyond the house was green with young plants. A man who had been bent over hoeing and weeding in it looked up. Seeing them coming down the slope, he stopped and watched them, his hoe balanced in his hands rather like a weapon.

"Is that her?" hissed Eucherius urgently.

"It must be," answered Marius uncertainly, "Gideon seems to know her, but she looks really different!"

The girl he had met the previous year had been dressed in a long unbleached tunic and trousers, and her golden hair had fallen freely down her back. The girl in front of them was wearing a long white Roman stola with a red stripe around the neckline and a high red girdle. On her feet she wore sandals, not boots, and her hair was piled high in an old-fashioned, very Roman hairdo. Around her neck hung a heavy gold chain with a locket suspended from it.

Nevertheless, judging by the dog's ecstatic reaction, it must be his Bissula.

But, such a difference! Nervously, the two tribunes approached her.

Theona looked up, a happy smile on her face. What miracle had brought Gideon back into her life? He was the same, but different, just like her.

She recognized Marius immediately, and hurried toward him. "You brought my dog back!" she exclaimed in Latin. Gideon chased after her, jumping in front of her to recapture her fond attentions.

Marius's heart was pounding. The girl had recognized him, and her welcome was everything he could have wished. She was thrilled that he had brought her back her dog. He felt once again like the hero he had been when they had first met. Little did she know that he was here to remove her from her pretty home. She would soon lose her enthusiasm for him, but he had this moment, and he would not be rushed.

"Hello, Theona," he said, warmly, a broad smile on his face.

For some reason, she blushed. The man who had been watching from the garden drew closer. He looked shorter and older than the tribunes, and very strong.

"How do you know my name?" she asked in wonder.

"Your father mentioned it in his letter to my friend's father."

"Oh," she said, turning to Eucherius, "and who might you be, sir?"

Eucherius looked oddly shy. "Flavius Eucherius, my lady."

He bowed, then frowned and stared at the ground. Marius grinned. Eucherius seemed to have lost his ebullient self-confidence.

Theona waited calmly for more, never taking her eyes off him. Eucherius stammered, "I am the good friend of Tribune Ausonius, whom you have met, and we have come to take you back to your father."

At this her companion strode forward to stand beside her, his head thrown back, the hoe held menacingly in front of his body. Ptolemy knew how to intimidate his opponents, and the two tribunes were well able to recognize his signals, even if the girl could not.

"If Theona goes anywhere, it is I who will take her, not you."

Marius squared his shoulders and tried to look taller. He gazed down at the man.

"Are you her husband that you speak for her?"

"No, Roman," he sneered, "but I answer to the one who is. This is my lady's home, for now, and Theona's intended wishes her to stay here in safety. If her father finally wants to see her, he should come to her here."

Marius turned to look at Theona. She was looking at the other man in alarm.

"Theona, we know of whom he speaks. Are you now betrothed to Prince Roderic?"

"Don't answer him," instructed Ptolemy.

"Because if you are not," continued Marius, "or even if you are, you will be far safer with your father. Their paths are moving apart."

"She is safest here. You know it."

Marius ignored him. "Your father desires to see you very much, Theona. He has been worried about you."

"It is a trick. Do not trust him."

Theona frowned at Ptolemy. "This man risked his life for my dog, and he showed kindness to me. Can a man change so much?"

Ptolemy looked at Marius and Eucherius scornfully.

"This is different. He is under orders now."

She looked uncertain. "What proof do you have?" she asked.

Eucherius reached into his pouch and pulled out the letter Pastor Rhodus had written.

"I understand you can read this," he said politely, holding it out.

Theona reached for the scroll, her hand shaking a little.

"Yes. We can offer you hospitality, at least. Come inside."

She turned and led the way, Eucherius followed, then Marius, and finally Ptolemy, still carrying the hoe, brought up the rear, treading too closely behind Marius, the hoe bumping roughly into his back.

They had to stoop to get through the first door, and stumbled as they stepped into the darkened inner room, blind for a few seconds after the sun's brightness.

An old woman was sitting dozing in her rocking chair, her long scrawny grey hair falling forward, a partly sewn wig dangling from one limp hand. She jerked awake when the extra sets of boots tramped into the room.

"Take those boots off immediately," she ordered, turning her sightless eyes toward the doorway.

Marius looked at Eucherius quizzically. Eucherius shook his head.

"We are on official army business, lady. We have to keep them on."

"Soldiers!" she said with satisfaction. "It's about time! Have you beaten that rascal Radagaisus yet?"

"No, lady. Not yet. Very soon, we hope."

"Granny," protested Theona in Goth, "please do not talk like that. You know I have many friends and loved ones with the High King."

"And no doubt all of them have become thieves and murderers, my dear," replied Granny in the same language. "You've heard the stories. The Goths will deserve whatever they get."

Theona shrugged, and ladled out two bowls of the soup that had been simmering over the fire. Silently, she gestured to the two visitors to sit at the table. Silently, they did.

"And what exactly do you two soldiers want," said the old lady in Latin. "I pay my taxes regularly. Much good it's doing me right now. This girl and my son are also innocent of any wrong-doing."

"We are here to take Theona back with us to her father."

"Don't trust them, Theona." The blind woman did not bother to switch from Latin. "The Romans are tricky. They never do anything good for anyone without a good reason."

Ptolemy, still blocking the entrance with the hoe in his hand, burst out laughing. He laughed so hard that tears began to trickle down his cheeks. Theona looked at him fondly and smiled, then glanced at the infuriated tribunes and smiled again, her cheeks pink. The old lady looked in the general direction of the gladiator, and her voice softened.

"Of all men, you must know that, my son. Look what they did to you, and did a single Roman come along to help? No," she answered firmly.

"They brought me a letter, Granny," said Theona. "From my father."

"Read it aloud, Theona. We'll see if it sounds genuine, or if it's a fraud."

Theona opened the scroll. Marius hastened to speak before she could begin reading it.

"It was not written to you, Theona, but to General Stilicho."

Surprised, she looked at him. The hazel eyes were looking at her with the same gentle concern she had seen on that dreadful November day so many months ago. The man really was sweet. She looked down, and, her throat tight with emotion, read the letter that her father had penned to the commander of the Western Roman Army. When she had finished, she looked at Eucherius.

"You are General Stilicho's son?"

Eucherius's face reddened and he nodded his head. Marius was chagrinned. He remembered that he had said that her father had written to his friend's father. It had been meant to disarm her, but now she would be on her guard. As would they all.

Theona turned to Marius. Her grey-blue eyes had gone steely. "And you have come to take me with you whether I agree to go or not, haven't you?"

Reluctantly, he nodded.

"And you used Gideon to find me." It was an accusation.

Again, he nodded.

"You *have* changed."

Her mighty protector, still standing by the door, smiled at that.

"We have not lied to you, Theona", Marius protested. "You read the letter yourself. There was a second letter that came with it. It was also written by your father. It was written to General Stilicho and signed by a number of chieftains. They want to distance themselves from King Radagaisus and become allies of the Roman Empire. General Stilicho wishes you to go with him to prove to these men that the Roman Army is willing to deal with them in good faith."

"And if you do not wish to go, then the kind General will make you go anyway," said Granny caustically.

"No, Mother," said Ptolemy. "That won't happen."

"I need a few minutes by myself, Ptolemy," said Theona. "Keep them in here. I'll be back as soon as I know what to do."

He nodded, used to her ways by now. Theona slipped out the door behind him while the two tribunes awkwardly ate their soup. The room was very quiet apart from the slurping noises they were making. The old lady sat straight and still in her chair while the man watched from the doorway.

"How do we know Bissula isn't running away?" muttered Eucherius quietly. "I'll never hear the last of it if she slips away on this my one and only chance to do something adventurous for my father."

"I don't think she will leave," whispered Marius. "Where would she go? Besides, we were going to take her to her father and her people. She must want to see them after all this time. Nevertheless . . ."

They stood up together and turned to face Ptolemy, who was eyeing them with amusement.

"We're going out," said Eucherius, pulling his sword from its scabbard on his belt. "Stand aside. She's been long enough." He advanced toward the door with Marius right behind him.

Ptolemy stood his ground. Granny chuckled.

"You won't get past him, boys. He's a gladiator."

"Move," shouted Eucherius, brandishing the sword. "Get out of our way."

Ptolemy's hoe came up and at him fast. He knocked the sword right out of Eucherius's hand, and flipped it neatly across the room where it landed beside the fire, just missing the pot of soup. Marius rushed at him furiously, his sword pointing straight at the man's heart. Ptolemy ducked and somersaulted out of the way, then leaping to his feet behind Eucherius, turned and pinned his neck back in a tight embrace. Eucherius squawked helplessly, while Marius tried furiously to unjam his sword from where it had got caught in the doorframe.

Granny said something in Gothic to the gladiator, and he eased his hold.

"I warned you, didn't I!" she declared. "Now why don't we solve this little problem my way? We keep the good General's son hostage with us here while the other young man goes to find Theona. She won't be far. Likely over by the lake, praying."

Marius looked at Ptolemy. Ptolemy looked at him, a grim smile on his face.

"If you are not back by the time I count to three hundred, this one gets his pretty face cut up."

"Count slowly then. Really slowly."

Embarrassed and furious, Marius gave his sword one last yank, released it from the door, and stalked out.

Theona was sitting over on the far side of the pond, her legs pulled up to her chin. One of her hands rested on Gideon's flanks, and occasionally she would stroke him. Her eyes were open, and she appeared to be talking to someone.

Marius stood beside the door to watch, counting slowly to a hundred. How long would she be? For his friend's sake he couldn't afford to wait much longer.

All joy had gone out of the day. He felt like an incompetent fool, an inexperienced boy facing off against a . . . gladiator.

He said a quick prayer himself, for her, for him, for Eucherius who was now a hostage inside this house. Poor Eucherius would have to report this disgrace back to his famously valiant father. He could just imagine how that would feel! What a pair of heroes they had turned out to be!

He wished Theona *had* run away. He would certainly like to do that himself now, but orders were orders, and his friend's life was at stake. He did not doubt for a second that the man inside was a gladiator—some of them had been brought in to give special training to the more advanced legionaries, and now he knew why. They were the best fighters in the world, some of them trained, like this one he suspected, since they were young.

He reached the second hundred and started walking toward the lake, then stopped. The girl had seen him. She waved, and then languidly began pulling the fancy hairdo apart, letting the curls down and undoing the braids. He knew what it meant. She had decided to come with them after all. He exhaled, and sent a quick prayer of thanks up to God.

When Theona reached him, her face was calm. She saw his anxious eyes and reached up to smooth out the furrow between his eyes, murmuring something in her own language. He looked at her questioningly.

"Thank you for taking care of Gideon," she said. "He is almost as good as ever."

"Forgive me," he murmured, ashamed.

Her lip started to tremble. She nodded abruptly and turned toward the door.

"My name is Decimius Marius Ausonius."

Theona looked back and smiled, then reached for the door handle.

Without thinking, Marius reached for her arm and turned her gently back to face him. This was his Bissula, the girl of his dreams. Intently he studied her face, memorizing it feature by feature.

Nervously Theona looked back, and somehow the intensity of his gaze brought her under the same spell. They became lost to the world around them as unconsciously he pulled her closer, and unconsciously she found herself letting him.

Gideon growled, bringing them back to reality. Marius roused from his trance and released her, and Theona, suddenly self-conscious again, turned and went in.

CHAPTER THIRTY-TWO

A PEACEFUL INTERLUDE

Bononia, Italia
(Bologna, Italy)
July, 406 AD

The long journey from Pons Drusi to Bologna was done in only three days. Theona rode in a closed carriage and was closely guarded. Her escort travelled quickly, slowing mainly to change horses. At night they stayed in Roman military hostels or gained admittance to the walled towns along the route.

From time to time the party would join civilian and military convoys for part of the journey. These were composed of columns of soldiers escorting merchants, smaller military units and important travellers to their destinations. People with family or business elsewhere in the country rushed to avail themselves of this opportunity to travel in safety.

The convoy they travelled with the longest had a large group of barbarian prisoners in tow, guarded by slavers who were taking them to the slave markets of Rome. They had been seized in places where there was still a modicum of law and order, and were a chilling sight for Theona as she trotted past in her carriage.

They passed mile after mile of ruined and abandoned farms and burned villages. The extent of the devastation horrified her; she grieved for the peasants affected, remembering her own acute shock and fear when the Huns attacked and destroyed her village. The soldiers she was travelling with appeared to be accustomed to such sights, and their attitude towards her was cool. Marius's appeal to respect her person was heeded, perhaps because he kept a scowling eye on his companions, but perhaps more because he was supported by the formidable presence of his fellow tribune, the only son of General Stilicho.

The two of them rode close by her carriage but seldom approached her except to enquire as to how she was faring. Their remoteness upset Theona. They seemed to have resumed the role of soldiers under orders. She felt abandoned by them, even deceived, especially by Marius although she could not think why.

She was particularly unhappy that at the last minute they had all made the decision to leave Gideon behind. When she left with the tribunes, they had had to confine the dog in the house, and as they descended the gully path to the plateau beyond, the three of them were silent, listening to his frantic barks and heart-broken wails. The spunky little animal had now lost both Marius and her, when all he wanted was to be with them. She knew exactly how painful that was, and felt more guilty about this betrayal than about anything she had ever done in her life, save leaving Wolfric behind. She tried to comfort herself with the belief that Gideon would be cared for well enough, once Granny got used to having him around; Ptolemy had promised.

The Roman Army had used him and abandoned him, and now they were going to use her and abandon her. Theona could not get to her father and her own people fast enough.

Late on the third day they reached Bologna, and the squad of men from the Seventh Alpine Cohort formally handed their prisoner over to the legate of the military base there. Legate Merula had received orders concerning her. It seemed that General Stilicho was determined to make a good impression on the Gothic chieftains he was soon to meet. She was to be treated well. Nothing else being deemed suitable, Theona was taken into Merula's own home.

The soldiers from the Seventh Alpine Cohort were sent to barracks and given time off to explore the town before their journey back to Pons Drusi. Marius and Eucherius were assigned a house on the base which offered luxurious guest accommodations to high-ranking visitors. General Stilicho would join them there once he received word that they had found Pastor Rhodus's girl.

The Base Commander's house was large and elegant, as befitted his status. Theona had the guest wing all to herself. Two guards had been assigned to her. Legate Merula told her that she could go for walks around the base, but she must not venture into the city, even accompanied by the soldiers guarding her, or she could be attacked by a mob. Numbly she nodded.

Legate Merula's wife, a broad-minded matron from an Equestrian family, and their two little girls lived with him on the base. The children, though warned not to bother their young barbarian "guest", were rather lonely. A young woman staying just down one of the hallways was a strong attraction.

The morning after her arrival, they found her in the peristyle sitting on the ledge of the garden pool, watching the carp swimming among the water lilies.

Theona spotted the little girls peering from behind two of the columns and called to them. Shyly they sidled over to her, looking at her through big, dark eyes. Their names, she learned, were Prunella and Zenobia, and they were four and six years old. Glad for the company, she played hide and seek with them in the garden and the guest wing, and then did their hair in two of the styles she had learned watching Granny.

When the children showed up for dinner that evening, they were still wearing their long dark hair piled high, and looked like self-satisfied miniature matrons. They were full of the stories the girl with the long yellow hair had told, and the fun they had had with her. Their parents were astounded and intrigued. The next day the legate sent word to her guards to request that "their young guest" join the family for the evening meal.

Theona declined—living with Granny and Ptolemy had not prepared her for dining with an Equestrian family in a gentrified Roman setting. Legate Merula subsided, but his wife rose up and decided to take Theona under her wing.

The second morning after Theona's arrival, Lady Juliana arrived at Theona's bedroom trailed by Prunella, Zenobia and a slave, a woman whose dark skin had Theona staring.

She was in the middle of doing her ablutions, and was using the chamber pot from an empty cubicle down the hall as a wash basin. Embarrassed, she snatched up her long white tunic and hid behind it, wondering what the matron meant by this unexpected visit.

The legate's wife was looking at her with curiosity.

"I know your name is Theona. You can call me Mistress Juliana. I understand you speak Latin."

The woman was tall and lean, and had kind amber eyes and black hair which she wore straight and loose. Theona noticed that the hair had a fringe across the forehead. She decided she liked it and wondered if she would ever work up the courage to try such a look herself—it probably took years for the shorter hair to lengthen out again. She reached up and fingered the two locks that Granny had cut short. They were in the wrong place for such a fringe.

"Yes, my lady."

"I don't suppose you've ever had a proper bath, have you? Put your tunic on quickly and follow me. The children and I are going to show you how to use the bathhouse."

She turned to the slave. "Take her clothes and match them up for size with the castoffs that are being collected by the church. The steward has them all. Bring the best ones here, and have hers laundered when you do your own."

The slave nodded and passed Theona, gathering up Granny's castoffs as she went.

Mistress Juliana turned to Theona. "Put on your tunic and come right away. We will wait for you down the hall. We won't have long. In another hour the men will be waiting to get in to use the bathhouse."

Theona dried herself quickly, threw on the long white tunic Granny had given her, and hurried down the hall. Prunella, the youngest child ran to meet her and seized her hand. They followed Zenobia and Mistress Juliana to the far side of the big house where the bath complex was located. This area could also be entered from the garrison street outside. It served the needs of the officers on the base and their families.

A slave unlocked the door from the other side, and they passed through a vestibule with a modest black and white marine floor mosaic and a few statues of athletes. Beyond it was another small room where the family and their guests could hang their clothes on wall pegs and leave their shoes on the floor beneath. A latrine bench ran along one of the walls here, and the steady stream of water flowing underneath the seats and in the trough in front provided a pleasant background sound.

Mistress Juliana and her daughters stripped off their clothing. Theona was astonished to find that all of them wore loincloths, and the woman even wore a breast band.

Theona had only the one garment to hang on the peg, and she wondered if Mistress Juliana would think she was too poor or too ignorant to dress properly. She had never watched Granny dress and the old woman had never commented on Theona's clothing, since she had never laid eyes on it. She had, however, eventually offered her some of her own clothing, garments she had kept for decades. These Theona prized. A castoff, however old, was, in her opinion better than a stolen garment, however new and beautiful. It was a question of honor.

Naked, they walked into the next room. This was the tepidarium, a steam-warmed room where a couple of slaves stood chatting together beside chairs and long benches.

Mistress Juliana continued on through a doorway into another room. In the center of this one was a deep, round pool. Marble steps led down into it. Mistress Juliana warned Theona that the water would be cold. This was the frigidarium.

The three Romans lowered themselves into the water and clambered out quickly, shivering. Theona followed more slowly, finding it not too bad: she had been in colder water than this when bathing in alpine lakes and rivers. At Mistress Juliana's insistence, she climbed out after a couple of minutes, and followed the other three back to the tepidarium to warm up. Following Mistress Juliana's example, she submitted to having a female slave oil her body and then scrape it down with a long strip of metal, wondering what her father would say about such a situation.

Among her own people she had often bathed in public, but one did not submit to having another person touch one's body in that vulnerable state, not unless one were married. The very thought made her uncomfortable, but she braced herself, trying to think of other things while the slave worked on her. Even the little girls seemed to be totally at ease with the procedure, but Theona was uncomfortable throughout, and glad that, so far at least, there was no one else there but the four of them and the slaves.

When they had all been oiled and scraped, they headed through another door where there was a much larger pool, an oblong one. Her companions appeared to be most excited about showing her this one, which they called the caldarium. Theona saw steam rising from the water and grew alarmed. Even the floor seemed warm here. To her, this pool seemed subversively designed to cook any unwary girls who ventured into it. She remembered old Gothic horror stories of unearthly creatures that breathed fire and kidnapped young maidens, and wished she had never listened to them.

But she was a Christian girl: she needed to be brave. She tested the waters with her feet and watched as Juliana and the girls immersed themselves in it and invited her in. Their skin seemed to be turning rosy.

"Does it burn?" she asked anxiously.

"No," laughed Mistress Juliana. "It's lovely. Your body gets used to it. When you get out, you pour some of the cold water from that," she pointed to a large marble basin at the end of the room, "onto your head to cool you down again. Then you dry off, and get dressed."

Theona wondered what on earth would make these Romans abuse themselves so much with all these unnatural experiences, but when the whole thing was over, she had her answer. Her body and her mind felt refreshed and relaxed. The stress of the trip down the Adige Valley and across the plain to Bologna seemed to have been washed away along with the grime.

After the bath, Prunella and Zenobia clamoured for her to do their hair again. This time they went right into the family's own living quarters, and the children fetched their mother's combs and brushes. Theona gave them a fourth-century hairdo which they all admired, and then Mistress Juliana conducted her and the children to the triclinium.

Here, Juliana taught her the basics of dining Roman-style. With the children participating, she made a game of it, showing Theona how to climb gracefully onto the long couches, how to prop herself up on her left elbow and then reach with her right hand for the food on the central serving table, how much water to add to your wine, how to imperiously summon a slave, when to excuse herself, when she should offer an opinion, and when she needed to keep her opinions to herself.

That evening she nervously dined with the family for the first time. Mistress Juliana presented her with a large bleached napkin and told her to keep it—she would need to bring it with her if she ever went out for dinner in any other Roman setting. It was a preposterous idea, but she played along, a twinkle in her eyes.

For the first time in her life, Theona faced an array of fancy foods on fancy dishes. Most of the food she did not recognize. Some she liked and some she wanted to spit out. Legate Merula and Lady Juliana encouraged her and corrected her throughout the ordeal, and after that first dinner, she was pronounced ready to dine with the 'almost-best'. That was Merula's little joke, and they all laughed.

Everyone had supposed that Theona would usually eat her meals alone in her own wing of the house, but after that first night she was almost always included, even when there were guests to dinner. The guests, once they had accepted her presence and the fact that she could speak Latin, were always curious about her and eager to hear her story. Usually she had to endure their frustrated tirades about the sufferings of the Romans due to the presence of Radagaisus and her fellow barbarians. Theona bit her lip and suffered through the humiliation, and usually the guests would stop once they deemed she had been sufficiently punished for the sins of her people.

Most mornings she spent with the two children. One day Zenobia asked if she knew any children their age. Her first thought was of Wolfric, and she became tearful. Prunella climbed onto her lap to give her a hug while Zenobia ran to fetch a handkerchief and her mother. They demanded to know why she was so sad. The children were too little to hear the truth, so Theona instead told them about Anarilka, the Queen of the Danube River. That was not much better; she could not help wondering what the little girl was living through now, or if she would ever see her again. War was no place to bring up a child, any child. Rilka was in her own fiery furnace now.

That evening in the triclinium, Theona worked up the courage to ask the legate if he had any news about Radagaisus and the members of his family. She learned for the first time that Anarilka's father, Vitiges, had been killed in a battle against an army of Huns.

Theona was stunned. Huns in Italia? They had fled their land to escape the Huns. What were the monsters doing here? And how was it that they were working with the Romans? She couldn't imagine the Huns she had seen working with anyone.

The next day a messenger arrived from the High Command with the news that contact had been made with the defecting chieftains. General Stilicho was already on his way to Bologna. Arrangements for the historic meeting had been made, and she would be handed over to her father and the barbarian chieftains in two days.

Theona was in a fever of excitement. Legate Merula and Mistress Juliana were dismayed by the fire that lit her eyes. She couldn't sleep, and she couldn't stop smiling.

Gently they tried to tell her that a future with her people was doomed, that if she wished, they would tell General Stilicho that she had decided to stay with them, but her enthusiasm was unquenchable. If she had only a short time to live, she wanted to spend it with her loved ones.

They looked at each other, and sadly agreed.

The next day General Stilicho arrived at the base with some of his aides. That evening she was not invited to dinner. Legate Merula was hosting a feast for the great Generalissimo and his party, and had invited his officers and the elite of Bologna.

Theona supposed Marius and Eucherius would be included among the dinner guests. She dressed carefully in a blue stola that Mistress Juliana had given to her and did her hair, expecting to be summoned as usual, but she was not. Her guards told her that if she was lucky, she might meet the great General the following morning. He would be among the party taking her to the assignation with the chieftains. They expected her to be comforted by that, but she was not.

She took off the stola, shook out her hair, and went to bed.

CHAPTER THIRTY-THREE

TREATIES AND DECLARATIONS

Ad Silarus, Padus Valley
(A village on the Via Aemilia east of Bologna)
July, 406 AD

T heona was awakened early the next morning by one of her guards. He handed her the lamp he was carrying and left her to finish her preparations and final packing. Thanks to Lady Juliana's intervention, she was leaving Bologna with a much finer set of castoffs than when she had arrived.

Mistress Juliana and the two girls showed up to see her off. They accompanied her to the street outside their home where the same two-horse carriage she had come in stood waiting. The children embraced her, and Mistress Juliana handed her a picnic basket. Legate Merula helped her inside the carriage, and she waved goodbye to them all as it set off down the road. Now she was alone, cut off even from her driver. Her bag was stowed in front, but she had kept the picnic basket and placed this on the seat beside her.

It was still dark. No one had told Theona how long the journey would be, or what the plan was to hand her over to her father and her people.

The family's parting gesture gave her courage. The surprising kindness of this Roman family had helped the days of confinement pass quickly. She hoped she had done the right thing in refusing their generous invitation to stay with them.

The next stop would bring her back among her own people.

All winter she had worried and wondered about what was happening to her father, to the people from her village, to Duke Helerix and Bishop Segeseric, to Roderic and Rilka, and to all the others she had come to know on the journey here. Soon she would be finding out. Beyond that reunion, the future was an impenetrable fog. She only knew that there were turbulent waters ahead.

Her dinner conversations at the legate's house had convinced her that the Romans would demand revenge for the damage done to their homes, their land and their fellow citizens. If the Romans beat them, the Goths and their allies would be made to suffer greatly, and Theona's journey to Bologna had shown her all too clearly that that punishment would be well-deserved.

She did not know what she would say to Roderic if she met him again—he was Radagaisus's son! Would the Romans execute him along with his father? If she was his wife, what would be her own fate? What would happen to Vitiges's widow, and to Anarilka, for that matter? They had a closer connection to Radagaisus than she did.

Many months had passed since the last time she and Roderic had been together, months in which both of them would have changed significantly. Ptolemy had assured her that the Prince was happy she was in a safe place and would come for her or send for her when the time was right. Roderic seemed to take it for granted that she would marry him, even though she had not yet agreed. If so, he had not learned much from the situation they had lived through at the wine merchant's house in Bressanone. As long as she remained a Christian, King Radagaisus was a danger to her. But she was now heading back towards them both, and perhaps they would meet again. If they did, she did not know what she would do.

The carriage stopped for a few minutes and she heard men's voices talking around her, among them Marius's and Eucherius's.

"Is she in there?" was all she was able to pick up before other noises drowned out their voices. Then the procession was on the way again. The journey smoothed out, and became an interminable clatter of hooves and shaking of bones.

Theona fell asleep in spite of the jouncing her body was receiving. She woke up when a tall man whose face she had never seen before pulled open the curtain and peered in at her. He had a strong face with a wide firm mouth, prominent blue eyes and silver blond hair. They looked at each other, and she guessed that this was General Stilicho, Eucherius's famous father.

He pulled open the door and held out a hand to help her down. She took it, smiling, and he said in Vandal, "Why the smile, princess?"

She looked up at him—he was as tall as Roderic—and answered him in Latin. "You offered your hand more like an officer compelling me to get out, than a gentleman helping me down—I wondered if your wife ever felt that way."

His pale eyes glittered. "Serena has said that! We are taking a brief respite. Perhaps you would like to stretch your legs and use the latrines here."

She looked around. They were standing in the enclosed courtyard of an inn. It was bustling with people, mostly legionaries who were watering their horses, chatting in groups, or heading into and out of the inn. Some of them eyed her and her companion curiously. She looked around for Marius and saw him standing beside a grey horse only a dozen feet away. He was watching her.

He saw her looking at him and smiled, but she would not smile back.

"Well?" General Stilicho had turned to look in the direction she had been staring.

"Oh yes. Thank you."

"Come with me then."

He led her across the courtyard towards the inn and shouldered his way through the crowded doorway. Theona followed in his wake toward the kitchen area where the latrines were located.

"Let the lady through," he shouted. "And disappear, you lads. Give her some space."

Theona, pink with embarrassment, and well aware of the men's curious glances as they fled away, hurried over to the quickly emptying open latrine bench. The General turned his back on her, frowning at the curious kitchen staff. He stood there forbiddingly, his tall presence and folded arms speaking volumes. Theona gratefully used the latrine and washed up in the trench of clean water flowing in front of the open seat. As she walked past him, she paused and looked up at him.

"That was thoughtful."

"I have two daughters," he said.

"Oh behalf of all daughters, I thank you," she replied.

He took her straight back to her carriage, and made her get in.

It was a while before the rest of the cavalry escort were mounted and ready to leave again. Theona sat inside her carriage listening to the commotion outside and wishing she could get out and talk to Marius, to Eucherius, to the General, to the driver, to anyone, but clearly that was not going to be allowed. She was an enemy hostage, in spite of the courtesy they had shown her.

As her carriage pulled out of the courtyard of the inn, she saw that the road they were taking to the east was filled with cavalry and military wagons as far as she could see. The General's party was part of a huge convoy of supplies being brought into the area. General Stilicho was laying his groundwork.

Dejectedly, she reached across to the picnic basket and opened it up. On top of the food and flask of wine was a package wrapped in cotton cloth. She undid the wrapping. She recognized one of Zenobia's toys, a delicately carved wooden doll wearing a white linen tunic with a woven red stola over it. Underneath was a thin scroll with some words written on it by Mistress Juliana: "Zenobia wanted you to give this to your other little girl."

Tears sprang to Theona's eyes, and she began to laugh. She hugged the doll for the rest of the journey.

The church of St. Sabas the Martyr was located on the banks of the Silarus River, many miles east of the city of Bologna.

The convoy reached the village of Ad Silarus in the early afternoon. General Stilicho's bodyguard, along with Theona's carriage, split away from it and travelled up a dirt road toward the church. A large detachment of cavalry remained behind to wait for them at the main road, while the rest of the convoy carried on toward Rimini.

Theona heard a series of loud notes from a horn blare from somewhere nearby. General Stilicho shouted, "HOLD." Her carriage stopped.

Theona peered out and saw only the soldiers in her own escort, but she overheard comments about the Goths having already arrived. The General's men had decided that the horn had been blown to let the Gothic leaders know that the Roman delegation was approaching the host church.

A quarter mile farther they rode into the courtyard of the church, a large wooden structure which resembled some of the Great Houses Theona had seen. She could see warriors running for their horses. By the time the Romans had come to a stop, the barbarians had mounted and were in formation, their leaders mounted in front of them. She recognized Duke Helerix, Duke Rumbert and Duke Arnulf among them, and felt her spirits lift.

The Roman cavalry formed their own lines, and stared haughtily across at the warriors facing them.

Two men walked out of the church. One was in the robes of a cleric. The other was a thin, greyhaired man with a lined face. His eyes were fixed on the lone carriage.

General Stilicho and a big blond officer dismounted and walked forward to meet them. They spoke briefly, and Stilicho's companion walked back to let Theona out of her carriage. She stepped down onto the dusty ground feeling a bit shaky. Her father cried out and ran towards her, oblivious of the Roman soldiers all around her. She shouted, and took off toward him, hoisting her skirts to keep from tripping. They embraced in tears, hugging as the soldiers on both sides watched.

"Take your daughter and go into the church," ordered General Stilicho. "My advisors and I will meet your leaders inside there as well." He turned to face Duke Helerix, who had dismounted and was coming over to them, a welcoming smile on his tanned, intelligent face.

Stilicho straightened to face him.

"Welcome, Duke. Everyone must leave their weapons outside the building. My men will check your men, and your men can check us."

Arm in arm, Theona and her father strolled into the church. They could not take their eyes off each other, and more than one man on both sides of the conflict had a lump in his throat, watching.

Inside the shadowed building they embraced again.

"You look well, my sweet," Pastor Rhodus said as the door closed behind them. "God has taken good care of you."

"You look worn out, Father," she said sadly. "Life has been harder for you than for me. I should never have left. I am so sorry I trusted Cantarcchio. I tried for days to find you afterwards—I still do not know how we missed each other."

"God works in mysterious ways," he reminded her. "We never stopped praying for you. You and I may be here for some time while these men work out what they are going to do. Tell me everything. How do you come to look like such a Roman lady?"

She told him about her reluctant flight with Cantarcchio, and about Granny and Gideon, her encounter with Tribune Ausonius, Roderic's rescue, Radagaisus's threat and her flight, Ptolemy's adoption, and the skills she had learned over the winter. He listened eagerly and laughed at times with delight.

"Prince Roderic will not recognize you."

"Have you seen him? What news do you have?"

"Yes, I have seen him. Quite often, in fact. Once we reached the plains, we divided into smaller groups again and went off in different directions. Radagaisus ordered Roderic and his men to continue on as messengers among the various factions. The prince has dropped by our camp several times to meet with our leaders. He never fails to seek me out.

"Our chieftains have been mostly keeping to the wild lands to the east of these mountains. We live off the land as much as possible. All of our leaders were in agreement that they preferred to find the most honorable course through this hideous adventure. It is a good thing, too; we were always being watched. That man you came with would have no tolerance for the kind of behavior we heard was happening elsewhere."

"But what about Roderic? Does he know about today? Does he know I am coming? Does he know you and the chiefs with you have left your camp to meet with General Stilicho?"

"No. We could not take that chance. Asking the young man to keep such information from his father is asking too much. All of our people are still at the camp and a few of the leaders as well, just in case the prince or one of the other messengers came by."

"The lords here today want to negotiate with General Stilicho for land to settle on—as Alaric managed to get for his people in southern Pannonia. They waited for months for King Radagaisus to reach out to the Romans, or the Romans to us, but things quickly got out of control, as they always seem to do. Our chiefs are now persuaded that the King does not seem to have any real interest in talking. It may be too late for him now. He and many others among us are living without honor."

"Where is Darric? Is he back at the camp?"

Pastor Rhodus shook his head.

"I hope you won't take this too hard, Theona. Darric hated what he saw going on, as I do, so he left. He decided that he would rather face God with a clear conscience and be killed by Huns back home in Gothia than wander in this land doing the devil's work. He always thought this was a hopeless cause we have undertaken. The dream is truly a nightmare. We have not lost to the Romans, but we cannot go on as we are. He has left us altogether, but I could not leave without knowing that you were safe.

He abruptly gripped her arm, "Oh! Do you remember Puella, the Pannonian woman to whom you gave the red cloak? Well, she left with Darric, along with his mother, Anna. He was going to see her as far as her home, and she was going to try to help him get safe conduct across the bridge at Carnuntum. Apparently her cousin is the governor there."

Theona was glad. She hoped Puella would be able to find her children again, and rebuild her life. She remembered the woman's pitiful appearance when she first arrived at their caravan with her captor. After that, it was all downhill until her cruel master had been killed by the Romans. She and her children deserved some happiness.

"So, Darric is gone," she said slowly. "And Edrica?"

"She has married one of Duke Rumbert's men and is expecting a child."

Theona was astonished. "It seems life goes on, doesn't it?"

"Not for me, child. At least, not until now. For the last eight months, I have been holding my breath. Now that we are together again, perhaps I can begin to breathe again."

The church door opened and the Gothic priest walked in, followed by the Gothic chieftains, General Stilicho, the blond officer who had fetched her from the carriage, Eucherius, and several other men. They were a tense group. They did not talk as they passed, but headed grimly through the nave towards a door at the other end of the church. Duke Helerix waved, but never broke stride.

They watched the last of the leaders disappear and the door close behind them. Two Roman soldiers and two Gothic warriors lounged against the walls nearby, eying each other and talking softly together.

"What do you think will happen to Roderic?" she whispered.

"I don't know. You had better prepare yourself, though. The Romans may want these men to seize him and turn him over to them to ensure that his father complies with their demands. General Stilicho might suggest it as a gesture of good will such as the Romans showed in turning you over to our side."

"I wasn't important. He is."

"You are very important to me," he said.

"I am a common girl. He is Radagaisus's son! They will kill him!"

"If he surrendered to them, they might let him live, but if he stays with his father to the end and they get him, then he will indeed die."

"We can't let that happen to him, Father. He's a good man."

"It is out of our hands, Theona. It will be his choice."

"If someone could persuade him to join this coalition . . ."

"I doubt anyone but you could do that, Theona. He has come to me more than once to plead his case for your hand."

"Is he willing to listen to the Gospel of Christ?"

"He says no. I think he feels it would be a betrayal of his father and his heritage. He wants you, and he wants his father's approval. Only he thinks he can have both. I have told him a little about our Lord. He seemed a little put out when I told him that Jesus was the King of kings and Lord of lords." He chuckled.

"What should I do?" Theona heard the hesitancy in her own voice.

"This is an unusual situation, dear heart. If you ask me, you will not marry him. Not because he is not a Christian, but because there are dangerous implications for you if you do marry him. I cannot contemplate *that* with any courage. I just got you back!"

"Did you know the Prince sent me a gold chain with an icon of Jesus on it?"

"No!" he exclaimed, surveying her bare neck, "Where is it?"

She pulled it from her pouch and he gasped. "Put that away immediately. That thing is worth a fortune!"

"Where do you suppose he got it? Ptolemy says he bought it from one of his men."

His look darkened. "I have heard that he has led some raids himself, my sweet. It is probably stolen, and who knows, someone may even have killed to get it."

"That is why I do not wear it often. And if I should marry a man who can do such things, I do not think I could be happy, even if I do love him."

Marius's earnest face had just flashed before her eyes. But that was even more fantastic.

Her father sighed. "Well, you may have to make up your mind sooner than you wish. No doubt he will be eager for your answer when he learns that we have you safely back. How we are going to explain that, I don't know. Telling the truth would mean telling him about our defection to his enemies. I could almost wish you were still with that old woman!"

They strolled out the door of the church and stopped. A warm moist breeze blew drizzle in their faces. Crows cawed in the cypress trees nearby, while a hundred horses shifted their feet. There was a low murmur of conversation from both sides of the enemy divide as soldiers and warriors waited for their leaders to emerge.

Marius had inched his horse slightly away from his companions to get a better view of the door of the church. Theona spotted him immediately.

Impulsively, she said, "I want you to meet someone, Father."

She pulled him right through the buffer area toward the ranks of Roman cavalry. The murmur of conversation on both sides increased sharply, and then hushed. Theona would have turned back, but it was already too late. Her cheeks pink, her eyes lowered, she tugged her father toward Marius. He straightened up in the saddle and watched them come, his own face a study in discomfiture and anticipation.

Theona stopped and looked up at him.

"Marius, this is my father. Father, this is the man who saved Gideon's life, and then found me for you."

"My son, may God bless you for that," said her father in Latin.

"Thank you, Pastor. For your daughter I would do much more."

Marius couldn't believe he had said that. Theona looked at him in amazement, as did her father.

"It is ill times we live in, Marius," said her father at last. "Take care of yourself, son. Someday, you may live to be of service to her once more."

Around them, listening legionaries were grinning.

Theona grabbed her father's hand again and led him away. He was beaming. She was blushing. It was a long walk back behind the Gothic lines.

"That was interesting, Tribune," mused one of General Stilicho's bodyguard. "Your grandfather would certainly approve. We'll have to keep our eye out for that one when we whip the Goths. She could soon be your very own Bissula! I suppose you've thought of that?"

There were a few chuckles from riders nearby. Marius laughed too, elated that at last he had had the chance to say something to Theona about these crazy feelings he had been experiencing for the last couple of months. Life was beautiful. She was beautiful. He was in love. It would all work out somehow.

The leaders did not emerge for another forty-five minutes. When they did, they saluted each other cheerfully, and headed for their horses. The Goths rode out first, with Theona once again in her carriage, this time driven by a Goth. It was a final gesture of good will from General Stilicho.

The Romans dismounted and stretched, their first chance to do so since their break at the inn.

Marius hurried over to Eucherius.

"How did it go?" he asked.

"Quite well. Some of them are very decent chaps. Father and Sarus are excited to have them join the army. They've got big plans for the future."

"But what's the plan for their defection?"

"They will rejoin Radagaisus and try to recruit others to leave with them. When we march on Florence, at a given signal they will desert the king, and after that we will close in on the rest of them."

"And what do they get out of this agreement?"

"Their lives and the lives of their family members," replied his friend. "Their warriors will join the Army and fight under our officers, but they will be able to stay together in their own fighting units, and their families will be allowed to stay together nearby."

"What about the others?"

"What others?"

"What about the men, women and children who are not warrior class, or are with the chiefs who will not cross over to us?"

"The usual. We only need the warrior class, Marius. If you're worried about our Theona, I'm sure she will be safe. Maybe her father is considered one of their warriors. Perhaps he will become a chaplain to Sarus's Goths. If not, I guess I'll have to buy her and present her to you as a slave girl in a deliciously ironic repeat of history. "

Marius whirled on him. "That is not funny, Eucherius!"

His friend looked at him soberly. "Don't get too attached, my friend. It would be most inappropriate, almost as inappropriate as my jumping ship on the princess and marrying into your lovely family. Theona's a Goth and a heretic, not quite the patrician beauty an Ausonius would be expected to marry. And I doubt very much if your mother would approve of any other type of arrangement with her."

CHAPTER THIRTY-FOUR

THE PUSH TO MONTEFIESOLE

Ticinum Military Base on the Ticino River
(Modern Pavia)
July, 406 AD

Back in Pavia, Marius learned that his request for a transfer to a cavalry unit had come through. After that, he was back in training again, this time doing something he quite enjoyed—spending much of his time in maneuvers out on the broad flatlands of the base. At the back of his mind was Prince Roderic's spectacular leap from his horse, sword in hand, ready to take on the Rhaetian soldier who had abducted Theona. It would take a lot to impress the girl who had witnessed that!

By mutual agreement, he and Eucherius had given General Stilicho and their housemate, Jason, a severely abridged version on how things had gone when they had taken Theona into custody. They mentioned no details that might lead to awkward questions about exactly how they had handled, or mishandled, the situation. Soon the matter was forgotten, and the only news Marius received about the Wodenvale coalition was that the chieftains who had signed the treaty had moved from a largely unsettled coastal area inland toward Florence. After that, he lost all trace of Theona's movements.

Eucherius was busy at headquarters. The plans for the march on Florence were coming along fast. His friend shared what he knew which was more than Marius would have learned any other way, but Eucherius said nothing about the High Command's main battle strategy.

One day a letter arrived from his godfather. He opened it impatiently.

My dear godson, it read.

I send you my fondest greetings, and trust you are in good health and enjoying your adventures during this, your time in the army.

I had business affairs to attend to in Trier a while ago, and spent an afternoon with your family. Paulus and your brothers are well, and busy as usual. Your sister has changed since I last saw her—she is taller and fuller than I remember from your send-off party last summer. Your mother has more grey hair than she did a year ago. (I've noticed that women do seem to age faster than men though. However, as the doctors tell us, their body temperatures are cooler than men's bodies—hence, of course, the difference in gender. Perhaps they have to work harder to stay warm, and that is the reason they get older faster than we men do.) I hasten to add that your lovely mother looks well and seems happy enough.

I have been anxious for news of you, and for news of what is going on in Italia these days. Everyone in Arles and Southern Gaul is constantly on the lookout for travellers, especially soldiers on leave. The stories we hear are appalling! I, for one, have been expecting to learn every week that the counterattack has begun, or is even over, but no such news has come to relieve our anxiety. I confess I am now deeply worried about the state of our Empire.

Your family told me you are well and have made a new friend. That is very good news. I was wondering if you would be so kind as to indulge me with some account of what you see and hear around you, especially given your connections with the people who ought to be in the know. I am not asking just out of curiosity, dear Marius. I have a friend, an army officer from Gaul who now serves in Britain. We met recently in Reims at the home of Bishop Nicasius, and my friend expressed his own concerns about the delay. He sent contingents of his own soldiers over quite a while ago, and according to him, they are hanging around Pavia waiting for orders. He needs them back in Britannia.

Why do you think the High Command is waiting so long? This is, after all, Italia that is being devastated, the homeland of our beloved Emperor Honorius! My friend was anxious that I use all my connections to try to find out the truth, and I shall be sure to pass on any news you can give me to him and to other loyal patriots in the province.

I believe your family is expecting you home for leave soon. If you should happen to come overland through Gaul, I will be pleased to offer you the comforts and hospitality of my home in Arles. I am sure Sebastianus would want to say the same. He has a lovely daughter of about your age whom I am sure you would enjoy meeting.

Your affectionate godfather,

Jovinus

Marius made a rude noise, threw the scroll onto the floor and stamped on it. He would write to reassure his godfather, but he would say only the most insipid, un-insightful things he could think of. Sebastianus's daughter indeed!

However, his godfather's remarks stuck in his head. They were what everyone had been wondering for months. The people of Florence were said to be in desperate straits. The harvest everywhere in the Po Valley would be sparse this year. Food shortages were affecting even the invaders now, and gangs of barbarians had started spreading farther south. Eucherius confided that General Stilicho had received many nervous envoys from the Roman Senate demanding an account of his plans.

It was, as Theona's father had said, ill times they were living in. The sooner they could begin the counterattack the better. He and his fellow soldiers were raring to go.

Towards the middle of July, they heard that the last units of infantry the High Command needed had arrived just across the mountains in Gaul. They would reach Pavia in a few days. This would bring the field army up to more than thirty regiments, enough troops finally to be able to defeat Radagaisus and his undisciplined and scattered followers. The pace of preparations picked up dramatically. Units of infantry marched off east, accompanied by cavalry to provide protection for the marching men and the wagon trains that accompanied them.

Marius left for Bologna with his cavalry unit soon after. They were to wait at the base outside the city until the order came to press on toward Florence.

Cohorts spread out and began attacking caravans, laagers, and settlements of barbarians. Local militias, encouraged by the activity of the Army, initiated their own offensives. Roman roads that had been constructed for military purposes became military thoroughfares once more. The battle was about to begin.

Only in the distant east and north-east were barbarian groups ignored; the Roman Army would take on Radagaisus and his warriors first, and deal with the others later.

Florence

All the months of wandering and plundering had come down to this moment. The Roman Army had waited almost a year to come after them, but now they were on their way. All the barbarians by now knew much more about the Romans and their history than they had in the first flush of the invasion. The Romans were stubborn and vengeful. They might lose a battle, but they had never considered defeat a long-term option. If history was anything to go by, the invaders would have a real fight on their hands.

Panicked caravans retreated across the Apennines or fled eastward from the regions of Pisa, Lucca and Genoa. Those that tried to turn back found escape cut off behind them. Flight in the direction of Rome or Arezzo[49] south of Florence was also blocked. Caravans that had been active in those areas were instead fleeing back to seek refuge with the Gothic king and his men. The area around Florence filled up with caravans of Goths, Suevis, Vandals and other barbarians seeking sanctuary with their leader.

Radagaisus had to release his pressure on Florence and find a defensible position all the people could get to quickly. To the south of the city lay a vast marshy area. Roman roads were blocked in every direction. They were trapped. Only the hills behind Florence seemed a viable option for the thousands upon thousands of men, women and children fleeing into the area. Higher ground would also give the warriors an advantage in a Roman attack.

The king chose Montefiesole, a mountain directly behind the city and within easy reach of it. Montefiesole stood a thousand feet high at its crest, and was sixteen miles in circumference. Most of it was covered with forest, but there were also rocky patches, pasture land, accessible water and many olive groves and vineyards. The crest commanded a good view of the roads into the area, including the Via Flaminia Minor from Bologna. If the worst happened, one of these roads might provide an escape route.

The King issued the order for his warriors to abandon their positions around the walls of the city and get the people to the heights of Montefiesole.

A couple of miles east of Florence, Theona and Edrica were splashing and laughing with a group of children in a mountain stream. It meandered past the village they were occupying, one of many small farming communities in the hills of this area which had existed since Etruscan times. The peasants who had lived here had barely held their own under normal conditions, let alone during the periods where waves of aggressors had swept through. Today it was the turn of the Goths to control the area.

When the Wodenvale coalition arrived from the east, they found the homes already deserted. A few of the families moved into the abandoned hovels here, while the remainder of the caravan looked around for other places to settle.

---

[49] Arrezo, formerly Arretium, is in Tuscany 50 miles southeast of Florence.

Some of the olive trees and grape vines had been there for countless generations. The women and children made an attempt to look after the gardens and the cash crops by hauling water to the plants and chasing away vermin.

The July morning was hot. The two girls and the children in their charge had already spent two hours weeding and watering the gardens, but the relentless heat and hard work had driven them all to the stream bank to cool down and have some fun.

The girls were looking after sixteen Goths and one Roman child. The Roman child, now happily splashing water on two screaming little blond girls, was a boy of about five who had begun coming into the village soon after they arrived.

He had shown up from somewhere over the hills, his dark eyes large and hopeful. No one knew what had become of his parents, or where he went at the end of the day, but Edrica had begun feeding him when she fed herself and her husband, and the little boy had been staying longer and longer.

Only Theona and her father knew enough Latin to talk to him, and they had learned his name was Thaddeus. He was shy with all the adults, but just the day before had scraped his knee badly in a fall and allowed Edrica to comfort him. Everyone in the little settlement now accepted his presence among them.

In the middle of the happy giggles and splashes, they heard a rider pounding down the road below them, and ran to look. Theona recognized one of Roderic's messengers. He turned up their dirt road, and reined in his sweaty horse beside them.

"Where are your leaders?" he demanded.

Theona pointed to the end of the village where a group of archers, her father among them, were having a target practice. The men were taking turns shooting their arrows on the run past the target, and then retrieving the arrows and changing strategy.

"Is anything wrong?" asked Edrica.

"The Romans are down the road and marching fast," the rider answered tersely, and spurred his horse in the direction of the men.

Theona and Edrica looked at each other with alarm. Quickly they marshalled the children back toward the little cluster of hovels, watching while the archers stopped to listen to the messenger and then started to run.

"Pack up," shouted her father. "We have to leave immediately. There are Roman troops coming this way. The messenger says they were coming fast. We have to get to Florence immediately. Take only what Bagautus can carry, the necessities and food. Hurry."

Bagautus was the old horse he had been given for the trip to St. Sabas the Martyr in Ad Salaris. Helerix had allowed him to keep it.

The girls told the children to go find their parents right away. Frightened, they ran off toward the little hovels they were staying in. Thaddeus looked at his scared playmates and started to cry.

"What do we do with him?" asked Edrica quietly.

"I don't know," muttered Theona. "Leave him here, I guess. I don't suppose the Roman soldiers will hurt *him*."

"Someone's got to get that child back to his family, if he has any," said Pastor Rhodus. We can't just leave him here. It's not right. Find out where he lives. I'll take him on Bagautus."

"I don't think you'll find anyone," Theona protested, but he kept going toward the pasture where Bagautus was grazing with several other horses.

"Come," she said to Thaddeus, "I need to talk to you. You can watch me pack."

They hurried into the little house where she and her father had been staying. Feverishly she went through their possessions.

Fear propelled her. All of her people would be hurrying toward Radagaisus's camp, now, rushing for safety and a new place to stay. Those with the lightest loads were more likely to go quickly. They must take the tent! And blankets! She needed to make her choices fast. Food, a few clothes, cups and plates, a pot, money or things to trade with, the Gothic Bible, knives, flint, her slingshot, Roderic's gold chain . . .Making the necessary choices was an agony. How could they carry everything they would need for food, shelter, cooking and self-defense?

And then there was this little boy. Thaddeus had been watching her anxiously.

She threw up a prayer to God and sat down, pulling the little boy onto her lap. He was trembling and gulping, and buried his head against her breast. His dark eyes were wet, his nose streaming. He understood. They were all going to leave him alone again. She held him for a minute to settle him down, and her mind flashed back to Nerthus's priestess, cuddling the doomed little lamb. She pushed the memory angrily away.

"Thaddeus," she said stroking his hair away from his eyes, "Who lives with you?"

"My brother."

"How old is he?"

He shook his head. He didn't know.

"Do you live far from here?"

He shook his head.

"Where are your parents?"

"Dead," he whispered. "Some people killed them and took all our chickens."

Theona rested her head against the top of his, a lump in her throat.

"I am so sorry, Thaddeus. Do you have any grandparents?"

"Yes. Nonno and Nonna."

He had grandparents—that was good. "And where do they live?"

Outside she heard shouting and running, and then the creak of wheels and the clip-clop of hooves.

"Theona!" Her father burst through the door. "We've got to go. Is he ready? Are you?"

Thaddeus tensed up in her arms.

"Where do your grandparents live?"

"On a big farm."

"Do you know how to get to there from here?"

"Yes."

Theona breathed a sigh of relief. "You must go home right away, Thaddeus. Get your brother and then you should both go to Nonno's and Nonna's home right away, and stay there for a while. There is going to be trouble around here, and you and your brother both need to be somewhere safe. Do you understand?"

His lip started to tremble again. "We don't like them very much. They have a big goose and he chases us, and Nonna is mean to us. She doesn't like children."

This was not going well.

"Who do you know in the area who would let you and your brother stay with them for a while?"

He sniffed. "There is an old man who lives at the top of our mountain. His children are all gone away. He sometimes gives us chestnuts. He doesn't have a goose, but he's sick. He coughs a lot, and my mama used to tell us to stay away from him."

She hugged him. "Dear boy, you must be brave. Goose or no goose, you must leave and go to your Nonno's house. You cannot stay with us because you will not be safe. Soldiers are coming to chase us and hurt us. You must go where your own people will be able to look after you. I will pray for your safety. Now you must go."

"Can I come with you?" His dark eyes were pleading.

"No. GO!"

He burst into tears and ran out of the little house just as Edrica and her husband arrived at the door.

"Thaddeus," exclaimed Edrica, "Look what I have for you!" She handed him the rest of their morning porridge in a beautiful ceramic bowl. "Take this home with you, boy, and be good. Don't forget that Jesus loves you."

He accepted her gift and ran off, his little body shielding the bowl as he headed to the end of the village and the path that led toward his home. Pastor Rhodus pursed his lips, watching the little boy run. He had brought Bagautus up to the little hovel. Theona explained about the child's grandparents.

He nodded. "Okay, let's go."

Just before the Roman child was about to disappear over the hill, he stopped and looked back at them. Edrica waved, and Theona waved him on, but Thaddeus just stood there, dipping his fingers into the porridge and scooping up mouthfuls, his sad, dark eyes on them all.

Pastor Rhodus and Athanaric began to load the old horse with their belongings. Neighbors ran down the street toward them, begging them to allow the horse to carry some of their things as well. When Bagautus was covered with burdens, they set off down to the main road and turned toward Florence. Pastor Rhodus walked ahead, leading the horse, while the neighbors followed with hand carts. Some families were dragging their tents piled high with their food and possessions.

Throngs of people filled the road. Close to the city the king's men intercepted them with instructions to take one of the roads to the top of Montefiesole and find a place to settle. Looking up they could see several hamlets and farms on the slopes, and a little town at the top. It was going to be a long, hard climb to get there. Theona looked at Edrica with concern. Her friend's pregnancy would be an impediment.

As they started up the narrow road leading to the top of the mountain, people coming from behind began to push past them, hurrying to stake out their place to stay. Everyone had seen the limited number of homes up there. Once those were gone . . .

Theona looked anxiously at the other three and the old horse. Bagautus was already tired.

"You girls go on." said Athanaric. "I'll help your father with Bagautus. See what you can find up there. Perhaps Duke Helerix has already set aside an area for us."

She and Edrica began the climb. Below them, long lines of wagons snaked along the roads toward the mountain. Thousands upon thousands of people were coming up this mountain. It seemed quite big. Would it be big enough?

About a mile up the mountain they passed a cathedral. It had been raided many times by Radagaisus's followers, and much of the artwork inside was gone. Only the ceiling showed the original beauty of the building. Several families had already staked out their living quarters in the basilica, and their men were guarding the door. No more families would be allowed in.

They continued climbing for another hour. Edrica, looking pale, leaned on Theona's arm more and more. She had to stop to rest frequently, and kept looking back down the road for Athanaric. Theona was becoming impatient.

As they approached the top of the mountain, they could see ahead the edge of the town of Fiesole[50]. It was perched just under the southernmost crest of the mountain. Already the air was not as blisteringly hot as it had been at the bottom.

They rounded the final bend and walked right into the town forum. It was already crowded. The horses and mules that had made it to the town stood panting, their heads hanging. A few were munching on whatever grasses and flowers they could reach along the verge of the road and in the little gardens.

Radagaisus's men were everywhere. A few of them stood guard at the entrance to the main buildings around the forum, while others tried to direct newcomers to their leader's campsites.

Theona and Edrica recognized a few people from the Wodenvale coalition and called out greetings. Duke Helerix was in the middle of the square talking to some of the King's men. They waited until he was free and approached him.

"Where do you want us all to go?" Edrica asked.

He pointed up one of the streets at the far end of the forum. Several cobbled streets exited from there. Most headed further uphill. Men and women shouted and shoved as they carried their belongings up and down the hillside streets looking for a vacant home or some other building to shelter in.

"We have been assigned an area on an eastern slope about half a mile that way," he said. "We have a pasture and an olive grove. If there isn't enough room for us, we have been told to cut the trees down. Keep going up that street and when you get to the top of the hill, one of my men will tell you where to go."

They stood in the forum a little longer waiting for Pastor Rhodus and Athanaric, but Edrica was exhausted, so they headed towards the town amphitheater on the other side of the forum. Many of the benches were already filled with mothers with babies and young children, the elderly, the ill and the exhausted. Some were resting, while others ate. A few enterprising vendors were already walking up and down with objects to sell and prepared food to eat.

They found a seat and looked around. Just beyond the amphitheater were extensive gardens containing Roman baths, including a long narrow pool. The aqueduct that brought the water in from the hills across the valley loomed above them. At the more distant end of the gardens they could see several pagan temples. On the hill to their right, some of the town's houses straggled up nearby streets. Across the gardens and behind them were other homes on several levels.

"Do you suppose all of those houses have been taken already?" asked Edrica.

"Probably," said Theona. It was comforting to know that Duke Helerix had their site already.

They sat there resting for a while.

"We had better go back to see if we can find the men," sighed Edrica at last. "There was a fountain in the middle of the forum. I need a drink. Help me up."

They went back into the forum. Duke Helerix was no longer there.

They headed toward the fountain Edrica had seen. People were crowding around it with buckets, jars and amphorae. The ones who had already reached the fountain were throwing water onto their heads, slurping it down from their open palms, and filling their empty vessels with water to carry away. Some of them had buckets to water their thirsty animals.

Theona and Edrica waited their turn, creeping forward when someone at the front left the crush. It would be a while before they reached the water, so they kept watching the corner where Rhodus and Athanaric were expected to appear with Bagautus.

---

[50] In Roman times Fiesole was known as Faesulae. It is several miles from Florence and overlooks it..

One of the most prestigious looking buildings in the forum was directly across the street from them. The door opened, and King Radagaisus walked out onto the spacious porch followed by three of the chieftains. Phaedrus came out last, his eyes scanning the crowded square while he kept one ear on the argument the four men were having.

Theona hunched down behind Edrica as they inched forward. Two big blond women, sisters by the looks of it, moved out of the way with their heavy amphorae balanced on their heads, and it was finally their turn to drink. She bent down and scooped the water into her hands, and blissfully drank, and then washed her face and neck. One more drink and she would leave.

She bent down again and felt someone smack her arm. She looked up questioningly and saw Edrica discretely pointing toward the corner they had been watching.

Instead of her father and Athanaric, she saw Prince Roderic coming around the corner leading his horse. He looked tired and dirty.

Her heart leaped. It was the first time she had seen him in months.

Edrica was frantically scooping up another drink, her eyes on the prince. He was leading his horse purposefully toward the fountain.

Phaedrus had observed him too. He left the King and hurried down the steps to intercept the prince.

Theona stood staring too long. She had forgotten to drink and shield her face. Prince Roderic's eyes widened. He stared back and quickened his steps just as Phaedrus reached him. She and Edrica turned and plunged through the crowd behind them.

They hurried toward the street Duke Helerix had indicated. It sloped upward and bent out of sight. Just before she turned the corner, Theona could not resist looking back. Roderic's eyes were on them. He was talking to Phaedrus in some agitation, then turned around and led his horse back toward where his father and the chieftains were talking.

She and Edrica continued on up the road until they saw Duke Helerix's man standing at an intersection. They followed his directions to the campsite.

The warlord and many of the Wodenvale people were setting up camp on a lower slope some distance away from the center of the village. Tents in various stages of assembly were everywhere. They could hear the sounds of trees being chopped down somewhere below. Some horses were grazing on the edges of this new camp.

They hurried over to talk to him.

"My lord," panted Edrica, "Is it possible for us to move farther away from the village to somewhere more secluded?"

"Why? I was directed here by the King's own men. It would look suspicious if I refused to take one of the best spots on the mountain. There is a spring here, and the ground is reasonably level."

"We saw the King and Prince Roderic in the village. Phaedrus was with them. Theona thinks Prince Roderic saw her. This area is too close to them."

Duke Helerix frowned. He looked back up the hill toward the village and then turned to Theona.

"I heard about the King's threats to hurt you. Is that story true?"

She nodded. There had been many witnesses that morning.

"I think, Theona, that you and your father will have to stay somewhere else this time," he said. "As you can see, I am responsible for many people now. When things get tough up here, as they surely will, King Radagaisus is going to be looking for someone to blame. I fear it will be you Christians, and especially you and your father."

Theona shivered. Duke Helerix was right. The king had wanted to harm her once before. Perhaps he still wanted to. His surviving son had been willing to defy him and marry her. He would surely blame Theona for that. And then there was that harrowing incident with her father at the Grand Council—Radagaisus was not a man to forgive or forget.

"Sometime soon," continued Duke Helerix, "The king is going to learn that many of us are not as loyal as he thought. Until then I dare not risk arousing his suspicions. For all I know, the king himself assigned this area to us. We were told to camp here, and here we will stay."

He looked at Edrica. "You and Athanaric will remain, of course. Neither the king nor his son will be looking for you."

Theona was devastated. She felt close to tears. Edrica was angry.

"Where they go, I go," she said proudly.

Marriage had softened Edrica. In recent weeks she had become a friend and a confidante, no longer a rival prickly with jealousy. Her stubborn words gave Theona courage.

"Edrica, I am truly grateful for your loyalty," she said, "but this is the best place for you and your baby. There is water here, and safety. Father and I will be alright. God will take care of us."

"If he can take care of you, he can take care of all of us together," said Edrica firmly. "I'm sure Athanaric would say the same. We are family."

Duke Helerix grinned. "That is very brave, Edrica, but not very sensible. The fewer people who know where Theona and her father are, the safer they will be. How do you suppose they will get the news? Or provisions? Or warnings? You can serve them best by remaining right here. I promise you, when we get the signal from General Stilicho to march out, I will make certain that Theona and her father are notified."

To Theona he said, "I trust you understand that I cannot offer you and your worthy father proper protection, though. Not here, and not now."

It was another hour before Pastor Rhodus and Athanaric finally arrived with Bagautus. They left the horse grazing with the others near the camp.

The two of them were already tired, hungry and dispirited. The news that Pastor Rhodus and Theona would not be allowed to stay with the Wodenvale coalition was very worrying, especially since all of the inhabitable parts of the mountain had already been assigned. The four of them were quiet as they set up Athanaric's and Edrica's tent and ate some of the food they had brought.

After they had eaten, Pastor Rhodus, Theona and Edrica's husband left her behind to rest inside the tent, and they set off to find a place for Theona and her father.

They decided to avoid the town and all the camps anywhere near the village, especially those that were led by allies of Duke Helerix. Beyond the amphitheater and the area where the thermal baths and temples were located, they found a road that sloped gently downhill. Alongside it and bracing the temple gardens just above them, was an ancient wall built with colossal rectangular blocks. They started here and followed it downhill for some distance. Scenic vistas opened up the Tuscan countryside on their right, and footpaths descended from the road to levels below. None of them presented much hope of a viable place for them to stay; they were all too open to view. They kept going until the road turned a corner and seemed to be circling back toward the forum. This area, too, was filling up with people, so they left it to follow a footpath to the crest of the mountain.

They emerged into a peaceful place where the trees were tall and there was a beautiful view of the city below. There were no other people up here yet, but the area still seemed too accessible.

Theona noticed a woodpile near the edge of the hill. It seemed an oddity in this location—there were no houses near it—so she went around it and found yet another path down the mountain side. This one headed sharply down and ended at another one, a horizontal footpath that probably had served local residents as a short-cut into the town or down to the cathedral.

The three of them eagerly followed this horizontal path in the other direction, towards the back of the mountain. This area, like the crest they had just left, was covered by forest. They kept following the trail until it became overgrown and increasingly difficult to follow. Finally it seemed to stop altogether.

"I guess that's that," said Rhodus, quietly. "We can try going the other way, I guess."

"There's got to be a reason why it came this far," mused Theona. "Maybe we missed a turn-off."

They began checking back along both sides of the path. She was right. There was another path a little farther back that began just below it and descended through the forest. They started down. Some distance below them, Athanaric drew their attention to the crest of a fig tree.

"It looks like there's some kind of little building there," he said in excitement. "I think I see a roof."

"Let's go!" said Pastor Rhodus eagerly.

"Watch out for wasps then," admonished Athanaric. "Fig trees attract them."

The tree was at the end of the path and the start of a little clearing. People had lived here once, or at least worked here. There was, as Athanaric had seen, a small stone building, and in front of it an ancient charcoal kiln. The land was almost level here, too. They would be able to pitch their tent.

At the edge of the clearing someone had built a bench. Pastor Rhodus headed over to it. The view was spectacular.

"This will do nicely," he said with satisfaction.

Theona dragged open the door of the stone building. It was damp and chilly inside, and had not been used for a long time. A few vent holes near the roof allowed some air to circulate, but had also allowed bats to take up residence. Rotted black straw covered the floor, and tools for the camp-fire, the kiln and a garden leaned against the wall. She wrinkled her nose at the terrible smell, and hurriedly shut the door. The tent would do for now.

They spent a few minutes exploring the area. There wasn't much else to see, but as expected, another of the steep paths descended through the woods from the clearing to the gentler slopes below. Here they found a meadow with an abandoned vegetable garden in it. Animals and birds had done some damage, but some wilted produce struggled on among the weeds. They watched as a fox trotted across the far end of the meadow and entered the woods above them. Lower, much closer to the road, they could see a tiny settlement and vineyards.

All of this would have needed water. Where had the owners of that vegetable garden and those vineyards obtained the water for the crops now shriveling in the hot July sun? They needed water now, and they would need it every day. They separated to search for a source, but came back empty-handed.

"We had better go back and get our tent and supplies," sighed Pastor Rhodus. "I'd like to get settled in."

Athanaric looked at the sun. It was beginning to turn golden.

"Why don't you wait here," he suggested. "I'll get some of our people to carry your things as far as the woodpile and leave them there. You can carry them here. It will be faster. I'll bring back water. You can look for stuffing for your mattresses, fetch some of that fire wood, and decide on the right place to pitch your tent. I don't suggest you put it anywhere near that tree!" He swatted at an inquisitive wasp.

When he had left, Pastor Rhodus and Theona sat on the bench to look out over the golden hills to the west. Above and behind them soared the mountain. There must be tens of thousands of people on it by now, but you would not know it from where they sat.

Across from them the countryside spread wide. To their left they could see the river and a corner of the beleaguered city, and farther away, glimpses of the dark marsh. They could even see a stretch of the winding road they had climbed to get to the top of the mountain. People were still trudging up it. Warriors swarmed like ants to dismantle the wagons that were collecting at the bottom of the mountain, and create barricades along the roads and accessible slopes. Defense was now the priority.

And then two new things happened.

Directly below them, a group of wagons lurched unsteadily across the lower slopes and stopped near the tiny settlement they had seen. From this distance it wasn't possible to say whether they were Goths or some other group, but now they had neighbors.

"Those people are going to have to come higher up the mountain," remarked Pastor Rhodus. "They cannot get in the way of the King's men and the warriors. They are too close to the road there."

That meant that those neighbors would likely be climbing the hill.

At the same time, a long column of riders and wagons appeared below on the road from Bologna. The Roman Army had arrived.

CHAPTER THIRTY-FIVE

NEIGHBORS
~

Florentia, Italia
(Florence, Italy)
July, 406 AD

Marius was tired and saddle-sore. His unit was approaching Florence now, part of the van-
guard of an army that had been travelling for two days. They were going slowly, alert for any
surprise attacks from warriors still loose in the hills around them.

As they emerged from the last valley before the city, Montefiesole towered on their left. It was
to here, they had been told, that the Goths had retreated. He could see a few people moving up
there, and then a large field full of tents on the upper flanks. Barricades of wagons stretched across
roads, paths, pasture land and gardens. Behind them he could see the tiny figures of barbarian warriors, armor clad and armed with weapons they had seized over the last year. He knew they would
be watching him and his comrades as intently as he and the soldiers with him were watching them.

Behind him stretched miles of wagons, infantry and more cavalry. Their destination was close—
they would soon reach Florence and then the real work of the day would begin. Many of the wagons
winding through the hills behind him carried food for the starving people of Florence.

He wondered if the other armies had arrived yet; two more were approaching from different
directions. His orders were to secure the city gates and then clear the way through the streets for
the wagonloads of food to get into the city center. Some of the other units had orders to guard the
bridges and control the roads nearby. The first units of infantry were going to sweep through the
suburb across the Arno to look for barbarians and clear them out.

Marius had lost track of what they were all doing; there was so much that had to be done in
these first critical hours. He wondered if and when he would be able to get some sleep.

One of the soldiers shouted and pointed towards another road, a higher one to the southwest.
Another long column of soldiers was approaching Florence on it. His men cheered, and he grinned
with satisfaction. The more the merrier. Radagaisus and his chiefs were in for a surprise or two.
General Stilicho had coordinated the arrival of his armies so that the barbarians surrounding the
city of Florence would have nowhere to go but up.

Theona and her father watched the two armies draw close to the city. The cavalry they had first seen had disappeared out of sight around a bend, but they were followed by a long string of wagons and by miles of marching soldiers. One battalion left the column and went behind their mountain instead of continuing on around toward the city with the other units. Curious, they went down the path to the meadow and worked their way across to a different vantage point. In the distance they could see the tiny figures unloading some of the wagons and beginning to lay out a campsite on the back slopes of their own mountain. As they walked back to the clearing, a second campsite was being set up on the hill opposite them.

In the center of the clearing, they found a large jug and a bucket of water. Athanaric had been back and left again. Theona pulled her cup out from her leather pouch and filled it with water for her father—he had had none since the morning. Pastor Rhodus eagerly drank four cups of it before they left to hurry back to the crest of the mountain to fetch their belongings.

Athanaric was sitting against a tree near the woodpile, guarding their tent and supplies. The other men had gone back to their camp.

The three of them took turns standing guard and lugging everything back to the stone house clearing. When it was all safely there, Athanaric left. Even he looked worn out, and he had to give his report to Duke Helerix.

Theona put together a supper for the two of them, and they sat together on the stone bench eating it. There was a golden haze in the western sky; the hot sun was hovering over the mountains to the west.

As Pastor Rhodus had predicted, the people they had seen moving their wagons across the lower slope had decided to move higher on the mountain. They watched the men push and steady the wagons up the flanks of the mountain while the women followed, their arms full with pallets and boxes and bags. A dozen little children struggled up the hillside behind them, aided by their older siblings. It seemed that the clan leaders had decided it would be advisable to get as far away as possible from the range of Roman catapults and cavalry charges.

They chose an area about two hundred feet below where the forest ended, not far from the meadow where Theona and her father had seen the vegetable garden. As they began to set up their tents again, Theona and her father could hear indistinct voices. From their dress and hair styles, they deduced that the group was Suevi.

It grew dark at last. The air was cooling off and the quarter moon was rising. Birds in the forest around them twittered and went silent. Bats passed over their heads, and disappeared into the forest below. Exhausted, they crept into their tent and fell asleep.

As the Roman Army approached the gates, the guards watching from the walls of Florence raised a hoarse cheer and waved their spears high in the air. A trumpet blasted forth to alert the people of the city that rescue had come at last. Soldiers scrambled down from the parapets to help the guards at the big main gates get them open again, and a messenger left to advise the civic rulers and the bishop that their deliverers had arrived.

All over the city, people came staggering out of their homes. Most of them were now so weak that they had to use staffs to help them move along the cobblestone streets. They had only one thought on their minds—food. Everyone was desperate for food. Food meant life. Nothing else mattered just yet. With returning strength would come fresh thoughts, like burying their dead, grieving their losses, reclaiming their lives, and revenge.

Marius and his fellows dismounted a little distance away from the main bridge across the Arno and left their horses there under guard. As they reached the gates of the city, they were unprepared for the stench that filled their nostrils. Piles of bodies had been pitched over the city walls and lay at the bottom. Some of them were still recognizable. He faltered and almost vomited on the spot. Several of the men with him went white and did throw up. He left them there to recover, and led the way grimly forward.

The gate stood open, and the first of the wagons of food was just coming along the road towards it. He and his men saluted the thin guards inside the gates and looked around. Bodies littered the streets as well. Their job was to clear a path for the waggoners with the food, and that meant removing those bodies. Meanwhile the streets were filling up with Florentines streaming towards them—skeletal men, women and children, crying and shaking with weakness and relief. The sight of their emaciated figures horrified Marius.

"Unload the first five wagons out on the bridge," he ordered. "We need them to carry these bodies out of the city, and it will also get some of these people out of our way."

"Aye, Tribune."

It was almost dark by the time the first of the food wagons was able to finally rumble through the gates and press on toward the main forum in the center of the city. More wagons were directed to other town squares and forums. Marius's orders had included sending food wagons to the public parks as well, but these had been filled with stacks of bodies. The air was rife with decaying flesh.

Each wagon was accompanied by a group of guards. The Army had expected rioting, looters, gangs of thieves, and stampedes from desperately hungry people. They were not prepared for the silence and listlessness of the emaciated people who managed to shuffle as far as the wagons. Marius had been told that his soldiers would stand guard by the wagons to keep the distribution orderly, and that the task of handing out the food would likely be done by local leaders. It was not to be—they were as desperate as the poorest citizen by now. It was all any of them could do to show up.

The soldiers had to take on both tasks. More and more soldiers arrived to help, and as each food wagon emptied and left, other wagons crept through the streets to replace them.

Marius was on the move the whole time. Anger burned hot within him whenever he had time to look at the dull eyes and gaunt bodies around him and remembered their loved ones lying in undignified piles outside the walls and abandoned on the streets of the town. All the men working with him were equally distressed. He heard constant oaths and furious remarks about what the men intended to do to the people who had inflicted such suffering on their fellow citizens.

He overheard an irate young Spanish soldier talking to a thin waif of a girl who stood before him with her hands out. "Don't worry. We'll get those devils for you, I promise!"

She looked at him with dull eyes and said nothing. Her whole body was trembling with the effort to hold the packages he was handing her.

How do you recover from something like this? worried Marius. *What was she like before?*

A man with a long white beard pressed through the crowd toward him.

"Tribune, I am the bishop of this city. Could some of your men take food door to door with the members of my congregation? There are many people who cannot make it to any of your distribution centers. Unless something is done right away, some of them won't make it through the night."

"I can't do anything until this crowd thins out," replied Marius, wearily. "But if you can provide guides to the homes of the direst cases, I will do what I can. After that my men need to rest. We have come a long way over the last two days. We need to be ready for our main task which is to face the barbarians who did this to you."

"My people will be glad to take over from you once they have had some nourishment," replied Bishop Zenobius. He started to weep. "God be praised that you are here at last."

He staggered away clutching several packages of food which Marius had placed in his arms, and entered a beautiful house on the far side of the square.

Sometime later, a messenger arrived from General Stilicho ordering Marius to report to him. The Generals had set up their headquarters in a private home right beside the bridge in the suburb. It had a garden that overlooked the river and a good view of the walled city across the way. He was led to a large room where General Stilicho and his advisors were enjoying a late supper while they listened to the reports coming in. Junior officers acted as escorts and intermediaries. One of them had the plans for where all the military camps were to be set up, and he informed Marius where to find his cavalry camp.

The generals listened grimly as Marius reported on the conditions he had seen in the city. He left with several dozen fresh troops and headed back to the forum. He went straight to the bishop's house and knocked on the door. When the old man opened the door, he had thirty people crowding behind him who declared that they were ready to go. The bishop calmly ordered Marius's soldiers to carry all of them on litters, while other soldiers walked behind pulling handcarts loaded with packages of food. Marius watched them head off in different directions.

Depressed, and famished almost to the point of faintness, Marius trudged down the main street and out of the gate of the city. Off to his left he heard soldiers begin to cheer. He hurried onto the bridge to look in the direction of the commotion, and saw a third army approaching from the northeast.

He glanced in triumph up at the mountain, black behind the night sky. Campfires burned up there, and lamps twinkled in some of the homes. He imagined the barbarians, perched on rocks and hilltops, cooking their food and sharpening their axes while they looked out over the countryside. They were cornered now, and probably afraid. But they had food—not like those poor beggars in the city. Radagaisus and his barbarous people would deserve whatever they got.

And then he remembered Theona and her father. They were up there too. They were good people. There must be other good people up there as well. It was a troubling thought.

Theona woke up to the sound of birdsongs and the gentle rustle of leaves in the trees overhead. She became aware of something crawling on her out-flung arm and shook it off quickly. She sat up. Her father was asleep on the pallet next to hers, and the long-legged spider had landed on his chest. She picked it up by one of its legs, and crawled to the entrance to flick it away across the grass.

It was very early and peaceful. The morning air was still cool, the sky cloudless. Theona poured some of the water Athanaric had brought into her cup and drank deeply, then poured more into a pot to wash herself. She fished through her clothing for something clean to wear. She now had more Roman clothes than barbarian ones. Oh well, she and her father were alone up here; she might as well wear the Roman clothing while no one was up and about on the mountain so she could wash her dirty tunic and trousers with the same water she had used to wash herself.

She smiled, remembering that first evening at Granny's house and her attempts to wash her clothes in the old washtub and dry them on the nails in the loft. She wondered how the old woman and Ptolemy were getting along these days, and was glad that Gideon was safely with them.

Theona worked the clothes for a while, and then hung them on some branches to bleach in the morning sun. After that, she crossed to the bench to look out.

The Roman Army had entrenched themselves already. The hills and valleys close to the city and stretching up the Via Flaminia Minor were dotted with eight-man tents. Soldiers were already busy with their responsibilities in the camps. Wagons of food were still drawing close to the city. The food distribution seemed to be uninterrupted since the evening before. Around the base of the mountain, barricades set up by the Roman soldiers now faced the barricades of Radagaisus's warriors.

Her father crossed to join her. She pointed at the soldiers and horses passing briskly along the road below.

He nodded absentmindedly. He was looking at the Suevi camp below them.

The Suevis were also up and out. Theona could see more than twenty of them already.

A man with light brown hair and a grey-haired woman were standing together on the meadow and looking up towards them. She and her father stepped hastily back. She looked behind her, wondering if the fig tree was visible from where the couple stood, or perhaps the roof of the stone house.

"They're going to be coming up here to look around," she gasped. "And then they are going to want our figs. What are we going to do?"

"What Jesus would want us to do," Pastor Rhodus replied. "Share."

He set off down the hill. She saw him emerge onto the meadow below and raise his hand in greeting. The couple started towards him.

Theona watched anxiously as he went to talk to the two of them. A crowd of their people gathered around to listen, and many eyes looked up towards the clearing. Her father waved and started back up the hill. All the others followed him. Theona glanced down at her Roman clothing, wondering how to explain that to them. It was too late to change—some of them were already running up the path.

So much for privacy and secrecy, she thought ruefully. Any one of them could have the loose lips that would unleash the king's men in their direction.

"God save us," she prayed, and put on a welcoming smile.

A dozen of the Suevi crowded into the clearing, looking curiously at the kiln, the little stone building, and their tent. The leader, a man her father introduced as Wieland, was in his thirties. He had large twinkling eyes and several missing teeth. He looked down at her with grinning admiration. The woman, though, after looking swiftly around, seemed disappointed. "Too small for us," she muttered to Wieland as though Pastor Rhodus and Theona were not there.

"Yes, but exactly the right size for my daughter and myself," replied Pastor Rhodus. "You are welcome to visit us, though. There is some shade from the hot sun here, and as you can see, there is a fig tree if you don't mind wasps. We do expect you to respect our need for privacy, though. No one is to come too early in the morning or after sunset."

One of the men, as tall as Wieland, but bigger, stuck his lower lip out and scowled. The woman's mouth thinned. Pastor Rhodus returned her gaze calmly. There was a short silence.

"What's in there?" demanded the second man, gesturing toward the stone house. He seemed to be the least friendly among the visitors.

"What's it to you, Meinrad?" demanded Wieland.

"Maybe we can store things in there," Meinrad replied. Theona noticed he had one blue eye and one brown one. His mouth, like the other man's, was large, but there was no twinkle in his eye or friendliness in his voice. "Food will keep longer where it's cool. Isn't that right, Ma?"

"That's right, Meinrad," said the older woman. "That's a good suggestion." She patted him on the arm and turned to Pastor Rhodus. She, too, had one blue eye and one brown one. Theona realized she must be the mother of the two men.

"Would you permit my family to keep food in there, sir?"

Theona had had enough of their rudeness. "It is cool in there all right, lady," she said quickly. "But I suspect food will spoil quickly. It's very dirty and the air smells bad. It hasn't been used for a long time except by mice and bats."

"Oh that's alright," answered the woman insolently. "We'll clean it up."

Theona stiffened.

Her father smiled broadly. "As it is ours, we will help you with that. Show Mathilde the inside of the building, daughter. You, sir," he said to Wieland, "might be interested to know that there is a path a bit farther up the mountain. I think it leads around to the village forum. Would you like to see it?"

The rest of the crowd followed him and their leader. Theona led the older woman to the stone house, and together they tugged open the heavy door. The dank air flowed out at them. The woman stepped inside and looked around.

"I see what you mean, but we've used worse," she commented. "I'll get my girls up here this morning to start work on it. We've been worried about keeping our food from spoiling in the hot sun. What's that you're wearing?"

"It's a Roman tunic," answered Theona, feeling a flush begin in her face.

The woman reached out and fingered the material.

"That's a quality one," she approved, looking at Theona with respect for the first time. "I have several so far, but they aren't as fine as that one. You must have plundered some great man's house!"

Theona did not reply. The gulf between them would take a miracle to cross.

Soon after, Mathilde left to go back to her camp.

A while later, her father and the rest of the Suevis came back from the path. All of them, even her father, were carrying logs. It would not be long before the woodpile itself disappeared and the path behind it became exposed.

Mathilde was back an hour and a half later with her cleanup team. The stone house was attacked with furious energy by five women and girls, and before long the dank air was lifting, logs were being laid to allow the circulation of air underneath the food, and straw was drying in the sunny field below. Several of the boys and girls swarmed up the fig tree and began detaching all the fruit they could reach, dropping it to eager hands below. The wasps battled back to no avail.

Theona went to sit by herself on the bench. She sighed forlornly.

"God, you are our refuge and our hiding place," she prayed. "Keep us in the shadow of your wings."

One of the older girls came and sat beside her to nurse a young baby. She smiled at Theona, but did not break the silence. Meinrad walked past with a scowl. The girl looked at Theona apologetically, and eased her body away. Meinrad seemed to find Pastor Rhodus's friendliness suspicious, and her own distant politeness threatening.

Theona sighed, and ignored them both.

All of the clan members now began to climb the hill and use the path, venturing even as far as the village. After a while, they didn't even bother to acknowledge her or her father, but crossed through the clearing as though the two people staying there did not exist. Theona's heart sank as Meinrad and a few others grew bolder in their manner, and less cautious in their display of contempt toward the father and daughter who lived alone in the clearing.

The Suevis were curious, but not yet too curious. What would happen when they found out that she and her father were hiding from the High King? All they had protecting them now was the cautious respect of the leader, Wieland.

Athanaric arrived in the afternoon with two more heavy jugs of water. He was astonished to see several boys racing past him on the path, two more up the fig tree and Theona sitting alone on the bench while half a dozen women carried their supplies into the stone house.

"What's going on?" he bellowed.

Surly glances took in his strong body and angry glare. The clan matriarch stepped out from inside the stone house and faced him, her fists on her hips.

"Who are you?" she challenged.

"I am Athanaric, envoy from the warlord Duke Helerix, and this is an outpost of his camp. These people are under his protection. Who are you? And under whose authority are you people?"

"My name is Mathilde, and my son Wieland is our leader. We are doing nothing wrong here. We were invited to come by this young woman's father."

Theona leaped angrily to her feet.

"Is that true?" Athanaric asked Theona anxiously.

"We did not give them permission to overrun our campsite!" she protested. "We offered them traditional hospitality, but they do not seem to understand traditional limits!"

Mathilde glared at her.

"Where is your father?" asked Athanaric.

"He went off with her son in that direction." She pointed towards the back side of the mountain.

Athanaric face turned red. He took a shuddering breath. "He is supposed to stay here!" The clan matriarch looked surprised.

"Her son Wieland said there was a young woman whose baby had died over in the other Suevi camp," said Theona apologetically. "She is one of his sisters, I think. Father went to visit her."

"Well then, I'm in charge here," said Athanaric. "Scat, all of you," he shouted. "You can come back later when Pastor Rhodus is back if that is his wish. No doubt our warlord will be over soon to sort this out with your son, madam."

Theona winced. She wished he had not referred to her father as a pastor, although Rhodus would never have denied it if any of them had asked him directly. She wished they had been able to think all of this through ahead of time, but they kept being corralled by new challenges.

Sullenly, the woman ordered her family members out of the clearing. The children followed her down the hill and back to their camp. The last to depart was the young mother who had shared the bench with Theona. She scuttled past them holding the baby in her arms.

Athanaric settled his much larger bulk on the bench. He seemed glad to have a chance to relax. Theona thanked him.

"What's been happening?" she asked. "How is Edrica?"

"She's fine. She's going to try to teach a couple of your classes for as long as she can. Two of the other women have promised to help her. There seems to be quite a bit of excitement about the reading lessons. Even pagans want to learn. She tells them she will be using the Bible, but nobody seems to care. Many of them have picked up Roman books over the last year, and they want to learn how to read them. They may change their mind when they find out that their scrolls are written in a different language," he laughed.

"Duke Helerix has sent his greetings to you both. I told him where you are staying and he will come over when he can. I must speak to him about these Suevis—I suspect they are a lawless bunch. He will want to know—he is a very good man, Theona. The bishop believes he is close to the gate of God's Kingdom, and we are praying he does not get frightened away, or delay too long."

"Have you seen Prince Roderic?" Theona heard a slight quaver in her voice.

She had thought of the prince constantly, and was fairly certain he had recognized her in the Fiesole forum. It was frustrating to know he was so close, and she would not be able to see him or explain why she and Edrica had left so quickly. She hoped he knew that it had to do with Phaedrus, and not him.

"Prince Roderic?" Athanaric looked at her in surprise. "That's right. Edrica said you would ask. He came down into the camp yesterday evening and asked for you. He even spoke to Duke Helerix who said he did not know where you were camping, but that you were no longer with him. After he left, that pagan priest came down into the camp too, and wandered around. He did not say much, but Edrica thinks he was spying on Roderic. You will have to take care that the prince does not find what he is looking for, because that man will be right behind him."

CHAPTER THIRTY-SIX

TRAPPED!

Faesulae, Italia
(Fiesole, Italy)
Late July, 406 AD

During the first days of the liberation of Florence, the army's main focus was on setting up their camps, bringing relief to the people of the area, and clearing bodies from the streets, walls and parklands of the city. Very soon though, there was another focus.

Theona woke up. It was the second morning she and her father had spent in the little clearing on the side of Montefiesole. He was lying beside her, snoring lightly. Outside the tent she could hear the usual early morning bird songs, but today there was a new sound. This was the one that had woken her.

At first she could not identify it; the noise was faint and far away, but it was deep and repetitive. She hurried over to the bench to look downhill.

At the bottom of the mountain she could see that both the Roman barricades and the barbarian barricades were fully manned. Along the Via Flaminia Minor, wagons were lined up, and hundreds of soldiers stood in line at the wagons to receive something that glittered in the morning sun. She thought at first they must be weapons of some kind, but the men moved off and took up positions between the road and the Roman barricades all along the base of the mountain as far as she could see. She became aware again of the sound she had heard; it was a drum beating a steady rhythm. The soldiers who had taken up their positions began to dig in time with it.

Dig! What were they doing? Her father came up beside her and watched, too, his brow furrowed.

"What are they doing?" she asked.

"Making sure we can't get away," he replied.

She stared at him, frightened. All of a sudden the mountain seemed much smaller. She watched the tiny ant-like creatures below bend and heave, bend and heave.

"We have to get away." Her voice shook.

"We can't. We're trapped here," he said gloomily. He put an arm around her shoulder and they stood watching.

Boom

Bend and dig.

Boom.

Heave and toss.

Boom.

Bend and dig.

Boom.

Heave and toss.

The dull and constant drum beat was the sound of fate. From now on they had to stay in the camp and listen to it all day, every day.

As Theona had seen, General Stilicho had issued the order for a wall of circumvallation that would prevent the trapped barbarians from escaping the appropriate punishment he had designed for them.

The first step was to dig a ditch right across the base of the mountain, one that was wider than a horse could leap, and deep enough to make it difficult for horse or man to climb out of. To make this ditch even more of a deterrent, the soldiers placed sharp stakes at angles all across the bottom of the trench, and then fill it with water.

Thousands of soldiers, peasants and army slaves took shifts working as archers stood behind them ready to release a volley of arrows at anyone getting too close. As one shift tired, another line would move in and take over the digging, removing the debris, and planting long sharp stakes along the bottom of the lengthening trench. The water would come later.

The people on the heights of Montefiesole wandered from vantage point to vantage point, watching the show going on below. The word spread that the ditch-digging was happening even at the back of their mountain where forest-clad hill met forest-clad valley. The trees were coming down to create a buffer zone, and the shovels were active. It looked as though the Romans planned to encircle the entire mountain.

Duke Helerix had ordered Pastor Rhodus and Theona to stay put in their clearing for their own protection. There was little to do there other than sit and watch, so sometimes her father went down to visit their Suevi neighbors. He was too restless to stay cooped up, and too much of an evangelist not to go where he perceived lost souls. At such times, Theona stayed alone. She was much less willing to embrace her neighbors.

From their bench they could see sections of the ditch being connected. Soon a second phase began. Along the lowest slopes of Montefiesole, the soldiers began to dig horse traps in the lowest fields and meadows. These were huge pits placed in irregular rows to prevent the elite warriors from being able to mount a successful charge. At the bottom of these traps, too, the army planted the sharp, angled stakes. Farmers from the surrounding areas drove into town with wagonloads of hay and sod. These were laid on top of the pits to disguise their presence. Seen from the various campsites high on the mountain, they blended in with the uneven ground nearby, and before long, few people could remember exactly where all of the traps were located.

Simultaneously the army engineers began construction of the real wall of circumvallation. They built this one right behind the ditch.

It was twelve feet high and had watchtowers at regular intervals and parapets. Such circum-vallation walls had been used effectively by the Romans centuries before by Julius Caesar in Gaul, and by Titus Caesar in Jerusalem. When it came to winning wars, the Romans had adopted and adapted ferociously in their determination to dominate. No cost would be spared if they could defeat Radagaisus without risking serious losses themselves. They were preparing for a lengthy siege.

The people on the mountain were no longer placing bets on when the Roman Army would be ready to fight them. They knew now that there would be no glorious battle. Gloom descended on Montefiesole. Too late, the people realized that their enemies were planning to give them a taste of their own medicine—starvation, slow and steady. The spectators became as mesmerized as a bird watching a snake creeping toward it.

The chiefs urged the king to begin the fight before the ditch could be completed. The King agreed. They began to dismantle part of the makeshift wagon barricade in preparation for the assault. The Roman barricade was already being dismantled as the ditch and the wall became effec-tive barriers.

Early in the first week of the siege, Radagaisus ordered a cavalry charge. The warriors led their horses down the access roads to the lowest pastures and mounted. As the great horn blared out, thousands of them dashed towards the Roman line, howling and waving their weapons. They were met with a wall of arrows and carroballistae bolts long before they could reach the ditch. Some of the horses at the forefront were driven into the great pits by the warriors pounding along behind them. They were impaled on the sharp stakes, their riders hopelessly crushed or impaled with them.

A few riders made it as far as the ditch, but the horses balked and threw their riders or fell into the ditch, unable to stop their rush. Others, charging behind them, toppled in, and the horses and riders who survived became impaled on the stakes or died from the rain of arrows and jave-lins pouring down on them. Many of the warriors chose to mount their charges in areas where the ditch had not yet been started. This strategy failed, too. The ground here was rougher, riskier for the horses descending towards the Roman barricades. It was also where the Romans had placed some of the disguised horse traps, and massed carroballistas and archers.

Radagaisus ordered a second cavalry charge. This was better organized, more cautious. It failed as thoroughly as the first one. The warriors retreated back to the heights of Montefiesole, while the Romans plodded on with the ditch and the wall. The level of fear in the camps increased dramati-cally. It did not help that the Roman Army had not lost a single soldier.

The King had taken over a villa on the edge of the village. It overlooked the road up the hill from Florence. Radagaisus stayed there with Prince Roderic, his daughter-in-law Clothilde, and Anarilka.

It was a short walk from here to the forum, and the Fiesole Curia had become the main meeting place for the king, his allies and their advisors. During the day, at least at first, the building was a busy place. Chiefs, messengers, petitioners, and the leaders of the king's bodyguard came and went. Meetings were usually held in the council chambers. The King intended to use the Fiesole amphi-theater for larger meetings.

From the beginning, the meetings in the council chamber were stormy affairs. One of the main sources of friction was the placement of campsites. The king's men had assigned many of these, and they were not all of equal quality. There were few places to get water on the mountain. The closer your tent was to one of these, the better. You could live without food much longer than you could live without water.

Everyone complained that they had not been given enough time to find sufficient food for an extended stay on the mountain. Already people were begging their neighbors for help. For a chicken or a bag of grain they would offer fancy clothing, fine jewelry, children's dolls, mirrors, quality ceramic plates, Roman coins and bronze statuettes. No one needed such things now. Everyone had plenty of them. Food and good campsites were the barter of choice.

To get to the water, you had to have food.

Another major issue was the assignment of sections of the mountain each leader had been asked to patrol and defend. Some of this territory was much more difficult to protect than others. Sometimes the chiefs who had the campsites farthest from the water sources also had the most diffi-cult terrain to guard. There were accusations of favoritism. Old rivalries surfaced. The chiefs argued and shouted at one another, and frequently vented their anger even on the High King.

The leaders were expected to attend Council meetings every day or two. After the failed cavalry charges, some of them no longer bothered to come.

Duke Helerix and the men who had signed the treaty with General Stilicho were usually silent while the storm raged around them. They faithfully attended the council meetings, and diligently guarded their territories, but when they met privately, they would discuss their fellow leaders' char-acters and degrees of loyalty to Radagaisus. They began courting some of the other chieftains with a view to including them among the defectors. The more people who could be saved, the better.

Roderic and his messengers were the glue that held all the factions together in spite of the growing tensions. It was their job to visit all the camps on the mountain and act as intermediaries between the King and his allies. They went everywhere on foot now. Their horses were useless on the rough terrain and spent their days grazing with the rest of the animals in the increasingly scarce pastureland.

Radagaisus had warned Roderic to be on the lookout for signs of revolt. He was counting on Roderic to keep the chiefs happy and him informed of any dissatisfaction and disaffection. The King could be roughly voted out and replaced if enough of the chiefs lost faith in his leadership. Worse still, the uneasy alliance among the various groups present on the mountain could disintegrate into feuding and mutually destructive warfare.

Prince Roderic was unaware of any subversive plots, but he could not ignore the complaints and dissatisfaction. There were too many to report, and they were coming at his men from everywhere.

People complained to the messengers about their campsites, their leaders and their neighbors. They wanted to know what was going on elsewhere on the mountain, and demanded to know what the plans were to save them from catastrophe. They were also eager to share their opinions about their leaders and any other groups who seemed to be doing better than they were.

Roderic received all these messages from his men, and dutifully passed them on to his father. King Radagaisus listened at first, and then stopped listening.

The High King had not trusted Roderic since that early morning Council meeting in Bressanone. He had little faith in the loyalty of his fellow chieftains either. Since Vitiges had been killed by the Huns, he had lost much of his fire. At night when Roderic tried to discuss some of the growing animosities and issues his men were reporting, his father roared at him that there was nothing he could do. He would storm up to the forum and wander around the town talking to people instead.

Each morning he spent time on the lower slopes of the mountain visiting the warriors on the barricade. Sometimes he wore his bearskin costume to remind the people of their proud tradition of liberty from Roman domination and shared ancestral values. He harangued them about the need for courage and loyalty, and the warriors on the barricades listened with varying degrees of tolerance and contempt.

Sometimes he took Rilka with him. Rilka alone seemed to give him comfort and peace. When the king was in a particular kind of mood, even Clothilde, the six-year-old's mother, could barely get access to her daughter. When he came home for meals and to sleep, he would not talk to Roderic or Clothilde. Radagaisus would hunt for Anarilka and play with her. Her innocence and liveliness diverted him from the scope of the deepening crisis.

The King's obsession with his granddaughter worried her mother and her uncle. So did his growing isolation and unreasonableness. The prince and Vitiges's widow had grown closer during the time since Vitiges' death. Clothilde knew all about Roderic's feelings for Theona. She even knew that he thought she was on the mountain somewhere.

Seeing Theona in the Fiesole village forum had been a profound shock for the prince. When he first laid eyes on her, he had been startled by how much the girl at the well looked like Theona. His pace had quickened so he could get a closer look at her. He hadn't really believed that it was his sweetheart until the girl had fled with the other woman. He had tried to follow, but Phaedrus had intervened.

What was Theona doing on Montefiesole? Where was she staying? Where was Ptolemy? His orders to the gladiator had been clear. Stay with Theona and keep her safe. Don't bring her any further into this disastrous invasion.

He had thought she was safe in the mountains to the north and would be there waiting for him when the day came that he managed to get away from his father and go for her. It had been a secret consolation to him, one he had not shared even with Clothilde.

Perhaps Ptolemy had not made it back to Pons Drusi. Perhaps Theona had already left by the time the gladiator got there.

However she came to be here on Montefiesole, she must not be seen. Roderic's father had made it very clear that he would never accept her into the family, and if Roderic persisted with the courtship against Radagaisus's wishes, it would be a simple matter to get rid of the girl. And then some of his men had warned him that they thought Phaedrus was following him. Roderic would be doing her no favor to persist in pursuing her.

Back in Pannonia she had said something that seemed to have gone deep into his heart. He had asked her what she wanted.

"A home and peace," she had said. "No fighting. No wagons. No running."

Those words haunted him now. They were a chant marching through his tired mind. It had become his dream now, too. This had all been a terrible mistake. If only he could start over afresh with Theona by his side. He yearned for her and would not rest until he found her.

His job took him all over the mountain. He would visit every inch of it and then he would decide what to do.

One morning in the second week of the siege of Montefiesole, Theona woke up find her father gone. She heard voices and looked out. He was seated beside Wieland on the bench, part of his Bible open on his knee. He seemed to be trying to explain something—his hands were busy creating a picture in the air. Wieland was listening earnestly.

Theona pulled on her trousers and her old barbarian tunic. The little white cross was rather grubby now, and the yellow threads in the centers of the flowers had lost their color completely. The garment was a little too loose, still, but was rugged enough to still have some wear in it.

The early morning air was chilly. She reached for Roderic's jacket and pulled it on.

She crawled out of the tent and crossed to the stone house to get some grain for their morning porridge. The heavy door stood partially open. Surprised, she pulled it open the rest of the way, and startled Mathilde in the act of withdrawing a portion of grain from her and her father's supply.

"Stop," she shouted. "That's our food!"

Mathilde whirled around, her eyes defiant.

"You're doing alright, it seems. You can spare this," she rasped. "We need a lot more food than the two of you do."

Pastor Rhodus sprang up and rushed over, followed by Wieland. He took one look at Mathilde, standing over their supply of food, and glared at the man.

"Were you trying to keep me occupied while your mother helped herself to our food, Wieland? You led me to believe you had an interest in your own eternal salvation. Shame on you!"

He turned to the woman, his eyes still blazing. "Lady Mathilde, my daughter is right. We have graciously allowed you the use of this place to store your own food, and you return the favor by stealing ours. If the time ever comes when you have no food left and we still have some, we will gladly share with you and your children, but what you are doing is wicked. It is stealing."

"Put it back, Mother," said Wieland, wearily.

"Have you forgotten the number of mouths we have to feed?" she snapped. "Are these Goths more important to you than your own family? Stand up to him and be a man."

Wieland said nothing.

Mathilde sneered. "You're a fool. You think the girl will marry you if you defy me? Do you think I would permit that? Think again. That will never happen. Not in my lifetime."

Surprised, Theona and Pastor Rhodus turned together to look at the Suevi. He went red.

Pastor Rhodus frowned.

"Do not embarrass or disrespect your son, Mathilde," he said. "Wieland wants to do what is right, and so should you. You may keep the food you have taken, but I will be informing Duke Helerix of your behavior. If any one of you tries to steal from my daughter and me again, we will bring a charge against you. You will have to face the Grand Council."

He wouldn't dare! thought Theona, fighting a smile. Facing the Grand Council with an appeal for justice after the last one they had attended would not be very prudent, but then, prudence was not a quality she would normally ascribe to her father.

Insolently, the woman poured the grain back into their bag, then bent over and spat into it. She straightened up and smiled at the three of them. Shocked, Theona slapped her. Both men swore, and took a step forward. Mathilde scowled and held her stinging cheek.

"You'll pay for that," she said.

She left the stone shed, and started down the path toward their camp. Wieland shook his head and followed, with an apologetic look backward at Theona and Pastor Rhodus.

"I'm sorry, Father. I should not have done that."

"You did not exactly turn the other cheek," he agreed, "but she is a dreadful woman. Very provoking."

"And she has surely fixed it so that Wieland will no longer be visiting you to hear the Gospel," said Theona.

"That must have been a pretext," he muttered. "I should have suspected that he had his eye on you. He told me that his wife died during the journey down here. He is a lonely man, and under the foot of his mother. Meinrad, the younger brother, has a jealous eye on the leadership of that clan, but it seems to be Mathilde who holds the power."

They watched as the couple emerged onto the meadow below. They appeared to be arguing. They continued watching while the women and older children did their chores and the men emerged from their tents, dressed for duty on the barricades. A number of the younger children raced around the meadow, playing. The silence in the stone shed clearing pressed in on them.

Pastor Rhodus stood up.

"I cannot stay here doing nothing," he fretted. "And I will not go back. Surely I am needed somewhere else."

"Athanaric and Duke Helerix say you have to stay here."

"But this is a wonderful chance for me to talk to people about the Lord. I know many who have been afraid to listen up till now. They may not get off this mountain alive, or if they do, their families will be separated and their lives will no longer be the same. I would not be worthy of my calling if I did not at least try to tell them about the Kingdom of God. If they have Jesus Christ in their hearts, they will still have peace and purpose when everything else is gone. If I let them die without sharing the good news, it will be on my own head! You know that!"

She sighed. "I will prepare porridge for us then. Just promise me you will go only where you will be safe."

He looked uncomfortable. "I'm not hungry."

He seized an empty water jug and hurried up the path toward the crest of the hill without looking at her.

Annoyed, Theona watched him go. She went over to the shed again, and delicately scooped out the grain that the woman's spittle had spoiled. She was about to toss it into the forest, but stopped. She would rinse it off and cook it for her own breakfast, nauseating though the prospect seemed. Every grain of food would matter.

She prepared her porridge and added figs to it to give it more appeal, brushing away the wasps that followed her to the bench. She forced the food down, gagging several times until it was gone. It seemed even quieter in the clearing now that her father had left.

Theona wanted to get away too, but someone had to stay to guard their food and the few possessions she and her father owned. The Suevi children passed through this clearing all the time, and if she left, it would not be long before Mathilde found out that there was no one there. She resigned herself to waiting for Athanaric to come.

The Romans were hard at work at the base of the mountain. Across the valley she could see peasants at work in their fields. Her glance lit upon the vegetable garden in the meadow below. It was in sad shape, its crop wizened and dying from lack of attention. The Suevis had ignored it. Perhaps she could coax it back to health.

She got up and fetched several of the garden tools and the rest of the water, and started down the path. The Romans wanted them to starve. She would fight back.

It wasn't long before someone from the Suevi camp climbed the hill to join her. It was the girl who had sat with her on the bench nursing her baby when the Suevis had first moved into the area. She was carrying the baby in a sling across her chest, and greeted Theona shyly.

"Mathilde sent me up here," she said. "She asked me to come and work with you in the garden. I hope that that is all right?"

"I would be glad of your company," replied Theona warmly. "It will take work to bring this garden back to life, but maybe we can get more food for all of us. I am Theona. What is your name?"

"Gerlinda. Meinrad is my husband. This is Detlof." Carefully she laid the baby in the shadow of a bush beside the garden and left him to sleep.

They hoed and weeded, digging around the parched roots and watering them. Theona's one jug of water was soon gone. She did not know how she would answer if Gerlinda suggested that they go into the village for more water, but Mathilde decided the matter for them. The clan mother climbed the hill, looked around at the garden, and went back to her camp. A short time later every child in the Suevi camp who could carry a container was sent up the hill through the clearing and along to the village. An hour later they were back with water. Each shriveled plant was given a drink. Then the children headed back to the village again. They did not seem to mind—the outing was something to do, an adventure, and they had picked up some of the local gossip.

All the barbarians in the area around Florence had managed to make it safely onto the mountain on time, but only a minority had brought food enough to last for more than a few days.

Many of the men had gone hunting and laid traps in the forested areas all over the mountain. They were looking for any signs of wildlife—deer, squirrels, foxes and birds. Even mice habitats had been noted. Every garden in the village and elsewhere on the mountain had been raided. The crops in the olive groves and vineyards had been noted and left to ripen. Many people had been exploring the woods in search of berries, fungi, edible leaves and roots. Everything on the mountain was now being assessed as a potential source of food.

According to the older children, the people they met were now faced with the decision of standing guard over their food supplies within their campsites, going searching for new sources of food, or standing guard over what they had found. Fights had broken out over holes in the ground and berry patches.

The council of chiefs had issued warnings about the consequences of stealing. People would be hanged if they were caught—there was already one body suspended from a tree in the forum. But this deterrent was expected to have little effect when the shortage of food got worse.

This was worrying news to the girls. Who would protect their garden from human predators once it was discovered? Theona knew her father certainly wouldn't. He would give the vegetables away rather than keep them for himself. She wondered if she should have a chat with Mathilde or Wieland about this, and then felt guilty for being selfish.

She and Gerlinda climbed wearily back up to the clearing and sat on the bench to rest. Gerlinda nursed Detlof.

"Tomorrow we should start earlier, Theona," she said in her soft, timid voice. "The water will work better if the sun doesn't suck it up so fast."

"We will have to get the water to the plants sooner, then," said Theona. "Do you think the children will help us again?"

"I will speak to Mathilde," replied Gerlinda. "The children will do what she tells them."

Pastor Rhodus returned in the late afternoon with Duke Helerix. The warlord looked around the campsite with pleasure.

"Not bad!" he said, stripping off his jerkin and shirt, and settling himself on the bench. "Solitude, shade, and a great view. I think I'll bring Rue over and we'll move in."

He grinned at Theona. "We may have to! I've just become a Christian!"

She leaped at him and hugged him. "Oh, that's so exciting. How wonderful for you!"

"Yes," he beamed. "I feel like a new man. In fact, I am a new man. Now, all I have to do is be baptized."

"Sigeseric and I have worked it all out, Theona," said her father. "The Christians in the camp will be doing what they can to share the Gospel with anyone who is willing to listen, and they can come here for their baptismal instruction and baptisms. Isn't that wonderful? It will give me something to do."

"That's the only way I could get him to agree to stay out of sight!" grinned Helerix. "Your father swore that as long as he had strength in his body, he would not give up the work God has called him to do. I am beginning to understand why you Christians are so passionate about your God. Everyone I look at, I want to speak to. I have to be careful to control my excitement or the whole camp will get suspicious. After all, this is not exactly a happy situation we are in."

He stood up abruptly and pulled on his shirt and jerkin again.

"I'm staying for dinner, Theona. Your father is going to baptize me tonight. We brought you some fresh horse meat and a satchel of grain. I suggest you find a cave or some other place to hide it. Meanwhile, I'll see what I can do with those people down there."

He started briskly down the hill toward the Suevi camp. Tears sprang to Theona's eyes—whether tears of relief, or gratitude, or anxiety she could not tell. She sat down on the bench and sobbed.

CHAPTER THIRTY-SEVEN

THREE LITTLE SCROLLS
༼

Florentia and Faesulae
(Modern day Florence and Fiesole)
Early August, 406 AD

More and more sections of the ditch were connected until one day water began to flow through Florence's aqueducts to the trench using a series of pipes.

Only the forest at the back of the mountain still offered a possible way in or out, and given the speed with which the Romans were cutting trees down to create a no-man's land, this area, too, would soon be blocked. Until then, this last passable frontier would bristle with soldiers and warriors eying each other through the trees.

By the sixth day, many of the families on the mountain had run out of food and were beginning to starve. Panic gripped some of the men and women and slowly began to spread. Within hours panic was taking hold. Families who had food posted guards or hired toughs to guard their dwindling hoard of grain. The horses of the warriors on the barricades became food for their families, or were led off during the night to more isolated parts of the mountain to be killed. Anarchy was also taking hold.

And on the sixth day Prince Roderic of the royal Amali line and the house of King Radagaisus, finally found Theona.

One morning early in the siege he had gone into the amphitheater to sit by himself for a while and look out over the eastern hills. He noticed a small group of women from Duke Helerix's caravan were sitting together near the bottom. A girl stood in front of them handing out tablets. Her belly was swollen with a child nearing term. The girl was talking to the others and appeared to be leading a class of some sort. She seemed vaguely familiar. He remembered that the girl fleeing with Theona that first day on the mountain had been pregnant. That was the only thing he had noticed about her at the time; his attention had been on Theona.

As he studied her, puzzled, he suddenly realized that she was the sister of Theona's other suitor, the one she had called Darric. He had not seen that man or thought of him for a long time. Was Darric's sister the one who had been with Theona? It seemed quite likely.

He asked around, and learned that her name was Edrica. Later that day, he saw her walking through the forum with a man who was carrying two big jugs of water and talking to her. Could this be her husband? Roderic followed them almost to the Wodenvale camp, and saw them enter a tent together. So, they were married. He had another lead.

Three days later while on his rounds, he spotted Edrica's husband ascending a path toward the crest of the mountain. Once again he was carrying water, a jug in one hand and a bucketful in the other. What was he doing bringing water here? Roderic followed him slowly to the top of the mountain and looked around the area. He could see nothing but trees and a small woodpile. The man had disappeared.

Frustrated, he stood there listening and idly looking out toward the city of Florence. He heard children's voices from somewhere below him. Behind the woodpile he found a dirt path that led steeply downhill. He descended quickly, hoping to find some sign of Edrica's husband. On the path below he hesitated. Which way had the man gone?

The children he had heard were coming towards him from the direction of the village. They, too, were carrying containers of water. Recognizing him, they bowed slightly and scurried past. Roderic waited for a minute and then followed them to the end of the trail. The children's voices could now be heard coming from somewhere below him.

He found the path they had taken and made his way down it with mounting excitement. Soon he entered the little clearing with the stone house, the old kiln and the bench.

Someone was staying here. That was obvious because a tent had been set up in the middle of the clearing. There did not seem to be anyone about. Roderic walked to the tent and peered inside. There stood the jug of water the big man had been carrying. He could not see the bucket, though.

He settled himself on the bench to watch. His men had never mentioned this place. If this was where Theona was staying, perhaps he could creep back here at night and find a way to talk to her.

He saw the children emerging from the trees some distance away. Their destination was a small Suevi camp, one his men *had* told him about. This was a renegade clan that had been cast out by the main group because of a conspiracy to overthrow the current chief. They were none too popular with their own people. The site they had chosen was also well off the main routes used around the mountain.

Below and over to his left he could see two women working in a garden that lay in a meadow above the Suevi camp. One woman was watering some plants. The other was in conversation with Edrica's husband. He felt a surge of hope. Could that be . . . Theona? The girl was too far away to see clearly. He decided to go farther down and hide among the trees near the bottom to get a closer look, but the man had turned and was heading back up the path.

Roderic retreated behind the stone shed, hoping Edrica's husband would keep going through the clearing and on back to Duke Helerix' camp. It would be awkward if he decided to stay for a while.

He did not. He kept going right back up past the tall fig tree and on out of sight.

Roderic went back to the bench. He kept studying the two women, more and more convinced that one of them was Theona. He was on edge, afraid that Pastor Rhodus would return, or the children or some other adult would come through the clearing and recognize him. This was ridiculous! If this was where Theona was staying and none of his men had discovered it, then chances were it was the best place for her. He should leave and forget the whole matter. He just wanted to be certain.

The two girls working in the garden stopped their work and stood chatting. The girl he thought was Theona picked up the tools, and the other one picked up a baby that had been lying in the shade of a vegetable mound. They started up the hill together toward the clearing.

It was Theona. Roderic's heart raced.

She seemed taller than he remembered and a bit fuller, more of a woman than a girl now, he supposed. Her golden hair shone in the sun, and her arms and face were tanned. In spite of her dirty clothes and hands, she carried herself like a queen. Last year he would have rushed to reach her. This year he was much less certain of what he should do.

The best thing that had happened to him since leaving his home in the distant north was meeting Theona. The air she breathed seemed to be purer, sweeter than the air elsewhere. Her natural sense of humor, plain decency, and kind heart had soothed his. At first he had admired her and merely wanted to impress her. He was used to that from many of the other girls around the wagon city.

He had not meant to fall in love with her, but he had. The thought of marriage to Theona had grown like a healthy plant. Very soon Roderic knew that he wanted to be with the young woman, get to know her, protect her, and perhaps raise a family with her. He believed that having her as his life's partner might even make him happy!

But, perhaps not. Every time he looked in the mirror, he saw his own sad eyes looking back. He was ashamed of the man he had become and wanted to hide that from her. He had led his men in a few raids. He had stolen goods in his possession. He and his men had hurt and killed the people who resisted them. They had even destroyed homes and barns and ruined people's livelihoods. What would Theona think of that?

At the time he had just done what he knew others were doing, but over the months his heart had sickened at the destruction and suffering he and all his people had caused. There had not been any real satisfaction in this entire ambitious adventure. He looked at the goods he had stolen and hated them. He looked at his men and hated himself for what they had become simply by following his own orders. He had become ashamed of his father, something that he tried to conceal even from himself.

He wanted to see Theona, to claim her even, but he was not the same man he had been. He was torn between his desire to see Theona, and his desire to keep her safe. And he no longer felt that he deserved her.

Sighing, he slipped away before Theona could reach the top of the path.

Four days later, Marius and Eucherius crossed the main bridge from the suburb of Florence and walked through the city gates.

It had been ten days since the army had first arrived. The streets were beginning to look almost normal again. The heaps of bodies had been removed and buried outside the town and there were more people in the streets. Some of the Florentines were becoming strong enough to pick up their social and business obligations again, but the life of the city was still sadly diminished.

Once proud citizens waited near the city gates or went to the churches to beg for alms. Children followed the soldiers down the streets, their big eyes appealing. Mothers held out their babies to them. Old men with tired eyes displayed their war wounds and held out their hands for a few coins, and emaciated girls tried to work up a wink and a smile.

Many of the soldiers had got into the habit of carrying small coins with them every time they entered the city, enough to get them through the growing lines of beggars. Now Marius and Eucherius pressed a few coins into the hands of the nearest hopeful faces and pushed on through the crowd.

Their destination was a large bath and gymnasium complex that was once again in operation. This was the first chance they had had to be together since arriving in Florence, and all they wanted to do was to have a good soak and shave, and maybe a massage.

They reached the block where the bathhouse was located and started across the square towards it. Suddenly something bumped hard into Marius's legs. He whirled around and saw Gideon standing behind him, his tail waving and a bright-eyed welcome on his furry face.

Marius dropped to his knees in delight.

"How on earth did you get here? It is so good to see you, my friend!"

He gently rubbed the dog's head and stroked his body. Gideon's eyes half closed in appreciation.

"That can't be . . . ," said Eucherius slowly.

"It must be. He knows me, and you know what happened to all the dogs and other animals in the city. But how did he get here?"

"Ptolemy!"

Both of them whirled and scanned the faces up and down the square. The gladiator was nowhere to be seen.

They heard a shrill whistle from somewhere.

"Grab him." said Eucherius urgently.

"What? Why?" Marius tightened his hold on the dog. "He seems to be well-treated. He looks well, a little on the thin side, but in good shape. And you know we can't keep him right now. What's the idea?"

The whistle came again. They looked around wildly. Several streets and alleys opened into the square. The sound could have come from any of them.

"Let him go," said Eucherius quickly. "We need to follow him."

Marius loosened his grip on the dog. Gideon turned and ran off.

Eucherius started after him. "It's fate, Marius," he called back. "Ptolemy is Roderic's man. We need to know what he is up to here."

"If Ptolemy *is* here, what do you expect to do when we catch up with him?"

"I don't know yet. Let's at least find out where he is staying."

They raced after Gideon. When they reached the street he had turned down, they saw him just turning a corner ahead. Ptolemy was with him. He was dressed in a new tunic and sandals, and had grown a beard, but it was plainly him. The tribunes followed the gladiator and Gideon through the narrow streets for several blocks before they disappeared down a lane between two apartment buildings.

Cautiously, the tribunes approached the entrance to the lane. The gladiator might have seen Gideon with them, but had he recognized them? There were a lot of soldiers in the town.

Gladiators were notorious for being "thugs for hire". They already had a healthy respect for his prowess, and neither of them wanted a thrashing at his hands.

There was no one in the lane. At the end of it they entered a small courtyard, filthy with refuse, including the skeletal remains of domestic animals.

Several doorways opened into it. There being no other exit, Ptolemy had to have taken Gideon through one of those doorways.

They hurried back through the city gates and across the bridge to the large villa which General Stilicho was using as his headquarters.

He was there, and he had a guest. The Legate from the military garrison at Bologna had arrived, and Stilicho was briefing him on the local situation. He held up a warning hand to stop Eucherius from interrupting.

"How many more days before the wall is finished?" asked Legate Merula.

"Another two weeks, I've been told," Stilicho replied.

"And the barbarians are just sitting there, letting it happen?"

General Stilicho smiled. "It seems so. They tried charging us a week ago, but now they just sit and watch all the time. It's almost as though they have lost their initiative. We don't know how much food they've taken up there, but it can't be much. They pillaged the whole area mercilessly long before they all fled up there."

"When are you going to let the chiefs who signed the treaty defect to you? My wife is very worried."

"That's been my main concern, too," replied General Stilicho. "By now the warlords we met in Ad Salaris will be wondering if I am a man of my word. Every day that goes by, they will see their people getting weaker and more desperate, and I expect some will die. The army engineers have told me the soldiers are going as fast as they can—I have told them to go faster. I also have to make sure we have everything in place to receive the elite warriors and their families.

"We don't have to wait until the whole wall is finished to get them out. We just have to have everything ready on this side so we can receive them. Then we'll just reinforce our troop density at the point of exit. But I *would* like to make contact with the chiefs I met so that they don't lose hope."

"Father!" Eucherius burst out. "I think we may be able to help."

General Stilicho raised an eyebrow.

Eucherius grinned. "We just saw Ptolemy in town with Gideon."

"Gideon? Oh, the dog!" said his father. "But who is Ptolemy?"

Marius discretely poked his impulsive friend in the back.

Before Eucherius could answer, Legate Merula cut in. "I know who he is! He is the gladiator who lived with Theona and the old Gothic woman north of Pons Drusi! He is Prince Roderic's man, isn't he?"

He sounded excited.

General Stilicho looked confused. All of them plainly expected him to share their enthusiasm. "What's he doing in Florence, then?"

"He may be here to try to help his master or Theona. We know where he is staying," replied Eucherius smugly. "We followed them."

Stilicho was silent. They waited.

"Good work!" he said at last. "He must have been one of the gladiators who escaped from the area outside Savaria. Before we bring him in though, I need to know more about him. Check the records. Send investigators to talk to people who know people in his business. I'll wait until we know a little more about the man before I decide how to use him. Let's see if we can find a way to persuade him to help our side, or at least find out why he is here. Until then, I can assign some soldiers to keep a discreet eye on him."

"There's no need to wait, general," interjected Legate Merula. "I can fill you in on the man's background. Theona told my wife and me a few things about him."

"Well then," said Stilicho to the two tribunes, "Take a few men and go get him. You can fill me in, Merula, while we wait. Would you like some dinner?"

The little courtyard where Ptolemy had his room swarmed with soldiers.

Gideon started to bark.

Marius knocked on the door he had heard the barking coming from. His hands were sweating, and he discretely wiped them on his trousers.

As soon as Ptolemy opened the door, Gideon launched himself at Marius, thrilled to see him again. It was impossible for his newest master to slam the door shut again without badly hurting the dog.

He looked from Marius to Eucherius, standing just behind him, and then took in the courtyard full of armed men. He looked at Marius with amusement.

"What do you want, Roman."

Gideon was still dancing around Marius excitedly. Marius stood stiffly at attention, his eyes on Ptolemy's. "General Stilicho wants to talk to you."

"Why?"

"You are a known associate of King Radagaisus. He may have a job for you."

Ptolemy looked skeptical, but came along to headquarters quietly enough.

Half a dozen spears were pointed at his back as they went through the streets toward the main gates of the city. The little procession picked up a following along the way. It wasn't every day that so many soldiers came to apprehend one man! The muscular prisoner must be a real villain!

Marius and Eucherius led the way with Gideon. They had brought a collar and a rope. This gave the dog no end of annoyance. He kept trying to bite at the rope and drag Marius back to walk beside Ptolemy, clearly torn in his loyalties.

General Stilicho, Legate Merula, and Commander Sarus were waiting for them at the villa. Several of the General's Hunnic bodyguards were there as well. This seemed to give Ptolemy some measure of satisfaction. They all surveyed the prisoner, who stood sullenly waiting.

Stilicho approached the gladiator and stopped in front of him. He towered over the man by several inches and was unimpressed by the gladiator's attempts to look intimidating.

"Young man, I understand you are a runaway slave, and you now serve King Radagaisus."

Ptolemy shifted his feet and stared at the general blankly.

"Both of those are serious offences. By rights you should be lashed for the one, and executed for the other."

Ptolemy's eyes flashed. Stilicho looked unworried.

"But you are in luck. I have something you can do for me."

There was absolute silence in the room.

Still Ptolemy said nothing, but Marius, watching his eyes, could see he was speculative.

"In return, I will grant you pardon for your crimes, and see that you get your freedom."

Some of the tension went out of the gladiator's body. He looked at General Stilicho suspiciously.

"I do not serve King Radagaisus," he said haughtily. "I serve Prince Roderic."

General Stilicho nodded slightly. "Yes, that is what I have been told. Perhaps you will do what I ask if I tell you that it will help Theona get off the mountain, and possibly save your master's life."

Ptolemy stared at General Stilicho.

"That is what I came for. What do you want me to do?"

There was one patch of forest at the back of the mountain that had not been cleared yet by the Romans or the Goths. It faced an almost vertical slope that ended at a cliff. So far this area had been left untouched by both sides, and this was thought to be the only way the Romans could now smuggle Ptolemy onto Montefiesole.

His assignment was to haul himself up this near impossible slope using the trees both as cover and as an aid to climbing, and then either scale the cliff to the top, or find a sideways route below the cliff into barbarian territory.

He carried with him three letters, messages to three individuals on the barbarian side of the siege. These were in the form of scrolls. Two were official. One was for Duke Helerix as head of the treaty chieftains. The other was for Prince Roderic.

The third scroll was very short. It was for Theona. Marius had diffidently requested permission to put his own note in with the other two. General Stilicho had read it quickly, and agreed.

In Ptolemy's presence, Stilicho personally dictated the two main letters to a scribe, and then had taken a chance. Ptolemy could not read, and he was by nature a suspicious man. Stilicho had released the gladiator with the papyrus scrolls in his possession, assuming that Ptolemy would try to find someone to verify that the notes said what the General had said they said, and that, reassured, he would come back for the attempt to get onto Montefiesole.

His gamble worked. Ptolemy was back and dressed for action just before sunset that evening, and he had brought Gideon with him. Marius was delighted to take charge of the dog again. He suspected David would be, too.

The first difficulty Ptolemy would face would be in getting through the buffer zone between the Roman soldiers and the barbarian defenders.

By now the Romans had a pretty good idea which areas of the mountain were patrolled by men belonging to the coalition, and which were not. Ptolemy was taken to the east side of the mountain and shown an area where the Romans believed Duke Helerix's camp was located. Unfortunately they could not be sure how far over his authority extended, or where the next warlord's began, so Ptolemy would have to work his way over to Helerix's territory without being discovered. Once he reached the Wodenvale camp, he would be in a position to safely hand over General Stilicho's letter to Radagaisus's surviving son.

Three days later there was a brilliant and beautiful sunset, one of those memorable spectacles that can mock suffering, or bring joy to the soul.

In the east the moon inched above the horizon, barely noticed by those watching the changing colors in the opposite direction.

Ptolemy was one of the few who did not notice either one. He was guided to the limits of the territory controlled by the Romans close to the slope they wanted him to ascend. After that he was on his own. The Romans melted back into their territory. It was already dusk in the forest.

Ptolemy had to move silently on the difficult terrain. He dared not alert the warriors patrolling this area. Most of them were above him. The Romans did not know whether these people were part of the coalition. He had been told only that they were not Goths.

As a fighter, Ptolemy had had to learn stealth and cunning. He had survived by outwitting many of his opponents he had faced in the arenas. Now he crawled slowly along the ground, stopping every few seconds to listen. The area he was working his way through was a trench no wider than the Roman ditch out by the road. Ahead of him the ground was starting to rise sharply on both sides of him. Warriors would not be patrolling the lowest levels here—it was too narrow and too exposed. The defenders on both sides would keep to higher ground, but the area would be watched. He inched along on his belly until he had to stop and wait for his chance to rush up the slope on his right.

From time to time he heard movements and voices. There were men above him, and occasionally he heard hushed voices and muttered conversations. He recognized the dialect they were speaking as Vandal. He had heard that most of the Vandals had left with the Alans to head west with King Respendial and his son Goar. This must be one of the few Vandal groups that had stayed with King Radagaisus.

As the sun reached its brilliant crescendo, he heard the warriors' replacements beginning to arrive, and distant conversations between the men leaving and the new arrivals. This was the chance he had been waiting for. He rushed up the steep slope, and began to haul his body up using the weirdly angled tree roots. His movements were covered by the growing darkness and the movements of others. He had to get high up fast so that he was out of the range of the area where the guards would be looking.

It was difficult going. Low-hanging branches and rocky patches hidden by the trees forced him to change direction frequently.

Strong and agile as he was, he soon made it above the area patrolled by the Vandal sentries. He kept climbing all the way to the top of the slope. He could still hear the sentries moving off through the forest back to their camps. Behind him, the moon was growing brighter as the sky in the east deepened to azure. Just above his head the cliff soared, pale in the moonlight. If he tried scaling it, he would be visible to anyone who happened to be looking that way, and swarms of warriors would be waiting for him at the top.

That choice was out. Ptolemy was glad. General Stilicho and the others had assumed that a man of his courage and strength would have no trouble with that twenty-foot rock climb. Ptolemy had not disillusioned them. He had not wanted to admit it, but he was afraid of heights. It unnerved him just to look behind.

For a long time he continued hauling his body across the mountain. He lost any sense of where he was and just kept going. Then a gap opened through the trees below him, and he saw the Roman wall at the base of the mountain. There were guards walking along the parapets. The figures looked tiny, and he looked away quickly. He should be well past the buffer zone by now. It was time to get down to where the going was easier. Quickly Ptolemy scrambled down the hill, not caring what noise he made. When he finally reached flat ground, he stepped out into the full light of the moon. A man appeared from the darkness of a cluster of bushes, his sword pointed straight at Ptolemy's heart.

"Identify yourself."

"Ptolemy, servant of Prince Roderic."

The man hooted, and three other men converged on them. They were all armed and wearing body armor, something Ptolemy was not.

"Wait here," said the first man, and ran off into the dark. The others kept their eyes and weapons on him while they waited. Ptolemy sat down on the ground. A few minutes later Duke Helerix climbed down the hill with several of his henchmen.

"Welcome, Ptolemy." He turned to the man who had brought him.

"It is him. Carry on as usual. We'll notify Prince Roderic that he is here."

To Ptolemy he said, "Come this way then. I can give you safe conduct as far as my own camp-site. You can wait there while my men find your lord."

Ptolemy followed closely behind Duke Helerix and his men to the Wodenvale campsite, another twenty minute walk away. People were still up, but it was quiet. Everyone he saw was thinner than he remembered, even Duke Helerix, although the man seemed in good spirits and as calm as ever.

He sat down beside the campfire with the other men and looked around. Rue came out of a tent where a child was crying. Tears were streaming down her face. She turned away when she saw him among the men around the campfire, but when Helerix called to her, she brought Ptolemy a goblet of water to drink.

The Duke spoke quietly to one of his men: "Find Prince Roderic without drawing attention to yourself, and tell him to meet us in the amphitheater. Just mention the name 'Ptolemy'. Make sure he knows to come alone."

The man nodded and left.

"I presume you came from the Roman side?"

"Yes my lord."

"And did you bring messages?"

"Yes, my lord. I have a letter for Prince Roderic." He looked pointedly at Helerix's men, all of whom he recognized. He did not know how much the warlord had told his people about the treaty. Helerix looked at one of the men, who nodded and rose. The rest got up and went off as well.

"Who are the other letters for?" he asked, when they were alone.

"You, my lord, and there is one for Theona."

"I will see that Theona gets hers. She and her father are not in my camp, but I know where they are staying, and the way there is complicated. Come. We had better be off to meet Prince Roderic."

Ptolemy looked around him with interest as they entered the back streets of the village. Here, too, people were up. He heard a few murmured discussions and more children crying. Phaedrus walked past on the other side of the street. He stopped when he saw them, and turned back toward the forum.

They went down a side street to reach the amphitheater. A number of people were sitting there quietly. Helerix led Ptolemy to a section where no one else was seated. The light from the moon was now strong enough to read by.

"My letter now, please. And the one for Theona," Helerix held out his hand.

Ptolemy opened his waist pouch and took out the scrolls. He looked at them, frustrated. He could not read. He had memorized some of the marks on them, and their relative lengths, but it was still hard to tell which was which. Except for the note to Theona, of course. He looked anxiously at the other two.

"I can read now, my friend. Let me help you," assured the warlord.

Ptolemy shook his head stubbornly, his lips tight. He did not want to give the warlord the wrong letter, but then it occurred to him that Prince Roderic could not read, either. He did not know of anyone in the High King's entourage who could read except, perhaps, Phaedrus, and that would never do. He glanced around the amphitheater and was relieved when he did not see the man. Reluctantly he handed over the first scroll. He would have to trust the duke.

Helerix bent over the scroll and slowly mouthed the words.

"I think this one is for Theona," he said. He opened the second one, and once again bent over the letter to mouth the words. "This one is for me," he said with pride.

"Read it aloud," urged Ptolemy. "The general told me what was in all three of them, so I know which one is yours."

Helerix looked dubious. "What does it say in the one for Theona, then?" he asked.

"Bissula, I am praying for you. Your devoted servant, Marius."

The duke nodded. It had been a very short letter. "Who is Bissula?"

"Someone Theona knows, I guess." Ptolemy had privately decided that it was a code name between Theona and one of the Roman tribunes she had left with, but he was not going to suggest that to the warlord.

"And who is Marius?" The voice was Prince Roderic's. He had come down the steps from behind them, and was alone.

Ptolemy stood up, a smile cracking his somber face, and bowed.

"My lord!"

"It is good to see you, Ptolemy. I received the message that you were here. It is a miracle that you got onto the mountain.. You must tell me how you did it. Why are you here? Is everything all right?"

He was looking at Ptolemy strangely.

Ptolemy knew what he was asking. He became embarrassed. "Yes, my lord, but she is not with the old lady anymore. She left several weeks ago."

Roderic's look turned cold. "And did you go with her?"

"No, my lord. She went with some of General Stilicho's men. They had a letter from her father."

Roderic was shocked. He would not have suspected Pastor Rhodus of having had any contact with the Romans.

"Couldn't you stop her?"

"It was her decision to go, my lord," said Ptolemy defensively. "She knew one of the men who came to get her. They had met before. She said she trusted him, and she seemed to believe the letter was real."

The Prince was hungry and short-tempered. "I told you to stay with her and protect her."

"That is why I am here," said Ptolemy with dignity, "I followed them."

"And it was Roman soldiers who delivered her father's letter to her? Pastor Rhodus has had dealings with them? Are they the reason you are here?" His voice was rising.

Duke Helerix interrupted. "It seems the Romans found out that Ptolemy was trying to reach you, your highness. They did help him get here. Ptolemy has brought a letter for you from General Stilicho. Perhaps you should read it. The Romans may be trying to appeal to you to save our people from starvation with an honorable surrender."

Roderic looked at him with dawning suspicion. Duke Helerix's eyes were very serious.

"You will excuse me, Duke Helerix," he replied. "I will speak to you about that matter later. Right now I would like to deliver the letter for Theona. I know where she is staying."

He held out his hand. Helerix placed Theona's letter and the one for the prince into it. Roderic glanced at the two of them.

"Which one is the one for me?" His mouth was tight and he was barely civil to the two of them.

"The bigger of the two, my lord," replied Ptolemy.

Roderic nodded and started up the stairs again, shoving the scrolls into his jacket. He stopped suddenly and looked back at Ptolemy.

"Ptolemy, it would be wise if you stayed with Duke Helerix in his camp. I would rather not have to explain your presence to my father, not after such a long absence."

He hurried away, leaving the other two anxiously watching him go.

CHAPTER THIRTY-EIGHT

DISCOVERIES AND DISCLOSURES
❧

(Montefiesole, Italia
Early August, 406

Theona had watched the sun set and then the moon rise. The horrible rhythmic beat of the Roman drum had stopped several hours ago, and in the trees around her she could hear the comforting sound of birds preparing to sleep. It was a glorious evening, but her whole body was aching today, and she felt a little shaky. She knew she was getting weaker. She and her father were down to two small meals a day now. If she went to bed, she could conserve her strength and perhaps sleep would stifle the angry twisting within her stomach. Her plan was not working. She lay inside the tent on her pallet, wide awake.

Gerlinda did not have enough milk to give Detlof anymore, and the sound of his crying was driving them both crazy. The crops were coming back to life, but they still were not ready for harvesting. The children no longer had the energy to do more than one trip into town a day. Theona turned a blind eye when they, and even Gerlinda herself, had pulled up immature vegetables and gone off with them.

She wondered how Edrica was doing these days. The last time they had seen each other was the day they had ascended the mountain together. Her friend was supposed to be eating for two, and probably did not have enough food now for one. Athanaric had not come by that day. Theona hoped that Edrica and the baby were still alright. How long could this situation last?

There were very few domestic animals left in the pastures on the mountain. Even the King's men were now slaughtering their horses for food. The horses had been losing weight—there had been no rain for so long and there were just too many of them grazing in the same area. In hindsight, people were saying that they should have killed the horses first because they ate so much, but the chieftains and the elite warriors would never have agreed to that.

The fig tree still had some fruit on its branches, but there was nothing within reach. The remaining fruit was so high that climbing to that area became dangerously insecure. The grape harvest in the vineyards around the mountain would have been ready in another week or two, but people had not waited for them to fully ripen. The clusters had been stripped from the vines already. The olive crop would be ready in a few weeks, if they lived that long. Theona supposed someone somewhere was trying to use the unripe olives as food, too.

All day long she had been thinking about Anarilka. Of all the children on the mountain, Rilka probably had as much food as she needed. She was, after all, the High King's granddaughter, and the one person Radagaisus truly seemed to love. While all the other children were becoming malnourished and catching infections, Rilka seemed to be still alright. Athanaric said he had seen her in the village square with her mother a few times, as well as down at the barricades with the Gothic king. That was all he knew.

People who made it to the Stone House Clearing for their baptisms had said, usually a little spitefully, that Anarilka was doing just fine, better than the other children on the mountain, but Theona was still uneasy about her. The child was at the epicenter of King Radagaisus's unravelling empire. Who was helping Anarilka keep her balance in the middle of all this? She remembered that first morning after the massacre in her own village. When the adults were overwhelmed, the needs of the children could take second place.

She still possessed the carved wooden doll that Zenobia had wanted her to give to "her other little girl." It was still wrapped in its cotton cloth and, although she and her father were certain their tent and possessions had been searched, the doll had not been stolen by Mathilde and her kin. Perhaps, she thought, the Suevi children had plenty of Roman dolls of their own.

Anarilka probably had many dolls too, but this one, a gift from another child meant especially for her, might still be welcome. It would suffice, anyhow, to give Theona a way to comfort the child. She could hand it over to someone, Athanaric or Duke Helerix perhaps.

That decided, she tried to go back to sleep. It was impossible. She was too wide awake. She got up, felt around for her clothes in the dark and got dressed again, then crawled out to go sit on the bench for a while. Her father and Wieland were already there, talking quietly.

The nights had become Pastor Rhodus's busiest time of the day. Wieland had begun coming up to see him again in the evenings after those who had come for baptisms or baptismal instruction had left. The Suevi man's original pretense at an interest in Christianity seemed to have become sincere.

To Theona's amusement, Gerlinda had asked her on Mathilde's behalf what was going on in the clearing in the evenings—were they having a party? Did Theona and her father have a source of food that they had not shared? Theona laughed, and began to tell Gerlinda her Bible stories whenever they had a break in their work together. Gerlinda had never heard any of them, and listened eagerly.

She went back into the tent, gathered up the wooden doll and crawled out again. If she couldn't sit on the bench, or sleep, she would deliver the doll to someone in Duke Helerix's camp herself. At this time of the night, she should be safe.

She startled the two men on the bench with her unexpected appearance.

"I have an errand to do," she said to her father. "I'll be back as soon as I can."

"Where are you going?" he asked, alarmed.

She showed him what she was carrying. "I'm going to try to find someone to get this to Rilka."

"Can't it wait until tomorrow? Athanaric can take it."

"I can't get to sleep. If I go now, it won't be as hot as during the day and I won't get as dizzy." That last comment was for Wieland's benefit.

"I'll wait up for you," her father said. "Be careful."

"Would you like me to go with you, Theona?" asked Wieland anxiously.

"Thank you," she smiled. "It's not necessary. I won't be long."

She hurried away to the other side of the clearing and started up the path through the woods. The trees overhead that so sheltered her during the day made the ground under her feet almost pitch black. She heard sounds in the forest nearby and jumped. Some animal was still alive on the mountain. It was unnerving, even for a country girl. It occurred to her that if animals were up at night, hunters might be too. Her father's warning echoed in her mind.

Once she reached the path around the side of the mountain, the strong moonlight painted it white and made the walking easier. She reached the place where she had to climb to the crest of the mountain, and clambered up it using both hands, trying not to dirty the cloth the doll was wrapped in.

At the top, she stopped to catch her breath before starting into the deeply shadowed forest. Almost nothing of the woodpile was left. The moonlight streaming through the tall trees created an alien world of silver shavings, shiny leaves, black-and white tree trunks and leafy shadows. It was an unearthly beauty. Theona shivered and almost turned back. She dreaded leaving the moonlit edge of the woods here to head into the deeper shadows. If she did not go now, though, she did not know if she would ever have the strength to go again. Resolutely, she set off through the trees toward the far side of the crest where the descent began to the roads into the town of Fiesole.

When she reached the other side of the crest, she was startled to see a man coming up the path from the road straight toward her. He was walking heavily, his head down. She pulled her shawl up to cover her hair and withdrew into the shadows to wait for him to pass.

When he reached the top of the path, he looked up, and the moonlight lit his face. She was astonished to recognize Roderic. He was holding something in one of his hands and looked pensive.

Gladdened, she stepped out into the moonlight and waited for him. "Welcome, Prince Roderic. What brings you to my forest?"

"Theona!" He was as astonished as she had been.

He hurried the last few steps to join her, and they moved back into the shield of the shadows.

There they stopped and regarded each other, beaming.

"I am glad to see you, Roderic."

"But you ran from me in the town." His words were accusing, but his voice had that light note in it that had so charmed her.

"I ran from Phaedrus, not from you."

He nodded. He had thought that might be the case. "Who is Bissula?"

Theona looked puzzled. "Bissula?"

"Yes. Who is Bissula and who is Marius?"

"Marius?"

"I have a letter for you from someone called Marius."

Her eyes widened in shock.

"Marius is one of the names of the Roman tribune who saved Gideon's life. I told you about him. He came to get me to take me to my father."

That was more truth than Roderic had expected. He handed her the letter and watched her face.

"He sent you this. It's for someone called 'Bissula'. Is that you?" He waited.

She frowned, and absently handed him the doll while she opened the scroll.

"What's this?" he asked.

"It's a doll for Anarilka. A little girl named Zenobia wanted her to have it."

He waited for her to explain, but she moved away into the moonlight to read the note.

"That's not a Gothic name," he accused.

"No. Zenobia is Roman," she murmured. She looked up suddenly. "You are heaven sent, my prince. I was on my way to try to get it to her." She bent her head again and scanned the little note.

In the moonlight he saw a smile touch her face, and felt a jealous pang. "What does it say?" He was still testing her.

"Bissula, I am praying for you. Your devoted servant, Marius." She rolled the scroll up again pensively.

"Ptolemy brought that letter. He said it was for you, so who is Bissula?"

"Ptolemy is here?" Theona was astounded.

"Yes, he is back at Duke Helerix's camp. That was one of three messages he brought from the Romans. One of them," he said casually, "was for me."

She looked pleased. "What did the letter to you say?"

Roderic shrugged. "I haven't read it, yet. I wanted to know who Bissula was."

Theona moved back into the shadows close to him. He still cared.

"I don't know who Bissula is, or why the tribune would think I knew her. He knows my name is Theona. He always called me that. He probably thought I would know where to find this other girl."

They stood looking at one another awkwardly. Neither of them knew what to say next. They had not seen each other for months. Now neither of them could see the other's face in the leafy shadows.

"Thank you for the locket," she ventured at last." Ptolemy told me that the little picture in it is of Jesus. I was thrilled by the thought that you would do that for me."

"I bought it from one of my men. I thought you would like it." He sounded pleased.

"There was no message with it."

"I couldn't exactly tell Ptolemy what I would have said to you, could I? And I still cannot write."

"It's been a long time since we were together, Roderic. Would you like it back? Is there another girl you would like to give it to instead?"

"By the gods, no," he growled. "You're the one I want. That hasn't changed."

Theona felt a thrill pass through her body.

"It's been a long time," she said softly. "I'm more ready to marry now than I was then, but this is not the easiest time or place, and we still have much to talk about."

She saw him cock his head to see her better. She took his hand and led him through the woods to the much dwindled woodpile. There was enough light here so that they could see each other's face clearly, and much more privacy than on the other side of the hill. He looked down the hill appreciatively. When he looked at her, she could see how weary he was. He seemed to have aged a lot over the last year.

"Theona, it is dangerous for you to be with me—I know that now. I was selfish and thoughtless when I insisted I could take care of you. I will not put you in danger again even if it tears my heart out. I only came tonight to find out who this man Marius is, and to hope that he, at least, is worthy of you."

"The Roman is kind and brave. Handsome, too," she grinned. "But he is not you. Do you . . . not want me any longer?"

He did not answer.

"Roderic?" She took a step toward him, her face upturned.

He opened his eyes again and let her see the pain in them.

She reached up to cup his face between her hands and her shawl fell back onto her shoulders. Moonlight touched her hair and her face.

He let out a long, shuddering breath. "Theona . . . My love. . . Don't do this. It's cruel."

"It seems I must."

She pulled his head down and gently kissed his mouth. "You are turning me into quite a hussy, Roderic."

"Stop!" He pushed her away and pinned her hands with his own, keeping her at arm's length.

"I meant it when I said you're the one I want, but that does not mean you should have me, Theona. I would never ask you to marry me now. Last year when I told you I had finally made up my mind to marry you, I was a presumptuous fool, but I still had hopes and dreams and a good opinion of myself. I thought I was a good man, a worthy match for you. In fact, I wondered if you were a worthy match for me!

She could feel his eyes burning into her and knew she must let him finish what he had to say.

"You do not know the kinds of things I have done this last year. I look in the mirror, and I hate the man I see. I look at our people, and I see killers and thieves. I look at our children, and I see despair. I look at Rilka, and I feel like a failure. I look at my father, and I despise him. There are times I feel like hanging myself."

His voice was tight with grief.

"I've come to realize that you deserve someone far more worthy than me, and your father would agree."

Theona felt the Holy Spirit touch the top of her head. Roderic must be ready.

"You say you are not worthy of me. None of us are worthy, Roderic. We've all done things . . . I do or think things every day that are unworthy of my Lord and lower my good opinion of myself. But that is why God sent his son to take all of that shame and wrong thinking from us. God can make you 'worthy' again, if that is truly what you want."

"I cannot," he said. "I cannot abandon the old ways and the old gods."

"Do you see any other way forward?"

He was silent. "No."

"Then why don't you at least listen to some really good news. My Lord Jesus can give you a brand new start, in fact a brand new heart! He has done it for many others and now he wants to do it for you."

He looked at her in surprise. She looked so confident now, and she was smiling at him with a tenderness that was breaking his heart. He wondered if there could be anything in what her religion offered that would allow him a glimmer of hope.

Theona saw he was wavering. "Come with me, Roderic. My father can explain it better. I only know that our Lord can take away the burden you are carrying and clean the stains from your soul."

"I don't deserve that, but I guess I could at least listen. It will give me a chance to be with you at least a little longer."

She could feel him relax. He let go of her hands.

"Follow me then," she said.

"Wait. First. . ." He embraced her, kissing her face and hair softly, holding her against his body. They stood together quietly, contentedly and then began to kiss. Roderic could not believe the joy he was feeling. Theona was here in his arms, eager and loving. He could not believe he was feeling happiness.

"Let's go," he said at last. She nodded, and pulled her shawl back over her head to cover her hair. She was surprised when he started down the steep path and held out his hand to her.

"You've been here before," she accused.

"Once in person," he grinned, "and since then several times in my dreams. I followed Athanaric."

Pastor Rhodus was still up, waiting for her to return. On the silvery slopes below, a small dark figure was just entering the Suevi camp. Rhodus stood up and stared at the man who followed his daughter out of the darkness into their camp. The prince was now carrying the doll.

"Prince Roderic! Welcome. I hope you have come in peace?"

"Yes, sir. Theona brought me here so that you could tell me more about your God. But I also have a few questions for you, and a letter I need you to read to me."

They beamed at him, and then at each other and back at him. Rhodus was amused.

"Of course," he said. "Theona, you go to bed. Leave the young man and me alone. He will make a more clear-headed decision if you are not around."

"Yes, father." She skipped off to the tent and started to pray. After a while she fell asleep, a smile on her face.

The two men talked until the moon began to sink and the darkest part of the night settled over the countryside. By the time Roderic left, it was very late and very dark. Theona's father walked with him as far as the path to the village. They embraced, and went their separate ways.

Roderic could hardly believe the lightness in his own heart. Hope buoyed him again. The wonderful moments he had stood with Theona in his arms, the lifting of that heavy suspicion about Marius, and the frank and fruitful conversation he had begun with her father had brought him back to life.

Nothing had changed yet. He and his people were still desperate. The Roman wall below him had made it impossible for them to escape the mountain; food was almost gone, even for his own family; his men were becoming tired and sullen; and now the Romans were building slave pens in the hills across the way. But somehow he had changed. He had options, and he had love.

He kicked his legs up into the air and laughed aloud at himself, and then walked sedately the rest of the way home.

As he neared the house, he saw that a light was on in the kitchen. Someone was still up. He stood outside for a moment, composing himself. He hoped that it was not his father.

Clothilde was in the kitchen. She was sewing a number of large pieces of bleached linen squares together. A pot of water with some chunks of horse meat in it simmered over the fire. Roderic had had to kill his own horse and share the meat with the families of his men. There wasn't much left, even of this, but he couldn't face eating it.

"You've been gone for hours," she said, irritably. "I got worried and waited up for you."

She took a second look at him and her eyes sparkled. "You've been with that girl, haven't you?"

"What girl?" His face had gone hot and he was unable to control his smile.

"Oh, don't be tiresome, Roderic. You don't usually stay out all night, and you don't usually come in fresher than when you left. I mean your Theona no harm, even if she is a Christian. If you have found her, I am glad for you. In fact, perhaps we can get Rilka to her some time. It would do her good to hear one of the girl's stories instead of listening to a bunch of old men bragging and arguing in circles." She sounded bitter.

"I'd like to get Rilka away from Father, too."

He had so much to tell her now, and so many reasons not to.

"Do you think we should surrender?" The question popped out of his mouth before he had time to think.

Clothilde looked at him in surprise. That subject had been taboo in the house.

"Do I think we should surrender and take what's coming to us?"

She calmly began to unfold the item she had been working on, and stretched it out on the floor. Roderic saw that she had stitched thirty of the linen squares together.

"I have five to go," she said.

"What is it?" he asked. "It's kind of big, isn't it?"

"I hope so," she said. "I want the Romans to see it."

He looked mystified.

"It's a white flag, Roderic. I've been working on it for weeks."

He stared at her, stunned. Everyone but him seemed to have plans these days.

"I started it while we were back in Florence. I think it will show clearly over the back wall, don't you?"

"What are you thinking of! Put it away. What if my father sees it?"

"He's asleep now. I've told him I intend to stuff it with goose feathers and sew the sides and ends together and turn it into a bed covering. Don't worry. He has never seen the whole thing assembled, and he won't." She began to fold it up again.

"So, you think we should surrender while we can?" he said slowly.

"If we don't, and we are too weak to resist, they will come and do what they like with us. I know it seems disloyal to the King, but I can't help worrying about Rilka. I am so afraid they will take Rilka from me. It has been bad enough trying to raise her without Vitiges, and with your father always so ornery. What if the Romans kill the two of us? Who will look after her then?"

Roderic put an arm around her and gave her a quick hug. He had thought about that for months, but he had no answer to give her. Anarilka's fate, and their own, would soon be out of his hands.

"Speaking of Rilka, someone gave this to me for her today," he said nonchalantly. He handed over the cloth-wrapped doll.

Clothilde unwrapped it. "Another doll!" she exclaimed. "It's a nice one, but you know we have too many already. Why did you accept it? What do you expect Rilka to do with it? She has more than I can count."

Then she noticed the look on his face. "It's from her, isn't it?"

Roderic just smiled.

"Oh well. If it's from her, Rilka might like it. Can you please try to eat some of this soup?"

He nodded. He had a reason now.

CHAPTER THIRTY-NINE

DIVERGING PATHS

∾

Montefiesole, Tuscany
Mid-August, 406 AD

The Romans weren't making any attempt to get onto Montefiesole, so standing guard in the relentless sun for hours every day seemed like a useless exercise. The barbarian warriors sat most of the time in the shade of the wagons. Sometimes they would take aim at songbirds that landed within reach of their slingshots. It helped to pass the time. So did speculation on various strategies to get off the mountain, but the Roman preparations had them all ultimately baffled. There wasn't much to do except watch whatever the Romans were doing.

Twelve miles of the circumvallation wall had been completed. Only a section along the back of the mountain was still open, but it was closely guarded.

The Romans were now busy building a network of pens along the roads outside the city. They looked like the kind used for animals, but these had watchtowers on each corner. They were slave pens. Slavers always followed the army, eager to take defeated enemies away and sell them. Emperor Honorius's coffers would benefit, and the barbarians' new owners would be able to exact lengthy, personal revenge on their new slaves, as well as exploit their labor.

The sight of these exposed, comfortless accommodations made the living arrangements on the mountain look almost humane. On the other hand, anyone being held in the holding pens would presumably be fed.

King Radagaisus had ordered that only the warriors be fed now. The food was distributed down by the barricades at the beginning and end of every shift change, but even the warriors were experiencing dizziness and periods of weakness. Many of them smuggled at least a portion of what they were given back to their families. The effect of prolonged lack of food was now affecting everyone. They had gone from aching muscles and irritability, to listlessness and mental confusion. Everyone had lost weight and many had lost interest in living. They were all dying.

The day after Ptolemy's arrival on the mountain, something new happened. A squad of soldiers accompanied an officer riding a large white horse from the city to the heavily fortified gate in the wall near the long road that led up the mountain. The gate was opened and a bridge was pushed through it and dropped across the ditch by the muscular soldiers. Then the soldiers walked across the bridge and stood at attention. The officer followed leading his white horse. He led the animal into the grassy area between the ditch and the nearest horse trap, and stood there for a few minutes, brushing the horse's gleaming white sides and conversing with the soldiers who had accompanied him. After a while he led the horse and the soldiers back across the bridge to the Roman side, and the bridge was pulled back across.

Word of this strange incident spread quickly. Some of the watchers swore that the officer was General Stilicho himself. They thought his appearance on the white horse was a signal of some kind. Others thought the General had planned to do something, and then had changed his mind. But whatever it was, it heightened the tension on the mountain.

Duke Helerix went from camp to camp to visit the co-signers of the treaty and give them the instructions he had received from General Stilicho. These chiefs, in turn, quietly visited the others whom they had been cultivating. This time they spoke plainly. Their fellow chiefs listened and considered what the treaty signers had to say, and then quietly left to speak with their own advisors and families.

Duke Helerix's last visit was to the clearing where Theona and Pastor Rhodus were staying. There was no sign of either of them. He crossed to the bench and looked out. Theona was working with Gerlinda in the garden below. He heard snoring from behind him, and looked inside the tent. Pastor Rhodus was asleep. Helerix shook him awake.

"Good news," he said, squatting at the doorway of the tent. "I've received a message from General Stilicho. We're getting off this mountain tomorrow."

Pastor Rhodus sat up quickly. He almost fainted and lay down again.

"I didn't get a lot of sleep last night," he groaned. "Prince Roderic was here for a long time. He showed me his letter. It didn't say that, though. General Stilicho offered him a commission if he would lead his men in the service of Rome."

"I knew he was coming here. He was very agitated and suspicious when he left me. I have been worried."

"It's fine." Rhodus gingerly tried sitting up again. "By God's divine appointment, he met Theona on the way here. I think they are finally ready to be married. They were as happy as a pair of otters in springtime."

"But you both told me he could not marry her because he would not listen to the gospel!" protested Helerix. "And you know the king hates both of you. I won't have it!"

"His whole attitude was different last night. He had a lot of questions, and he has a long way to go, but he understands his need for what Jesus came to give him now, and he is sincere about needing to change. It was genuine. I would have been suspicious about his motives, but the Holy Spirit was here with us. I did not feel led to ask him to make a decision to become a Christian, though. He has to consider the cost, but we have agreed to meet so that I can continue teaching him."

Helerix slapped his thigh with pleasure. "That *is* good news. Did you speak to him about our agreement with General Stilicho?"

Pastor Rhodus nodded. "He asked me to read his letter, and then asked me to explain how I happened to become involved with General Stilicho. I told him about the meeting where Theona was returned to me—he knew about the tribune who brought her—but I did not mention the names of any of the chiefs who were present."

"He must suspect me. It was I who gave him the scroll. What odds would you give that he may be willing to come with us now?"

"Better, perhaps, than before. He has divided loyalties now. He had a very hard time forgiving his father for threatening Theona and not handling the invasion better, but he is a deeply worried man. He is worried about his father and the rest of his family, and all the people who will be left behind. Roderic could choose to go either way. Help me up. I have something to tell you myself."

Helerix went to sit on the bench to wait for him. Pastor Rhodus emerged from the tent a short time later and went to join him there.

"I'm not going to leave with you."

"What?"

The pastor gestured towards the Suevi camp and then broadened his wave to indicate the whole mountain.

"You know what the treaty says. General Stilicho wants the elite fighters only. I have been troubled by that from the beginning. When the warriors go, they will be leaving thousands of people behind, men, women and children who are not warrior class. You know what will happen to them. They are destined for the slave market. Families will be separated. Men, women and children will be dragged away by their owners and put to work in God knows what circumstances doing God only knows what. I can't leave the mountain when I know that so many lives will be torn apart. They are still valuable in God's sight. They must know that He loves them even if man does not. I need to try to reach as many as possible while I can, or the blood that Jesus shed on the cross will not cover their souls. They will suffer throughout this life and suffer even more in the next."

"Rhodus! We need you too! If you stay, you may die. And years of good work among us in the future will be lost forever. And think of Theona! She won't want to leave without you. Don't you think she has suffered enough loss?"

"My son, Theona will have Prince Roderic, and you now have the Holy Spirit and the scriptures. There are many believers out there who can help you learn how to take those early steps in the Kingdom of God. They will teach you how to hear God's voice and find God's will."

"Prince Roderic could decide not to come, too," Helerix objected. "If he is not willing to leave his father, the king, Theona will have no one."

Pastor Rhodus shook his head. "You think I have a choice, Helerix, but I don't. As St. Paul said, 'I am compelled to preach the good news in season and out of season.' So long as there is strength in my body, I must reach as many as I can before they die. In the end I think Theona will understand."

❧

A knock came on the door of Radagaisus's villa. The king was not there. He had taken Rilka, as usual, down to the barricades. Roderic hurried to open it. It was one of Duke Helerix's henchmen.

"Yes?"

"My chief would like to talk to you in the amphitheater."

Roderic suddenly remembered Ptolemy. He hadn't given the gladiator a thought since the previous evening. He hadn't been very gracious to the man either.

"Clothilde," he shouted. "I have to go meet someone in the amphitheater."

He heard her sighing as he shut the door. She was almost always alone these days.

At the amphitheater Duke Helerix was sitting in the middle of a row by himself, his head bowed. There was no sign of Ptolemy.

He strode quickly down the rows to join the Wodenvale lord.

Helerix noticed him coming and looked around the amphitheater. No-one was sitting close to them, but he stood up as Roderic approached.

"Let's go for a walk in the garden," he suggested.

They crossed to the bottom and left the amphitheater for the gardens, heading towards the temple area.

"Did you see the white horse?" asked Helerix.

Roderic nodded. "It was the signal, wasn't it?"

Helerix nodded. "I know Ptolemy brought you a letter from General Stilicho last night," he said. "What did it say?"

Marius was evasive. "I'll use my influence to help Theona whenever I can," he replied. Roderic remembered the warlord's parting words to him—something about 'accepting an honorable surrender for the sake of the people'. Helerix must be one of the chiefs who had signed the treaty with General Stilicho.

He was silent for a minute, considering what to say.

"It is an invitation for me to serve the Roman Army as an officer in the Gothic corps."

"And what have you decided to do?"

"I have not decided. May I ask what you know about this? Are you one of the chiefs who is planning to leave with your warriors?"

"I cannot say, my lord."

They were both being too cagey. Roderic badly needed someone to talk to.

"What would you advise me, then?"

The question could be a trap. Helerix nevertheless had already decided how to answer this one.

"My advice is to accept. The Romans will let you live if you agree to defect with your men. Already too many of our people are dying. You know that they will continue to die even if they receive food today—they are too far gone. It is time to save those we can. We have lost, Roderic. The Romans are justifiably angry with us. I am afraid that they will not spare your father, the king, but you do not have to die alongside him. You have your own life ahead. Why not accept their offer, even if it comes with hard strings attached. This may well be God's will for you."

Roderic stiffened and stared at the man sitting beside him. Was Duke Helerix telling him that he had become a Christian?

Helerix looked at him, a smile in his eyes, and added "I have just been with Pastor Rhodus. He told me you were with him last night, and that you and Theona may have marriage plans. Do not worry. I am a believer now, and I am very happy for you and Theona. If God is giving you a new life, Roderic, don't turn away from it because of old loyalties."

Roderic did not know what to think. "You know more about this than you have told me," he said quietly.

"Ptolemy brought me a letter too, Prince Roderic, and I did not need to go to anyone to help me read it. I have learned to read by myself." He stood up. "If you want to talk about this further, come find me. Ptolemy is staying with me at my tent. I must go now."

After Helerix had left him, Prince Roderic sat on the bench for a long time, thinking. After a while he got up and left, heading toward the Etruscan road to go to the Stone House Clearing. Too much was happening too fast. He needed to be with Theona. Perhaps she would be able to help him sort out the chaos of shifting loyalties he was seeing around him, and put his priorities into their proper place.

He did not notice Phaedrus following him.

King Radagaisus climbed back up the hill pulling Anarilka behind him. He was puffing. She was carrying her new doll and dragging her feet. She stopped suddenly, forcing her grandfather to stop, too.

"Please, grandfather, could you carry me? This mountain is getting too big."

The king looked irritably at her. Two men with yellow and green armbands were coming down the hill toward the barricades. He recognized them both as Roderic's men. He and Anarilka waited until they drew close.

"Gapt," said the king to the younger man, a freckled redhead with several missing teeth, "Kindly carry my granddaughter back up to my house. She's tired."

A look of resentment flashed across the young man's face.

"Yes, sire."

Gapt bent low so that Anarilka could clamber onto his back. The little girl took a step toward him and stopped, weeping helplessly. The other warrior hastily picked her up, and planted her on his friend's back. Slowly Gapt straightened up again.

Anarilka latched on to his neck and pressed her face into his back, her new wooden doll pressed tightly in one of her arms. Gapt winced, and started slowly up the hill again. She continued to cry, her tears wetting his tunic.

Radagaisus and the older warrior watched them go.

"Rilka is my good luck charm, Wolfram," confided the king. "If I die, and Prince Roderic dies, I trust that you men will see that she and her mother are kept safe and provided for."

"Surely your majesty does not think the Romans would take revenge on a little girl?"

"You think they will respect her because she is a child? She is my grand-daughter, the future of my branch of the Amalis. I would rather she were dead than in the hands of the Romans," replied the king flatly.

He noticed the man's surprised stare. "What news do you have this morning?"

"Sire," said Wolfram. "We were looking for Prince Roderic. There is something going on in a few of the camps. People are more guarded today. They're staying away from us, and they're less friendly than they have been before. A few of the messengers have reported that people stop talking when they come into the camp. With the news about the white horse going around, we suspect that there has been unauthorized contact between some of the chiefs and the Romans. We came to tell Roderic and get instructions as to how to proceed."

Radagaisus was alarmed. "Which camps?" he demanded.

"Duke Helerix's, my lord, and the chieftains who travelled with him."

"Any others?"

"We are still checking, sire."

"Tell Gapt to find Phaedrus and tell him to come see me in the council chambers. Don't wait for my son. I need you to alert his men to notify the leaders that there will be an emergency Grand Council at mid-day today. If they ask, tell them it is to discuss the Roman's latest strategy. Hold your tongue about what you suspect," he ordered.

At the top of the path, Gapt was crouching to let Anarilka climb down. Once the other two had reached them, the messengers left to carry out the king's instructions.

Radagaisus turned to the child. "You've got to stop crying, Rilka" he said sourly. "It sends a bad message to everyone. Remember, you are an Amali." He took her hand and marched her into the house.

"Clothilde," he shouted.

His daughter-in-law hurried into the room.

"Where's Roderic?"

"He's gone to the amphitheater to meet with someone."

"I'm going to go find him. Give this child something to eat. She's getting too thin and cranky." He hurried back outside, and left the two of them standing in the kitchen looking at one another.

"I can't give you more food, Rilka. You'll get some soup tonight. Would you like me to tell you a story?"

"Yes, mama."

Clothilde sighed. She was not a gifted story teller. Nevertheless, she knew a few.

She began to retell the story she had first heard from Rilka herself a year ago. "Once there were three young men who were seized from their own country and taken far away to the country of a bad king. Their names were Shadrix, Meshix and Arminius."

Phaedrus walked into the forum just as Radagaisus was nearing the entrance to the amphitheater. He found the king standing near the back wall and looking around. "Good morning, sire. Are you looking for someone?"

"You, my friend. And my son. I need to talk to him," muttered Radagaisus.

"He was here earlier with Duke Helerix, and after they had talked, he went to find that girl he fancies."

"That Christian girl? But she isn't here. Is she? I heard she had been left behind!"

"She is here now, sire, and so is her father."

Radagaisus turned to look at him. The priest had an unusually smug look on his face.

The king's expression was turning from astonishment to rage. "Are they staying with the Wodenvale camp?"

"No, sire, but I know where they are. I can take you to them."

The king bellowed. Five of his men came running into the amphitheater from the area around the bath house and the gardens. He ordered them to fall in behind them.

"Lead on, Phaedrus," he said grimly. "Let's destroy that viper's nest once and for all."

Theona was not in the clearing when Roderic arrived. Neither was her father.

He crossed to the bench and looked down toward the garden that she and the other girl had been tending. They were there, all right. Pastor Rhodus was arguing with a man and a woman, people Roderic had not seen before. Theona stood beside him. She seemed agitated. She was glaring at the girl whom he had seen working with her. A dozen children stood close together, watching fearfully.

Roderic hurried down the path through the trees, and strode towards them across the meadow. The argument stopped abruptly as they watched him coming.

"Is there a problem here?" he asked.

"They've dug up all the vegetables, Roderic. The garden is empty. They haven't left a thing for my father and me to eat, and it was I who started taking care of this garden in the first place."

"This is our garden, your highness," said the woman with dignity. "This girl has been tending it for us. We have no obligation to give her anything. She lives alone with her father and they are well-provided for by their warlord. They even have a little house and shade, but look at us. We have no protector. We look after ourselves, and we have many mouths to feed. Our children are young and helpless—you can see that they need the food more than she does."

Roderic looked at them. They were all waiting for him to pass judgment. He knew the truth of the matter, but had to pretend otherwise.

"Did she do this work?" he asked the woman.

"No, your highness," she replied promptly. "She worked with my daughter-in-law, Gerlinda, and the children, these children," she pointed to their thin brown faces, "made numerous trips into the village to fetch the water for the plants. It is because of them that the plants are ripening now. It is the water that they brought that has allowed that to happen."

"What promises were made between you?" he asked Theona softly

"None, Roderic. I trusted that they would be fair to me. As I told you, it was I who began to look after this garden in the first place."

"You know him?" cut in Mathilde sharply.

"I am doing the questioning, madam," responded the prince. "Yes, she knows me. Theona and her father were in the caravan I travelled with for a short while. Now, if I may."

He looked at the girl with the baby. She looked close to tears.

"You must be Gerlinda."

She nodded.

"Tell me the truth. Did Theona start this garden?"

Meinrad took a step toward Gerlinda and made a fist. She glanced nervously at him.

Theona glared at her. "Gerlinda?"

"Gerlinda!"

The girl shot a quick glance at her husband and then stared miserably at the ground, her eyes lowered.

"Do you threaten this woman every time she says something that you don't like, sir?" demanded Roderic.

"No, my lord," mumbled Meinrad.

"Yes he does," called one of the younger boys, indignantly. "He hits her. He hits us all. He's telling her now that he will hit her again if she does not say what he wants her to say."

"Do *you* think that this girl deserves a share for her work in the garden?"

The children nodded their heads. Gerlinda glanced at them briefly before raising her eyes to look the Gothic prince in the face.

"Theona and her father should get some of the vegetables. She is not our servant. She is my friend."

She turned defiantly to Mathilde and Meinrad. "They have been kind to us!" she said, her voice quavering.

"Hush, girl. You are making things worse for yourself," reproved Mathilde calmly.

Roderic glared at Meinrad. "If I hear that you have beaten your wife for telling me the truth, she will be taken away from you," he threatened.

Meinrad's jaw dropped, and his big fist clenched. "You can't do that. She's mine."

Mathilde raised her arm and stepped in front of him.

"You have no right to say or do that, *Roderic*," she sneered. "We are not Goths. We are Suevis. We have our own laws. Our clan chiefs will not permit that to happen."

"Your clan chief is Siedric, and he has told me he wants no part of you. I would not count on much sympathy from the Suevis, lady. And do not call me Roderic. Theona may do that because she is going to be my wife. All of you, please deliver a decent portion of the harvest to my bride-to-be and her father before the day is over. Quality ones will make me the happiest. Rhodus, Theona, I need to talk to you."

The Suevis all stared at Theona in astonishment.

Theona walked past the two bullies to Gerlinda and embraced her.

"You have a good heart," she whispered. "Don't let them belittle you or bully the children. Ask God for boldness and wisdom."

She and Pastor Rhodus followed the prince back to the path. As soon as they were out of sight and climbing the hill, she reached for him, her eyes sparkling

"Thank you," she exclaimed. "That was magnificent timing. You seem to be rather good at that!"

"And no wounds for you to tend to this time, curse it!"

They were all smiling when they finally reached the top of the path.

Radagaisus was sitting on the bench waiting for them. His face was black with fury. Several of the king's men were also there.

The door of the stone shed stood wide open, everything in it spilled and scattered on the ground.

The tent they had been sleeping in had been ripped to shreds. Phaedrus stood complacently on top of the ruins, Pastor Rhodus's knife in his hand. On the kiln a fire had been laid. One of the warriors was feeding Pastor Rhodus's Gothic Bible to the flames, one section at a time.

"Roderic," roared Radagaisus, jumping to his feet. "I forbade you to be with this girl. I warned you before about that. You have disobeyed me. Now I find you are consorting with her father who is a viper within the bosom of our people.

"There is also treason on this mountain, and Phaedrus tells me your gladiator showed up last night with a letter for you. If I find that you are collaborating with the Romans, you will die alongside your beloved Theona and her contemptible Christian father.

"Guards, take my stubborn and wayward son back to the council chambers and lock him in the jail. He will have to answer to the Grand Council when it meets. They will soon find out whether he is a traitor to our cause. Keep these Christians here in this shed until I have time to deal with them as they deserve."

He turned and stormed off up the path toward the higher level. Phaedrus smiled at Pastor Rhodus, and made the sign of the cross. He bowed to Theona and wheeled to follow the King.

Three of the men closed in on Prince Roderic, whose face was ashen. He was looking at Theona and Rhodus with indecision.

"Get in there, Theona," said one of the other two warriors anxiously. "You too, sir."

The man who had been burning the Gothic Bible poked Theona in the back with his spear, propelling her toward the open shed. The darkness yawned before her; the mess the king had left covered the floor inside. Radagaisus's choice had been quick and callous. Being locked into the miserable little building was Theona's worst nightmare.

Rhodus reached out his hand for her. "Come on, Theona," he said softly.

She hesitated and threw a panicky glance at Prince Roderic. The warrior who had poked her lowered his spear and shoved her hard. She flew through the door and fell to the ground, landing hard on the garden tools. She cried out in pain. Her father rushed in after her. Roderic shook off his guards and ran toward the shed. The warrior who had pushed Theona slammed the door shut before he could reach it, and the other guards toppled him to the ground.

"Where are you? Are you alright?" Her father's voice was above and behind her. He must be standing just inside the door.

Theona groaned. Her side and leg hurt, her jaw was bruised, the pain in her nose was excruciating, and her wrist was sprained. Her hair was full of straw, and her clothes were filthy. There were recent bat droppings on the floor. Her mouth tasted blood.

"No," she said.

"Stay down until you feel stronger."

Theona sat up. She felt dizzy. Her body was sore where the tools had pressed hard into her flesh. There would be bad bruising there, but no cuts. She looked around and saw her father's legs a few feet away just inside the door. He must not dare move farther until he knew where she had landed. It was very dark inside the shed.

There were air vents near the roof which allowed the bats to come and go at night, so they had some air and a little light. There were probably spiders and other crawling creatures as well as the bats, but the place was not as horrifying as it would be at night, or as damp and infectious as it had been when she and her father had first arrived. They were in no danger of running out of air. There was even a little food here, scattered and trampled on the floor, though no water.

She wondered how many guards had been left outside, and when the king would send for them. Phaedrus's parting gesture terrified her. She would not allow herself to think about his threat of crucifixion. The king had been very angry, and Phaedrus would not let that fire go out.

But it was the thought of Roderic that filled her with despair. He was alone now, and about to pay the price for disregarding his father's commands. She almost wished she had not met him the night before and brought him to her father to hear the Gospel message. They had put the prince in almost as much danger as they were in themselves.

How naïve she had been. How naïve they had all been! And Roderic had been so tender, so broken-hearted, so in need of hope and a better way to live. His father had certainly arrived on the scene just in time to crush that possibility.

Her father was speaking in a quiet voice. She recognized the words he was saying as one of the psalms.

"He who dwells in the shelter of the Most High will rest in the shadow of the Almighty. I will say of the Lord, 'He is my refuge and my fortress, my God in whom I trust'.

"Surely he will save you from the fowler's snare and from the deadly pestilence. He will cover you with his feathers, and under his wings you will find refuge; his faithfulness will be your shield and your rampart.

"You will not fear the terror of night, nor the arrow that flies by day, nor the pestilence that stalks in the darkness, nor the plague that destroys at midday. A thousand may fall at your side, ten thousand at your right hand, but it will not come near you. You will only observe with your eyes and see the punishment of the wicked."[51]

His quiet voice soothed her. God's peace reached her fearful heart. The Lord was here, in this horrible shed, in this terrifying nightmare. She listened for a while and then joined her voice to her father's.

"'Because he loves me,' says the Lord, 'I will rescue him; I will protect him, for he acknowledges my name. He will call upon me, and I will answer him. I will be with him in trouble; I will deliver him and honor him. With long life will I satisfy him, and show him my salvation.'"

[51] Psalm 91

She struggled to her feet and took a step toward the door. Her father's arm reached out for her, and she went and stood close to him. How strange if this should be the end of their terrible journey!

She had heard somewhere that the lion shook its prey to numb them before killing them. The peace they both felt was ridiculously misplaced, but most welcome. If God was giving His peace to them so that they would be strong for whatever came next, she would take it.

Her sandaled foot crunched on the messy floor. The Suevi clan's grain supply had been spilled, too. She and her father began groping around in the dark shed to straighten up the mess as best they could. She found the sacks and bent to see if she could gather up any of the grains on the floor and put them back into the bag. It was going to be impossible. She couldn't tell what was grain and what was broken straw and dirt. They would have to leave it, but at least the Suevi clan would have the vegetables.

CHAPTER FORTY

THE LAST GRAND COUNCIL

Montefiesole
August, 406 AD

At mid-day the warriors and chieftains began arriving at the Fiesole amphitheater.
Attendance was high. All the chieftains who were defecting the next day had come with their chief henchmen. Most of the others leaders had managed to come as well. Conditions were so bad in their camps that this might be the last Grand Council meeting some of them would be able to get to, but the news about the officer on the white horse had brought them to hear what King Radagaisus had to say. They had had precious little guidance from him for months, but if he had a new plan, or news about the latest Roman initiative, they wanted to know.

The king's men had placed his throne on the floor of the amphitheater. Chairs for his advisors had been placed alongside and behind it. There were no thrones or chairs set up for the other leaders, but the area was small. The leaders went to sit on the stone benches with the other spectators.

Radagaisus arrived from the village dressed in his bearskin regalia and crown, and carrying his shield and club. He was followed by Phaedrus, his other advisors, and his top military commanders. All of them had waited in the street outside while dozens of armed warriors in chain mail streamed in from the garden beyond and the street above to take up positions around the amphitheater. The chiefs and their companions watched uneasily.

A chorus of hah rahs began. Radagaisus strode down the stairs and across to his throne. There, he held up his hand for silence, and began the opening ceremony.

As usual, he hit the shield with the bear's head hard with his club. The sound rang out and echoed around the town. As soon as the echo had died away, he hit it again. The people began to stamp their feet. Some of the spectators dutifully hit their shields to begin the build-up to the blowing of the great horn.

One of the Marcomanni chieftains suddenly shouted out. "King Radagaisus, do we really have to go through all this?"

The people near him stopped their rhythmic clangs and waited. Encouraged, the chieftain stood up and called louder: "Do we really have to go through all this? I have neither the time nor the strength to sit through an entire Grand Council. I came here to find out the meaning of the white horse, and if you have any plan for me and my people to get off this mountain. And what is the meaning of all these armed men? I was not told of any special threats."

He sat down.

"Guards," shouted Radagaisus, pointing his club at the man who had spoken, "Arrest that man."

There was a surprised murmur from his audience.

"On what charge, your majesty?" called out one of the Gothic dukes.

"Treason. He is part of a conspiracy to defect to the Romans."

There was an excited buzz around the amphitheater.

"That is ridiculous," exclaimed the Marcomanni warlord. "I never even heard about that before today."

His words brought the buzz to a tense silence. Even Radagaisus looked surprised to hear his suspicions confirmed. Several of the chiefs cast surreptitious glances at Duke Helerix.

The Wodenvale chief made a wry face and stood up. "Permission to speak, sire?"

Radagaisus looked at him coldly. "Permission granted. Do you wish to come forward?"

"No, sire." Duke Helerix stayed where he was. "I do not believe that this man you wish to arrest has no connection with any conspiracy. He is just tired of pretending that everything is normal. As we all know, it is not!"

Duke Helerix turned to face the crowd. "How many of you men would give your life for your families?"

All over the auditorium hands hit shields, and feet stamped in agreement.

Phaedrus made an urgent gesture to the king, who ignored him. He was watching the Wodenvale leader, his face tense.

"And how many of you are ready to let your families die for this man here?" Helerix pointed to the king.

There were a few clashes of metal and stamped feet. These soon died away, and there remained an awkward silence.

"What are you trying to do, Duke Helerix?" roared the king, getting to his feet. "Is this treason I smell?"

"Treason, your majesty? My first loyalty, like the rest of my brothers here, is to my family and my people. When I agreed to serve you, my wish was to keep them all safe from danger. I trusted that you, Sire, would be the man to help me do that. Yet today all of us are trapped here on this mountain. Our wives and our children are dying, along with the rest of our kin, our friends, and our people. This invasion has turned into a disaster. You have not reached out to the Romans, but have spent the last year antagonizing them.

"For once you are right—there is a conspiracy, and I am at the head of it."

There was a sharp gasp at such open rebellion. A few people tried to leave, but the guards along the back walls prevented them.

"Guards," shouted Radagaisus. "Arrest the lord of Wodenvale at once."

Some of his men started down the stairs. The men who had accompanied Duke Helerix and the other conspirators stood up and blocked their path.

"Let him speak," called the Marcomanni chief who had first spoken up.

"Yes, let me speak," roared Helerix angrily, "And *then* you can judge whether what I have to say is treasonous."

The crowd settled back onto the stone benches. The Wodenvale lord stayed on his feet.

"We mean no harm to any of you," he shouted, looking around the amphitheater. "Not even to the man who has forged this disaster. But some of us saw long ago where King Radagaisus's leadership was leading us. We decided then that we could not sit back and let our people turn into outlaws and earn the hatred of the Romans. That was never our goal. We need the good will of the Romans if we are to make a home within their Empire. Today we are no closer to peace and a good life than we were when we started. That is the result of the king's leadership. He has failed us and I say he no longer deserves to be our leader."

There was a defiant pounding of shields and stamping of feet, much louder now.

Helerix held up his hand for silence. "As you can see, we now have no choices left. If we want to leave this mountain alive, it means serving the Romans either as soldiers or as slaves. The terms now are much harder than they would have been had the king reached out to the Emperor when we first entered the Roman Empire. We all bear a share of the blame for that.

"However, the Romans were still willing to make a deal with us that would save many lives. I and the others within this conspiracy have agreed to their terms, and there are still more of you who support us in this view. If that is treason, then so be it. Who is with me?"

He looked around the amphitheater.

Duke Rumbert stood up, followed immediately by Duke Arnulf. The other leaders who had signed the treaty stood up as well, and then, one by one, those who had secretly pondered joining the defectors rose to their feet.

Radagaisus paled. More than half of the leaders were on their feet.

"Arrest all those men," he whispered hoarsely.

Phaedrus shouted to the guards. "Arrest those men, all of them. Immediately."

One of the guards laughed, ripped off his yellow and green armband and threw it onto the ground. Others followed his example. Some of the men who had moved to obey the king's order looked at them in shock and stopped. The more determined ones faced a wall of defiant people guarding their leaders. The crisis passed with embarrassingly little response to the King's order. Radagaisus sank back onto his throne.

"Tell us, Lord Helerix, about this agreement you have with the Romans," called one of the chiefs.

"It is not what we wanted," admitted Helerix, "nor is it what we had in mind when we first reached out to General Stilicho, but he is a very angry man. After the damage all of us have inflicted on Pannonia, Noricum, Rhaetia and Italia, it is the best deal the Romans are going to give us.

"Our elite warriors will join the Roman Army and serve as a unit under Roman and Gothic officers. Their families will be given a little land to farm, and they will stay together in a number of settlements guarded by the Romans. The warriors can visit their families when they are not away training or fighting against the enemies of Rome. When we have proven that they can trust us, we will be allowed to advance within the Empire in the same way that Alaric did. That is it."

He sat down. The chiefs pondered this in gloomy silence.

Radagaisus looked at the somber faces, and stood up again.

"That is no life for you or your families," he shouted. "That is a life of shame, barely above the existence of a slave. Duke Helerix, you are asking these men to give up everything they have won, including their freedom and dignity, and get nothing except a little land on which to grow a garden and the chance to fight against Rome's enemies. We are Rome's enemies. The warriors who leave with you will be fighting against their own kindred, or sent far away to die in foreign lands. That is why the Rhaetian soldiers deserted to us. Where is your pride, my brothers? You, Duke Helerix, and all your cowardly followers are a disgrace to your people and our glorious tradition of valor and loyalty to the death."

There were growls of agreement from some sections of the amphitheater.

"Is it less shameful to watch your family die here on the mountain, sire?" shouted Duke Arnulf angrily.

"Yes," shouted Radagaisus. "My family and I will die together as true Goths. And who will stand with me against these cowardly conspirators?"

There was no rally to his battle cry. The chiefs and their advisors sat there, dazed, as they were forced to choose between two bleak futures. Radagaisus sat down, defeated.

"Helerix!" shouted one of the chiefs in the audience. "Hail Helerix, our new leader!"

Helerix waited while others took up the cry, and then raised both hands for silence.

"Thank you for the honor," he replied. "It is indeed time to choose a new leader. I realize that it is hard to elect someone when we may all be dead or separated soon, but perhaps we can agree to offer the position of leader to the king's own son, Roderic. He is of the royal line, an Amali. I am not. Where is your son, your majesty? Why isn't he here?"

"He is in the jail awaiting trial for treason!" shouted Radagaisus. "As you should be!"

"The king had him arrested for treason," explained Phaedrus. "He believed that Prince Roderic had betrayed him. His Majesty was going to put him on trial here as soon as he had exposed your conspiracy and dealt with it."

He smiled wryly. Duke Helerix did not return his smile.

"Prince Roderic has not betrayed his father," he said loudly. "He is a good man, a brave one, and he has been overly loyal to his father the king. He has never had a part in our treaty with the Romans, although I know that General Stilicho would like him to work with them. He has the chance to be an officer and lead our warriors. Perhaps the rest of you can persuade him to accompany us off the mountain. I was not able to. We leave tomorrow. That is the significance of the white horse."

He raised his fist high. "Hail Prince Roderic, our new leader."

"Prince Roderic, our new leader. Hail Prince Roderic." The chant was picked up and grew strong.

Helerix led a crowd of men up the aisles, out of the amphitheater and on to the jail.

The king, shattered, turned to look at Phaedrus. The priest was not there. He had left with the others. Radagaisus sank back onto his throne, and stared moodily at the cobbled stones of the empty amphitheater.

The men guarding Prince Roderic looked at the determined crowd of leaders and warriors advancing towards them, and hastily released Prince Roderic. He and Duke Helerix hurried together to the clearing with a number of the duke's and Roderic's men following.

The warriors who had been left to guard Theona and her father were the same two who had forced them into the shed. Prince Roderic pushed past Helerix and charged at the man who had shoved Theona so hard. He flattened him, and then tugged open the heavy door of the shed. The other guard took to his heels down the path toward the Suevi camp.

Theona and her father stumbled out, shielding their eyes against the onslaught of light.

"Are you alright?" asked Roderic anxiously.

"Yes!" she said. "Yes, we're fine except for some sprains and bruising and the smell of bat dung. It wasn't too bad. We were worried for you. Hello, Lord Helerix," she said as she recognized him. "Is it to you we owe this rescue?"

"To me and to many other people who wanted a change of leadership," he said. "Roderic has been asked to take over as leader of the Goths. The chiefs are waiting for him at the Grand Council now, but he insisted on coming personally to set you both free."

"Well, your highness, congratulations, and my deepest gratitude," exclaimed Pastor Rhodus. "I was not looking forward to your father's plan for us."

Roderic had Theona in his embrace. "You should be alright going back to Duke Helerix's camp now, Pastor. My men and his will make sure you are both safe until you can get off this mountain."

The malicious destruction the king and his men had inflicted on all their belongings meant that there wasn't much Theona and her father were able to take with them when they left the clearing for the last time. Wieland and Gerlinda showed up carrying armfuls of vegetables. Theona and her father filled their water buckets with some of these for Edrica and Athanaric, and left the rest in the shed.

When they reached the Wodenvale campsite, Theona bit her lip when she saw her friend, large of belly, but skinny of body, waving to her. Athanaric and Edrica would not be allowed off the mountain. Athanaric was not one of the elite warriors.

"We've brought you vegetables," she said, as they hugged. "There is more back at the shed. They should keep you going for a while."

"That's wonderful!" exclaimed Edrica. "I'll start preparing them right away. What do you think, Pastor Rhodus? Fire-roasted, or boiled?"

"Boiled," he said. "My teeth are getting a bit loose. The softer the better."

Theona filled a bucket with water and washed her hair, then refilled it and cleaned up inside Edrica's tent. She was forced to put on the clothes she had been wearing as she worked in the garden that morning, and ruefully reflected that she owned less now than she had when left her village. She knew that God had been with them in the shed, though, and had delivered them. He must have a plan in mind and would look after their needs one way or another. It gave her comfort for the future.

It was an emotional evening on the mountain. Everyone now knew that a large number of the best fighters among them would be leaving the next day with their families.

Those who were going to be left behind faced continuing starvation with either death or slavery at the end. The great assembly of barbarian peoples that had crossed the Danube determined to wrest a secure kingdom within the Roman Empire was dissolving in the bitterest way possible. The news that King Radagaisus had been rejected as the High King and his son, Prince Roderic, had become the new leader of the Goths meant little to any of them now. The story spread that General Stilicho had offered Prince Roderic the chance to lead the defecting warriors. It was widely assumed that he would accept the offer. His name was cursed, along with his father's, the Romans, and the warlords who had betrayed them.

Even the people who were leaving were not happy. They had misgivings about what lay ahead for them as individuals and as families, and guilt about all the people they knew whom they were leaving behind. Overriding all that, though, was relief that they and their loved ones would once again receive food, and live for another day.

Duke Helerix and Rue joined Theona and Pastor Rhodus, and Edrica and Athanaric after their meal of boiled vegetables. For the most part they sat quietly and reminisced until Prince Roderic arrived to join them.

His eyes lit up when he saw Theona wearing the heavy gold chain and locket. They sat together in contentment, his arm around her, her head on his shoulder.

"What's happening with your father, Roderic?" asked Pastor Rhodus.

"He's at the house," he answered shortly. "He won't talk to me. In fact he won't talk to anyone. I wanted to send Rilka to see him, but Clothilde would not let me. I expect he is preparing for the worst, now. All the fight seems to have gone out of him."

"I am glad to hear that Ptolemy is staying there with you, Prince Roderic," said Helerix.

"Yes. I expect I need a bodyguard now more than ever."

There was an awkward silence.

"Are you going to come with us tomorrow?" asked Rue. Theona straightened up and looked at Roderic. His fingers stole under her hair and caressed her neck. He smiled at her.

"No, Rue. Today I was elected as leader over all these people. Until all of them can leave, I will stay."

"The Romans offered you a position as an officer!" exclaimed Helerix. "Did they give you any reason to believe they will hold the offer for you if you do not come away with the rest of us tomorrow?"

"You can inform General Stilicho that I intend to accept his offer. If they want me, they will wait for me," said Roderic. "I will come as soon as I can persuade the rest of the chiefs to surrender. Perhaps General Stilicho will be willing to take their elite warriors, too."

"Well, Prince Roderic," said Edrica shyly. "I am grateful that you are staying. It makes me feel a little less terrified."

Theona looked at her friend with concern. "The thought of you and Athanaric and your beautiful baby alone here once the warriors are gone, and with so little food left anywhere on this mountain frightens me, too, Edrica. I would do anything I could to get you off this mountain."

Edrica smiled at her. "Your vegetables will help a lot," she said patting her belly, "and God willing, the three of us will survive. Athanaric and I are realists. He chose not to be a warrior, and I chose him. I believe my mother and Darric would both be happy with our choices. I would like them to know about us, though."

No one commented. That seemed highly unlikely.

"Pastor Rhodus," said Edrica, "If by some miracle Athanaric and I are allowed to remain together as a couple," and this time a tear slipped down her cheek, "we intend to continue the work your family always did."

"My dear, we will work together. At least here on the mountain. I am staying as well."

"What!" Theona looked at him aghast.

Rhodus's blue eyes were apologetic. "You know I have to stay, Theona," he chided gently.

"You can't leave me too, father," she said sharply. "I couldn't bear that. I cannot leave here alone."

"Can I leave God's children without the comfort of a pastor at a time like this?"

"I am beginning to hate heroes," she exclaimed angrily. "Suppose I decide to stay too?"

"That would be childish," snapped her father, "and a waste of your life. Prince Roderic and I have very good reasons to stay. You do not. I do not believe God would be pleased by that choice, so don't even think about it."

They glared at each other.

"Knowing you are safe and waiting for us will give your father and us courage, Theona," said Roderic. "We will have one less reason to worry, and one more reason to fight to live. I don't intend to be a martyr. I swear I will come to you as soon as I can. You know me, I'm just a moth to your flame," he teased.

"Right now this flame feels like it's about to go out," she said dispiritedly.

"I will try to persuade the other leaders to surrender as soon as possible," he promised.

"You do that!"

He grinned and kissed the top of her head.

"What if the Romans won't take me if I'm not accompanied by at least one of you!" she said suddenly.

"You will be Helerix's and my oldest daughter," promised Rue firmly.

"Besides," added her husband, "I think General Stilicho would make an exception for you. You were an essential part of his treaty."

CHAPTER FORTY-ONE

THE END

⌒∾

Montefiesole
August, 406 AD

The next morning Duke Helerix led the way out of the Wodenvale camp, up the hill, and into the town. He and his children carried a few of their possessions with them, while Rue carried the youngest child. One by one Duke Helerix's elite warriors with their wives, children and close relatives fell into line behind them. The commoners watched them go in glum silence.

Next to come would be Duke Rumbert, Duke Arnulf, and the other treaty signers with their people, followed by those whose leaders had only recently decided to join them.

Theona and her father walked with the people of Wodenvale accompanied, at first, by Edrica and Athanaric. They walked together in a heavy silence until they reached the back streets of Fiesole, where they stopped to share one final prayer together. Theona, her face wet with tears, hugged the girl who had journeyed with her all the way from their village home. At last Athanaric drew Edrica away, and the couple turned back towards their campsite, their arms around each other.

"May God bless you and keep you," whispered Theona as she watched them go.

In the village people were in the streets everywhere, just as on that first day on the mountain, but now everyone she saw looked weary and weak. Packages of food and other items changed hands as the families that were leaving gave away whatever they had left. She spotted Wieland and Mathilde down one of the streets checking out newly vacated houses. Evidently they meant to move into town and find living quarters closer to a water source.

The Wodenvale procession reached the forum and headed into it. The large central square was crowded with people watching them leave, or waiting to join the procession. They passed the fountain where Theona had first seen Prince Roderic,

and turned the corner at the far end of the forum to start down the road to Florence. Everyone would have to find the strength for the long walk down to the Roman wall. Some of the people she saw were so malnourished that Theona feared they would not make it to the bottom. A few of the luckier ones had relatives to support them, or carry them on makeshift litters.

Radagaisus, still wearing his crown and amber-eyed bearskin, stood outside his villa watching them come. His arms were folded across his chest and his mouth was unsmiling. He seemed determined to show the defectors his disdain.

Prince Roderic was not with him; he would be waiting for her near the base of the mountain. He had told them all that he wanted to say goodbye to the elite warriors and their wives before they crossed the bridge to the Roman side and went their separate ways. Ptolemy was nowhere in sight; Theona supposed that he had gone with the prince to protect him.

Clothilde stood beside her father-in-law holding Anarilka's hand. Theona was shocked at the woman's appearance. Her gown was so loose that she was using one of her large jeweled pins to close her neckline to keep her gown from slipping off her shoulders, and in spite of the August heat, she was wearing a shawl.

Anarilka did not look much better. She was taller now, and much thinner. She stood between her grandfather and her mother clutching the doll Theona had given her, her large eyes watching the people coming toward her.

Duke Helerix strode past Radagaisus and his family without looking at any of them. Radagaisus did not appear to notice; his eyes were fixed on Theona and her father with such hatred that Theona felt momentarily sick. Her father reached out and put a comforting arm around her shoulder. Some of the Wodenvale men moved closer. They were all armed, and would remain so until they had to surrender their weapons to the Romans.

"Theona!"

Anarilka darted forward, waving her doll. Radagaisus's muscular arm shot out to grab her.

"Let me go, grandfather," implored the girl in her high-pitched voice. "I need to ask her what to call my doll."

"Zenobia," said Theona, huskily. She raised her voice. "Call her Zenobia, Rilka. She is named after a great warrior queen who fought against the Romans but later went to live with them."

"Zenobia," echoed Rilka, pleased. "A warrior queen. How exciting! Thank you for her!"

Radagaisus stared at the child in shock. He snatched 'Zenobia' from her and hurled the doll hard at Theona. One of the Wodenvale men caught it, and, with an ironic bow, handed it to Theona. Rilka wailed and tried to break free from her grandfather's grasp to retrieve it.

"It's alright, Rilka," called Theona. "I will keep her for you, I promise."

"You will never see my granddaughter again," roared Radagaisus. "Nor my son, I promise *you*."

He pushed Anarilka toward the door of the house with a sharp word to her mother. Clothilde scowled at him. Defiantly, she waved to Theona and followed her daughter inside.

With a stern look back at Radagaisus, Pastor Rhodus gripped Theona's arm and hurried her on.

They continued down the long, winding road as far as the cathedral and stopped to rest under a tree. Below lay the city of Florence. They could clearly see the variety of army constructions looming below, including what were undoubtedly holding pens for prisoners. The duke's men who had accompanied them bade them farewell here, and moved away to rejoin their families.

Pastor Rhodus looked at his daughter with deep sadness in his eyes.

"I've got to go too, Theona," he said. "If I go any farther, I won't be able to make it back up."

Theona took a step back to look at him. His hair was long now, and thinner, and his clothes hung loose. The blue eyes were still kind and loving, and if his back was a little stooped, his mouth was still firm. The smile he was giving her was full of tenderness.

"I know," she said, "and I really do understand, Father. I have been dreading this moment. I can't imagine my life without you there beside me. I have never told you how proud I am to be your daughter.Please take care of yourself. If not for your own sake, then for mine."

Her earnest eyes drew his reluctant nod.

Impulsively she embraced him. "If this is goodbye, . . ."

She noticed his eyes were moist.

"Thena, you have been the best daughter I could ever have hoped for. I have been so grateful to God for the joy and privilege I have had as your father. Take heart. We don't know yet how all of this will turn out."

He turned to leave and then stopped.

"I wasn't going to tell you this in case it meant nothing, but I had a dream about you last night. You were in a palace. There were an awful lot of people with you. I don't know what it means. It wasn't all good, but Jesus was there with you. Pray for all of us who are remaining up here. God willing, we will meet again."

She stayed under the tree and watched him go, feasting on the sight of his retreating figure. He stopped several times to rest. The uphill climb was already taxing his strength.

Alone, she started downhill again. The land began to level out, and the going became easier.

Farther down, Duke Helerix and his family were nearing the bridge where the first group of Roman soldiers waited. She passed the makeshift barriers the warriors had been manning. There were still men on them, but far fewer than previously. Here, near the bottom of the mountain, the heat was worse than it had been higher up. Theona stopped to wipe her face and rest, wishing she had brought water. The stream of people coming behind her flowed around her and continued on.

She saw Prince Roderic not far below standing near a growing pile of shields, chain mail and weapons. He was surrounded by men and women who had come to pay their respects and say goodbye.

Theona left the road and went to join him. The prince turned with relief as she arrived.

"I was wondering if you were alright," he said. "I saw Helerix and his family go by quite a while ago."

"I'm not as strong as I thought," she admitted. "I had to rest several times."

She handed him the doll.

"Again?" he asked, a smile in his eyes.

She grinned at him. "Your father threw it at me as soon as he discovered I was the one who had given it to Rilka. I'd like to give it back to her. Hide it until it's safe to give it to her. It will be a comfort to both of us."

"Clothilde will know where to put it," he said thoughtfully.

"Your sister-in-law looks very frail, Roderic. I am afraid for her. Could you ask Edrica for some of the vegetables? Athanaric can fetch them. It might help you all get through this. I'm afraid she will die if you don't. And Rilka is only a child!"

He nodded morosely.

"Clothilde and I have talked endlessly about how to get her safely off the mountain, but my father watches their every move. He told me flatly that he would rather Rilka was dead than in the hands of the Romans. He's bragged all along about how he wants us all to die like true Goths." He made a face.

"He may have a point, though. Even if they could both get away, we don't know what would happen to them. They're not protected, and General Stilicho might make an example of them. Clothilde made the decision to wait and see if I could intervene with General Stilicho, if he is still willing to accept me, that is."

At the bottom of the hill they could see Duke Helerix moving around the crowded confusion of barbarians and Roman soldiers. He was with a Roman officer. Theona recognized him as the son of General Stilicho.

"I have just had an idea!" she exclaimed. "This locket you gave me is worth a lot of money, isn't it? It might be useful if anything happens to Rilka and her mother . . ." she faltered. "Perhaps you should take it back."

Roderic understood. "I doubt the general would let me buy my own sister-in-law and niece," he said grimly. "We don't even know if he will still be willing to accept me onto his staff once this is all over."

"If I can get it to Tribune Marius," she said, "I am sure he will help us. He promised my father that if he had the chance to help me again, he would. He is probably our best hope to save them."

The prince's looked at her speculatively, and then he nodded. "If you can get the chain and the locket to him, tell him it's my betrothal gift to you," he said firmly. "And don't let him or anyone else woo you away from me. I'm coming for you!"

"Of course!" she smiled. "But you needn't worry." She stepped into his arms for a last, lingering kiss.

Ptolemy was climbing the slope toward them. Another group of warriors was approaching the weapons heap too.

"Duke Helerix is waiting for you, Theona. It's time to go."

Theona broke away from the prince's embrace. "Keep an eye on my father, Roderic," she said. "I need you both."

She hurried down the hill, waving goodbye.

Duke Helerix stood near the gate with several of the other chiefs and officers from the Roman Army. Nearby were rows of tables where military scribes recorded the names of the defecting warriors and their family members. As each man approached, his warlord would call out his name, and the warrior would walk across the bridge with his family members to be separated on the far side.

When Theona reached the area, Duke Helerix came over to escort her to one of the tables.

"Theona, daughter of Pastor Rhodus of Wodenvale," he informed the scribe.

"Is Rhodus a warrior?" the man asked, glancing at her curiously.

"Indeed he is!" said Duke Helerix. "First class!"

Theona nodded emphatically, her heart swelling with pride. She stumbled away from the table and headed toward the bridge, quietly wiping away the tears that were threatening her composure.

Marius and Eucherius were waiting for her and smiled as she approached them.

"Did you get my letter?" asked Marius nonchalantly.

She shook her head.

"You wrote to someone called Bissula," she answered. "I didn't know who that was. I'm afraid I kept it."

"Good," said Marius evenly. "It was meant for you."

"It's a family tradition," commented Eucherius with a smile.

She raised an eyebrow, but they would say no more.

"Thank you for your prayers," she said quietly. "Please don't stop now." She looked around at the growing crowds of armed soldiers and desperate people who pushed and scrambled through the confusion.

"Once you told my father that if I needed help again, you would give it if you could. Did you mean it?" she asked.

A slow smile began at the corners of Marius's mouth and spread to his eyes.

"Of course I did." The look he gave her caused her to look away in confusion to the distant form of Roderic, watching from the hillside.

Carefully she lifted the gold chain from around her neck, and handed it to Marius.

"I need you to keep this," she said steadily. "Prince Roderic gave it to me as a betrothal gift. It is possible that his young niece and sister-in-law will not be protected by the terms of the treaty General Stilicho offered to some of our leaders. If that is the case, could you sell this and use the money to take care of Anarilka and her mother, Clothilde?"

The two tribunes looked at her with dawning consternation.

"Radagaisus's granddaughter and Vitiges's wife?" gasped Eucherius.

Theona nodded. The little girl is only six, and she is a friend of mine. Her mother is a gentle woman, and only wants to protect the child. So does Prince Roderic, of course."

She saw the apprehension on their faces, and seized their hands.

"Please!" she begged, glancing from one face to the other imploringly.

Two burly soldiers exclaimed and moved in to pull her away. Eucherius held up his free hand to prevent them coming any closer.

Marius took the chain and looked at it, a bemused expression on his face. "This is infuriating, Theona! I can't seem to say no to you!" he exclaimed ruefully. Eucherius chuckled and nodded.

Theona sighed with relief.

"Thank you, my friend. I am very grateful."

She started across the bridge.

"I don't need your locket, though," said Marius hastily. I've money of my own. However, I'll keep this for you. Someday you might need it back."

Theona smiled. "You are the kindest man I have ever met!"

"If I am," he replied with that same warm look, "it's because you make me so."

She didn't reply, but headed across the bridge, conscious of their eyes following her.

"I hope you know what you are doing," my friend, said Eucherius softly. "What happens to the Gothic king's family is out of your hands."

All day long the procession continued. The road remained crowded with thousands of people, and the area near the gate through the wall filled up with men, women and children waiting their turn to cross the bridge and pass through to the Roman side. Since all of them had to be identified, their chiefs and clan leaders would remain at the bridge the whole day.

Theona was escorted to one of the women's corrals and left there. She searched for Rue and for other women from the Wodenvale caravan, but she had missed all of them.

The women with her were the family members of Gothic warriors. Even though they were treated better than those destined for the slave market, they were not treated well. The Romans had only to look at their fashionable Roman clothing to recall why they were there, and to want to keep punishing them.

Soldiers brought food and water regularly, but rarely entered the crowded quarters. Instead, they left the food and water near the gates. Theona got some of it some of the time, but it wasn't much more than she had had on the mountain.

For days the army sorted through, and dealt with the needs of the tens of thousands of people. In all, twelve thousand warriors with their closest family members, at least seventy thousand people altogether, approached the bridge family by family to be registered and assigned to their new accommodations.

The process was not at all straightforward. The Romans suspected that 'warriors' who were not warriors, and 'family members' who were not related to the elite warriors had been smuggled off the mountain. Widows of dead soldiers were suspected to have become instant wives to unattached men. Children of couples who were not among the elite warrior class were taken in by families that were.

Once the last individual protected by the treaty had crossed over into the hands of the Romans, General Stilicho gave the order to draw the bridge back through the wall and secure the gate. For the barbarians on both sides of the barrier, it was a bitter moment.

Marius and Eucherius lost track of Theona. The guards on watchtower duty had no idea who was within their pens. Theona was just one of thousands of barbarian women waiting to be assigned a place to go.

Marius even took Gideon to prowl the perimeter of the pens, hoping that the dog might be able to detect his mistress among the crowds of women hostages. The attempt failed. All he was able to accomplish was to deposit Theona's gold chain in his newly acquired treasury box with a banker in the Florentine forum.

For Theona, it was the lowest and most degrading period of her life. The crowded pens, the desperate conditions, the broiling sun, and the competition for food made the long hours of the day and night miserable and interminable. Ever mindful of the work her father was doing at the top of Montefiesole, she told her stories to the children and shared the Gospel with anyone who would listen. Sometimes she crawled to the wall of the corral to seek shelter from the sun. Occasionally she was able to find a place to stretch out, and tried to sleep.

What they all craved as much as nourishment and shelter was news. They knew nothing about what was going on outside their own corral—on the mountain, or with their brothers, older sons, husbands and fathers presumably departing to train as Roman federate soldiers.

About Prince Roderic and his family, she heard nothing.

One day they saw a massive fire up on the mountain. It looked as though the barbarians had built a funeral pyre and were burning their dead. The stench reached even the bottom of the mountain.

On August 23, the news spread through the barracks and the pens that Radagaisus had been captured alive trying to escape over the back of the mountain. He had apparently been guided by an Egyptian gladiator who claimed to be working under orders from General Stilicho.

Roman troops watching for such an escape took the former king in chains to their Supreme Commander. Radagaisus was forced to lie down at General Stilicho's feet so that the triumphant victor could place his foot on his neck, the traditional sign that an enemy of Rome had been vanquished. A soldier stepped forward and beheaded the Gothic king on the spot. His gory head was stuck onto a pole and displayed high above the wall of circumvallation. The people still on Montefiesole learned the hard way that their former leader had tried to desert them, and now was dead.

Shortly after, the people at the base of the mountain saw a white flag draped over the back wall of the house they knew to be the residence of the deceased Gothic king. It was presumed that the flag had been draped there at Prince Roderic's request.

Once more the Roman Army opened the gate in the wall to lower the bridge. Soldiers ascended in huge numbers to force the rest of the barbarians to the base of the mountain. The surrender was complete.

The survivors became fodder for the slavers. They were carried off to slave markets all over Italy. There were so many slaves on the market that prices dropped to rock bottom. Buyers recoiled when they saw how wasted and sickly their new slaves were. Restoring such weak specimens to health would take months, and a good deal of money. They were too weak to perform their new duties in the butcher shops, fields, brothels, households of the poor, and work details of the towns and cities of Italia. Many souls had gone too long without food, and continued to die.

CHAPTER FORTY-TWO

NEW BEGINNINGS
∾

Florentia, Italia
(Florence, Italy)
September, 406 AD

Marius soon found out that keeping his promise to Theona was going to be a challenge. The army clerks told him that the members of Radagaisus's family were not protected by the treaty General Stilicho had signed, regardless of what Prince Roderic decided to do.

He eventually discovered that Clothilde and Anarilka had been sold to one of the most influential slavers in the Western Empire. The man had paid more than double the usual price for the two of them, and had gleefully expressed the opinion that Prince Vitiges's widow and the granddaughter of the dreadful Gothic King would bring in a hefty price at auction. The slaver expected competition for the two of them to be fierce and attract the interest of wine merchants from Spain, members of the Senate, and probably the slave brokers who pandered to the desert sheiks of Africa and Egypt.

With no time to lose, he needed to seek the help of General Stilicho.

These days the man was very hard to find. As soon as the last barbarians on Montefiesole had been rounded up, the General had left for Ravenna to report to the Emperor.

Eucherius promised Marius he would let him know as soon as his father was back. He had almost given up hope of finding Theona, too, by then, and dreaded having to tell her that he had failed to save Clothilde and Anarilka.

On the first day of September, Eucherius found him in one of the horse barns talking to a groom. General Stilicho had arrived back and was presently by himself at the house on the Arno River. He would be delighted to see Tribune Ausonius.

Marius hurried to headquarters. An officer pointed out the room in which Stilicho was working.

The generalissimo opened the door and waved him in.

"My son tells me you want to see me," he said with a friendly smile. "Good. I wanted to see you, too. He tells me you have taken turns looking for that Gothic girl, Theona. Have you found her yet?"

"No sir."

"Take a team of your men and go right away to every pen in the area. Have your men line up every young woman who fits her description. You and Eucherius know her by sight. You should be able to find her.

"Legate Merula's wife is on her way here to collect the girl, and I would like to get Theona cleaned up before they meet or that woman will give me an earful that her husband wouldn't dare!"

"Yes, sir," said Marius with a grin. "Is she going to go back to Bologna with Lady Juliana?"

"I haven't decided yet. Lady Juliana and Legate Merula did want her, but I've talked to Prince Roderic a few times and he wants to marry her. If she is married to him, she would normally be sent with the other wives and children to one of the hostage villages we are setting up."

"Where is Prince Roderic, sir? No one around here seems to have seen him."

"He's away with Commander Sarus learning the ropes," replied the general evasively. "He's not far. I can get to him when I need him. What was it you wished to discuss with me?"

Marius explained about Theona's request that he purchase Clothilde and Anarilka.

"Are you taking orders from that young woman, tribune? May I remind you that you are under my authority, not hers!"

Stilicho's smile softened the stern words. "Prince Roderic asked me about them both, of course. I did not know where they were at the time, and frankly, I did not care. I have enough to do. He seemed disappointed and worried. What have you found out about them?"

"Clothilde and Anarilka have been handed over to one of the slavers. The man believes he can expect a high price for each of them. Sir, we cannot let the wrong kinds of people get hold of that little girl! And it would be a tragedy to separate the child from her mother after everything she has been through.

"Theona says the woman is worth saving in her own right. She is a noblewoman and a good mother, whatever you might think about her husband and King Radagaisus. I am sure that Prince Roderic would be grateful if he knew we had rescued them."

"And suppose you manage to buy them both, what do you expect to do with them?"

Marius paused. He had been unable to come up with an idea that he thought might be acceptable to General Stilicho or the Roman people.

"Send them to my mother and father, I guess," he said heavily.

General Stilicho's mouth twitched. "Tell me, young man, what kind of a hold does Theona have over you anyway?"

Marius smiled. "She turned me into a hero, and I would like to live up to that. In fact, she inspires me. Whenever I have been with her, I feel capable of taking on the world. I know that sounds crazy, General, but I think of her as my muse."

"Hmm. That's rather a good sort of love."

"I didn't say I loved her, General."

"Ah, but perhaps you'd like to!"

Stilicho started to pace, and then stopped and looked at Marius, his light eyes gleaming.

"I have an idea. As you know, Tribune, I have met Theona and would like to oblige her. I will send for the slaver who bought them from the army, and give him back double his money. He won't give me any trouble, especially if I send a squad of my men back with him to fetch the woman and her daughter. Then I will assign the two of them to Roderic's home in one of the hostage villages. That should certainly earn me his gratitude, and you Theona's."

Marius felt his spirits lift. Consulting General Stilicho had been an inspired idea.

The Supreme Commander was not finished.

"Prince Roderic says he has no objection to working with me and the Roman Army. He is of enormous stature right now, and the chieftains who have joined us esteem him highly. At the moment they will follow him wherever I direct him. It makes Theona a very worthy hostage. I will condescend to let him keep Clothilde and the little girl with him at his home in the hostage village.

That should earn his gratitude and cooperation, but that is not enough. I need to keep him firmly under my control as well. All things considered, I think I will take Theona home with me to Rome. Legate Merula's wife will be disappointed, but she cannot object to that!"

Marius stared at him, and then his face split in a huge grin. "That is brilliant, General. She will live at the palace in Rome?"

Stilicho smiled. "Yes. And I have a more personal reason. Prince Roderic told me that her father did not survive his time on the mountain. He was too weak at the end to make it, even when we tried to give him food. As one Vandal father to another, I would like to help his daughter. I can keep a distant eye on her if she is in my own household, and I know my wife will be kind to her. She will get on well as the companion of my youngest daughter, Thermantia, and may even interest Princess Galla Placidia when she comes to visit. I will let Prince Roderic have her from time to time, of course, and you can see her when you come to visit with Eucherius."

"Yes, sir!"

Marius saluted and turned to go.

"One last thing, Tribune. Ptolemy tells me he would like his dog back as soon as possible. He wants to go home."

The two horsemen waited among a clump of trees beside the road in tense silence. It was mid-day, and they had been waiting for over an hour for the carriage to arrive.

The younger man was thin, still hollow-cheeked from his recent ordeal. The older man was bigger. Although they both wore Roman military uniforms, they were both Amalis, members of the most distinguished clan among the Gothic nation, although their positions in life were now very different from each other.

"I hear them coming," murmured the younger one.

They urged their horses forward, and moved into the center of the road. The older Goth noticed that his companion's hand holding the horse's reins shook a little.

A large, elaborately decorated military carriage came into sight, accompanied by a squad of soldiers.

The older Goth held up his hand to bring the mounted escort to a halt. Recognizing the crimson coat of a superior officer of the Roman army, the members of the detachment saluted. The officer in charge dismounted to approach the two Goths.

"Good day, Commander Sarus. I was warned I might be intercepted somewhere along this route." He smiled.

"Good day, Tribune Ausonius. We appreciate your cooperation. This won't take long. My new optio wishes to see his betrothed before she disappears into the palace beyond his reach."

"Yes sir. She's in the carriage with Lady Juliana."

"Would you kindly request that Lady Juliana step out for a few minutes and give these two lovers a few moments alone?"

"Yes sir." Marius turned to walk past his men to the carriage.

"Wait!" called the younger horseman.

Marius turned back to face the Goth who had hurriedly dismounted and was walking towards him. The man's face was lined, but still handsome, and he lacked the brash self-confidence Marius remembered from the last time he had seen him north of Pons Drusi.

"Are you Tribune Marius Ausonius?" The man's words were diffident, his accent strongly Germanic.

Marius nodded. "I am."

"I wanted to thank you for what you did for my sister-in-law and my niece," he said haltingly.

Marius's shoulders relaxed. "Are they well?"

"Not well, but getting stronger."

They looked at each other with mutual curiosity.

"Who is Bissula?" asked the young Amali at last.

"My grandfather was a poet. He wrote a poem about a Suevi slave girl named Bissula."

"So Bissula is what you call Theona?"

"Sometimes."

"My betrothed is not a slave. She is a hostage," replied the prince haughtily.

"Yes, of course. She will be well-treated, I am sure."

"Tribune Ausonius?" Sarus was becoming impatient.

"Yes, sir." Marius walked to the carriage and opened one of the doors. Lady Juliana, wearing a long robe and dark cloak, calmly stepped down from the carriage onto the road. She seemed unsurprised by the interruption to their journey. Commander Sarus gave her a courtly bow, and took her arm. The two of them walked a little way down the road making conversation, while Roderic climbed inside to join Theona.

There was a surprised exclamation, and then a whispered conversation in Gothic with occasional long silences. Marius waited nearby, trying not to listen.

Fifteen minutes later, Roderic re-emerged, a happy smile on his face, and Lady Juliana got in again.

The young Goth stopped in front of Marius again. "Tribune, take care of Theona for me until I can claim her as my wife."

Marius nodded, surprised. "If I can."

"She says she trusts you."

"She can."

"Can I?"

Marius was evasive. "I'll use my influence to help Theona whenever I can," he replied.

"She's going to be all alone now except for that God of hers."

"God seems to have taken good care of her so far," said Marius. "I don't think you need to worry too much."

The Goth was thoughtful. "I told her once I could protect her better than her God. I've changed my mind."

He struggled for the words he wanted. "It's strange. Once I offered to give her a palace. Who could have guessed I would give it to her this way!"

His smile was ironic.

He saluted Marius and strode away to remount his horse.

"Satisfied?" asked Sarus, as the carriage and its military escort disappeared around a corner on its way to Rome.

Roderic nodded. "Thank General Stilicho for me, will you? Let's go."

GLOSSARY

WORD	DEFINITION
Amali	The name of one of the ruling clans among the Gothic peoples.
Barbarian	The term was originally Greek and meant anyone who was a foreigner.
Barbaricum	The "uncivilized" area outside the Roman Empire.
Caldarium	The caldarium was the hottest of the pools in a Roman bath house.
Carroballista	This was a heavy, cart-mounted bolt and arrow throwing piece of artillery. It was usually manned by two people and pulled by a mule.
Circus	The Roman circuses were large, open-air public venues for horse races, chariot races and large scale entertainments.
Cohort	The basic tactical unit of the later Roman Army, several of which would have comprised a legion. The manpower strength of the cohort is not clear for this time.
Consul	In the late Empire, the consul was nominated by the Emperor and held the honor for one year. It was awarded for superlative public service.
Cuirass	A piece of armor made of one or multiple pieces of metal that protected the torso, and sometimes the back.
Diocese	In the late Empire, Rome's vast territory was broken up into more manageable pieces, the largest sections being the diocese, and within these a number of provinces.
Equestrian	One of three titles used in early Roman society to classify its people. Patricians were at the pinnacle of society and plebeians were at the bottom, with Equestrians often representing members of the merchant class able to afford a horse. By the Fifth Century AD, many of the high ranking army officers came from this class, but all of them were of much less significance than in previous centuries.
Frigidarium	The frigidarium was the coldest of the plunge pools in a Roman bath house. It was usually entered after the bather had had his pores opened via the tepidarium and caldarium, and was sometimes kept cold with snow.
Garum sauce	Garum was a favorite Roman condiment made from the intestines of small fish that were salted, left to ferment in the sun, and turned regularly for three months. The clear liquid was strained off and sold.

WORD	DEFINITION
Germania	The Roman term for the area between the Rhine and the Vistula River. The people here were could be Celts, Slavs, , and German speakers.
Gladiator	A gladiator is an armed combatant who entertained the Roman public in exhibitions. Most were slaves, brutalized, isolated and marginalized, even in death.
Grammar School	Grammar teachers schooled boys especially in both Greek and Latin using a close analysis of classical literature as the basic curriculum. A few would go on to the next level, that of rhetor.
Great House	A large building used by a community as a meeting hall.
Legate	A General in the Roman Army who was in charge of a fortress or double fortress.
Legion	By the fourth century AD the size of a legion had shrunk from 4,000 – 6,000 men, to between 1,000 - 1,200 men.
Mead	An alcoholic beverage brewed from honey and water which can also have spices, fruits, and other grains included in the recipe.
Mulsum	A Roman beverage with white wine, water and spices such as anise.
Mile (Roman)	A Roman mile was a thousand paces, and each pace was two steps or strides. The Roman mile in our terms would be 4,851 feet or 1,479 meters.
Onager	An ancient war engine for hurling stones. The word derives from the Latin word for wild ass.
Optio	An optio was a soldier in the Roman Army who was selected by his leader to act as his lieutenant. Our word "option" derives from it.
Ornatrix	An ornatrix was a lady's hairdresser, experienced in the use of the wire frameworks
Panegyric	A panegyric at this time was an uncritical, written eulogy in praise of a person or thing.
Peristyle	The peristyle was an open courtyard within a house which might contain a garden. It was surrounded on all sides by pillars that supporting a shady, roofed portico whose inner walls were often embellished with elaborate wall paintings
Praetorium	Originally this meant the tent of the commanding general. Later it had evolved to be the buildings around a central square courtyard which provided rooms for public and social functions, a drill area and private living space.
Prefect	Prefects, like tribunes, covered a wide range of responsibilities in the Late Roman Army.

WORD	DEFINITION
Principia	The administrative and spiritual heart of the legion. In a fortress, its main entrance, constructed on a monumental scale, lay near the center of the fortress and included the legion's Treasury, standards, flags and full sized statues of the emperors and their families.
Province	See Diocese
Stola	The stola, worn over a tunic, was a long, full dress gathered up by a high girdle, often with a colored border around the neck.
Tepidarium	The tepidarium was the warm bath room of the Roman baths. It was kept warm by radiant heat from the hypocausts under the floor.
Toga	The toga, originally worn by both genders and all classes, eventually became worn by Roman men for special occasions. It was a large piece of cloth, roughly semi-circular in shape (18 feet wide and 7 feet deep was most common), and had to be draped carefully around the body. It was made of fine, natural white wool that had to be cleaned frequently.
Military Tribune (Tribune)	A senior staff officer within a legion. There were many levels within this rank, from tribunis laticlavius, the legate's second-in-command, to a tribunis notarius, who would have clerical responsibilities.
Triclinium	Dining room, so named because there were three couches facing each other around a central serving table. Romans would recline on these on their left side while dining, and reach for the food with their right hand.
Trireme	The trireme was a Roman ship used mainly from the 5th to the 4th century BC. It had three banks of oars, each oar manned by one rower. In the later empire it was used in auxiliary service.
Via	Street, road
Viaticum	The money given to a soldier to defray his travelling expenses to his assigned military base.
Villa, Villa rustica	House, Country or farm house.

MAP I

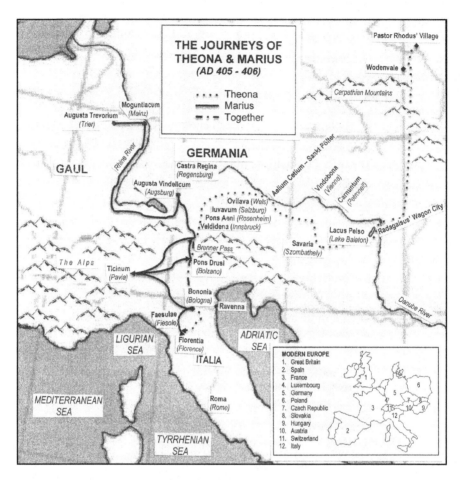

THE JOURNEYS OF THEONA & MARIUS
(AD 405 - 406)

· · · · Theona
——— Marius
-·-· Together

Pastor Rhodus' Village

Wodenvale

Carpathian Mountains

Moguntiacum
(Mainz)

Augusta Trevorium
(Trier)

GAUL

Rhine River

GERMANIA

Castra Regina
(Regensburg)

Augusta Vindelicum
(Augsburg)

Ovilava *(Wels)*
Iuvavum *(Salzburg)*
Pons Aeni *(Rosenheim)*
Veldidena *(Innsbruck)*

Aelium Cetium ~ Sankt Pölter

Vindobona
(Vienna)

Carnuntum
(Petronell)

Radagaisus' Wagon City

Savaria
(Szombathely)

Lacus Pelso
(Lake Balaton)

Brenner Pass

The Alps

Ticinum
(Pavia)

Pons Drusi
(Bolzano)

Bononia
(Bologna)

Ravenna

Faesulae
(Fiesole)

Florentia
(Florence)

LIGURIAN
SEA

ADRIATIC
SEA

ITALIA

MEDITERRANEAN
SEA

Roma
(Rome)

Danube River

TYRRHENIAN
SEA

MODERN EUROPE
1. Great Britain
2. Spain
3. France
4. Luxembourg
5. Germany
6. Poland
7. Czech Republic
8. Slovakia
9. Hungary
10. Austria
11. Switzerland
12. Italy

The Journeys of Theona and Marius

MAP 2

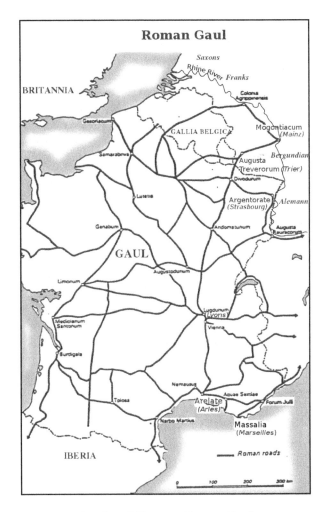

Roads and Towns in Roman Gaul

357

MAP 3

Roads and Towns of Roman Italy

CPSIA information can be obtained
at www.ICGtesting.com
Printed in the USA
FSOW03n1122090415
6331FS

9 781498 428729